A SONG TO SAY GOODBYE

Bee Rowse

ATHENA PRESS
LONDON

A SONG TO SAY GOODBYE
Copyright © Bee Rowse 2007

All Rights Reserved

No part of this book may be reproduced in any form,
by photocopying or by any electronic or mechanical means,
including information storage or retrieval systems,
without permission in writing from both the copyright owner
and the publisher of this book.

ISBN 10-digit: 1 84748 152 3
ISBN 13-digit: 978 1 84748 152 8

First Published 2007 by
ATHENA PRESS
Queen's House, 2 Holly Road
Twickenham TW1 4EG
United Kingdom

The characters within this book are purely fictional and any similarity to any
persons living or dead is purely coincidental and unintentional.

Printed for Athena Press

To my darling husband David, for his extreme love and devotion, and his encouragement in the writing of this book.

Each one of us has a purpose in life.
It is our duty, with all our heart and soul,
To discover exactly what that purpose is.

                                        Sophia Bertucelli (1943–)

Prologue

Harrington Hall
North Yorkshire
18 December 1988

My dearest son Jonathan,

It is exactly one week before Christmas and here at Harrington Hall, Sir Oliver is making extensive plans for Yuletide, which, this year, will be of great significance for me. I hope in my heart you will be able to join with us in all the wonderful festivities that will be taking place. I realise you may not be able to take time off from your vast touring schedule, but to have your presence at the Hall, and at Starbeck Row, as special guest at my Christmas wedding is more than I could possibly hope for. It would be tremendous for you to join me in my happiness, as I take you in my arms and tell you how deeply I love you.

Jonathan, there is so much I wish to convey. During the last few months I have had a considerable amount of time on my hands to reflect on the past, and it is therefore now, while in remission from the illness that has invaded my body, that I have written my memoirs for you, in the hope that I have explained all the questions which must run silently through your mind, but which, to date, you have been too polite to ask of me. I will present you with my life story on Christmas Day.

On the various occasions we have been together, I have not spoken to you at great length of your father. I hope my story will express the remarkable love he and I shared. Each day since you were born has been one of sadness in that you were taken from me at a few days old, through no fault of my own. I trust these memoirs will help you understand the circumstances of your adoption.

Life, unfortunately, does not allow us a dress rehearsal and we have to seize opportunities as they present themselves, living as dutifully as we can, hoping that not too many mistakes are made en route. Unfortunately my mistakes were many; but my life has been a fruitful if sometimes traumatic journey, with considerable lessons learnt. It is inevitable that I have countless regrets, but I have now reached one of the most contented, peaceful and loving periods of my life.

Although I am your birth mother, never lose sight of the fact that it is Robert and Catherine who have selflessly nurtured you since you were a few days old. They watched you cut your first tooth, utter your first word, dried your tears when you hurt yourself, helped and encouraged you with your schooling and supported you in your musical career. They are the parents who had many sleepless nights when you matured into the handsome young man you are today and began taking an interest in the female form and they in you. Love and treasure them as they have adored you.

I am extremely proud of you, my son, and also of your musical achievements, a gift we have both inherited from our Italian and English ancestors. May your success in your chosen career continue to flourish. I myself promised my darling mama, before her demise at a young age, that I would give my life to music. This I hope I have done. Maybe not in the way she had intended, but I do not have a single regret on this score, and I am exhilarated with the outcome of my efforts and the rich rewards which have been bestowed upon me.

Christmas this year will be the happiest of times for me, and my blessing is in knowing I can give myself in marriage to the one person who means more to me than life itself. I trust when you have read my autobiography you will share the contents with your grandfather, Marcus, Benedict and one day perhaps Freddie and Ollie.

Wherever life takes you, Jonathan, and whatever happens to you, please carry with you the thought that you, my darling firstborn, will be loved and treasured by me for all eternity.

Your adoring, proud and devoted mother,

Sophia Bertucelli

Chapter One

North Yorkshire, June 1948

'Sophia, darling, please concentrate on the work in hand.'

Mama peered relentlessly over my shoulder, reprimanded me and watched as my small fingers glided across the piano keys. 'Please stop! Now try again. This time I want to see evidence that you have been practising.'

Mama was a hard taskmaster, but I obeyed her without question.

'No, Sophia, you are not sitting correctly on the piano stool.'

I adjusted my position, straightened my small frame, swept my long, wavy, Latin-black hair from my face and paused, ready to perform the piece of music once more.

'Good! Now let me hear you play correctly this time!'

I proceeded once more.

'Pianissimo, Sophia! *Pianissimo*! Can you not read? This piece is to be played softly. You are performing far too loudly!'

I apologised for my lack of concentration, saying, 'I will practise more Mama, I promise.' But as I spoke I watched the sun's rays beckon me from the kitchen window, casting their warmth into the sitting room. I wanted desperately to follow normal childhood pastimes, behaving as any five-year-old would, skipping in the fresh air which blew gently across the fields at the rear of our cottage.

On completion of my lesson, Mama sat beside me, placed her arm around me, drew me close and rested my small frame against her body, softly saying, 'Well done, little one. You are an exceptional child prodigy.'

I did not understand the word but I knew I had a natural talent for playing piano and absorbing music far beyond my years.

'The more you practise and the more of your soul you give to your music, Sophia, the greater will be your success.'

Mama encouraged me continuously, hoping one day I would follow in her footsteps by attending the Royal College of Music in London. I turned toward her, gazed into her large, soft brown eyes which had once sparkled with life, but which now appeared glazed and tired. Her coal-black hair, always thick, shiny and neatly styled, was dull and lifeless.

Her lips and cheeks were ashen, her skin cold and clammy. It was not her usual perfume that gently teased my nostrils, but an offensive odour which lingered on her clothing and in my memory. My beautiful Italian mama looked distinctly older than her thirty-three years. She withdrew herself from the stool, moved gently across to the window and stood, surveying the scene outside. Her features were sad as she studied the huge Tudor building in the distance, enchantingly silhouetted against the blue sky, its immaculate lawns and flower beds adding a grace and charm to the ancestral home of Sir Oliver Harrington, his wife Mary, and her two sons. Sir Oliver had recently married Mary Hastings, a war widow, whose husband had served as a pilot in his RAF squadron. He had been killed returning from a mission to Germany, leaving sons Alexander and the newly born Benedict.

Harrington Hall had been handed down through many generations. The Harringtons were renowned wool merchants and carpet manufacturers in the area, sheep farming being the main production on the estate's thousands of acres. Extensive parkland was prominent, as were the magnificent knot gardens and maze, maintained in the style in which they had been designed.

The wedding of Sir Oliver and Mary Hastings had been a spectacular affair at the church of St Michael the Archangel in the grounds of the estate. Three months previously, I, with my mama, Anna, and papa, Alberto, had attended the wedding followed by an afternoon reception on the lawns, with estate workers and their families. It was a prestigious occasion. Mama had frequently entertained guests and dignitaries at the Great Hall within the Tudor building, captivating them with her musical repertoire, her reputation as a concert pianist well established by the exceptional public performances she had given both in the United Kingdom and abroad.

Mama returned to the piano. Holding her hand to her face, she appeared faint. She noticed the anxiety on my face as she cradled her head in her hands.

'Mama! Are you ill?' I trembled at the uncertainty of her balance.

'Do not worry, Sophia. Focus on your music, darling. During the coming week I want you to practise dutifully! Give your life to your wonderful talent.'

'I promise, Mama! I want you to be so proud of me!'

'I *am* proud of you, Sophia! Move over, dearest child, and allow me to play for you.'

I removed myself from the stool, watched Mama sit comfortably and begin to play Beethoven's *Moonlight Sonata* with expression and feelings only she knew how to give. It was beautiful and it touched my soul. Then, without warning, Mama collapsed, slumped forward and hit her head on the frame of the piano, before coming to rest face down on the keys.

'Mama! Oh, Mama!'

I was in a complete state of shock as blood trickled down her face. She gave a distressing cry and then became silent. What should I do? Suddenly I remembered the instructions she had once given me: 'If you ever need help, go to Harrington Hall.'

'I will get help!' I cried. As fast as my legs would carry me, I ran across the lawns and down the long path. In the distance I could see Roberts, Sir Oliver's chauffeur, driving the Rolls-Royce to the front of the building. The heavy oak front door was open. I rushed in, running headlong into the legs of Sir Oliver Harrington.

'Steady, young lady! Steady! Where do you think you are going?' he remonstrated.

He caught my arm and held me securely. Looking up, I came face to face with this tall, lean, handsome man of about forty, his features enhanced by greying hair, huge brown eyes and a handlebar moustache. He was dressed in a neat grey suit.

'It's Mama!' I sobbed. 'She is ill!'

Realising my distress, and hearing the urgency in my voice, Sir Oliver's mood became sombre. He called his young chauffeur. Wiping my tears on his neat, crisp handkerchief, he took my hand. Together we hurriedly returned to the cottage, followed closely by John Roberts. I stood at the cottage door, crying. My body shook as Sir Oliver rushed inside. He approached Mama and gently lifted her into his arms. There was blood on the piano keys which had trickled from her face. As he cradled her against his body, his white shirt, tie and grey suit became blood-stained. Placing his lips close to her, he asked, 'Dear Anna, can you hear me?'

There was no reply. He placed her on the sofa and covered her fragile body with a rug, saying, 'Anna! Can you hear me? Please speak to me!' but there was no response to his request.

'John!' he shouted frantically. 'Take the child to the Hall and telephone for an ambulance immediately. Ask Alexander to fetch Alberto Bertucelli from his violin workshop at Doggett's Barn, and explain to him his wife has been taken ill.'

John took my hand and hurried me along, but I frequently turned to view the cottage, sobbing, 'Mama! Mama!' I swept away with my other hand the tears that rolled down my cheeks. Inside the Hall, John

Roberts entrusted me to his young wife, Edith, cook to Sir Oliver, while he telephoned for an ambulance. Then he summoned a blonde, curly-haired boy to fetch Papa. In what seemed an eternity, I heard an ambulance bell. I was informed it had left with Mama on board, accompanied by Sir Oliver, for a hospital in Leeds. Papa arrived shortly afterwards and was taken to the hospital in the Rolls by John. I waited nervously for news. Finally, Edith Roberts grew tired of waiting for a telephone call which never came. She took me to number four, Starbeck Cottages, her residence, where I finally found sleep, enveloped in her arms.

The realisation I would not be going home from the Roberts household for several weeks did not dawn on me initially, but after a while the truth hit me. As Mama fought a courageous battle against the demon illness which had invaded her body, Papa, during the day, crafted his violins and repaired others for various clients, then visited Mama in hospital by night. How little he smiled! He appeared to have the troubles of the world on his shoulders. I asked to visit Mama, but it was explained to me that I was too young. Being parted from my beloved parent for so long seemed intolerable, but I was well cared for by Edith and John. It could not have been easy for the childless couple to entertain a weepy, anxious little girl, but they carried out their promise to my parents to attend to my every need with compassion and oodles of love. I could not have been in more capable hands, and began to adore the wonderful couple who had taken me to their hearts. As it was summer, I whiled away mornings in the kitchen at the Hall, helping Edith prepare food for the Harrington family. I feared I was more of a hindrance than a help. During the afternoons, John would amuse me with walks around the estate, when he wasn't needed to chauffeur Sir Oliver. For outings, I would sit quietly in the front seat of the Rolls as John ferried the Squire to various meetings. Sir Oliver insisted on sitting in the rear of the vehicle with mounds of paperwork, in a briefcase, to occupy him.

The only visitor to the kitchen was Lady Harrington, a tall, slim, neatly dressed woman of attractive appearance, with smooth blonde hair and blue eyes, who gave the impression of being unassuming, yet extremely likeable. She brought along the daily menu, smiled sweetly as she greeted me and asked after Mama's progress. She would then disappear. Sir Oliver, on the other hand, was officious, businesslike and troubled, continuously puffing on his meerschaum, opening the nearest window to expel clouds of smoke which penetrated the rear of the vehicle. John told me the Squire was a most kind, philanthropic employer to the estate workers and villagers or, as he frequently remarked, 'a damn kind, humane and generous fellow.'

As I travelled in the Rolls, I sensed Sir Oliver's eyes fixed on me. This made me feel uncomfortable, sending shivers up and down my spine. He spoke little, except to inform me that Mama was progressing well. He visited her on countless occasions when his commitments allowed, armed with flowers and various titbits to encourage her appetite, or perfumed bath oils to give her a sense of dignity and well-being. I was given to understand Mama was in a private ward at an exclusive Leeds hospital, paid for by Sir Oliver. I continually drew her pictures and wrote little notes which Papa took to her. He always returned with the same message: 'I hope you are practising every day, Sophia! I love you dearly and will see you soon.'

Unfortunately, I had not been practising. The piano in our cottage had been removed. One morning Sir Oliver entered the Hall kitchen and announced I could use the Steinway baby grand piano in the drawing room for an hour or two each day on which to practise. I was thrilled! This made life more bearable, and I extended my one-hour session to two hours, in an attempt to show Mama I had made a great improvement on her return. I practised far harder than I had previously done. On one occasion, Sir Oliver sat in on a session while I played Mozart. Afterwards he shouted, 'Bravo, Sophia!'

I was embarrassed. On another occasion he accompanied me on the violin. He was an extremely accomplished musician.

John and Edith were tearful when the day arrived for me to return home. Mama was due to reach the cottage at two in the afternoon. Papa and I worked tirelessly in the rooms, filling them with flowers from our small garden. We ensured each room was neat and tidy. Our cottage had, at one time, been two, when Grandpapas Tipaldi and Bertucelli were alive; but after their sad deaths during the Second World War, Sir Oliver had instructed they be converted into one, to allow substantially more room for Mama's piano.

I was surprised at how thin and gaunt Mama looked on her arrival home, and my facial expressions must have portrayed how disappointed I was at her lack of improvement. A small bed had been brought down from an upstairs room and conscientiously aired. A tiny table was placed carefully at one side, housing a lamp and several personal items.

Papa spent less time at his workshop and more at the cottage, catering for Mama's needs. On arrival she had gone directly to her bed, where she stayed. I talked and comforted her at every opportunity when not playing piano at the Hall. Sir Oliver visited the cottage regularly, armed with flowers from the Hall gardens, or vegetables and fruit from the magnificent walled garden and produce from the farms. Edith would send delicacies she had cooked with tender loving care. We were informed by Sir Oliver that if Mama needed anything at all, we only had to ask and it would be provided.

Over the following two weeks, Mama did not appear to improve in health, although on occasions she sat on a chair in the kitchen, by the cooking range, to warm herself. Those times became less and less frequent. One evening, when Papa had settled Mama, Sir Oliver appeared at the door. He and Papa drifted into the kitchen to talk and I retreated to my bedroom. They were conversing for ages and when I thought they had said all that needed to be said I crept quietly downstairs to say 'goodnight' to Mama. She was sleeping soundly, possibly the effects of the large amounts of medication she was taking. I gently kissed her forehead and was on my way to my room when I heard my name mentioned.

'You are going to have to tell Sophia soon, Alberto. You cannot leave it any longer,' I heard Sir Oliver say.

Papa seemed to be agonising over Mama's situation. He said, 'It is so difficult. I would not know where to begin.' He was obviously distressed.

'I must get you help, Alberto. You and your little one can no longer cope with this situation you find yourselves in. I know neighbours and friends are kind, but you need a live-in nurse to cater for Anna's needs.' Sir Oliver was adamant. Papa reluctantly agreed.

'Anna has lasted far longer than the hospital anticipated. I want her to have the finest care money can buy in her remaining days!'

My heart sank at this astonishing admission. I could not believe what I'd just heard. No one had had the courtesy to explain that my darling mama was terminally ill. I was dumbfounded, and stood shaking uncontrollably at the bottom of the stairs. Once the gravity of the situation had been absorbed, I ran upstairs, making the most awful din. I slammed the bedroom door, launched my body onto the bed, buried my head in the pillows and sobbed hysterically. A hand rested on my shoulder. I realised Papa had come to comfort me and I lifted my head. There, on my bed, sat Sir Oliver, casting an eye over my fraught expression. He wiped my tears.

'*Go away!*' I shouted, '*I want Papa!*'

Sir Oliver placed his fingers to my lips and whispered, 'Quiet, Sophia, you will wake your mama. Please, I want to help you! You obviously heard what Papa and I were discussing. Your mama is very ill.' He again wiped my tears as he continued, 'I am sorry you have had to find out this way. Your papa was going to tell you but found it difficult to find words to explain the situation. You are going to have to be a brave girl, Sophia, over the coming weeks. Keep smiling for Mama. She does not know she is dying.'

I looked into his tear-filled eyes and sobbed once more. I cradled myself into his muscular arms. He held me tightly, looking like a man who did not know what to do with a small child, let alone a broken-hearted one. He comforted me as best he knew how and asked that I leave Papa for a while. Papa was grieving and needed time to analyse his feelings. Sir Oliver bade me stay in my room while he fetched Edith from their cottage nearby. She stayed with me that night and comforted me. On parting, Sir Oliver informed me he would contact a nursing agency the following morning. A private nurse would arrive to care for Mama, Papa and me.

Chapter Two

Green eyes glared at me as I opened the door. The private nurse stood tall and upright, her lean figure clothed in an immaculate navy suit and white blouse. Her long auburn hair was neatly gathered in a coil and secured on top of her head. She hovered in the doorway. Sir Oliver had escorted her and stood behind, ready to introduce the nurse who was to attend to Mama's needs. I moved to one side allowing her to enter the room. First impressions were that this young, extremely attractive woman was the personification of efficiency. As Sir Oliver introduced Mama and me to Miss Maura O'Connor, she knelt in front of me, took my hand and stroked my long hair.

'What a beautiful child,' she murmured in a soft Irish accent. 'You must be so proud of her. Isn't she gorgeous?'

Mama commented that I was her precious daughter, Sophia. Miss O'Connor continued to fuss over me. She charmed Sir Oliver and Mama with her pleasant demeanour, while John Roberts struggled upstairs with mountains of luggage. He returned and directed her to her room, allowing Miss O'Connor time to unpack. Sir Oliver gazed at Mama and muttered, 'Charming woman.' Mama nodded in agreement.

'You will be taken good care of, Anna. I am sure Miss O'Connor will have you on your feet in no time,' Sir Oliver said reassuringly, but Mama returned his comment with a shake of her head. She was no fool, and to all intents and purposes was aware of the inevitable situation facing her. She quickly beckoned me to her side while the nurse settled in. Sir Oliver kissed Mama's forehead and said, 'I will call to see you later, Anna, when everyone is familiar with the situation.'

Mama grasped his arm. 'If anything—'

'Ssh, dearest Anna!' he whispered. 'All will be well. Sophia will always be taken care of – of that you can be sure.'

Having given Mama some peace of mind, he returned to the Hall, a sad figure of a man. I sat on the bed and began reading one of my books to Mama. She encouraged me with my reading. It was part of our daily routine, allowing us time to be close to one another.

'*Get off that bed!*'

The instruction resounded across the room. I almost jumped out of my skin. Maura O'Connor stood, hands on hips, and announced, '*Sophia*! That is not something I allow! We have to run a tight ship here.

It is necessary we get off to a good start by you adhering to my rules and regulations. Sitting on the bed is something I will not tolerate!'

She moved swiftly across the room, drew a chair to my side, pointed to it and bade me sit. I did so without question. Although weak, Mama was about to comment, but Miss O'Connor interrupted her by announcing she was sure we would all get along just fine. Smiling sweetly at us, she instructed me to go and tidy my room, which I did without hesitation, although I knew it to be spotless. I climbed the stairs, glancing into her room as I passed by. There was a box on her bed containing books. My curiosity overcame me as I nosed at the reading matter. Romantic novels! I lifted them out one by one and discovered the bottom of the box to be covered with bottles – whisky, brandy and gin! I imagined they were for medicinal purposes connected to her work. I carefully placed the books back to cover them. I was not sure I was going to like Miss O'Connor and her sugary smile or her ridiculous rules and regulations.

Papa returned from his workshop early in the evening. More introductions were forthcoming. Maura seemed thrilled she had entered a musical world. In no time she had coaxed Papa into a discussion on violins. He seemed impressed with her charm and wit. They were deep in conversation for some considerable time. She prepared him a meal. After supper and before bed, Mama explained she had been a concert pianist and that I too could play piano, and practised daily at the Hall.

'You must take me with you, Sophia, to hear you play! What nursery rhymes do you know?' Maura asked, as Mama smiled.

'Sophia can play Handel, Mozart – in fact her repertoire covers the works of many famous composers!' she explained.

Why did I think Maura was more intent on getting her foot inside the Hall than hearing me play? I did not like Maura O'Connor. Something about her troubled me greatly.

On my arrival down to breakfast the following morning, Mama and Miss O'Connor were deep in conversation. As I approached the room, Maura was enquiring of our musical heritage. She was introduced to the memories of my grandparents, the Tipaldis and Bertucellis. Mama explained that I frequented the Hall each afternoon for piano practice. 'Oh! How I would love to play the Steinway grand piano once more in the Great Hall. It would be my dearest wish,' she sighed as Miss O'Connor served breakfast on a tray.

'Out of the question!' was the reply. 'You really are not well enough for such an escapade. Put it out of your mind, Anna! May I call you Anna?' she asked, smiling her sickly smile.

Mama said, 'Yes,' but the look of utter disappointment on her face spoke volumes.

After Sunday lunch, happily swinging my music case, I skipped across to Harrington Hall, where Haynes, the butler, accompanied me to the drawing room.

'The piano is all yours, Miss Sophia,' he said and raised the lid as I offloaded my sheet music from the case. He positioned it on to the stand for me. I thanked him, and practised my scales before settling down to a new piece I wished to perfect. How I wished Mama could have been there to instruct me! Ten minutes into my lesson, Sir Oliver appeared and insisted on listening to me play. Apart from a few observations, he sat quietly until I had finished.

'That was excellent, Sophia! You played with such expression. You will surely become a famous concert pianist one day with your immense talent.'

'Sir?' I asked sheepishly. 'You told Papa if Mama needed anything we only had to ask and you would arrange it…'

'Correct! What exactly is it that Anna needs?'

'I heard her talking to Miss O'Connor. Her wish was to play piano in the Great Hall. Miss O'Connor told her it was not possible.'

'Of course it is possible, Sophia! In fact we will do it today – before it is too…' He hesitated, but I knew what he meant.

As soon as my practice was over, Sir Oliver beckoned his chauffeur, who brought the Rolls to the door. The journey to the cottage took seconds. He entered, surprising our private nurse, who was sitting in the kitchen consuming a glass of alcohol. She promptly and sheepishly removed it to the sink.

'Miss O'Connor, Sophia tells me Anna has expressed a wish to play piano at the Hall. I am here to collect her. Please see she is dressed immediately!'

'Oh, what a wonderful idea! It will be so good for her,' the nurse commented, contradicting everything she had previously uttered to Mama. 'I will fetch her suitable clothing and then accompany Anna to the Hall.'

'That will not be necessary, Miss O'Connor. John will drive Anna, Sophia and me.'

From the look on her face Maura was not pleased with the rebuff from Sir Oliver and appeared startled and angry. She shot a glare in my direction which frightened me. Maura prepared Mama for the short journey and Sir Oliver, John, Mama and I returned to the Hall. On arrival, Sir Oliver gently lifted Mama with his strong arms, carried her to the Great Hall and placed her on a chair, then made the piano stool comfortable for her use. The look on Mama's face was one of considerable pleasure. Helping her across to the stool, he positioned her at the piano. She looked so frail and doll-like, her hair cascading over her shoulders, just as she had worn it so many times when playing to an audience. Mama settled herself. As if by an unforeseen energy force, she began to play. It was moving to watch and listen to her. I detected great sadness in Sir Oliver's eyes as he watched her perform what could possibly be her last piece on the magnificent Steinway grand piano.

'Please go to the kitchen, Sophia. Ask Mrs Roberts to send a pot of Earl Grey tea and an assortment of cakes,' Sir Oliver requested.

I did as asked, leaving Mama to entertain Sir Oliver with his favourite piece of music, the *Moonlight Sonata*.

Edith was in the kitchen baking something delicious.

'Sophia! How lovely to see you, lass! You would like tea? Why, of course! You shall have some of my finest cakes too. I baked them only this morning. How is Mama?'

'Poorly, I am afraid. Thank you for asking,' I replied. 'She is in the Great Hall playing piano for Sir Oliver.'

'You can tell Sir Oliver I will send tea in soon.' Edith kissed me on the cheek and I threw my arms around her roly-poly frame in an affectionate gesture and then hurried back to be with Mama and Sir Oliver. As I approached I observed an unusual scene. Mama was no longer playing. Sir Oliver was holding her tenderly in his arms.

'Anna, my darling! Please don't cry. You and I have travelled a long road together through our love of music. I do not regret one single moment of that journey with you.'

'Nor do I, Oliver. Nor do I. Not one single moment. It has been a most wonderful experience. Please forgive me for all my mistakes of the past.'

He lifted her head as she gazed longingly at his features, exploring every contour with her huge, brown eyes. She somehow knew this would be the last time she would play for him.

'Dearest Anna! You do not need to ask for my forgiveness, and I promise you I will keep a close watch over Sophia. She will want for nothing. But, dear God, how I am going to miss you, my love!'

'Thank you, dearest Oliver! You know exactly what my feelings are for you. No one else could love and adore you the way I do. Please make sure Sophia continues with her music. She has such great potential.'

He lifted Mama once more into his arms and set her down on the chaise longue so that she was at ease. He knelt down in front of her, placing his head in her lap as she lovingly stroked his greying hair. He looked up and kissed her on the lips in a long, lingering kiss. I had never seen Papa kiss Mama in such a way. I thought how strange grown-ups were in the way they demonstrated their feelings for one another. I expected Sir Oliver was saying his goodbyes. I moved toward them, placing my feet noisily on the floor. Sir Oliver arose from his kneeling position immediately and stood upright with his hands clasped behind his back as I made my presence known.

'Mrs Roberts is sending in tea and cakes,' I announced.

'Good girl.' Sir Oliver patted my head as I sat on the floor by Mama. He focused on me and with a captivating smile announced, 'One day you will be able to entertain dignitaries here in the Great Hall, Sophia. It will be a wonderful experience.'

'Yes, Sir!' I said, but music was far from my thoughts at that moment. My head was in a spin. I could not truly comprehend what I had seen or heard, but the memory of those few precious moments would stay with me for always.

That evening, Papa seemed impressed with the dominant Maura O'Connor and her interest in his work. Once more they became engrossed in conversation. With Mama sleeping peacefully, I was instructed to wash and retire to bed. I wanted to spend time with Mama and Papa, but Maura insisted I had an early night, so I did as she wished.

'What a delightful child!' I heard her tell Papa as I left the room. Once again Maura O'Connor, from Dublin, Ireland, disturbed me, but I could not establish why.

With summer holidays over, I returned to St Catherine's Roman Catholic school, a distance of twelve miles from home, travelling by special bus. I disliked school immensely; the nuns were strict and thoughtless at a time when I needed comfort and understanding.

Mama had two extremely restless nights. I hugged her as I left for my day at school. She'd been drowsy, but opened her eyes, lifted her hands and cupped my face within them. Kissing my cheeks, she had murmured, 'I love you, Sophia. Please practise daily. You have such a great gift.' She slumped back on the pillows as I made my usual promise that I would devote my life to music, and I saw a contented smile creep over her pale features.

'I love you too, Mama!' I croaked, fighting back tears. Then I looked at the clock, excusing myself to catch the school bus. Papa escorted me and was less chatty than usual. He waved farewell and then disappeared into his workshop. In the rear seat of the bus I sat and cried silently.

The first day was fraught with activities I hated and lessons I had little interest in. The nuns were austere and unforgiving. I couldn't wait for the day to end. The school bus waited in its usual spot and I climbed aboard, anxious to see Mama, hoping she had improved; but the journey home seemed endless. On arrival at the cottage I dashed in.

'Mama, I—!' I stopped in my tracks and viewed the room. The bed in which she had spent so much time of late was gone, along with all her possessions she'd had at hand. In one fell swoop there was no evidence whatsoever Mama had been there.

Maura appeared.

'Where is Mama?' I asked tearfully.

She took my hand, placed me on the sofa and sat beside me saying 'Your mother died this morning, just after you left for school.'

She sounded so cold. Her breath had a strange odour, like Papa's had when he had been drinking alcohol at Christmas. I cried and Maura offered me a handkerchief. I did not want to accept the news and ran to my room, launching myself at the bed. Why hadn't Papa met me from the bus to console me? I needed his presence.

He arrived shortly after my return and came to my rescue. I was heartbroken and empty inside. He cuddled me, spent time trying to explain it was for the best, as Mama had been in terrible pain, and that she was brave in hiding her discomfort from us all.

I needed her and wanted her there: those loving arms, the gentle touch – my darling Mama. That evening I took my teddy bear, Rupert, to bed. He was the last gift she had given me. It gave me great comfort as the tears flowed. I hugged it, caressed it and talked to it about my pain. Gradually tiredness overcame me and I fell asleep.

When I awoke, after a disturbed night, it was ten o'clock. It was obvious school was not scheduled for the day. There was a dampness on my skin that bothered me a great deal. As I pulled back the bedcovers to investigate, I was shocked and horrified to find my bed was soaked. Then the realisation dawned that Mama was no longer with us, and I began crying once more. It must have been the trauma of losing her that caused me to wet the bed, something I had never done in my short life. I descended the stairs in my damp pyjamas to find Papa, but realised he must have gone to make arrangements for Mama's funeral. I heard Maura in the kitchen and had no option but to approach her.

'Maura, I have had an accident in my bed,' I confessed.

She turned and, wiping her hands on her apron, said, 'Never mind, Sophia. We had better investigate.' She followed me to my bedroom and stood, surveying the wet sheets, my pyjamas and Rupert bear.

'Come here, Sophia,' she said sweetly. 'Be a good girl. Help me take these sheets off the bed.'

I assisted her and muttered, 'Sorry, Maura. I am really sorry.'

'Now, don't you worry. We'll soon have this mess sorted.'

She picked up the sheets and the bear and asked me to remove my pyjamas for washing. I was so pleased to be rid of the smelly items. She bade me follow her to the kitchen. She piled the sheets into a heap, tossing them into the corner of the landing, and descended the stairs with Rupert bear and my pyjamas in her arms. I followed closely until we reached the cooking range. My body was naked and I was trembling with cold. How good of her to wash the bear Mama had bought for me.

'Now! We must sort Rupert out! Good old Rupert Bear!'

She sneered as she waved the bear in my face. With her comment she opened the door of the range to expose the fire inside and promptly threw the bear, and my pyjamas in to burn.

'Goodbye, Rupert!' she mocked. 'And good riddance!'

'Please, Maura! No, you cannot...!' I begged, but she had already carried out the awful deed. I wanted Rupert so much. He was my last contact with Mama, and she knew it. I launched myself forward to rescue him, but she screamed, '*Sophia!* Go upstairs *now!*'

Her voice was menacing. I was too scared to do anything but obey. She returned with me to the landing and ordered me to stand in the corner. I did as requested and she draped the wet sheets over my head, ordering me to stay there until I was told otherwise. Tears streamed down my face but she showed no compassion or kindliness, leaving me in a state of utter humiliation. I do not know how long I stood there, crying and shaking with cold and fright. Later, I heard her running a bath, and then her footsteps vibrated along the wooden floor of the landing. I knew she was close by. She dragged the sheets from my head and pulled me by my hair into the bath. I was too terrified to react. My whole body was scrubbed with a loofah and masses of shampoo roughly rubbed through my hair. She dragged me out of the bath so brutally that I thought my arms would break. I was pushed into my bedroom without being dried or clothed, and she locked the door. Shaking, wet and scared, I searched through the drawers and found a winceyette nightdress to put on. My long wet hair had to be left to dry naturally.

If Mama had been alive she would have coped with the situation and not chastised me in this awful manner, but would have held me close and comforted me. How I missed her! I needed her and her tender touch! Hopefully, now we no longer needed a nurse, Maura would leave. Then Papa and I would be happy once more. The sooner Maura

O'Connor departed the better I would like it. For a moment I wanted to die and join Mama in heaven. At teatime Maura unlocked the door and stood there defiantly. I cowered as she said, 'You tell your father what happened today and I will beat you!'

She waved her spindly finger in my face. I believed her. I would say nothing for fear of repercussions.

'You are a very wicked little girl! The devil is after your soul, and you must ask for forgiveness! You will pray every night he does not come and take you! Do you understand me?'

I indicated that I did, but I could not understand how I had been so wicked as to need such dreadful punishments.

'Go! Get your tea!' she snapped. She pushed me toward the stairs. I moved quickly to the kitchen, where a meagre portion of sandwiches had been placed along with a glass of water. There was no smell of newly baked cakes forthcoming to stimulate my taste buds, and none of the refreshing lemonade Mama used to make and which I'd grown to love.

Papa appeared at six o'clock, surprised to see me in my nightdress and ready for bed. He had been finalising arrangements in town for Mama's funeral.

'How is my favourite girl?' he asked moving across to me, placing his arm around my shoulder. He held me gently to him. 'Has Maura been taking good care of you?'

'Yes, Papa, I am fine,' I lied. I could see the shadow of Maura lurking in the kitchen doorway. I dared say no more.

'Ah, Alberto! Do come and have supper,' Maura offered. 'I have prepared you a delicious meal.'

Her gushing attitude sent shivers down my spine.

'If you could give me a few moments with Sophia, there are things I wish to discuss with her,' he explained.

Papa sat me on a chair and pulled another close to me. He stared into my eyes as he said, 'Mama requested a small service in the private baroque chapel in Harrington Hall. Father Pierre will take this. The funeral is on Friday and we will attend. In the afternoon there will be a requiem mass for Mama in the church of St Michael the Archangel in the grounds of the Hall, so that dignitaries, estate workers and friends can attend. She will be buried in the churchyard. We can visit her grave often.'

'How wonderful, Papa! Mama will seem closer to us. She had many friends who will want to attend. I will play her favourite piece of music.'

'Good girl, Sophia!' He patted my hand and turned as Maura hovered above us.

'Excuse me, Alberto, I could not help but overhear your conversation. Sophia is too young and not in a fit state to attend the funeral. She is too vulnerable at this time. I hope you will forgive me for interfering, but I have the child's best interests at heart.'

Her smile made me cringe. They adjourned to the kitchen and discussed the matter further. The conclusion was that I would not attend the funeral, and no matter how hard I tried to persuade them otherwise, Maura was adamant.

I met Edith Roberts as she walked across the lawn to her cottage.

'Hello, Sophia lass!' She opened her arms and I threw myself into her warm, enveloping embrace.

'Sir Oliver was asking after you and how you were coping. You were obviously in no fit state for piano practice with the passing of your dearest Mama. I suppose you have had a lot on your mind.'

I let the tears flow as she kissed me.

'Maura will not allow me to go to Mama's funeral,' I blurted out. 'I want to go so much. What can I do?'

'I will speak to Sir Oliver. He will sort it,' Edith replied, looking shocked. She was a ray of hope in a dim world. Papa seemed to go along with every word Maura uttered. He was spellbound by her yet, she was so manipulative and cruel.

'Edith, I miss Mama so much!'

'I am sure you do, lass. Leave it with me. I will be seeing Sir Oliver later.'

Suddenly I felt relief creep over me. I knew Edith would do what she could to help.

I hurried to the Hall to practise, and I sat at the piano and played until my fingers ached. During this time the drawing room door opened and a young, blonde-haired lad of approximately eleven years of age stood there.

'I am sorry to interrupt you. Please excuse me!' he said.

He smiled, turned and was gone. I vaguely remembered seeing him at Sir Oliver's wedding and believed him to be Alexander Hastings, the son of Sir Oliver's new wife.

Later, Sir Oliver arrived at our cottage, looking extremely severe. Papa opened the door as Maura lurked in the background, ready to interrupt at the earliest opportunity.

'Do come in, Sir Oliver. Have a seat,' Papa said.

'I have come to discuss funeral arrangements,' the Squire announced. 'I am arranging flowers for the private chapel and also the church. I wish to talk to you about the service, Alberto, for the celebration of Anna's life.'

Sir Oliver looked across at me and gave a sly wink. Papa explained about musician friends who wished to take part.

'Sophia will no doubt want to play at this service,' said Sir Oliver.

Maura immediately interrupted, forcing an opinion that was not asked for and certainly not wanted. 'I have told Alberto, Sophia is not in a fit state to attend,' she declared with a smirk.

'You have, have you, Miss O'Connor? Well, have you asked Sophia what she would like to do?' he asked.

She shook her head and looked totally embarrassed by the line of questioning.

'Sophia, would you like to take part in the celebration?' he asked.

'Yes, Sir, I would. I want to play one of Mama's favourite pieces of music!'

'Then it is settled. You shall most definitely play! We have several people who are taking part. I will prepare an order of service!'

Sir Oliver arose from his seat. 'There is nothing more to be said. Arrangements will be made.'

'I will bring Sophia to the private chapel, Sir,' Maura interrupted, but Sir Oliver explained there was no need as John would fetch me.

'Edith and John are Sophia's close friends. They will take care of her, and her papa will be there too,' he added.

I made myself scarce by going to my room. I do not think Sir Oliver was as enchanted with Maura O'Connor as he'd first led us to believe: neither was I! Many times I had discovered her drinking from bottles carefully hidden around the cottage. This exacerbated her behaviour to animalistic proportions, bouts of which I would later experience.

The quietness of the private baroque chapel in the east wing directed one's senses to the magnificence of the venue, with its fine wall paintings, architecture and sculptures. The brasses at the altar gleamed. Papa, to my left, held my hand tenderly, while Edith and John, to my right, offered love and support in what was an emotional setting. Sir Oliver, his wife and her sons, Alexander and Benedict, were also in attendance, as were two of Mama's closest friends from the music world. It was an intimate gathering. Father Pierre conducted the service. As it ended, a quiet tranquillity filled the chapel and I realised Mama was finally at peace from her suffering. There was a feeling of spiritual uplift which helped me through the day, and I prayed silently that Mama's soul was finally at rest.

The church of St Michael the Archangel bore witness to the most wonderful musical celebration of Mama's life. Violins, horns, a double bass, oboes – all the members of the symphony orchestra who had accompanied her at so many of her concerts were in attendance. The church rang out with music of a bygone age whose appeal remained timeless. There were readings by friends, poems by farm workers and scriptures read by the children of estate workers. I played one of Mama's favourite pieces of music, accompanied by Sir Oliver on violin. The congregation focused on every single note. It was mesmerising and emotional, and I thought I detected tears in Sir Oliver's eyes.

Mama was laid to rest under an oak tree in the churchyard, close to the graves of members of the Harrington family. I dropped a single 'Peace' rose from our garden on to the coffin and whispered, 'Goodbye, Mama. May you rest in peace.'

She was gone but her memory would live on in the hearts and minds of so many people. For me it would live on in my heart for always and in my music too. Mama was one very special person.

Chapter Three

'Alberto, I do not think you will require Miss O'Connor any longer. Do you?'

Sir Oliver confronted Papa as he arrived at the Hall to hear me practise on piano.

'I have been thinking about this myself, Oliver. It is important Sophia has a woman about the place when she arrives home from school, someone who will nurture her as Anna did.'

That someone was not Maura O'Connor! I loathed the woman, but was too frightened to speak out for fear of retribution when Papa was not at home.

'I see!' said Sir Oliver, puffing on his pipe. He murmured, 'Very well. I will have words with her and renew her contract for another six months. We will see how the situation progresses.'

Papa looked extremely pleased at the turn of events but I fumed inside at the thought of having to live with Maura for another second. She had two faces: one for the outside world and one for me! Men were putty in her hands but I could see through her façade.

A few months slipped by. I had no choice but to follow her demands and instructions implicitly. Bedtime was at seven o'clock. Food was scarce, whereas Papa ate well. He was generous with his money. I could only assume she spent what money I should have had for my food, on drink. Most of my spare time was passed in my bedroom. I played outside, alone, only on rare occasions, and did more than my fair share around the house. Maura hated any attention Papa bestowed on me and did her utmost to cause a rift between us. My only haven was during piano and guitar practice, which Papa occasionally taught me. I missed my mama terribly. I found kindness and affection in the presence of Edith when I managed to steal away from Maura. I was too frightened to tell her about Maura's drinking or about her dislike and punishment of me. I said nothing and kept all thoughts silently hidden within, but an unbearable situation was just about to rear its ugly head.

The announcement came from out of the blue. I couldn't have contemplated a more disastrous fate for myself, and Papa. I had been to Sunday mass, at Maura's insistence, at the private baroque chapel. There was only a small, intimate congregation, comprising Sir Oliver, his wife and her sons, Papa, Maura, me and several estate workers. Father Pierre was most gracious, enquiring after my welfare and how I was coping with the sad loss of Mama. He was a warm-hearted man with a pleasing, caring personality. He had considerable humanity toward his flock and was exceedingly approachable.

We hurried along to the cottage after mass. I helped Maura in the kitchen, but considered myself in the way as she agitatedly pushed past me. On completion of all the necessary food preparations, I joined my Papa in the sitting room.

'Sophia, I want you to sit here with me. There are things I need to explain to you.'

I stared at him as he patted the cushions for me to rest against. It was good; Papa and I were alone for once, but in no time we had been joined by Maura.

'Will you tell her, Alberto, or will I?'

He looked at Maura scornfully and muttered, 'Leave it to me!'

She sat on a chair in front of me, her arms folded menacingly across her chest. I wondered what was happening, but at least I knew she would soon be gone. Her six month contract had almost expired.

'What is it, Papa?' I asked, fearful of what was to come.

'Well, Sophia,' he said, 'Mama, God rest her soul, has now been gone six months. Dear Maura has looked after us exceptionally well, hasn't she?'

He gazed into my eyes, but I looked at the floor with no intention of praising the spiteful, manipulative woman.

'I miss Mama so much,' I said, tears welling up in my eyes.

'I know, Sophia, darling. That is why I have made a decision which is going to affect the rest of our lives.'

As I lifted my head, I recognised a smirk on Maura's face!

'I have asked Maura to become my wife and a dear mother to you!'

The words stabbed at me like a knife penetrating my heart. How could Papa possibly believe she could replace my mama? She shot me an evil glance. I was terrified of her.

'Please, Papa. You cannot do this! *No, Papa! No!*' I sobbed and dashed for the door.

Through my tears I ran until I could run no further. I charged across the footpath, straight in front of Sir Oliver on his horse, Caesar. He brought the horse to an abrupt halt, dismounted and tied the reins to a tree. I launched myself at a bank of wild flowers and sobbed. Sir Oliver stared down, not knowing how to approach me or what to say. He lifted me into his arms and returned to Caesar, who was snorting and agitated at being tethered.

'Sit here, Sophia!' he instructed and lifted me onto the saddle of the horse, then mounted it himself. He rode toward the stables, where his trustworthy stable lad, Jimmy, took Caesar. Sir Oliver dismounted and lifted me carefully down.

'Come with me, Sophia,' he said, leading me by the hand to the Hall.

Alexander came to greet us and was instructed to hurry to Starbeck Cottage and inform Papa I was safely at the Hall. Inside, Sir Oliver summoned Lady Harrington. Together they joined me in the drawing room, offering me milk and biscuits, which I readily consumed. Hunger took over from my emotions.

'Now, Sophia, what on earth is wrong?' Sir Oliver asked.

'It is Papa, Sir; he is going to marry Maura!'

'Marry Miss O'Connor? Are you sure?' He seemed shaken by the announcement.

'Yes. He told me this morning!'

'And you are naturally upset...' he said thoughtfully.

'Yes, I am, sir. *I hate her!*'

'That is an awful thing to say, Sophia!' reproached Lady Harrington.

'She is an awful woman!' I sniped back.

Sir Oliver looked at me and asked, 'In what way, Sophia?'

I was at the mercy of Maura. She would severely punish me if I uttered one word against her. 'She just is,' I whined.

'It must be dreadful, having lost your beloved mama, but you need a woman in the house. Maura will be a stabilising influence. I am sure you will get used to the situation in time.'

Why was he taking her side?

'She will *never* be my mother! Mama was good and kind. I want her back!' I sobbed.

'We all wish she were here, Sophia,' Sir Oliver replied sympathetically.

'Yes, Oliver, but all the changes, all the emotional upheaval, cannot have been a pleasant thing for the child. I remember when Douglas died. It was such a traumatic time for Alexander. Sophia must be feeling so vulnerable and lost.'

Lady Harrington had challenged her husband's mode of thinking and appeared concerned for my feelings.

'Look, this is getting us nowhere,' he snapped. 'Sophia,' he said, looking at me and twirling his moustache between thumb and forefinger, 'I am afraid you are going to have to be a good girl. Try to see the situation for what it is. You will be fed and cared for, and I will see you are found a reputable piano teacher to further your musical career. Dry your tears. Be a pleasant girl for Papa!'

As I departed, I heard Lady Harrington say, 'It is far too early for Alberto to take another wife.'

'I agree, but what can we do? It is his choice. I cannot imagine how he thinks he will ever replace Anna.'

I walked to Starbeck Cottage, thinking of Mama and how cross she would have been that I was at the mercy of Maura; but I had to learn to be on my best behaviour from now on. On my return, Papa took me under his wing. By suppertime he had convinced me his forthcoming marriage was in both our best interests.

The wedding of Maura and Papa was a subdued affair. He wore a dark suit; she was in a pale green and white outfit with a bouquet of spring flowers. Unfortunately I could not attend due to an extreme headache, which unexpectedly disappeared shortly after the ceremony began. They honeymooned in Scarborough for a few days. I stayed with Edith and John, who treated me with extreme kindness. There were times when I wanted to confide in them as to the nature of the beast, Maura, but was too terrified to do so. They took me to a piano recital in Leeds, which was an absolute treat; but all good things must come to an end and in no time Maura and Papa had returned. I was ecstatic at seeing Papa but devastated at the return of my new stepmother. She asked in front of Papa that I call her 'Mother'. No way would I grant her request. I would die first. Papa resumed work immediately on his violins. I was thankful I was at school during the day and had only a short time during the evenings to contend with her presence. Maura began going through the contents of the cottage with a fine-tooth comb, removing anything of Mama's she could find.

One afternoon, on returning from school, I found Maura in the garden. A bonfire was blazing. She was attending to it. I arrived as the last few items were alight but took little notice. Later in the evening, after piano practice, Papa and I decided to plant a row of seeds in the garden at the rear of the cottage. We would grow Mama's favourite flowers, which, when fully grown, would be cut for her grave. Papa collected tools from the garden shed as I opened the seed packets.

'Sophia! *Come here immediately!*' shouted Papa. He was angry as he emerged from his shed, clutching numerous papers. 'What do you know about these?' he demanded, pushing musical scores and torn photographs at me.

I was speechless. All Mama's treasured sheet music had been torn to shreds and her photographs were defaced. Looking at the carnage, I could see photos of Mama, taken by press photographers when in concert, or with Papa.

'Well, Sophia, do you know anything about these?'

'No, Papa, nothing!' I declared, absolving myself from any blame.

'Someone does!' he said and marched into the cottage to address the situation with Maura. They were obviously the items she had been burning on my return from school. My presence had prevented her from finishing that which she had set out to do. I heard a loud exchange of words before Papa reappeared, looking enraged.

'You are a naughty, naughty girl, Sophia! How could you lie to me? Maura has informed me that on returning from the village shops she found you tearing up these items. When she approached you, you threw a fit and stated you never want to play piano again. Is this true?'

'No, Papa! *No!*' I could feel my cheeks burning with anger that Maura had the audacity to make such accusations. It was obvious she had every intention of trying to turn Papa against me, and she was succeeding.

'I don't believe you, Sophia! Maura tells me she tried to burn the evidence so as not to get you into trouble!'

'It is *not* true, Papa. I haven't *touched* them!'

'I know you are hurting inside, Sophia, and do not approve of me marrying Maura, but acting like this to get attention is not the way forward. I am prepared to forgive you this time, as you have been through so much, but this behaviour must end!'

I stood silent but infuriated.

'Now go! Get ready for bed. I do not want to hear another word from you. *Go!*'

I turned on my heels and fled into the cottage.

'Sophia, dear!' Maura stretched out her arms, sneering as she did so. I rushed past her, ascending the stairs like a bat out of hell.

'You see, Alberto,' I heard her say, 'I try so hard to be a loving mother but she just won't cooperate!'

'Calm down, Maura. She will come round eventually,' he soothed.

I lay on the bed, thumping my pillow, chanting, 'Evil old witch, evil old witch!'

I would not cry. I could not cry. Every tear I possessed had dried up.

Later that week, Papa and Maura were to attend a violin concert for a charitable cause, in Leeds. This was an exceptionally glitzy occasion, with dinner to follow. Maura was ecstatic at the invitation and spent all day trying to look beautiful. Mama would not have had to spend time on her appearance; she was a natural beauty. At six o'clock, Maura descended the stairs in a ravishing white sequined gown. On closer inspection I realised it was one of Mama's designer gowns she had worn at a piano recital. Papa looked superb in a dark suit, white shirt and bow tie. The realisation that Maura was wearing clothing of Mama's suddenly dawned, and the expression on his face was enough to freeze the North Sea.

'*Take the gown off!*' he demanded. 'It's not yours to wear!'

She fumed. An argument ensued, and neither of them attended the concert. Maura walked out in temper and Papa retreated to his workshop, taking me with him.

A frosty atmosphere in the cottage lasted several days, but the arrival of Papa with a gold necklace, matching earrings and a huge bunch of flowers, accompanied by a profound apology, saw them conversing once more. Days later I watched Maura load all Mama's beautiful gowns into cases and take a taxi to town, where she offloaded them at a pawn shop. The money received bought a green sequined dress and numerous bottles of spirits.

On occasions I would secretly venture to Doggett's Barn, Papa's workshop. It was a marvellous experience watching him craft violins. Wood from the spruce, willow, maple, pear and poplar was carefully stored. Violins for repair lay on the workbench in various stages of careful reconstruction. New violins were completed with the utmost dexterity and precision. Papa played for me and we laughed and had fun, unbeknown to Maura. I loved those precious moments, but they were few. On my last visit, Papa coughed continuously and I was worried for his health. He had looked ashen-faced of late and seemed continually tired. The violins Papa crafted sounded magnificent. He would hang them for at least a month in the workshop before parting with them. He explained that during this time his soul would enter the instrument, making it very special to play. I truly believed him and considered, as did so many others, that he was the greatest violin maker in the country.

When I managed to escape from my stepmother's clutches, I would walk to the nearby lake, sit on the bank and watch the fishermen cast their lines, waiting for a bite. Today was the exception, for there were no fishermen, only the glimpse of three boys playing in the distance, teasing one another and having fun. I sat and watched them for a while. As they drew closer, I recognised the older boys as Sir Oliver's stepsons. I had briefly set eyes on them at the Hall but did not recognise the younger one. The oldest boy walked toward me and spoke, saying, 'Hello, you are Sophia Bertucelli, aren't you?'

'Yes,' I shyly replied.

He held out his hand, saying, 'I am Alexander Hastings-Harrington. This is my brother, Benedict.'

I greeted them. Alexander was a moderately built, good-looking lad with blonde curly hair, vivid blue eyes and pale skin. He had the loveliest captivating smile and was eleven years of age. Benedict bore no resemblance to his brother whatsoever. He had brown straight hair, hazel eyes and a ruddy complexion. He was well built, and aged seven, like me. As I jumped up from the lakeside, Alexander extended his hand to help me to my feet, in a gesture of friendship.

'And this is our friend, Marcus Walker,' Alexander announced, pushing forward a sullen, bespectacled little lad with straight black hair, huge brown eyes and an attitude. 'He is living with us at the Hall for a while!' explained Alexander, and Benedict nodded in agreement.

I held out my hand, but Marcus put his hand behind his back and glared over his spectacles. He was an unhappy little child, seemed frightened and withdrawn, yet possessed a demeanour which could only be described as enchanting.

'I am afraid it's going to rain!' said Alexander, pointing to black clouds overhead. 'You may join us on the walk back to your cottage, if you wish.'

I nodded approval and pondered on how he knew where I lived. I followed in pursuit of the brothers, leaving Marcus dawdling behind, kicking anything in his path.

'I have seen you play piano at the Hall!' said Alexander, adding that he thought I was extremely competent. I thanked him, and was given to understand both he and Benedict attended the Grange Roman Catholic Boys' School as day boys, in the next village.

'Your father attends to all our musical instruments,' explained Alexander. 'Sir Oliver and I play violin. Your father has given me many lessons.'

I felt so proud of Papa.

'He is a wonderful craftsman. Father says no one in this country can make violins as superbly as he does,' Alexander observed, and I agreed.

We hurried along as rain began to fall. Alexander was an extremely friendly boy. Benedict said little, but agreed with his brother on all matters. Being an only child, I was shy, but Alexander had a great gift for making one feel completely at ease in his presence.

'Hurry up, Marcus. Keep up with us!' he pleaded. I turned to see the little one grumpily dragging his feet. 'Mrs Roberts will have tea ready and will not be pleased if we are late.'

Marcus dropped his head, peered nonchalantly over his spectacles and began kicking the grass underfoot. Suddenly the heavens opened and rain poured down. We rushed for the nearest tree. Turning round to help Marcus to shelter, I discovered he was nowhere to be seen.

'Alexander!' I screamed. 'Marcus isn't following us!'

We turned and together ran toward the lake, to see the small boy disappearing under the water, then reappearing, his arms waving frantically. Quickly and without thought I removed my cardigan and skirt and jumped into the water. All I knew was I had to rescue the little child, and immediately my life-saving skills, taught to me by the nuns at school, came into play. (The nuns were most determined we learnt these, as a pupil at school had drowned on a seaside holiday the previous year.) I swam strongly toward him, managed to grab his sweater and held on desperately. With my hand under his chin I raised his head above the water line. He was breathing but in a state of shock. I swam powerfully toward the bank. The two boys assisted in dragging Marcus out of the water and then me. Marcus, lying prostrate on the grassy bank, coughed and spluttered. I was so relieved he was alive, as were the boys. He lifted himself up and clung onto me as if his life depended upon it. He wouldn't allow Alexander or Benedict to fuss over him. Benedict, under instructions, returned to the Hall for help, while I removed the small boy's jumper. Alexander removed his own shirt for me to dry Marcus on and then wrapped him in my cardigan. He placed his little arms around my neck, sobbing. I sang, trying to calm him, but he wept into my cardigan repeatedly saying, 'Sorry, sorry!'

Sir Oliver appeared on the scene in record time, followed by two estate workers.

'Damn you, Alex! I told you Marcus was to stay at home!' screeched Sir Oliver. 'Don't you listen to a word I say?'

'I apologise, Father, but he wanted to join us. I am sorry!'

'In future, damn well do as you're asked. He could have drowned. What would your mother have done? It would have killed her! She and I have a huge responsibility for this boy!'

Alexander shrugged his shoulders, looked totally embarrassed, and apologised once again. He immediately departed with his stepfather close on his heels. No one recognised the fact I existed through the entire trauma, or that I was drenched in lake water. A worker took Marcus from my arms and carried him sobbing up to the Hall. He turned around to look at me and held out an arm, but I shook my head and blew him a kiss. That was my first meeting with the boys of Harrington Hall. Although it left its mark, I cannot say I was impressed by the episode.

Papa was in bed, asleep, when I arrived home. He had suffered chest infections and coughed continuously, but refused to see the doctor. Maura, on her usual good form, ranted and raved at me as she ripped off my wet clothing in the outhouse, which was attached to the cottage. She took Papa's leather belt to me which hung on the wall and punished me for returning home wet. I gritted my teeth, determined I would not show her how deeply she hurt me. She would not allow me to explain what had happened. Beatings were one of her more severe forms of physical punishment.

'Tell Papa what I have done and I won't just beat you next time, I'll kill you! You evil child. The devil is after your soul!'

I was so frightened that I crept to my bed, without tea, my back and buttocks sore from the belt. I buried my head in the pillow but would not allow myself to cry. If Mama had been there she would have taken me in her arms, praising me, but she wasn't. I was at the mercy of the wretched woman. I hated her! She took great care to leave marks where they would not be seen. I tried to visualise Mama's angelic face, but could see nothing but Maura looming over me. I hid my face under the sheet and eventually fell asleep.

Sunday morning arrived. Papa was feeling decidedly brighter and arose early. The bedroom door swung open and there stood Maura. She closed the door quietly and sat on the edge of my bed. I hoped she had come to apologise, but her face had a thunderous look.

'Listen here!' she dictated, waving her finger in my face. 'You will stay in bed today! No arguments! You will keep well covered and say nothing to your papa, except that you are tired. Do you hear me?'

I whispered an incoherent, 'Yes.'

'Do you hear what I am saying?' she repeated, 'Or you know what will happen. One word to your papa…'

'*Yes*!' I said, raising my voice.

The door opened and Papa stood in the entrance. I was so relieved to see his handsome smiling face although he appeared tired and pale.

'Maura tells me you were off-colour when you arrived home yesterday afternoon and you were wet.'

'I was, Papa,' I replied feebly. 'I am staying in bed today,' I pulled the bedclothes up around my neck. Papa moved forward to kiss me, but Maura stood in the way.

'Leave her, Alberto. Let her rest!' She ushered him out of the room.

I was confined to bed, at her mercy.

Papa was different now. I reflected on the days when I was younger. We would play games, have fun and he would rough up my hair, take me in his arms and sing me to sleep. Now, the only contact I had was when he gave me guitar and piano lessons during the week. He taught me the repertoire he had learnt from Grandpapas Tipaldi and Bertucelli in his youth. Papa constantly commented that I was a natural musician, but I did not fully understand his comments. All I knew was I treasured those precious moments we shared together. Maura was determined to destroy even those.

Lunch consisted of a morsel and was served in my room on a tray. It left me with feelings of immense hunger, having missed supper the previous evening. This state of affairs was now my regular way of life. After lunch I heard voices at the front door as Maura answered the knock.

'She is in bed, unwell!' I heard her arrogant voice say.

'I am so sad to hear this, but if we could have a word with her, it would please us greatly!'

I recognised the voice as that of Sir Oliver.

'She is not having visitors!' Maura insisted.

'If she is ill after yesterday's episode we must fetch Doctor Marsden.' Sir Oliver was extremely firm in his reply.

'I am a nurse, and know what is best for Sophia!' Maura said.

I heard the voice of Alexander exclaim, 'Yes, but Doctor Marsden knows better!'

For one moment Maura was actually at a loss for words. 'Well, you may come and see her for a moment, but only a moment!'

Maura had succumbed to the Harringtons. She dashed ahead, climbing the stairs two at a time. On entering the room she shot a glance at me that said it all. *Say nothing or else…*

I huddled under the sheet and blankets as the Squire, Alexander and Marcus entered the room. Marcus made a beeline for my bed, climbed up and placed his arms around my neck.

'*Get down, Marcus!*' Sir Oliver's loud voice sent Marcus crashing to the floor. He dusted himself off and stood quietly with Alexander.

'Well, what have you to say to Sophia?' He addressed his question gruffly at Marcus.

'Thank you, Soapy!' he said as he tried to get his tongue around my name. I wanted to smile, but Sir Oliver immediately corrected him. 'Her name is Sophia!'

Try as he may he could not pronounce my name. I insisted it was fine for him to call me 'Soapy'.

'I am so thankful you are fine after yesterday, Marcus,' I said.

He looked shyly over a different pair of spectacles to those he had lost in the lake and hid behind Alexander. Alexander moved forward, saying, 'You were extremely brave yesterday. We wanted to bring you this present. Here, Sophia, this is from the family to say thank you. We hope you will like it and always wear it. It was our stepgrandmother's and is very special.'

His eyes sparkled. His manners were impeccable. I opened the box. An old, solid gold locket faced me. Alexander opened it for me and it took the shape of a shamrock. Inside were photographs of Sir Oliver, Marcus, Benedict and Alexander. It was one of the loveliest gifts I had ever received. I thanked them graciously saying, 'It is beautiful. I will always wear it! I will treasure it for ever!'

Sir Oliver moved forward and fastened the locket around my neck.

'Wear it with pride, young lady. It was a wonderful thing you did yesterday, saving young Marcus. Lady Mary and I will always be grateful to you.'

'Saving the boy? What is this about?' Maura's inquisitiveness had got the better of her.

'Did Sophia not tell you? She saved Marcus from drowning in the lake yesterday.' Sir Oliver looked straight into her green, glaring eyes. For a moment Maura was unable to speak. Then she escorted the family to the door, explaining that I needed to rest.

'Before I forget, Sophia, I am having a birthday party next week,' Alexander explained. 'You will come, won't you?'

'I would love to,' I said.

'We will send you an invitation.'

'I doubt she will be able to attend!' said Maura. 'Sophia has so many things that she does and will have so little time.'

'But you must come. We insist!' said Alexander. 'We will look forward to your attendance.'

'Yes, young lady. The party will not have the same impetus if you are not there,' explained Sir Oliver, as he opened the door to remove himself from the room. 'Come on, Alexander. You too, Marcus! We will see you at the party next week, Sophia!'

As quickly as they had arrived, unannounced, they departed. Marcus waved from the door and they were gone.

Chapter Four

Papa had tried his utmost to ensure I looked respectable and was worthy to attend the birthday party at Harrington Hall, but as usual he and Maura had words.

'The child should not be attending frivolous birthday parties at her age. They are not her kind of people,' Maura snarled.

'It would be most impolite – no, downright rude – for Sophia to refuse the invitation,' retorted Papa.

He had made his point. Papa had sent Maura to buy me a dress we had spotted in a shop in town. It was dark green velvet, finished with a white Peter Pan collar and sporting a green satin sash tied in a large bow at the back. It was enhanced by my Latin-black, wavy hair, which cascaded over my shoulders. With my new white socks and black patent shoes I thought how proud Mama would have been of me. I was so excited at being able to attend Alexander's birthday party. To complement the outfit, I wore my locket with pride. I viewed myself in the long mirror in my bedroom and was extremely elated by what I saw.

As I stood in the Screens Hall, tightly clutching my birthday gift, wrapped in decorative paper, I heard Sir Oliver's austere voice ring out in my direction.

'Hello, Sophia! We are so thrilled you could attend the party. Do come this way!' and he escorted me into the Great Hall. I was nervous but he soon made me feel at ease by commenting, 'What a beautiful dress, Sophia! You are as pretty as a picture!'

I blushed, but thanked him. The Hall had been tastefully decorated with balloons and bunting. A large sign said:

HAPPY BIRTHDAY ALEXANDER

Tables were laid with a magnificent assortment of food and a chair had been placed for each child. I was certainly going to eat well on this occasion. Children had gathered in a swarm. Looking around I could see no one I knew, until Ben and Marcus arrived. They escorted me to sit with them at the table. Alexander was nowhere to be seen. I settled myself comfortably on the chair. Suddenly everyone stood, and in walked Alexander, extremely smart in grey trousers, white shirt and a red bow tie, his blonde curly hair immaculately groomed. The children sang a chorus of 'Happy Birthday to You'. I took it upon myself to leave my chair and walked to where he was standing, clutching the birthday gift I had brought for him. I trembled as all the children stared. I wanted so much to give him the present Papa had kindly obtained for me. He looked at me intently with his soft blue eyes penetrating mine and smiled a captivating smile.

'A present?' he enquired.

'F-f-for you,' I stuttered, my mouth dry with nerves.

'How kind of you, Sophia! What on earth can it be?' he asked, shaking the package.

'Have a look! I am sure you will like it!'

He undid the wrappings to an audience of children gathered around asking, 'What is it? What is it?'

Finally reaching the box, he stared at the labelling and the contents.

'Rolling stock!' he exclaimed. 'Look, Father! Sophia has given me rolling stock for my trains. How thoughtful of you! How on earth did you know I had model trains?'

Oliver Harrington moved to his stepson's side to view the present, which impressed him greatly.

'My papa asked Sir Oliver what your hobbies were,' I explained.

'Thank you so much, Sophia!' called Alexander as I was escorted to my chair by a servant.

'What a charming child she is!' I heard Sir Oliver say to Alexander, but I did not hear the reply.

The party was an enormous success. Marcus insisted on shakily passing plates of food in my direction and consumed large quantities himself. The games were different to any I had known. A clown arrived to make us laugh and entertain everyone. A magician also attended, and performed the most amazing tricks with doves, paper flowers and rabbits pulled from a hat. I really couldn't understand how on earth he did such extraordinary things, but I enjoyed every moment of the afternoon. It was a wonderful party, and I certainly did not wish to return to the cottage. As the children departed, Sir Oliver asked if I would stay for a while, as he wished to speak to me. Alexander, Benedict, Marcus and Sir Oliver remained in the Screens Hall while Lady Harrington disappeared for a short while to organise staff.

'Sophia, I wondered if you would play a piece of music before you depart. My wife has not heard your great gift in action. It would please her greatly. We would all enjoy it.'

'Yes, Sir, I will play for you,' I said.

He led the group to the grand piano in the Great Hall. The room was by now immaculate. Staff had worked laboriously to make sure every trace of the party had been removed. Lady Harrington appeared and she, the Squire and the boys, seated themselves comfortably to listen to my repertoire. I looked around and observed two large glass cases, containing a collection of magnificent old violins, some of which had been crafted by my Italian ancestors. The grand piano Mama had frequently played stood gleaming from the care and attention it had received. The Great Hall had a vast amount of my family's influence in it. It seemed to penetrate every aspect of the superb room, and I could feel the atmosphere surrounding me.

'What would you like me to play for you?' I asked, feeling nervous at being viewed by people awaiting my performance.

'Alex, while Sophia prepares herself, can you fetch Edith and John Roberts? I am sure they would like to hear Sophia play too.'

Alexander retreated to find my dear friends.

'What shall I play?' I asked once more.

'I will leave the decision to you, Sophia,' Sir Oliver replied.

I seated myself on the piano stool, preparing for my performance in mind and spirit, just as Mama had taught me. Sir Oliver seemed mesmerised by me as I sat there. From the corner of my eye I observed his eyes fixed on my every movement. It was almost as though he had seen a ghost. Edith and John hurried into the Great Hall and were instructed to sit between the boys. There was silence. You could hear a pin drop. I announced I would play a piece of music Mama had taught me, which was close to her heart. I began to play the *Moonlight Sonata*, which I had practised so intently since her passing. I knew it to be a favourite of Sir Oliver's too. I was not as note perfect as Mama, but I knew I had mastered it to a great degree. Mama had always insisted I put my soul into every piece I played. Then without warning, Sir Oliver pushed his chair backwards and fled from the Hall as though ill. I carried on playing, as Mama would have. At the end of my performance, everyone except Lady Harrington, who had gone to attend to her husband, clapped and called, 'Encore!' But I was anxious for Sir Oliver, and said I could play no more. I received praise and rose to ten feet tall, but I hurried from the room in the hope I could find him.

I bumped into Lady Harrington and asked about Sir Oliver's condition.

'He is fine, Sophia. He seems to think he ate something at lunch which may have upset him.'

I acknowledged her explanation, but knew differently. It was my choice of music that had upset him. It was the last piece Mama had played for him. He was grieving for her as much as I was. Her friendship must have meant a great deal to him. I tinkered a little on the piano and Marcus joined me, toying with the keys; but without warning Sir Oliver returned, made a beeline for the piano and abruptly closed the lid. Fortunately Marcus and I managed to retrieve our fingers.

The look of disappointment on little Marcus's bespectacled face was upsetting, but I instantly realised that Sir Oliver and young Marcus had very little rapport with one another, and the Squire had no patience with this free spirit.

Papa was sleeping soundly next morning while I made myself presentable for the first day of the school week. Maura insisted I did not disturb him as he'd had a restless night, coughing and with chest pains. I ran for the school bus, which waited for me on the corner of Baker's Lane. I was anxious in my mind, knowing all was not well with Papa. I did not want to leave him but Maura ordered me to attend school. I concentrated very little on lessons, and Sister Phoebe took a ruler to my knuckles when I could not answer an English literature question that had been directed at me, my mind being at Starbeck Cottage. The other pupils thought it hilarious, me being made a laughing stock. I was angry and intimidated. With the painful punishment over, I dashed at full speed out of the classroom. How would I get home? I didn't know, but was not prepared to stay. I heard Sister Phoebe's voice shouting, 'Come back here!' as I passed by Sister Brigit and Sister Clara in the corridor. Sister Brigit tried to grab me as I ran, but I would not be caught. I could not stay in the building a moment longer to be hurt and humiliated.

I had enough problems at home. I hated the whole world at that precise moment, and wanted desperately to see Papa and know all was well; but I could not brush away the traumatic feelings of hopelessness I encountered within myself concerning his immediate welfare. I needed to know if he was recovering from the coughing fit he had experienced during the night. I ran, finally reaching the town centre, trying to decide how I could travel home, when I spotted Peter Smyth, a farm worker from the estate, in his truck. He had been collecting horse feed from a local warehouse. I managed to draw attention to my plight by waving my arms frantically in the air. He noticed me and pulled his truck over to the side of the road.

'What are you doin', lass?' he enquired. 'Shouldn't you be in school?'

'Please, Peter, take me to Starbeck Cottage!' I begged.

'Get in, Sophia!'

He opened his door and jumped out and lifted me into the passenger seat. 'You're in a hurry, lass!' he said, a questioning expression on his rugged face.

'I need to get home to see Papa!' I explained that he'd had a distressing night.

'I see.' He looked at me and said, 'I saw Doctor Marsden's car at your cottage this morning. Your papa can't be at all well.'

'I expect Sir Oliver sent for the doctor. He is the Squire's private physician. I am so worried, Peter.'

He engaged gear. We moved off in the direction of Harrington Hall and travelled swiftly through the town and down country lanes, gathering momentum, until we turned into Baker's Lane and the gatehouse to the Hall. Peter Smyth thrust his foot on the brake, sending me flying toward the dashboard.

'Sorry, lass,' he said, and had the presence of mind to prevent me from hitting the windscreen by placing his left arm across my chest. An ambulance, bell clanging, rushed past us, and I shouted, 'Papa! Papa!' I knew in my heart they were taking him to hospital. I turned to look at the ambulance but it had disappeared from view.

Outside the cottage, I alighted from the truck and thanked Peter, who shouted, 'Take care, lass!' and seemed genuinely anxious for me. Doctor Marsden's car was parked by the gate. I ran up the path and opened the door. I was hot and trembling. My heart was beating in my throat. Maura stood in the room and greeted me with, 'How did you get home so quickly? It is not long since Sir Oliver sent a car to fetch you.'

I did not intend explaining the circumstances to 'the dragon'.

'Where has my papa gone?' I protested.

Doctor Marsden approached me, taking my hands in his. 'I have to tell you, Sophia, your papa has been taken to a sanatorium on the coast, near Whitby. I am fairly sure he has tuberculosis. Lots of tests are going to be carried out on Papa, you and Maura. Firstly, I will need to examine your chest and breathing by listening to your lungs with my stethoscope,' he explained. 'Then you will have X-rays.'

'Is this all necessary, Doctor?' exclaimed Maura, wringing her hands on her dress.

'I am afraid so,' he insisted. He examined us there and then. Maura, for her part, cooperated with him. With his inspection of her over, his warm eyes and calm expression concentrated on me.

'The child is all right! I would know if she had any problems!' Maura said nervously. 'As you can see, she is full of energy. I would soon be aware if all was not well.'

My stepmother appeared anxious and erratic in her behaviour.

'If I may be so bold, Maura, you did not exactly notice the deterioration in Alberto that you should have. I am sorry, but it is extremely important that I examine Sophia.'

He looked caringly at me and said, 'Please be a good girl and remove your top clothing!'

I removed the things he requested and stood shyly with my arms folded across my chest.

'Goodness! What on earth has happened to you, young lady?' Simon Marsden's face was grim. His eyes looked as though they would pop out of their sockets.

'Where on earth did you get all those bruises and marks?' he asked, viewing my thin damaged frame.

Maura interrupted, saying, 'She fell downstairs – didn't you, Sophia?'

I nodded, knowing it was a lie.

'Look at the stairs!' she said, pointing. 'We've all tumbled down them at one time or another. They are extremely dangerous. Sir Oliver needs to do something, before one of us has a fatal accident.'

The doctor asked me to breathe in and out slowly and then hold my breath while he put the cold stethoscope on my back. I tried to do as requested, but he could see I had discomfort and was having difficulty in carrying out those tasks.

'Did you fall down the stairs, Sophia?' he asked looking at me with a deep frown on his solemn face. His large, honest eyes fixed on me. I could not make eye contact with him and stared at the floor as I whispered, 'Yes, sir, I did.' I was confused and scared. The devil was after my soul. I would go to hell if I lied to the doctor and be in absolute hell if I didn't. Hell seemed the lesser of two evils.

'Fair enough!' he said, but his tone did not reflect a jot of belief in what I said. He took samples of blood and left, stating he would organise chest X-rays for us. The samples would be tested immediately.

'Doctor Marsden, can I see Papa?' I asked, tears forming in my eyes.

'Not yet, Sophia! Tuberculosis is a very infectious disease. Hopefully we have caught it in time to halt its progress. When your papa is stronger and *you* have been given the all-clear – and I stress this – you *may* be able to visit. Let us wait for the outcome of all tests, shall we?'

I wanted to see Papa so much, just to see his attractive face, his smile and to hear his gentle voice. I began to cry. Strange though it may seem, Maura was actually pleasant to me, but I felt it was a show of togetherness for the sake of the doctor.

She did not seem too bothered that Papa was in hospital, and I couldn't understand why. Maura frequently drank, but Papa was wonderful to her, pandering to her every whim. I would try to reciprocate with caring feelings toward her. Perhaps she would continue to respond in a like manner. Little did I know I was stepping into the lion's den as I had done so many times in the past.

After ten days, Maura and I received the all-clear from tests and X-rays, but were informed we would need three-monthly check-ups. It was then Alexander arrived at the cottage to enquire as to my state of health. Benedict accompanied his brother and brought a delightful bunch of flowers for me. I was so enthralled to see the boys. For once I could not stop chatting to them.

Papa was making slow progress. I knew he was having excellent care taken of him, generously paid for by Sir Oliver. With such excellent news I began to feel extreme relief. Maura, by now, often encouraged me to walk out with the boys and insisted on one occasion that I did not return for two hours, while she did housework. We meandered along the path toward the woods and Alexander asked after my papa. I explained he was slowly improving.

'My father,' remarked Alexander, 'considers your papa to be one of his most trusted and respected friends, and misses him greatly.'

'My papa is wonderful!' I reiterated.

Benedict, Alexander and I threw stones into the beck, skimming the water, a favourite pastime of ours. Alexander took me to one side, out of earshot of Benedict.

He said, 'Are you happy living with Maura, Sophia?'

'Yes!' I quickly replied, but not convincingly, wondering why he had asked and what would transpire next.

'Doctor Marsden came to see Father. I am afraid I eavesdropped on the conversation. I heard him tell Father he was extremely worried about you. He said you had weals and bruises over a great part of your body. You had told him you had fallen downstairs, but Simon is not convinced!'

I turned sheepishly away.

'You see, Sophia, if you are having problems, you can always talk to me. I would like to think we are the best of friends. My parents, my brother, Marcus and I, well, we all like you so much and...'

'I am all right Alexander, *really*!' I insisted.

I walked off in the opposite direction not wanting further questions fired at me. I was far too afraid to answer for fear of what Maura would do. 'I am going home, back to the cottage!' I announced. I ran along the path and reached our gate. I turned to see Alexander standing with his hands on his hips. I waved and he waved back, then I opened the door and went in. Maura was nowhere to be seen. I hunted in the kitchen, in the garden and the outhouse, where the dreadful belt hung. I re-entered the cottage and climbed the stairs, suddenly disturbed by noises coming from the parent bedroom. I opened the door and stood there, horrified at the scene confronting me. Maura, naked, lay across the bed. One of the farm workers I knew only as Greg was kneeling between her legs, kissing her breasts. He too was naked, apart from a gold chain dangling from his neck. He immediately stopped what he was doing. Maura leaned up on her elbows with such a look of hate in her eyes that I scurried to my bedroom and bolted the door. I had interrupted her once before in a similar situation with Papa, and unbeknown to him had received a beating. This time it was with another man, and I hated her!

I saw no more of her until nine o'clock in the evening. She barged against my bedroom door with such a force that it broke the small bolt. I was sleeping but woke startled and bewildered. She threw a huge jug of water over me. This time she was fully clothed and dragged me by my hair down the stairs to the outhouse. I screamed and pleaded but she beat me mercilessly. I crouched in the corner, trying to protect myself from the raining blows, my arms taking the brunt of her brutality. My nightdress showed signs of blood. Not satisfied with giving me the beating of my life, she locked me in the outhouse, screaming, 'If you ever breathe a word of what you saw to anyone…!'

Yes, I thought, I know, you will kill me! By then I felt as though she had almost succeeded. My body ached and bled. I was terrified. I buried my head in my burning arms and sobbed. Strands of my hair, which she had furiously pulled out, lay on the floor. I stayed there all night, cold, hungry and terrified.

Alexander called at the cottage on three consecutive days. Each time the excuse was that I was not well and had 'flu-like' symptoms, so I could not be allowed visitors. Maura could lie for England. On the fourth day, having not attended piano practice, or school, and being confined to bed, nursing my injuries, Maura found it necessary to make a trip to the village to collect some shopping. There was no food in the house, although minimal amounts had been given to me. She took off, on foot. I was threatened with another beating if I opened the cottage door to anyone. I crept out of bed immediately she had gone and viewed myself in the mirror. I was horrified at what I saw. I did not recognise myself. The injuries she had inflicted covered me from head to toe. Many bruises had become discoloured. Within five minutes of Maura leaving, I heard a noise on the window pane. Someone was throwing stones at the glass to attract my attention. I hid behind the closed curtains, peered through a gap in the centre and saw Alexander, accompanied by Marcus. I drew back from the window in the hope I had not been seen.

'I know you are there, Sophia! I am coming in!'

Alexander was determined, but I said, 'Go away! Please go away! I cannot see you!'

All appeared quiet. Then I heard the downstairs front sash windows squeaking. Alexander had prised opened the catch and pushed Marcus through. The little boy, under instruction, dragged a chair to the front door and stood on it, opening the latch to give Alexander access to the cottage. Once inside, they rushed up the stairs to my room. I will never forget, as long as I live, the look on Marcus's face. His jaw dropped and I could see tears brimming in his eyes. Alexander, his lip quivering, rushed to help. Every bone in my body ached and my flesh hurt when touched.

'Sophia! What on earth has your stepmother done to you? Marcus, go and fetch Sir Oliver immediately. Please hurry!'

Marcus, still in shock, tears rolling down his cheeks, turned on his heels, and holding the stair rail, carefully padded down the stairs. He did not attempt to open the door, but climbed through the open window, knocking over a plant in the process. He did not stop to attend to it, but rushed for help as instructed. Meanwhile Alexander bathed my wounds until his stepfather arrived. He was so gentle and caring.

'Maura did this, didn't she? Oh, Sophia, why didn't you tell us what was happening? We are your friends. We want to help you.'

All I could blurt out was, 'I couldn't. She would have killed me!'

'My father will not let her touch you. Not ever again! Wait until he sees what she has done.'

I did not know whether to be scared or relieved. Alexander suddenly brought calm into an otherwise manic life. He was so attentive and respectful of me.

Marcus reached the Hall and dived into the study, saying, 'Come, Sir. Soapy's got black things all over and blood!' he gasped. *'Come on!'* He took his godfather's hand, dragging him from his desk. Sir Oliver knew from the child's behaviour and tears that something needed his urgent attention. Summoning Lady Harrington, they all rushed back to Starbeck Cottage. I had never seen a man so enraged as his tall frame towered over me. Lady Harrington burst into tears as Marcus enveloped her legs with his tiny arms in an attempt to comfort her. I noticed a distinct twitch of Sir Oliver's moustache, which I recognised as anger. He picked me up gently from the bed, as if I were a china doll. With Lady Mary and the boys running behind, he strode across the lawn with me in his strong arms. The servants were called and pandered to every instruction.

Doctor Marsden was summoned, and I was comforted in the most sumptuous bedroom I'd ever seen. A four-poster bed stood regally in the room. Plush drapes hung from the top and sides. The servants were extremely kind, and in no time I realised they were there for my comfort and safety. Millie Dexter, a maid, was so distressed by my injuries that she began to cry. Sir Oliver took her to one side, bade her dry her tears and proceed with the job of making me comfortable. How wonderful it was to be away from 'the witch', who I detested! Sir Oliver asked me what had happened for me to have sustained such injuries. Alexander, fussing around with fresh drinks and fruit, said I should tell the truth. I did as he suggested. I explained I saw Maura and Greg on Papa's bed, with no clothes on. As a result, Maura had beaten me, leaving me all night in the outhouse. Then she confined me to bed for four days, with little to eat or drink. I related how she beat me for the least little thing, and often. Doctor Marsden provided the necessary medication and treatment. Sir Oliver and he spoke at length. Both were angry and upset at the state of affairs, the Squire all the more so because he considered he had failed in his promise to Mama to take good care of me.

Chapter Five

Sir Oliver Harrington was my first visitor the following morning, accompanied by his wife.

'How are you, Sophia?' he enquired, placing two tapestry chairs at the side of the bed. They sat and gave me their full attention, Lady Harrington viewing me through half-spectacles.

'Much better today, thank you, Sir!' I answered.

'Did you sleep well?' he asked, smoothing his moustache with thumb and forefinger.

'I did, thank you, Sir. This is a wonderful, comfy bed!' I announced stroking the luxurious covers.

'Comfortable, Sophia! Comfortable!' Lady Harrington corrected my pronunciation of the English language.

'Hush, dear!' Sir Oliver said, putting his wife firmly in her place. She gave him a coy smile. There were no points for guessing who was in charge in the Harrington household.

'We have good news for you, Sophia.' The Squire looked extremely pleased with himself. He related how he had waited for Maura's return from shopping to confront her about my ill-treatment. 'I told her that we knew everything concerning her behaviour towards you. She had the audacity to refuse to leave the cottage. When I insisted, she threatened to take you with her. After an exchange of extremely harsh words, I assured her that if she came within a mile of you I would not be responsible for my actions!'

'Where has she gone?' I pleaded, nervous that she would reappear in our lives.

'Back to Dublin! You will never have to worry about Maura again! She packed her cases and left early this morning. She has gone for good. Have no fear that she will trouble you again.'

Sir Oliver had organised her departure with tactical precision. No wonder he had been a Wing Commander in Bomber Command during the war.

'What is happening to Papa?' I enquired, asking for knowledge of his state of health.

'Well, I am afraid he does have tuberculosis, but he is having an operation tomorrow to remove the diseased part of his lung. He will recover in no time. You may stay with us, Sophia, until he returns home. Then you can join him at the cottage.'

I dearly wanted him home, but did not know if I could face the cottage again. I did not voice my fears to the Harringtons.

'We have decided against telling Alberto about Maura and your injuries until he is well on the way to recovery,' Lady Harrington informed me.

I toyed with the precious gold locket around my neck and cupped it in my hand. Perhaps it would bring Papa and I luck from now on.

'Please can you telephone the hospital and tell Papa I send my love?'

Lady Harrington readily agreed and scurried away to make the call, followed by Sir Oliver. So I could stay at the Hall until all was well with Papa. There would be delightful food, kind people and a comfortable bed. It appeared as though I had died and gone to heaven. I opened my locket and viewed the photographs. It would be jolly good fun having playmates so near. I would no longer be lonely. With these happy thoughts, I fell soundly asleep.

The day was warm and sunny. I was feeling considerably better. Millie Dexter prepared a reclining chair for me to laze on, in the knot garden. With a rug around my legs I looked every inch like someone's forgotten grandma as I basked in the sun's rays. I was joined by Alexander, who seemed to appear out of thin air. He looked uncomfortable and not his usual smiling self. A servant quickly produced a chair. He sat beside me, glancing at me and then at his shoes.

'Sophia!' He hesitated and focused on the ground. 'Sophia... oh, this really is no good! Father thought that as we are good friends, I should talk to you, but I... I really cannot do this.'

'Do what? What can't you do, Alexander?' I queried.

He lifted his head, his sad blue eyes focusing on me. He straightened his shoulders, trying to be as manly as possible. I wanted to smile, but he looked extremely serious. He took my hands in his. As I began to pull away he said, 'Please, Sophia. Do not make this situation more difficult than it already is. Father thought the news would be far better coming from me!'

'What news? You are talking in riddles, Alexander!'

He clutched my fingers tightly. 'It is about your papa,' he blurted out. 'He died last night!' His face was sombre as he delivered the news.

'*No, no*! He can't have! Don't be ridiculous! You've got it all wrong,' I pulled my hands away and shook my head frantically.

'Listen, Sophia! Your papa was much worse than they first thought. The operation was far more extensive than expected. He died in theatre! Please, please...'

I struggled up from the recliner, demented and ranting at the news. 'Papa has gone? *No!* It's not true!'

I repeated it over and over as I ran around the lawn like a headless chicken. My mind told me life would never be the same again. I did not know what would become of me. There would be no more Starbeck Cottage, no darling Papa. I wanted him with me so desperately. I needed to feel his loving arms around me. Maura was right: *I was a wicked girl*. That was why so many awful things were happening to me! The devil was after my soul. Feverishly, I pulled my locket from my neck and threw it across the lawn. I hated everything and everyone. I too wanted to die. I hit the ground with a great force.

When I awoke in my room, Sir Oliver, Lady Harrington and Doctor Marsden were peering down at me.

'Thank God you are all right,' muttered Sir Oliver, his wife nodding in approval that I was back in the land of the living.

'You gave everyone such a fright!' added Doctor Marsden.

My eyes were sore from crying and my heart ached even more. I did not wish to talk and made it obvious by hiding under the bedclothes. I surfaced when Sir Oliver announced that Papa's funeral would take place on the following Friday at the church in the grounds of Harrington Hall.

'Your papa requested to be buried alongside your mama. We are carrying out his last wishes. We thought it in your best interest that you do not attend, Sophia. You are not well enough.'

'Sir, *I want to go! I am going!*'

'Please, Sophia, it is not advisable,' said Lady Harrington. 'We can send your papa's favourite flowers on your behalf.'

'I do not want flowers sent,' I insisted. '*I want to go to his funeral. I must say goodbye to Papa!*'

Simon Marsden glanced at the Harringtons and nodded toward the door. They understood and beat a hasty retreat. Simon sat on my bed.

'I know you are upset, Sophia, but the Harringtons took your papa into their hearts. They paid all his medical bills and those of your darling mama. I feel you should at least try and behave sensibly toward them. This situation is not their fault, any more than it is yours. Try and be a reasonable girl, Sophia!'

'It *is* my fault! The devil is out to get me!' I sobbed.

'Who on earth filled your head with such rubbish?' Simon queried.

'Maura! And she's right! He's after me and all my loved ones!'

'Absolute nonsense! You can get those stupid thoughts out of your head *now*! I will talk to Sir Oliver and Lady Harrington and convince them you should go to your papa's funeral on Friday. I am asking you to be a brave and considerate girl. I know you are only eight, but I want you to be extremely grown-up for me!'

He kissed my forehead and was gone.

Friday arrived. The Harringtons had ordered me a dark blue dress which I wore with pride. I asked Alexander if he would take me to Starbeck Cottages. He agreed. I entered and tears overcame me. He comforted me with a friendly arm around my shoulder. I entered my old bedroom alone and hunted through my dressing table drawers. Maura had taken so many of my personal possessions; little things I held dear. She had not realised under the drawer's lining paper I had hidden Mama's last Christmas present to me. I removed it and placed it in my pocket. Alexander waited to escort me back to the Hall. As I turned around to view the sitting room, I noticed a piece of paper resting against an ornament. It was Maura's new address and a small note saying that one day I might possibly need her. There was no way I would need her, not in a million years! I tore the address and letter into tiny pieces and placed it in the bin.

Within minutes the funeral cortège arrived at the Hall. I entered the car with Sir Oliver, Lady Harrington and the boys. I thought it sad Marcus should have to accompany the family but his behaviour was impeccable for a small child. The Harrington influence, no doubt!

The requiem mass was very moving, with no sign of Maura, although she had been notified by Sir Oliver of Papa's sudden demise and the funeral arrangements. After the service we gathered around the grave side. Marcus handed me a red rose to place on the coffin. Then I dropped the small gold charm bracelet featuring six musical instruments (which Mama had given me as her last present) onto the coffin. It was all I had to give Papa as a token of my love. I stood tall, as Mama would have wished.

The Harringtons had arranged a wake at the Hall and many people attended.

Alexander, Benedict and Marcus were superb. Marcus followed me everywhere, holding my hand. This little three-year-old did not realise what comfort he gave me on such a sad day.

Edith caught my arm as I left the dining room one morning.

'Sophia, Sir Oliver wishes to speak to you in the study. Please hurry! They do not like to be kept waiting.'

I turned and walked swiftly to the study door. As soon as I knocked I was asked to enter.

'Hello, Sophia!' Sir Oliver greeted me, and Lady Harrington acknowledged my presence with a nod and a smile. I made myself comfortable on a chair in front of the desk.

'Are you happy here?' Sir Oliver asked, lighting his meerschaum pipe. He puffed clouds of smoke into the air.

'Very happy, Sir. Thank you both for your kindness.'

'Good!' he muttered, sending further clouds of smoke into an already laden atmosphere. 'I understand you do not like your school.'

'No, Sir,' I admitted.

'Umm!' He coughed. Lady Harrington glanced in his direction and handed him a glass of water. He sipped it and settled once more, appearing deep in thought.

'There have been arrangements to make on your behalf, Sophia. Before we make any final decisions concerning your future I would like to put some ideas to you.'

'What ideas, Sir?' I asked.

'You say you are happy here. How would you like to live here permanently with us?'

I could not believe my ears and shouted, '*Yes! Yes, please!*'

'That sounded like an enthusiastic answer!' he said, laughing at my response. 'Well, I think you can remain here and be part of this family, if you so wish,' he announced.

'Thank you, Sir! Oh, thank you! I cannot think of anywhere I would rather be. You are such wonderful people!'

Lady Harrington interrupted. 'We know you do not like the school which you presently attend. We are therefore arranging for you to be transferred to a small private Catholic school in the village. You will be a day girl. Will that please you?'

I nodded with great eagerness.

'Good! The school is small and is only a short distance from the Hall. Sir Oliver is on the committee. The teaching nuns are excellent! Music takes up a good part of the curriculum, so that will hopefully make you happy. I want you to come to us if you have any worries or problems. We will do our utmost to help. We are always here for you, Sophia!'

'Thank you, Lady Harrington,' I replied gratefully.

What a wonderful life I would have from now on! I was happy to the point of euphoria.

'Run along, Sophia! Leave us to sort out the necessary arrangements. We want you to have a happy life here. There are rules and regulations but I am sure there is nothing you cannot cope with. Bless you. Now, off you go!'

I removed myself from the chair and hurried to the door. All my Christmases had come at once. I was the happiest girl alive. The boys were waiting for me in the corridor and seemed aware I was to be part of the Harrington family. They were thrilled that I would be an element in their daily lives and Marcus, unable to reach my arms, clasped his arms around my legs in a gentle hug, letting me know he was as ecstatic as I was. I would be his playmate and friend.

Once I was integrated into the Harrington household, life changed dramatically. Millie Dexter, my maid, was assigned to assist with my daily routine. She was a sweet little thing; twenty-two years of age and courting one of the farm workers. Millie insisted on attending to my needs with great care and devotion. I adored her and found her extremely easy to communicate with. Slight of build, with unruly hair and plain features, she had a tremendous sense of humour. I found myself laughing for the first time in a long while as she related stories of life within the farming community. In retrospect, it was delightful having clothes neatly set out on a daily basis. Shoes shone like army boots awaiting kit inspection. My hair was washed and groomed until it shone like velvet. Personal hygiene became a twice-daily ritual. The bathroom cabinets were filled with containers of talcum powder, bottles of expensive eau de toilette and fragrances with exclusive names I could only have dreamt of, had life stayed as it was. I had become quite self-sufficient during my time with Maura, and this personal attention did not sit comfortably on my shoulders; but Millie was so dedicated to her work that it would have been discourteous not to praise her daily for her fondness and devotion of me. Food was delicious and plentiful, thanks to Edith Roberts, and it arrived at regular times. I noticed in no time at all my very thin frame began to take on a different shape. I considered myself no longer a little child, but a young lady. The servants were exceedingly affable. Within a short while I assured myself I was part of the fixtures and fittings of the imposing Hall I had come to regard as my home. I was no longer 'lass' to the staff, but 'Miss Sophia'.

Benedict was a mischievous lad, intent on having fun. He led me into trouble on numerous occasions, enjoying the chastisement I received from Lady Mary and Sir Oliver. Alexander kept a close eye on me, seeing I adhered to the rules and regulations of the household. He was a good friend. I liked him tremendously. He was delighted to receive instructions from me on how to improve his piano playing, although the violin was his first love. He was interested and attentive during piano lessons, not at all uncomfortable at being tutored by a girl four years his junior. He appreciated my help, and I his. Marcus, a cute, stubborn child, followed on my heels continuously, and persisted in addressing me as 'Soapy'. His enthusiasm in attempting to follow me into the drawing room to try and play the piano was overwhelming. His usual comment was, 'Play me blues, Soapy!'

Would I dare? Sir Oliver would never have allowed it! It was classical music in the household, or nothing. Sir Oliver was an extremely reasonable person, but often brusque in speech and manner. Underneath his stern persona lurked a kind heart. He gave me a monthly allowance in proportion to that administered to Alexander. Benedict, being my age, received the same amount as me. This was an exceedingly welcome and generous amount, I having had nothing like this in the past. I opened a savings account with the help of Sir Oliver. A great proportion of my allowance was deposited there on a monthly basis. For me, the greatest experience was having three congenial boys of different ages as playmates. Our popular game was that of hide-and-seek around the Hall. Behind the oak panelling in several of the rooms, we discovered, quite by chance, disguised holes where priests had once been hidden by Sir Oliver's ancestors during the troubled period of the abolition of the monasteries in Tudor times. Sir Oliver and Lady Mary were not aware of the existence of many of these places. We children came upon them during our games. It was exciting, finding new ones, but proved traumatic on occasions when Marcus became lost in these hiding places and panicked when we could not find him. He turned into a hysterical, sobbing heap! These situations lead Sir Oliver to forbid us to use these rooms again. At all times it was instilled in us that there were priceless objects within the Hall, and certain areas were considered out of bounds, especially to Marcus, who seemed accident prone. Marcus's favourite occupation was collecting tadpoles and sticklebacks when in season, and of course, frogs!

'Where are you going with that frog, Marcus?' I would ask.

'It's a secret, Soapy, can't tell you,' he would answer.

Fair enough. He had no wish to tell me, so I questioned him no more but soon discovered after bathing and climbing into bed, a weird, slimy creature climbing up my nightdress. This led me to the realisation that the said frog had been placed between my sheets. It sent me into a state of panic. Screams could be heard emanating from my bedroom and echoed round the Hall. Millie arrived and quickly removed the amphibian. Sir Oliver was not amused. Marcus was 'frogmarched' into my room to say, 'Very sorry, Soapy! Won't do it again.'

I wanted to laugh at his big, brown eyes peering over his tiny spectacles and for the mispronunciation of my name, but in the presence of Sir Oliver, I refrained.

Snails were his other love. He would help 'Old Arthur', the head gardener, collect as many as he could in his little red bucket. As with any task he undertook, his interest span was short, so as an incentive, I suggested I gave him a halfpenny for every snail collected. Within ten minutes of searching he returned with twenty snails.

'What shall I do with them, Soapy?' he asked, peering intently at me.

Having spotted a large Kilner jar in the nearby potting shed, I suggested he put them in it. He readily offloaded the snails and went in search of more. During the following two hours, he had brought in snails by the bucketful. I could see my monthly allowance being depleted at a rate of knots. It was then I realised Marcus had been recycling the snails he had found earlier. I was paying for the same snails time and again! I was tickled pink at his little scheme and went along with it. He made his own pocket money at my expense on several occasions.

Sir Oliver insisted we all learnt to ride. It was my first lesson, and Marcus's too. He looked cute in jodhpurs and riding hat.

'Soapy, come, we go to horses,' he said, grabbing my hand. He appeared excited at the thought of his lessons, but I was apprehensive. Richard Hamilton, Sir Oliver's horse trainer, had volunteered to teach Marcus and me all he could during our daily lesson. We approached the stable block. Alexander and Benedict were waiting with their respective horses tied to a post. Storm, a beautiful white gelding, was saddled up and ready for the off. Alexander looked handsome in his riding apparel. Benedict stood by a gelding named Titus, which was also ready for the short hack we were to take to Hardy's Wood. Ben and Alex helped with the reins and saddle of a small pony Marcus was to ride, which was aptly named Brownie, because of its warm brown coat. My horse, a bay mare called Zippy, was tethered to a post, waiting the arrival of Richard Hamilton, but had not been saddled up.

'We'll put her saddle on for you, Sophia,' chanted Alex and Ben in unison, 'and her bridle and reins.'

How wonderful, I thought, and I thanked them for their help. They were efficient, having handled horses since they were both six years old. They lifted Marcus onto his well-behaved pony. He looked a picture sitting there, and appeared quite a 'natural' on a horse. Alexander said, 'Here, Sophia! I will lift you onto Zippy.'

I went to him and obeyed his instructions. He showed me where to place my hand on the saddle and how to place my foot in the stirrup.

'Now lift yourself up and place your leg over the saddle,' he explained.

I did as instructed. Without warning the saddle slipped and I ended up hanging under the belly of the horse. Alexander and Benedict burst into uncontrollable laughter. They were in stitches and their bodies ached. As I hit the ground I wanted to cry, but I managed to stop myself.

'What on earth are you boys doing?'

Richard Hamilton appeared and rushed to my rescue. He lifted me up and dusted me down, his expression one of anger.

'What on earth have you lads been doing to Sophia?'

He examined the horse and saddle. 'Well, which one of you deliberately failed to do up the girth strap? Own up or I will go immediately to Sir Oliver about your little escapade!'

To my amazement, Alex admitted to doing the deed as a joke. Both boys apologised profusely and I accepted. A lecture from Richard ensued. With everything in order, we set off on the short hack. Gosh, I ached! But I enjoyed the ride. Although Marcus and I had no knowledge of horses, I knew that with a great number of lessons, he and I would come to enjoy the riding experience. We came to a gate leading to an open field. Ben opened the gate to allow us through. He closed the gate behind us. As he approached me, he whacked my horse on its flanks with his riding crop. She reared up and set off across the field, like a hopeful Derby winner. I was petrified. I held on to the reins and saddle for dear life, but eventually, with my feet having left the stirrups, I worked my way up over the saddle and onto the horse's neck. As I passed everyone, Alexander shouted, 'Stop showing off, Sophia!' and laughed. I held on tightly as my short life flashed before me. The horse came to a sudden halt at a fence. I swung round its neck and fell off. I was terrified, upset and angry, but determined not to show it. Alex and Ben would not get the better of me! Richard Hamilton was the first on the scene, followed by Alex.

'What on earth startled your horse, Sophia?' asked Richard.

I looked at Alex and then in the direction of Ben, and said, 'I really don't know. I think she may have heard a shotgun go off in the distance.'

Alex and Ben looked relieved that I was not hurt, and even more thankful I did not set out to cause trouble for them by explaining what actually happened. I was determined they would not deter me from riding. Somehow I would fight to become a good horsewoman in what appeared to be a man's world and I would eventually be as competent as the boys. Richard Hamilton helped me on to my horse, remounted his, and, holding onto my reins, escorted me back to the stable block. The other ponies followed. My first riding lesson was over and what a lesson it was!

Chapter Six

Alex approached me as I walked along the road leading from my school.

'Here, Sophia, this is for you!' He handed me a small neatly wrapped package.

'What is it?' I asked, expecting it to contain a spider or something equally as horrid.

'Open it and see!' he urged.

I carefully removed the wrapping paper and discovered a small blue velvet box inside.

'Well, open it, Sophia!' he insisted.

I did, quite reluctantly. 'Oh, Alex, it's my locket! I thought I would never see it again. It is so kind of you!'

'I had to save my allowance for a new gold chain, Sophia,' he explained. 'I am so glad that you are pleased with it.'

I squeezed his arm in an affectionate gesture. 'I am over the moon with it! Thank you *so* much!'

He insisted on fastening the clasp for me so I could wear it immediately.

We walked across the lawns together to the Hall. My fingers constantly fiddled with my necklace. I was thrilled to have it returned. It meant so much to me. Alex carried my satchel – ever the young gentleman. He was a true friend. We walked through the knot garden, savouring the perfume of roses planted to complement the various types of old lavender. In the distance the yew hedges had been, in years gone by, painstakingly planted into various lines and curves to form a maze of passageways with only one route into the centre. In the middle was a summer house where Ben, Marcus, Alex and I often ventured, inventing plays about knights and damsels in distress. Alex was my knight in shining armour, rescuing me from the jaws of the mighty dragon – Marcus! Marcus was so cute draped in a length of green curtain material, making the most awful roaring noises. He was the first dragon I knew of who wore spectacles! Ben was always the village yokel and excelled at the part.

Alex and I sat on a pine seat, facing the small hedges which formed the knot garden.

The precise shapes, interplanted with excellent choices of colourful flowers, had never looked more beautiful.

'You are fond of Marcus, aren't you, Sophia?'

The words came unexpectedly as we sat and savoured the beauty around us.

'Yes, I am, Alex! He is like the younger brother I never had, but always wished for,' I admitted, smiling into his eyes.

'I am so glad. You see, he needs a friend to guide him. You seem to be just the person.'

Alex picked a Rosa Mundi rose, which had entwined itself into the seat, among the lavender. Its romantic striped crimson and white petals gave out a profusion of perfume. Alex knelt down on one knee and cheekily presented me with the flower.

'A rose for my lady,' he said, chuckling.

'Thank you, kind sir,' I murmured, accepting the gift.

He returned to sit beside me. He was so charming and thoughtful.

'Marcus has had such a poor start, Sophia,' Alex explained. 'I should not be speaking out of turn. I wanted you to know of his situation. It will help you understand him a little better. I know what I am about to tell you, you will never discuss with anyone.'

At that precise moment I could see Alex too had a great affinity with Marcus that he did not have with Ben. Benedict was a charming, genial boy, but somehow the brothers did not gel as Marcus and Alex appeared to.

'You see,' he continued, 'my mother had a dear friend, Frances, from schooldays. Frances met a Canadian pilot who was stationed in England during the war and was in Sir Oliver's squadron. They lived together in this area. After the war he chose to stay in England. Marcus was the child born from the relationship.'

'I see,' I declared, finding the story fascinating.

'They moved to London. When Marcus was almost two, his father returned to Canada, leaving them behind, for a reason I know nothing of.'

'Gosh, Frances must have been devastated!' I could not even begin to understand the sorrow of the situation.

'Mr Walker said he would send for them both, but never did. Mother kept in touch with Frances, knowing she had become extremely depressed. She offered her and Marcus friendship and accommodation but it was refused. Mother and Frances wrote and spoke regularly.'

Alex paused, despondency creeping over his features.

'When the communication stopped, Mother went to the apartment in London and could get no answer. Mother contacted the police and they immediately forced an entry and found Frances lying unconscious on the floor, with Marcus huddled against his mother's body. Frances died within hours of being discovered. She had overdosed on pills and alcohol. Marcus was removed into care. His father was traced but could not accommodate him in his life. Mother and Sir Oliver arranged that Marcus should be removed from care and live with us.'

I could not contemplate what young Marcus would have experienced and could only envisage the trauma as a reason for his sullen moments, when he seemed, sad, shy, lost and vulnerable.

'He has never talked of that frightful day. Mother says he has wiped it from his memory deliberately.'

Together Alex and I made tracks to the Hall. We parted company and I was left alone to contemplate what I had been told about Marcus and his mother. As I entered, Sir Oliver summoned me to the library. He was deeply engrossed in looking through some old manuscripts, handling them with cotton-gloved hands.

'Hello, Sophia. Please come in. I need to talk to you about Doggett's Barn.'

I understood from a previous conversation with Sir Oliver that all the violins Papa had taken in for repair had been returned to their owners. Papa had willed the remaining musical instruments in his collection to me. Several of these had been purchased many years previously, or had been crafted by my Italian grandpapas.

'I would like you to accompany me to the barn, Sophia. We're going to have to decide where we are going to move the instruments to. They cannot stay there indefinitely. They are extremely valuable and need a place of safety and security. Therefore we need to discuss what the next move will be.'

'Yes, Sir,' I agreed. 'I have ideas about what I would like to do with them,' I added.

It was arranged that we meet at the barn the following afternoon at 4.30 p.m.

I arrived at Doggett's Barn early. I had dawdled across on my return from school. Sir Oliver was punctual. We entered the building. It was an emotional time for me. Everything was just as Papa had left it. I experienced a tight feeling in my throat, as though I would choke. At one stage I thought I could not keep my emotions under control, but I managed, although at times I felt as if I could not breathe. I looked around at the tall cupboards and my curiosity got the better of me. I opened them, to be faced by sheet music, papers and photographs, all of which needed to be sorted. The tools Papa had graciously used to craft his beloved violins were all neatly laid out.

'What will you do with this barn, Sir?' I asked.

There had been a violin workshop there since the late 1920s when Grandpapa Tipaldi had moved from Italy to Yorkshire.

'I am not sure what I am going to do with it at the moment, Sophia. We are desperate for barns in which to store animal feed. We may need to use it for that. My main concern is that these instruments are well taken care of. They can be stored safely within the Hall for your use, should you need them at some stage in your musical career. The Steinway grand piano in the Great Hall, which belonged to your mama, is also part of your inheritance.'

In various places within the barn we found cases containing violins, a banjo, a mandolin and two guitars; one of these I had already learnt to play, and the other Mama had brought home from America for Papa, as a present, after having appeared in concert in New York. The first violin case I opened housed a prized violin which had belonged to Grandpapa Bertucelli. I heard Papa play this instrument once. He played a Mozart violin concerto and gave an enthralling performance which had always remained uppermost in my mind. I had a specific purpose for the instrument.

As we returned to the Hall I met Edith, who asked if I would collect some strawberries from the walled garden. I was anxious to please and went in search of the luscious fruit. I returned along the path to be met by Ben.

'Humpty-Dumpty wants to see you in the drawing room!' he announced.

'Who?' I asked, but he ran off to find Alex, chuckling as he did so. I handed the strawberries to Edith so she could put the finishing touches to her pavlova, washed my hands and hurried to see what it was Ben was talking about. I was on a collision course with Sir Oliver as our paths crossed outside the library door.

'Ah, Sophia, I was coming to look for you. Bodil Larson, your new piano tutor, is awaiting you in the drawing room. She has turned up unexpectedly. Follow me!'

I did as requested. On following Sir Oliver into the room, I came face to face with a small middle-aged woman, whom one could only describe as looking like an Easter egg on legs. However, after introductions I discovered that she was delightful. She was a small bundle of emotional energy, set to instil in me the beauty of the piano and the awe-inspiring works one could create and achieve with it. Miss Larson could not wait to see what stage I had aspired to. Sir Oliver and my new tutor took a seat to watch my performance. This made me nervous and uncomfortable, so I gave myself a short while to prepare before beginning to play. I began with great enthusiasm and gusto. As I finished, there was complete silence. I turned and looked intently at Miss Larson. She looked at Sir Oliver and he returned her gaze. She then stared straight at me.

'Play something else for me, Sophia,' she said in a sombre voice. 'Off you go!'

I did as requested. What had I done wrong? As I drew to the end of the following piece, she struggled up from her chair and placed her hands on my shoulders.

'Magnificent! Such grace! Tremendous feeling and soul! Why, before long this child will be teaching me! What else can one say, Sir Oliver, except that the child has the most exceptional talent it has been my fortune to witness!' she excitedly concluded.

Sir Oliver and Miss Larson then spoke at great length and it was agreed she would tutor me until such time that I no longer required her help. I was extremely happy with this arrangement, and reckoned Miss Larson would be a most helpful, kind and dedicated tutor.

Lady Mary and Sir Oliver took tremendous interest in my education. My small school in the village was a decidedly calmer, more personal place with excellent, caring, teaching nuns and classes of no more than twelve children. I noticed after a short while that my work improved considerably and continued to do so. I excelled in subjects that before I'd found difficult to grasp. Music was a great part of the curriculum, and I adored those lessons. I joined the school choir and immediately became interested in singing. I was also asked to play piano at school concerts, and was given solo parts in the choir. Life was extraordinarily happy and contented.

As August 1953 approached, Harrington Hall was a hive of industry. Extensive plans were under way. Sir Oliver was expecting guests from a great distance. It was midsummer holidays, and we siblings were given to understand Sir Oliver was to entertain old RAF comrades from his squadron. A huge dinner and dance had been arranged for the Saturday evening. Two people were arriving a few days ahead of the reunion, from Canada. Lady Mary advised it would be in our best interests to be on good behaviour and we should, at all times, be polite and well-mannered.

On the Friday morning, John Roberts drove Sir Oliver to Heathrow Airport to meet his guests who were arriving on the long flight from Toronto. On board were a Mr Bruce, an ex-Canadian Air Force pilot, and his thirteen-year-old son, Michael. Mr Bruce had frequented these shores a great deal during wartime. For Michael, it was his first visit, and we were asked if we would entertain him while Sir Oliver and Mr Bruce discussed important business matters. Although we anxiously awaited their arrival, it was not until Saturday morning breakfast that we had the pleasure of meeting them both.

As we sat at table, they approached the dining room and I was awe-struck at how tall Mr Bruce was. He had a dark mop of hair and was handsome in features. He was a quiet, subdued fellow about thirty-five years old and was most congenial. His son bore no resemblance to him whatsoever. Michael was three years older than me, fair of face and hair, quite charming and friendly. We all stood up from the table. Marcus hid behind my dress and viewed, with suspicion, the tall stranger and his son.

'This is Mr Bruce,' Sir Oliver announced. 'This is his son, Michael. I hope you children will make sure my special guests receive kindness and attention from you all.'

We burst into a chorus of 'Yes, Sir!' – except for Marcus, who clutched tightly at my clothing and scowled over the top of his spectacles; but I am sure Sir Oliver allowed for the fact he was so young and very shy.

'Hiya, how ya doin'?' Mr Bruce asked in a strange accent.

We politely said, 'Very well, thank you, sir.'

Sir Oliver introduced each one of us individually. Mr Bruce seated himself beside Sir Oliver. Michael made tracks for the chair next to me, which did not suit Marcus. He pushed Michael aside with such ferocity that he almost landed on the floor.

'*Marcus!*' bellowed Sir Oliver. '*Enough!* Let Michael sit next to Sophia. Then he can tell her about Canada. Go and sit next to Alex.'

Marcus sloped off, staring down at the floor, sidled up to Alex and slithered onto the chair like a slimy snake, viewing me from across the table with a tear in his eye, obviously jealous I had a new friend. I did my utmost to include him in the conversation.

'You see, Bruce,' said Sir Oliver, 'I think Marcus is joined to Sophia at the hip. He only leaves her at bedtime or when school beckons.'

They smiled at one another and continued breakfast.

Edith buzzed around like a bee round a honeypot, serving the most delicious food.

She was complimented by Mr Bruce, which pleased her greatly. Alex flashed me a captivating smile and winked. I returned the smile. I asked Michael, 'Where is Canada?'

Sir Oliver looked at me as if I should have known. Michael informed me it was at the northern end of the United States of America, at which Marcus asked, 'Are there any cowboys and Indians there?'

'There were, once,' replied Michael, but before we could enter into any further conversation Marcus shouted, 'I am going to be an Indian one day, Soapy!'

He had the guests roaring with laughter.

'Why does he call you Soapy? asked Michael in a loud voice, as Marcus chased his bacon, sausage and egg around the plate.

I began to whisper when Ben shouted out, 'Because he cannot say Sophia!'

He taunted Marcus, who threw his fork on the table and ran from his chair, heading toward the kitchen.

'Go and fetch him, Sophia,' ordered Sir Oliver, 'and pacify him!'

'Don't be hard on him, Sophia,' Lady Mary pleaded.

I excused myself from the table and went in search of Marcus.

'Do you see what I mean, Bruce? I heard Sir Oliver say. 'They are stuck to one another like glue.'

Evening arrived and we children were asked to retire early. Sir Oliver and Lady Mary had arranged a reunion dinner for Sir Oliver's wartime RAF squadron personnel. There was food, drink and dancing. The Great Hall rang out with laughter. Millie Dexter allowed the boys into my room for a short while. No one would have heard us giggling and having fun, as the merriment from down below was quite overwhelming. Michael made several attempts to sit next to me on the chaise longue but he was squeezed, nipped or pushed off the end of the furniture by Marcus, so that he himself could sit and hold my hand. In the end, Michael withdrew graciously.

Over the following days we played cricket, rounders, boules and croquet on the lawn, went riding and were treated to an excursion to the zoo by Mr Bruce. Marcus never left my side. Michael was nevertheless charming and I liked him an awful lot. When asked about other members of his family in Canada he was non-committal and did not mention his mother.

On Friday morning, the day prior to the departure of our Canadian guests, we had a massive tour of the estate. Lady Mary drove one of the Land Rovers, taking Ben, Michael and Alex. Sir Oliver drove ahead in his vehicle with Mr Bruce, Marcus and me. Mr Bruce was amazed at the vastness of the estate and concluded he had not realised on his visits during wartime just how extensive it was.

'Excuse me, sir,' I asked 'if you were here during the war, did you know my mama?'

He looked at me intently, saying, 'Yes, Sophia, I most certainly did! I knew her well. Gee, she was the most beautiful woman I've ever seen. You're gorgeous, just like your mama,' he observed. 'and she was a brilliant pianist. I guess you have her gift.'

I blushed as Marcus cuddled into my side.

'Oliver, can we go down to the lake where—'

Sir Oliver interrupted. 'Of course, Bruce!' He drove to the lake and pointed to the spot where I had rescued Marcus a few years previously.

'You were a brave girl to have rescued your little buddy, Sophia!' Mr Bruce said turning to look at me. 'I'm sure we'll forever be grateful to you!'

'I just did what I had to do,' I explained.

Sir Oliver drove away hastily, followed by Lady Harrington. He took us to Hardy's Wood, where we picnicked on food Edith and the kitchen staff had prepared. Mr Bruce sat on one side of me, Marcus on the other, suspiciously viewing the large man over his spectacles.

'Do you like living at the Hall, Sophia?' he asked suddenly.

'Very much, sir,' I replied.

He turned to Marcus and said, 'And what about you, young buddy?'

Marcus stared at the ground, clutching my arm tightly.

'Mr Bruce is talking to you, Marcus. It is rude not to answer,' I said, prompting a reply.

'I love it! I love Soapy. We are best friends. I always want to be with Soapy,' he murmured, and dropped his head once more.

'And what about your schools? Do you like your schools?'

'Yes, we both love our schools and we go riding and have fun together. I look after Marcus because he is my best friend too,' I admitted.

'I am so glad, young lady. You both seem very settled at the Hall. Sir Oliver has given you both an excellent home.'

I paused and said, 'Yes, sir. Sir Oliver is strict but kind, fair and very generous. We want for nothing.'

'Good!' he replied, and handed around a plate of scrumptious sandwiches. We ate and drank far in excess of what we should have. Marcus ran hurriedly behind the trees to have a pee.

Later that evening I went to say goodnight to Sir Oliver in the drawing room, Marcus close on my heels.

'Goodnight, Sophia,' he said standing at the drinks cabinet, pouring Mr Bruce a whisky. 'And go straight to sleep! No reading until late!'

I promised I would not read. Marcus stepped forward and shyly said, 'Goodnight, Sir!' to which Sir Oliver replied, 'Goodnight, Marcus. You have been a good boy today. Off to sleep, and no playing with your cars.'

We turned to Mr Bruce and in unison said, 'Goodnight, Mr Bruce!'

In an unexpected move, he lunged forward, shook my hand and kissed me on the cheek, saying, 'It has been a great experience knowing you, Sophia. You are a credit to Sir Oliver.'

Without warning, he threw his arms around Marcus and drew the surprised child to his chest. 'Young buddy – it has been a wonderful experience getting to know you. You are gonna be a great guy when you grow up!'

As he released one very surprised little boy I noticed a tear in his eye. Were all Canadians emotional people? Marcus left the room post-haste. As I retreated to say farewell to Michael, I heard Mr Bruce say, 'You were correct, Oliver. How could we possibly split them up? I think the decision made is for the best. They seem so happy.'

'I agree, Bruce. Let them grow up together here.'

In an instant, I concluded that Mr Bruce was either from a children's home or a Canadian adoption agency. I wanted to stay at my beloved Harrington Hall, not go to Canada. I was anxious about the situation for weeks. Mr Bruce did not return to collect me. I had heard considerable numbers of orphans had been despatched to Canada and Australia during and after the war by the British government. I did not wish to become one of the statistics.

Chapter Seven

'They are so gorgeous, Sophia!'

Marcus and I sat in the straw which lined the barn floor. I held a tiny bundle of black and white fluff in my arms, gently stroking its coat. It was one of five strong, healthy puppies. Sally, our youngest sheepdog, and mother to the litter, looked up in concern that Marcus and I could harm her offspring, but we reassured her all was well. She continued surveying us with a cautious, relentless stare. Marcus was besotted by a particularly handsome puppy. Handling it gently, he treated it to oodles of tender loving care.

'Is it a boy?' he asked inquisitively, trying to investigate its tiny 'credentials'.

On closer examination I could see it was a male.

'Sophia, do you think Sir Oliver will let me have one?'

He was obviously smitten with the little animal. The puppy appeared to have a rapport with him too as it huddled against his sweater.

'I think not, Marcus! Sir Oliver likes his border collies to be trained for a specific purpose – that of rounding up sheep. A dog in the house is a definite *no*. Winter is not a good time to house-train a puppy, either!'

He stared at me, his sad, vivid, chocolate-brown eyes speaking volumes. I could see he would make an excellent owner, but Sir Oliver was adamant about animals in the Hall. Dogs on the estate were there to earn their keep and nothing more. We returned the pups to Sally and walked casually toward the Hall.

'Why is Sir Oliver against everything I want to do, Sophia?' With his hands in pockets, shuffling his feet, Marcus was obviously depressed by my remarks.

'I don't know. It is nothing personal against you, but at eight years of age you are too young to take on the responsibility of a dog, Marcus. Sir Oliver has great responsibility running this estate, overseeing the carpet factories and other business commitments, so he has his mind on far more pressing matters and would consider a dog an encumbrance.'

Disappointment was written over his face. A dog would certainly provide the companionship Marcus desperately needed.

'Come on, Marcus, we have lots to do. We promised Sir Oliver we would help pick holly and mistletoe in Hardy's Wood.'

Christmas loomed. Workers at the Hall were involved in preparations for the festivities. There was to be a staff party the following day. It was a time I particularly enjoyed, when the family met with the estate workers and their families, for a superb get-together and traditional dancing. As we approached the stable block, Sir Oliver roared toward us in the Land Rover, coming to an abrupt halt.

'Get in, Sophia! I need your help to buy Mary a Christmas present in York.'

'But Sir,' I protested, 'I am not dressed for the city.'

'You will do fine! I have a ten thirty appointment with Jacob Godber at Witherington's, so hop in! Marcus – take two estate workers with you to the wood and collect the holly and mistletoe, please!'

'Yes, Sir!'

Following instructions, Marcus sidled off. I hopped into the vehicle as requested.

'This is the season for rushing about, Sophia. Sometimes I think Christmas is too much of an effort these days. It is moving away from the fundamental event which it is supposed to celebrate. It seems to be all presents, presents, presents and spend, spend, spend!'

'Sir,' I asked gingerly, 'can I give Marcus one of Sally's puppies for Christmas?'

The look of horror on his face at the suggestion was unbelievable.

'Most certainly not! You know how I feel about dogs in the Hall!' He was adamant.

As we travelled along, I wondered how I could get him to change his mind. Ah, tears! He always succumbed to Lady Mary's tears, and had occasionally melted at mine.

'What are you snivelling for, Sophia?' he asked, handing me a clean handkerchief. 'Here, wipe your tears!'

I blew into it several times, showing my upset at his refusal.

'Now, pull yourself together, Sophia! There is no need to be tearful. Dogs leave hair everywhere. We have priceless furniture and treasures in the Hall. Try to understand why I am saying "no" to you.'

I blew my nose and sniffed dramatically. How could he resist my request?

Sir Oliver insisted on lecturing me on the pros and cons of keeping a dog and was adamant that it was a lifelong commitment. As we approached York I said, 'I know Marcus would be an excellent owner to the puppy. He'd take good care of it. The pup could have a kennel outside. We have a spare one!'

He rapidly changed the subject but I continued to sniff until York Minster drew closer.

Jacob Godber gave us an exceptional welcome, but then we were invaluable customers. Sir Oliver ordered an exquisite watch for Lady Mary, encrusted with diamonds (to be delivered by special courier), which she could wear on special occasions. He then bought wristwatches for Alex and Ben, and an expensive character alarm clock for Marcus in the hope he would, in future, arrive at school on time.

Shopping completed, we strolled through the Shambles. Sir Oliver insisted on taking me to an exclusive restaurant for lunch. I was embarrassed that I was not dressed more fittingly, but Sir Oliver was not concerned and seemed extremely well known in the establishment. He was shown to a table he had obviously reserved. He introduced me to the owner and staff as Anna's daughter. The waiters almost fell to their knees at my presence.

We ordered. As we waited for our starter to arrive, Sir Oliver commented, 'You know, Sophia, I am not sure Marcus would care for a dog on a long term basis!'

'Oh, but he would, Sir! Marcus does not make friends easily. He is so shy. A dog would give him the confidence he needs.'

Sir Oliver changed the subject once more.

The food was delicious. As we ate, the question of my lessons with Bodil Larson, my Danish piano teacher from the Conservatoire in Copenhagen, arose.

'Miss Larson tells me you have completed further music grades, passing with honours. I will enquire about a scholarship for you at the Royal College in London.

'Oh, *no*, Sir! Please do not send me away from Harrington Hall. I do not want to leave you, Lady Mary and the boys. I could not bear it. I don't want to make music a full-time career! I love farming, horses and cooking and I adore my school. Edith lets me help her in the kitchen and teaches me many dishes.'

He glanced at me disapprovingly but commented no further. Nor did he mention the puppy again.

Before leaving York, we walked quite a distance around the walls encompassing the minster. A short history lesson ensued. Sir Oliver was well read on the history of the city. Our expedition completed, we returned to Harrington Hall.

The following day, Lady Mary drove me to Leeds. We visited a large department store. Not for me the children's section any longer; I was introduced to a charming assistant who furnished me with items of clothing to try on. Lady Mary made a selection of garments for everyday wear and chose a beautiful long pale blue dress for me to wear on

Christmas Day. There were stylish shoes to accompany it. I was allowed dainty ones with heels now I was almost thirteen.

Embarrassment came in the lingerie department when I was measured for my first bra, but on viewing the range, I was taken aback at the sensual way in which they were designed, and Lady Mary purchased four for me, with panties to match.

I began to feel I had changed from a tomboy into a presentable young lady, especially when flounced nightdresses and sheer silk stockings were obtained for me. The word bandied around the store by the assistants, as I tried on more dresses was 'gorgeous' and 'very beautiful', but I was shy and did not comment.

In the evening, the boys and I helped load enormous amounts of parcels into both the Land Rovers and we were driven by John Roberts to a large house outside the village, accompanied by Sir Oliver and Lady Harrington, each driving one of the fully laden vehicles. As was customary each year we visited 'Sunny Bank', a children's orphanage which Sir Oliver had purchased with his own money during the Second World War. He had given his childhood nanny, Miss Pearson, the authority to run it, until her passing some years previously. It was now in the capable hands of Matron Baldwin, a jolly figure of a woman and every inch a motherly figure to the children, having four of her own. Here, in the huge sitting room, we stacked the gifts under a huge flamboyantly decorated pine tree presented by the Harringtons. The children had aptly added their own contributions with handmade ornaments. Edith had cooked excellent fare to add to the cook's already bulging larder. It was obvious that the residents of 'Sunny Bank' would lack nothing at Christmas. Villagers had also contributed parcels to the huge array of goodies that we delivered.

We stayed for two hours, meeting the residents, who were an affable bunch, and joined them in carol singing and a feast of mince pies and hot cocoa before returning to the Hall. It had been an excellent evening and extremely worthwhile.

The Christmas party for estate workers and their families proceeded with great gusto. Alex, dashing in a dark suit, bow tie and white shirt, along with Sir Oliver, who looked extremely handsome, was there to greet the guests. Lady Mary, Ben, Marcus and I greeted the workers, wishing them a Merry Christmas and every good wish for the New Year. Food was plentiful and all sorts of games were played. The afternoon and evening festivities ended with traditional dancing and music. Marcus and I had organised a Christmas song. He wrote the words, I wrote the music. He sang and I played piano. Lady Mary and

Sir Oliver were proud of the performance we gave, which was note and word perfect.

'Sophia, you have worked wonders with Marcus. To think he wrote the lyrics to the song. Well done!' Sir Oliver was ecstatic.

'He has worked very hard, Sir, to make this a success.'

I wanted Marcus to receive the acclaim, but Sir Oliver had only praise for me.

I related his words to my young foster-brother, but he shrugged his shoulders and walked away. If only Sir Oliver could have spoken to Marcus and not me alone.

Waltzes were the last event of the evening. Workers and wives embraced as they floated across the floor, happy in each other's arms.

'Will you please dance with me, Sophia?'

I turned to find Alex staring at me with his vivid blue eyes. I suddenly felt uncomfortable, but the word 'please' swayed my decision. I nodded. Alex took me in his arms and we moved around the floor in complete unison. For the first time in my life, as I gazed up at this striking young man, I began to experience feelings too difficult to understand. I saw him as a person far removed from the family, a young man in his own right, with all the charm and loveliness of manhood. He chatted as we danced and commented on my ability to channel Marcus's energies into the song we had composed together, and said he thought it an amazing feat.

At the end of the dancing, each family received a hamper of wine, fruit, pâté, cheese, a ham, home-made pickles and a capon. Each woman received a special gift; each child a present befitting their age, and a bottle of spirits for the men. Sir Oliver and Lady Mary distributed these, adding their seasonal wishes.

With the guests having departed, the staff moved in quickly to clean the Great Hall. It was 9.30 p.m. I met Alex in the doorway to the Great Hall, after he'd bid the remaining guests farewell.

'You look so lovely tonight, Sophia!'

'What a sweet thing for you to say,' I replied, meeting his eyes.

What would he think of the dress I was going to wear on Christmas Day?

'Oh, look!' he remarked pointing above my head.

I peered up at a huge sprig of mistletoe. As I returned my gaze he kissed me on the lips.

'Merry Christmas, Sophia!'

With one kiss, he was gone. I stood, trembling at what had happened. I spotted Marcus hiding behind the Hall door. He frowned, peered over his spectacles and disappeared, grunting disapprovingly. I lay in bed, tossing and turning, unable to find sleep. I could not understand the feelings running through my body; feelings I had not experienced before. I thought of Alex's lips on mine and wanted the moment imprinted on my memory for ever. If only his kiss could have lingered a while longer! It was the loveliest Christmas present I could have wished for. What on earth was happening to me? He was a member of my family, and it was imperative that I controlled my emotions.

Early on Christmas morning, with a small present for each member of the family neatly wrapped and placed at the bottom of my bed, I bathed. With the help of Millie, I dressed. Breakfast was always an hour earlier to allow food to be digested at leisure before the family gathered around the magnificent tree for present opening.

I needed to place my gifts in position. I crept out of my bedroom, at 7 a.m., my arms laden with goodies, to be confronted by a large, holed, cardboard box. I heard a noise coming from within. Placing my presents on the floor, I investigated. Inside was a small bundle of living, breathing, black and white fluff! It was one of Sally's puppies, the one Marcus favoured. Sir Oliver must have asked Robert, the shepherd, which one Marcus adored, and had collected it early for me to give to him. Dear, kind, abrupt, caring Sir Oliver! What a man!

I took the box to my room, removed the pup and placed him in the adjoining bathroom until he was needed, notifying Millie of his existence and asking her to keep a beady eye on him. I hurried downstairs and placed my presents under the tree.

Breakfast was a family affair. Lady Mary had asked Edith and John Roberts to join us for the Christmas celebrations, in thanks for all their kindness to me in the past. This was wonderful news, as we adored them.

Sir Oliver was enthralled at handing around the gifts lurking under the tall, sparkling Christmas tree, and he watched attentively as we opened our gifts. He was delighted with the pipe rack I had an estate carpenter craft for him. Alex appreciated the new train track I bought him; Ben enthused over his geometry set; Lady Mary cherished her embroidered handkerchiefs; Edith was ecstatic with her dressing table set I had crocheted; and John could not wait to try his new driving gloves on. Marcus surveyed his tiny parcel, wondering what the package contained. He smiled on discovering two Dinky racing cars to add to his ever growing collection.

Sir Oliver winked in my direction. It was time for me to collect the puppy. I returned post-haste, holding the large cardboard box carefully.

'Here, Marcus, this box is for you!' I announced.

Everyone focused on the young sibling. Marcus, wide-eyed and curious, laid it on the floor, thinking it was a joke. He knew I loved to tease him. I have never seen such joy on his face as when he opened the lid and a black and white head appeared. The head yawned and Marcus carefully lifted the pup from inside.

'Marcus! There is a kennel outside!' explained Sir Oliver, but Lady Mary insisted the pup stay inside for the day, as long as he was regularly toileted.

'Thank you so much, Sophia!' Marcus leapt up and quickly kissed my cheek.

'I think you should thank Sir Oliver,' I instructed. 'He fetched the pup from the barn for you!'

Marcus turned, said a big, 'Thank you, Sir,' and proceeded to ask me what we should call the pup. Alex suggested Prince, Ben proposed Sabre and Lady Mary considered the name Winston.

'What do *you* think I should call him, Sophia?'

I thought for a moment. 'How about *Deefa*?'

'*Deefa*?' he queried, 'What does it mean?'

'Well, it's D for Dog,' I replied.

Everyone chuckled.

Marcus called out, 'Deefa!' The pup held its head to one side as if recognising the name, so it was decided it would be Deefa, and one very happy young boy was having a joyous Christmas.

How could Sir Oliver and Lady Mary have been so heartless?

It was my thirteenth birthday. Breakfast was well attended and I was showered with a huge selection of cards. To my absolute amazement I received one from Maura, a neat card with words inside.

'Please forgive me for my behaviour toward you, Sophia! I wish I could make amends.'

I dare not inform the family that I'd heard from her. It would have caused an atmosphere on what I hoped was a special day. I hid the card. It was the Easter school break, and Alex, Ben and Marcus were at home for my exciting day. I was not sure if it was the lure of Edith's delightful breakfast which had them racing down the stairs, or their enthusiasm at wanting to wish me a happy birthday. Marcus delighted me with the gift of a new riding crop, my old one having been lost in Hardy's Wood. Ben showered me with perfume newly on the market, and Alex appeared empty-handed except for a card. He had obviously forgotten I had reached my teens. Lady Mary and Sir Oliver did not have a present for me and then Lady Mary hit me with a bombshell!

'Oliver and I and the boys are going out today, Sophia!'

I choked on my kipper. Ben slapped my back.

'We thought you would like to help Edith and staff prepare goodies for your party.'

Sir Oliver nodded. I was speechless. For the first time since residing at the Hall, I was totally excluded from the day's activities.

'Sir Oliver is going over to Wetherby to conduct some business. The boys and I are going along for the ride. We hope to return in time for your party. Millie will attend to you and help you dress. Games will take place in the garden and courtyard, as it is such a pleasant day.' Lady Mary gazed at the sunshine through the leaded windows as she spoke. I looked at the boys for some kind of comment, but they sat, heads bowed, staring at the tablecloth. They didn't care about me, either!

'Sophia, don't look so glum! I have to go today. It is the only available time I can meet with this person to do business!' Sir Oliver explained.

He could see indignation welling up inside me. Without an 'excuse me', I pushed the remains of my kipper to one side, rose from my chair and, head in the air, abruptly left the room. I raced to my bedroom, too angry to shed tears. I sat for ages, staring out across the lawns. In the distance I saw Sir Oliver disappearing in his Land Rover, Lady Mary and the boys with him. Why on earth did he have to do business on my birthday? It was my first lesson in real anger! I made my way to the kitchen.

'Hello, Edith, is there anything I can do to help?' I asked, determined to control my feelings and be helpful.

'Happy birthday, Sophia,' chanted the kitchen staff.

'So you are thirteen today! Congratulations!' said Edith.

She rushed to kiss me and give me one of her glowing smiles.

'Thank you!'

She produced a small present from her and John. I unwrapped it, saying, 'You are both so kind to have bought me this.'

The box contained a beautiful brooch, crafted in the shape of an 'S'. I kissed her. The kitchen staff showered me with flowers. I was overcome by their kind thoughts.

Edith produced items from the pantry and in no time my sleeves were rolled up. I succumbed to making cakes and other culinary delights for my party.

The time flew. I admit I enjoyed myself, although I did get messy. The staff were full of fun and we laughed away the hours. Millie called me at 3.30 informing me that I had one hour to bathe, dress and be ready to greet guests. I untied my apron, picked up my flowers and brooch, bade farewell to Edith and her helpers, and prepared myself for the party. Lady Mary, Sir Oliver and the boys had not returned. I felt pangs of anxiety creeping over me. Then Alex appeared!

'I am so glad you are home, Alex! Where are Sir Oliver and Lady Mary?'

'They will be here soon, Sophia. You look exceptionally nice in your new dress,' he commented.

'Thank you. Will you help me greet my guests?'

He agreed. We welcomed ten enthusiastic friends from my school, who seemed more intent on flirting with Alex than meeting me. I moved along the terrace and into the garden for games. Sir Oliver, Lady Mary, Ben and Marcus arrived at last to complete the picture. Sir Oliver organised the proceedings. There was a present for the first child to complete walking through the maze in both directions. Marcus won, hands down.

After sandwiches, jellies and all manner of party food, Sir Oliver suggested we all go to the courtyard to play blind man's bluff.

We did as instructed. As it was my birthday I was the one to be blindfolded. I had to wait while guests gathered in a group. Meanwhile, Alex blindfolded me and led me carefully into the centre of the courtyard. He spun me around many times and I became dizzy. With arms outstretched, I staggered in search of any child nearby. The guests screamed with excitement at the thought of being caught. Alex directed me to 'move left, go forward, and turn right'.

I obeyed his commands. Suddenly my hand touched something soft. I removed my blindfold to see who had been caught. Directly in front of me was the most gorgeous bay mare, fifteen hands high. I could hardly believe my eyes and stood with my mouth wide open. Sir Oliver, holding the reins, stepped forward and announced, 'Happy birthday, Sophia! This is your present from Lady Mary and me!'

I stood there, mesmerised, then flung myself at Sir Oliver, kissed him and said, 'Thank you, Father! Thank you so much!'

He looked at me in amazement. It was then I realised I had inadvertently called him Father. Sir Oliver took my hand and stroked my cheek with his fingers.

'I am sorry, Sir,' I apologised. 'I was so overcome with my present that I forgot what I was saying.'

'Please do not apologise, Sophia! I am thrilled you have referred to me as Father. It shows you feel you are part of our family and realise you truly belong here. Do please cease calling me "Sir". I know Lady Mary would wish for you to call her "Mother"!'

I was genuinely pleased at the turn of events. Sir Oliver was now *my* father too!

'What are you going to call the horse, Sophia?' Marcus asked.

'I must give it some thought!' I said.

There were many suggestions from the guests. After consideration, I said, 'I will call her Petronella.'

Everyone agreed it was a splendid name. Alex appeared with his present. I rushed to open it. A super riding hat was contained within the box. I immediately tried it on. It was a perfect fit.

After the party, I changed into jodhpurs and hacking jacket and rode with Alex to Hardy's Wood, to give my new riding crop, hat and Petronella a road test. She was great. I knew she and I were going to bond together just fine. It was a birthday I would always remember.

'*Sophia*! Where are you?'

I could hear Father's voice reverberating around the Hall. It was obvious he was angry.

'I am here!' I called, following the direction of his voice.

'Where is Marcus?' he asked. 'Have you seen him?'

'I did see him earlier. He has gone across the fields with Deefa.'

'That damn dog! I have told him before if he does not keep it under control it will have to go!'

'But Father, you can't do that! Deefa is his friend and companion.'

Father raised his eyebrows and said, 'I have had old Arthur here. He insists Deefa has dug holes in the flower beds in the knot garden!'

'How he can say that, Father? There are lots of rabbits about!'

'Not in our knot garden, young lady,' he retorted.

'Marcus keeps Deefa under control. He has trained him well. I think the dog is not to blame,' I insisted.

'Trust you to rise to Marcus's defence! You have an excuse for every bit of trouble he gets into.'

'And I think you're too hard on him! You always blame Marcus for everything that goes wrong!'

'Don't be insolent, Sophia! It does not become you!'

I apologised and retreated. Father fumed and made his way to the library. I had to find Marcus and warn him that Father was looking for him. Marcus sat by the beck, skimming the water with stones, Deefa lying quietly by his side.

'Father wants to see you! He thinks Deefa has dug holes in the knot garden. He is very angry!'

'He didn't, Sophia! I know how picky Sir Oliver is, so I keep him under control at all times. When he's not with me he is on a long chain in the courtyard.'

'I believe you, Marcus. I suggested the holes were dug by rabbits. Father says there are no rabbits in the garden.'

'I saw one last evening at dusk!'

'Father has cages set for them,' I said. 'How could there possibly be?'

'Goodness knows,' Marcus said, frowning.

We walked back to the Hall. Marcus faced the wrath of Father, bursting into tears as he left the library. Father summoned me. I listened to him fuming about Deefa's behaviour.

'I think it's about time young Marcus started taking up a hobby or some pastime instead of wrapping himself up in that damn dog. What do you suggest, Sophia?'

'I don't know what to suggest, Father,' I replied.

I sat there for a while as he puffed on his meerschaum, giving the situation some thought. Marcus had outgrown his love of snails and amphibians. He was now almost nine years old.

'Well, Sophia!' exclaimed Father, expecting me to devise a mind-blowing suggestion on how to amuse my young foster-brother. 'Where do we go from here?'

'He could join the Boy Scouts, well, the Cubs!' I suggested.

'Could you see Marcus sleeping in a tent? I think not!' said Sir Oliver sarcastically.

'Well, he does like music,' I ventured.

'Don't I know it! I lie in bed at night, listening to that infernal music he plays on his radio! Time and again I've suggested he should listen to classical records on the gramophone, but will he? He now likes "skiffle" music.'

'Well, I could teach him piano and encourage a love of classics! What do you think?'

'Will you have time with your other studies, Sophia?'

'Yes, Father! I would love to teach Marcus. It would encourage me to see if I would like to become a teacher of music when I leave school.'

Father insisted I consider attending the Royal College of Music. I ignored his suggestion. I have to admit there was plenty of encouragement for us children to follow the careers we wished to follow, and not what Mother and Father thought we should do. They offered helpful advice, but in the end the final decision rested with us.

'See what you can do with him, Sophia!'

'I will, Father, but please let him keep Deefa. He loves the dog dearly!'

Father agreed, and I walked away quite happily.

It was dusk as I crept into the garden.

'*Gotcha!*' I shouted.

Lily Phillips, the parlourmaid, almost jumped out of her skin. 'Oh, Miss Sophia, you frightened me!'

'Lily, you are naughty, persistently springing the rabbit cages! Do you realise Deefa was blamed for the holes dug in the knot garden? It was the rabbits, wasn't it? You have been releasing them!'

'Yes, Miss Sophia,' she cried. 'I love the creatures. I hate seeing them caught!'

'Well, this time I will not tell Sir Oliver, but if you attempt to do it again, I will have to. Do you understand me?'

'Yes, miss! I understand!'

'Good! Then off you go. Remember what I said!'

With the chastisement over, Lily disappeared into the servants' quarters, having received my message loud and clear.

The most wonderful part of life on the estate was between January and May, which was the lambing season. The pregnant ewes were brought down from the fields if having more than one lamb and housed in a large pen so they could receive extra food. When the lambs were born, the ewes were placed in separate lambing pens with their young, enabling us to observe them bonding and feeding their lambs successfully. Alex called me when he was helping with lambing and asked if I would like to assist. I readily offered to go with him. The ewe we attended was having two lambs. Alex and I stayed with her. When delivery was imminent, I had no idea what would happen at the birth. Suddenly she delivered this exquisite young one, encased in a sac. The ewe released her young lamb from this, cleaning and protecting it. It was the most wonderful, unbelievable experience.

It was then that Alex explained to me how babies were born. I thought he was joking, but he was almost eighteen and knew about such things. I knew nothing. He suggested I should ask Mother about the subject. She could explain circumstances in more detail. I was embarrassed, but he considered there were issues I should know about and he'd had reproduction explained to him by Father. He had been told about 'procreation', and it was very interesting! He had a huge smile on his face. I remembered the word 'procreation' and chanted it all the way to the Hall, then wrote it on a piece of paper in the hope of asking Mother about it the following day.

Mother was at the village hall sorting out items for a jumble sale she was organising for an African appeal.

'Hello, Sophia darling, what brings you here?' she asked, delighted to see me.

'There is something I need to ask you!' I ventured. 'I am not sure this is the time or place!'

'If I can help I will,' she said, sorting items of crockery.

By now other female helpers were eavesdropping on the conversation.

'It's Alex! He thought I should ask you about procreation!'

She looked up at me, startled. The helpers stared and nudged one another.

'Oh, he did, did he? For what reason did he suggest you talk to me about this?' she whispered, looking indignant.

'Well, last night I went to help with lambing. While the ewe was giving birth, Alex said I should ask you about procreation. He said Father had explained it all to him!'

'Keep your voice down, Sophia!' she murmured. 'People are listening. Sophia, this is a difficult subject. I really think you should ask Father. Now run along. I am very busy this morning.'

I walked dejectedly home and searched for Father. Haynes, the butler, directed me to the study where Sir Oliver was engrossed in paperwork.

'Come in, Sophia. Shut the door behind you. What can I do for you?' he asked.

'I am sorry to interrupt you, Father, but I need to ask you about procreation!'

My statement was followed by a coughing fit!

'Umm! Aah! Well…' he muttered, taking sips of water from a nearby glass. 'Your mother is the person to ask about this!'

'She said I should ask you!'

'Oh, well, umm… it's a very involved subject. I do not have the time to explain it at the moment because…'

'Alex said you explained it to him!' I demanded.

'Oh, he did, did he? Well, I am busy just now, Sophia. We will discuss this at a later date. Now off you go!'

I was disgruntled. Why were they being so evasive? All I wanted to know was what Alex already knew. It certainly was no big deal, so why all the fuss?

I decided to ask Sister Augusta on my return to school the following Monday.

Monday arrived, and during mid-morning break I entered the staffroom in search of Sister Augusta. She was sitting in a comfortable chair, surrounded by other nuns.

'Hello, Sophia! Have you come to see me?' she asked in her sweet, sensitive manner.

'I want to ask you about procreation,' I announced.

You could have heard a pin drop as all conversation in the room ceased. The nuns viewed me with disdain. What had I said? I had never seen Sister Augusta leap from her chair so athletically. She took my hand, led me from the staffroom and into the classroom, where we were attempting biological experiments on dead rats. She fingered through a case of books, finally resting her hands on a large volume of information on the subject.

'Here you are, Sophia! I will lend you this book. You must return it when you have finished reading it. Please do not show it to the other girls. Treat it with great care. This should explain everything you wish to know, from the beginning, to the end result.'

I thanked her kindly and placed the thick book in my locker.

After Marcus's piano lesson, I retreated to my room where I studied the contents. I could see why Mother and Father were loath to talk to me of such matters. There were situations in there I found difficult to comprehend. I spent days reading, but it opened my eyes to the physical relationship between male and female and it explained why I had experienced such intense feelings when Alex had kissed me, and why my heart leapt when in his company.

Chapter Eight

Arrangements were in full swing for a fiftieth birthday celebration for Father. He had requested a dinner with family members and a few long-term friends from RAF days, accompanied by their respective wives. He was in the study, when, after breakfast I caught up with him and handed him a birthday card. He was thrilled, putting it in a place of honour on his desk, so he could view it throughout the day.

'Would it be possible for you to leave your paperwork?' I asked. 'And accompany me to my room?'

He looked inquisitively at me, saying, 'I suppose these papers can wait, Sophia!'

He left his desk and escorted me to the staircase, where he bade me climb the stairs ahead of him. I entered my room. He followed.

'This is to wish you a very happy birthday, Father! I would like you to accept this gift from me!'

He looked puzzled as I pointed to a large, wrapped present on my bed.

'What on earth can this be, Sophia?'

'I do hope you will like it,' I said, watching as he began removing the wrapping paper. He viewed the violin case within. He stared at me and said, 'I cannot take this, Sophia! This violin was bequeathed to you in your papa's will. I know this was a treasured possession of your Grand-papa's.'

'I know, Father, but I would like you to accept it with all my love and affection! You will take good care of it I know and give it a good home, along with your other violins. Mama and Papa would have wanted this for you on such a special birthday for all the care and kindness you have shown me. *Please* take it!'

'Sophia—'

I interrupted him. 'It would really make me very happy!'

He carefully removed the violin from its case, gently stroked the wood and admired the wonderful finish. He placed it under his chin, removed the bow from the case and played a succession of notes. The sound was magnificent.

'I will treasure this and protect it with my life, Sophia, I promise you. It is a truly wonderful gift. I will forever be appreciative of your wonderful gesture.'

He returned it to its case, with a tear in his eye. He kissed my cheek and held me close to him. It was the first time he had shown me such fondness and I was mildly embarrassed. It reminded me of the love Papa had shown me, years previously.

'You are a lovely young lady, Sophia and have a special place in my heart,' he said.

His comments made me truly happy and he seemed euphoric with the violin.

'I will arrange for Haynes to remove it to my display cabinet. We will house it there until I play it!'

He eyed the violin once more in disbelief. We returned to his study, where I said farewell and I ventured to meet Ben and Alex for a morning ride.

Mother had approached me a few days earlier, asking if I would like to play a piano solo for Father and his guests after the dinner party. I was elated and said, 'Yes.'

Alex had been asked if he would play a piece for violin. He accepted the task graciously. The menu was a delightful one, chosen by Mother and prepared to perfection by Edith and the staff. The special crested family china and Waterford crystal wine glasses were taken from the cabinets. The table was exquisitely decorated with displays of fresh flowers and fruit, with ivy intertwined. Superb silver cutlery graced each place setting. The guests began arriving early and were greeted by the family.

Several ex-RAF personnel affirmed that they had known Mama and how delightful she was and an extremely gifted pianist. This instilled in me immense pleasure. I knew I had to give the performance of my life, in her memory. I would not be playing the *Moonlight Sonata*.

Dinner was cooked to perfection. Marcus was on his best behaviour and acted impeccably at all times. After dinner, guests moved into the Great Hall for the musical evening. Alex was the first to perform. He showed an exceptional talent for the violin.

When my turn came I stepped forward and seated myself at the piano. I heard Wing Commander David Hughes say, 'Oliver, I have never seen a young woman so resemble her mother. It is as if I have seen a ghost. Why, she is the image of Anna, and every bit as beautiful!'

Father nodded. I settled and played *Ave Maria* by Schubert and then the theme from *Romeo and Juliet* by Tchaikovsky. The officers and their wives clapped loudly and begged me to continue. I finished my repertoire with Chopin's Nocturne in E flat major. As I finished, Father arrived on stage with the violin I had presented to him earlier in the day and played 'My Heart and I', a 1940s song that was his favourite during the war. The guests sang along. Mama had favoured this too. She had taught it to me at an early age, so I accompanied him on piano. I watched tears roll down his cheeks.

After the guests had departed, Father declared it was the greatest and most enjoyable birthday he had experienced. Our family cheered loudly and sang 'For He's a Jolly Good Fellow', and after consuming bedtime drinks we all retired to our rooms, happy and contented.

A family meeting had been arranged for the following morning. We all trundled into the study, where Father presided. Both Mother and he looked sad and appeared in a sombre mood as he spoke.

'I have called this meeting today to inform you all of significant changes taking place at the Hall,' he announced.

We all looked at one another, wondering what the changes would be.

'I am hiring a new estate manager at the end of the month,' he declared.

Eyebrows were raised in amazement. It had always been accepted that Alex would take over the day-to-day running when he had finished his higher education and gained the necessary experience. Raising my arm to interrupt the meeting, I said, 'What about Alex? He was going to take up this position at a later date.'

Father looked at me, explaining, 'This is the next point I am coming to, Sophia! Alex has decided, after lengthy talks with his mother and me that he is going to follow in his father's footsteps and train as a pilot in the Royal Air Force. He has taken an entrance exam and passed with flying colours.'

I could feel anger welling up. Alex and I had walked from the village on a daily basis, meeting en route from our respective schools. Not once had he mentioned the fact he had thought of joining the RAF. He and I were supposed to be the dearest of friends, yet here I was, learning of his life-changing decisions in a family meeting. I was bitterly disappointed.

'What is it, Sophia?' Father demanded as I raised my hand again.

'Father, how on earth will we run this estate without Alex? The workers hold him in high regard, and his casual work here has been of the highest standard. He cares about the farm workers and their families, the animals and this estate.'

Alex turned to look at me but I evaded his glance.

'I know, Sophia, but the new estate manager comes highly recommended. He was in my squadron during the war and has since trained in management. He's a genial fellow, thirty-seven years of age, and very capable. His name is Stephen Howard.'

I didn't care a damn what his name was! It would not be the same as having Alex around. I had Ben and Marcus for company, but I could not share my innermost thoughts with them as I could with Alex. Ben was always so indifferent. Marcus, almost five years younger, was delightful when not in one of his stubborn moods. I adored teaching him piano, but his mind was not on the classics, but on folk, blues and rock and roll. He was a determined little monkey and not easily swayed from what he adored.

Father continued the meeting while Mother sat there saying nothing. You could sense Alex's decision was causing her heartache, especially as her first husband had been killed after a bombing mission over Germany. Many memories must have been flooding through her mind, and here was her eldest son going off to train as a pilot. I knew how sad it was for her, to some extent, because I was feeling sad too. I thought of all the times, good and bad, we had shared together. Now all this was to change, and my heart was heavy. It was at that moment I realised how much I adored him.

Alex stood up to speak. It was as though he could read my thoughts.

'Dear family, I am going away, but not too far. I will be home whenever weekend passes allow, and of course there will be leave. You will still see me frequently.'

Marcus rushed toward Alex, throwing his arms around him and saying, 'I don't want you to go, Alex. I will miss you too much!'

That was an understatement. They hugged, and Alex tried to reassure the emotional boy all would be well. When he was not following me around, Marcus was a companion to Alex. Life was not going to be the same ever again, and I knew it was my mission to watch over Marcus and try to replace the care Alex had shown him, a task which would be impossible to follow.

Alex approached me as we left the study. Taking my arm, he said, 'Please, Sophia, we need to talk! Come into the garden with me!'

I was reluctant to agree and still fumed at the fact he had not informed me of his decision. I had lived at the Hall now for seven years and had become increasingly fond of him. We were close, and I would find his absence hard to deal with.

'I really cannot accept these changes at present, Alex. I do not want to talk about it!' I snapped, behaving like a spoilt child.

'Please, Sophia!' he pleaded. 'I need to talk to you!'

Without further ado we set off down the winding paths, and he declared, 'I am sorry I did not ask your advice, Sophia, but I was scared Father would find out my intentions before I had a chance to make enquiries about my suitability as a trainee pilot officer!'

'But we could have talked things over in confidence, Alex. I would have told no one.'

'I know, Sophia, but if I had failed my entrance exams it would have caused lots of heartache for no reason. I thought it better to wait until I had been accepted; but Father found out when the RAF contacted him!'

'I see!' I said, a tear rolling down my cheek. 'I am going to miss you dreadfully, Alex. You were always my lifeline, taking care of me and watching over me. I cannot relate to Ben as I can you, and I know Marcus is devastated.'

He wiped my tears, saying, 'I know! I am going to miss you dreadfully too, but I know you will take good care of Marcus for me.'

'Of course I will watch out for him, but you will be a hard act to follow.'

He took my hand and we walked around the gardens, nattering about his future, and he stated that once he was a trained pilot, he would earn substantially more than he would as an estate manager. There would also be a chance to travel the world. At this point I realised we were all growing up, and would eventually go our own separate ways; but I was settled at last after a traumatic time during early childhood and did not want the good times to end.

'I wish you every success in whatever you do!' I said, the words choking me.

He acknowledged me, and made the future parting a little easier by saying, 'You and I can get together and have fun when I have leave.'

I was suddenly quite happy to settle for that.

'Before long you will be having boyfriends queuing to take you out, Sophia. You are a beautiful young lady.'

I blushed, thanked him for his kind comments, and explained I was not interested in the opposite sex, but he laughed.

'Then there will be your move to London to attend the Royal College. Father wants you to go there so much!'

'But *I do not*, Alex! I want to stay here at the Hall. I love this place with all my heart. I cannot think of anywhere I would rather be!'

'But Sophia, you have such outstanding talent. You must follow in your mama's footsteps and become a concert pianist. You promised her faithfully that you would.'

I looked at him with sad eyes. He could see I was not happy with such a suggestion.

'No, Alex! I am going to stay here and help on the estate with lambing and cooking and riding. My music will take a back seat. I never want to leave Harrington Hall!'

We parted on good terms. I learnt that he would be departing in approximately two weeks, enough time for Mother to arrange a farewell dinner, which had to be a very special occasion. Marcus, Ben and I shopped for lots of little things Alex would find useful in his new environment. His life was about to change dramatically, and ours with it.

Life seemed strange with Alex gone. I had looked forward to our walks from the village to the Hall, after school, when we'd exchanged news and gossip, but I now had to contend with Ben, who was intent on annoying me as often as possible. We were the same age, yet he seemed so childish, playing tricks and generally getting up to mischief at my expense. Marcus had been transferred from his boys' school in another village, where he had not been progressing well. He was now at the Grange with Ben, and joined us every afternoon for the walk home. I found him to be more talkative than Ben, and decidedly more mature for his years. He always seemed delighted to see me, and as we talked, the subject would always be something to do with music, which Ben had no interest in. We talked of Alex frequently, wondering when we would see him. There had been little communication from him by letter, and even less by telephone, but Mother insisted that initially there were large amounts of physical training and study to contend with. We accepted her explanation but missed not being able to converse. We did not have an address where we could write.

When a few weeks had passed, Marcus dived out of school one afternoon, his satchel swinging off his shoulder. He was one of the tallest boys in class, and by far the most pleasant looking, with his black hair and big brown eyes. There was something almost mystical about him I had not noticed before. He ran toward me waving a postcard.

'Look, Sophia, I have a message from Alex! The postman gave it to me as I left for school!'

'I am so pleased for you, Marcus!' I said, feeling dejected. Alex hadn't written one word to me.

'He says he misses me, Sophia!'

'Did he mention me?' I asked.

'No, I'm afraid not!' he said, looking at me with those large eyes.

'Oh, well!' I commented as though it did not matter. 'I am not bothered. I am sure he will write when he can!' I hurried ahead, not wishing Marcus to see my disappointment.

'I expect he will write soon,' he soothed.

'Yes! Come on, Marcus. We must hurry and get your piano lesson into full swing.'

'Sophia, will you be disappointed if I miss it today? Several lads in my class want me to play cricket with them on the village green!'

'If you must – go ahead! Father will not be pleased if you are not taking your music seriously,' I said disapprovingly.

I wanted Marcus to go for a game of cricket as he had few friends. I was pleased he had been asked to join in the game, but anxious for his company.

'Please cover for me,' he asked.

I agreed but did not feel happy about the situation. I suddenly began to feel pangs of utter loneliness and isolation. Mother was busy with all her fund-raising activities for the charities she supported, and Father was continually tied up with estate business or visits to the factories. I fought back tears and made my way to my room to attend to my homework. As I entered the main door, Father called, 'There you are, Sophia! Come and meet Stephen Howard, our new estate manager, who I hope is going to relieve me of a great deal of the work around here.'

Good! I thought. Perhaps then we can all begin to behave like a family again!

Father asked me where Benedict and Marcus were. I excused their absence by informing him they had after-school activities and stated they would be returning soon.

'I wanted them to meet Stephen, but there will be plenty of time.'

He opened the study door. Stephen Howard stood up and extended a hand. Father introduced me as his daughter. I reciprocated by shaking hands with the brown-haired, smiling, tanned thirty-seven-year-old with attractive features and hazel eyes. He gave the impression of being able to charm anyone in his immediate vicinity.

'So you are Sophia!' he remarked. 'I have heard so much about you from your father.'

'Some good things, I hope,' I said modestly.

'Why, of course! Your father tells me you are an extremely competent young lady, especially when it comes to the piano. I would love to hear you play sometime.'

'There will be plenty of time for you to hear Sophia, Stephen. She plays daily!' said Father, lighting his meerschaum and settling down at his desk.

'Well, run along, Sophia. Get your homework finished, and then after tea you must practise! Can you call at the kitchen and ask Edith to send tea, sandwiches and a few of those cakes she has been baking?'

'Consider it done, Father! Goodbye, Mr Howard. I expect our paths will cross again soon.' He stood up from his chair, shook my hand once more and said, 'I hope so.'

With my farewell, I left the room. At least there was a new face around the estate. He seemed a pleasant enough person, and Father seemed relieved to have help in running the estate, so it looked as though everyone was happy with their little lot except me!

Days passed and on arriving home one Thursday afternoon I went in search of Mother to ask for help with a sewing project I had been given at school. I heard her talking in the drawing room. As I entered I realised she was conversing on the telephone and waited outside the door.

'How wonderful, Alex! This weekend? Why, of course you can!'

At the mention of Alex's name I moved closer to the door and listened naughtily to the conversation.

'Yes, you know you can bring a friend home. I will make sure one of the guest rooms is prepared. I am so thankful you have found people you can get on with at the base.'

Mother sounded delighted that Alex would be gracing us with his presence. It was twelve weeks since he had set foot in the Hall. He was at last coming home for a long weekend, accompanied by a friend.

I couldn't wait for the following evening to arrive. After piano practice I bathed, donned a new dress Alex had not seen before, asked Millie to style my hair in a more ladylike fashion, and sat in the drawing room, awaiting his arrival. Marcus was over the moon at the thought of having Alex's company over the weekend and joined me to listen for the sound of his car roaring up the drive. Mother popped her head around the door and announced that cocoa was made and ready for us in the kitchen. We departed to drink this, and were told that as Alex had been delayed we should not wait any longer but retire to bed. Marcus and I were extremely disappointed and began to plead with her when we heard Haynes answer the door. It was Alex! I heard his voice. Without further ado, Marcus, Mother and I hurried into the Hall to greet him. He looked so handsome in his uniform, but I suddenly stopped in my tracks. Behind him was a girl – a long-haired, blonde, slim, beautiful girl of about twenty years of age. She slipped her arm through his and moved forward to greet Mother, Marcus and me – when I had finished giving her a once-over. Alex had brought a young lady home for the weekend!

My first reaction was one of horror, but I had to admit to myself she was extremely sociable, and in no time at all decided I liked her immensely. Her name was Lucy. She was attached to the NAAFI on the base. Marcus was not so entranced by her. I think he considered her a threat to his relationship with Alex.

'Gosh! You seem to have changed an awful lot in the last few weeks, Sophia!' Alex noted as we hugged.

'You too, Alex,' I replied. 'You look very handsome in your uniform!'

He smiled his intoxicating smile. My heart leapt. Mother ordered refreshments and we all congregated in the drawing room. Father and Ben joined us, welcoming Lucy, although they too seemed surprised Alex's friend was a girl. We chatted for ages, asking about training and life in the RAF. We then nosily asked Lucy about her life on the base and how they had met. She was an open, honest and friendly girl, with no airs or graces. She and Alex seemed well suited to one another. He was ecstatic in her company. She fitted readily into our way of life. I could do no more than be happy for him in his choice of lady friend, but I had to admit to myself I was jealous of their relationship. It was late before the niceties of the evening ceased and we retired at midnight. It was wonderful having Alex home. Before departing to bed, he called me as I was halfway up the stairs.

'How about an early morning hack, Sophia? I hope you have been looking after Storm for me!'

I turned and announced, 'Storm is in excellent condition and yes, I would like to join you. Seven o'clock too early?' I asked.

He laughed and replied, 'No! Seven o'clock will be fine! See you at the stables!'

'I'll be there!' I laughed and then, addressing Lucy, I said, 'Please will you join us? It would be wonderful if you could come along too!'

She thanked me for my invitation but declined, saying she had never ridden and was not interested in horses. I bade her goodnight and climbed the stairs. As I reached the last stair and turned toward my room I watched Alex take her in his arms and kiss her tenderly on her lips. Alex was head over heels in love!

He was on my mind as I crept into bed. I was determined to be at the stables for seven o'clock so I could at least spend a couple of hours with him before breakfast.

He was saddling up Petronella for me as I arrived and greeted me with, 'Come on, lazybones! I was going to go without you!' But I laughed, and knew he was teasing.

I donned my riding hat, and with the saddle securely in place I mounted Petronella. He mounted Storm and we trotted slowly toward Hardy's Wood.

'It is so good to be home! You all look well. You, in particular, Sophia, seem to be changing, in looks and shape.' He had noticed.

'I am almost the tallest girl in class now!' I remarked. 'Which is strange, as Mama and Papa were both of average height. I must favour other Italian ancestors.'

'It suits you,' he remarked.

'Thank you. I am so glad you have found yourself a charming girlfriend. Lucy seems extremely pleasant from the little I have seen of her.'

'She is a great girl! Very lively and full of fun. I adore her!'

'I can see you do!' I observed.

'Marcus does not seem pleased with my new friend.' He chuckled.

'You know Marcus! He thought he was going to have you all to himself this weekend.'

'He is growing so fast, Sophia, and will soon be towering above us all. I understand from Father that his piano playing has shown signs of great improvement, with your help. It will be an achievement in itself if you get anywhere with disruptive young Marcus!' He laughed.

We stopped and tethered Storm and Petronella to a tree and sat on a nearby grassy bank to continue our conversation. Alex explained a great deal about his training in the RAF, but there were things he was not able to discuss and I did not pry. I realised he had chosen a career which satisfied him and gave him a sense of purpose. He was more contented than I'd had seen him in a long while, although I had to give Lucy a certain amount of credit for this state of affairs.

'I thought I would take you, Marcus and Lucy out for the day tomorrow in my car. I had thought of going to Brontë country. What do you think?'

'We'd love to, Alex, but surely you would rather be alone with Lucy.'

'Lucy and I see each other almost every day, but I do not see you and Marcus often. Please say you'll join us!' he pleaded.

'If the arrangements are satisfactory with Lucy, then we would love to. I know Marcus will be enthralled just to have a ride in your new car!'

The decision was all but finalised. He would consult Lucy, but he could not foresee any problems. We mounted our trusty steeds and galloped further into Hardy's Wood and out on the other side.

Excitement took over. At breakfast Marcus and I could hardly eat a thing. Father lectured Alex about taking great care in his new car, and to have great respect for other road users and passengers alike. I think he had forgotten Alex was maturing and in a few years would be flying bombers on missions around the world, when required.

Lucy dressed appropriately for the journey to Haworth, sporting jeans and a sweater and a scarf for her long blonde hair, which she had dressed in a French pleat. I wore an almost identical outfit, except, to please Mother, my long black hair cascaded over my shoulders in its usual fashion. I took a headscarf with me in case I needed it. Marcus insisted on sitting in the front of Alex's Riley convertible sports car. Lucy and I squeezed into the seats at the back, which gave us little room, but we viewed the countryside and breathed in the fresh air of the Yorkshire Dales.

The conversation was typical, cars!

'What model is this, Alex?' asked Marcus, running his fingers over the red leather upholstery.

'It's the Riley RMD series. It is superb, isn't it?' Alex replied, obviously very proud of his acquisition, bought by Father as an eighteenth birthday present, soon after he passed his test.

'How fast can it go?'

'Around one hundred miles an hour!' Alex boasted.

'Gosh! Can we do that speed today? Please, Alex!'

'I think not, Marcus! We have to appreciate we have two delicate young ladies in the back. We don't want to scare them, do we?'

'Spoilsport!' moaned Lucy.

We all laughed hysterically as we ventured across Ilkley Moor in the magnificent cream sports car.

When we arrived at Haworth there were scores of visitors milling around the various gift shops lining the cobbled main street leading to the parsonage where Emily, Charlotte and Anne Brontë had lived with their father when he was parson at the church. I had recently read *Wuthering Heights* and as I stopped to view the bleak Pennine moors I could feel and experience the backdrop for this famous novel. After an interesting visit to the parsonage, we stopped in the cobbled street at a tea shop and afforded ourselves cream teas, before walking to the local railway station, where we boarded the steam train and had a tour of the Keighley and Worth Steam Railway. It was so exciting.

The Riley proved a draw to the visitors. After answering numerous questions about the vehicle, Alex drove us back across Ilkley Moor and introduced us to one of his favourite haunts, the Biggest Fish and Chip Shop in the World. He slowed down and pulled into the car park. The thought of us having fish and chips for our Sunday meal did not impress Lucy one bit, until we entered the building. I had never experienced anything quite like it. Instead of linoleum floors there were plush red and gold carpets and instead of strip lights, chandeliers. Beautiful crisp white tablecloths adorned and there was a waitress service where the girls wore black dresses, white aprons and caps. I sat at the table staring around me, eyeing the large mirrors, watching waitresses bring pots of tea and bread and butter to the tables to accompany the meals. It was a sight to behold. I was totally mesmerised. The fish was delicious. I had never tasted anything so wonderful, not even from the hands of Edith Roberts. We finished with a range of delicious desserts.

Lucy and I sang fifties hit songs by Buddy Holly, Bill Haley and Elvis as we were driven homewards. Alex and Marcus made meowing sounds as we perfected our harmonies. I don't think any of us had laughed so much in a long time. Marcus was totally taken with rock and roll, and to say we had fun was an understatement. I fell into bed, warm, happy and pleased. Alex was home again to bring some laughter into our lives, but in twenty-four hours he would be gone. I would miss him, and Lucy too!

Lucy was a fantastic person: friendly, warm, charming and helpful. She brought all the fun ideas of a twenty-year-old growing into maturity in the late 1950s. She arrived in my room on Monday morning as I finished dressing. Mad about hairstyles, make-up and fashion, she took Millie, the maid and I into a realm that had, until then, lain virtually undiscovered to us.

Mother was averse to changes in fashion and styling, preferring what she knew to be comfortable, hard wearing and good value for money, whereas Lucy lived for the moment and dressed as the mood took her on any particular day. Together Millie, Lucy and I had great fun experimenting with hair and make-up, but Mother cast a disapproving eye on me at lunch on the first occasion I decided to sport a bouffant hairdo.

'I do not think your new look is quite you, Sophia!' she exclaimed, frowning as she moved to examine the hairstyle. She moved cagily around me as though at any moment a creature, which she imagined lurked within, would rear its ugly head and attack.

'How on earth do you keep it up in the air like that?' Mother asked quizzically.

'Backcombing!' I replied, leaving her looking intrigued, but still objecting to the style.

'Ricardo, at Tresses, my hair designer in York, would never conjure up such a monstrosity, Sophia, and I suggest after lunch you return your hair to its usual style, darling.'

Of course Tresses wouldn't do such a design. They were what one might call 'terribly old-fashioned'! Father, always deep in thought, sat himself at the table, acknowledged each one of us without glancing at us individually, and appeared not to notice my new look. When he did discover it, during the consumption of his first glass of wine, he almost choked on the contents of the glass.

'*Good God*! I didn't realise there had been a hurricane today! You obviously got caught up in it, Sophia!'

That amused Alex, Ben and Marcus immensely, but not Lucy. Much tittering ensued.

'A little too much make-up around your eyes, too!' Mother noted. 'You have lovely eyes, Sophia. No need to emphasise them to such a degree!'

I made no comment, but Ben winked at me in fun and puckered up his lips as if to give me a passionate kiss. I kicked him under the table for his efforts. I was quite happy with my look, so to me it was all that mattered, but after Lucy had departed I couldn't maintain the art of styling my hair, and my new regime fell by the wayside even though Millie tried her hardest to assimilate what had been taught her.

Chapter Nine

Alex rested his elbow on my shoulder and together we surveyed the assembly of the marquee on the front lawn. It was an enormous feat for the labourers, but it looked marvellous once in place. The drinks tents were then added to the sides. Mother had arranged for her favourite florist from Leeds to arrive with massive stands of spring flowers to decorate the inside of the marquee. Small decorations had been ordered for each table to complement the 'Spring Flowers' family china. Looking up at Alex, I said, 'I am so delighted for you that you and Lucy have decided on a spring engagement followed by a summer wedding. You really were made for one another.'

'Thank you, dear Sophia. She really is a super girl and I know she will be a marvellous wife. I am thrilled too that you and she get on so well.'

He smiled his captivating smile – the smile I knew so well – and I was overjoyed at the thought of his engagement the following day. I wanted him to be truly happy.

Several cars appeared in the distance and drove slowly in a convoy along the driveway leading to the Hall.

'I have to leave you, Sophia. My guests are beginning to arrive. I want to greet them and ensure they are comfortably settled in their rooms.'

Alex patted my arm affectionately and departed, leaving me staring at the work in progress. I suddenly returned to my senses from my daydream and thought that I ought to see if I could be of help to Edith.

On arrival at the Hall, Mother was bustling around like a woman possessed, making calls to various establishments and trying to finalise arrangements. It had been decided by Alex and Lucy, when invitations were printed, that they would ask that guests wear fancy dress for the evening ball. This had taken Mother and Father by surprise, but they embraced the idea simply to please the young couple. The theme was to be that of the Tudor period. Father had informed me, in confidence, that he was going as Henry VIII, and Mother as Elizabeth I. They had visited a theatrical costumier in Leeds and hired the most fabulous clothing.

One of the large barns had been scrupulously cleaned and prepared for Elizabethan dancing, in keeping with the theme, but no doubt a few modern waltzes would creep in. A small orchestra of the finest musicians had been engaged. The barn was in the process of being tastefully decorated to simulate the period it represented. Workmen were busy putting finishing touches to the scenery. Edith was working to full capacity, catering for the event. A banquet in the marquee was to begin the engagement celebrations and, following speeches and toasts to the young couple, guests would change their attire for the fancy dress ball to commence at 8 p.m.

I approached Edith and asked if my services were required. I was set the task of making an assortment of food for the following day. There was staff bustling around the kitchen who I had never met. They had been called in from the two adjoining villages. We all worked hard and long, and eventually Edith had the vast menu under control.

I had hired a costume myself from Leeds and was pleased with my selection, but revealed to no one what I had chosen. Marcus and Ben chose to dress as court jesters, and with the help of library books, Lucy, Millie and I had managed to make two suitable costumes for the boys to wear. I thought how appropriate their choices were.

Lucy disappeared early on the Saturday morning to collect the dress she would wear for the banquet. Several days previously I had gone through my wardrobe and discovered a dress I had worn only once before. With Lucy's help I had altered it and added decoration to give it the appearance of something I had recently purchased.

I saw little of the family during the day. They all appeared to be scurrying around, each with an important task to carry out. I set eyes on Marcus on a couple of occasions, and he seemed to have adjusted to the fact that Alex was to become engaged to Lucy. He, like me, was extremely fond of her.

At three o'clock Millie called me to my room to help me prepare myself for the meal. I bathed and groomed myself with her help. I wanted to look particularly attractive for this special occasion. Millie had learnt a host of new hairstyles from Lucy which particularly suited my long black hair, and she took great care to arrange it on top of my head in a cascade of curls, with small white artificial rosebuds entwined throughout. They matched the decoration on my dress. I was just sixteen, and realised that womanhood was fast approaching as I slipped into the long, pale blue silk dress Mother had once purchased for my role as bridesmaid to one of Father's god-daughters. Lucy had carried out the exceptional task of helping me alter it. We had lowered the neckline – rather daringly – and the back too, adding a swirl of tiny rosebuds which reached from the back, across my shoulder and down to the front of my dress. I viewed myself in the mirror, and with my make-up perfected, could not believe the change which had taken place in me.

The finishing touches were a string of pearls Father had bought me the previous Christmas, with a new evening bag and shoes. Millie said I looked a million dollars. Father called me from the foot of the staircase, asking if I was ready to accompany Mother and him to the banquet. Millie answered by announcing that I would be along in a few moments. He waited patiently with Mother until I put in an appearance.

I stood elegantly at the top of the flight of stairs. As I began to descend Father remarked, 'Sophia? Is it really you? What a transformation. Why, I have never seen you look so becoming. You astound me, young lady!'

It was praise indeed coming from Father. I blushed and carefully concentrated on walking downstairs in my new, fashionable high-heeled shoes.

'Darling, where on earth did you buy that delightful dress? It suits you to perfection!' Mother commented, radiating a huge smile in my direction. 'It really is quite something! Did you get it in Harrogate?'

I shook my head and realised that dear Lucy and I had made such an excellent task of the changes that Mother had not recognised the garment. I had so much to thank Lucy for. Over the past year, with her help, I had matured into an attractive young lady!

Edith had exceeded all expectations when it came to the catering. The food was expertly prepared and presented. All the staff worked unstintingly to give the marquee a tremendous boost with ribbons and balloons, all tastefully positioned. Gorgeous perfumed flowers provided the finishing artistic touches to an impressive scene.

Father gave a wonderful speech, welcoming Lucy and explaining about the joy he and Mother knew she would bring to both Alex and to our family, how fond we were of her and how delighted we all were that arrangements were being made for a forthcoming summer wedding. Expensive champagne of an excellent quality flowed, and first-rate wines were also consumed. Alex gave a long, sentimental speech, portraying what a wonderful life he had had at the Hall, and recalled comical instances from our childhood, which had guests greatly amused. He thanked Father for his love and devotion to Ben and himself after the loss of his father, Douglas, and of his mother's unconditional love for us all. He spoke of how his life had been enhanced by his brother, Ben, and by Marcus and me. He thanked Lucy for agreeing to become his wife and assured everyone that he would treasure her during their lifetime together. I detected Mother choking back tears, quite unsuccessfully. This made us siblings quite emotional too.

After the lavish meal, speeches, drinking and general chatting, Ben,

Marcus and I presented Lucy and Alex with Waterford crystal glasses for their bottom drawer. They were delighted with the gift. I asked to be excused and hurried across to the Hall, where Millie had prepared my outfit for the evening of dancing and merriment. She redressed my hair in a suitable style and helped me into my gown and accessories. It was quite sensational, with all the bead trimmings. I resembled the royal lady I was supposed to be likened to.

The small group of musicians, engaged to entertain a large group of the most illustrious guests from far and wide, were already playing when I entered the barn. Each guest had made a special effort to dress in a costume of the Tudor period, and had embraced the spirit of the occasion. The atmosphere was one of happiness and frivolity. Father looked splendid as Henry VIII, the outfit enhancing his masculinity, but with so much shoulder and bodily padding, I was fretful he would not be able to dance and converse with guests; but he did so in his charming, yet inimitable manner. Mother, as Queen Elizabeth, wore a dress of ivory silk, embroidered in a gold floral design, the pleats of the skirt fitting over a farthingale. It greatly enhanced her figure. Ropes of costume pearls draped the bodice. Two strings of pearls were worn around her neck.

Dear Alex arrived as Sir Walter Raleigh in a delightful outfit, complete with fake beard and moustache. Accompanied by Lucy he looked so handsome. She was dressed as Catherine Howard, and wore a French hood with white under cap and black velvet trailing from the back to below the shoulders. Her gown was full black velvet with gold embroidery and white and gold wrist frills. She looked amazing with her beautiful blonde hair and flawless complexion.

I, as Mary, Queen of Scots, wore a red French hood with a crimped edging and pearl and jewelled billament. My dress had a long square neckline edged with pearls. The dress was rich orange/red brocade in a pomegranate pattern. The velvet cuffs and under-sleeves were of white damask and were held with jewels.

'You look so regal in your costume,' Marcus commented as I turned and faced him and Ben. I wanted to laugh, but held back my amusement. They looked so devilish in their court jester outfits. I smirked and commended them accordingly. I watched Alex and Lucy as they mingled with the guests. They were extremely happy in one another's arms and smiled as they gracefully danced across the floor. I knew without a doubt that Lucy would be a splendid wife and fit perfectly into RAF life, following Alex wherever his postings took him.

Turning around, I saw Stephen Howard arrive, dressed as a falconer, and within minutes he had the ladies flocking around hoping they would be asked to dance. There were enormous bowls of punch and flagons of ale, and in no time the guests were merry and relaxed. I stood chatting to some of them when I was startled by a hand resting on my shoulder. A voice apologised for the interruption and asked, 'Will you dance with me, please, Sophia?'

I turned around to be faced by Stephen Howard.

'Thank you, I would like to,' I replied.

'I hope you will not be offended if I tell you that you look beautiful, Sophia,' he said, smiling at me, as he took my hand and led me onto the dance floor.

'What a kind thing for you to say, Mr Howard,' I remarked coyly. 'I will treat it as a very nice compliment.'

'I saw you from a distance during the meal and I thought what a stunning young lady you were in your blue dress, and now you are a picture of enchantment in your beautiful costume. Your parents must be very proud of you!'

'I hope they are, Mr Howard.'

He held me close and gave me his full attention as we joined other dancers. I thought how polite and considerate he was. He was delightful company, a superb dancer, and made me feel quite at ease considering the difference in our ages. He seemed young-minded and talked about so many interesting subjects. I danced with him for a considerable time until we were interrupted by Alex, asking for a dance. Excusing himself, he took my hand and led me away in a different direction.

'You really need to socialise with more guests, Sophia!' he said reproachfully. 'You have spent far too much time dancing with Mr Howard. Young men are queuing up to be with you.'

'I am sorry, Alex, but I find him a very interesting person!' I explained.

'And he seems to have an unhealthy interest in you, Sophia!'

'I do not know what you mean!' I snapped.

'I saw how closely he held you and how personal he was! Why, he is old enough to be your father!'

'What an awful thing to say, Alex! He is a very kind, well-mannered man. I like him.'

'Yes, and he likes you too – too much, as far as I am concerned.'

'Alex,' I chided, 'don't be so ridiculous! He is simply being friendly. You are imagining things.'

'I hope so, Sophia! I really do hope so!' he muttered as he swept me across the floor. 'You are looking far older than your sixteen years tonight. In fact, you are so damn beautiful you are setting several hearts aflutter, from comments I have heard. Just be careful, Sophia!'

'Alex, please do not worry. I am quite capable of taking care of myself.'

'Are you, Sophia? I don't think so…'

The dance ended and he took my hand and kissed it gently. This small, close gesture of his sent exciting feelings down my body as I thanked him for partnering me, and I retreated outside to allow myself to get some fresh air. Father appeared, joined me on the lawn and commented, 'I notice that you have danced with Stephen Howard a great deal this evening, Sophia! There are other guests needing your attention.'

'Yes, Father, I have – much to Alex's disgust.'

'You must not be annoyed with Alex that he is acting like a big brother towards you.'

He had obviously informed Father that Stephen had paid me considerable interest. Petulantly I said, 'I do wish Alex would stop treating me as though I were a child.'

'No one could possibly mistake you for a child, Sophia, after seeing you tonight,' he commented. 'You have been maturing into a stunning young woman right before our eyes. You are very beautiful, like your mama. You are a mirror image of Anna.'

'Thank you, dear Father,' I said shyly.

'Alex considers himself a man of the world now he is in the RAF, and wants to protect you. You must allow him a certain amount of consideration for the way in which he concerns himself about you.'

'I do, Father, but I am capable of taking care of myself. Stephen is a perfect gentleman. He was simply being kind and friendly. He is a very pleasant man. I find his conversation stimulating.'

'Well, he is a good estate manager, but please don't take a person at face value. You have a lot to learn about life, Sophia! Stephen is definitely handsome and enchanting, but with these advantages I cannot understand why he has never married. There are plenty of sweet eligible women in his age group.'

'I imagine he hasn't found the right one, Father,' I interjected. 'Can we go back to the barn? It is rather chilly out here.'

He returned me to the party, where he took me in his arms, dancing me around the floor. It was wonderful, dancing with Henry VIII, with the man who had plucked me out of an impossible situation and given me love, kindness and stability.

He was a good man, and I knew he loved me just as much as he did his other children, and being a girl, I realised he spoilt me far more than he did the boys.

I stood in the corner of the barn once more, politely chatting to guests when a familiar voice whispered, 'This is the last dance. Will you please accompany me?'

I turned to see Stephen with a smile and a pleading look on his face. I agreed to dance with him once more.

'When the party has finished, I would be pleased to accompany you back to the Hall, if you will allow me.'

I accepted his kind offer, and after bidding numerous guests farewell, I left with Stephen. We walked across the lawns, he helping me whenever the high heels of my shoes sunk into the soil. It was a laughable time and we talked light-heartedly. His opinion was that the engagement banquet and dance had been a huge success, to which I wholeheartedly agreed. I reached the steps leading to the entrance to the Hall. He thanked me once more for dancing with him and bade me goodnight.

'I will wait until you are safely inside,' he offered.

I thanked him and turned to climb the last two steps when my heel caught in the hem of my dress and I lost my balance. Stephen rushed forward to save me from falling and caught me in his arms when...

'*Get off her! How dare you touch her!*'

From nowhere Alex appeared. Without waiting to discover what had happened, he punched Stephen heavily on the jaw, sending him tumbling down the steps to the ground below.

'*Stop it, Alex!*' I screamed as he launched himself at Stephen once more, in an attempt to deliver more blows to a defenceless Mr Howard, who had begun to lift himself up. I ran to his aid. The look on Stephen's face told me that he was extremely angry. I could sense the start of a fight. Thankfully, Marcus, Ben and Lucy arrived, stepping in the way.

'I am so sorry, Stephen,' I said apologising for Alex's behaviour. I really don't know what got into him!'

Ben and Marcus dragged Alex into the Hall, with the help of Haynes, who had by now arrived on the scene. Lucy and I inspected the damage inflicted on Stephen. He was going to have severe bruising, but would hopefully soon recover. After I had apologised once more, he left. Lucy and I entered the Hall, where we had intended giving Alex hell, but the boys had seen that he had gone to his room in disgrace.

Lucy and Alex returned to the base the following afternoon, but not before Alex had received the wrath of Father. He kept a low profile during the day and certainly did not come within yards of me not even to apologise. I was still infuriated by his behaviour and had never known him act in such a manner. Lucy excused it by suggesting Alex had had too much to drink. He certainly hadn't appeared intoxicated to me, but was simply being overprotective. Thank goodness Marcus and Ben arrived when they did, or I dare not contemplate what would have happened. It would have spoilt an otherwise magnificent day. In future I would not divulge to Alex any relationships I embarked on for fear of a repetition of the previous night. I would not want to watch Alex exercise his right hook as he had done in anger at what he thought he saw happening.

Summer was fast approaching and the wedding loomed. I had decisions to make about my future and what I intended doing with my life. I had a choice of applying for a scholarship to the Royal College of Music, working for the family businesses, or staying at school for another year. I had no intentions of going to London, which provoked Father to become grumpy and disappointed in me, reminding me of my promise I had made to Mama; but he eventually gave me carte blanche to do as I thought fit with my life. I decided that my next course of action was to work within the estate. I had decided I would leave school at the end of the summer term having sat GCEs but would not venture on to the advanced courses. I loved my work with sheep and horses, and adored the invigorating air of the Dales. We had experienced, in recent years, some pretty poor winters when food supplies had to be flown in, but we somehow managed to survive during that time thanks to the preservation of many fruits and foods undertaken by Edith during the summer months. A fair number of sheep had been lost due to extreme weather conditions.

   A new type of flooring had appeared on the domestic market, and there was not such a demand for carpeting that there once had been. The industry dwindled a little. There were times when Father looked extremely harassed, but he never breathed a word to any of us what it was that made him look so sad, or what financial situations there were to contend with. Life seemed to carry on as normal, although I could sense that all was not as well as we were led to believe. I heard him having harsh words with Stephen Howard on several occasions.

   Marcus settled down to his piano lessons and tried to come to grips with the classics that I taught him, but without any enthusiasm. I helped him with a great deal of music theory, which I hoped would stand him in good stead for the future, but Father still complained continuously that he heard him listening to awful rock music into the early hours. Father had purchased a black and white television. Marcus was glued to

Six Five Special on a weekly basis to watch and listen to bands and groups perform their latest music, but if Father was in the vicinity he would steal in and turn down the volume or turn off the set completely.

Ben decided to continue with his education for another two years. Then he hoped to get a place at Cambridge University.

Lucy's parents were attached to the NAAFI in Gibraltar, so most of the wedding preparations fell squarely on Mother's shoulders, not that she objected. She was in her element. Lucy's mother and father had been unable to attend the engagement party, so the wedding would be the first time they would be introduced to our family. They had planned their two weeks' annual leave to coincide, which in turn would give them a chance to familiarise themselves with the Hall, church and our family. We were looking forward with great excitement to meeting them.

Alex and Lucy arrived four weeks prior to the wedding, Alex having his annual leave. Lucy and I and the two other bridesmaids attended a bridal shop in Harrogate to try on our dresses, which had been ordered and needed final fittings. Mother drove us there. Lucy's friends, Sarah and Elizabeth, and I, tried on our shimmering pink dresses. They were dresses to die for. We were to have fresh flower headdresses to complement the bouquets. Lucy allowed me to see her wedding gown, but only me. She looked incredible in gorgeous white silk, but she found fault with so many aspects of the dress. At the end of the fitting I began to think that she was one very sad young lady.

We returned to the Hall for afternoon tea. I chatted with the two bridesmaids about our excitement at the visit to Harrogate, while Lucy disappeared to look for her beloved Alex, who was helping around the estate. I hoped his path had not crossed with that of Stephen Howard, who had still not forgotten the incident at the engagement party. He promised me most implicitly that he would not confront Alex over the episode, and as far as Stephen was concerned he had forgiven Alex. The two bridesmaids had to return to Lincolnshire by train, and John Roberts transported them to the station in the Rolls. I searched for Marcus to give him his piano lesson. It was then that he informed me he had written some lyrics to a song, and I was so impressed by his efforts I promised I would show him how to write music to accompany the lyrics. He was thrilled. After his lesson I retreated to my room for some well-earned rest. As I passed the door to Lucy's room, I heard a noise and investigated what I thought were sobs. As I entered her room, I found her lying face down on the bed. She looked up and I could see tears streaming down her cheeks.

'Goodness, Lucy! What on earth is the matter?' I asked, distressed at seeing her in such a state. She asked me to leave her, sobbed and turned her head away, but I could not go.

'Has Alex upset you?' I asked. 'He seems to be behaving so erratically these days.'

She turned and laid her head on my lap, as I sat on the bed. Then she whispered, 'No, Sophia!' and began sobbing again, this time far more uncontrollably.

'Then have I upset you?' I asked, wanting to know what it was that had hurt her so.

We were so close and I was feeling her pain.

'You have not hurt me, my dear friend. You have always been so wonderful to me. You and I are like sisters. I adore you.'

'Then what is it? You can tell me anything, but if you do not tell me what the problem is, I cannot help.'

She looked at me and with swollen eyes said, 'It is me, Sophia. I *cannot* marry Alex!'

I frowned in disbelief at the words she uttered and stroked her shiny blonde hair in a comforting gesture. She cried into the fabric of my dress.

'Lucy, please don't say such a thing. You love Alex so much. I know you do. He loves you dearly too. You will break his heart.'

She looked at me and made an attempt to dry her tears. Greatly distressed, she seemed to need a friend and confidante, and I was there to comfort and help her in any way I could.

'I do love him, Sophia, but it would be absolutely pointless to marry him. You see, it is not me he loves!'

'Of course he does! He is head over heels in love with you.'

'I am afraid not! If we marry in three weeks we will both regret it for the rest of our lives.'

'You are being silly,' I told her. 'I think you are having prenuptial nerves. Everything will be fine! Everyone has silly notions at a time like this.' But Lucy would not listen and continuously shook her head.

'You see, Sophia, he says he loves me, but I know that he loves someone else…'

I could not believe the words she uttered. I tried to think of girls I had known him associate with but none were more than friends. No one had attracted him other than Lucy, unless there had been another woman at the base, unbeknown to me, and I think he would have confessed to me about it.

'You are wrong in your assumption. Alex has never looked at another woman in the way he looks at you! You are the love of his life.'

'If only that were true,' Lucy sighed.

'Then who is it? I asked 'Do you know her?'

'Yes, I do,' she whispered sheepishly, trying to evade the question.

'Then tell me, and we will see if we can sort this out!'

Lucy turned away, but I insisted we discussed the matter fully and decide on a course of action.

She returned her gaze with sad eyes, focused on me and said, 'Sophia, he is in love with you!'

'*No! No, Lucy*! Please don't be ridiculous! We are like brother and sister and nothing more. I have never encouraged Alex in any way. He and I have grown up together.'

'I have seen another side to Alex. He never stops talking about you, Sophia. He continually sings your praises and why do you think he punched Stephen on the night of our engagement?'

'Because he thought Stephen was taking advantage of me!' I said.

'If only that were the case! Alex attacked Stephen because he was insanely jealous that he was with you! I watched Alex throughout the evening. He couldn't take his eyes off you. He wanted to be with *you*, but it was Stephen who danced with you and walked you home. That move upset him more than you could imagine.'

I was dumbfounded at these revelations and began to focus on the events of the night in question.

'I am sure you have the whole episode out of context. There is no way Alex and I will ever be part of one another's adult lives, except as friends.'

'Nor he and I, Sophia! Not now! Not ever! I have thought it through and I must go and speak to him and explain to your parents that I am calling the wedding off!'

'Please, Lucy, reconsider your decision. Alex will be devastated – and my parents too!'

'I must. I cannot live a lie. Please don't be concerned, Sophia. I won't tell anyone what you and I have spoken of today. As far as anyone else is concerned I have simply had a change of heart.'

I watched as she dried more tears. My heart ached for her, but I am sure she had got the whole scenario wrong, and after talking to Alex I was sure they would sort out any differences they had; so I tried to console her until she departed to search for him. I returned to my room, and after shedding tears myself, thought of the blow it would cause to Alex, to Mother and Father and to Lucy's parents. I concentrated on the times Alex and I had spent together. He had always been the perfect gentleman and treated me with a great deal of respect. Admittedly he

105

kissed me once under the mistletoe, and I admit to having had strange feelings, just as I did when he kissed my hand on the night of the engagement; but I had never encouraged him or led him to believe we were anything other than family. I mulled over many thoughts in my mind and tearfully drifted into a deep sleep, missing the evening meal.

I was woken the following morning by a hand on my shoulder, shaking me. Lucy stood over me, her face still bearing the sadness of the previous day.

'Sophia, I have come to say goodbye,' she said softly. 'John is taking me to the station. I am going home by train.'

Grabbing her hand I said, 'Please don't go. I am going to miss you so much.' I hugged her tenderly.

'I haven't slept a wink, Sophia. I am going back to the base. Alex has decided to stay here for a while. I think he needs to be with you all at the moment.' She sighed.

'Have you really made up your mind? Is this the end of it all?' I tearfully asked.

She nodded.

'I am sorry things have not turned out as expected. I have come to love you as a sister. You will always have a special place in my heart,' I promised.

I released her from my embrace and she sat beside me on the bed, shaking uncontrollably.

'I promise I will stay in touch, Sophia. I will write and hope you will answer my letters.'

'Of course I will. Your letters will be so welcome, and perhaps we can meet for a meal and a chat one of these days. I will be anxious to know how life treats you!'

I looked at her sad features. Gone were the sparkly eyes and the bubbly personality.

'I must go. John is waiting for me, and I'll miss my train if I don't hurry!'

She kissed my cheek, stood up, wiped away a tear, turned and walked toward the door. I called out, 'I wish you all the luck in the world.' She held up her hand in acknowledgement and was gone.

I watched from my bedroom window as John drove the car toward the village. He disappeared through the archway and into the distance beyond the Hall. I returned to my bed, buried my head in my pillows and sobbed. I'd lost a very dear friend whom I'd grown to love and admire. Hopefully consolation would come through her letters, and I hoped she would survive without Alex.

Lying there, I decided a good remedy for my sadness was to savour the fresh air, and I washed, dressed quickly and made my way into the knot garden; but following closely on my heels was Marcus.

'Sophia!' he called. 'Wait for me!' He caught up with me and said, 'You were not at the evening meal and you missed breakfast. I have been worried about you!'

'I am fine, Marcus,' I lied. 'I thought I would give myself a walk through here and catch a breath of fresh air.' I stopped to smell the roses.

'Thank goodness you were not at the meal last evening! It was an awful time. I guess you have heard about Lucy and Alex!'

'Yes, I have, but I really do not want to talk about it! It is too sad for words!'

'Mother and Father are beside themselves. Alex is heartbroken. He really is taking it all very badly.'

I could hear the anxious tone in Marcus's voice as he spoke of Alex and I tried to console him by saying, 'I am sure he will get over it given time.'

'I do hope so, Sophia! He missed breakfast this morning.'

'I bet *you* didn't,' I teased, trying to change the subject. He looked at me over his spectacles and gave me a sly grin.

'I thought not. You love food too much. It makes me so jealous to think you can eat whatever you wish and not put on an ounce. Why, look at you. You are slim, and becoming so tall!' I had delicately changed the subject.

'You are not doing too badly yourself, Sophia. You are tall, and attractive too.'

'Maybe, but I will never catch up with you, Marcus. You are like a beanpole, and when I first met you, you were a little dumpling.'

I patted his tummy and he laughed. We were interrupted by footsteps. As I turned I saw Alex making a beeline for me.

'Can you excuse us, Marcus?' I asked politely.

He waved at Alex and disappeared. Alex hurried across to where I was standing.

I began trembling at what he might say to me, but I tried to keep calm. I had to face him at some stage, so what better time than now?

We walked together through the garden and into the maze. Ambling slowly he rested an arm around my shoulders, saying, 'I expect you have heard the terrible news.'

He looked so forlorn.

'Yes, I have. I am so terribly sorry, Alex. I don't know what to say to you to bring comfort to your topsy-turvy world.'

'Just you being here for me and being able to talk to you, Sophia, is enough. You always seem to understand.'

'I am always here for you, Alex. If you want to share your heartache, then I am a good listener.'

He asked if I had seen Lucy before her departure and I admitted that she had visited my room.

'Did she say anything to you?' he asked.

'Only that she was sad your relationship had to end and that she would keep in touch.'

'Is that all?' he queried.

I explained that it was. I hated lying to him, but could see no sense in divulging her reasons and breaking my promise to her.

'I do not understand her, Sophia. One minute she was happily shopping for a wedding gown. Then in the next breath she was informing me that the wedding was off.'

I commiserated, and could sense the heartache he was feeling. He took my hand as we strolled, holding it tightly, and showing his emotions in every squeeze he applied.

We reached the summer house where Ben, Marcus, Alex and I had frequently played as children. We sat and chatted at great length about what he would do in the future. He had no plans other than to work hard at RAF college and hopefully qualify as soon as his training was over.

'I think it will be a long while before I venture out to meet another girl. You females are so complicated. I will come home more often on my forty-eight-hour passes and annual leave. At least I know you are here to talk to. Perhaps we can take in a show or the cinema from time to time. What do you think?'

'That would be splendid,' I said.

'You are a good girl, Sophia! By the way, I didn't take you out or buy you anything special for your sixteenth birthday. How about I take you to the Royal Ballet in London on my next long weekend leave?'

'I would love that, Alex. I have always wanted to go to the ballet,' I said excitedly.

'Then it's a date! You are super. One day you will make someone a fantastic wife!' he mocked.

I smiled, and we returned through the windings of the maze to the Hall.

I think that unburdening himself to me had helped. The next task was to face Mother and Father and help with the process of cancelling flowers, dresses and the proposed honeymoon in the Bahamas. Perhaps one day he would take a honeymoon with a new woman in his life, but in his delicate state I feared it would be a long time off.

Chapter Ten

Alex was true to his word. On his next weekend leave he drove me to London in the Riley to see *Swan Lake*. Father thought we should ask John to drive us in the Rolls, but Alex wished to speak of personal matters, and couldn't do that with John in attendance.

I was enchanted by the slender figures of ballerinas and their sylph-like movements, mesmerised by the performance, and had a wonderful evening in Alex's company. Afterwards he and I dined in a charming little restaurant a short distance from the theatre.

The return journey to Yorkshire was long and arduous. We arrived home at an ungodly hour to find Father pacing the drawing-room floor.

'I have been extremely worried about you both! You might have considered telephoning me to advise that you were safe.'

'Yes, it was thoughtless, Father. I am truly sorry!' apologised Alex.

'I suggest you make yourselves a bedtime drink and then get some sleep,' Father said curtly, climbing the stairs in his dressing gown, pyjamas and slippers. 'It is extremely late!' Muttering, he retired to his room.

Alex and I ventured into the kitchen where I prepared milk for our bedtime drinks.

'I'll just have hot milk,' Alex requested.

I prepared it and made some cocoa for myself. He disappeared, and when I turned around he stood there, clasping a bottle of Father's finest Scotch. Pouring a quantity into his hot milk, he smiled at the astonishment on my face.

'What is wrong, Sophia? Don't you think I should have a nightcap?'

'Yes, but do you need such a large amount of whisky?' I asked coyly.

'How do you think I've coped with events of the last weeks? I go down to the local with a few guys and we drink each other under the table most nights – that's how!'

I was disgusted and said, 'Oh, Alex, you really shouldn't, especially when you are training the following day.'

'It keeps me sane, Sophia, especially with so many exams on the horizon and I have countless thoughts going on in my mind!'

'I imagined you would have got over your separation from Lucy by now.'

He frowned at me, saying, 'I have, but there are other demons occupying my feelings. Since Lucy and I parted I have realised she was correct in her assumptions. It would have been stupid to have married her! Here, have a drink!'

He poured another whisky, downing it immediately, then poured me a tot, but I refused it on the grounds that Father would be livid if he knew I had touched one drop of 'the hard stuff'.

'Come on! One little drink won't hurt!' he insisted.

Alex added a drop of soda water to make it palatable. I gulped it down, pulled awful faces, and he laughed hysterically. He downed another tot.

'Ssh!' I teased. 'You will wake Mother and Father. If he knows I have been drinking he will be furious. He considers me a child when it comes to alcohol.'

'Then his eyes are not open, Sophia. You are not a child. You are a beautiful young woman, sensual and sweet, with all the loveliness of—'

I interrupted him, chastising him for having had far too much to drink, and I suggested we retire to our rooms. Deep inside I did not want to go to my room. I wanted to stay, talk, and be close to Alex, comfort him and…

I placed my unfinished cup of cocoa in the sink and walked toward the door. He followed and took my hand in his as I reached the staircase.

'Thank you for accompanying me to the ballet, Sophia! You looked radiant. I adore the way your hair curls around your shoulders,' he said, stroking my dark tresses.

'Thank *you* for taking me to London, Alex. I cannot remember when I last enjoyed myself so much,' I said as I began my ascent of the staircase.

'Sophia,' he whispered.

I turned and he placed a soft kiss on my cheek, saying, 'Thank you for your friendship. It means so much to me.'

I smiled and hurried to my room, my heart beating fast in my chest, my body trembling. What on earth was happening to me?

Father, as Squire, was Master of the local hunt, a position he cherished. I have to admit that although he was heavily engaged in fox-hunting we siblings had no inclination to join in such thoughtless escapades. I would not allow myself to be drawn into the debate surrounding the archaic sport. He had had more than his fair share of hunt protestors at Saturday morning meetings. Several had caused mayhem, which infuriated him immensely. Annoyance on his part toward protestors, escalated when he spotted Marcus and a school friend marching along with a banner which read, 'BAN FOX HUNTING! SAVE THE FOX!' Father was livid with Marcus's antics and he was severely reprimanded; his monthly allowance was docked considerably. This angered Marcus as he had been hit where it hurt most – in his pocket! Father lectured him on the fox's ability to destroy vast numbers of livestock on our estate and neighbouring farms.

The day of the yearly hunt ball arrived, and it was due to take place within the Great Hall. It was to be a splendid affair attended by landed gentry, dignitaries and their guests.

Edith was appointed to oversee the arrangements and planned the most delicious menu, which was nothing short of a mouth-watering feast. She toiled away happily in the kitchen with numerous staff to assist and carry out her instructions. Other hired staff quietly and diligently prepared tables with the finest cutlery, china and splendid flower arrangements. Harrington Hall had come alive with the preparations for the evening function! Mother delightedly watched the progress. Father strutted around, organising, as if briefing a crew for a bombing mission. Nothing had been overlooked.

While these plans were taking place, Marcus and I went riding to Hardy's Wood and beyond. I was aware he was far from happy we were entertaining hunt members, but I tried to explain that England was a free country, and although neither of us liked certain situations in life, Father and Mother were at liberty to choose what sports they endorsed without us showing disdain. He did not comment further on the subject.

It was a wonderfully, bright, crisp morning. We enjoyed our ride, chasing one another across open fields and through wooded areas. It was exhilarating and life-giving. We returned to the Hall refreshed and happy. As we entered the rear of the Hall, I could hear sobs – loud, soulful sobs – coming from the kitchen.

'What on earth is the matter, Edith?' I exclaimed. She was sitting at the table, nestling her face in her hands, tears flowing down her cheeks.

'Oh, Miss Sophia, it's Deefa! He has been in the kitchen, pinched a whole salmon and scoffed the quails' eggs I had prepared for this evening. What on earth will I do?'

I placed my arms around her shoulders, drew her to me, consoling her in her plight. I assured her I would make good the loss. Deefa would be greatly chastised for his behaviour. Marcus stood, red-faced, and sympathised with her.

'*Who is crying?*'

I turned. Father stood in the doorway, hands on hips. He had heard the commotion Edith was making and arrived to investigate what was amiss. Edith explained what had happened. Father's face turned scarlet, his moustache twitched. '*Marcus*! Go and find that damn awful dog! I have warned you time and again about his behaviour! He will have to go! I will have him put down!'

I had lost count of the number of times Father had threatened Marcus, but nothing ever came to fruition. More tears followed, this time from Marcus as he hurried to find his beloved dog. I assured Edith I could manage, if Father would drive me into Leeds, to get replacements for the food Deefa had devoured, and told her we could replace all that had been eaten. She stopped crying as Father went to fetch the Land Rover. I changed from my riding gear into something suitable for the city and met him at the entrance.

The journey into Leeds was not a happy one. Father constantly moaned about 'that bloody awful hound'. I did not intend getting into serious arguments with him, and simply stated that he could not think of having Deefa exterminated.

We collected a huge salmon, plenty of quails' eggs, and then returned to the Hall. As we approached the entrance, a small crowd of hunt protestors, knowing it was the day of the hunt ball, gathered outside with banners and placards stating:

BAN FOX HUNTING. DOWN WITH THIS CRUEL SPORT

Father was absolutely livid. He leaned out of his window and insisted on giving them a piece of his mind!

'Bugger off!' he shouted, waving his fist. 'Go home and leave us in peace!'

They were so angry I thought he would be bodily dragged from our vehicle, but I knew he was a match for any one of the group. We managed to drive through the small crowd, our Land Rover receiving the brunt of their anger. Once inside the Hall, Father used a few choice words before telephoning the police to have the activists removed. The police handled the situation well. No protestors were local, and most had travelled some distance.

Edith prepared and cooked the salmon in preparation for her mousse. I attended to the quails' eggs. Marcus had disappeared, and I assumed he had taken Deefa and walked across the fields, far away from Father's wrath. Father was still extremely angry and behaved like a wild man at the very mention of the dog's name.

Evening approached. I prepared for the ball and was asked by Mother to accompany her and Father in welcoming guests. Marcus had no intention of attending, and was nowhere within the vicinity. Just as guests were due to arrive, Haynes drew Father to one side. I heard him say, 'You must come and see this, Sir.' He pointed to the entrance. 'The protestors have infiltrated the grounds of Harrington Hall.'

Father's face was like thunder. He called me to his side and said 'Come with me, Sophia. You will see what I have to contend with! I don't want Mother upset, but I am afraid the hunt saboteurs have finally got to us!'

I was upset and fearful for him and did not want a well-planned social function to turn into a free-for-all. I accompanied him to the entrance. Outside, carefully placed to one side, was a huge banner, fastened to poles, stuck into the lawn. It read:

PRESERVE WILD LIFE! PIKEL SIR OLIVER

Father was furious, but I have to admit I wanted to laugh.

'See, Sophia?' He pointed to the banner, his moustache drooping downward in disgust. 'This really is not funny!' he said, as I stifled a giggle. 'The clown who instigated this needs a good beating. I wish I could lay my hands on the offender!'

He called Haynes and requested that staff remove it immediately. His wishes were dealt with promptly and the banner was taken down. I returned to the Great Hall with him and stood as the first guests, Sir Robert and Lady Bartholomew-Childers arrived. Steady streams of people were introduced to Father, Mother and then me. They were decked in the most dazzling finery, ladies sporting their exquisite jewellery. As the last guests arrived, Father turned to me and said, 'You look really stunning tonight, Sophia. I am so proud of you!'

He kissed my hand and as he turned to walk away he muttered, with a twinkle in his eye, 'Oh, by the way, when you catch up with young Marcus would you give him a message from me?'

'Yes, Father!' I promised.

'Please tell him that you spell pickle P-I-C-K-L-E and not P-I-K-E-L.'

Having delivered his comment he strode away, grinning to himself.

My dearest Father. No one could fool him, not even Marcus.

During the week, when Marcus and Ben were at school, I helped around the estate in whatever capacity I could. I spent considerable time in Father's study in the smoke-laden atmosphere he generated with his pipe. His secretary, Mrs Tindale, the dedicated woman she was, suffered with me. We perfected a filing system even he could operate, and the study took on a tidier aspect.

One morning, I discovered our postman had not called to collect mail, which was unusual. Father asked if I would take it along to the village post office and hand it over the counter to catch the late morning collection. I hunted out my old bicycle, which I used infrequently, and pedalled down to the village. I could not put my finger on what it was, but there was a distinctive atmosphere as I approached the shops, which were grouped together in a row. People seemed to be huddled in small groups, talking. At first I thought they were talking about me. They turned around and stared as I passed by. I reached the area where bikes were parked and chained my cycle to the rack. Looking across in the direction of the post office, I saw three police cars parked. Mrs Danvers, the village gossip, walked across the road to where I was unloading letters from my bicycle basket and said, 'No good you taking those letters in there, Miss Sophia. There has been an awful robbery.'

Knowing Mrs Danvers as I did, I remembered she was prone to exaggeration. I politely asked her what had happened.

'It was this morning. Simon Phillips was found lying on the floor in the back room, battered and bleeding.'

'I hope he is all right,' I interrupted.

'He's dead, Miss Sophia! Mrs Robinson, his assistant found him! A fortune was missing from the safe!'

'Goodness, how awful! I must go home and notify Father. He and Mr Phillips were golfing chums,' I exclaimed, not fully understanding the extent of the situation.

I left her standing on the spot, returned the mail to the basket, un-chained my cycle and pedalled furiously back to the Hall. Hurrying up the drive, I dashed into Father's office, leaving my bicycle strewn across the lawn. I sent Haynes flying in my attempt to carry the news. I approached Father, who was deep in conversation on the telephone and tried to attract his attention.

'*Wait, Sophia*! I am speaking to the police!' he groaned.

When the conversation had finished I was informed by Father of the news I had intended telling him.

'It's Simon Phillips, he's been found battered to death. I cannot believe it, Sophia! Mrs Robinson found him when she opened the shop. He had been lying there all night. The police are convinced the attackers knew their way around the village and knew of Mr Phillips' movements and routine.'

'How dreadful!' Mrs Tindale and I said in unison.

'Furthermore, the police think there were two robbers. Mr Phillips had taken his Alsatian for a walk, as he always did last thing at night. He returned, unexpectedly, disturbing the burglars. They think he recognised the robbers. That is why he was attacked and killed. The blighters got away with a substantial sum of money. I have offered a large reward for information leading to the capture of these men.'

'What a generous thing to do!' I said. 'I expect there will be extensive investigations.'

'A reward was the least I could offer for a friend, somehow. Until these men are caught, the village will not be at ease. No one will sleep peacefully at night. I think it will take a considerable time before this dreadful tragedy is erased from the hearts and minds of the residents.'

I agreed, and hoped the murderers would soon be apprehended.

I savoured the herbs in the walled garden, with their intoxicating aromas, and collected the vital ingredients Edith needed to add to her next sumptuous dish.

'Miss Sophia, your father needs you urgently,' announced Haynes as I watched him approaching across the grass.

'Oh, dear! Is it really urgent? I have a project here. Edith is waiting for the produce.'

'I am afraid it is. The police are waiting to interview you, Miss Sophia!' Dismay crept over his solemn features.

'Then I must go. Will you please inform Edith where I am. Ask if she can send one of the kitchen staff to collect the herbs, fruit and vegetables I have not managed to pick, and take her this basket, please!'

'Of course, Miss Sophia.'

I hurried along to the Hall, removing my gardening gloves as I did so.

The police! What on earth could they want with me? After removing my wellingtons and replacing them with shoes, I tapped on the study door. Father bade me enter. I did and met a haze of tobacco smoke swirling round the room. He introduced me to a detective from the Leeds Constabulary who, though pleasant, had arrived on a very serious mission.

'Miss,' he said, 'I am detective Alan Greengrass, investigating the post office robbery and murder. I'm afraid we are no further forward in apprehending the guilty persons.'

'Please, have a chair!' I insisted.

'I will leave you,' Father said. He explained he had been interviewed but detective Greengrass would be returning to interview estate workers at a later date. He shook hands with the officer and departed.

'Now, miss, I have to ask you some questions.' Producing a notebook from his pocket, he asked, 'Where were you on the night of the twelfth?'

'Goodness!' I exclaimed 'I will have to think!' I sat and pondered. 'Yes, I remember! My brothers and I visited a cinema in Leeds. Alex was on a weekend pass from the RAF. He wanted to take us to see a newly released film, so we all went along.'

'What film was that, miss?' he asked viewing me suspiciously.

I gulped. 'You will have to ask the boys the title,' I explained 'I only went to keep Alex company, but the boys enjoyed it. It was a war film, not something I care for. It was at the Odeon!'

'What time did you leave?'

'About ten o'clock,' I muttered.

'Did you return here?'

'Yes, we returned to the Hall and went to the kitchen, where we had snacks and our usual bedtime drinks. You are not suggesting my brothers and I had anything to do with robbery and murder?'

'No, miss!' the detective replied. 'But I need to eliminate you all from our enquiries. We know there were two men. The postmaster, we think, recognised them. That is why he ended up in the unfortunate situation. We suspect it was someone local.'

'You cannot believe my father would have anything to do with this, surely!'

'No, miss, of course not! Your father played golf with Mr Phillips. I wondered if he knew any friends who may have had money worries.'

'Doesn't everyone?' I snapped.

He ignored my remark. 'I have to interview everyone on the estate, so I will return. I may need to interview you again!'

'You must have evidence from the scene,' I remarked.

'The thieves were thorough. No fingerprints we could decipher as being those of the murderers. They obviously wore gloves. There is no evidence pointing to a specific individual, other than there was more than one involved. We are continuing our searches until they are caught. This was a particularly nasty crime!'

He said goodbye, adding he would be returning the following day to continue his interviews.

I exited the study and bumped into Stephen Howard.

'Hi, Sophia!' He greeted me with his usual charm.

'Hello, Stephen. I have been through the third degree with a police officer asking me where I was on the night of the murder.'

'I don't think you have anything to worry about!' He chuckled. 'Don't look so glum. I am sure they do not suspect you.'

'I couldn't remember the film I watched with the boys on the night in question.'

'I don't expect you could. What night was that?' he asked.

'The twelfth.'

He thought for a moment. 'Sorry, I can't help. I'm not an ardent picture-goer.'

'Well, I hope you can remember where you were, Stephen. They will want to know when they return tomorrow.'

'Don't worry,' he said, laughing. 'I go to my girlfriend's house in Leeds most evenings, so I would have been there. Occasionally I stay overnight, but not often. I will have to consult my diary.' He found it amusing. 'Take care, Sophia. I'll see you around.'

'I am sure you will. I must dash.' I left him chuckling to himself as we said farewell. What a super person he was! So he had a girlfriend in Leeds! No wonder I saw him frequently drive off after supper. He was noticeably 'taken' by her, judging by the many visits he made. It looked as though there could be wedding bells on the estate before too long.

The police returned in force when I arrived at breakfast the following morning. The place was swarming with officers of various ranks. Workers were being lined up for interviews. Marcus approached me and explained he had to attend for questioning before school. He wanted me to accompany him. Detective Greengrass was waiting in Father's study as Marcus and I entered.

'There is no need for you to be here, miss,' he announced as we walked through the door.

'But there is! I insist on being present while Marcus is interrogated,' I replied firmly.

He did not argue but beckoned us to the chairs by the desk. We sat there like lambs going to slaughter. He spoke to Marcus. I wondered what an eleven-year-old could possibly say or do to help the police. He basically wanted confirmation that we had attended the cinema on the night in question. We were notified that Alex was being interviewed at his base in Lincolnshire to confirm our stories. Marcus was decidedly upset by the questions and thought it an affront to his integrity, but he immediately remembered the name of the film we had seen, the row we had sat in, and even produced stubs of the cinema tickets he had saved as a memento of time spent with Alex. I marvelled at him.

After the interview was concluded, Marcus and I spoke for a few moments, mostly about arrangements for our piano lesson, and then he departed for school, walking hurriedly across the lawns. I saw Father later in the day and discussed the interviews. He mentioned that the workers were upset at being included in the police questions, but he had explained it was necessary to eliminate them from their enquiries. I could not contemplate such a person in our midst. Knowing the staff of the Harrington estate, I was reassured not one of those, in mine or Father's opinion, could have been the perpetrator of such evil deeds.

Chapter Eleven

The year was 1960. Life on the estate could not have been more contented.

It had been almost a year since Lucy and Alex had gone their separate ways.

Alex came home when RAF leave allowed it. He, Marcus and I had super trips to Knaresborough, Aysgarth Falls and Fountains Abbey. Ben rarely accompanied us; he had his head continually buried in books, studying for exams.

Alex, on annual leave, wished to view work in one of the fields. We sped along the farm track in his Riley.

I asked, 'Please Alex, teach me to drive!'

'Certainly not, Sophia! You are sixteen and not allowed to drive yet.'

'I'll be seventeen soon. You could teach me on the estate roads. Please! I have driven the Land Rover. I want to become mobile,' I pleaded.

'You *are* mobile! You have got Petronella. You can ride her anywhere you need to,' he joked.

'Don't be an old grouch,' I protested. 'Just a few lessons, Alex – please! Then, when I am seventeen, I can take my test and go wherever I wish.'

'OK, I will teach you, Sophia, but you must not tell Father. He'll be angry. I'll teach you in the Land Rover; then my new car will remain unscathed.'

I punched his arm in fun. Alex retaliated by tickling me.

We motored over to the vehicle maintenance section and bumped into Stephen.

'Hello!' he said cheerily, but Alex ignored him. I nudged him and he gave a disgruntled, 'Hi!'

'What can I do for you both?' he asked pleasantly.

'We would like to borrow a Land Rover, Stephen.'

'And where are you going in that?'

Before Alex answered, I put my foot in it by saying, 'Alex is going to teach me to drive.'

'Well, we had better find you a battered one,' Stephen commented, laughing.

He found a suitable vehicle, and Alex, without a thank you, drove me in the direction of the farm road.

'You were silly to have told him I was going to teach you to drive. He will tell Father!' Alex was unhappy.

'I don't think he would do such a thing,' I said.

'Well, Sophia, I am glad you have more faith in him than I have,' he muttered.

I could not understand why Alex was so against Stephen. I reckoned he was jealous because I liked the man.

'Now, I want you to absorb all I tell you, Sophia. Remember, the rear-view mirror is not for applying make-up!' Alex joked.

I listened intently to all I was told and all that was asked of me. During the two weeks Alex was home, I am sure I was driving as competently as any male.

We had fun, we had arguments! I got out of the vehicle and walked through mud to prove a point. I cut my nose off to spite my face on several occasions, and Alex dumped me on a farm track more than once when I became impossible to teach. At the end of the fortnight it all ended with laughter as we looked back on times spent together. Marcus and his music lessons were neglected but it didn't seem to bother him too much. He carried on writing lyrics and doing music study, which, at that particular time, was what seemed to keep him happy.

The comment came unexpectedly from Alex.

'Now, Sophia, as a special treat I am going to let you drive my car.'

I could not believe my ears. I jumped for joy that he thought me competent enough to handle his beloved sports car. He removed himself from the driver's seat and I climbed across. We were on a farm track at the side of a field full of haystacks. In a few weeks I would be seventeen. Then I could have a few lessons with an instructor and take my test.

'Sophia, remember you are sitting in the driver's seat of a very expensive sports car. I will kill you if you as much as put a scratch on her,' Alex said, running his fingers along the paintwork.

'I understand implicitly, sir,' I said, saluting.

He suggested I should stop mucking around and become serious.

I was told that the Land Rover had differently positioned gears from the Riley and that I should take this into consideration. No problem! I knew everything there was to know about driving now! I set off, doing a steady twenty miles an hour, when a pheasant flew up across our path. I intended braking at this point, but put my foot on the accelerator by mistake. The Riley shot forward at a dreadful speed and Alex grabbed the steering wheel, shouting and turning it at the same time. We veered into the field. Looming large in front of us was a haystack.

'Put your bloody foot on the brake!' he screeched as we hit the stack.

The straw tumbled down and completely buried us. We had come to rest.

I pulled straw out of my hair, face and clothes. When I turned and looked at Alex he was a complete replica of a scarecrow. We burst into laughter at the sight of one another. He was anxious that I might be hurt, but soon realised otherwise. He began picking straw from my nose, face, eyes and hair. I brushed straw gently from his face.

He looked at me with a tantalising smile. I returned his gaze. Our faces moved closer together. He kissed my lips – not as he had under the mistletoe, but a passionate, lingering kiss I did not want to end. I could hear Lucy's words echoing in my brain: 'He loves *you*, Sophia. He is not in love with me!'

Shivers of delight raged through me as he moved his body closer to mine. I knew what we were doing was wrong, but I could not stop the feelings that stirred inside me. I realised quickly that Alex felt the same. The flesh of his arms was warm and inviting. The scent of aftershave wafted gently from his skin, teasing my nostrils. His hands caressed my long silky hair. He pulled my face closer to him. I could hardly breathe, but I was in heaven and wanted this tender moment to last for as long as possible. Unfortunately this was not to be. A farm worker came rushing across the field to our aid. Alex released me quickly and whispered, 'Another time, another place, Sophia.'

We were assisted in the recovery of his beloved sports car from the giant haystack.

Father released me from duties around the estate at times when Alex was on leave so I could keep him company. His sports car was in need of urgent attention after my escapade. He and I took a bus from the village to Knaresborough to visit Old Mother Shipton's wishing well. We had a marvellous time. It was our intention, after lunch in one of the riverside cafés, that we would walk along the banks of the River Nidd to Harrington Hall. Alex was so attentive. We had a superb lunch, hired a small boat and rowed on the river.

Walking home, we watched in amazement as the water cascaded over rocks, followed twists and turns of the sloping ground, and meandered into the distance. It was late summer. The river was at its most beautiful. Warm rays of the sun beamed down on the water, adding another dimension to the scene. Droplets of water suddenly appeared as if by magic, sparkling like diamonds on the rocks. I breathed in the glorious air. It was fresh and invigorating. Alex and I dawdled, holding hands, caring for each other's welfare, savouring the wonderful moments together. We were deeply in love. He was my life, and I his! I adored his personality, looks, voice, and his gorgeous body. He was every young girl's dream and he was in love with *me*! Alex was vibrant and outgoing, popular with the estate workers, and greatly admired in RAF circles. He was twenty-one; I was seventeen.

We mischievously chased one another over rocks, wetting our feet, drenching our clothes and acting as if we were two demented otters. Life was exquisite, and so was he. Climbing up the bank, Alex gave me his hand. I stumbled. He laughed heartily. I was cross at the fun he found in my misfortune, but his impromptu sense of humour soon had me giggling. He helped me to my feet. As I straightened myself he took me in his arms. Looking into my eyes, he murmured in a soft voice, 'I love you, Sophia. You are so beautiful! God, how I love you!' Placing his lips on mine, he kissed me excitedly.

'I love you too, Alex. More than you could imagine,' I whispered, gazing into his vivid blue eyes.

Hand in hand, we walked toward a nearby wood. My heart beat fast inside my breast in anticipation of what I knew would happen. We both knew we wanted one another, needed one another. We sat on the ground. He removed his wet jeans and hung them on a nearby branch to dry. Throwing off his shirt, he suggested I remove my skirt, which dripped with river water. He hung all the clothes on the nearby tree, allowing the sun to work its magic. I began trembling as he put his powerful arm around my shoulders, stroked my long, dark hair and then gently kissed my neck. His mouth moved along my shoulders toward my breasts. I experienced his warm breath on my skin as we slid toward the dry, leafy ground, caught in a soothing embrace. Desire for Alex raced through my body as he looked lovingly into my eyes.

'You really are special, Sophia, and so tantalising! I have wanted you for so long. Those large brown eyes of yours penetrate the very depths of my soul. Your olive skin is so soft and delicate. You drive me wild. I can wait no longer.'

He caressed me with such intensity that I couldn't resist him. I did not want to resist him. He stroked my face, cupped it in his hands and explored my mouth with his tongue. This excited me. A tingling sensation travelled down my body to my toes. I could feel a throbbing sensation as he pressed his body close to mine. My heart raced. He searched for the buttons on my blouse, removed it, and then my underwear. I searched for his remaining garment and removed it; we now lay naked (except for my beloved locket and chain), enveloped in one another's arms. My nipples were firm against his muscular chest. I took his hand and kissed his fingers. Suddenly I heard Maura's voice whining in my head: 'You bad child. You disgusting creature! You need badness beaten out of you! The devil is after your soul!'

I wanted to cry but fought back tears. She was no longer part of my life. I did not have to succumb to her threats. How could this all be wrong when it felt so right? My body was urgent for the touch of the man I loved. I was anxious to please him. In a world of our own, lovemaking became a new, wonderful experience, beyond my wildest dreams. My soft moans vibrated gently against his cheek as warm scent of aftershave drifted softly from his skin. Alex's hands caressed my back, my breasts and my nipples. He gently slid his fingers down my slim hips, along to my thighs, pressing me hard against his excited body. I kissed him passionately. He responded, his hands exploring the tops of my legs, desperately wanting me. Every movement, every touch gave me such pleasure and an increased awareness of delight. Feelings flowed through me with an urgency I had never known. He parted my legs, exploring my womanhood with such tenderness, and then, longingly, with all his manhood he entered me. The sky disappeared into oblivion. I sighed with sheer excitement as we moved in harmony, our bodies as one. It was a love that would never end, could never end. We demonstrated passion in the noises emanating from our lips. Alex moved with an erotic strength. I could tell he loved me, body and soul. The discomfort I should have experienced, I did not. We were as one, giving ourselves to each other. It was not sex alone. It was a special kind of love. I did not know if it was his first sexual experience. I did not ask, but somehow I do not think it was, and I did not care.

His love suddenly flowed into me like a thousand shooting stars erupting across the heavens. It was the most beautiful experience my body had ever known. I melted into his arms. I wanted him to remain inside me for ever, but Mother Nature had other ideas. In one passionate encounter my childhood had ceased. I was now a woman, a real woman! We lay together for what seemed like eternity, wrapping our warm bodies around one another, drifting into a satisfied sleep.

How long we slept I do not know. Distant voices awoke us. We quickly dressed, our clothes dry from the sun's rays. We walked slowly, hand in hand as if innocent and virginal. Alex smiled and murmured, 'That was so special, Sophia, so very special!'

We were intoxicated by the moment.

'We will marry, perhaps in a couple of years. We are going to have to talk to Mother and Father about our feelings for one another. How they will accept it I have no idea, but I will approach them soon.'

'I want to be your wife and have your children!' I told him.

'You will, darling, you will! I promise!'

We continued our long walk toward the estate.

Part of me was frightened; frightened of Father and what he would say about our relationship. I dreaded the revelatory moment, but for now I would not worry. I was no longer a virgin. I was Alex's special woman and he my lover and friend. It was all that mattered. The rest could wait.

As Alex and I approached Harrington Hall, he drew me into his arms and lovingly teased my hair into tresses around my face.

'That's better. You look half-decent now!'

He straightened my beloved locket and chain, the collar of my blouse, patted my bottom endearingly and smiled at me saying, 'See you later, darling Sophia!'

He kissed my lips for a long lingering moment and then escorted me toward the Hall.

On arrival Alex departed swiftly to his room. I knew Marcus would be waiting for his afternoon music lesson. I was late – twenty minutes late! He waited impatiently for me to make an entrance, pacing the room, observing his watch as he did so, and sighed loudly with disapproval that I had kept him waiting. I stopped by the nearest large mirror, adjusted some loose strands of hair, smoothed my creased clothing and joined him by the piano. Did I look guilty at the outcome of my day's activities? I certainly hoped not.

'Ah! There you are, Sophia! You are late! I have homework today. I am afraid I cannot allow you more than forty minutes of my precious time!'

Marcus had spoken. I was not the happiest of souls at his comment.

'I see! Well, Marcus, let me tell you now, I have hurried back to be with you and cut short what was an enjoyable day with Alex. Young man, you are becoming far too self-absorbed. I suggest you take stock and realise the world does not revolve solely around you – Marcus Walker! Not everyone is here for your specific benefit.'

I sounded so much like Father!

He stared at me in disbelief. How could I be so direct? His vivid brown eyes peered at me over heavy rimmed spectacles. He seemed at a loss for words for a while.

'I am sorry, Sophia! I did not mean to be rude and upset you. I have an essay on the Tudor period which has to be handed in tomorrow. I should have completed it days ago.'

'That is typical of you, Marcus! Father would be cross if he found out. I suppose you have been writing lyrics again instead of doing history homework. Knuckle down to your music lesson. Then I will help you with your homework.'

'Will you, Sophia? You are the greatest! I will work really hard for you on piano. I have been practising scales and have written lyrics to another song. Perhaps you will read them?'

'Later, Marcus,' I said. 'At the moment it has to be Chopin!'

He scowled, but smiled when I added, 'But if you are really proficient at your playing maybe – just maybe – we'll have twenty minutes of rock and roll, if Father is not listening.'

'Thanks, Sophia! Where do I begin?'

'How about the piece we practised last week?'

Without more ado, Marcus removed some sheet music from his case, placed it on the stand, adjusted his jacket, cracked his knuckles (an infuriating habit he had) and began to play. Marcus had improved dramatically, therefore blues, folk and rock and roll looked set to appear on the agenda, and they did, for a full thirty minutes.

At the end of our music lesson I accompanied one grateful boy to his room where we engrossed ourselves in his homework. On finishing, I was given a little lecture on Elvis Presley. Marcus was fascinated by his singing and the way he performed. He was totally captivated by his style. I had to admit I enjoyed his songs immensely, and on occasions Marcus and I watched him on television and were astounded at the way in which girls continually drooled over him.

During the following two months, Marcus made enormous strides in his understanding of the transposition of music from one key to another. I found myself devoting more of my time to him than usual in my quest to bring his exceptional musical talent to the fore.

In early October, on a fortnight's leave, Alex was involved in laborious work around the estate, coming into frequent contact with Stephen Howard, who tried to be a sociable member of the workforce. Alex was having none of his charm or friendship. He was adamant. I frequently told him he was being silly in carrying on his vendetta, but he would not listen. Alex and I saw less of one another than usual, but the moments when we did meet were precious and special. Meanwhile, Marcus flourished with the attention I provided. Within Harrington Hall he played Beethoven and Chopin. Of all composers under discussion, Chopin appeared to be the one Marcus had the greatest appreciation of. With the lesson completed we would collect our sheet music together sit in the drawing room and discuss composers further. Deefa accompanied Marcus everywhere and rarely left his side. Father would occasionally allow him in the Hall as long as he sat quietly beside Marcus. Marcus, having now reached the age of twelve, had an excellent understanding of the piano, but extreme happiness was reached when we discussed folk, blues or rock and roll. I had to draw the line at times for fear Father would find us intent on studying 'that kind of music' and not the classics. I could see this was the direction Marcus wanted to follow, but he was going to have to wait until he was considerably older before embarking on his preference. On one occasion I had written some lyrics called 'Only Child, Lonely Child'. I explained to him, 'I think you will find the words in this song I have written sum up the great affection I had for my mama and papa, and how I had to come to terms with my loss. I feel, when writing good lyrics, they have to contain what we feel from within, rather than what we see for ourselves from without! Do you know what I am saying, Marcus? I have tried to put my soul into this song!'

He looked at me intently, appearing to understand completely what I said.

'If you read my lyrics you will see I do it too, Sophia! I say what I feel in my heart and soul!' he remarked.

I stared into his huge eyes and said, 'I think my life with you all at Harrington Hall is the most important relationship I have ever experienced, apart from that with my beloved mama and papa, and I feel it has a great bearing on my music.'

'Definitely, Sophia! Harrington Hall would certainly not be the same without you. You fill the place with so much love.' Marcus shyly dropped his head toward the floor, explaining, 'I appreciate in every way what you do for me, Sophia. You always seem to be able to negotiate a better life for me with Sir Oliver. He is so strict, but you have him eating out of your hand. I respect what you are able to achieve on my behalf.'

I looked at him. For the first time in our friendship I realised we were very much alike. He related to me the circumstances that took him to the Hall after the death of his mother, but I did not confirm that Alex had already told me of this. Marcus's voice became choked with emotion. He removed his spectacles and wiped a tear from his eye. This was Marcus at his most vulnerable. 'So here I am, Sophia, at Harrington Hall, with Lady Mary and Sir Oliver acting as foster-parents, and you guiding me in the direction I want my life to take. I am so fond of you all. You have all given me so much. I do love you so much, Sophia,' he said timidly.

'And we all love you too, and know that the family would not be complete without you, Marcus. You are certainly a great part of my life, believe me!'

We explored the lyrics of my song and discussed them with a view to putting music to the words. We were a team musically, Marcus and I. For us, music was about reaching the deepest part of our souls and laying bare our absolute true feelings, whether sad or happy. As we approached the end of our discussion of 'Only Child, Lonely Child', I could see Marcus was impressed by the lyrics. He said that when I had written the music, he would like, with my approval, to add it to his repertoire at the November concert at the Grange Roman Catholic Boys' School. I wholeheartedly agreed, but wondered how Mother and Father would react, when invited to a classical concert, to see with pride their budding pianist son play my song, and his, and forgo Chopin and Beethoven in the process. He handed me his latest set of lyrics and we toiled together to write suitable music to accompany 'I Wanna Stay a Child', words written by a talented boy desperately trying to come to terms with his impending teenage years, growing up with an authoritarian, but deeply caring, foster-parent, Sir Oliver.

I read:

I Don't Wanna Be a Man

(I Wanna Stay a Child)

I don't wanna be a man,
I wanna stay a child.
Not responsible or sensible,
I'd rather stay just wild.
Why should I be rational?
Why can't I be free?
Why must I be someone else?
Why can't I be me?
I don't wanna be a man,
I wanna stay a child!
I often wonder who I am,
This notion drives me wild!

Do I have to be a puppet?
I'd rather stay afloat.
Do I have to run with the sheep?
I'd rather stay remote.
Must not have an opinion,

Have to accept others' views,
Do I live the life *they* want –
Or live the life *I* choose?
I know I sound complaining.
You can tell it in my tone.
Need I agree with others' thoughts?
Just wanna have my own!
I don't wanna be a man.
Just wanna be a child,
Help me keep my sanity,
Just let me run free awhile.

Marcus Walker, aged 12, 1960

This sounded to me like a cry for freedom of expression! Father would hear this for the first time at the concert. Would he be impressed? *Would he listen?*

I feared he would not.

Chapter Twelve

The Grange School concert was an outstanding affair. Father, having given a substantial sum of money toward the building of the 'Theatre for Classical Music Studies', as it was called, was to give a speech on opening night, before and after performances by pupils. Programmes accompanied each ticket purchased. There were one thousand seats in all. Father looked in anticipation at the programme's contents and smiled with approval, until he saw that Marcus and I were daring to perform our own compositions.

'The creation of your own music must excel, Sophia! This is an extremely important evening. There will be the educational hierarchy, numerous well-known patrons and dignitaries, and a great number of people from the surrounding villages attending and of course heads of various school departments.'

'I am sure we will not let you down, Father,' I promised.

'Good, but I'm not sure about Marcus! He does not have his heart in classical music,' he complained.

I leapt to his defence, explaining, 'He tries so hard, Father! Classical music comes naturally to me. With Marcus it is different, but he is continually discovering his abilities. It may not be what you want him to play but it is right for him! We should not stifle his creativity. Please, Father, give him a chance,' I pleaded. 'Marcus *will not* let you down.'

'We will see on the night, Sophia. We will see!' he replied cagily.

Father was not prepared to change his opinion, but we would hopefully be instrumental in doing so.

John and Edith were given Friday evening off so that they could attend the concert and were genuinely excited at the prospect.

Marcus appeared extremely nervous on the day, unable to settle to anything, but his school was closed an hour early to prepare for the concert. He dashed home to put in a bit of practice before the performance. We pottered around the Hall collecting up sheet music and prepared the evening wear we were to take with us. I had decided on a long, shimmering pale green dress Mother had purchased for me in Harrogate. Marcus was to wear his maroon school blazer, white shirt, tie and grey trousers.

Father drove Mother, Marcus and me, in the Rolls to the school. Ben had a previous engagement and was unable to attend. Alex had written us both a letter, sending his love and wishing us a truly successful evening. He too was unable to attend due to extensive studies. As we approached school we were met by a barrage of photographers and reporters from various Yorkshire newspapers. Flashguns 'popped' in all directions. Marcus and I managed to squeeze through the crowd and headed for the dressing rooms, changed our clothing and prepared for our performances.

He looked handsome in his school uniform. I suppose it was due to the fact that for once he was actually wearing a tie and had neatly brushed his hair. We peeped cautiously through the gap in the fire curtain to watch hundreds of people taking their seats. Father was nowhere to be seen, nor was Mother. I imagined they were being introduced to guests before taking their seats on the front row, along with other school governors, wives, and the mayor and mayoress. I looked at my watch. All those who had purchased tickets had arrived. There was not a vacant seat in the theatre.

Father and Mother appeared with the governors. Father was shown to the stage and introduced to the audience. After a warm welcome, he spoke of his gratitude to everyone who had given money so generously to allow the building of the theatre. He commented on the exceptional quality of classical music taught at the school, of the formation of the orchestra and choir in years gone by and how well the orchestra had progressed, winning a national award, and how the choir had travelled to New York, in the USA, on an exchange visit that had proved hugely successful.

Speech over, Father took his place. The curtain arose to the strains of 'I Vow to Thee, My Country'. Every boy was dressed in school uniform, looking immaculate. En masse, they sounded like a choir of angels. They sang several songs they'd performed in America.

Peter Danvers played trumpet; Robbie Squires thrilled the audience with his violin concerto, and the Smyth twins sang 'An English Country Garden'. All performers were brilliant by any standards. As the evening progressed I glanced at Marcus.

'Sophia – I am terrified I am going to let you down,' he admitted.

The moment had arrived for him to play the theme from Beethoven's *Moonlight Sonata*.

'You will not let me down, Marcus! You are more than capable of this,' I whispered. 'Go out, sit quietly, compose yourself and give of your best! And he did!

He was given rapturous applause and bowed before leaving the stage. Marcus was in his element, lapping up every ounce of praise. Father was overjoyed by the response. During the interval I approached Marcus and gave lashings of praise. He accepted it graciously. He was on a 'high'. Father walked towards us and congratulated Marcus on his performance, but commented, 'You could have played with considerably more sensitivity.'

'You were fantastic!' I interjected as I watched the smile disappear from his face.

Why, oh why, did Father do this to him? Continually disparaging him at every opportunity?

After the interval, our parents returned to their seats. Mother blew a kiss as we peered from the wings. We reached the part in the second half where Marcus and I were to perform our songs together. We were announced onto the stage by the conductor of the Grange School orchestra, Alec Markham. The orchestra retained their positions on stage. Marcus took his seat on a chair, held his guitar comfortably and looked attentively at me. I placed myself at the piano with the microphone close by. The next few moments astounded me.

Marcus, always quiet and shy, suddenly stood and announced, 'Ladies and gentleman, Sophia and I have written the lyrics and music for the following songs we are about to play and sing. This could not have been achieved without Sophia's dedication to my love of music. She has passed on to me the great knowledge she has, enabling me to achieve what I have and has spent a considerable amount of time encouraging me. I invited her to attend tonight so that she receives the kudos to which she is entitled. We are aware this is an evening of classical music and would not consider our songs as such, but one day they may be regarded as modern classics. Thank you so much, Sophia.'

He stared at me and I gazed toward Father, looking for a reaction. There it was! He wriggled uncomfortably on his chair, stroked his moustache and turned a crimson colour. I am sure he expected Marcus to rock and roll his way through the next two numbers, but our songs were beautifully written and musically great. While Marcus and I played, we also sang in harmony. We received a standing ovation. Father and Mother clapped enthusiastically, enjoying every single minute of the adulation. Breathing a sigh of relief and wiping his brow, Father smiled at us. Mother gave a regal wave of approval.

After the clapping had died down, I stood centre stage and announced, shaking slightly, 'For our final performance, which you will not find listed in your programme, we have chosen the works of Giacomo Puccini. We are so fortunate to have the Grange School orchestra to accompany us. This piece is for a very special person in the audience, to express how much he means to us, and to thank him for his care of us both over the years.'

I watched Father's face. It was a picture of amazement as he realised that the song was for him. If only I had had a camera to catch the moment.

'Ladies and gentlemen,' Marcus announced, 'for Sir Oliver and Lady Mary Harrington, I would like to play piano, and accompanied by the orchestra, Sophia will sing in Italian, Puccini's '*O Mio Babbino Caro*', 'O My Beloved Father'.

I experienced a contraction in my throat. All emotions I felt for this beloved man welled up inside, but I knew I could not let Marcus down. Weeks of practice meant I had to perform it well. From somewhere within, strength came. It was as if Mama were with me. I sang like I had never sung before. From the corner of my eye I saw Father wiping away tears. Mother consoled him discreetly. We finished, and the orchestra stood as Marcus and I bowed. The audience rose to its feet, clapping and shouting, 'Encore! Encore!' It was another standing ovation. As the audience returned to their seats, we performed the song once again to more cheers. Flashbulbs from the newspaper photographers popped from all around the theatre.

Father walked onto the stage and enveloped Marcus and me in his arms, hugging us. In turn, Marcus embraced me. Trembling with emotion, Father spoke of the ecstatic evening. The audience applauded loudly. He mentioned with absolute pride his musical family and exclaimed how taken aback he was at our performance, and hoped many more concerts of the same sort would be forthcoming. There was further applause. Father complimented the choir, orchestra and performers on their exceptional contribution. In conclusion, he thanked the teachers, pupils and all those involved who had ensured that the evening was an undeniable success.

After the audience had departed there were more interviews with newspaper reporters. When we were finally able to leave, Marcus and I crashed into the back seat of the Rolls as Mother and Father conversed happily in the front.

I was elated to see the Hall in the distance and couldn't wait to fall into bed. It had been such a hectic but extremely pleasurable time. I could happily sleep the weekend away. On reflection, I realised how exhausted my darling mama must have been, giving piano recitals to large audiences around the world. I imagined a pianist's life was a lonely one and not the route I wanted to take with my life, despite my gift. My teacher, Bodil Larson, had already confirmed that the life of a concert pianist was a difficult one. Father drove us swiftly along the approach to the Hall when we experienced a thud at the side of the Rolls.

He observed his rear-view mirror and snapped, 'Damn foxes! I hope my car isn't damaged!'

I glanced through the rear window and shouted '*Stop, Father! Stop!*'

He brought the vehicle to an abrupt halt. I opened the door, lifted my dress and scurried to the scene. Marcus followed. Together we huddled over a heap of fur lying in the driveway, not red fur, but black and white.

'Goodness!' I screeched. 'It's Deefa! He's badly hurt.'

Marcus was speechless. He bent down, cradled the injured dog in his arms and began crying hysterically as Father walked toward us.

'Please, Father,' I begged, 'send for a vet! Deefa has been hurt!'

'Move, Marcus!' he ordered. 'Let me have a look!'

Marcus, upset and crying, moved away. Father bent down and examined Deefa who whimpered in pain. His conclusion was that Deefa was dying and he coldly announced that the dog would have to be put down.

'No, Father! Please! I am sure there is something to be done!' I wailed.

He pointed at the animal. 'Look, Sophia! *He is dying*! Can you not see?'

'I hate you!' shouted Marcus, aiming his grief at Father. '*I hate you!*'

'Enough, Marcus!' yelled Sir Oliver.

I tried comforting the distraught boy and held him in my arms as he sobbed.

'You won't let him put my dog down, will you, Sophia?' he pleaded. Then he bent down and cradled Deefa once more.

'It is the only way. He's suffering!' stated Father.

'*No! No!*' screamed Marcus. '*I hate you!*'

Father fumed. 'That is enough! Go to your room immediately!'

As I knelt, Marcus placed Deefa gently into my arms, took to his heels and ran across to the Hall in the dark, crying hysterically.

'Leave the dog, Sophia!'

'No, Father!' I retorted.

'I will get my gun and put him out of his misery.' He turned, got into the car and drove off with Mother. I was sure Deefa was not fatally injured and would never allow Father to shoot him! Leaving the dog, I ran to number two, Starbeck Cottages, where Stephen lived. I could see a light shining through a gap in the curtains. I knocked frantically on the letter box.

'Please help me, Stephen,' I gasped as he cautiously opened the door. I quickly explained what had happened. He picked up an old blanket from the cupboard, followed me to where the injured dog lay, obviously in great pain, and covered in a quantity of blood. Stephen placed Deefa in the blanket and helped me carry him to the rear of the Hall. We crept quietly up the servants' staircase to my room. Father was nowhere to be seen. He had clearly gone out with his gun to end Deefa's suffering. We put the dog in my bathroom. Stephen carefully examined him. His limbs were not broken, and it seemed his injuries were external, but he was not totally convinced Deefa did not have internal injuries. He insisted I watch certain aspects of his behaviour. Stephen helped me bathe the wounds and Deefa finally stopped whining. I thanked Stephen for his help, and promised that I would not inform Father he had been instrumental in helping me. Then he departed down the back staircase and disappeared into the night.

I went to look for Father who had returned from his search. I explained that the dog was in my bathroom. He was furious and insisted Deefa be shot.

'I will not allow it, Father!' I said, trembling.

'Young lady! How dare you speak to me in that manner? I suggest you calm down and do as you are told!'

'I have no intention of letting you shoot him! Marcus is broken-hearted, and I am going to do everything in my power to save the dog!' I persisted, turning my back.

'Come here, Sophia! Do as I tell you! I demand respect from you! *Do you hear?*'

I turned and faced him. His features were livid, and his hands were resting on his hips.

'You cannot demand respect, Father! I am not in your squadron! I am your daughter. You have to *earn* respect!'

With that he slumped into the nearest chair. I realised I had hurt him deeply.

'How dare you?' He banged his fist on the table.

'I am sorry, Father. I didn't mean to be rude to you, but I cannot let Deefa die! He and Marcus are great pals. He would be lost without him.'

He looked at me and sighed.

'I think I have lost sight of the fact you are no longer a child, Sophia, but a young lady with a mind and spirit of your own.'

He thought for a few moments, and then said, 'I will give you a week. If the animal is not greatly improved by then he has to go!'

Father made his intentions perfectly clear. 'He stays in the bathroom and must *not* sleep on your bed!'

'I promise, Father!'

'Off you go, Sophia, but remember, one week!'

I moved forward to kiss his cheek but he dismissed me with a wave of his hand. He was extremely angry with me.

My next port of call was Marcus. I knocked on his bedroom door, but no answer was forthcoming. I heard a noise inside and called, 'Marcus, please let me in!'

He shuffled to the door in his pyjamas, trying to disguise his tears, and bade me enter. The room was in semi-darkness.

'Here, dry your tears!' I said, and I passed him my lace handkerchief. He gazed sadly at me as I whispered, 'Follow me! I have got Deefa in my bathroom!'

'Is he dead, Sophia?' he asked dreading my response.

'No, of course not! Father has given me a week to return him to health.'

He threw his arms around my neck and hugged me. We searched out a large dog basket, took it to my room and laid his beloved pet gently in it. He was amazed at how different the dog looked without traces of blood coating his fur. Deefa was in pain, but not complaining too much. It warmed Marcus's heart to see his friend. We settled him for the night. Marcus and I chatted at length about how we would tend the animal. I agreed Marcus could sleep in my room on the chaise longue, and I searched for covers for him. We agreed we would take turns in looking after Deefa during the night.

'You are so caring, Sophia! Here you are, coming to my rescue yet again,' he sighed.

I placed covers for Marcus so he could curl up inside. Father would be furious if he knew he had set foot in my room. I insisted he told no one of our arrangement.

'I hate Sir Oliver,' he whispered as he bedded himself down on the sofa.

'You are not serious, Marcus. You are angry because it was Father who knocked Deefa down. What was he doing, roaming around the grounds?'

'Sophia, I always put him on a long chain in the courtyard when I am out. His collar was firmly fixed to the chain,' he assured me.

'There was no collar on him, Marcus. The collar is still attached to the chain. I noticed it when I came home. Who on earth could have released him?'

I covered Marcus and tucked the blankets around him so he would be warm. We agreed I would do the first shift and wake Marcus when 2 a.m. arrived. I kissed his forehead, stroked his cheek and he was asleep.

When I looked at him during the night he was sleeping soundly. I really could not disturb him. The weekend approached, and there was plenty of time for Marcus to dog-sit his beloved Deefa. I lay on top of my covers and checked on the injured animal several times during the night. Deefa's eyes followed me around the room, but he did not attempt to get up so I let him rest. I thought I saw his tail wag at one stage. I sat in bed, pondered on who could have released the dog from his lead, and for what reason. Perhaps Marcus had upset someone or was it a prank that had gone horribly wrong? I really couldn't fathom it out, and had no answers to the questions roaming around in my head.

Marcus and I spent the weekend caring for Deefa. On one occasion Marcus disappeared, returning with a small glass of Father's expensive brandy, and spoon-fed tiny drops to Deefa in warm water. I considered it harmful and said so, but strangely the dog began to thrive on it, so it became a twice-daily ritual. By day three I was able to feed him chicken and rice, kindly prepared by Edith, while Marcus was at school. After his return he took over the duties, pleased to see a marked improvement in the health of his dog; but I am sure Deefa was slightly tipsy!

I continued my musical studies with Miss Larson. The week saw Marcus forgoing piano lessons in favour of watching over his precious dog. He continued sleeping in my bedroom at night, unbeknown to our foster-parents. Deefa improved daily. Within six days he was up, walking and not wishing to be confined. By day seven I approached Father to explain that the dog had greatly recovered, and could be returned to his kennel. Father was extremely surprised at his rapid recovery and begrudgingly congratulated me.

'Just the person I am looking for!'

I spun round as Father struggled to control a mound of paperwork he had secured in his arms. The whole lot looked in danger of dropping. I rushed forward to assist and relieved him of a great deal of it. His study was a mass of paperwork and I wondered how he made sense of anything he tried to do. I placed the papers on a table.

'Are you busy, Sophia?' he asked.

'Not really. Why? What is the problem?' I enquired. After speaking those words I thought what a futile comment I had uttered.

'This is the problem!' he retorted, holding up a handful of business papers and bank statements. 'I am afraid poor Tindy is off sick again,' he muttered. 'She has another cold or something similar. I advised her not to return until she is fit. I don't want to catch any germs.'

'No, of course not!' I laughed, watching him light his new

meerschaum. I am sure we would all die of smoke inhalation long before being infected with the common cold.

'What do you find amusing, Sophia?'

'Nothing, Father!' I smirked. 'How can I help?'

He thrust papers and chequebooks into my hands. 'Can you sort these for me? I need entries on the statements to coincide with the cheque stubs.'

I told Father I would deal with the backlog of three months' statements immediately and withdrew to a small table in the corner of the study. It was quite a simple task. Father lacked patience in anything pertaining to accountancy. He knew how to make money and spend it, the rest was left to Tindy and the accountants. She was his guardian angel at all times, except when she was ill, which these days was a frequent occurrence. She had worked for the family for nigh on forty years. I worked my way through the paperwork, safely securing documents into neat piles with clips.

'Any problems, Sophia?' Father asked as I placed the last pieces together.

'Just one small problem, Father. You are paying £400 a month into an account in Dublin. I have no paperwork to substantiate this. It is a regular sum. It goes out on the 28th of each month.'

'There is no problem!' he said abruptly. 'I am aware of it. It is business, Sophia. Business! There is nothing more I wish you to do,' he added, relieving me of the papers and locking them in his desk drawer. Then he smiled. 'You have done a marvellous job, young lady. Well done!'

He dismissed me and I ambled down to the kitchen to see Edith. I had been an enormous help to him in Tindy's absence, and would possibly be required to do more paperwork until she returned.

It was a cold, damp, exceedingly frosty morning as I walked into the churchyard, clutching flowers I had purchased from La Petite Fleur, the florist's in the village. I stood gazing at my mama and papa's grave. Father had had a beautiful white Italian marble stone erected. The carving of a woman in a flowing dress with roses in her long tresses, positioned on the side of the large headstone, reminded me of my darling mama. The inscription was beautifully carved, and a marble edging around the perimeter of the grave secured green chippings within. In the centre of the chippings was an ornate marble flower pot, bearing the inscription, 'To darling Mama and Papa. May you always rest in peace. Sophia.' It was there for me to fill with the flowers. I had made a wreath of holly collected from Hardy's Wood. I'd decorated it with nuts, slices of dried fruit and a large red bow. I had followed some instructions I'd seen in *Country Life* magazine; it was a Christmas decoration popular in the USA. The grave looked magnificent in its entirety. Christmas was three weeks away. I knelt on the kerb, arranged the flowers, placed the wreath and then spoke softly, saying, 'Mama, darling, I hope you are looking down on me and can hear me. Please help me! I find myself in an awful predicament! I do not know what to do or which way to turn. I have discovered I am carrying Alex's child. Please do not be disappointed in me, because I love him so much.' A tear trickled down my cheek as I continued. 'If I go to Simon Marsden, he will insist I tell Mother and Father. I could not bear for them to discover this. It would be devastating. Alex will be home soon. I hope and pray with all my heart he will not be angry and will know what to do. I want this child so much. Please help me!'

Tears flowed and I bowed my head in shame. What would Mama have thought of me? She would have been disappointed, I am sure. I had promised I would give my life to music and had not fulfilled my promise. Why would she want to help me? I knew my mama was a wonderful, forgiving soul, and prayed she had heard my plea. Tears flowed once more. Wiping them from my cheeks, I stood up feeling calmer than when I had approached the grave. It was as though Mama and Papa had heard. A peace I had not known in the last month descended on me. I threw back my shoulders and meandered through the rows of graves. I walked down the path in the direction of the Hall. In two weeks Alex would be home. I would speak to *him*. I hoped our problems would be sorted out satisfactorily and we could rear our darling child together in a loving, safe environment.

Chapter Thirteen

The Christmas tree Father had ordered stood tall and stately in the drawing room. Haynes had collected a large box of delicate ornaments from the store cupboard, and as I climbed the ladder to put the finishing touches to the decorations I heard the familiar noise of a car engine. I was confused, as Alex was not due home on leave for another two days. I ran to the entrance and peered outside and came face to face with the Riley. Alex was struggling to remove mountains of luggage from its interior.

'*Sophia!*' he exclaimed. 'How wonderful it is to see you.'

'You too, Alex. This is a marvellous surprise.' I threw myself into his arms and we discreetly kissed. He looked so healthy and fit in his superb uniform.

'This is going to be the most exciting Christmas this family has known,' he chuckled, as he attempted unloading mounds of presents from the seat of his car. I stared in amazement. He handed me several parcels and joked, 'These are not all for you, Sophia, just seventy-five per cent of them!'

Enthusiastically, he followed me into the Hall and I placed the presents under the tree.

'Gosh! The tree looks so magnificent! Did you decorate it? If so you have done a splendid job!'

I nodded.

'Christmas is just a week away, Sophia, so no opening any presents yet.' He laughed as he carefully placed the beautifully wrapped gifts in place. 'Now, promise me you will not open these.'

I giggled and promised him that nothing would be touched.

'Good girl! Be a poppet and let Mother, Father and the boys know that I am home!'

He patted me affectionately on my bottom, saying, 'God, I have missed you so much, Sophia!'

'When can I talk to you, Alex?' I asked, a forlorn expression on my face.

'Later, darling! I am tired from the journey. We have two wonderful weeks together when we can walk, talk, and make love,' he whispered cheekily.

I smiled, hiding my worried look.

'I will fetch Mother and Father. They are so excited at you being home for Christmas and New Year, and have organised so many celebrations.'

'I am excited too,' chirped the unmistakable voice of Marcus.

The lads embraced. Alex stood, eyeing the youngest sibling and said, 'I hope that Sophia has been taking good care of you!'

'She has been marvellous to me, as always,' Marcus replied.

Alex stood back from him and said, 'Goodness! How much taller are you going to grow? You are thirteen, and yet are almost as tall as me. Are you ever going to stop growing?'

'Nope!' replied Marcus, and laughed as they disappeared to catch up on life in general.

I wandered off to find our parents. What I had to tell Alex could wait. I had kept my secret for more than two months, so another day would make no difference.

After an excellent family supper, we withdrew to the drawing room. Alex and Father huddled around the enormous log fire and opened a bottle of the finest malt whisky, while Mother, Ben, Marcus and I amused ourselves with a game of Monopoly. Ben bought several properties from Marcus, leaving him virtually bankrupt. Marcus, angry in the extreme, put his hand under the board and upturned it in temper. Father raised his eyebrows as if to say, 'There he goes again!' Marcus and Ben spent the following half-hour trying to retrieve pieces of the game from the drawing-room floor and furniture, while Mother and I chatted. The log fire, cosy as it was, did nothing to warm us. It became increasingly cold during the evening. Marcus and Ben were sent to bed at 10 p.m. amidst complaints of 'It's not fair!' leaving Mother, Father, Alex and I to catch up on estate and village gossip.

'Have they found those maniacs who killed the postmaster?' asked Alex.

'No, the police are no further forward in their enquiries,' Father said. He had formed the opinion that it must have been intruders from further afield, and stated his reasons for why he considered it to be the case.

'Sophia told me in her letters that you had a tremendous grand opening night at the Grange School Theatre,' said Alex, winking in my direction.

'Marvellous!' Father insisted, his chest swelling with pride. He quickly produced some newspapers from the rack by his chair, carefully opening page after page of photographs and reports for Alex to inspect.

'You looked adorable, Sophia. Goodness, is that Marcus? He looked smart for once in his life!' He laughed. 'What a marvellous write-up you received from the press! The critics consider that you both have a wonderful future ahead of you in the entertainment world.'

'No thank you!' I grimaced. 'Give me life at Harrington Hall any day.'

Father was not amused by my comments and showed it in his facial expressions.

I thought it wise to withdraw to the kitchen and offered to make everyone their nightly cocoa. Alex followed me to assist. Making sure no one was within view, he wrapped his arms around my waist and drew me affectionately to him.

'You cannot imagine how much I love you, Sophia. Tomorrow I am going to take you to do a spot of Christmas shopping in Harrogate. I need to get something for Mother. What do you think?' he asked.

'I do not care where I go, Alex, as long as I am with you,' I admitted.

'Tomorrow it is, then! You can help me choose a present for her.'

He kissed my face and neck, sending shivers down my spine. He kissed my lips in such a tender manner. It was an enthralling feeling being close to the man I loved. I did not want to leave him and go to bed. He released me, and I prepared my parents' cocoa and took it to them in the drawing room, where they were engrossed in listening to some music by Tchaikovsky. I bade them goodnight and returned to Alex. We sipped our drinks together in the kitchen and he held me close, saying, 'I really have missed you dreadfully, Sophia. No one will ever come between us. We are going to be together very soon, I promise you, darling!'

He kissed me passionately and I explained that I was retiring to bed.

He clasped my hand and said furtively, 'Sophia! When Mother and Father have gone to bed, please come back to me down here. We can have an hour together alone. Please promise me...'

I vowed I would and he released me from an intimate caress so that I could go to my room. I lay in bed listening for Father's footsteps, but it was 1 a.m. before I heard him climb the staircase and turn out the lights. I crept quietly downstairs in my nightdress and joined Alex on the sofa. He took me gently in his arms, kissing me softly and caressing my breasts.

'Please, Alex, can I talk to you?'

He glanced at me with a puzzled frown and said, 'You look troubled. What is wrong?'

He released me and gave me his undivided attention. Holding my hand, he stroked it lovingly and caressed my cheek with his fingers. I was unsure of how to approach him although I had rehearsed time and again what I would say. Now, faced with the situation, I was at a loss for words. I looked demurely at him and blurted out, 'I am pregnant.'

The look on his face was one of astonishment. He seemed shocked and taken aback.

It frightened me, as he was absolutely dumbfounded at my announcement. After a short time of contemplation, he murmured, 'Did you say pregnant, Sophia?'

'Yes, Alex. I am three months. I am so sorry!' I cried, tears welling up in my eyes.

'Darling,' he whispered, drawing me close to his warm body, 'Please do not be sorry. It is I who should apologise for placing you in this predicament.'

'Are you very angry, Alex? I do hope not!'

He dried my tears. 'Angry? Of course I am not. To be truthful, Sophia, I am absolutely thrilled. My love for you has produced this little life that you are carrying. What worries me most is how we are going to tackle Mother and Father.'

'It worries me too. I have thought about it, and I am so scared that I will have brought shame to the Harrington household after all the love and care they have shown to me!' I said.

'Please, darling,' he said soothingly, wiping away more of my tears, 'do not cry. We will find a way through this.'

I tried to explain that Mother and Father might possibly send me away from Harrington Hall for fear of scandal and the recriminations that would ensue, but Alex insisted he would not let this happen, and would take me to Lincolnshire to be close to him so that we could share our lives. We talked softly at great length about the future of our child, and Alex seemed genuinely pleased that he was to become a father.

'What has Simon to say about your pregnancy?' he asked, smoothing his hand gently across my tummy.

'I haven't seen Simon. I was scared he would tell Mother and Father.'

'But he cannot, Sophia. He is bound by the Hippocratic oath. Please don't worry. I am here now and I will take good care of you. No one and nothing will keep you, me and our child apart. We will bring up this little life in a loving environment. I promise you, Sophia! We will take the bull by the horns and speak to Mother and Father after lunch tomorrow afternoon.'

He held me closely to him, his arms protecting me from the outside world and all its expected opposition. All my terrible worries seemed to melt into oblivion and I relaxed into his strong arms, tired yet relieved. I cuddled into his athletic body for a few moments, but in a while began to shake with cold. He retrieved a mohair rug from the arm of the sofa and placed it around my body. In no time I drifted into a sound sleep.

Alex woke me at 3 a.m. and insisted I return to my room. He was fearful Father would discover us lying on the sofa together the following morning, before he had a chance to explain about our relationship and the pregnancy.

The air was chilly and the embers of the cosy fire had disappeared. I crept quietly up the staircase, Alex following. As we went off to our separate rooms, he whispered, 'Sleep well, darling. We will speak to Mother and Father later today. I am sure that all will be well.' We kissed and went our separate ways.

During the following hours winter came to the Dales with a vengeance. I was restless in bed, experiencing coldness around me. My room was far below its usual comfortable temperature. I jumped quickly out of bed, searched for a warm, cosy dressing gown to wear, and snuggled down into bed, pulling the covers around my face. My extremities were frozen but gradually I managed to warm myself sufficiently to fall asleep. I finally awoke and glanced at the bedside clock, which revealed that it was 8 a.m. and time for breakfast. Late nights were certainly not favourable for me in my condition. I staggered out of bed to the bathroom to bathe myself, and hoped that morning sickness would not intervene. I ran a hot bath and soaked myself until my skin began to crinkle. I dried myself and dressed rapidly, before my body temperature dropped once more. I pulled back the heavily-lined brocade curtains, a task usually given to Millie, but she had been given the weekend off to spend with the man in her life. In amazement I stared out across the Dales, not comprehending fully the scene that confronted me. The harsh winds had blown the unexpected falls of snow into huge drifts, and the whole area surrounding the Hall appeared like a scene from a Christmas card. We were going to have a white Christmas! I wondered if Alex was awake and had seen the snow. There would be no shopping expedition to Harrogate to buy presents for Mother, but a family day building snowmen and having snowball fights with the lads as we had done in years gone by. Then there would be the dreaded meeting with Mother and Father after lunch. My heart jumped at the thought.

My unborn child was obviously hungry as I reacted sharply to the aroma of bacon wafting up from the kitchen. Dressed warmly I made my way down to the dining room to converse with the family but there was no one to be seen.

'Where on earth is everyone?' I asked as Marcus appeared.

Looking at me pensively he replied, 'Sir Oliver, Alex, Ben, Stephen and a number of estate workers have gone in search of sheep stranded in snowdrifts. Alex has taken Sally and two of the other border collies. They also have help from Mountain Rescue.'

He appeared deeply concerned for the sheep. I wanted to see Alex to discuss our afternoon meeting with Mother and Father, but would obviously have to wait until his return.

'They have been gone since five o'clock,' announced Marcus taking his place at the table.

I thought of dear Alex not getting to bed until three. It would have been horrendous him having to get up again at an ungodly hour to go in search of the stranded animals in atrocious weather conditions, but I guessed that as a trainee pilot he would be expected to rise at any unsociable hour when needed. With my plate of cereal I joined Marcus at table, sitting opposite him.

'Tell me, Marcus, do you think everyone will be safe up on the ridges in such terrible weather?'

Marcus tried to alleviate my fears by saying, 'Of course they will, Sophia. They are used to extreme weather conditions and will soon have the sheep rescued. We really cannot afford to lose any more after the poor lambing season last year. Please, Sophia, don't fret!'

I was reassured as Marcus leaned across the table and placed his hand over mine, patting it gently.

'I did offer to help Sir, but he explained that I was too young and inexperienced to be of use.'

I replied, 'Perhaps he was wise not to let you go, Marcus. You can be of more use here.'

We chatted as he tucked into his usual breakfast of bacon, eggs and an assortment of other delicacies, but I exited the dining room abruptly, leaving my breakfast untouched. Marcus stared in disbelief.

'Don't forget my lesson this afternoon, Sophia!' I heard him shout as I hurried from the room. Piano lessons were the furthest thing from my thoughts as I hurried to the bathroom. Marcus was oblivious to the reason I had so hastily departed.

'Are the men back?' I asked, as Marcus waited patiently for his lesson in the drawing room that afternoon.

I approached the piano. His music sheets were perched on the stand, but he looked fraught as he commented, 'No, but they should be returning soon.'

'Come on, Marcus, let's get this piano lesson into full swing,' I said.

He pointed to the music saying, 'I have been practising this piece all week. I am so anxious for you to hear it, Sophia. Shall I begin?'

His enthusiasm was a joy to behold and an excellent performance was forthcoming. He had developed terrific expression, wonderful timing and played with immense feeling. Father's appearance was not so well timed. He strode through the door, tired, soaking wet and with a concerned expression on his face.

'Marcus! Sophia! Come into the study, I wish to talk to you both immediately. I am going to remove these wet clothes and change into something warm. Then I will be with you. Marcus, fetch Mother! Ask her to hurry down immediately. She should be in her room having an afternoon nap.'

He disappeared. Marcus went in search of Mother while I made my way to the study.

What on earth was the problem? Whatever it was, he was in a distressed state! Mother returned, looking anxious, and asked what the meeting was about. I looked around to see if Alex and Ben were going to join us and realised they were not there. I guessed that there must have been substantial numbers of sheep lost in the blizzard. Father returned, bade us sit and collapsed into the chair by his desk, exhausted. He was never one to gloss over circumstances, good or bad. He simply said, 'I am afraid it is bad news! Alex has had an accident.'

At the sound of Alex's name I experienced anguish as my stomach turned and my heart sank. Looking across at Mother, I could see she was anxious and in a state of shock. She began to utter words but they eluded her. I jumped up, placing my arms around her and embraced her.

'What on earth has happened, Father? *Please* tell us!' I begged.

He looked grim. His complexion had assumed a grey tint. Marcus was extremely restless and asked for more news. Father explained, 'The snow was deep on High Ridge. Several ewes were stranded. Against my wishes, Alex insisted that with Sally's help he could manage, before Mountain Rescue arrived. Stephen Howard followed to lend Alex a hand in what was deemed a tricky situation – again, against my wishes! We watched them disappear. In no time Stephen had returned to inform us that Alex had taken a fall from off High Ridge in a freak accident and had hit his head as he tumbled down. It was lucky that Mountain Rescue had just arrived to help get the sheep in. Together we all managed to find Alex. Sally had faithfully climbed down to stay by his side until help arrived. Her barking led us to the scene. Stephen Howard was wonderful in the way he helped with the rescue. Without him I do not know what we would have done. I have to give credit where credit is due. Ben accompanied Alex to the hospital.'

There was no time for more questions and my heart sank further. Father insisted we don our warmest clothing and endeavour to get to the hospital as swiftly as possible.

I have never seen a family move so quickly. Father brought the Land Rover to the front entrance and we all piled in. Snow chains around the wheels were a great asset as we travelled along the roads, which were almost impassable. Eventually Leeds came into view and we alighted from the vehicle at the hospital entrance.

Alex had been examined at the accident and emergency department and tests had been carried out. On Father's instructions, he'd been admitted to a private ward. We all sat in the waiting room, fearful and frightened. No one spoke but we all looked solemnly at one another. I wanted to burst into his room, tell him how much I loved him and that I was there for him no matter what, but he was unconscious and badly injured. The medical staff awaited instructions on what the next procedure would be.

A neurological surgeon had been sent for. Father saw that no expense was spared for the return of Alex to his old self. He consoled Mother to the best of his ability, but she could not be comforted for any length of time. Marcus hugged me and then held my hand. Together we consoled Ben, who must have gone through hell on the journey to the hospital, watching Alex in his injured state. One hour led to two as medical staff moved to and fro. At last, evening arrived. We watched Alex being ferried from his room to the operating theatre. The surgeon approached Father and Mother. I heard him say, 'I am sad for you both. Your son has a haematoma which necessitates an operation. We will inform you immediately there is anything to report on his condition. Please use the facilities of the rest room and restaurant while you and your family are waiting for news. It could be a long wait before we are finished in theatre.'

The emotions I experienced at that moment were indefinable. I was in an anguished state, but tried desperately to hide it from Mother. I suddenly encountered a strange sensation in my tummy, like butterflies floating around. My child was moving. I hoped the little one was not trying to explain that one life was beginning as another was ending. I tried to dismiss these negative thoughts. I knew I could not live without Alex. *I did not want to live without Alex!*

We sat, staring into our cups of coffee and dismissed plates of sandwiches everyone thought they ought to eat but did not want. I excused myself to go to the bathroom to have a weep and say a prayer. As I returned I am sure the family noticed my inflamed eyes.

Marcus looked totally bereft, staring into space, hoping upon hope that good news would come. Ben paced the restaurant and Mother wept into her handkerchief.

Father tried to maintain a stiff upper lip and endeavoured to comfort each one of us in turn. He too looked as though he was going to break down at any moment.

Simon Marsden appeared after several hours, having investigated the procedures taking place. He was able to inform us that the operation had been carried out and that the next few days would be critical. No one could possibly understand what we were feeling. Simon suggested that we could do nothing by staying at the hospital and insisted we drove home. We would be notified immediately there was any change in Alex's condition. We returned to Harrington Hall but none of us slept as we waited for a telephone call which never came. I hoped 'no news was good news'. By morning, Father had telephoned the hospital and was told that there had been no improvement in Alex's condition and that we should visit later in the day, but only two visitors at a time were allowed. I attended to the lads while Mother and Father attended the hospital. I had intended visiting with Ben and Marcus later in the day.

On arrival at the hospital room, Marcus, Ben and I could not believe the changes that had taken place in Alex. He had aids to assist breathing, and drips were in place. Heavy bandaging covered his head. Marcus squeezed my hand tightly. I could see tears appearing in his big brown eyes. Ben, totally lost for words, left the room and wept silently in the corridor. We did not stay for long. Each moment was one of torment for us, so we returned to the Hall, where Mother waited in anticipation for good news.

When it was not forthcoming she developed a weeping frenzy. It took Father and me a considerable time to calm her. He rang for Simon to attend to her. Simon arrived promptly to administer a sedative, after which Mother retired to her room. This routine developed into a general pattern each day. Visits to Alex, every member of the family extremely upset, sedatives given to Mother, Father at his wits' end, and us siblings in tears most of the time.

Christmas loomed. Mother and I attempted with every ounce of strength to assist Father with the distribution of goodies and presents to the orphanage in the nearby village, where so many youngsters depended on Father's generosity for their Christmas cheer. Father insisted that we could not neglect them, despite our own misery; so with bravely worn smiles we attended, as we did every Christmas, to bring cheer and comfort to under privileged children. I played the piano and we sang carols and joined the young ones for hot mince pies (which Edith had made) and cocoa before leaving. We were thanked for our efforts at such a traumatic time, and were assured that everyone at the orphanage was holding a daily vigil of prayers for the return of Alex to his old self. For this I was extremely grateful. My child so desperately needed its daddy; I needed Alex; and the family were lost without their lovable member.

As Christmas Day arrived, presents were left unopened. Late on Christmas night, when everyone had retired to bed, I crept down to the drawing room and removed from under the tree the presents which Alex had brought home for me on his first day of leave. There was a large silver box containing the most beautiful white silk nightdress and negligee, which I would store carefully in my room to wear on the night we married. A huge box of exclusive Belgian chocolates was the next present, followed by a sequined bag, a necklace and earrings to complement my new black velvet evening dress. Another small box contained my favourite perfume. Last but not least was the tiniest package I almost missed which was carefully planted under the tree with a small card attached which read, 'To dearest Sophia'. I removed the wrappings to find it contained a blue velvet box. Would it be more earrings, perhaps? Alex knew how much I loved earrings. I opened it to find an exquisite solitaire diamond ring and a small note which read:

> To the love of my life, Sophia. Please accept this ring as a token of my undying love for you. A love that will last for all our life together and beyond. Alex.

I placed it on my engagement finger and it fitted perfectly. I kissed it, placed it in its box and took it to my room to hide in a safe place where I could keep items Alex had bought until a time when I could wear them for him. I lay on my bed, wept countless tears, and after mulling so many thoughts over in my mind, I fell asleep.

★

The new year, 1961, approached. We continued our daily visits to Alex in his private room. I sat for ages every day, holding his hand, but I soon realised that he was going nowhere fast. He remained in a coma. This had been his existence since the operation.

We were told he was unconscious, unresponsive and in a persistent vegetative state. This news took its toll on the family, and it was difficult dealing with everyday life, no more so than for Father, who had so many other responsibilities on his shoulders.

Edith and John visited, but were so heartbroken they did not attend again. Marcus and I continued visiting together. He found the scenario difficult to handle and wrapped himself in his music even more. Mother became dependent on Father. That added to the enormous strain on him. I helped where I could, but realised I needed to begin thinking about making arrangements for the child I was having. What on earth would I do with no Alex to support and care for me? I could not imagine!

Stephen Howard was faithfully supportive to us. On evenings that Marcus did not accompany me, Stephen insisted on taking me to the hospital in the Land Rover. I was grateful of the company and had to admit it was more agreeable than facing the journey alone. He was a sympathetic fellow, constantly expressing a wish that he could have accomplished more to have prevented Alex's accident. I explained that he should not carry such guilt on his shoulders, and that no one was to blame except the extreme weather conditions.

In the new year, the weather improved dramatically, although it remained extremely cold. I busied myself around the estate, but my mind was a million miles from the work I engrossed myself in. Marcus and I continued faithfully with our music, which Alex would have approved of, but somehow our hearts were not in it. We made excuses some days not to have to practise. Marcus and I talked over the prognosis for Alex and what the future held for him. We could not see an immediate future. The only future in the frame was for my child, the unknown factor in all this that no one could be allowed to learn about. Father and Mother were already desolate, without having more traumatic news placed upon them.

Chapter Fourteen

Father Pierre distributed hymn books along the pews. He lifted his head and acknowledged my presence in church, saying, 'How good it is to see you, Sophia!'

He stopped, walked toward me and gave me his undivided attention.

'Father Pierre,' I whispered, not making eye contact, 'have you a moment of your precious time to help me? I need to talk to you, in confidence.'

'I always have time for you, Sophia! Is it a confessional you want, or do you just wish to talk?'

'I need to unburden my soul, but I also need advice and help, in a delicate matter. I am relying on you for complete discretion.'

'We will retreat to the vestry where you can talk to me privately. We will not be disturbed by anyone wishing to use the church.'

He accompanied me to the room and cleared a chair for me which was stacked with papers. It resembled Father's office at the Hall – untidy!

He seated himself opposite me. With hands clasped he awaited my revelations. I stared at him, thinking what an exceptionally kind, caring man he was. I hoped he would be sympathetic and understanding of my plight.

'It is difficult to know where to begin, Father,' I admitted, fiddling nervously with my watch.

'What is troubling you, child?' he asked.

'Well, you see…' I began, shedding tears.

'Dry your tears, Sophia. Nothing can be so dreadful to make you this upset. Let me help you with your problem! What is wrong?'

'Will you promise me that whatever I tell you, Father, you will treat in the utmost confidence and not disclose it to another soul?'

He looked puzzled. 'I do not know if I can, Sophia!'

'Then I cannot tell you, Father!' I removed myself from the chair.

'Come, Sophia. Sit!' he begged, beckoning me to return. 'You are obviously frantic, therefore what you tell me will be in the strictest confidence.'

At this promise, I returned to sit opposite him.

Wiping tears from my cheeks, I admitted, 'I'm pregnant, Father Pierre.'

'Oh, Sophia, you poor child! Who did this dreadful thing?'

'Father Pierre, I am deeply in love with the father. This child is the result of our love for one another.'

Frowning at me, he said, 'You know how wrong this is, as you are not married. Who is the young man who has left you in this state?'

I explained I could not name the father and was already six months pregnant. I had to make speedy arrangements for the birth and future of my child.

'I understand, Sophia, but have you not approached Lady Mary and Sir Oliver?' he asked. 'I really think you should!'

'No, I cannot tell them. They would be so ashamed of me – and you must not tell them, either! It is such a delicate situation, especially with all the worries they have on their shoulders. It would break their hearts if they knew the whole story.'

'My goodness, you have got yourself into an awful mess, my child.'

I asked what I could do. He sat there tapping his fingers on the desk as he pondered on what advice he should offer. Suddenly, he asked, 'Do you ever hear from Maura these days?'

'No, Father. I had a card on my thirteenth birthday. She wrote a note asking me to forgive her for having ill-treated me. She said I would always be welcome at her home, but I cannot forgive her. Sir Oliver and Maura have had no contact with each other since he dismissed her from the cottage. He cannot abide her.'

'We all have to forgive at some stage in our lives, Sophia. I think she wants to make amends. She has written to me frequently asking forgiveness and explains she has given up the "demon drink". Maura may be your light at the end of a very dark tunnel.'

'How can she possibly help me?' I asked.

He explained he had letters from Maura wishing to heal the rift between us. She was sadly dejected at not being able to mend old wounds and move on with her life.

'I could write to her to see if she would have you stay for a short while. You could have your baby there and then decide what you wish to do when it is born. Perhaps you could have it adopted.'

'No, Father! I am going to keep my child. *It will not be adopted.*'

'That is your decision, Sophia, but it will not be an easy journey bringing up a bastard child. It will suffer for your sins, of that I have no doubt!'

'I will protect it, Father, with my life. If I have to move from place to place, away from prejudice, then I will.'

'You are a brave girl. Leave it with me. I will contact Maura by letter. We will see what she says, if that is agreeable to you.'

I reluctantly consented. 'Maura must not be allowed to breathe a word of this to my parents or anyone!' I insisted.

'I will be adamant about that, Sophia, when I write.'

I thanked Father Pierre and agreed to wait for any communication from Maura. The meeting was concluded. He took my hand, advised me not to worry, as it was not good for the child I was carrying to experience stress.

Three weeks passed. I became increasingly agitated that the written communication from Father Pierre to Maura had been lost, or she had chosen to ignore our request for help. When I had given up hope of receiving word, a letter arrived. The priest summoned me to his cottage.

'Sophia,' he beamed, 'come in, child. You are looking well. Take a seat.'

I entered the quaint room. He moved books so I could be comfortable on a chair.

'You will be pleased to hear I have received word from Maura, and it is good news.'

My heart leapt as he picked up an envelope and removed the contents. Unfolding the paper, he read:

'Homelea
Priory Street
Dublin
26 February 1961

'Dear Father Pierre,

'How charmed I was to receive your welcome letter, but sad to read the news contained therein. What a dreadful state of affairs Sophia has found herself in. My heart aches for her. She is vulnerable and in need of our help. I have searched my heart and know I have much to do to make amends to the child for past misdemeanours. It is therefore my intention to offer my home to her and assist in any way I can. I am still Sophia's legal guardian, and have made enquiries on her behalf. I am pleased to inform you there is, outside Dublin, a convent where they will take Sophia, when the birth is imminent. She will be supported afterwards with work and accommodation so she may contribute to the life of her child and the daily working of the convent. Her child will be assured of a good home and religious upbringing.

'I understand this situation must remain confidential. I can assure you I will respect this.

'Thank you for turning to me in Sophia's hour of need. I will do all in my power to assist in this sad state of affairs, if agreeable to Sophia. Please contact me at your earliest should you wish to take up this offer.

'Yours sincerely,

'Maura Bertucelli.'

Father Pierre passed me the letter. I sat quietly fingering the pages. Memories of her behaviour flooded into my brain. Maura appeared to genuinely regret the heartache she had inflicted on me in the past. She needed to make amends, offering help when it was desperately required. On reflection, I had nowhere else to turn. It was then that in my wisdom I agreed, with the assistance of the priest, to accept her offer.

Father Pierre would acknowledge the letter and organise my arrival in Dublin. He would advise when plans were made. He showed extreme compassion for my predicament. I thanked him for his constructive help and decided I would tell Mother and Father I was leaving Harrington Hall once final preparations had been made.

'I have visited Alex often,' Father Pierre said as I rose to leave. 'I am distraught that you have to leave the Hall at a time when your parents need your utmost support.'

Feelings of guilt ran through me. The priest went on, 'Poor Alex. It must be a dreadful time for you all. I am sad he is not making progress but can assure you my flock and I pray daily for a miracle.'

I thanked him for his dedication toward Alex, my parents and us siblings, and prepared to leave.

'Take care, Sophia! I will contact you when Maura answers.'

'Bless you, Father. I will wait to hear from you,' I concluded.

I walked to the village several days later. I could hear footsteps following closely. I turned and caught a glimpse of Father Pierre's cassock.

'I'm relieved I have seen you, Sophia,' he gasped, breathing laboriously. 'I have received a communication from Maura. She is preparing for your arrival in one week's time.'

'Gosh, Father!' I exclaimed. 'That soon? I'm going to have to speak to Mother, Father and the boys today and tell them I am going to a convent to work.'

He handed me a piece of paper on which was written Maura's address.

'Now, don't forget, Sophia! One week today! She is expecting you.'

I thanked him graciously for his efforts. Having wished me well, he departed leaving me to face my family with an explanation for leaving.

'Why do you consider it necessary to leave at this time, Sophia? Has it something to do with Alex?'

I was horrified by Father's line of questioning. He had sent for Mother. Together they began their inquisition into why I found it imperative to go to Ireland to work. I wondered if they had noticed that I was pregnant, but I had carefully disguised the fact in my mode of dress. I hoped not. I do not know how I would have faced them.

'Are you leaving because you are finding it difficult seeing Alex in such a state, when you visit him?' Father asked.

'I suppose I am,' I replied trying to hide the reason for my departure.

'I need time away to find myself, discover who I am, what I intend doing with the rest of my life. It is time I stood on my own two feet and unearthed my capabilities and weaknesses. After all, I am almost eighteen!'

Mother interrupted. 'You believe Ireland is the place to do this, Sophia?' She looked forlornly at me as if she was about to cry at any moment.

'Yes, I do. There is a convent where I can work and pray and decide what my future holds. Please try to understand. Maybe I will follow a career caring for the sick. If the convent proves unsatisfactory I will return home immediately.'

'What about your musical career, Sophia? You promised Anna you would follow in her footsteps,' said Father in a disgruntled fashion. He was far from happy with my decision.

'Many times I have explained to you, Father, that I do not wish to be a concert pianist. The life is not for me,' I explained, trying to convince him my decisive step was the correct one.

He looked at Mother and then rested his eyes on me.

'If this is your way forward, Sophia, so be it. I want you to promise me, should you not find the answer or the fulfilment in your journey of discovery, you will return home forthwith. This is your home. Never forget that.'

'I will not forget the Hall, I assure you and I will miss you both terribly, but I will write when I can to let you know I am well. One day I will make you proud of me.'

Lies flowed from my lips like water from a tap. How could they be proud of me? I was about to bring shame to their name and the love they had shown me. I realised at this point the devil had taken my soul. I hated myself immensely and knew somehow I would be punished. It was agreed I should leave for Ireland as soon as I could prepare for the journey. Once installed in the convent I would inform them I was settled. Ben thought I was crazy. He tried unsuccessfully to persuade me not to leave.

He was angry, upset and called me 'foolish' and 'ridiculous'.

I was aware daily of the life inside me as the child moved and kicked. This precious one needed me. I visited Alex two nights before my departure. Though he lay there comatose I sat by his bed. Placing his hand in mine, I poured out my heart to him, explaining I loved him deeply but had to go to Ireland to have our child.

'I cannot tell Mother and Father. It will destroy them. They will hate me for what I have done. I so want our child, this treasured part of you, conceived out of our undying love for one another. I will care for it, love it with all my heart, just as you would have done, darling. Forgive me for leaving you. I have no choice and I will miss you dreadfully.'

There was no movement, no indication he had heard a single word. He was my darling Alex in body only. His mind was aeons away in some remote place, far removed from the world in which I and his child were barely surviving without him. I was helpless and bewildered. Dear God, why was this happening to us? Was this the price to pay for loving a man so deeply?

Marcus was the most difficult member of the family to contend with.

'You are mad, Sophia! Why do you need to shut yourself away in a convent in Ireland? You have such great musical talent.' He was fuming.

'You see, Marcus…' I tried to explain, but it was no good.

'I don't want to hear! You're crazy.' He put his fingers in his ears so that he couldn't listen to the explanation I had to offer. I began walking away. He ran after me and grabbed my dress. 'Don't go, Sophia! Please don't go!' he begged. 'What on earth will I do without you? You are my best friend. Life will be nothing without you.'

'Please try to understand,' I implored. 'I have to go. I cannot explain why! I just have to!'

'Go then! See if I care. I hate you, Sophia Bertucelli!'

The words struck me like a knife penetrating my heart. I began to cry, turned my head and walked away, so he could not see. He was correct. I was turning my back on vulnerable, sensitive, talented Marcus, who needed me as I needed him to share my innermost thoughts, feelings and music with, but this time I could not explain my dilemma to him. He would not have understood and would have hated me for what I had done. In seconds he caught up with me, twirled me around and gazed at me with his piercing brown eyes.

'I apologise, Sophia! I did not mean to say such hateful things. I cannot bear to think of life without you.'

'It won't be for ever, Marcus. I need to sort out my life, and before you know it I'll be back.'

I was lying again, but how could I hurt him more than he already had been? The devil was certainly working his magic! He had me in his clutches. Marcus calmed himself and professed his undying friendship. We hugged one another on our infinite bond of attachment. What would I do without him and my music? Perhaps I would be allowed to play piano at the convent. I knew little about the place other than what Father Pierre and Maura had explained. I hugged Marcus once more and requested we meet in the drawing room at 7.30.

The evening was spent playing piano and going through songs we had written. I knew it would be the last time we would play music together. I dared not dwell on these thoughts. My heart ached yet I had not set foot outside the estate.

Farewells on the following morning were emotional time bombs. I could not tell when or if I would see my family again. Father was first to set foot in the dining room. I followed in his footsteps. He insisted on holding an audience with me in his study.

'Here, Sophia. Take this money!' he said, clutching what I perceived to be my train and ferry fare to the port of Dun Laoghaire. 'I want to know you have sufficient funds to see you through!'

I looked in amazement as I fingered the bundle of banknotes. 'This really is too much, Father,' I protested.

'Sophia, there may be things you need. Please take it.'

I thanked him wholeheartedly. As I placed my hand across the table to shake his and bid him farewell, he pulled me close and affectionately kissed me.

'Take care, darling, and please keep in touch.'

Turning abruptly, I avoided showing him the emotion that had overpowered me. I managed to control myself until outside his study. How I would miss the dearest man who had unstintingly taken care of me for the last nine years. I wanted to return to the study, throw my arms around him and confess my pregnancy. He would have listened but I could not hurt him or Mother. I was on my own. Knowing Alex's prognosis, but still managing to be a tower of strength to the family, Father needed no more ordeals placed upon his shoulders. I hurried to the Screens Hall where Mother waited for me, with Ben by her side.

'Please, darling, take care!' she insisted. 'Make sure you eat properly.'

She appeared anxious, fiddling with her handkerchief.

'I will, Mother. Do not fret!'

'When you discover what it is you want to do with your life, come home. We will talk about it. We are here to encourage you in whatever you have in mind.'

I promised her I would and explained I had so many things to think about. I stated I would contact them from time to time to let them know how I was progressing. She and Ben embraced me, but were interrupted by Marcus, who arrived and pushed his way forward. He held me so tightly I found it difficult to breathe.

'Don't stay away long, Sophia. We want you back here soon,' he pleaded.

I walked away once his vice-like grasp had been released. I shed tears as John arrived to carry my luggage into the Rolls. I hopped in and was keen to be gone before I made a fool of myself with more tears.

John drove me swiftly to Liverpool where, after another emotional goodbye, I boarded the ferry as a foot passenger for Dun Laoghaire in Ireland, and my short journey to Maura's house in Priory Street, Dublin.

'Sophia! What an absolute transformation. Is this the eight-year-old child I left in Yorkshire?' she commented, feasting her eyes on me. She moved her gaze up and down my frame as the taxi driver squeezed past and deposited my luggage in the hallway. She led me into the lounge.

'What a picture! I cannot believe it is you. How you have grown! So tall and slender and what a magnificent head of hair! You are a sight to behold. Pregnancy suits you. You certainly cannot tell you are having a child!'

Maura's greeting was extremely welcoming. She had aged a great deal over the past nine years but dressed smartly and wore her hair in an attractive style. She had prepared food for us, befitting a special occasion. Her house exceeded all expectations. The rooms were spacious and exceptionally well furnished. I noted the presence of a well-stocked drinks cabinet, which seemed strange, her having supposedly given up the 'demon drink'. I took it to mean she either socialised frequently or was still hitting the bottle, but it appeared to have no bearing on her behaviour toward me. I thanked her sincerely for coming to my rescue. Her answer was, 'The pleasure is all mine, Sophia! I need to make amends for the past. This is one way I feel I can do this.'

We ate and then spoke of what had happened in our lives during the past nine years. She questioned me as to the father of my unborn child, but I was not forthcoming. This conversation was the first sensible one I had had with Maura. It was enlightening and stimulating. She was amiable and considerate of my needs. I could not believe this was the Maura under whose regime I had received punishment as a child. She continued to allude to the fact I had grown into a beautiful young woman.

'The Harringtons should be proud of their upbringing of you. You are an adorable young lady!'

I smiled at her observations, but explained I was exceptionally tired after my long journey and would like to retire to my room, if that were possible. Maura led the way and familiarised me with my room and bathroom. She had discouraged me from carrying my case upstairs, and suggested I unpack just what I needed for the night. I did as directed and settled myself in my room. The money Father had given me was in my bag, along with my bank book. I would need every penny for buying the items a baby would require for its daily upbringing. I wanted to ensure it was kept safe and not carried in my purse. I hunted for a secure hiding place. Recalling all the things of mine that Maura had stolen years previously, I decided not to put temptation in her way. I found the safest place was under the carpet below my bed, and placed the money and bank book there so it was accessible to me only. Maura appeared after I had washed and donned my nightdress, carrying a large mug of my favourite cocoa. What a memory – except that I was never indulged by her as a child! A glass of water would have had to suffice. It was explained to me that a priest, known as Father Anthony, would call to see me the following morning to explain details concerning the convent. I bade Maura goodnight. For the first time in ages, I prayed for forgiveness and slept completely free from stress.

Father Anthony arrived promptly at ten o'clock the following morning. A short, brown-haired, ordinary-looking man, aged about thirty-five, he had come on a mission of mercy. He was a distant relative of Maura's, connected to the convent in an administrative position. During our introduction I had a distinct impression his eyes were exploring every contour of my body. I endured his stare, but was extremely uncomfortable in his presence.

'Are you packed, Sophia? I can take you to the convent immediately!' he announced.

I was astounded at the curt way in which he spoke of his intentions. I had been given to understand that I would remain with Maura until the birth of my child was imminent. It appeared that arrangements had been made for my immediate admission. I did not want to jeopardise my chance of antenatal care, and agreed to be packed and ready within five minutes.

'Now take care of yourself, Sophia darling. I will visit you at the first available moment after baby is born. It will not be long.'

Maura embraced me affectionately as Father Anthony loaded my case into his car. 'Be good, Sophia! It has been marvellous seeing you again after so long! I know what I have arranged for you will be just what you need.'

I hugged her, saying, 'Thank you for your help, Maura. Please visit me and my child as soon as you can. You have been so kind.'

She smiled one of her sugary smiles of old. As she waved, she called, 'You are far too beautiful for your own good, Sophia!'

What on earth did she mean?

I asked Father Anthony if he could stop at the nearest postbox. I sent a postcard to Mother and Father which I had penned the previous night. I climbed back into the car, when suddenly I remembered my money and bank book stashed under the carpet.

'Please, Father Anthony, can you take me back to Maura's house? I have left something behind.'

'It's not possible, Sophia. The traffic is far too heavy. We are expected at the convent now. Sister Florence does not like to be kept waiting.'

'But I will need it…' I begged.

'There is nothing you will need. You work and everything is provided. You will want for nothing!'

I thought the process through quickly and realised my money and book could be retrieved after my child was born. I would walk out and visit Maura on my time off.

Father Anthony was decidedly quiet on the journey. When he did speak he began each snippet of conversation by touching my knee. Something about him annoyed me intensely. I shuddered at his touch. As we approached the convent I realised I was homesick, and petrified.

Chapter Fifteen

The convent loomed large and eerie against the backdrop of tall trees and cloudy skies, its façade cold and uninviting. The high, ivy-clad stone perimeter wall with large wrought iron gates, lent a prison-like quality to the structure. I wondered why the gates were locked and had to be opened by Father Anthony. I observed a huge bunch of keys hanging from his waist and was intrigued as to what they were for. The large key, I discovered, unlocked the main gate. Were the gates to keep intruders out or patients in? What kind of establishment was this? Father Anthony and I were greeted by Sister Catherine, an elderly nun with lived-in features and a certain difficulty in walking. Her limp reverberated on the cold, tiled floors. She showed us to the admission quarters. I was taken to a room, where Father Anthony deposited my case and left me with the words, 'Be a pleasant, hard-working girl, Sophia! I will see you when the baby is born.'

I sat on a wooden chair in a half-tiled room, awaiting the arrival of a young nun, who introduced herself as Sister Florence.

'You must be Sophia,' she said briskly. 'Remove your clothing and take a shower!' She pointed to an adjoining room.

'I had a shower this morning,' I insisted.

'Do as you are asked, Sophia, and we will get along fine.'

I did as requested and returned, wrapped in a rough towel. She thrust a button-through brown serge dress at me and was adamant I put it on. It was designed for a person much larger than me, which I pointed out, but to no avail. I was about to return my precious gold locket to my neck, when she snatched it from me, stating, 'Jewellery is not allowed in here.'

I protested angrily, but was informed in no uncertain terms it would be kept safely 'until I needed it'. No amount of pleading would induce her to return it to me. I *did* need it! I wanted to view it nightly. My only photos of Father, Ben, Marcus and my beloved Alex were contained within. My mind raced to Alex, wondering how he was progressing. I wondered if perhaps the good Lord had seen fit to take him from us. I began to feel terribly lonely and frightened but could sense this was not an establishment where emotions were entertained. I did not think love or sentimentality were part of any agenda.

'Now, Sophia, we are going to take your case. Remove your underwear from it. We will store everything else safely. You will not need the contents. These brown dresses are your working uniform and these are your shoes.' She handed me the most dreadful clumsy black footwear. I was handed a thick nightdress and told it was all I would require.

'What will I wear during recreation time?' I asked.

'*Recreation time*? Sure, you won't have time for recreation! You are here to work until your baby is born and after.'

Sister Florence was not forthcoming with information and seemed to view me with a degree of disgust. Dressed in my brown uniform and black shoes, I was taken with a few items deposited in a cardboard box, to Sister Josephine, a sour-faced, middle-aged nun with an aggressive attitude. In her office I placed the box on a chair.

'*Stand there*, Sophia Bertucelli!' she demanded, pointing to a spot a short distance from her desk. She circled around me, viewing every inch of my frame. I began to feel as though I were a criminal. She roughly touched my long black hair.

'This hair must be dressed in a more manageable style!' she demanded.

She plaited it, piled it on my head and fastened it with pins, saying, 'So you are seven months pregnant? Shame on you!'

'Yes, Sister Josephine.'

'*You*, young woman, have committed a mortal sin! You know that.'

'Yes, Sister Josephine,' I whispered, hanging my head.

'*Speak up child*! *Do not whisper*! Do you know what this place is, Sophia?'

'I do, Sister. It is a convent,' I replied.

'This convent is where young shameless girls, like you, who have given in to temptations of the flesh, are brought, to make amends for their wrongdoing! Look at me, Sophia, when I am talking to you!' she bellowed.

I lifted my gaze from the floor as she circled around me once more and stood within inches of my face, fixing me with her cloudy eyes. How old and wrinkly she looked! My immediate thought was, No man would want her flesh, even if it were offered on a plate. I don't suppose she knew what a real man looked like, let alone having had the experience of a loving and fulfilling relationship.

'This, Sophia, is the convent of St Mary Magdalene. Listen carefully to what I have to tell you! You will then understand why you are here.'

As she returned to her desk, her eyes became fixed once more on mine. She began quoting chapter and verse the reason for my stay.

'I am the Sister in charge here! You will obey me at all times! Understand that, and we will get along fine!' she shouted.

'I am to be addressed at all times as Sister Josephine! The philosophy here is simple. You will do well to adhere to it. We believe in the cleanliness of mind, body and spirit at all times and hard work! Do you understand?'

'Yes, Sister Josephine,' I answered, raising my voice a few decibels.

'Through the power of prayer, it is hoped you, as one of the fallen, may find your way back to Jesus Christ Our Lord and Saviour. Mary Magdalene, as you know, is the Patron Saint of sinners. Did you know, Sophia, that she was a sinner of the worst kind?'

I nodded my head.

'Mary Magdalene gave her flesh to depraved and lustful humans, for recompense. Filthy money! She only received salvation by paying penance for her sins, as you will! She denied herself all pleasures of the flesh, as you will, and of course sleep! Mary Magdalene worked beyond human endurance. She could then offer up her soul to God to enter the gates of Heaven and live in life everlasting! This is what you will do!'

'But, Sister, I have not—' I began, but she barked, 'Do not interrupt me!'

She explained that I would share a dormitory with many other girls, and there would be no talking. They had all been, or were, in a similar situation to myself.

'You will rise at 6 a.m. Breakfast and prayers are between 6.30 a.m. and 7.30 a.m.

'At 7.30 a.m. you will commence work. While you are pregnant you will work in the sick bay, caring for those who are ill, or cleaning the corridors. After your child is born you will work in the laundry.'

'But, Sister, I do not understand. When my child is—'

'I have not asked if you have any questions!' she snapped. 'Therefore, do not speak! The first thing you will learn here is that you do not speak unless asked to do so. *Do you understand?*'

'I understand perfectly, Sister Josephine!'

'Well, Sophia! Follow our rules and you will not have problems. Remember when you enter the laundry, the linen is not ordinary linen, it is an earthly means to cleanse your soul from all the sins you have committed. You will have a chance to redeem yourself. God willing, you will save yourself from eternal damnation.'

She finished lecturing me. I wanted to yawn! She rang a small brass bell on her desk. Sister Florence entered the room.

'Go with Sister Florence. She will show you to your dormitory and take you for a medical examination. Afterwards we will put you to work. I do not want to see you in my office for any reason! Behave and it will not happen!'

It was blatantly obvious I would hate every moment spent in this hell-hole. As soon as my child was born I would leave. Maura would fetch me. To think this was the 1960s! This dreadful establishment existed and the narrow-minded views of the Church, and families, were all too prevalent. Carrying my box containing my few allowable pieces of clothing, I reached the dormitory at the top of the building. It was bleak. No pictures adorned the walls. There were rows of beds on either side of the room, each with a thin mattress and the minimum amount of covers. So this was where I would sleep! Certainly not for long, if I had my way. I would leave at the earliest moment. At the first opportunity after my baby's birth I would be gone.

The gynaecologist was a sanctimonious man named Brendan Flatley. He was rough and unrelenting in his examination of me. After a medical had been carried out he declared me a fit, healthy young woman who had eaten well and been taken care of 'unlike girls who normally passed through his hands,' as he put it.

I began to wonder how I would cope with another two months in this godforsaken place when I had only just arrived. Examination over, the nuns immediately engaged me in work, washing walls and paintwork in the corridors. Time seemed endless with the repetitive work. I and two other girls were watched over continuously by a nun seated at the end of the corridor. Speaking was definitely out of the question, but I noticed the two girls were in a similar situation and due to give birth soon.

I crept into bed and had my first 'meeting' with Niamh O'Leary, an attractive twenty-year-old, due to give birth within the month. Our friendship took place across the space between our beds, late at night when other girls were asleep. Niamh was a super girl, but exceedingly thin. She had been dismissed from her family when they realised she was having a child. Niamh was sent to the convent, where she had been for five months. She explained that to prevent recriminations, the father of her baby had sailed to Liverpool. It was the last time she had seen or heard from him. She horrified me when she explained there were women who had been in the convent for years after having given birth.

'It happens here, Sophia,' she whispered. 'They take your child away and then you spend the rest of your life here. Didn't you know?'

'I am not staying here, Niamh! I will leave as soon as my baby is born!'

'No one leaves here, Sophia! Once here it is for life. You must have heard of the Magdalene Laundries?'

I would not accept this was to be my life from now on. Like me, she desperately needed a friend. We offered one another help and support. Each night, after an exceptionally long day, we would hold hands and whisper of our hopes and dreams, which seemed to fade as each day passed. I told her about Mother, Father, Ben, Marcus and of course darling Alex. I also explained about Maura, whom she dubbed 'the wicked witch of Dublin'. She listened as I explained about the accident Alex had had and the consequences. She was sensitive to the situation as I spoke. I could no longer release my emotions with tears. I was changing fast, residing in the convent, and could find no time to weep, but to be defensive and fight my way through each day. Niamh, in turn, explained how she'd grown up in a large Catholic family in Dublin, a life far removed from the loving home I had experienced at Harrington Hall.

Each morning began with a wake-up call at 6 a.m., when we were directed to our prayers and breakfast. Niamh had explained how little we had to eat. I experienced it at first hand. The aroma of bacon, eggs and home-made bread made one feel hungry, but we saw nothing of this on our table. The nuns stuffed their miserable faces with food while we made do with a small bowl of porridge and dry bread. I watched as they ate bacon, eggs, bread, butter, jam, and an assortment of food. We were hungry. It was like a scene from one of the Dickens novels I had read. This prompted me to anger. Someone had to do something for the poor, frightened, half-starved girls, who needed substantially more food. I gave Niamh my plate of porridge one morning so she would not be hungry, but Sister Florence came down on me like a ton of bricks and insisted I took back the half-eaten plate of 'stodge' I had given to Niamh. I flatly refused! I pointed out, without being asked, in as loud a voice as possible, that the nuns seemed to be eating heartily and could easily spare each one of us food from their table. The girls sat silently, heads bowed. I was instructed to leave the table. The girls were extremely frightened, but I did not care. I was simply stating a fact.

I was marched to Sister Josephine's office and ordered to stand in front of her like a naughty child. She fumed as she screamed, 'How dare you answer Sister Florence in such a manner? How dare you ask for more than your allotted rations?'

She moved to the back of me as I said, 'You nuns are eating all kinds of hearty food—' but before I could finish she administered a blow across my back, sending me reeling. I managed to regain my balance, turned and saw Sister Josephine wielding a leather strap at me, just as Maura had done years previously. I held my hands up to protect myself as she delivered more blows. Six in all! Screaming, she administered her punishment. She announced, 'You will not speak to me in such a manner! Do you understand? I will not tolerate your behaviour!'

I was fearful for my unborn child and apologised immediately. What kind of hell was this? My back hurt terribly. I made up my mind, there and then, that I would escape at the first possible opportunity. Unfortunately, Niamh and I received only half our normal daily food rations from then on. We were both continually hungry, but we soldiered on together. The situation did not improve for the other girls. At least we knew at night we could whisper words of comfort to one another from our beds.

One morning, after breakfast, I was sent to the sickbay to work. There I met Sinead. She was in a single room and grabbed my hand as I passed by her bed to fill her water jug. As she took my hand and held it tightly, I looked at the bandage around her wrist. Her other wrist was bandaged also.

'Oh, dear,' I whispered, 'have you hurt yourself?'

She stared at me, her eyes possessing a wild look. She held on tightly to me, but gradually released her grasp and began to cry. I was appalled to see her in such distress and wanted to comfort her, but a nun appeared.

'Hurry along, Sophia! You will get nothing done if you are slow!' she said curtly.

I left the room immediately but intended returning at the earliest moment to comfort my new friend.

During the week I gleaned snippets of conversation from Sinead. She had given birth to a little girl and was forced, by her parents, to give it up for adoption. As a result she had tried to commit suicide by slashing her wrists. I thought how terrible it was, but promised myself no one would part me from my child. By the end of the week, Sinead had disappeared. I learnt she had been transferred to an asylum! I was devastated! 'Mentally insane' was the diagnosis. This was her punishment for trying to end the heartache of having her child taken away! What kind of uncaring, unfeeling monsters were they who ran this convent? Here was one teenager they would not force into submission. That was something they would soon learn about Sophia Bertucelli!

As I washed the walls in one of the empty sick bays one morning, I had the most excruciating pain. I could not understand it. My child was not due for another month. After a series of more severe pains, I was dragged along in agony to the delivery ward for examination.

'You are having your baby!' announced Doctor Flatley. He stated, 'Labour has begun.'

The pain was unbelievable. All cries for pain relief were dismissed as being totally unnecessary. I was observed regularly. How I wished Alex could have been there to comfort me! Sister Ursula examined me occasionally, as did a very pleasant nurse from outside the convent called Mary O'Connell. On one occasion, Sister Ursula, unsmiling and unfriendly, attended to my screams and asked, 'Is the pain you are suffering hour upon hour, worth the five minutes of pleasure it took for you to conceive this child?' But I ignored her catty remarks and gritted my teeth. I bore whatever pain Mother Nature decided to dish out.

Labour continued. I knew in my heart something was wrong. As the hours passed, Doctor Flatley appeared and announced a forceps delivery was required, and amidst screams I endured the worst barbaric procedure one could imagine. At one stage I thought I was going to die, and wondered how on earth Mother and Father would cope with my demise and the circumstances under which it would have taken place. As I reached my lowest ebb, I heard a voice say, 'It's a boy!' and, bending over me, Nurse O'Connell announced, 'Sophia! You have a son! He is beautiful! We have to take him to the special care unit. The forceps have made a mess of him!'

I had no chance to hold him in my arms. When approached by her for a name I realised I had had no one to discuss it with. I wondered what Alex would have chosen. As drips were placed in both arms, I asked Nurse O'Connell what my son was like.

'He is gorgeous! Lots of black hair like yours! He reminds me of the son I lost last year,' she explained sadly.

'What was his name?' I asked.

'It was Jonathan!' she replied.

'Then would you mind awfully if I call him Jonathan?'

'Sophia, I would be delighted!' she said emotionally. She patted my hand. I realised at that moment I was the happiest girl alive, and could not wait to hold my darling son!

It was almost three days later before Jonathan was brought to me. I had become anxious as to his whereabouts but was assured that he was having good care taken of him. Swaddled in a small blanket, he was handed to me. I carefully uncovered him in the privacy of my room in the sick bay and held his tiny, warm body close to mine. I detected the delicate perfume of baby talcum powder, masking the overriding smell of dried baby milk on his clothing. Against my express wishes, the nuns had seen fit not to allow me to breastfeed him but to place him on formula, hence the delay in holding my precious little one. It was obvious I was going to have no say in his daily welfare. As I held the tiny

6 lb bundle secure to my breast, his head nestled close to me. His mouth opened in search of my nipple. He wanted to suckle. I wanted to form a bond with this most wonderful gift of life, my darling son Jonathan, our son – Alex's and mine. I wondered if he knew who I was. I had read somewhere that paediatricians had stated a child could recognise its mother purely by body odour, so perhaps he did recognise me. I hoped so. He was gorgeous, with his dark hair and delicate ivory skin. I gazed at him and softly called his name.

'Hello, Jonathan, my precious one, I am your mummy. I love you with all my heart. When we leave here I am going to show you all the blessings of life. I will cherish you all my days. I do wish Daddy could see you now. Perhaps one day he will. He would be so proud of you. You have his handsome looks.'

My tears fell on his small hands. I marvelled at his tiny fingers and his perfectly formed nails, and held his hands gently in mine. He was like porcelain. I stroked and kissed them. His face searched once again for my overfull breast and without further ado I decided I would feed him. My breasts were so heavy and uncomfortable but I was soon relieved of the fullness as he contentedly suckled. It was the most wonderful, fulfilling feeling any new mother could possibly experience. I knew the bond between Jonathan and me could never be taken away. I watched the door. The nuns were moving to and fro in the corridor. Sister Philomena arrived with a bottle and pushed it in my direction. I grasped it. After her instructions of, 'Here, take this! Don't be all day,' I waited until she had disappeared before going to the sink to flush the contents of the bottle away. There would be no bottles for my son. I would feed him with my milk, of which I had plenty. We could carry on our bonding process, in spite of the nuns and their stupid rules.

Oh, how Jonathan favoured Alex in looks! If only I could have visited Alex and taken Jonathan with me, but it was impossible. I was a prisoner in this hell of a place, and had to do as instructed or be severely punished. I hoped Maura would fetch us soon. She had been notified of Jonathan's birth, but had not appeared but she no doubt would. No one would answer the questions which lay heavy on my mind. If I attempted to query anything I was told to keep quiet. It was two months since I had entered this place. There were no means of communication. I did not have my beloved locket to view my photographs. Sometimes I woke at night in utmost panic and could not visualise Alex's features. I would cry myself to sleep, wondering if he was still alive or had left this world. Were Jonathan and I totally alone? I feared isolation so much.

Sister Philomena relieved me of my baby. I was sent to wash floors and walls in the corridors once more, until the next bottle feed was due. I had an overriding feeling of not being well and wished desperately to climb into my bed and stay there. My throat hurt, my head was heavy. I was running a temperature. I was allowed to continue sleeping in the sickbay and had the company of Niamh, who had given birth to a beautiful baby girl, Angelique, born the day after Jonathan.

'You must tell them you are not well, Sophia!' she whispered, 'otherwise you will be ill if you do not receive treatment. You will not be able to feed your son.'

I took no notice. I was too wrapped up in the wonderful experience of having my beloved son with me and for me to breastfeed him when no one was around. Niamh was my lookout.

During the night I awoke feeling extremely ill. In the distance I could hear a baby crying. I knew it was Jonathan. I could recognise his cry above all others. He was in a room where cots were placed side by side. It was dark except for a light in the corridor. I had to go to him. He needed me. I shivered with cold as I left my bed. My chest was wheezy and I was decidedly worse than I had been the day previously. As I took a step forward, my legs would not hold me and I fell into a crumpled heap on the floor. Jonathan continued crying. I wanted to crawl to his side and comfort him in my arms as only I knew how. I remember nothing more and do not know how long it was before I awoke, finding myself in my bed. My head throbbed and every joint ached. I was burning like a fiery furnace but remember calling, 'Jonathan! Jonathan!' No one heeded my cries or brought him to me. I found difficulty in breathing and was forcibly fed medication, given injections and slept hour upon hour. This daze continued, but I remember being given a blanket bath and having my hair combed. Two figures arrived at the end of my bed, but I could not make out their faces. There had been so many figures there in the past days. I did not know if I was hallucinating or if they were real. A voice said, 'Hello Sophia! I am Father Anthony. You must remember me. I brought you here. Maura is with me!'

'Sophia, darling, I have just seen your son! He is gorgeous.'

I could not distinguish the face but recognised the voice as that of Maura.

'I want to come home!' I whispered, as I tried to lift my head, but swimming sensations invaded my brain. I flopped against the pillows.

'Quiet, Sophia! Listen to Father Anthony!' Maura insisted.

I felt too ill to listen to anything the priest had to say. I turned my head away. I needed to feel better, but they traumatised me.

'Now, Sophia, you know your child is a bastard child,' he said.

His voice drifted in and out of my consciousness. I coughed but it hurt desperately. My chest ached, my ribs were sore. At one stage my body appeared to float to the ceiling. I could view myself lying in bed.

'You are very sinful, Sophia! Jonathan will pay for those sins all his life. Are you listening to me?' Father Anthony asked.

I heard him but I did not want to. I could not comprehend where this was leading.

'Can you understand me, Sophia?' he asked.

I shook with cold and then burned. My body was sore from needle punctures.

'Sign here, Sophia. Jonathan will have a good life!'

A paper was thrust at me. Once more I tried to lift myself up on pillows, experiencing dizziness as I did so. Maura assisted me as I tried hard to read the form. Father Anthony placed a pen in my hand but I was too weak to hold it.

'Sign here!' he insisted, as Maura directed my hand.

'If I sign… can we leave here… come home to you?' I asked.

'Of course you can, darling, as soon as you are well,' Maura promised.

I was so relieved. She guided my hand, and I signed where directed and then slumped back on the pillow. I was going home to Maura's house and taking my son. I closed my eyes, but although they were talking I was too ill to listen.

Chapter Sixteen

I knew where the devil's disciple was – in his office! No doubt he was filling in more forms that poor innocent girls would be asked to sign, so that their newborn babies could be taken away for adoption. I wanted my son Jonathan back and was determined to do all in my power to see he was returned to me. The bitch known as Maura Bertucelli would suffer for what she had done to me – somehow, sometime, somewhere. I stormed into Father Anthony's office unannounced, having absconded from my duties.

'Where is Jonathan?' I demanded, and watched as he lifted himself from his knees. He had been searching in his bookcase for some literary masterpiece.

'How dare you barge into my office!' he shouted, shooting me a worried glance. 'Calm down and sit here, Sophia. We will talk. You are naturally upset.'

'Upset? *Upset*? I am not just upset; I am livid, angry, and *frantic*! I want Jonathan back! You made me sign the adoption form under false pretences.'

I stood with arms folded, staring angrily into his eyes, but he turned his head away from my face and could not look at me. I banged my fist on his desk.

'Let us talk this over rationally, Sophia,' he said, seating himself behind his desk, with its usual bundles of paperwork.

'There is nothing to talk over, Father Anthony. You have stolen my baby son. I want him returned to me forthwith!'

'Don't be ridiculous, Sophia. You signed a form to have your child placed in a good Catholic home with loving parents. He has gone to good people.'

'He is *my* son and I love him with all my heart. He is not yours to give away! You tricked me! *I want my son back now*!' I screamed.

'Stop this behaviour this minute, Sophia! He is not coming back to you, and the sooner you get that idea into your head the better.'

'You are wicked, Father. If you do not have Jonathan returned to me I will—'

'You will do what, Sophia? What will you do? There is nothing you can do!'

'*Nothing*? We will see!' I shouted.

Where had the calm, composed, reasonable Sophia Bertucelli gone? She certainly no longer resided in the convent.

'I can do this!' I roared and I swept my arms across his desk, sending books, papers and pens flying to the floor and then began tearing up any paperwork within my reach. He rushed to try and stop me but not before I had almost emptied the contents of a bookcase onto the floor. Holding me roughly, he opened his office door and called for help. Sister Florence appeared like a bat out of hell and between them they pushed me to the floor. As I struggled, they insisted I clear up the awful mess. I flatly refused. No amount of hitting me would entice me into doing it, so I was dragged downstairs to Sister Josephine's office.

'You evil child!' she snapped, when told of my behaviour.

Without thinking, I spat at her. She was furious as she wiped the saliva from her immaculate habit. She said, 'You will pay dearly for this behaviour!' She shot me an evil glance.

So what, I thought. They couldn't hurt me any more than I already had been.

She summoned help from Sisters Catherine and Florence, who held me down on a wooden chair, screaming and shouting. With dressmaker's scissors at the ready, she unplaited my long, black hair and hacked it off, nicking my scalp in numerous places as she did so. There was blood all over my dress and bruises over my arms, legs and body where I had been held. I continued hissing and spitting at them, like a caged animal. They could try and break my spirit but they would never get my soul. Eventually, my wounds were dressed. I was taken to a room with just a bench in it. Solitary confinement was my further punishment. I spent the night there being told to 'calm down'. I wanted to cry, but would not. I muttered continually, 'Jonathan, I want you back!'

When Niamh spied me in the laundry the following day with my hair hacked off, she was visibly moved but unable to comfort me. After supper and prayers, we settled down for the night in our dormitory beds. My head ached, was sore and still bled from the cuts which had been inflicted the previous day. I tried desperately to make my hair look decent and encourage it into a style, but it was impossible. I could do nothing with it and would have to wait until it grew. Niamh clasped my hand across the space between our beds and tried to comfort me. It was wonderful to have such a dear friend and confidante. I wanted to talk long about Alex and the loving relationship we'd had and how he'd had hopes and dreams of becoming a pilot like his father before him. She and I realised there was very little hope that if I returned to Yorkshire one day, Alex would still be alive. She was caring and soothing when I wanted to show emotion, but somehow tears evaded me more and more, especially after all I had experienced. I was becoming a rebel and my tears were all spent.

I detected Niamh crying on several occasions. She seemed to have accepted the fact that Angelique had been taken from her, but she did not have the love of a family to return to. I would make sure she had my family to share if we escaped from the convent. We were both young unmarried mothers who had been parted from their beloved babies, and together we grieved. There was little consolation we could offer one another, but at least we were aware of each other's suffering.

Work in the laundry was unbelievably exhausting, with long hours, little food and constant prayers. Every day became a trial. It was then I decided I would add a little spice to the daily proceedings. Marcus and Ben would have been proud of me.

On my first assignment with the ironing board, I 'accidentally' put scorch marks on numerous items of laundry brought in from outside. Holding them in the air, I could see straight through the holes from Dublin to England! I was punished with a beating.

Woollen items needed careful washing so that there was no shrinkage, but really hot water had a marvellous effect, in that it shrunk most garments to half their original size. Again I was beaten! It was worth it to see the expressions on the faces of the nuns. The girls giggled, unnoticed by those in charge, but they became frightened for my welfare. On one occasion, as a punishment, I was stripped naked and, along with two other girls, was given a cold shower via a hosepipe. Two nuns administered the water and laughed hysterically as they watched us shiver and shriek. I managed to snatch the hosepipe from the nuns and turned it on those who had laughed at us so heartily.

They laughed no more when they were drenched. We three received yet another beating. I was determined that while I was there I would leave my mark, but unlike many who had succumbed to the convent way of life year after year, I was not going to be browbeaten or intimidated. My main concern was that I would try to escape as soon as was humanly possible and find my son. If Niamh wanted to go with me I would take her to Yorkshire. I had to wait, watch and observe whatever I needed to know in order to contrive an exit from the prison I was in. When the time came for me to leave I would ensure the name Sophia Bertucelli resounded around the corridors for years to come.

The months flew by. I often wondered about Harrington Hall and what had happened in my absence. Daily, I would wonder if Mother and Father had coped with Alex's illness. Would he still be with us, or would he have left this earth? Certainly the prognosis had not been good. Ben would have gone to university at Cambridge, no doubt, and Marcus would soon be approaching his fourteenth birthday. I could not imagine the tall, lanky teenager and wondered if he was progressing with his music without me to watch over him and encourage his talent. My eighteenth birthday had been spent in the laundry. It was like any other hard-working day, with no respite from the awful conditions: no nice dress to wear, no Millie to style what was left of my hair. She would have been disgusted if she could have seen the state of it, but at least it was in a style. Niamh managed to 'borrow' scissors when cleaning Sister Josephine's room and trimmed my hair neatly. Then she returned them before they were missed.

I was busy in the laundry when Sister Florence came looking for me.

'Take your apron off, Sophia! Father Anthony wants to see you in his office!' she ordered. 'Make sure you do not cause trouble. You have been warned that if you persist in your behaviour you will be transferred to an asylum!'

I removed my apron and hurried along to his office in the hope that the priest had news of my son.

'Come in!' he announced. Father Anthony's dictatorial voice echoed around the room. I entered his office.

'Hello Sophia, sit here!' He pointed to a wooden chair positioned in front of his desk.

I sat with expectations that he had news of Jonathan. He took one glance in my direction and seemed visibly shocked by my appearance.

'Good gracious!' he exclaimed 'You have been in the wars! I understand you have been misbehaving a great deal. What on earth has happened to your beautiful hair?'

I stroked my fingers through my lank, greasy locks; a poor excuse for what should have been a woman's crowning glory.

'Sister Josephine, with some help, hacked off my hair with dressmaker's scissors as a punishment!' I snapped.

'There, there! Don't be so aggressive, Sophia! It does not become you.'

What would he know? He did not have to work in the godforsaken hole, in such dreadful conditions, just to survive.

'So, have you called me here to tell me you are returning my son to me?' I asked. 'Because if you haven't, then we have nothing more to say to each other.' I stood up in an attempt to leave.

'Sit down, Sophia!' he ordered.

Uncharacteristically, I obeyed his command. He left his seat from behind the desk and stood behind me. I could feel his hot breath on my neck. His fingers stroked various cuts and bruises on my neck and face. I turned my face away from his hand. He fondled my short hair as I gritted my teeth. He could feel my muscles tense as he touched me. He returned to his chair, saying, 'You are making life difficult for yourself, Sophia! If you were to cooperate you would not receive the punishments being meted out to you.'

'I want my son back now!' I screeched.

'Stop that, Sophia! He is not coming back to you. Why won't you understand?'

I stood up and hit out at the papers on his desk, scattering them. It seemed he had anticipated my reaction and sat there, doing nothing to retrieve them from the floor. It was useless trying to provoke a reaction from him so I slumped into the chair.

'The Sisters here are at their wits' end with you! You are disruptive on a daily basis. No amount of punishment seems to make a difference. They are talking of sending you to an asylum. Is that what you want?'

'If I cannot have my son, I don't care! Give him back to me and I will behave.'

'We have been through this, Sophia! *He has gone.* He is not coming back!'

The finality of the situation suddenly hit me. I began sobbing uncontrollably.

He paused for a while until I had collected myself and said, 'Sophia, I can help you! I really can!'

I listened but did not know how. Something had to change dramatically. Not just for me, but for all the other forsaken girls in that dreadful laundry. Maybe he was a ray of hope in such an awful place.

'I can get you things you find necessary,' he promised.

'My son? Can you get me my son?'

'Let's not go over old ground again! You know what the position is with Jonathan! I know you would like your locket to wear and I can see you have it. You also need more food for yourself and the girls.' He finally admitted we were starving. 'You and the girls in your dormitory need better working conditions. I can get all these things improved for you!'

He stood up from his chair, moved around the desk toward me and turned my chair abruptly sideways to face him. He knelt in front of me and took hold of my hands. I tried desperately to pull away but he grasped my fingers tightly in a vice-like grip. He looked intently at my face as he said, 'Be nice to me, Sophia!'

'I do not understand you, Father Anthony. The girls are overworked, badly treated and hungry. What do I have to do to change this?'

He placed a hand on my knee saying, 'You are a gorgeous young woman, Sophia. You are more refined than other girls here. A man in my position has difficulty being celibate. I have needs, Sophia, like any other man. Those needs become urgent! All I am asking is that you satisfy those needs.'

'Are you mad, Father Anthony! What kind of woman do you think I am?'

'A whore!' was the reply. 'Why else would you be in here?' He smirked.

I raised my hand to slap his face. He held my wrist tightly before I could make contact.

'Just what I like, Sophia! A woman with spirit!'

'Father,' I announced, 'I do not know what you have been told about me but I have had a relationship with only one man. We were in love and hoped to have married, but life dealt him a cruel blow and I have ended up here.'

He towered over me as he stroked my hair. 'Do not dismiss what I have said out of hand, Sophia. I can make life easy or difficult for you – it's up to you. Think about it. The ball is in your court.' He lifted me up from the chair saying, 'I will send for you in a few days, when you have given my offer some thought.'

Leaning over, he tried to kiss me.

'Don't touch me!' I pleaded.

Standing, I moved the chair and sidled backwards toward the door which fortunately was not locked. I opened it quickly, removed myself from the room and closed the door behind me. I trembled with fear. Returning to the laundry, I donned my apron and began working, feeling dirty, betrayed and hopeless. I looked around me at the sad faces. Was this hell on earth to be my life from now on?

That night, although extremely tired I could not sleep. Niamh could see I was disturbed. During our night-time chat she whispered across the space to me, 'Sophia, what's wrong?'

I explained about Father Anthony and how he approached me on the subject of concessions for the girls if I would please him.

'He wants you to have sex with him, doesn't he?' she moaned.

I was aghast at the way in which she came straight to the point.

'How do you know?' I asked feeling ashamed.

'Because he has approached most of the girls in this dormitory. You would be amazed at how many have succumbed to his promises of better conditions. They never amount to anything. His promises are like piecrust. They crumble.'

Niamh sounded degraded by it all. I suspected she had been a victim of his assurances of better conditions herself.

'Please, Sophia, don't be drawn into his web. He deviates from what is normal,' she explained. 'He likes to be tied to his bed while having sexual acts performed on him.'

I was horrified at her portrayal of this man of the cloth. I could not believe what she was saying. She explained it was called 'bondage', and I imagined all the young women in the laundry who must have been subjected to his evil demands. How could a priest act in this way to satisfy his lust? I realised I had led a sheltered life, within the world of Harrington Hall and the estate, and knew nothing of such practices.

Elizabeth O'Brien, in the bed next to my own, said, 'Ssh!' and complained she could not sleep with us whispering. We stole under our covers and tried to sleep.

I knew little of Elizabeth. She was a blonde, blue-eyed girl of slight build with a ruddy complexion, having spent a considerable time outdoors. She possibly had family in the farming community. Elizabeth had no child and was simply detained at the convent for having been caught in a compromising situation with a neighbour's son.

One night when I found sleep difficult, I observed what I thought to be a strange situation. Elizabeth removed herself from her bed. Quietly and carefully, she floated across the floor when the other girls were sleeping. She walked toward the dormitory door. My immediate thought was that she was sleepwalking. I arose from my bed with the intention of gently stopping her in her tracks, turning her around, returning her to the direction of her bed. Before I could stop her she had reached the door. I was amazed when she opened it. It was constantly locked when we were in residence. I could not understand how the nuns had been careless in leaving the door unsecured.

Elizabeth walked through and began closing it behind her. I caught up with her, and realised she was not sleepwalking but absconding from the dormitory.

As I faced her she said, 'Sophia, go back to bed! Don't follow me. It would be a big mistake.'

I reluctantly did as instructed and she was gone. I lay there, imagining she had conjured up an escape plan and was bringing it to fruition. It bothered me if she were caught there would be tremendous repercussions for her and for us all.

Two hours passed before the door opened. Elizabeth was back in the dormitory. What on earth had she done? Where had she been? She didn't realise I was awake as she climbed into bed. I could hear her crying. I wanted to comfort her, but Elizabeth was a private individual, not used to outbursts of emotion. With her back toward me I heard continual sobs for what seemed like hours. Eventually, as they ceased, I fell asleep.

Morning arrived. We were woken and taken to prayers, then breakfast. At the table, Elizabeth's chair was vacant. Sister Florence asked of her whereabouts. It was unlike Elizabeth to miss breakfast. Food was desperately needed to give us strength to work.

Niamh was asked to return to the dormitory to find her and bring her to the table immediately. She did as requested but returned within minutes, ashen-faced and hysterical. She asked Sister Florence to leave her hearty breakfast and accompany her back to the dormitory. Elizabeth O'Brien had been found by Niamh, hanging from the beams. She had hidden rope we were issued with, for pegging laundry on to, and had used this to end her life. We were all in a total state of shock! I could not understand why she had been so desperate. She hadn't had a child taken from her. Could it possibly have been something that happened to her the previous evening? Guilt overtook me. I had not attempted to comfort her when she was distressed. Elizabeth, an introvert, would possibly not have let me comfort her or confide in me about her plight. I could only pray and mourn for this poor lost soul. Within hours, her bed had been changed and a new girl moved in. Nuns went about their business as if nothing had happened. Did we all mean so little to this establishment and its staff? We prayed silently for Elizabeth and attended to our daily chores. Morale was at an all-time low. We would miss her greatly.

As Niamh and I lay in our dormitory beds one night, cold and unable to sleep, I asked, 'Would you like to escape from this hell?'

She faced me and asked, 'What have you in mind, Sophia?'

I explained quietly of a plan, carefully worked out in my head. After revealing my idea I watched a huge smile appear on her face and noted the start of a giggling fit, which she stifled. It was a joy to watch and was the first occasion I had seen any sign of happiness in the time we had been friends.

'I am with you in whatever you do, Sophia! Do you really think we can escape from here?' she whispered.

'Yes, Niamh, I do!'

'Then we will carry out your plan! We will be successful, won't we?' she asked, fear creeping into her voice. We knew what our punishment would be if the plan did not succeed. It did not bear thinking about. It *had* to succeed.

'We will work it out like an army exercise and get to Dublin, unscathed,' I assured her; but I knew what I was planning bore no resemblance to an army exercise. I reached out and touched her hand in an act of reassurance. Hopefully there would not be many more nights we would have to sleep in our awful beds.

We were hurriedly woken at 6 a.m. During the morning, Sister Florence approached me announcing that Father Anthony wished to see me. Niamh looked up from her ironing board, winked in my direction and I acknowledged her with a nod. The first part of the plan had begun. I wiped my hands, removed my apron, smoothed away the creases in my brown dress and walked to his office on the first floor. I knocked loudly. There was no reply, so I knocked again.

'Come in!' Father Anthony was staring out of his office window, admiring the countryside beyond.

'Hello Sophia! Sit down. Make yourself comfortable. I have been observing how far we are from the nearest houses,' he said, pointing out of the window. 'No one escapes from this place, you know. Once here, you are here for life.'

I took in the point he was making. As I watched him I noticed another door in his room which led to a fire escape. It was extremely handy for his unauthorised comings and goings.

'Have you thought any more about the proposition I made to you?' he asked, turning to look at me, studying my reaction.

'Yes, I have given it considerable thought, Father Anthony.'

He moved from the window and sat at his desk. 'And what conclusion have you reached?'

'I am not sure, Father. I have little knowledge of sexual matters,' I confessed.

'Well, Sophia, I could teach you! You would soon learn what makes me happy.'

He stared into my eyes and I felt exceedingly uncomfortable.

'When would you need me to visit you?' I asked, staring at the floor.

He paused for a few moments, consulted his desk diary, and no doubt fitted me in between meetings with Sister Josephine and the signing of adoption papers.

'How about Thursday at 11 p.m. after prayers and lights out?' he suggested. 'I will make sure the dormitory door is unlocked!'

The penny suddenly dropped. I realised what Elizabeth O'Brien had been subjected to, the night before her dreadful demise. Father Anthony had drawn her into his evil web. This man had to be stopped! It would please me greatly if Niamh and I could bring about his downfall.

To his delight, I agreed to the arrangement. Discreetly I observed his surroundings, knowing the knowledge I gleaned would be of great help during a future liaison.

'You are a very sensible young lady, Sophia. Keep me sweet and I will see Sister Josephine gets off your back. What concessions you receive depends on how good you are to me. Do you understand what I am saying?'

'I understand perfectly, Father Anthony,' I said.

Under my breath I whispered to myself, 'If only you knew what plans I have for you!'

He gave me permission to leave. As I stood he moved to within inches of me.

'Good girl. I will see you on Thursday at 11 p.m. Please, Sophia, remember you are to say nothing of this to anyone, or the concessions will not apply.'

'I will say nothing, Father. This is our little secret,' I whispered.

He tried to touch my breasts through my brown dress but I moved away. He made my flesh crawl. I retreated to the corridor. I walked along with the biggest smile on my face the convent had seen in over a year.

'Oh yes, Father Anthony, you will have a night to remember!' I giggled and returned to the laundry.

Chapter Seventeen

Thursday evening arrived. Niamh and I conferred at length about our plans. I was extremely scared and knew our scheme had to work. We could not afford to have our plans go awry. The wounds on my face had healed well and I was able to wash my hair without undue discomfort.

In my long nightdress, I slid silently across the dormitory floor, not waking a soul. The door was open as planned. Niamh quietly followed with our serge dresses and shoes tucked under her arm. It was her intention to hide in the alcove outside Father Anthony's door, should the impending situation be deemed out of control.

Niamh hid as I tried the office door. It was unlocked. I gulped, took a deep breath and entered. Father Anthony was nowhere to be seen. I heard muffled movements in a side room attached to his office and I investigated. He sat on his iron bedstead, wearing a pair of striped pyjamas. I tried hard to control the tremors taking over my body. One false move on my part and our hope of escape would be thwarted.

'Sophia, dear girl, come over here!' he begged, beckoning me.

I smiled sweetly and moved toward him. Please don't let him touch me, I thought. I could not bear his hands on my skin. My body shook, but it was imperative I carried on with the charade, not simply so that Niamh and I could escape, but as retribution for all young girls who had suffered at his hands, with empty promises he made which never came to fruition; and justice for Elizabeth O'Brien *and* for the inhumane way in which he cheated me out of the chance to be mother to my precious son.

I stood innocently in front of him. He took my hand whispering, 'Sophia! You are cold. I feel you trembling. Come and warm yourself!'

He pulled back the bedclothes, inviting me to lie beside him. I sat uneasily on the edge of the bed. As I did so, my thoughts turned to Harrington Hall, to Mother and Father. What on earth would my father have thought of me if he could have seen me in this situation? Dear Alex came into my mind also. He would have been disgusted by my behaviour, but then under the circumstances, I think he would have understood. I wondered what had happened to him. If successful in my mission, I would return to Yorkshire and discover what had taken place while I'd been away. It was imperative I dismissed any further thoughts from my mind.

'You are such an attractive, inviting girl, Sophia! Now look at these!' he said reaching under his pillow. He produced four leather straps. I stared in disbelief.

'You look shocked,' he murmured, 'but listen, I want to be your prisoner. It excites me! You need to tie my wrists and ankles tightly to the bed frame. I will show you. After you have done this, I will explain what else I want you to do!'

He demonstrated how I should fasten the straps. I nodded, trying desperately to stop myself from quaking. He began removing his pyjamas and asked me to remove my nightdress. I did so, reluctantly, exposing my underwear. Father Anthony leered at me.

'Hurry, Sophia!' he said as he lay there naked.

I wanted to close my eyes, but I wrapped the straps around his wrists and ankles as directed and tied them to the bedposts as tightly as possible, trying hard not to look at his naked flesh. He looked a sight, the disgusting creature!

'Remove your clothing, Sophia!' he pleaded.

'I will, Father Anthony,' I cooed softly. 'I want to make tonight a night you will never forget, as long as you live!' I whispered sensually.

His eyes protruded. He looked at me lasciviously and immediately became aroused.

'Please hurry, Sophia! I want you so much. You can have so many things if you succumb to my wishes. Hurry!'

I left his side and looked around the room for his clothing.

'What are you doing?' he asked.

I ignored him, searching for the bunch of keys attached to his belt.

'Sophia! Come here this minute!' he ordered.

Again I ignored him. He continued making loud, begging noises, pleading with me. I moved toward him and quickly placed one of his smelly woollen socks in his mouth to quieten him. I opened the office door and softly called, 'Niamh!'

She entered. On seeing Father Anthony, she attempted to control her laughter. We donned dresses and shoes. He continued making muffled noises and wriggling motions from his bed. A vase of lilies graced his dressing table. I took one, removed part of the stalk and a piece of Sellotape from the dispenser. Shakily, I stuck the lily securely to his manhood. Niamh and I laughed hysterically. He was fuming but helpless. I pushed open the fire escape door and prepared for us to leave.

'Goodbye, Father Anthony!' I whispered. 'I am sure Sister Josephine will be *so* pleased to see you in your natural state in the morning, when she finds you are missing and looks for you!'

He tried communicating but every word was unrecognisable. His face was red with anger as he chewed on his sock, trying to spit it from his mouth.

'Sophia, we must go,' said Niamh, chuckling excitedly.

We departed by the fire escape door, closing it behind us. Climbing down heavy metal stairs we reached ground level and crept toward the large wrought iron gates. All I had to do was find a key which fitted, and if my memory served me correctly it was the largest one that opened the gate on the day of my arrival. I fumbled in the dark, found it and opened the squeaky gates wide enough for us to squeeze through. We locked them and disappeared into the night, tossing the keys into the shrubbery.

We set off across open fields. I couldn't help but think of Father Anthony and what a commotion there would be the following morning. Colour would soon appear in Sister Josephine's cheeks, enhancing her otherwise miserable, pallid complexion, and there would be even more embarrassment when she had to have him released. An enquiry was sure to take place and maybe he would receive another defrocking!

It was important we made our route to freedom in the dark, hoping we would not be spotted. Niamh, who supposedly knew the area, led the way. We fell in mud, bushes and ditches, but finally saw lights in the distance. We had not allowed for the fact the night air was cold. Having little clothing on, we soon became extremely chilled. We had no idea where we were and were ill prepared. As often as we could, we huddled together to keep warm. Tiredness and hunger were our running mates. It was soon apparent the lights were those of Dublin. Niamh knew the district where Maura resided. It was imperative we arrived at her house by morning. Maura had a lot of explaining to do and actions to answer for, and I did not intend leaving Ireland before she had experienced my wrath.

On the outskirts of town, we crept down alleyways and hid in doorways for fear we would stand out with our serge dresses. We would soon be reported as having absconded and did not wish to be arrested by the Garda and returned to the convent.

We reached the street where Maura lived and stayed hidden for a considerable time behind a fence. There was a familiar noise. Suddenly a police car screeched to a halt outside Maura's house. The Garda had arrived. We were frightened and could not risk being caught. It must have been later than we at first thought, as people were hurrying to and fro making early journeys to work. It was obvious that Sister Josephine had discovered Father Anthony, and the Garda were on our trail.

'What are we going to do, Sophia?'

I couldn't think and didn't answer. We watched as two policemen knocked officiously on Maura's front door. It was ages before she appeared, looking unkempt and weary. She was not her usual smart, sophisticated self. Without further ado, the officers pushed past her, uninvited. We could see them at the bedroom windows. Minutes later they reappeared, spoke to Maura and climbed into their car. Niamh was quaking in her shoes.

'Look, Sophia, we can't stay together. They'll discover us. It will be better if we split up.'

'No, Niamh, I want to take you back to Yorkshire with me!'

'I wouldn't fit into that way of life, Sophia!' she explained.

She held me close and said, 'We are best friends and always will be. I'll never forget you. We have been through so much together. I don't want to make things difficult for us. I have a friend not far from here. I'll go there. She's a good person and will take care of me. I'm going to find my Angelique, if it takes for ever!'

'Niamh!' I sighed. 'I shall miss you. Please write when you are settled. Let me know you are OK. It will find me at Harrington Hall, North Yorkshire! I am going home once I have dealt with Maura. I will find my darling Jonathan too!'

We hugged, and without further communication she was gone.

I waited, rubbing my arms with my hands, in the hope I could warm myself.

When I thought the Garda were long gone and the street relatively quiet, I dashed down a side alley leading to the rear garden of Maura's house.

I fiddled with the door and found it to be unlocked. I let myself in, crept across the kitchen and along the hallway. I discovered Maura, reclining on the sofa in her lounge, sporting her dressing gown and night attire. She was, on even a casual observation, drunk.

'Ah!' she slurred. 'You've turned up, like a bad penny. The Garda have been here looking for you. I will phone them!'

'No, you will not!' I stated pulling the phone wire from the wall. 'You and I have lots of unfinished business.'

She tried desperately to raise herself up from the sofa, but couldn't.

'There is nothing I want to say to you, Sophia... except—' She giggled. 'Look at you... you're a wreck!'

'And you are an evil old witch, Maura! You told Father Pierre in your letters that you'd given up drinking! That makes you a liar. To think we believed you had changed and wanted to help me!'

'*So?*' she said staring at me.

How I despised her! How could my papa have loved this woman, when he had once had my beautiful mama to love?

'I will never forgive you for having my son taken away from me! You knew what my fate would be when you organised my admittance to the Magdalene Laundry!'

'At least that brute… Oliver Harrington… has been deprived of a grandchild!' She laughed. 'I wanted to… make you suffer… like he made me suffer when he threw me out of Starbeck Cottage… and sent me away from the Harrington estate!' she mumbled incoherently.

'He sent you away because of your violent abuse of me! Sir Oliver is a good man. How dare you speak ill of him!' I screamed.

'Sir Oliver? You know nothing about the *real* Sir Oliver!' she sneered. 'Sure, he's no gentleman! Not Oliver Harrington!'

'Stop it, Maura, you can say nothing about him which will make me love him any less! He is a fine man! Leave him out of this conversation!'

'Your precious Sir Oliver,' she smirked, raising half a glass of whisky in my direction, 'is an adulterer!'

'How dare you! I'm not going to listen to any more of your lies!'

I placed my fingers over my ears but she continued to ramble.

'You need to… open your eyes, Sophia! Your papa told me… on our wedding night… Oliver Harrington… had an affair… with your mama!'

She wobbled unsteadily, trying to remove herself and her glass from the sofa. She was gulping down the whisky as though it were water. I wanted to take her in my hands and shake the living daylights out of her, but such behaviour would have reduced me to her level.

'Stop lying to me, Maura! *Stop!*'

'I am *not* lying to you!' she said, pouring a larger glass of whisky from the bottle, spilling a deal of it over herself. 'Your wonderful Sir Oliver,' she went on, taking a swig of whisky, 'is paying me £400 – monthly – to keep quiet about the fact! He did not want her Ladyship to find out his sordid little secret, or Alex, or Ben! D'ye now see what the bloody gentleman – Oliver Harrington – is like?'

She dropped her glass on the floor and passed out! I had no intention of seeing to her and could not have cared if she were alive or dead at that moment, as anger filled my being. She was a lying, thieving, manipulative, drunken excuse for a woman. It was lies, all lies, I was sure. Then I suddenly had a flashback to the day I had helped Father with his office accounts and queried the payments he was making to a recipient in Dublin. He had appeared reluctant to answer me, and had stated it was business! Was Maura lying? I really did not want to think about it! I rushed upstairs and entered the room where I had slept for one night. Exploring along the carpet under the bed I retrieved my savings book and the sum of money Father had given me on leaving Yorkshire, which surprisingly was intact. Then I rummaged through Maura's drawers and wardrobe for a decent set of clothing to wear. I found several new sets of underwear that would be useful and put them in a rucksack that lay in the bottom of the wardrobe. I could hear Maura snoring peacefully downstairs, so I ran a bath. How I would have loved to wallow in the water for a considerable time, but time itself was of the essence, so I hurriedly bathed and dressed in a sweater and trousers belonging to her, and covered my top in her navy blazer. Then I collected my things together, headed downstairs, and went out of the rear entrance of the house and down the alleyway, walking as fast as my legs would carry me. I hailed a taxi on the next corner and asked to be taken to the port at Dun Laoghaire, where I booked a ticket as a foot passenger for Liverpool on the next available ferry.

I was going home to Yorkshire.

I boarded the ferry and made myself comfortable, having bought an enormous assortment of sandwiches and soft drinks, which I devoured like someone who had not eaten well for a long time. They were delicious. I rested myself against the back of the seat and could not wait for my arrival in England. It was then I realised that not only had I left my darling son behind, somewhere, but I had also left my precious gold locket, with the photos of my family, at the convent. It was obvious to me I would never see either again. I hoped one day, by some enormous miracle, I would be able to find my beloved Jonathan.

When I reached the station at Liverpool I fumbled in my purse for coins to place in the telephone box, but I didn't have sufficient change to allow me to call Harrington Hall to notify Mother and Father I was on my way home. This came as a relief in many respects, for I had not prepared what I'd say to them or the explanation I would give for not having corresponded in over a year.

I looked at the station clock and realised the train was due to depart within five minutes. With the rucksack over my shoulder, I hurried to the platform and stepped on the train as the guard closed the door and waved his flag. The train left on time. I sat in an empty carriage and stared out of the window as we sped across the magnificent English countryside. The closer we travelled toward Yorkshire the more nervous I became. My thoughts went out to Niamh. Did she make it to her friend's house? Was she caught and returned to the convent? I would wait in anticipation for her first letter to inform me she was safe and well. Then I could rest peacefully knowing she had made her escape to freedom and a new life. Perhaps, too, she would find her beautiful daughter, Angelique. I would pray for this nightly and for my own search for Jonathan, hoping this would be successful as well.

I finally arrived at my destination. I walked across the road from the village railway station and stared into the prettily adorned shop window of La Petite Fleur, at the potted plants and exotic blooms. It began to rain. I had intended buying flowers for Mother, but as the rain continued I decided I should make tracks swiftly along the country lane leading to the Hall. How refreshing it was to breathe in the country air once again. It was great to be free. Vehicles on the road were few. I walked at a reasonable pace and moved over toward the grass verge as I heard the sound of a horse's hooves coming from behind. The rider was almost level with me when I heard, 'Sophia? It *is* you! I thought it was. How could I mistake that walk?'

I turned as the rider brought the horse to a halt. The sight of the handsome young man made my heart skip a beat.

'Marcus! Dear Marcus! How good it is to see you!'

I began to weep at the sight of him. He jumped down from the saddle and, holding the reins in one hand, put his other arm around my shoulders and hugged me affectionately. My head rested on his chest and I cried unashamedly into his jacket.

'Thank God you are home, Sophia! I have missed you so much! But what on earth have you done to your lovely long tresses?' he asked, stroking my hair gently, as he looked down and frowned at me.

Placing my hand on my head, I said, 'The convent didn't wish us to have long hair, so it was cut!'

'It will soon grow,' he said, flicking up the ends of my pageboy style. Then he remarked, 'You are awfully thin, Sophia! Didn't they feed you?'

'I had enough food,' I lied. 'Anyway, Marcus, you look great and I see you are exercising Alex's horse.'

'Yes, I'm riding Storm, so he will be fit for Alex to ride one day!'

'Oh, dear Alex! How is he—?'

Before I could continue, he said, 'I am afraid he is still in a coma. There has been no change since you went away.'

'Oh, dear,' I said mournfully, 'I long so much to see him!'

'We have been visiting him daily, Sophia, and Stephen Howard has been so good, offering his help and providing his services as driver when Sir Oliver or John are not able to take Mother to the hospital.'

'And what of Ben?' I asked 'Where is he?'

'He is at university in Cambridge,' he explained. 'He's in his first year. Now come with me, Sophia, before we both get drenched! Let me help you up onto Storm.'

He removed his riding hat and gave it to me. 'You can ride him to the Hall,' he offered.

I put my foot in the stirrup as Marcus held my rucksack and I lifted myself on to the gelding. It was great being back in the saddle.

'Sophia!' Marcus said, his large brown eyes penetrating mine. 'I am so glad you are home. So very glad.'

I looked at the tall, lanky teenager and realised just how handsome he was underneath those dark-rimmed spectacles. He would break a few hearts one day.

There were no words to describe how ecstatic Mother and Father were at my arrival home, especially Father. Mother fussed over me like a mother hen whose chick had returned to the nest. Father chastised me greatly for the lack of communication on my part, but I tried to evade the subject. Question upon question followed. I answered as honestly as I could, but some aspects of convent life I avoided like the plague. My hairstyle was disapproved of, and an appointment was made for me with Ricardo at Tresses. *Ugh*! Marcus asked me about Ireland and seemed interested in their folk music, but I explained I had been too busy working to hear any or have a social life. I couldn't wait to tinkle the piano keys.

'Not with hands like those, darling,' murmured Mother, examining my cut, calloused fingers. 'I have just the remedy,' she said, and disappeared to fetch me a very expensive jar of Swedish formula hand cream to soothe the offending fingers.

Father treated me to a tour around the Great Hall, pointing out two new oil paintings he had acquired in my absence. They were wonderful horse paintings by Sir George Stubbs. I admired them and immediately recognised his favourite. He called them his 'rainy day investments', and they would join countless other magnificent pictures.

Life around the Hall seemed to have taken on an air of normality since my departure.

Marcus appeared, and after I had applied some of Mother's super formula cream to my hands, we sat and played piano together. It was wonderful being home, and I noted that Marcus had been practising, for there was a tremendous improvement in his playing.

Father departed to attend a meeting with Stephen Howard. He was apparently discussing planning permission for barn conversions.

It was just like old times. Marcus, me and music!

At afternoon tea, Edith appeared, gave me an enormous hug and commented on my hair and thin frame.

'My frame will soon expand with your famous home cooking,' I teased, and she disappeared laughing, to tell John that the prodigal daughter had returned. Father brought Stephen Howard into the Great Hall as Marcus played and I listened. I turned, shook hands and thanked Stephen for visiting Alex and acting as chauffeur on numerous occasions. He explained Alex was still in a coma and that he was more than pleased to have been a source of help to my parents in their time of need.

'We mustn't give up hope,' Father reminded us. 'We need a small miracle.'

'Very true, Sir Oliver,' agreed Stephen. 'You have lost weight, Sophia,' he remarked, turning to me. 'What on earth made you cut your beautiful hair?'

'It's a girl's prerogative!' I snapped, wishing everyone would cease making comments. 'It will grow, Stephen! Can we please change the subject?'

Both he and Father looked at me in a strange manner at my unexpected outburst.

'Stephen has yet to hear you play, Sophia! Will you play something for him?' Father asked politely.

'Certainly. Do you have any requests, Stephen?' I asked.

'How about Dvorak's *New World Symphony*?' Father suggested. 'Yes, Stephen?' he said, looking for approval at his choice.

I am sure Stephen did not have a clue about classical music.

'Excellent, Sir!' he agreed.

They quietly took their seats. I played as Marcus, Stephen and Father listened intently. I turned my attention afterwards to the works of Tchaikovsky and Schubert, which met with great approval.

'I did not realise what a superb pianist you are, Sophia. That was truly magnificent!' Stephen seemed in awe at what he had heard.

'Thank you. Although I am rather "rusty", I am glad you enjoyed it,' I said.

'I think I speak for us all when I say we have all missed you greatly,' Stephen commented. Father nodded, Marcus too.

'I'm going to see Alex shortly, as Marcus and your parents have to attend a school meeting this evening. Can I give you a lift to the hospital?' Stephen enquired.

'That's a very kind offer. I could be ready for 6.30!'

'Good! I will collect you from the Hall. See you then!' He bade Father and Marcus farewell and was gone.

Thank goodness my parents had received support from the kindly, caring Stephen Howard during my absence. I was enthralled I was going to visit Alex, and Stephen arrived promptly to collect me for the journey to the hospital in Leeds.

He deposited me in the car park, as he had to attend to unexpected business in the city and would collect me at 8 p.m., which allowed me an hour with Alex on my own.

I hurried to the private room. There in bed was darling Alex, looking a shadow of his former self. His eyes were closed and he was oblivious to the procedures being carried out by nurses to make him as comfortable as possible. He was being artificially fed, and I waited until the nurses had finished their tasks in attending to him. I drew up a chair, sat by his bed and took hold of his hand. Father had thought it a good idea if we talked to him and tell him family news in the hope he could hear us. I observed there was no one within earshot as I explained about my experiences in Dublin, of Maura and her awful treatment of me once again and then related that I had given birth to our precious son, Jonathan, who had been taken away from me and adopted by a couple. I was very emotional. There was no movement, not even the flicker of an eyelid or any recognition he had heard one word of what I had said; but it was at least a good thing for me to have been able to unburden myself. I leant over the bed, stroked his cheek and kissed his lips. Still there was no response. It was torture, watching him and being unable to improve an already desperate situation. I slumped into the chair, sighed and watched as a nurse entered the room to check his feed. Smiling at me, she said, 'I am so sorry there is no improvement. It must be very difficult for you!'

I nodded as she pottered around the bed, filling in charts, and eventually she left.

I examined what she had written, returned the charts to their rightful place and sat quietly once more holding Alex's hand. The time dragged. I reflected on our walk along the banks of the River Nidd the first time we made love. How wonderful the day had been! It seemed like a lifetime ago. I decided as I could not be useful, I would leave. I kissed Alex and ambled along the corridors and into the car park, where Stephen was waiting in the Land Rover.

'Hop in, Sophia. I am going to take you for a meal,' he insisted.

'What a kind gesture,' I said, 'but I really cannot eat anything.'

'But you must! I know an excellent little Italian restaurant not far from here. You will love it, and the food is wonderful.'

Without further ado, he waited until I was seated comfortably and then drove us speedily into the distance.

I had to admit he was correct. The tiny restaurant was superb and the food exceptional. For the first time in a long while I ate a reasonable supper. Stephen was wonderful company, and endeavoured to make me laugh as often as possible; but I continually heard Alex's words ringing in my ears: 'He is old enough to be your father!' I did, however, enjoy the evening, and I thanked Stephen graciously when he returned me to the Hall at a reasonable hour and then went home to number two, Starbeck Cottages. He had been the perfect gentleman, and I could not have wished for a more affable, kind and considerate companion.

Chapter Eighteen

'*Sophia! Stop!*'

I turned to see Stephen racing across the farm track in the Land Rover with Father hanging perilously out of the window, shouting as loudly as he was able. They pulled up precariously alongside me, alarming my horse in the process, but using all my strength I managed to control her. Crouching down until I was in line with the vehicle, I asked, 'What on earth is wrong, Father? What is so important you have to chase me half-way across the estate?'

He looked concerned as he explained.

'The police are waiting in my study to interview you, Sophia. Edith is plying them with coffee and biscuits! Can you ride back and speak to them? It appears to be extremely urgent!' he gasped, catching his breath. 'They will not talk to me, and specified that they wished to talk to you and you alone.'

I looked at the puzzled expressions on their faces and was increasingly anxious to discover why it was that I was wanted for questioning. My heart sank as I asked, 'What on earth can they want, Father?'

'I haven't a clue, Sophia. I thought perhaps it was to do with the post office robbery, but the officer in charge said it was concerning Ireland. What on earth did you do that would have the police in pursuit of you?'

Stephen looked at me and laughed at Father's question.

'I have done nothing, Father' I said, my cheeks taking on a rosy hue. 'Please don't be so ridiculous.'

Father looked anxiously at me and frowned as I bid them farewell and galloped back to the Hall. I believed the Garda were on my trail for the commotion and upheaval I had caused at the convent, and couldn't see how I could endure their interrogation and actions without Father discovering all that had taken place. I was still grieving for the loss of my son, and questioning at this delicate time was something I didn't think I could face without showing all the emotions I had stored inside.

I arrived back at the stables and Jimmy relieved me of Petronella. I entered the Hall and removed my riding hat and boots before anxiously going into the study. Two police officers, one male, one female, were sitting there drinking coffee and tucking into Edith's home-made ginger biscuits. They looked up and stood as I entered. We shook hands, and the policewoman introduced herself as Sergeant Diane Lawson. The policeman was Detective Mike Barnes, and they were from the Leeds Constabulary.

'Please sit and finish your refreshments,' I said, my body trembling.

They sat and I nervously joined them, shakily pouring myself a cup of coffee. Sergeant Lawson looked enquiringly at me and said, 'I am afraid we are the bearers of sad news. Would you like a member of your family to be with you?'

I shook my head and gulped.

'I understand that your stepmother, Maura Bertucelli, lives in Dublin. Is that correct?'

Gosh, I thought, *she has reported me for stealing her clothes and other items when I visited her after escaping from the convent*. I looked sheepishly at them and after a pause, replied, 'Yes, my stepmother has lived there for about ten years.'

I tried to carefully place my cup on the table, trembling so uncontrollably that I thought I would drop it in the process, but managed to set it down satisfactorily.

'I'm afraid we have to inform you that Maura Bertucelli has been found dead,' said Sergeant Lawson, putting her plate down.

I sat still, and for a moment the shock of the announcement rendered me temporarily unable to speak. When I had regained my composure she continued by saying, 'She was found on the kitchen floor yesterday morning, by a neighbour. She had been lying there for approximately two days.'

'I d-d-don't understand' I faltered. 'You cannot possibly think I had anything to do with her death!'

'Of course not!' Detective Barnes cut in. 'She'd had an accident. There will be an inquest, of course, but forensics are sure it was purely an accident, and they do not suspect that foul play had taken place.'

The relief at these comments must have shown on my face, relief borne on the fact she could no longer hurt me or any member of my treasured loved ones again.

'What exactly happened?' I asked. 'Do you have any details?' I was anxious to know of all the events leading to her death.

'Well, from the information given to us, it would appear Mrs Bertucelli had been drinking heavily. She was sitting at the kitchen table supping large quantities of whisky – which according to neighbours was her favourite tipple! Apparently she drank large quantities of this on a regular basis,' said Sergeant Lawson.

Detective Barnes continued, 'She became drunk, and it would appear she knocked the empty whisky bottle onto the tiled floor, in her inebriated state. Although it was broken, she left it there. Mrs Bertucelli had opened another bottle, consuming a substantial amount from that also. Subsequently, when she finally passed out, she fell sideways off the kitchen chair. As she hit the floor she fell on the jagged bottle, piercing her carotid artery. She was found in a pool of blood, having bled to death.'

'I do hope it would have been over quickly and that she didn't suffer,' I said.

'I am sure it would have been!' was the reply.

I thanked them for notifying me, and they then revealed that Maura had seen a specialist a week previously and had been diagnosed with advanced stages of cirrhosis of the liver, and that her life expectancy had been reduced to a few months. They would inform me of the date of the inquest in case I wished to attend. Father appeared as the police officers were leaving. He and I removed ourselves to the drawing room as they departed.

'What on earth was that all about, Sophia?' he enquired.

I watched for a reaction as I said, 'Maura is dead! She fell on a broken whisky bottle and bled to death!'

He grimaced and said, 'How dreadful!' However, I noticed that relief rather than grief emanated from him. 'I am so sorry for you, Sophia!' he said.

'Don't be, Father. I'm not!' I said curtly. 'I will never forget what she did to this family, or to me! At least you won't have to pay her £400 a month any longer!'

The words simply slipped out from my mouth.

'*Ssh! Sophia!*' he said, dashing to close the drawing-room door. 'What on earth do you know of this?' he asked looking puzzled.

'I know she was blackmailing you, Father,' I replied.

He raised his eyebrows. His moustache twitched and he appeared decidedly embarrassed at my comments.

'Why was she blackmailing you, Father?' I asked bravely.

He stared at the floor and said, 'It really is none of your business, Sophia! It was an arrangement between Maura and me!'

I was going to say, 'If it concerns my mama, then it *is* my business,' when Mother walked in. Father's complexion turned a deathly white. He approached her and, without looking at me, hastily escorted her from the room, saying, 'I have some sad news to tell you, Mary. Let's go on a shopping expedition to York and I will explain all the details on the way.'

Mother bade me farewell and they disappeared from the scene, leaving me to contemplate what Maura had told me. One day I would ask him if it were true.

I loved my father, but there was a time and a place to ask and this was neither the time nor the place!

Looking at his desk, I noted the mail delivery and noticed several letters addressed to me, which I took to my room to read. The first was a letter from Lucy announcing she had married, and asking why I hadn't answered her wedding invitation. Little did she know I was in Ireland when her invitation arrived! She asked about Alex's progress and said she was upset on hearing he had shown no signs of improvement. I was overjoyed she was happy and settled.

The second letter was the one I had been anxious to receive. It was from Niamh. How thankful I was she had managed to find her friend and was now, with her friend's help, installed in an apartment in Liverpool. She had traced Angelique's father, and together they were searching records and agencies to see if they could find their daughter, but doors were closed in their faces. The hunt was proving too difficult to pursue, but she stated she would never give up her search. I too had made enquiries to various agencies, but again no word was forthcoming of Jonathan. It was explained that I had no rights and my son was now legally 'owned' by another couple, and I should not attempt to make contact; but, like Niamh, I would never forget my child or give up hope that one day he would find me.

As Marcus finished his piano lesson, he stared at me and said, 'I really don't want a birthday party this year, Sophia! I will be fourteen and a party is out of the question, so could you talk to Lady Mary and Sir Oliver for me?'

'What would you rather do?' I asked.

'Well, how about tickets to a rock concert?' he ventured.

'You must be joking!' I retorted. 'I can't see Father allowing you to go, can you?'

'Please, Sophia! I am sure you could persuade him. *You* could take me!'

'It's an impossible task you are asking of me, Marcus. Let's concentrate on your piano lesson, shall we? Father will ask how you are progressing, and although your heart is not in the classics you're becoming a fine pianist. Please don't give up. It is giving you a good grounding in music!' I pleaded.

He looked severely over his spectacles, but knew if I was to persuade Mother and Father to allow him concert tickets he had to be prepared to give me one 110% of his time and attention. A bargain was struck.

I approached Mother and Father for a few moments of their valuable time, requesting a short meeting with reference to a forthcoming birthday.

'Make it quick, Sophia! I have to meet suppliers in Halifax shortly,' Father replied.

He was on one of his usual speedy forays to his factories, and Mother was due to attend the hospital and sit with darling Alex within the hour.

'I cannot promise it will be a quick discussion, but I will get down to business immediately,' I announced. 'It's Marcus I wish to talk about!'

Mother stared at Father and he quickly returned her glare. Before I could utter another word, Father remarked, 'What has he done now?'

'Nothing,' I replied.

'That about says it all!' he remarked sarcastically.

'Father, what I am trying to explain is that Marcus has a fourteenth birthday approaching, and is asking if he can have concert tickets this year, rather than a party at the Hall.'

I watched a thoughtful expression creep over Father's face. Mother went into a huddle with him, and with heads together they quickly discussed the idea. Eventually he spoke.

'Well, Sophia, we think that concert tickets would be a good present. What does he wish to see?'

'He wants to go to a rock concert!' I said sheepishly.

'Is this a joke, Sophia? No child of mine is going to such a concert! We thought you meant a classical concert. *No*, Sophia! Definitely not!'

'But Father—' I pleaded.

He looked at his watch, saying, 'The answer is *no*, Sophia! Please do not ask again!'

He retreated from the room with his briefcase, and Mother placed her arm around me in a comforting manner, knowing how upset I was at Father's refusal. How could I face Marcus? I needed to isolate myself from everyone to think of a good birthday strategy for a soon-to-be fourteen-year-old. I slept on the problem, which was always a good ploy with me, and awoke the following day with a tremendous idea for a birthday surprise. It was still so fresh in my mind how I had been totally in awe when I received a horse for my thirteenth birthday. I wanted to let Marcus know how much I cared about him, about his aspirations and his dreams. Again I had to approach Father with what I had in mind, as I needed his approval and help. He had left for a business meeting in London at the ridiculous hour of 6 a.m. and I had missed him. I crept into his study, peered through his desk diary. I saw a space in it for 11 a.m. the following morning, and wrote, *Appointment with Sophia to last approx. one hour,* underlined it in black pen, and closed the diary.

Marcus was at the breakfast table as I walked into the dining room.

'I was hoping I would see you, Sophia! What did Sir Oliver say about concert tickets for my birthday?' he asked.

'I am sorry, Marcus, but the answer is no,' I revealed.

'See what I mean, Sophia? Sir Oliver is against everything I want to do!' he complained.

As he arose from the table I grabbed his blazer. 'Please stop, Marcus! Don't you dare run away! I am meeting Father tomorrow morning. He and I are going to talk things over!'

'What things?' he asked.

'I cannot say. It will be a surprise!'

'If it isn't tickets to a rock concert then I don't want to know!' he retorted.

'Stop feeling so sorry for yourself, young man, and get off to school! I will speak to you later! And don't forget you have a 4.30 p.m. piano lesson.' I sensed that my words fell on stony ground. Marcus was sulking!

The following morning I ate a hearty breakfast and then took myself off in search of Father and our impending 11 a.m. appointment. He was nowhere to be seen, so I ventured to his study. Miss Wilkins, Father's new secretary, who was replacing Tindy during yet another illness, was a tall, slim creature with fair hair pulled into a ponytail at the back of her head. I assessed her age as being mid-thirties. She was a timid creature, nervous of her own shadow and did not appear worldly-wise. She wore the most ridiculous half-moon glasses and peered continuously over them as if eyeing the remains of an archaeological dig. I found her surveying the desk diary. Her pale cheeks were flushed as her fingers tapped irritatingly on the desk.

'Miss Sophia, I'm so glad you're here! Did *you* write this eleven o'clock appointment in the diary?' she enquired.

I nodded, and without stopping for breath she said, 'Only I didn't see it, and therefore I did not tell Sir Oliver you were wanting to see him, and he has gone off riding in Hardy's Wood and—'

'Wait one moment and catch your breath, Miss Wilkins,' I broke in.

'I'm so sorry, only you see…' she gasped. She shuffled the pages, turning them over frantically.

'Don't fret, Miss Wilkins, I will go and change my clothing, saddle up Petronella and then ride over to Hardy's Wood to find my father.'

She surveyed me over her silly glasses and apologised yet again for her mistake, wringing her hands frantically. I accepted her apology and beat a hasty retreat.

How on earth Father stood her whining, I could not imagine. No wonder he had retreated to the wood. I had noticed too that Stephen Howard, the charmer, had paid Miss Wilkins a good deal of attention of late. What he was attracted to her for, I couldn't understand. Maybe men liked subservient women. If so, Miss Wilkins was an excellent candidate. I wondered how long she would last as a replacement for Tindy. Was I slightly jealous of her friendship with Stephen? I don't think so!

I rushed upstairs, changed into my riding apparel, had Jimmy saddle up Petronella and rode out to find Father, who had either not seen my diary jottings or had chosen to ignore them. As I approached Hardy's Wood I could see his horse, Caesar, tethered to a tree. Father was leaning against a magnificent oak, his binoculars raised to his eyes. I tied Petronella close by and walked toward him. Aware of my approach he said, 'Ssh, Sophia. There is a spotted woodpecker in that tree. Can you see him?' He pointed upwards but I couldn't detect the bird he was so intrigued by.

He handed me his binoculars and I managed to view the magnificent creature.

'He is such a beautiful specimen, Sophia, isn't he? Look at the brilliant plumage and the contours of his body. It is such a pity he's so nervous. I would love to view him at close quarters.'

I voiced my admiration for the perfect specimen and returned the binoculars to their rightful owner. I was intent on approaching Father on the subject I had uppermost in my mind.

'Are you trying to avoid me?' I asked, frowning at him.

He grinned and replied, 'Of course not, darling! As if I would!'

I explained I had posted a message in his desk diary in the hope of an audience with him at eleven o'clock. He simply smiled, and I knew emphatically that he had tried to avoid our appointment. His grin was so enchanting. I observed what a handsome fellow he was when not embroiled in arguments or business discussions. He looked reasonably relaxed as he held his face skyward, enjoying the sun's rays which filtered through the trees.

'What a beautiful day!' he remarked. Then, lowering his head to look into my eyes, he said, 'But the answer to your question is still *no*!'

We both laughed. Setting his binoculars down, he wrapped his arms around me. He looked deeply into my eyes and said, 'You know I am so very proud of you, don't you, Sophia? You have given our family so much love and attention since you've lived with us.'

I lowered my eyes in shame but he placed his fingers under my chin and lifted my head until my eyes made contact with his.

'I am a very lucky man, Sophia, in so many ways. I have a good wife and wonderful children. I am still so devastated at what has happened to Alex, but I pray daily for a miracle to happen. Perhaps it will. Who knows? But I love him and will always see that he gets the ultimate in treatment and care that money can buy.'

'I know, Father!' I answered, as tears began to fill my eyes. He hugged me closely for what seemed like ages and then he said, 'Sit with me, Sophia! Then you can tell me exactly what you want to discuss!'

He slid to the ground and I followed, plucking nervously at the bracken nearby.

'It is Marcus's birthday in ten days,' I began. 'I really would like to arrange something special for him. My thirteenth birthday was a day I will never forget, and I would like his fourteenth birthday to be just as memorable.'

'You are a strange one, Sophia! Marcus gives you trouble with his music, he gives his teachers a hard time during lessons and with me, well, he is always so defiant! I cannot seem to reason with him!'

'He isn't really defiant, Father. He is unlike Alex and Ben in his approach to life. He is a free spirit, with a mind and will of his own!' I protested. 'We cannot all be academic. Some of us are just more practical.'

'I understand what you are saying, Sophia, but I wish he would be more focused on something,' he replied.

I explained, 'He loves his music, Father. I know he tries hard with his piano lessons to please you and me, and there is constant improvement, but he prefers modern music.'

'I am pleased to hear the effort you spend on him is not wasted, Sophia, but I think you are far too loyal to him at times,' he replied curtly.

'I feel that you are far too hard on him, Father, trying to turn him into something he doesn't wish to be. He can never seem to please you!' I ventured.

I tried diplomatically to explain that Marcus would be unlikely to want to follow in Ben's footsteps, go to university and study management. He agreed. I introduced the fact that Marcus wished to become a singer/songwriter and musician, but not in the classical sense. 'But he would like to focus on the guitar,' I added. 'I mean modern guitar music.'

'*Guitar*? *No*, Sophia, *no*! I really cannot go along with that idea. Think of the awful noise he would make within the Hall.'

'I have thought about it very deeply, Father. I have a Gibson guitar

Mama brought Papa back from America when she was in concert there. I have it stored in its case in my room. Papa took great care of it and I would like to present it to Marcus for his birthday. There were only a few hundred made, and this acoustic guitar has the most powerful sound. I thought he and I could play together, as I have a guitar of my own. Papa taught me to play, and Marcus and I could experiment together – with the little knowledge I have.'

Father shook his head, but I continued, 'As for the noise factor, I know Doggett's Barn is no longer in use. I wondered if you would let us have this area in which to practise?'

'Doggett's Barn? You really are asking a lot of me, Sophia! This situation needs very careful thought.'

I dived in with, 'We would need a piano too – and several other bits and pieces! I have money in my savings account, and I have worked out figures and could fund the renovations and items we immediately need.'

Silence took over as Father seemed deep in thought. He pondered for a considerable time and then suddenly stood, brushed the soil and bracken from his jodhpurs, and held out his hand, helping me to my feet.

'Come on, Sophia, I will ride with you. We will go and look at the barn. You can show me what you have in mind and I'll see if what you suggest is feasible. I don't know what I am doing this for, but it seems, young lady, that you could charm the birds right out of the trees!'

'Even a spotted woodpecker?' I mused.

We laughed. He could see the sheer delight on my face at the thought that he was even prepared to consider my scheme.

'We must hurry, Sophia, if we are to sort out the arrangements for the birthday surprise. Ten days is not long!'

He untied Caesar and mounted him. I followed on Petronella.

Doggett's Barn was nothing like the barn I had remembered as a violin workshop. Of late it had been a store for animal feed. Father observed it needed expert cleaning, and I talked with him about my plans. He asked if I had sufficient money to carry out the task. I said I had, and he kindly offered to buy a small upright piano for Marcus to complete the necessary surprise. I kissed him and he raised his eyebrows as if to say, 'You have talked me round yet again! How did I let this happen?'

I thanked him from the bottom of my heart for being such a wonderful father to us all. He dismissed my words with a wave of his hand and said, 'I must get back to the Hall. I have an appointment.' Then he was gone.

The work at Doggett's Barn soon began in earnest. I approached, with Father's permission, estate electricians, carpenters and builders, in fact anyone who considered they had a little time to spare to carry out the required work. The thought of the renovations appeared to encourage their talents, and with the required workforce I quickly drew up plans I had devised in my head and presented my thoughts on paper to the workers. Some things were deemed unnecessary or out of the question, but they worked hard and long and were sworn to secrecy. In no time at all, things began to take shape. The barn received a facelift. It was soundproofed. Flooring was laid; wiring was put in place for electrical sockets and anything that needed power. A stage area was erected, and on inspection I could not believe the transformation which had taken place. It had shaped up far beyond my wildest dreams. Finally the finishing touches were put in place, namely the guitar and piano.

'Thank you with all my heart,' I said and shook hands with each tradesman and worker.

'It is our pleasure, Miss Sophia,' said Robert Howes, the head carpenter. 'We all feel rather privileged to be part of this enterprise.' The others nodded in agreement.

'I have come to pay you for your labour and materials,' I insisted, as they removed all the excess bits and pieces.

'There is no need Miss Sophia. Sir Oliver provided the materials from the estate store and we wanted to put in our contribution by working to get this finished on time. We all have a soft spot for Master Marcus, you know.'

'But I insist! The work is magnificent,' I commented, my eyes investigating every little detail around the barn. 'I am so thrilled with your workmanship. It is fantastic. Please take these.'

I tried to get the men to accept envelopes of hard-earned money to recompense their efforts, but my pleas were in vain. Somehow I would compensate them – if not now, then in the future. I went to my room and thought about how I would arrange the surprise the following day.

The birthday boy was down early to breakfast. He smiled as I entered the room and helped myself to a plate of scrambled egg.

'It's a lovely morning, Sophia!' he said, looking at me all wide-eyed and innocent.

'Yes, Marcus, it is!' I replied, sitting opposite him. 'What have you planned for today?' I asked.

He looked at me, his large, brown eyes flashing a note of distaste in my direction.

'Well…' he said, pausing to think of how he should answer.

'It's such a great day I thought I would go for a hack,' I said.

'It's a special day too, Sophia!' he murmured under his breath as Father joined us at table. Mother trotted into the dining room behind Father. They settled themselves at the table and received a look similar to the one I had fallen foul of.

'Here you are, Marcus, a card for you!' said Mother, passing a long envelope across the table. I put my hand to my mouth and said, 'Gosh! Is it your birthday, Marcus? I had forgotten all about it.'

I expected him to laugh and say, 'Stop teasing me, Sophia,' but he didn't. He angrily stood up, pushed his chair backwards, marched out of the room and left his card unopened.

'You are naughty, Sophia! Look what you've done,' said Father, chastising me. 'Go after him and put him out of his misery!'

I left the table and my scrambled egg and raced along to find Marcus. He was striding along the path towards the lake, kicking everything that happened to be in his way.

'Marcus! Please wait!' I shouted, but he was angry as he continued striding along, ignoring my calls.

'*Please wait!*' I called. I ran as fast as I could until I caught up with him. He was crying.

'Please forgive me! I am so sorry I teased you at the breakfast table. I didn't mean to upset you! Did you really think I would forget your birthday?' I asked.

He focused on me as I continued apologising for my behaviour, and I asked if he would walk with me in the direction of Doggett's Barn as I had something there I needed to collect. He reluctantly agreed. I wished him a 'happy birthday' and kissed his cheek. We strolled along, chatting and making idle conversation until we reached the barn. I produced a key to the door.

'Marcus, would you do something for me? I hate going into the barn. It has too many memories of Papa. Could you fetch me an item sitting in the middle of the floor in a case?'

He agreed as I unlocked the door. He entered and was gone for just a few moments. I crept in behind him.

'What on earth has happened to the barn, Sophia? Why, it's superb! Look at the stage area, the lighting and the piano! You are so lucky to have—'

'This is not for me, Marcus. This is for you! You can write, sing and play your songs without giving Father unnecessary trauma.'

I picked up the guitar case and handed it to him. His eyes looked enormous as he opened it.

'Sophia! This is for me?'

'Yes, Marcus. The guitar is for you. Please take great care of it. It is a monster of an instrument, as you will find out. Treat it well and it will serve you well in return.'

He smoothed his hands across the spruce top, looked at the rosewood bridge and the bound fingerboard with its mother of pearl arrow inlay. He was mesmerised by the 'flame' pick guard and the sunburst lacquer finish. Trembling, he said, 'This is all too much, Sophia!' Then he began to weep.

'The estate workers made this barn into an area for you to practise in. I hope you will invite me here too. We can play guitar to our hearts' content without raising Father's blood pressure. Father and Mother have bought you this piano and donated the materials which have made this place so excellent. I think you have so many people to thank, don't you?'

He nodded as his eyes surveyed the surroundings. 'How can I ever thank you for persuading Sir Oliver to allow this? He really must care for you an awful lot.'

'Yes, Marcus, and he cares about you too! You are his son now, and always will be! His bark is far worse than his bite. You must learn to have broader shoulders!'

He smiled – and what a smile! It was not seen often, but when it appeared, it was magical.

'You are a wonderful friend, Sophia! What would I do without you?'

He turned his head away and I detected more tears.

'Come on, young man! Let's get down to some serious practice. I have a book here with lots of useful tips in. Here, take it! This is the first day of your life as a "would-be" star.' I sat him down on a chair and showed him his first lesson in guitar playing: how to hold the instrument.

'You do know all famous musicians give their guitars a name, don't you? So you are going to have to think of a name for this,' I explained.

He was lost in thought for a while and then he looked up at me and said, 'I have a name for my guitar, Sophia.'

'What is it?' I asked.

With a twinkle in his eye he said, 'I am going to call it "Soapy".'

We reduced ourselves to fits of laughter. He was my *Happy Birthday Boy*!

Marcus was overwhelmed by his guitar. He spent every free moment in the barn. The piano lessons in the drawing room continued, and then we would retire for more music appreciation of a different kind. He stated that the guitar reminded him of me. As he worded it, it has 'a good projection, notable tone, is rounded well, has a long scale and is very classy.'

He usually received a clip round the ear for such comments. Marcus was keen, extremely keen! It was delightful to see the tremendous progress he made. He continually referred to his guitar as 'Soapy', which gave us a great deal of amusement. We had a planned weekly schedule for practice. On Mondays we would do method exercises and major scales; Tuesdays would be picking and strumming exercises, open strings and major chords; Wednesdays saw us working on more method book items; on Thursdays we did harmony and learnt work on our songs, and then we would begin the whole procedure again. On Fridays we let our hair down.

His enthusiasm was outstanding. Thanks to the enormous amount of encouragement he'd had in the grounding of music, he moved along in leaps and bounds, staying relaxed and focused. He knew exactly what he wanted to do with his life and was determined to reach his goal. He would do impressions of the American idol, Elvis Presley, who I liked immensely, imitating his gyrating hip movements. He combed his hair in an Elvis lookalike hairdo and removed his spectacles, making me laugh in the process. They were great days and we had tremendous fun. Marcus moved from beginner to intermediate player in no time at all, and we continued to write songs as often as the inspiration would allow. We had a budding star in our midst.

Chapter Nineteen

After my stay in Ireland, experiencing such levels of inhumanity among people of my own religion, it was with great sorrow I could not find it in my heart to trust anyone other than immediate family and people I had known since childhood. When Stephen approached me offering lifts to the hospital on a frequent basis (on his way to see his girlfriend in Leeds) I was reluctant to accept. Mother assured me Stephen was a man of principles and integrity, so I accepted. He was cheerful and forthcoming about his life, talking happily on our journey to and from the hospital.

'I do hate to see you sad during visits, Sophia!' he stated, glancing in my direction.

'Please don't be. I am coping with each day as it comes. I try not to think of anything other than Alex making some sort of recovery. I pray for this daily!' I explained.

'So you believe a miracle will happen?' he asked.

'We, as a family, have to! Otherwise we would not cope,' I explained. 'Marcus is particularly devastated. He and Alex are very close.'

Stephen looked pensive as he said, 'I hope for all your sakes Alex comes out of his coma. He has been in a vegetative state for a long while now!'

'Yes, but the consultant has told me people have been known to return from a coma after many years,' I replied.

We continued the journey to Leeds. I wondered what I could say to make light conversation.

'Father tells me you were an excellent pilot officer during wartime.'

'He did, did he? So you have been talking about me, have you?' He chuckled.

'Of course,' I said, 'but only to sing your praises. Father appreciates the work you do on the estate.'

'I am pleased, Sophia. I adore my work, especially at Harrington Hall. Your father is an excellent employer, and a very honest, generous and fair man.'

I agreed and asked, 'What made you settle in Yorkshire?'

He explained he had been brought up on a farm in Devon and his parents had been killed in a road accident when he was seventeen. He had always had a longing to fly. A maiden aunt saw that he received flying lessons. In 1940 he joined the RAF and was eventually assigned to

Father's squadron. He had stayed at the Hall, with other RAF personnel, on various occasions, and had adored the Yorkshire Dales. He praised Father's wartime heroics. After the war he returned to farming and trained in estate management. When a vacancy became available at Harrington Hall, he applied and was excited when offered the post.

'I really feel, at last, I belong somewhere, with wonderful people. You have all made me feel so welcome and at home!' he explained.

I acknowledged the fact we liked him a great deal and recognised how kind he had been to the family during our ordeal with Alex. During the final stretch of the journey we sat quietly. I viewed the busy road and could see the lights of Leeds in the distance. In no time we had arrived at the hospital. Stephen stopped briefly to allow me to hop from the vehicle and begin my nightly ritual of doing what I could for Alex.

As the months passed, Stephen drove me into Leeds on four evenings each week. I hoped on each visit I would see improvement in Alex, but none came. Stephen would wait for me in the car park and insisted on taking me to supper.

'I hope your girlfriend does not find this arrangement disagreeable?' I asked.

He escorted me to a reserved table, held my chair and seated me comfortably before replying, 'Good gracious, Sophia! Of course she doesn't. She and I are simply friends. We have known each other years.'

'Good! I would not wish to cause you problems.'

'You… cause me problems? Why, Sophia, you are a pleasure to be with.'

He smiled, asking caringly for an update on Alex's condition. I explained there was no change. He commiserated in his charming way.

The food was delicious. He explained that Father was planning barn conversions on the estate and had intentions of moving, eventually, from Harrington Hall into one of the conversions, and opening the Hall to the public. I could not think of anything more dreadful but was sworn to secrecy. Harrington Hall had been in the family since 1530. Elizabeth I had stayed there. The history of the Hall was phenomenal, but the thought of the project troubled me. It was Father's heritage but it looked as though he was going to lose it.

'Do you think my father has serious financial problems?' I queried, but Stephen was non-committal.

It was Saturday evening when I next visited Alex. Father and Mother had a charitable function to attend and Marcus was learning to play his beloved guitar, so Stephen offered his transport services and I graciously accepted. I walked quietly and listlessly up to Alex's room, pulled up a chair and sat by his bed and kissed his hand. There was no response. I talked to him, explaining all that was happening at home; how Marcus was playing guitar. I told him that I missed him desperately. I explained Ben was excelling at university and that I was playing piano and guitar each day with Marcus.

I watched darling Alex intently. He was extremely thin and his blonde curls had taken on a dull tone. How I missed his touch and his lips on mine! I looked at my watch. The time had flown so quickly during the visit. I stood up to leave and then heard a noise. As I turned around I couldn't believe what I saw. Alex had opened his eyes. He was staring at the ceiling! I pressed the emergency bell and two nurses swiftly appeared. One returned to summon the doctor on call. He returned immediately to the scene. After a brief examination he said, 'Young lady, Alexander seems to be returning to our world, but we must not be too hasty. The next few days will determine what is happening to him!'

My enthusiasm at supper was overwhelming. I could not contain my excitement.

'Did Alex say anything, Sophia?' Stephen asked.

'Not a word! He said nothing. He cannot speak, but his eyes are open. I think it will only be a matter of time before he begins to recover,' I announced, feeling more positive than I had for a long while.

'I must come with you next time you visit. I would love to see this improvement,' Stephen said enthusiastically.

Returning to the Hall, I waited for Mother and Father. No one could imagine the delight on their faces as I told them the news. Father immediately telephoned the hospital.

'Yes! It is a miracle!' he was told. 'But please do not raise your hopes too high. He has not spoken or shown any sign he recognises anything or anyone at the moment.'

Father assured Mother progress would be made and that his prayers and those of so many people had been answered. Marcus was extremely elated. A telephone call was made to Ben at his college in Cambridge, and Father, Mother and Marcus planned a visit to the hospital the following afternoon. I would attend in the evening. I hoped this was the beginning of a full recovery for Alex, and then we could re-commence our relationship and search together for our darling son. Mother and Father would have to understand our plight and agree to our relationship.

Days passed. Alex improved slightly. He continued staring ahead and did not respond to conversations or questions; I thought he was aware of my presence in the room but was told this was not so. As time progressed he began to respond to certain stimuli. I fed him with small amounts of liquidised food on a spoon. It was a messy process, but I considered I was participating in his very slow recovery. Then the blow came! Mother, Father and I were informed Alex had reached his recovery potential and was highly unlikely to improve further. I received this news by telephone as I was going on an evening visit with Stephen. He arrived and was startled as I piled into the Land Rover in floods of tears.

'What on earth is wrong, Sophia?'

'Please, Stephen, just drive!' I asked. 'I can't explain what upsets me at the moment.'

He drove off. After we had travelled a short distance, he pulled the vehicle off the road into a lay-by. Stephen switched off the ignition, turned to me and asked, 'What on earth has upset you, Sophia? Please tell me!'

'Mother, Father and I have been advised that Alex is unlikely to make further progress. The way he is now, is how he will remain!' I sobbed.

'Oh dear, Sophia!' He wiped away my tears with his handkerchief. 'How can I comfort you?' he asked.

'I don't know! I was holding on to so many hopes and dreams. Now they have all been dashed.'

'Please don't cry. It hurts me to see you in such turmoil!'

'Stephen, you are such a good man. What on earth would we have done without your support?' I asked.

He looked at me tenderly and said, 'I am fond of you, Sophia! You seem to have had such a rough deal! Now your brother is not going to recover—'

I interrupted the conversation saying 'Alex *is not* my brother! I am fostered by Sir Oliver. Marcus is too!'

I explained the circumstances. He listened attentively as I spoke of Mama, Papa and Maura, and the circumstances that led me to live at the Hall. He was fascinated.

'Whatever you tell me, Sophia, will go no further! It has been my policy to hear all, see all and say nothing all my life.'

While relating experiences, I was reduced yet again to tears. He held my hand, trying anxiously to console me. He was a good listener. It seemed I could tell him anything and I really did need to talk. I sobbed into his handkerchief.

'I have told no one what I will now tell you, Stephen,' I whispered. 'I would like it to remain strictly confidential. Please promise me you will say nothing!' I pleaded.

'Of course,' he said compassionately.

'I have a son,' I revealed. 'Alex and I have a son!'

He looked at me in astonishment and disbelief.

'Why do you think I disappeared to Ireland for over a year? My son was born there in a convent attached to a Magdalene Laundry. His name is Jonathan. While I was ill, my awful stepmother made me sign papers to have him adopted.' I cried.

Having given me his undivided attention, Stephen said, 'What can I say about these revelations? It saddens me to think you have lost your precious child!'

Stephen was exceptionally understanding of my predicament. I knew I could trust him implicitly with my secret.

'I have tried to trace my child, Stephen, but to no avail. I have been warned off trying to do so. If only I could catch a glimpse of him and know he is well, it would please me greatly!'

'I will help you, Sophia, if you will allow it. I will search on your behalf and contact various authorities in London and Dublin to see if I can throw light on where he may be!'

I had a mature friend at last; someone who would help. I squeezed his hand, indicating I would like him to follow any lines of enquiry.

After my visit to the hospital and supper with him at the Italian restaurant, my intention was to have an early night, when Stephen unexpectedly invited me to his cottage for a night-time drink. I had refused his invitations on several occasions, but this time I accepted. Out of the blue, he said, 'It is my opinion – for what it's worth, Sophia – that you spend far too much time on Marcus and his music.'

'I don't think so, Stephen. He needs all the encouragement possible with his music. He has a goal and I want to help him reach it. He is doing exceptionally well with the guitar. It certainly is his instrument, and I know that one day if he stays focused he will become a star.'

'I am sorry, Sophia, but I think you give him too much attention. Let the school teach him! And as for becoming a star, it's just a dream. You spend hours a week with Alex, helping with his rehabilitation programme, and he doesn't even recognise you. You are never going to be able to renew your relationship,' he added curtly.

'I have to try to help Marcus. It is what Alex would want me to do, and I must do my utmost for Alex too! One day I am sure we will be a couple again. He is the only man I ever wanted.'

'Life is passing you by. You are having no fun! I am sure Alex would want you to have fun.'

'I am fine. I don't want fun unless it is with Alex. Music is my other love, and I can share that with Marcus. He and I are a good team musically.'

He looked at me as he passed me my cocoa, with the kind of look Father frequently had when he was displeased.

'You sound exactly like my father when he is cross, Stephen!' I joked but he did not find my comment amusing.

'I hope you do not see me as a father figure, Sophia! We are friends. Perhaps we can be more than friends!' he said, seating himself beside me on the sofa.

He turned to face me, his dreamy eyes fixed on mine, waiting for an answer.

'I don't understand what you are saying, Stephen!'

'You look so sad, Sophia! You won't admit to yourself that Alex is not going to recover, but you must be sensible. Two years have gone by and he cannot lift a spoon to feed himself!'

'Stop saying such things!' I said, burying my head in my hands.

He placed his arm around me and drew me closer to him, resting my head on his shoulder.

'It was not my intention to upset you, but someone has to face facts!' he said.

'I know! I realise what you are saying, and it breaks my heart that he does not recognise me,' I said, sniffing.

He took me in his arms, stroked my hair, then my face and kissed me lightly. I dropped my head, focusing on the carpet. I did not want his advances.

'You must realise how I feel about you! I have tried to dismiss my feelings, but I cannot keep them hidden any longer. I love you, Sophia. Please say you care for me!' he said, lifting my head until my eyes came into contact with his.

'I don't know what to say. I like you – we all like you – I like you an awful lot, but I will always love Alex.'

He placed his lips gently on mine and kissed me.

'You are an exceptionally elegant young woman. I could make you happy if you would give me the chance.'

I was lost for words. Stephen had been very kind to me. I didn't want to hurt his feelings. I should not have allowed him to run his fingers through my hair and kiss me. Not once did he attempt to touch my body, and at least I respected him for that.

'I must go, Stephen,' I insisted. I stood up and made a beeline for the door. He fetched my jacket.

'Think about what I have said. I do love you, Sophia. You and I could have some wonderful times together.'

I collected my bag, put on my jacket and murmured, 'I will think about what you have said,' so that I could make a quick exit. Then I bade him farewell, assuring him I would be in touch.

Father was acutely agitated as I approached his study one Friday morning.

He and Stephen were searching for misplaced plans of barn conversions and could not ascertain their whereabouts. Having assisted him in sorting through various papers on his desk, Miss Paula Wilkins discovered two unopened letters. Father puffed his pipe uncontrollably, blowing circles of smoke into an already hazy atmosphere. I waved my hand, redirecting the cloudy mass in another direction. Mother constantly criticised his tobacco habit, pointing out in no uncertain terms that the paintings of various ancestors, hanging on the study walls, were in danger of irreparable damage and were in desperate need of cleaning.

'Bring in the experts,' was his perpetual reply.

I imagined that Mrs Tindale – his original secretary – had succumbed on many an occasion to his tobacco addiction. Her illnesses were now frequent, namely chest infections. 'Smoke inhalation' would have been my diagnosis. Father toyed with his letter opener and pulled one very official-looking letter from its envelope.

'*Oh, no*! This is all I need – Marcus's school report! How long has this been lying on my desk? Weeks, I would imagine!' he snapped.

Miss Wilkins, surveying Father over her half-moon glasses, made no comment and retreated to the library, before being reprimanded for the delay in bringing the letters to his attention. Stephen offered genuine excuses to remove himself from the study. He could see Father was about to blow a fuse. Father engrossed himself in the contents and exclaimed, 'Good God! What on earth are we paying those extortionate school fees for?'

I looked at his solemn face, the twitch of his handlebar moustache, and detected immediately that he was livid!

'Where is Marcus? Go and get him for me now, Sophia!'

I leapt to my feet and obeyed his order. His mood was fierce. I was worried that this time I would not be able to defend the actions of Marcus. There was no doubt as to where he was. I hurried across the lawns, weaving in and out of the flower beds.

Old Arthur, the head gardener, leant on his hoe and muttered, 'You lookin' for Master Marcus, Miss Sophia?'

I nodded.

'He be in Doggett's Barn, playing his music.' He pushed his cap off his forehead and raised his eyebrows. 'He in trouble again?' he enquired.

I nodded once more and continued toward the barn, where Marcus was practising.

Approaching with caution, I peered quietly around the door, not wanting to disturb the young genius during a moment of creativity. He spotted me immediately. Deefa padded over, wagging his tail ecstatically. From my body language, Marcus could see that all was not well.

'Your school report has been read by Father. He is extremely angry!' I announced.

I tried to smooth the path for what was going to be a tense time between Father and him.

'He is very cross with your results! You must tidy yourself and get over to his study immediately!' I urged. 'You will need to prepare yourself for some heated verbal exchanges.'

Marcus sighed, ran his long, thin fingers through his unruly hair, adjusted his spectacles and brushed some flecks of dust from his jacket.

'I have written the lyrics and music to another song, Sophia! Would you like to hear them?' he asked.

Helping him straighten his hair and clothing, I said, 'No, not at the moment. Perhaps I will hear your song later. *Please* hurry over to the Hall! Father has never looked so angry!'

He grunted and strode casually along behind me, hands in pockets, kicking objects that happened to get in his path, just as in childhood days, except that he was no longer a child. Deefa followed, weaving across our path. I paused as I crossed the lawn. Old Arthur had returned to his hoeing, but he stopped to stroke the dog. I faced Marcus with some friendly advice.

'Please don't anger Father. Listen to what he has to say. He's got his eye on you at the moment. Try to understand! He is under terrific pressure, and it will do no good antagonising him! I am always here for you, Marcus, but I cannot continue to bale you out of every difficult situation. You are a young man now, and have to stand up and be accountable for your actions. It worries me you and Father cannot see eye to eye on so many things. You being near him is like waving a red rag at a bull!'

For one moment I saw a faint smile creep across his lips, but within seconds his solemn look had reappeared. He was maturing into a tall, handsome lad. I knew that at fifteen, he had numerous female admirers, but he was not interested. His only love was music. Deefa ran ahead to Father's study with us close behind. I knocked nervously on the heavy oak door.

'*Come in!*' The command was severe.

'Marcus is here, Father,' I announced.

Deefa dived in, followed by his master.

'Sophia, get that damned dog out of here!' Father shouted.

I retrieved Deefa and led him to the door.

'Stay, Sophia! I want you here!'

'I would rather not, Father,' I protested, knowing the following episode would be one of humiliation for Marcus. My presence would only make a bad situation worse.

'*I insist!*' Father would not be swayed. '*Sit*! Both of you!'

We knew this was no time to argue. We pulled up chairs and did as instructed.

'And what, young man, have you to say about this?'

Standing, Father frantically waved the school report at Marcus. He towered over us, tall and intimidating. Marcus straightened his shoulders, sat up in the chair and threw back his head in a gesture of defiance. Battle was about to commence!

'Sir, I do not know what to say to you. I have tried to do my best, but it obviously is not good enough!' He swallowed loudly.

'Good enough? Of course it's not good enough! This report is disgusting! You achieved an E grade for mathematics and a D for geography, English and English literature.' Father launched himself into his chair, clutching the report and scrutinising its contents. 'Oh, and an A+ for music. Now why doesn't that surprise me?' There was a note of sarcasm in his voice.

'Then you acquired a D for history, and no mark at all for science subjects. Are you not ashamed of these non-achievements?'

Colour flooded into Marcus's pale cheeks. He was embarrassed.

'I am very sorry, Sir, but I am not academic!' he explained.

'You certainly are not! This proves it.'

Father reached for his pipe, packed it with tobacco and lit it. He disappeared in a haze as he slumped disappointedly into his padded chair.

'The headmaster's report states you are uncooperative, prone to fighting, do not concentrate and spend most of your time with your head in the clouds – when you attend school – but I understand from this you are playing truant!'

Marcus said nothing.

'You also write music and lyrics on the covers of your school exercise books. This is no way for a fifteen-year-old to behave. What have you to say for yourself?'

Marcus looked down at his feet as Father straightened himself and banged his fist aggressively on the desk. He did not answer.

'Well, I am telling you now, young man, if you do not seriously buck up your ideas and knuckle down to your school work in the new term, I am going to confiscate your guitar and any other musical equipment you may have, until further notice. What do you have to say?'

'But Father—' I interrupted, jumping up in defence.

'Quiet, Sophia! Sit down!' His voice echoed around the room.

Marcus stood up abruptly, a tear rolling down his cheek. He made an unannounced and hurried exit, slamming the door as he left.

'Come back, Marcus! Go and fetch him back, Sophia!'

I sat in my chair and calmly said, 'No, Father, I will not!'

The expression on his face showed horror. How could I have the audacity to disobey him?

'Look, Father,' I continued, 'I think you have humiliated Marcus quite enough for one day, don't you? You know he is only interested in one thing – his beloved music. Instead of giving him encouragement you continually knock him down at every opportunity. I know you are under considerable pressure, with Alex being so ill, but we are all emotional at this time. Each one of us handles our emotions differently. Can you not see that Marcus is tearing himself apart, inside? Alex and he were very close. The only way he deals with his feelings is through his music!'

Father listened objectively to what I had to say. I continued, 'I can cry at night when I am alone in my room with my thoughts. My heart aches for the sadness this family is being subjected to, not knowing what the outcome will be; but every morning we have to wake to a new day and live our lives the best way we can! That is what Marcus is doing. What is it about his music you dislike so much?'

'The whole thing, Sophia! The whole thing!'

'But I adore Chopin, Beethoven and Mozart, and yet I love rock and roll. It is the music of the era. Like Marcus, music is my life, my soul, we both live and breathe it! Please, Father, do not take away his music, or you take away his soul!'

'God, Sophia! You are the epitome of your mama!'

I glanced across the desk at the unexpected comment and observed him as he watched every expression, every movement I made. I thought about what Maura had told me at our very last confrontation. One day I would face Father with the revelations, but not today!

'I will talk to him and try to get him to work more conscientiously at school,' I promised.

'You will have a hard task, young lady.' He looked at me, his eyes softening, and the frown disappeared from his troubled brow.

'I care very much for the boy!' he admitted 'I really do, but he has to learn to be more responsible, otherwise what kind of adult will he grow into?'

'A very caring one,' I retorted. 'I have no doubts whatsoever! Underneath his sullen persona beats a heart of gold. I have watched him at close quarters and from afar. He is a very special person and has enormous talent and great potential. We have not seen it fully in action, and you are not intent on looking, Father.'

I left the study, giving my father food for thought and retreated to Doggett's Barn.

As I entered I could see Deefa sleeping at the foot of the loft ladder. I immediately knew where Marcus had hidden.

'I am coming up!' I called. I heard rustling as I ascended into the small space.

Marcus was sitting cross-legged on the floor, leaning against a trunk. He viewed me over his spectacles as I appeared. He had been crying.

'Is Sir Oliver very cross, Sophia?' he asked.

'Not so much as he is worried about you, Marcus! He has calmed down a great deal since I spoke to him!'

I sat next to Marcus and comforted him, resting his head against my face.

'I don't want to make him angry, but I need my music. I cannot live without it!'

There was intense emotion in his voice. He seemed far removed from the real world and had entered a realm of his own making.

'I want Sir Oliver to be proud of me.'

'He will be, one day, Marcus. He will be! Now, I have a proposition for you!'

He moved away and viewed me sceptically, but was intent on listening to what I had to say.

'Try harder at school and I will help you to enhance this barn even further, into a place where maybe you can record your music.'

His exceptionally dark brown eyes protruded as he absorbed my offer.

'And for every acceptable school report I will give you one of my papa's or grandpapa's beloved musical instruments, starting with the harmonicas you love so dearly.'

'You would really do that for me?' he gasped. 'I promise you with all my heart I will work hard and prove myself to you, and to Sir Oliver!'

'I will most certainly keep my end of the bargain, but there must be no more insolence or fighting. Anyway, what were you fighting about?'

He turned away and sheepishly mumbled, '*You!*'

'*Me*? Why me?'

'Do you remember when you last attended one of our school concerts? Several of the older lads made verbal sexual innuendos about you, to me, so I punched them!'

'That was very sweet, Marcus, you defending this young woman's honour, but I don't care what they insinuate. You shouldn't, either, so no more fighting!'

He turned to face me, hugged me tightly and scurried down the ladder with renewed vigour in his step. I followed closely behind.

'Come and see what I have written!'

He handed me several sheets of paper, excited at showing me music and lyrics to the new song, 'Brotherly Love'. My eyes filled with tears at the words he had written for Alex. I could feel a lump in my throat. Together we practised the song. He played guitar and sang. I played piano and sang harmony. This was Alex's song from Marcus: very special music and wonderful lyrics for the special person who we hoped would return to us one day.

Chapter Twenty

I was grooming Petronella when Stephen appeared in the stable. He took the brush from my hand and, swinging me around to face him, said, 'Will you marry me, Sophia?'

'Pardon me?' I asked. 'I thought you said, "Will you marry me?"'

'I did, Sophia! Please say you will!'

'But we know very little about one another.'

'I will get down on one knee if you will say "yes",' Stephen joked.

'Stephen, this proposal has come out of the blue. I am going to have to think about it very carefully. I cannot give you an answer now. There are many things to be considered.' I was so shocked by his declaration, and I rudely pushed past him and left him standing, brush in hand, wondering how I would react. He shouted, 'I love you, Sophia!' as I disappeared into the distance. Stephen was twenty-two years my senior. Although he was athletic, handsome, charming and young looking, I did not know what my feelings for him were. He was all any woman could want. It was obvious he wanted to marry me, which surprised me, but there was darling Alex to consider. Although he was so ill, my heart still belonged to him and always would. Marcus needed me too. I wanted to be there for him if anything should happen to Alex. He would require my wholehearted support. I retired to my room to contemplate earlier events. I sat by the bay window and gazed out across the Dales where Alex and I used to play, walk, talk and share our innermost secrets, hopes and dreams. There would be no more sharing of precious moments. Alex had gone, in all but body. Hospital staff were not sure how long it would be before his fragile frame deteriorated further. The inevitable could happen at any time.

I had a choice! I could spend each day, watching the man I loved decline before my eyes, or make a life for myself with a kind, caring soul whom Mother and Father admired and whom I liked immensely. I was confused. The following day I approached Father who, for once, had time on his hands. It seemed he knew what I wished to talk to him about.

'Father,' I said, as he watched me attentively, 'I have been approached by Stephen, asking for my hand in marriage!'

He was neither surprised nor shocked by the revelation.

'And you have come to ask me what I think, Sophia?'

'Yes, Father. This proposal has come unexpectedly. I need your advice and guidance before making such an important decision.'

He stared at me. 'Stephen spoke to me yesterday and disclosed that he wished to ask for your hand in marriage and needed our approval. Naturally, knowing him as we do, we decided to give our blessing. The final decision rests with you, Sophia!'

'I need to speak to you about my feelings, Father. Stephen is a good man, but I do not know that I care enough for him to marry him! How do I know if I am in love? How should I feel? It has been a traumatic time for us all of late. I feel I should be here for you, Mother, Alex, Marcus and Ben. I don't know if I can enter into a meaningful relationship with a man who needs so much of my time and attention.'

Father looked at me forlornly. 'I think it time you started thinking about your own life, Sophia. You spend much of your time at the hospital – to no avail – and you are wrapped around Marcus and his music. God forbid anything should happen to Alex, but it seems inevitable it will, and you will be lost. In a few years, Marcus will have his own life. What will you have? Nothing! You need to make plans for *your* future. You are a young woman who will want to have children. I know you and Stephen are good friends. Often a relationship can be fulfilling if you start off this way. You grow to love and respect that person.'

What made me think Father was referring to his relationship with Mother?

He continued, 'Stephen will take care of you. He is attentive and will no doubt be a good father. Think carefully about what I have said. Only you can come to the right decision. You must seriously consider *all* these points. You can still live at Harrington Hall, therefore many things will remain the same.'

I absorbed what he said, and thanked him for his time and his advice, which I promised I would consider carefully. Then I said, 'Farewell,' and continued with the daily business. My mind pondered on all the things discussed. I needed to make a decision!

I gave great consideration to Stephen's proposal and Father's words. Five days later I approached him, informing him that if he was still interested in me becoming his wife, I would accept his offer, making him as happy as I could. He lifted me up and swung me around, placed me down, embraced me and kissed me with tenderness. He was so thrilled. Father was in the drawing room, listening to music. He turned off the record and gave us his undivided attention. Holding my hand, Stephen announced, 'Sir, we have come to inform you that Sophia has consented to become my wife.'

Father stared at Stephen, then at me and rang the bell for the services of Haynes.

'Fetch Lady Harrington, Haynes!' he ordered. The butler disappeared to carry out the request.

Mother appeared on the scene. I could tell by her expression she knew an announcement was imminent. Father turned to Stephen and asked him to repeat to Lady Mary what he had said. He announced my intention to accept his proposal. Mother smiled sweetly at Stephen and then at Father, nodding approval in both directions.

'Stephen! Sophia!' Father said. 'You have our blessing. If you are happy, Sophia, then this marriage will please us.'

Mother hugged me while Father shook hands with Stephen. Stephen turned to me, put his hand in his jacket pocket and produced a small box from which he took a ring. He had anticipated my acceptance. He knelt, and as he did so, Mother and Father linked arms. Placing the ring on my finger, Stephen kissed me. I was transfixed by the magnificent solitaire diamond set in white gold. It was exquisite.

'Well, I think this calls for a glass of champagne!' Father said, ringing the bell once more for Haynes. He requested his finest, and the presence of Marcus from the barn, and Ben who, studying in his bedroom, was currently on vacation from Cambridge. Marcus appeared post-haste, followed by Ben.

'Sit here!' Father ordered, pointing to the sofa.

'What is happening, Sophia?' Marcus asked as Haynes returned with a tray containing a bottle of champagne on ice and glasses.

'Marcus! Ben! Good news!' Mother said.

Haynes poured the drinks as Father handed a glass to each one of us.

'Speech!' cried Mother.

Father smiled, raised his glass and said, 'It is a special day today. Sophia has agreed to become Stephen's wife!'

What a mixture of reactions I received. Ben said, 'Congratulations,' but was no more forthcoming. Marcus stood up and said, 'How could you, Sophia?' and marched out of the door. I asked to be excused so I could talk to him. Stephen shot me a disagreeable look.

Marcus was sitting at the bottom of the staircase. He frowned as I drew near.

'How could you, Sophia? How *could* you? He is old enough to be your father! I do not like him! Not one little bit.'

'Of course you do, Marcus! You told me only yesterday you liked him!'

'Well, I have changed my mind! I don't like him now!' He turned his back toward me, his arms crossed, his head down.

'Please come and join us, Marcus,' I pleaded. 'It will not be the same if you don't celebrate with us! *Please*! Come into the drawing room – do this for me!'

He was very put out. I began thinking he saw Stephen as a threat to our close relationship. I tried to convince him that when I married Stephen, I would never neglect him or his musical talent. I would always be there for him, no matter what. He took my arm and accompanied me back to the drawing room. On entering, I heard Mother say, 'We must have an engagement party!' But I did not want a great deal of fuss. Stephen and I settled for a dinner party to celebrate our engagement, with the attendance of a few close friends of my family.

None of Stephen's friends (whom I had not met) was available to attend the dinner party. I thought this was strange. It was a tremendous success, and a small informal affair as requested. Mother had organised outside caterers to produce the meal, allowing Edith and John to attend. Mr and Mrs Godber of Witherington's, the Jewellers in York, were guests with their daughter Caroline, an attractive twenty-year-old. Squadron Leader Harvey and his wife, Dorothy, arrived from Lincolnshire. He and Stephen had known each other during wartime. It was their first meeting in nineteen years, but they did not appear to converse. Marcus was stubborn and insisted he would not attend, but I persuaded him I would be so unhappy if he were not there. It appeared I was correct in my earlier assumption, as he admitted he considered Stephen a threat to our relationship, but I continued to put his mind at rest. Ben attended with a very pleasant, good-looking girl called Marianne. It was apparent to everyone there would possibly be another engagement once Ben had obtained his university degree. After a delicious three-course meal with champagne, wine and speeches, we had dancing in the Great Hall. Marcus was my first partner, but had two left feet. Ben shied away from me, spending the evening canoodling with Marianne, but Stephen was superb! He waltzed me around the floor, making me laugh and teasing me when I dared put a foot wrong. Marcus appeared extremely annoyed as Stephen held me close. Mother looked attractive in a royal blue evening dress, with matching shoes. The necklace she wore was exquisite; sapphires and diamonds sparkled in the artificial light. I admired them greatly.

'One day this necklace will be yours, Sophia!' she told me.

'But Mother... ' I gasped.

'Sophia! This necklace is a family heirloom handed down from one Harrington generation to the next. One day, as our daughter, you will wear it, as I do, on very special occasions.'

I explained that if Ben married, it should go to his wife, but Mother was adamant that Father wanted me to receive it. Stephen charmed his way through the evening, dancing with Mother, Edith, Mrs Harvey, then Mrs and Miss Godber. They were putty in his hands, and commented on what a wonderful choice of husband I had made. I think by midnight we were all a little tipsy. After the guests had bid farewell, I hurried to the kitchen and made the nightly cocoa for the family, helped by Stephen. He was so attentive and loving. I had to admit to myself I was beginning to look forward to my wedding. Mother wanted a huge affair, similar to the one she had planned for Alex and Lucy, but Stephen insisted on a quiet wedding in the baroque chapel. Father Pierre was no longer the priest in attendance, but a pleasant new man, Father Andrew, would officiate. Father was least pleased, and asked us to consider the church of St Michael the Archangel, in the grounds, but after considerable discussion on the matter, a chapel wedding was decided upon. It was set for 26 September 1964.

What I could not understand was how no one had woken up during the night.
Father had always been a light sleeper, and Mother had been an insomniac since Alex's illness. On retiring we had all slept soundly until at least eight o'clock the following morning. Perhaps it was an indication we had exhausted ourselves at the engagement party. It was Miss Paula Wilkins, Father's scatty secretary, who made the awful discovery the following morning. Traumatised by what she had found on entering the study, she screamed and ran about like a headless chicken between there and the dining room, looking for Father. He had just finished breakfast and was on his way to join her. On hearing the commotion he ran to her side, trying desperately to dodge her erratic movements.
'They've gone! Oh Lord! They've gone!'
'Slow down, young lady!' he said 'Gone? What have gone?'
She peered over her spectacles and shouted, 'The paintings! The paintings! They have gone!'
Father led her back to the study where I joined in the fracas to discover that many precious paintings and items had indeed disappeared from various sites within the Hall. Several equestrian paintings by Sir George Stubbs were missing, plus three pre-Raphaelite works of art, a Turner, a Gainsborough and a Titian. Elizabethan and Jacobean portraits of former Harrington ancestors were also taken.
'Call the police, Sophia! Get on to the Leeds Constabulary!'
I obeyed the order like clockwork. Stephen appeared, and Father

explained there had been a robbery. He was sent to investigate what else was missing, but advised not to touch anything, pending police investigations. Miss Wilkins was fraught. There was no controlling her behaviour until Father handed her a large brandy. She found consolation in the contents of the Waterford crystal glass and a comfortable leather armchair. Stephen returned to inform Father that Mother was heartbroken, having discovered that her sapphire and diamond necklace was missing – the family heirloom! She had retired to her room in an exhausted state and had not deposited it in the safe before retreating to her bed. The piece of jewellery was priceless and irreplaceable.

The police arrived swiftly. All the workers on the estate were gathered together, at intervals, to be interviewed. With Father's permission the police had commandeered the library. They were led in, either complaining or crying. It was an awful time, not only because of the loss of the valuable items, but because all the staff, with the exception of Miss Wilkins, were known to us and were trusted completely. As for Miss Paula Wilkins, she appeared frightened of her own shadow. She sat in the chair, sipping her brandy and sobbing into a tissue. Stephen approached Father saying, 'You know, Sir, you really should have updated your alarm system and the perimeter fencing. I did warn you some time ago I thought you needed a far superior security alarm, but you didn't heed my words.'

'I know, Stephen! I should have taken more notice. Changes take time to carry out. I have been so wrapped up with Alex, the estate and the factories. Who would have suspected another robbery after the post office raid? I am thankful my family did not come into contact with the thieves. Who knows what might have happened!'

Stephen anxiously agreed with Father's comments, saying, 'I hope they have more success in finding the culprits than what they have had with their post office investigations.'

Father nodded. The forensic teams arrived and were extremely thorough. Fingerprints were taken, and all aspects of the Hall were examined for points of entry. The site of access was determined. Wires around the perimeter fence had been sliced through with metal cutters. Vehicles had driven through the wood and past the lake toward the back of the main building. The burglars had disarmed the main alarm. For an unknown reason the back-up alarm had not responded. They obviously knew how to bypass it. One of the gang had entered by a large window, exposing the opulence of the Hall with its bountiful treasures. They painstakingly removed paintings from their frames, loaded candlesticks, clocks, silverware, figurines and porcelain, manuscripts and first edition books, as well as Mother's beloved necklace (without disturbing us) into their vehicles and returned from whence they came. All in all, a small fortune was taken. All were irreplaceable and lost to cunning thieves. Father's priceless art collection, which had taken a lifetime to assemble had gone in just a few hours. What upset Father more than ever was that police notified him there were numerous rotten art and antiques dealerships around the country that would be more than happy to fence the stolen goods to private collectors. Engagement party guests were interviewed, as were Stephen, I, Mother, Father and the lads. My parents were fraught, wondering what kind of reaction they would receive from the insurance company.

'I cannot understand it,' Father confided in me. 'I never sleep heavily, but last night I slept like a log. So did Mother. It is very strange!'

'Me too,' I added, 'but I am sure it was just a coincidence. Too much wine and champagne, I suppose!'

Inspector Wallace took Father to one side and notified him Scotland Yard would be brought in, as well as TV and radio. They thought the robbery bore resemblance to a similar one in Cumbria, by an East London gang. Father was satisfied that all that could be done was being done to retrieve the rare items and find the thieves. All antiques dealers known to Scotland Yard were contacted, as were antiques salerooms. All we could do was wait and hope items would be recovered.

'Come on, darling. We can do no more here. We have both been interviewed and must go and get on with work around the estate,' Stephen said as he gently took my arm. We left the crime scene, but not before I had given Father my word I was there for him always.

Several estate workers approached me during the day, expressing their sadness at recent events and assured us they had had no hand in any robbery. I explained that both Stephen and I had been interviewed thoroughly and everyone would be interviewed regardless, but it was not a slight on their good characters and was purely for elimination purposes. Marcus was upset at having to face the police, and would not answer their questions. Eventually Mother sat in on the interview until it reached its conclusion. Meanwhile Stephen and I tried to ensure the estate and its workers carried on as near normal as possible, but it would take considerable time to recover from this traumatic turn of events.

Over the following months, Marcus and I continued with our music lessons. Lyrics and accompanying music were forthcoming at a rate of two a week. The tremendous sense of achievement we both felt was overwhelming. I had such fun and happiness when Marcus and I sang and played together. His school reports improved continually. He received three harmonicas, a mandolin and a banjo from me. I purchased an amplifier for him. He had his eyes set on another guitar, a Gretch, and saved hard until it was his, but 'Soapy' remained his old favourite. Stephen was not too happy about having to share me with Marcus, but as he was involved with taxing work around the estate and trips into Leeds on business, it left Marcus and me plenty of time to improve our guitar playing.

Alex did not improve, which was understandable, but heartbreaking. Marcus and I visited regularly. Stephen accompanied me occasionally. I fought hard to pass my driving test and Father provided me with an Austin Mini to allow me mobility.

Father had his plans for the barn conversions turned down by the local planning committee. I was relieved. I hated the thought of my parents vacating the Hall and members of the public mooching around the rooms that had been our personal quarters, with all the wonderful memories they contained. Father had intentions of converting the gatehouse into accommodation for Stephen and me, once we were married, but the plans did not come to fruition. It was decided we would reside within the Hall, which pleased me greatly. Stephen, however, was not pleased about living in close proximity to my parents and to Marcus.

Summer approached. I knew by the way Marcus slouched around that he was despondent. With hands in pockets, head down and a gloomy look on his face he was approached by Father as he arrived in the dining room.

'Go and comb your hair, Marcus! Where is your tie? You do not sit at the table half-dressed!'

Marcus disappeared, mumbling under his breath.

'Sophia! What on earth are we going to do with him?' Father asked.

'Please leave him, Father,' I smiled. 'He is just a teenager trying to find his way in the world.'

'Do you know what he asked me today, Sophia?'

I was amused by his question. 'No, Father.'

'He wanted to know if I would allow him to go to the village hall on Saturday evening to play the guitar and sing until 11 p.m.'

I explained that most young people in the village would be there and that Marcus would have an excellent time.

'Not on your life, Sophia! He should not be subjected to that kind of debauchery!'

I giggled at his terminology, which did not please him, and explained I would be going to the dance myself.

'I assume Stephen will be escorting you?' he asked, frowning at me as he tucked into his cold roast beef and salad, washed down with his favourite wine.

'No, Stephen is going to a golf tournament at the weekend. I am going alone. Marcus can accompany me. I am meeting some old school friends there.'

The answer from Father was a definite 'No'. Marcus would not be attending, and that was an end to the discussion. However, Father thought it a good idea I spent some time with old friends, and that I should allow my mind to focus on other things other than Alex, for a while. Father retreated to the library as Marcus reappeared, fiddling with his tie, making it obvious he was uncomfortable wearing this particular article of clothing.

'I suppose you and Sir Oliver have discussed Saturday,' he complained, 'and the answer is still *No*.'

I admitted we had and that Father would not permit him to go. He appeared devastated at the decision, rolling his eyes in a manner that said, 'Am I surprised?'

'You see, Sophia,' he said staring at me with his sad, chocolate-brown eyes, 'I have been asked to front a band at the village hall. *Me*, lead guitarist, *and singer*! It's such an opportunity, and I can play my own material.'

I sympathised and explained I wanted to help, but didn't know how. Tucking into a bowl of strawberries from the walled garden, I focused on the situation for a short while and then told him I had a cunning plan! He looked puzzled.

'I know where there is a ladder that will reach up to my bedroom window,' I whispered.

'If you let me bid Father goodnight and leave by the front door for the dance, you could retire early and climb out of my bedroom window, down the ladder, hide it in the shrubbery, and make your way to the village hall.'

He thought it an excellent idea.

'We can stay out until some ungodly hour!' I giggled. 'I will help you climb in the window later. No one will be any the wiser. What do you think?'

'You're a trouper, Sophia! Let's do it! *Please!*' he said.

During the following few days we finalised our plans.

Saturday arrived. We hid 'Soapy' in the shed by the gatehouse and leaned the ladders against the bottom of the wall, below my window, hidden out of sight.

I dressed myself in a great skirt, with lots of petticoats underneath, teamed it with a matching blouse, waspie belt and a pair of fashionable winkle-picker shoes. I strutted out of the front door, but found the heels of the winkle-pickers continually stuck in the grass, so I took them off, carried them and waited in anticipation for Marcus to join me. He arrived in jeans, old shoes and an even older shirt. His patched jacket had seen better days, but I said nothing. His music would truly compensate for his lack of dress sense. We collected his guitar and hurried to the village hall.

We had a truly fantastic evening. Part of me wanted to sit and contemplate on Alex's non-existent recovery but another part of me needed to release the frustration and emotion building up inside. Dancing would do it. I was not short of dance partners among the young men. The majority wanted to know what I was thinking of, being engaged to a man twice my age, but I ignored their remarks and engaged in idle chit-chat. Marcus had the village hall buzzing with excitement at his playing and singing. Local girls tried to continually touch him, which did not excite him, but infuriated him instead. He seemed to have endless material to call upon, which he'd written. The band was good, but it was Marcus who stole the show. I joined him on stage for several duets, which were appreciated. We entertained until long after 11 p.m. Eventually the village policeman arrived to bring the dance to an end, which was quite a relief, as my shoes were killing me.

Marcus and I sauntered back to Harrington Hall in the dark, he with 'Soapy' over one shoulder and his other arm resting on me. I carried my shoes and bag, dirtying my feet on the earth in flower beds below my window. I dared not enter the Hall by the main door. Father would realise how late I'd arrived home and would be angry. We thought it wise to leave 'Soapy' in the shed and collect it the following morning. On finding the ladder, we tottered to and fro trying to gain our balance as we placed it against the bedroom sill. It was decided Marcus would go first, and when inside my room, I would follow. He would help me to climb through the window and then I'd push the ladder to the ground, returning it to its rightful place the following morning.

Up he went. He opened the window and climbed in. I followed and extended my hand, but he was not there to hold me.

'Come on, Marcus! Give me your hand. It's damn cold out here,' I moaned.

'Oh, it is, is it?' came a voice.

As I looked up, Father was leaning out of the window, waiting to grab me. I had never been so embarrassed. He gave me his hand (1.05 a.m.) and hauled me into the room. I was barefoot and dirty, and had my bag and shoes strapped to my waspie belt.

'Do come in Sophia! Welcome to Harrington Hall! Have you both had a good time?' sneered Father, wrapping his dressing gown tightly around his body.

I was speechless. Marcus made it worse by saying, 'Yes, thank you Sir. It was great.'

'Go to your room, Marcus!' Father shouted, and for once Marcus did as asked.

'I am ashamed of you, Sophia, leading him astray! I will talk to you both in the morning!'

Father slouched back to his room, twiddling his moustache. He was very angry. We were left to wonder all night what fate would befall us. Marcus was denied any outdoor activities for a week and deprived of one week's allowance. As I was now twenty, he considered it inappropriate to confine me to the Hall, but I had two weeks' allowance docked. It hurt us both, in our pockets. On the Sunday, the telephone rang incessantly with villagers congratulating Father on his talented children. What a fantastic evening everyone had had! They expressed a wish for it to be repeated, at a date to be agreed. All the praise did not stop Father meting out our punishments. My depletion of funds to the bank would not allow me new winkle-picker shoes, and Marcus was unable to purchase his coveted new harmonica.

September arrived. Mother began to panic about my wedding, which loomed. It was to be a quiet affair, with a minimum of guests, namely the immediate family, Edith, John, the Godber family and a few close friends. Stephen had no parents and no plans to invite his Leeds friends. I considered him outnumbered, but it did not concern him.

Mother engaged a dress designer to make my dress. It was a plain, long, slim-fitting, white silk dress with the minimum of decoration. My headdress was to consist of fresh stephanotis, ivy and gypsophila, with no veil or bouquet. A small shoulder corsage was ordered to match my headdress. We were to have a champagne reception in the Great Hall with a few extra guests. Then Stephen and I would leave for a honeymoon in Monaco.

On the night prior to the wedding Stephen stayed in Leeds. The wedding was to take place at noon in the baroque chapel. Mother busied herself in the morning making telephone calls and organising staff. The hairdresser, the beautician and Millie Dexter arrived to help me prepare for the ceremony. My hair, having grown considerably, was dressed into a most becoming style. My make-up was applied with exceptional skill and Millie, my maid, helped me into my dress. The floral headdress and corsage arrived and were ready to adorn me at the last minute.

'You look gorgeous, Miss Sophia!' Millie commented. There was general agreement.

'Could you leave me for a few moments?' I asked as they finished.

I was alone with my thoughts. I sat on the chair by the dressing table, deep in contemplation. I reflected on Alex in his hospital bed, and on the last time I had held my son. Stephen had made no move to find him, as he had promised. I wanted to hold Jonathan and Alex, but life had made it impossible. As I sat, immersed in thought, Father entered. He looked so handsome in his morning suit.

'Sophia, my darling, you look radiant,' he said, moving toward me. 'Well, this is your special day. You cannot imagine how much Mother and I want you to be happy. You are happy, aren't you?'

'What on earth makes you ask such a question? I am fine, Father, but I'm a little nervous!' I replied.

Father produced a bottle of his finest Scotch from behind his back and two glasses.

'Here, Sophia! I think we can do with a drop of this,' he suggested, and poured whisky for us. Handing me a glass, he said, 'You know, Sophia, if you want to change your mind about marrying Stephen, you can. Mother and I will not be cross. We want you to make the decision that's best for *you*. We will understand.'

I thanked him for his concern, but insisted I was content with my decision. We talked for ages, especially about Alex.

'Sophia, you are such a bright light in our family, and have been ever since the day you joined us,' he said. 'Each one of us has benefited from that loving nature of yours, and from your care and concern for us all. Have a good life, Sophia. Do not lose your own personality. You must not become simply Stephen Howard's wife, but retain your right to be Sophia Bertucelli, a young woman with so many talents. Mary could not have any more children after Benedict, but she has looked upon you as her daughter, as if you were her own flesh and blood. We have prayed daily for the blessing bestowed on us for having you as our daughter. I remember the day I carried you to the Hall, all battered and bruised. Now look at you! You are a beautiful woman, Sophia, with so much to give to life. My father was a tyrant, you know. He brought me up under a harsh regime and I was afraid of him. Having been a brigadier in the army, he thought he could order me around in my life, and I disappointed him continuously. I should have been stronger and faced up to him sooner, but it took a war and being taken prisoner by the Nazis to be able to face my demons and tell him what I thought. Maybe I have continued those traits that I learned from him in my dealings with

Marcus. I don't know. I have tried not to but I know I can be unsympathetic. I do love Marcus and I want him to be happy. I know I give the impression I have life weighed up, but I am not as strong as I lead people to believe. One day I will explain to you about my life, but today is not the day!'

He placed his glass down, looked at his wristwatch and said 'Goodness! The whisky is talking.'

He took me in his arms and held me closely, his body quivering with emotion.

My brain was filled with the thoughts of the first day he embraced me in Starbeck Cottage, when I was just five years old, explaining to me that my mama was dying. He did not know on that day what to do with a heartbroken child, but today he knew exactly how to comfort me. He held me close to his body, which I could tell was trembling. I cried, and made an awful mess of my make-up. The beautician was called to make good the devastation I had caused with my tears. The headdress was set in place, and my corsage too. I was ready for my marriage. I took my father's arm and gazed lovingly at him as he escorted me to my wedding.

The baroque chapel was splendidly decorated with white lilies. I entered to see Stephen standing a few feet from the altar rail. He smiled his charming smile, and as I drew close he whispered, 'You look wonderful, Sophia!'

We stood together, made our vows and exchanged rings, while Mother shed a few tears, Marcus fidgeted and Ben sighed. It was such a quick ceremony, and was finished almost before it had begun. Then the family, plus guests, moved on to the Great Hall for the reception, which was a subdued affair. Marcus entertained us on the piano with background music. In no time we were jetting off on our honeymoon. Stephen had purchased, with Father's help, a TR-2 sports car, and we set off for the airport and our flight to Monaco.

Chapter Twenty-one

Our honeymoon was a disaster! Stephen and I had had no physical relationship before our wedding. Our honeymoon night was fraught with difficulties, mainly on my side. When he took me in his arms I could think of no one but Alex and the wonderful times we had spent together. This caused complications in what should have been the happiest day of my life. Stephen seemed irate and angry with me, considering *his* needs above all else. When he demanded I act as his wife and insisted on his rights as a husband, I grew increasingly tense, to the point where I was unable to please him. This charade ended with him leaving me distressed and in terrible pain. I wanted to make love as I had with Alex, but the love between Stephen and me was not there. After the initial shock of what had happened, I avoided him at all costs. It was not a difficult thing to do, as he spent most nights quite happily at the gaming tables in casinos that were angling for his money. He won at poker a few times but lost substantial amounts at roulette. This exasperated him. I blamed myself for the state of affairs, when I realised he would rather be at the poker table than making love to me. I couldn't wait to return home. I spent most evenings after our meal seated at the bar in our hotel, alone, talking to guests or resting in my room. During the day, Stephen slept after his 3 a.m. arrival back at the hotel, while I walked and explored the wonderful principality of Monaco. I was relieved when the day finally arrived for our departure. I had missed Harrington Hall and my family greatly.

We hardly spoke on the return flight. Stephen returned to work immediately we arrived home and I soon realised that I would have to make a considerable effort to please my husband if our marriage was to survive; but I soon realised the Stephen I had previously known was not the Stephen I had married.

Within months, Stephen coldly announced, 'It has to be today, Sophia! The wheels are already in motion, and we cannot leave the situation unannounced any longer. We have to inform your parents we are emigrating!'

The news came as a shock to me. Stephen, rubbing the sleep from his tired eyes, had woken in a particularly strange mood. He sat on the edge of the bed, removed his pyjamas and staggered nonchalantly into the bathroom, leaving me puzzled at his comments. I collected my riding clothes for the morning hack with Ben, which I was going to take after breakfast.

'But Stephen, I am not sure that I want to live and work in Australia! We've not talked about this drastic change in our future sufficiently. You have not given me time to think anything through. I need time to consider the pros and cons, before coming to such an important decision. After all, this is going to affect the rest of our lives together.'

Stephen appeared naked at the bathroom door, a towel resting around his broad, muscular shoulders, his brown hair ruffled, his facial expression one of extreme anger.

'You bitch, Sophia! You absolute bitch! I've already decided! What is your problem?'

He moved to within inches of my face, staring intimidatingly into my eyes. For a moment I was frightened and could feel my body begin to tremble. I had not experienced Stephen in such a hideous temper.

'*When* are you going to stop revolving your life around your so-called bloody family? It's about time you grew up and started considering *me*! All I ever hear about is Alex, your parents, or Marcus! Wake up and realise they are no longer your world. *I am*, or am I?'

His voice reached fever pitch. He cupped his hand around my jaw and squeezed viciously. He pushed me backwards onto the bed, straddled his legs across me, and with his athletic body pinned me down! Grabbing my arms, he held them fast to prevent me from struggling. I wriggled frantically.

'But, Stephen…' I protested.

'*No buts*, Sophia! Am I your life, or am I not?'

Letting go of my arms, he removed the towel from his shoulders and placed it roughly against my throat. I could hardly breathe.

'Stephen! Please stop! You are hurting me!'

'I asked you a question!' he roared. 'Am I your life? Do you love me? For God's sake, you married me!'

Before I could answer, without hesitating he threw the towel to the floor and violently tore at my nightdress, exposing my breasts. He planted kisses on my mouth, face, neck, breasts and nipples. I wanted desperately for him to stop and attempted to push him away. He was rough, demanding and lecherous. I closed my eyes, stifled my tears and hoped he would stop. Suddenly he did. Abruptly, he jumped off the bed, laughing and taunting me as he returned to the bathroom. I sat up, adjusted my torn clothing and wiped away the tears. He continued his conversation as I experienced feelings of humiliation, worthlessness and of being used.

'*You*, Sophia, can get it into your bloody head you have no option but to go with me to Australia. After all, I know lots of naughty little secrets about you. I could tell Daddy an awful lot of things about you and Alex that he would be disgusted to hear. We are going to Australia together. *You are my wife*! You will do as you are told! I have a partnership in this cattle station. *You* will help me make it a great success! Do you understand what I am saying?' he bellowed.

'I understand perfectly, Stephen! I unburdened myself to you with my innermost thoughts and secrets, and now you are using these to blackmail me into doing things I am far from happy about. What I need to know is, why are you doing this?'

'You will find out in due course, Sophia! Now get dressed!'

Stephen shaved and showered as I listened half-heartedly to his plans for *me*, in which I had no say. If the cattle station were not a success, he said we could return to Yorkshire. A great part of me wanted it to fail before it had begun. I leaned against the frame of the bathroom door, shaking uncontrollably, awaiting my intended shower. Stephen surfaced, flaunted his naked body at me, wearing only the expensive aftershave I had given him at Christmas. As he passed by he grabbed my long hair, pulled me to his face and kissed me passionately. His tongue parted my lips, exploring my mouth. Suddenly I wanted to vomit. Why on earth was he acting so strangely?

'Now, be a good girl, Sophia! Get dressed, join me at breakfast and we will announce our intentions to the family. Remember, *you are mine now* – not the Harringtons – *mine*!'

Without a word, I entered the shower cubicle. My heart was heavy. I suddenly felt like a possession instead of a woman. Why did I not feel passion or any satisfying sensation when my husband of nine months touched me? The love I had for Alex, and he for me, was so different. It was difficult hiding the fact that I thought of Alex day and night. I began to realise I had made a terrible mistake in marrying Stephen. I continued to hope a great miracle would happen for Alex, when in my heart I knew it would not. I stood in the shower and let the warm water trickle gently over my hair, face and body. I began washing frantically, removing every trace of Stephen's touch from my flesh. As I did, the water washed away the tears rolling down my cheeks. I could not comprehend the strange mood swings that Stephen showed. Did he really enjoy humiliating me, or was he beside himself at the thought I could ruin his future plans? Why was it imperative that we go to Australia? My life and family were here at Harrington Hall. I wanted to stay where I was happy and contented.

Saturday morning breakfast at the Hall was a family affair. Everyone sat together to eat and discuss the happenings of the week. Father was first to arrive and took his place at the head of the table. Stephen left me to bring my emotions under control and join the family. Marcus, sleepy from a late night guitar session, slumped into his chair opposite Ben, who twiddled with his napkin, awaiting the arrival of Edith's delicious breakfast. Mother appeared looking her neat, presentable self. It was her day for charitable works at the local village fête. A vacant chair and place sitting were always in situ for Alex, in the hope he would one day be able to take up his rightful position at the table. I was the last to enter the dining room. All eyes were focused on me. I realised that everyone present was aware I was upset. Taking my usual place at table, I faced Stephen but directed my eyes toward the fireplace.

'Here, my dears,' said Edith, entering the room. With her warm intoxicating smile and jolly, plump figure she delivered a sumptuous breakfast. She spread dishes across the table with the help of kitchen staff. There were kippers, bacon, eggs, kidneys, mushrooms and sausages, an enormous selection of food. The family dived in as if they'd starved for a week. Ben on my right announced, '10.30 a.m., Sophia! Jimmy will have Storm and Petronella saddled up ready for our hack! I will meet you outside the stables.'

'Fine,' I whispered. I continued to stare at the fireplace. Father glanced down the table, realising I was not making conversation. He said, 'What is wrong, Sophia? You are very quiet this morning!'

I looked in his direction saying, 'I am all right, Father. Just sleepy, I suppose.'

'Eat up, Sophia. If you do not help yourself there will be nothing left.'

Gazing at Marcus's plate I could see what he meant.

'I am not very hungry,' I protested.

'But you must eat, Sophia darling! Especially if you are riding this morning!' Mother prompted.

Kind, caring Marcus passed me a plate of bacon and eggs across the table. I could feel an assortment of emotions springing up inside me. Stephen then spoke.

'Sophia and I have important news to tell you all!'

Every member of the family stopped eating and looked in his direction. I shot him a disgruntled look which said, 'Not now,' but he had no intention of heeding my wishes.

He was determined to disrupt the family breakfast. Mother nudged Father, then smiled at me with a foolish grin on her face. 'Is it morning sickness?' she enquired.

Before I could answer she asked, 'Are you pregnant, Sophia? Oliver, we are going to be grandparents!' She sighed deeply as she jumped to the wrong conclusion.

Marcus scowled.

'No, Mother, I am not pregnant.' I waved my hand, dismissing such a suggestion.

Mother looked disappointed. Marcus looked relieved and Ben said nothing, as usual.

Stephen raised his voice, determined to inform the family of his intentions.

'Sir, I have been offered a partnership on a cattle station in Australia. With my tried and tested management skills, Sophia's equestrian and organisational abilities, we can run the station to perfection. I have discussed it in great detail with Sophia,' he lied. 'Australia needs new blood. We have therefore decided to emigrate.'

It was the word 'emigrate' that caused shock and havoc. Marcus immediately stood up, sending his dining-room chair flying across the floor. He threw his plate defiantly across the table.

'I hate you, Stephen Howard! *I really hate you*! You cannot take Sophia away from us! She belongs here at Harrington Hall with us!' Looking severely at me, he added angrily, 'You cannot go with him, Sophia!'

Following this emotional outburst, he rushed to the door, slamming it as he left.

Father made no attempt to chastise him or call him. Mother burst into tears. Father, speechless, comforted her as she wept uncontrollably into her napkin. I stood up to console her, but Stephen leaned over the table, grabbed my arm, flashed an evil look in my direction and said, 'Leave her!' Stephen had handled the affair pathetically.

'I will talk to you later,' Ben whispered. He left the table, his half-eaten breakfast pushed to one side.

'Sophia, come here!' Stephen ordered me to his side. I stood up and meekly joined him as he said, 'Sir, excuse us. I will talk to you later about our plans.'

Father waved his hand disdainfully, dismissing us from the room. His manner was brusque as he comforted Mother. I desperately wanted to go to her, but I dare not. Father raised his eyes in disgust as we retreated from the room. Outside the door, Stephen confronted me saying, 'See what I mean about your bloody family? They want to own us body and soul! They are not going to own *me* or *you*!'

'I don't agree,' I meekly said. 'They are interested in our welfare, Stephen. Remember, Father has been extremely generous to you, footing bills for your expensive lifestyle.'

'Don't I ruddy well know it!' he snapped. He hurried me upstairs to our room, shutting the door behind us. 'At least in Australia I will have the freedom to do as I please.'

'You have freedom here, and plenty of it!' I reiterated.

Stephen had an exceptional lifestyle. Father had footed bills for his expensive sports car, drink, and golf membership fees, vets' bills for his horse, his flying club membership and his expensive taste in clothing. My husband liked only the best. Now he insisted in throwing this generosity back in my beloved father's face.

Suddenly his mood changed. He smiled.

'Sophia, cheer up! You and I are going to have a great life in Australia. Your parents and the lads can visit whenever they wish. We can fly home often. Don't be silly! You will love the outdoor life.'

The old Stephen was laughing and talking once more, the Stephen I had grown to care about. I was, by now, totally confused. He played games with my mind. On reflection, I could imagine my family flying over regularly, staying for weeks at a time. Perhaps it would not be so bad after all.

Ben and I ambled through woodland on Storm and Petronella, chatting about my intended move.

'You are not going to the other side of the world, are you?' he asked, appearing extremely downcast at the news.

'Yes, I am, Ben! Stephen is my husband, so I *must* go with him! This is a marvellous opportunity to make something of our lives.'

'What on earth are we going to do without you, Sophia? Father and Mother desperately need your support at this moment in time. Especially with Alex being so ill!'

'Oh, Ben! You are making me feel so guilty! I care about dearest Alex more than you could possibly imagine, but what can I do? Stephen is my husband and I have to follow him.'

I suddenly experienced coldness on his part as he began coming to terms with my decision.

'Just take care of yourself, Sophia! I cannot put into words what I feel, but I think you have made a big mistake in your choice of husband.'

I was flabbergasted at hearing Ben speak those words. He rarely commented on anything, yet he had decided to speak ill of my new husband. Stephen was charming, well-liked and normally affable. I put his erratic behaviour down to the fact he was anxious of our impending move and all the arrangements it entailed. I even began to think he was correct in his analysis. The family all wanted a small part of me. I loved them all dearly, but I needed a life of my own, away from the memories that continually haunted me. God knows, the last four years had been traumatic. Maybe this opportunity was the right time for me to move on. I was so confused.

'You will keep in touch with me, won't you, Ben?' I pleaded.

'I certainly will, Sophia. By the time I see you again I will be engaged to Marianne. You will be able to fly home for the wedding.'

'How wonderful! You will be the new estate manager too,' I mused.

'I know how you care for Alex, Sophia. I will keep you posted with any news that is forthcoming. I do wish you didn't have to go! We are all going to miss you so much!'

I fought back tears, but realised he had no indication of just how special Alex was to me and how much I would miss them all. We had a son somewhere in the big wide world. Not a day went by when I did not think of Jonathan or wonder how he was progressing. Going to Australia would mean I could not search for him. I hoped in my heart he was truly happy with his parents, and that they loved him as much as I would have. He would be walking, talking and exploring his little world now with a substitute mother and father. It hurt me deeply.

I awoke, startled at voices coming from downstairs.

'Mary! I am taking the Land Rover to the railway station! Damn you, Mary! Where are the keys?' Father shrieked.

There was urgency in his voice. I descended the staircase in my nightwear at the ridiculous hour of seven o'clock to find him anxiously pacing up and down the Hall entrance, waiting on Mother's every move.

'Damn the boy! Damn him, I say! He has brought nothing but upset since the day we took him into the family! Ah, Sophia – Marcus has gone! He left Mother a note. He has gone to London and taken a few clothes, his bank book, that wretched guitar you gave him and his harmonicas. I knew he would come to no good with his crazy ideas!'

Father was wild with anger, his cheeks scarlet with the fury which had built up within him. I could not understand fully why Marcus had left but guessed that his actions were a protest against my emigrating. By going to London, he thought this would prevent me from leaving for Australia, as he knew I would go searching for him. He was obviously incensed with me!

'He will be back, Father,' I said, trying to calm a volatile situation.

Father ignored me. He shouted loudly for Mother and she appeared, tearful and distraught, carrying the missing car keys.

'I will come with you to the railway station, Father,' I offered.

I wanted to prevent Marcus from carrying out the plan he had concocted to keep me in Yorkshire. Turning to ascend the stairs, I said, 'Let me dress myself in suitable clothes and I will be with you as soon as I can!'

I climbed the stairs two at a time, rummaged through my wardrobe and donned jeans and sweater. Stephen woke, raised his head, watched me dress and returned to sleep, oblivious of the drama unfolding. Father had parked outside the front entrance. Mother, wiping her tears on her handkerchief, proceeded to wring her hands together in a frantic motion. She grabbed me as I passed.

'Bring him home, Sophia. Please bring my Marcus home! I love him as dearly as if he were my own son!'

My heart ached for her! I felt anger toward Marcus, that he could consider bringing heartache to the woman who had loved and nurtured him as her own, since the age of three; but I realised it was *me* Marcus wished to punish, not Mother. She idolised him and, like me, encouraged him to follow his dreams.

'I will try, Mother! I will attempt to bring him back! Please dry your tears.'

I wanted desperately to hold her in my arms, offering comfort, but Father blasted on the horn of the Land Rover in an effort to hurry me along. I climbed into the vehicle. Father sped toward the village as though our lives depended on it.

'We have Alex lying desperately ill in hospital, then you disappear to Ireland for over a year without a word – and now you want to live with your new husband on some godforsaken cattle station in the outback of Australia! Then, to cap it all, our youngest decides to run away to London to follow his dreams. What on earth is this family coming to, Sophia?'

'I am so sorry, Father,' I commiserated.

He looked extremely sad. He had been a marvellous father to us all: strict but fair. He had been generous with his time, love and money, yet his children were fleeing the nest. The family were disintegrating around him.

'I am sure Marcus will return when things get tough in the big city,' I added, fearing that he had already departed for London.

'He never had one flicker of interest in farming. He has only ever been interested in that damn music. I blame you, Sophia!'

'Please, Father, I—'

He interrupted me as he continued driving like a maniac. 'You filled his head with nonsense, telling him he had talent! I have yet to see it.

The boy needs a good beating. My father would never have stood for such behaviour.'

'But he does have talent. If you had listened to him and encouraged him from the onset, he would have talked to you about his needs.'

'Needs? *Needs?* He belongs here at Harrington Hall, helping with the estate – God knows we can do with all the help we can get – not having him drift around in the city, knowing no one and associating with the wrong people.'

His face was like thunder, and revealed a man with tremendous problems and responsibilities.

'He will survive,' I said, determined to convince Father all would be well, but in my heart I was worried about Marcus. He was just seventeen years old, vulnerable and not at all worldly-wise. 'Marcus has always been a free spirit. You know if you stop him from doing what he wants to do, his spirit will die. He will return when he has fulfilled himself.'

Father frowned at me and continued, 'He will drift around London knowing no one. You know how tragically shy he is.'

In my heart, I knew Father was correct about his son's sensitivity. He *was* painfully shy, and I was concerned. He looked at me strangely, eyeing the expressions on my face. 'In some things you are wise beyond your years, Sophia, but in others you wear your heart on your sleeve, just like your beloved mama, Anna. You are the image of her, both in attitude and looks.'

What did he really know of Mama? I wanted to ask him this vital question but he was fraught with worry. He hurriedly changed the subject, saying, 'When I lay my hands on Marcus, his feet won't touch the ground.'

I hoped in my heart that Marcus had caught the early train for London. On arrival at the railway station entrance, we came to an abrupt halt. I jumped quickly out of the vehicle and followed Father. He hurried to the window of the ticket master's office. I ran onto the platform.

'Hello, lass! Can I help?'

I looked along the deserted railway track and in the door of the empty waiting room, and was confronted by a porter who was moving bales of newspaper, delivered by the early morning train.

'I am looking for a young lad, aged seventeen, six feet tall. He would have been carrying a guitar. Have you seen him?' I gasped.

'Nay, lass! 'Fraid not!' He stood, cap perched back, scratching his forehead. 'No one of that description has taken a train today!'

'Thank you!' I said, an air of sadness in my voice. I ran back to Father to hear the tail end of his conversation with the ticket master.

'Next train is due at 8 a.m., sir. No lad of that description bought a ticket here today! I know young Master Marcus. He's not been around here.'

Father thanked the man for his help and looked puzzled. He asked me, 'Is he in the waiting room, Sophia?'

'No, Father. Nor on the platform. No one has seen him. The porter says no one travelled on the milk train. Perhaps he has gone by road.'

We knew we were beaten. Neither of us had seen Marcus since the afternoon of the previous day.

After riding out as usual with Ben, I had gone in search of Marcus, as I was worried at his disappearance from the breakfast table, but was unable to find him. When I did eventually catch up with him in the afternoon, he was moodily waiting for his piano lesson.

'I have been looking for you everywhere!' I told him. 'I wanted to talk with you earlier, but we have to concentrate on playing piano at the moment.'

He looked at me with misery and disappointment written all over his face. I decided that we would practise Beethoven's *Pastoral Symphony*.

He glanced at me sadly, saying, 'Tell me that what happened at breakfast was all a bad dream, and I'm going to wake up and find all is well. You're not going to Australia with Stephen, are you, Sophia? I would die if you left Harrington Hall! I simply couldn't bear it! I know you're not in love with him!'

I explained that I had no intention of discussing the subject of Australia before our lesson, and said I would talk to him about it after we had finished. He placed his music on the stand, seated himself at the piano, cracked his knuckles infuriatingly and began to play. He played the beautiful piece of music with such gusto that it was obvious his heart was not in what he was doing and he was intent on annoying me.

'Pianissimo, Marcus,' I whispered in his ear, 'pianissimo!'

At my comment he turned, glared and shouted, '*Fortissimo! Fortissimo!*' and banged his fingers down on the keyboard in an act of defiance. He played the following pages as loudly as possible, then stopped, slammed down the lid of the piano with incredible force, and before I could utter one word, raced past me out of the room, leaving his music and case behind.

'How childish,' I murmured.

I imagined he had gone to the lake to sit and sulk, or over the fields with Deefa to cool off. I had not realised Stephen's plan to leave England would have had such an impact on this exceptionally talented young man. He was nowhere to be seen, and missed supper, which was very unusual.

Father climbed into the Land Rover. The journey home began in silence. En route he suddenly asked, 'Are you really happy, Sophia?'

'I am fine,' I replied.

'You see, I noticed on your wedding day there were times when you looked awfully sad, and not how a young bride should look at all. You seemed detached from the proceedings. You have not been your usual happy, bubbly self for months.'

'I suppose it's because I am constantly anxious for Alex,' I said.

Father was genuinely worried for my well-being, but how could I tell him my innermost secrets and my true feelings for Stephen? I was also bothered by what I had learnt of my father from Maura, if it were at all true, which I was sure it wasn't. It would have killed him if I had approached him with it, and I would never have forgiven myself. Then there was my love for Alex, my pregnancy and my search for Jonathan. From now on I had to live the only way I knew how. Under the circumstances, if it meant going to Australia with Stephen, then so be it. I knew emphatically that I could no longer trust Stephen with any secrets. He appeared to be quite blasé about my whole situation. I was beginning to dislike my husband immensely.

'Please don't worry about me, Father. I am happy,' I lied.

He observed, 'Stephen seems a hard-working fellow. I know he drinks too much and loves to fabricate a story, but I think forty-three is a sensible age for him to take on the responsibility of a cattle station.' Father glanced at me and I agreed.

'He is very lucky to have this opportunity, Father,' I said.

'No, Sophia! He is very lucky to have *you* to love and support him!'

'When we are settled you will come and visit, won't you?'

'Of course! You just try and stop us! We are all going to miss you dreadfully. You are the daughter Mary and I never had and which she so desperately wanted. We will be over to watch your new enterprise grow and help where we can. Stephen is going to tell me your new address and we will write and telephone often.'

He squeezed my hand affectionately, saying, 'We know Alex is not going to make any further progress, but how long he will continue in this state, I do not know. The prognosis is poor,' he added, choking over his words. 'I haven't a clue how Mother will react if anything happens. It bothers me greatly. I dread waking up, not knowing what the day will hold.'

'Please keep me informed, Father. I will fly home when you need me. Alex has always been *so* special to me. I would want to be there for you and Mother. I do hope you understand what this family means to me! You are my life, but Stephen needs my support with his new venture, so I must go with him!'

He said he understood, but I am not sure that was the case. He stated that as Ben had completed his course at university he would be joining the estate team soon.

'Good, reliable Ben,' he sighed. 'What would I do without his help?'

I wanted to weep for Father, for the man who had taken me into his family and his heart. For a moment he looked as though he were out of his depth. My biggest regret was that I would be 12,000 miles away if news came of Alex. As much as I tried to contain my feelings for Alex in the back of my mind, those feelings continually surfaced. I still loved him very deeply. At night, when Stephen roughly took my body and demanded his conjugal rights, I obeyed, not because I wanted him, but because it was my duty as his wife – something he continually reminded of me in no uncertain terms. He did not treat me tenderly or care for me as Alex had. Stephen satisfied his needs and then slept by my side almost begrudgingly. Not for me the soft, warm, caressing touches I had experienced with Alex, but lustful self-satisfaction on Stephen's part, leaving me cold and dissatisfied with his sexual advances. This had become a way of life.

Perhaps in Australia things would be different. I invariably cried myself to sleep, thinking of Alex and then Jonathan, realising the two most precious people in my life were no longer part of it. Now there was Marcus too! How I missed him. His moods, his talent and our banter. I wondered where he and 'Soapy' would be laying their heads at night in the lonely city of London. Oh, Alex! Darling Alex! Why had fate been so cruel to us both? I was about to commence a new life in Australia, while he could possibly be coming to the end of his life in England.

Chapter Twenty-two

The following few months were apprehensive times. A passport needed arranging, medicals were taken, injections given, numerous interviews took place and paperwork needed attending to. I asked little about our plans. Stephen continually snapped at me. He seemed under increasing pressure with the estate, showing Ben the ropes and seeing to arrangements for life in Australia. Alex's condition remained the same but there were several anxious moments when he appeared to deteriorate. We heard nothing from Marcus. I missed him constantly and was annoyed he could have been so inconsiderate, but I thought that that was how he possibly viewed me – uncaring and indifferent. I wanted to see him, to know he was well and surviving, but Stephen would not allow me to go in search of him. I asked Stephen about our home, and what furniture we would require for the removal firm to pack and seal in crates. He supplied me with a list and advised me to take what I thought we needed and tell him later. Father thought it was a bad idea to ship the Steinway grand piano out. I agreed. I did not think a piano of such magnificence should be subjected to such a long and arduous journey by sea. I would leave it in the Great Hall to play on my many trips home. Father had bought a beautiful upright piano for me to take delivery of. It was a late twenty-first birthday present, so I could continue with my music. I was enormously grateful, and made my feelings known to my wonderful parents.

    The day I dreaded finally arrived, the day of our departure for Australia. I knew the hardest part was yet to come, with farewells imminent. This was a situation I had been warily contemplating for weeks. Ben was the first to visit, with Marianne. They explained they would holiday with us as soon as his workload on the estate decreased, perhaps for their honeymoon. I would miss them both. Marianne had become a great friend to me. After breakfast, dear Edith came to visit me in my room. We hugged for a considerable time, and she promised to write to me regularly with all the news and gossip on estate and village life. I sensed her becoming emotional as she walked toward the kitchen. She turned, raised her hand and was gone. Mother and I entered the Great Hall. I played the *Pastoral Symphony* for the last time on the Steinway. The walls were dull now Father's precious paintings were missing. We heard nothing about any arrests. Although the robbery had been reported numerous times on television and in the national press, no news or clues were forthcoming. Mother did, however, mention that she'd heard from Marcus. I was elated by the news. He was 'finding his feet' in London. What a relief! I expressed a wish that she should tell Father of the communication to put his mind at rest, and explain that Marcus had left no forwarding address. I asked if she could notify Marcus of my new address, should he contact her further, and she agreed. The telephone then rang, and it was a while before Haynes answered it. He entered the Great Hall, saying in hurried tones, 'The hospital has just rung, my Lady. They wish for you to go immediately. It is most urgent!'

Mother turned a deathly white colour as she received the news. I stood silently in despair, as she dismissed Haynes to go and search for Father. I desperately wanted to go to my beloved Alex. I had said my goodbyes only the evening before and tried to feed him, but he was uncooperative and unaware of what was going on around him. I had kissed him, explaining tearfully about my departure to Australia the following day, but he was unresponsive. If there had been a single glimmer of hope that he was aware of me, I would have stayed. Regardless of the outcome, Stephen could have gone to Australia alone, but there was no response from Alex. The staff informed me it was simply a matter of time. My heart was breaking!

'Darling Sophia! I must go to the hospital now!' Mother said, interrupting my train of thought. She threw her arms around me, hugging me tightly, then rested her head in my neck. I could feel her body trembling at what she knew would be facing her at the hospital.

'*Please*, Mother, I want to come with you!' I pleaded. 'I need to!'

'No, Sophia, you must go with your husband! You saw how Alex was last night, and know you cannot do anything! I am sure this is...' She bowed her head, saying, 'Please go to the airport with Stephen. Your plane will not wait!'

I shook my head. 'Mother, I have to come with you! I have to, please!'

'Sophia! Don't make things harder for me than they already are. Get on the plane for me, *please*, darling! You have to begin your new life in Australia! You can do nothing by staying here.' She pleaded with me until I agreed.

Father appeared, looking desperate. 'Come on, old girl,' he said, enveloping Mother in his arms. 'We had better hurry to the hospital.'

He paused, released Mother, looked straight at me and I fell into his arms, burying my head in his jacket. He smelt heavily of tobacco, but at that moment it was the most beautiful smell in the world. There was so much I wanted to do, to say, and to ask, but I knew time was of the essence. I cried into his shirt as he stroked my cheek and held me close.

'Sophia,' he whispered, 'do not forget me, darling. Write to me as soon as you get there, and remember that Mother and I will always love you.'

'Forget you, Father? How could I ever forget you and Mother? I absolutely adore you both. You are my life! You are exceptional people,' I said and began to cry again.

'I will miss you all and the Hall and staff so much.'

I glanced over his shoulder and watched the tears flow down Mother's cheeks. 'Stephen gave me your new address last night, darling. We will be over to see you as soon as possible,' Father promised. He released me, took Mother's hand, and with head bowed he escorted her to the door. Neither of them turned to look back. I watched them, two very sad people who'd had more than their fair share of heartache.

I dried my eyes and attempted to finish packing. During the morning I could not concentrate. Stephen had decided to work until the last moment, handing all aspects of the estate over to Ben. He had already inspected items which had been selected to be shipped to Australia. The removal firm designated to handle this had already arrived to carefully pack the items, which were assigned for delivery to a warehouse in Perth, Western Australia. I assumed from this we would be living somewhere near Perth. Paula Wilkins, Father's temporary secretary, came to wish me a safe journey and after shaking my hand, made a beeline for Stephen, who had arrived back from his meeting with Ben. He looked happier than I had seen him in ages. They spoke quietly for a few moments and then she departed. He had obviously worked his charm on her. Within the hour, John Roberts arrived at the front entrance with the Rolls, ready to take us to Heathrow Airport. John placed the matching luggage into the car, and as he did so, a succession of staff members came to bid us farewell, wishing us a safe journey and a happy life in Australia. Tears were shed, but I assured them we would return for a visit as soon as it was practical to do so. I stared out of the car window looking up at the façade of the Hall. It had never looked more beautiful. The tremendous old Tudor building, with all its secrets and memories of past times, stood gracious and stately against the blue sky. How I would miss it and the wonderful people within. The staff lined up at the entrance and waved as John started up the car. As we approached the gatehouse, I turned to look through the rear window. I saw Haynes running behind, waving frantically in our direction.

'Stephen!' I exclaimed. 'Haynes is trying desperately to attract our attention. He must have received a telephone call from Mother and Father. We must go back and see what they want!'

He stared defiantly at me and said, 'You must be joking, Sophia! We have a plane to catch!'

Waving his hand imperiously, he ordered John to continue driving. 'Get us to the airport as soon as possible!' he demanded.

'But Stephen—' I argued but he interrupted.

'Be quiet, Sophia! Alex is dead! You know he is! It had to happen. Why do you think your mother and father were sent for? That is an end to it! You can do no good, so sit back, relax, and for goodness sake calm down!'

I realised this was fact but I stared out of the window, my eyes streaming with tears. I discreetly wiped them, concealing their presence from Stephen. I assumed a trance-like state so I would not have to ponder on the misery Father, Mother and Ben were experiencing. Several times I noticed John watching me in his rear-view mirror. The journey to the airport was not without difficulties. Large volumes of traffic had built up, but John finally arrived with about two hours to spare before the departure of our evening flight. Stephen had explained we were flying first to Singapore, where we would stay for a night. Then we would be flying to Adelaide. I thought perhaps he had got his information wrong, but I had learnt not to contradict and accepted what he told me. John found a luggage trolley, loaded our suitcases onto it, and escorted us to the check-in desk. He bade Stephen farewell and turning to me, took my hands and held them tightly.

'Well, Miss Sophia, the wife and I are going to miss you! We have known you since you were a baby. To us you are like the daughter we never had.'

'I know, John. I have such great affection for you too. I will never forget the love and kindness you showed to me during and after Mama's illness and since. Please take care of Mother and Father for me, won't you?'

He said, 'I most certainly will. They are fine people! Do come back and see us soon!'

'I will, John,' I promised.

He released his grip on my hands, turned and walked away. I watched as he removed his handkerchief from his uniform pocket and held it to his eyes. He disappeared into the distance. Stephen and I checked in, had our luggage weighed and received our seat allocations. We had approximately thirty minutes before our flight was due to be called, and found comfortable seats to rest on. Stephen left me guarding our hand luggage while he went to fetch snacks, newspapers and confectionary for the journey. My mind whizzed through the events of the day. My heart was so heavy I wanted to turn on my heels and run, run as fast I could, leaving Stephen to go to Australia alone. I looked for the nearest exit. I could return to my beloved Yorkshire to give comfort to Father, Mother and Ben. Suddenly a voice from behind startled me.

'Hello, Sophia!'

I turned, and much to my surprise came face to face with dearest Marcus!

'Oh, Marcus, how wonderful it is to see you!' I held out my arms as I fought back tears. I was totally shocked by his presence but ecstatic that he had arrived to bid me farewell.

'Mother told me when your flight was. I had to come and see you. I just had to!'

He lunged his tall frame at me and enveloped me in his arms. He buried his head in my neck and cried quietly so as not to draw attention to himself.

'I am so pleased you are here, Marcus. I have been so worried about you. Where on earth have you been?'

He moved his head and looked down at me, his eyes penetrating the very depths of my soul as he explained, 'I have been in the big city, Sophia! I met three lads who are as crazy about music as me! We have formed a group – Marc Walker and the Dream Catchers – and we are trying to book gigs. I have also done a bit of busking. It helps to pay for food. Life is a bit rough. We are in a squat, but I'm OK.'

'I am so glad Marcus. I have been going frantic, thinking about you.'

I wanted so desperately to tell him how thankful I was he was surviving and how much he meant to me.

'You need a haircut, young man,' I observed, running my fingers through his unruly black hair. As I drew my hand away, he clasped it close to his cheek and kissed my fingers tenderly.

'The hairstyle is my new image,' he informed me. 'Got to look the part!'

'And are these patched jeans and jacket part of the image too?' I asked.

A smile crept to the corner of his mouth. 'I'm afraid so!'

'Are you eating properly?' I enquired. 'Because you look very pale and thin!'

He seemed to have grown taller since the last time I had set eyes on him.

'I am OK, Sophia.'

'You are not taking drugs, are you?' I asked.

'Of course not! I wouldn't do that!'

His black look made me realise I should not have suggested such a thing.

'Well, it is the sixties,' I said in my defence. 'You know, sex, drugs, rock and roll – and you are in London.'

He grabbed my arm tightly and fixed his eyes on mine in a penetrating stare.

'Sophia! Please, I am begging you, don't go to Australia! Stephen doesn't need you. I have watched the way he treats you. He doesn't love you and I know you do not love him! I need you! I cannot make it on the music scene without you.'

I tried desperately to explain to Marcus that it was imperative I went, but he did not understand my reasons and I could not unburden myself to a teenager who would not have comprehended how complicated my life had become. Holding me closer, he said, 'Sophia! I am begging you not to go! I really do need you here. We were such a good team musically, and I know between us we could make a huge success of our songs – but without you Sophia, I am nothing!'

'*You* are everything to me, Marcus!' I said, choking on the words.

I tried changing the subject but I could see the emotional state he was in. As difficult as it was, I endeavoured to keep my emotions under control.

'Look, Marcus, please promise me you will let Mother know your address so she can tell Father. He really cares about you and is worried for your safety.'

'I can't, Sophia! If Sir Oliver finds out where I am, he will take me home and then I will never be able to follow my dream of becoming a singer–songwriter.'

He looked so forlorn, so vulnerable; more so than I had ever seen him before. My heart was so sad for him. Here stood the boy I had grown up with for the past fourteen years. I was tempted to tell him Mother and Father had been called to the hospital urgently, but I was sure Mother would tell him about Alex when they were next in contact. I didn't want anything to spoil those few precious moments we had together.

'Just follow your heart in what you do, Marcus. You have terrific talent, you really can make it and without me!'

He shook his head.

I opened my handbag and pulled out a notepad and chequebook. I wrote a name and address on the notepad. I passed it to him and said 'Here, take this! There is this man in London who used to be Mama's manager. Tell him I sent you. He may be able to put you in touch with people who can help you further your career, or point you in the right direction. He has so many musical contacts in and around London.'

He observed the note, folded it carefully and placed it in the pocket of his worn jacket for future reference.

'Thank you, Sophia! I will contact him, but…'

'Take this too,' I said leaning on a nearby table to write.

'What is it?' he asked inquisitively, as I handed him a folded piece of paper.

'It's a cheque, Marcus. I want you to take it. You are going to need a lot of things to help you until you get on your feet.'

He unfolded it and stared in amazement saying, 'I cannot take this Sophia! It's far too much money!'

'Please, Marcus, you must take it.' I insisted. 'It was money left to me by Mama for the furtherance of musical studies, and this is exactly what it will be used for. I can think of no one who is more deserving of it. It will help with all the things you find yourself needing in the coming months.' I popped the cheque into his pocket to join the address. 'And while we are on the subject…' I hunted in my bag and found what I was looking for. 'Look! Father gave me this money so I could get a plane ticket home in an emergency; but I won't need it, so please take this too and use it wisely and well.'

'Oh, Sophia!' More tears clouded his eyes.

'Ssh! Just take it!' I begged. 'I will worry about you far less if I know you have "rainy day" money to fall back on, should you need it.'

I could no longer control my emotions and tears trickled down my cheeks. He tenderly wiped them away with his fingers. As he stood there, I wondered what was happening to the child Marcus whom I had known since the age of three. He was a young, handsome, oversensitive lad, with the capacity to become a star, if only he could channel his energies into his voice, his music and his lyrics. He stood tall, his scruffy hair growing out of control. His spectacles were well worn, his shoes and clothes unkempt. The next time we met he would be a man.

'I do wish you wouldn't go, Sophia!'

He tried pleading again, hugging me so firmly I thought my arms would break.

'Stay here! Leave Stephen, and I will go home with you to Harrington Hall!'

'I have to go, Marcus! One day I will explain why. It's too difficult to speak of now!'

He looked at me with an inquisitive expression, unable to understand.

'Come on, Marcus Walker,' I chided. 'You are going to be a star. You have all the qualities. Do it for me!'

'Have you heard the folk singer, Bob Dylan?' he asked. 'He's great, Sophia. Sings these protest songs about life in the USA! I love his lyrics!'

I feared I hadn't heard of him and said so.

'You appear not to be keeping up with the scene since I left, Sophia!'

I admitted I hadn't and for a moment we laughed.

An announcement was made, calling passengers for the flight to Adelaide via other destinations.

'Please come and see me when you can, Marcus. I will visit England as often as possible.'

'Give me your address so I can write!' he pleaded.

'Mother and Father have it! Ask Mother. Write to me often and I will answer immediately.'

Stephen appeared suddenly and took my arm. He noticed Marcus standing there but chose to ignore him. He dragged me away, saying, 'Hurry, Sophia! We will miss our flight if you don't get a move on!'

He marched me toward the departure lounge. I turned and shouted, 'Goodbye, Marcus. The next time we meet, I want a copy of your first number-one hit!'

'You will, Sophia! You will have a signed copy!' he promised.

'Come on, Sophia! Hurry! Our flight will not wait! *Come on!*'

I turned to see Marcus standing there, lonely and sad. I wanted to rush back, throw my arms around him and tell him just how much I cared for him. This was going to be the last of the Harrington family as we had known it. It was breaking my heart. Inside, I was in complete and utter turmoil.

'Don't forget, Marcus! Talk to Father. At least let Mother tell him you are surviving, even if you do not tell him where you are!' I shouted.

He nodded, wiped away his tears, turned and disappeared into the crowd. Stephen and I made our way to the departure lounge for boarding the aircraft which would take us to Adelaide, Australia.

Chapter Twenty-three

Stephen and I hardly spoke to one another during the long, arduous journey to Australia. I had not anticipated how far I was being distanced from those I loved, and homesickness overcame me. There were numerous stops for refuelling and I tried to sleep, but my thoughts continually returned to Harrington Hall, to my distraught parents and then to the sad scenario with Marcus at Heathrow. His face was imprinted on my mind. I had never seen him look so frightened or lonely. How on earth could I have left him and set foot on the aircraft with the uncaring control freak sitting next to me who I called my husband? Fear can play havoc with one's emotions. I was constantly apprehensive of what Stephen could – and *would* – do! I looked around the aircraft wondering what secrets other passengers had that had led them to leave England for a remote country thousands of miles away. Stephen had no difficulty sleeping, which suited me fine. I had nothing I wished to talk to him about, and if life was not a success at the cattle station (and I hoped it wouldn't be) we could return to Yorkshire.

As we approached the airport in Singapore, Stephen was more forthcoming about his intentions. He explained that we would be staying there for two nights in preparation for his meeting with a business associate. Arriving at the airport, we were transferred to our hotel by taxi. Temperatures were in excess of anything I had ever experienced. I was euphoric at being able to have a long soak in the bath to refresh myself after such a tiring journey. Stephen announced that he wanted to sleep, and being exhausted myself I thought it an excellent idea. He ordered snacks via room service, and after consuming the delectable food we crashed into oblivion. Neither of us woke until 9 a.m. the following morning.

We breakfasted in the hotel restaurant, during which time Stephen suggested he take me shopping to the fashion houses to buy me an evening dress. He wanted me to make a stunning impression on his business colleague that evening.

The fashion houses were enchanting and the dresses magnificent, especially those in Thai silk. Everyone was most helpful and charming. Stephen sat and watched as I tried on numerous items. *He* finally chose the little number I would wear. I admit his taste was excellent and I loved the shiny, smooth feel of the material with the added tasteful decoration. There were shoes and accessories to match. Our next visit was to find a lightweight suit for my husband, which had him looking businesslike. We returned to our hotel with our exciting purchases. Stephen was exceptionally attentive and kind and had reverted to the charming man I had married. I visited the hairdresser and manicurist within the hotel complex, while he settled for a sauna and massage. I realised, as his wife, that I was expected to do my utmost to encourage him in all his business affairs.

Our guests were waiting as we breezed into dinner. I was introduced to Edmund and Adele Remington, Australians who had homes in both Singapore and Perth. Adele was a charming middle-aged woman whom I gelled with immediately, but her husband was officious, overweight and balding. During dinner he made small talk with me, constantly boasting of his business interests in Australia, but I could not determine what those interests were. After our meal, Adele and I retired to the lounge bar to sample the famous 'Singapore Sling' while the men propped up the bar itself, discussing things they considered were of no interest to us females. I watched my husband as he downed numerous glasses of whisky. He was handed a large envelope from Edmund, for which he gave a large envelope containing banknotes in return. Edmund swiftly counted these and promptly concealed them about his person. Meanwhile, Adele and I talked about our families, and pangs of home-sickness overcame me once more. I was given to understand her husband was an antiques dealer and entrepreneur with fingers in numerous pies.

Stephen returned to me at 10 p.m. We bid his associate farewell. I was exhausted by the heat and returning to our hotel room, prepared myself for bed. He sat in a chair, pondering on the contents of the envelope, but said nothing about his business discussions with Edmund, and I did not ask. The atmosphere was peaceful and I didn't want to rock the boat. I crept into bed, leaving him perusing official-looking documents. I soon fell asleep and did not realise Stephen had left the room, but I was woken by his noisy return at 4 a.m. after a night of drinking and gambling. He slept most of that day, while I sat by the pool, taking in an occasional swim. Our flight was due to leave at 10.15 p.m., and we left our hotel in time to catch our flight to Adelaide.

Adelaide was a beautiful city. The river Torrens meandered through the centre. Although the airport was small, staff was friendly and helpful. We booked into a hotel for one night and explored the charming city. I could not understand why we hadn't flown out to our cattle station but Stephen explained that it was in the Northern Territory, many miles from Adelaide, and we would fly to the nearest airport, Darwin, the following day. After a short rest and shower, he ordered a delightful meal in the hotel restaurant. We wined, dined and took in a little dancing, but my heart was in the Yorkshire Dales, fretting over my parents. I slipped between the sheets at 11 p.m. exhausted, while Stephen once more disappeared to drink and gamble, not returning until the early hours. I attempted to put a telephone call through to Yorkshire via the hotel reception but was told that no outgoing calls were to be made, on the strict instructions of Mr Howard. I was astonished at this declaration and could not understand the reason for Stephen's behaviour. On his return he slept a while, and then we packed our cases and headed for Adelaide Airport. As Stephen struggled with our luggage, I said, 'I will hand our passports and papers in, if you wish.'

Abruptly he answered, '*No*, Sophia! I am quite capable!'

He had woken in a wretched mood. As we prepared to board our flight to Darwin, I had the distinct impression he had lost heavily at poker. All the signs were there. He handed in the necessary documentation. With our luggage safely weighed in, we received boarding passes from the clerk and the return of our passport.

'Thank you, Mr and Mrs Masters,' he said.

'Did you hear what he called us?' I queried, 'He called us Mr and Mrs Masters.'

Stephen placed his arm around my shoulders and roughly ushered me through further airport checks and then on to the departure lounge.

'But Stephen, he—'

'Shut up!' he snarled, squeezing my arm. 'I will explain shortly!'

I found seats for us and we quietly awaited our flight. People milled around looking for places to sit.

'Now listen to me, Sophia,' Stephen whispered. 'There is something I need to tell you.'

'What is it?' I asked noting his worried look.

'I didn't want to worry you before now, but when I was in England, I got into serious problems with gambling and owed substantial amounts of money.'

I began to speak but Stephen placed his fingers on my lips as if to silence me and continued, 'I used to go to Leeds to gamble, especially when you were visiting Alex in hospital. I became addicted. Then it was time for me to settle my gambling debts. I could not meet my commitments so I thought that to spare you and your family the shame, we should emigrate.'

'But Stephen, if you had confided in Father I am sure he would have helped.'

'I couldn't, Sophia! I still have my pride, you know! I thought if we came out here we could make a new life for ourselves.'

'I see. Well, what can I say? But why did the airport call us Mr and Mrs Masters?'

'Edmund Remington had a new passport and immigration papers falsified for us. No one can now trace us to collect their debts! We are now Mr Christopher and Mrs Maria Masters! Do you see what is happening?'

He grabbed my arm firmly as if to squeeze a 'yes' out of me!

I nodded reluctantly but I did not understand.

Once on board the aircraft, I sat quietly in my seat and tried to get my brain around the confessions Stephen had made. I was unable to comprehend what kind of gambling debts he had. I couldn't bring myself to ask. He sat quietly in his seat. I looked at my husband, the charming cad, and wondered how, if he had such awful debts, he had managed to buy a share in a cattle station? When did he arrange the false passport? How did he pay for the expensive hotel bills and the luxurious evening wear? I was scared as I reclined in my seat. I imagined the sentence for obtaining and travelling on a forged passport was a heavy custodial one, if caught. I had been thrown into a living nightmare from which there was no escape. I wanted to run away from him as far as possible – but where to? I would write to Father once we arrived at our new home to see what solution he could offer. I was sure he would settle Stephen's financial problems. I had given my lifeline money to Marcus at Heathrow and did not have a clue if our real passport still existed. I could only travel on the forged one as an escort of my husband. What on earth would I do? Stephen was certainly playing a game of cat and mouse with his creditors and with me.

The journey soon came to an end and the aircraft arrived at our destination on time. Darwin was a pretty place, though the temperatures were excessive. Stephen handed in our forged documentation as I stood by, trembling with trepidation. After extensive scrutiny of our passport, papers, luggage and facial features, we were free to go, much to my relief. We hailed a taxi and were driven to a remote area outside Darwin. In among some eucalyptus trees stood an old dilapidated homestead, badly in need of extensive restoration.

'Surely this is not our new home?' I queried, looking horrified.

'Don't be ridiculous, Sophia! This is the home of my partner in the cattle station. Walter Symonds is his name.'

It was Walter who walked out to greet us. I was far from impressed. He was an obese, scruffily-dressed man with untidy hair, tied back in a ponytail. He sauntered over, a huge cigar in his mouth. His features were well worn and rugged. I took an instant dislike to him. He was a 'touchy-feely' person whose behaviour reminded me of Father Anthony. I knew instantly, from lessons learnt in the past, that I should keep my distance. Removing his cigar from his mouth he planted a smoky kiss on my cheek.

'G'day,' he said. 'So you are Sophia! Stephen certainly knows how to choose a beautiful sheila.' He called out, 'Lizzie! Our guests have arrived. Get your butt out here!'

A young woman in trousers and T-shirt appeared and struggled with our cases. I insisted on helping her. With his arm around Stephen's shoulder, Walter ushered him into his home, which was as run-down and unkempt as the exterior.

My husband and Walter were deep in conversation. I retired to a room which I assumed was the kitchen and chatted to Lizzie. She was Walter's live-in girlfriend, very friendly and yet rather naïve. I noticed bruises on her neck and arms, but refrained from asking how she received them. We had a salad lunch and then Wally and Stephen retired to the verandah to talk business and drink Northern Territory rum, which I understood was considerably stronger than other brands. Lizzie showed me around the land attached to the homestead. I marvelled at the exotic birds with their awesome colours. There was a barn, the broken-down remnant of days gone by. Lizzie insisted I visited it with her. I could hear strange noises from within. As we peered around the door, we saw a bitch of indeterminate ancestry allowing three puppies to suckle. They were delightful. My heart immediately went out to them. As I carefully picked one up, it snuggled into my clothing, happy to nestle against my warm body.

'What breed are they?' I asked, stoking the soft fur.

'I think they're part German shepherd, part border collie, with a few other varieties thrown in,' Lizzie explained.

'They are lovable,' I admitted.

'Take one,' she insisted. 'Wally will drown them once he has to buy feed. If we do not find them homes, they will be gone within a fortnight!'

'How cruel!' I gasped. 'Surely Wally will not carry out such an awful threat?'

'Wally does what he damn well wants! You will soon learn about Wally,' she explained.

I had no idea what Lizzie was trying to convey to me. I was more interested in the welfare of the small pup. We walked toward the homestead. I spotted Wally and Stephen reclining on the porch, both inebriated by their consumption of rum.

'Look, Stephen!' I said smiling and holding out the pup.

'Good God, Sophia! What on earth have you got there?' he muttered.

'This puppy is only six weeks old! Can I keep him?'

Stephen laughed. 'If it's going to keep you happy, then yes, you may! We will take him with us tomorrow!'

'Tomorrow? I thought we were leaving today!' I commented but I could see by his drunken state he would not be taking me anywhere.

I returned the puppy to its mother and then helped Lizzie prepare an evening meal.

We dined quite late. During our meal a woman of about thirty-five years of age put in a brief appearance. I did not get a close look at her, but she appeared quite sophisticated compared to the likes of Wally and Lizzie. She stayed for a few moments, and Stephen went to greet her. I was not introduced. Her presence rather disturbed me. If I hadn't been so tired, I could have sworn I had seen her somewhere before, but that was not possible.

After an uncomfortable night on camp beds we prepared for our departure. I thought Stephen would have forgotten his promise that we could take the puppy, but he was quite happy for me to have the little bundle, so I collected it from its mother. Stephen had loaded numerous supplies into Wally's truck. We were driven to an airstrip, with me nursing the whimpering pup.

'I am going to call him Heinz!' I announced.

'He'll need regular small feeds,' dictated Wally. 'About every three hours!'

I agreed as we continued across the airstrip, and then came to an abrupt halt. In front of us was an aeroplane capable of carrying four passengers. It was old, slightly battered, but in excellent working order. Stephen was in his element.

'Meet Silver Lady,' he said, looking at his prized acquisition. 'She is going to take us to our cattle station.'

'How on earth can we afford her?' I asked.

'She comes with the property,' he explained. 'She is our means of quick transport in and out of the territory. She is going to be my lifeline to the outside world.'

He stroked the paintwork and said, 'Come on, Sophia! Let's load up and be on our way.'

I couldn't contemplate how far from civilisation the cattle station was, if it needed a plane and not a car for transportation. I realised it was not wise to challenge the decisions Stephen made. With Heinz carefully placed on the front seat, I helped with supplies. As we finished, Stephen started up the engine and I climbed aboard, placing Heinz on my lap. After routine flight checks had been carried out, we were airborne. I had never flown in such an aircraft and it was a frightening yet enlightening experience. I was informed it was a De Havilland Beaver, which meant absolutely nothing to me. I hoped Stephen would not attempt any of the stunts which had afforded him his RAF bomber pilot status during the war, and tried to relax.

During our journey, Stephen was more forthcoming about our new home. I almost collapsed when he explained that the cattle station covered almost 750,000 acres. I had no perception of such a vast area. It was almost 470 miles from Darwin by road and 190 miles by air! I was given to understand our nearest neighbours were more than one hundred miles away. I do not know what it was that perturbed me so about the situation, but my mind began working overtime. How could Stephen afford a partnership in the station? When I queried this, he simply said that with hard work from us both he could repay a large bank loan he had raised to fund the enterprise. Nothing he said seemed to ring true. Or was I still being paranoid?

As we approached what was now called 'Masters Valley', we flew over our land and property. It was a fantastic area indeed, although it was what many would consider a wilderness. Stephen cruised down the airstrip and came to a halt. His aviation skills had stood him in good stead. Our landing was perfect, sending up enormous clouds of brown dust in our wake. I later learnt that this was 'bull dust' and would be a plague to contend with on a regular basis.

'From now on in, you and I will be known as Christopher and Maria Masters. Have you got that?' he snapped. Stephen was most emphatic and stared at me with fiery eyes.

I did not understand but meekly said, 'Yes.' I was extremely nervous of my husband.

'I don't want my gambling associates tracing me. The more anonymity and distance we have from our former lives, the better I will like it. I do not wish to sleep with a gun under my pillow!'

What an exaggeration, I thought.

'Darling,' he smiled as he helped me down from the plane. 'Welcome home!'

Cuddling Heinz, I looked ahead as an enormous, muscular fellow hurtled toward us.

'I think this must be our head stockman,' he announced as the man bounded in our direction.

As the stockman spoke I immediately detected a Scottish accent. He extended a hand and said, 'Hi. I am Alfred McInnes, your head stockman, known to the workforce as Big Al. You must be Mr and Mrs Masters.'

He was a jovial giant of a man with red hair, a huge ginger beard and a great personality.

Shaking my hand keenly, I immediately knew I was going to like Big Al. He was bound to be a great asset. As we walked toward the house, Stephen suddenly relieved me of Heinz and gave him to Big Al and announced jokingly that he was going to carry me over the threshold. 'Come, darling,' he said softly, lifting me into his arms. 'This is our home, and I want you to be so happy and contented here. It is important to me.'

He carried me over the step and into the room, where he placed my feet on the floor. He continued to embrace me and kissed me passionately on the lips. Big Al looked embarrassed as he stood there holding Heinz. I then viewed the room as Big Al complained, 'We have a cook, but she really is no use. She is nothing more than an ornament. I apologise for the mess!'

It was obviously the kitchen that I had entered. It was in a filthy state. I relieved the stockman of Heinz and placed the pup in a handy cardboard box which lay in the corner of the room. I noted the flies using the dirty plates as a skating rink. Edith would have shaken in her shoes. The door opened and in walked what I could only describe as a tart, wearing the shortest skirt known to the female form, and a top of see-through material. She had long, painted fingernails.

'Who are you?' she demanded, smoke billowing from her cigarette.

'We could ask you the same question! We are Mr and Mrs Masters,' Stephen informed her.

'I am the cook,' she announced.

That figures, I thought. I said, 'Well then, perhaps you would like to help me clear this disgusting mess.'

She stared at me as I handed her the nearest available cleaning cloth. In no time, with my guidance she had grasped the idea of how to wash dishes, clean and run a tidy kitchen. She continued working as I made and fed Heinz scrambled egg. Stephen contented himself at the kitchen table and appeared deep in conversation with Al, but leered at the cook's legs and breasts as he did so. She and Stephen were soon 'bosom' pals. Her greatest talent seemed to be nail painting.

I soon discovered how intolerably hard life was. The cook was useless, there was a large workforce to cater for, and I rolled up my sleeves, preparing food almost non-stop. Within days I had asked Stephen to dismiss the cook, which he reluctantly did.

We were introduced to a new caterer, Bindi. She was an Aboriginal girl with a talent for laughter, fun and – most importantly – loads of culinary expertise. I adored her in no time. Her help allowed me to spend hours doing secretarial work or numerous important jobs as they appeared. I realised what a great weight of work she had lifted from my shoulders. I realised too that I desperately needed to contact home. I had to let Mother and Father know I was well and surviving. I wanted a visit from them as soon as was humanly possible. Our old Treager radio was useless for contact to and from the outside world. I could not understand what was being said through the crackle and static. I wrote asking my parents how they were. I asked about my beloved Alex's funeral, and wondered if they had organised a magnificent celebration of his life in the church and added that I was heartbroken not to have been there. I penned a confidential letter to Father explaining about Stephen's enormous gambling debts and asked if he could help in some way. The mail plane was due within days. I was sure the pilot, 'Sky-High Pete' as he was known, would post letters for me. I had written a long and detailed letter to Marcus pouring out my heart to him, telling him he was correct in his assumption about Stephen, and that I was not in love with my husband, but I was trying to make the most of a difficult situation, living with a Jekyll and Hyde character. I addressed it to Harrington Hall with the instruction 'Please Forward', in the hope Mother would do just that. Apart from mail and the dreadful radio, communication with the outside world was almost non-existent. Everything was so primitive compared to England, and far behind the times. Heinz brought me light relief as I fussed and fed him at regular intervals. I saw little of Stephen, but it suited me fine.

The mail plane arrived and I enthusiastically ran out to meet it. I had collected up my letters and a few dollars and ran out to introduce myself to Pete.

'Hi, I am Maria Masters,' I lied.

Pete was a really nice guy and pleasant, with a good sense of humour. He handed me a bundle of letters, and as I spoke to him I fingered through the envelopes, all of which were addressed to Mr Christopher Masters. There were none from Mother and Father in England, or Marcus and I considered that as being odd.

'Pete,' I asked politely, 'could you take these letters and post them for me?'

'Certainly,' he said, but as I handed him the letters a voice from behind boomed, 'I'll take those!' I turned round to be confronted by Stephen.

'Thanks,' he said, parting Pete from my letters. My heart sank as Stephen introduced himself to the pilot as Christopher Masters and then abruptly sent him on his way. I wondered when there would be repercussions. Stephen instantly tore open my letters. I tried to stop him, and although I made attempts to retrieve them he read the contents. Strangely, he did not react immediately.

'Oh, darling, what did I tell you about writing begging letters to your father?'

I apologised and simply said I wanted to help the monetary situation. Stephen smiled his charming smile and took my hand.

'Come with me, darling. Let's take a walk and talk about this.'

He led me along. Placing his arm around my shoulder as we ambled down the dusty road leading from our house, he said, 'You are a silly girl. We can work our way out of this mess. You and I can do it together. Fancy you writing to Marcus to tell him that you do not love me! Of course you do. You are just feeling homesick. I know we have our little arguments, but you *will* keep questioning my authority! It makes me feel inadequate when you do that! You must trust me, Sophia! During the next season I am going to want you to give your full attention in helping me muster the cattle. I will make sure you have a spectacular horse and we can do everything together, with help from the workforce.'

'I will do my best for you, Stephen,' I said trembling like a leaf caught in high winds. I glanced at his serious expression. He took my hand and we continued walking through a wooded area which led to a river bank. It was tranquil and peaceful, the only sound being that of the birds nesting in the trees. Unexpectedly, Stephen grabbed my hair and dragged me along toward the river.

'Ouch, Stephen, you are hurting me! Please stop!' I yelped, but he pushed me ferociously down on my knees until I was so close to the water I could see my startled reflection.

'You are a stupid cow, Sophia! Listen to me! You will not communicate with your family by letter or radio! You are with me! You are my wife! You will do as I tell you at all times! Do you hear what I am saying?' he screeched. 'You will not communicate with anyone!'

How could I not hear? His shrieking voice reverberated in my ears. My head was hurting and the arm he had pinned behind my back was painful. I fought back the tears. Just then I saw a dark shape in the river. It was a large, sinister reptile gliding silently toward me. It was a crocodile! My senses told me it was about ten feet in length.

'Do as I say or I will willingly feed you to these!' he snarled.

He pulled me back just as the crocodile attacked and I glimpsed the huge teeth as it missed me by a few feet. I broke away from Stephen's grasp and ran back toward the house. My legs were weak, my body shaking with fear. I could hardly hold myself upright and my legs did not want to support me. I could hear Stephen laughing as he ran and caught up with me.

You bastard, Stephen, I thought. You may think you have won, but one day I will get away from you and return to Harrington Hall, and you will wish you had never set eyes on me.

I sank hopelessly to the ground in a fit of hysteria, as he grabbed my arm and lifted me up, carrying me back to the house.

Chapter Twenty-four

During the following days I met the workforce of Masters Valley cattle station.

It intrigued me that we had Aboriginal stockmen and jackaroos under our auspices, as well as a New Zealand mechanic and a carpenter from Wales in the United Kingdom. Solomon, one of the Aborigines, lived permanently at the station. Thin of build, short, with jet-black hair and face, he was quiet and gentle, an expert hunter and tracker. I did not realise what tremendous skills he would be able to teach me over the following months. Those skills, after considerable practice, would stand me in good stead for the years ahead. Tim Hodges, the New Zealander, was a tall, good-looking, rough, hard-drinking guy. With a kind heart and good sense of humour, he was expert at his job, appearing punctually each day, poised for the work which lay ahead, repairing vehicles and machinery. Charlie Tungate was a different kettle of fish – thin, weedy and balding. I took an instant dislike to him, and was warned that he was not to be trusted. He was resident at the bunkhouse along with Tim, Solomon, Big Al and other members of the workforce, eating in the main building morning and night. He was Welsh, from Pontypridd and had been in Australia for more than twenty-five years. His carpentry skills ensured that fences, the homestead and the station were maintained in a good state of repair. He was lazy and constantly needed prompting.

Months passed and the wet season approached. The bull dust surrounding the house was ankle-deep. Dust storms leading to the wet season were an enormous problem, as they coated anything and everything. We could not see, breathe or speak without ingesting the wretched stuff. Then the wet season arrived, which was intolerable. It turned the bull dust into thick mud. The road to the station was impassable and mail deliveries were non-existent for eleven weeks while rain continued virtually non-stop. Many workers took to the nearest town to stay and drink themselves into oblivion. Big Al, Tim and Solomon stayed and Bindi continued to cook. The river swelled to an all-time high. Stephen and I lived a miserable existence, with him constantly moody and uncommunicative. He spent days drinking our hard-earned money, out of sheer boredom, while I sewed, making furnishings to enhance the rooms. Heinz had grown into a handsome dog. He was extremely protective of me and had a definite dislike of Stephen, snarling when he came within feet of us.

As the wet season progressed, I became unwell. I imagined it to be the environment and continual rain not agreeing with me, but soon realised I was pregnant. I told no one. I asked Stephen if he would fly me to Darwin when he next visited Wally, which he did, once the wet season had come to an end. He had to interview stockmen for the approaching cattle season.

While in Darwin I visited a doctor, unbeknown to Stephen, who was carrying out interviews. It was confirmed I was pregnant. Before returning to Stephen I entered a telephone box and attempted to contact my parents in England, without success. The operator tried numerous times to connect, but the lines were busy. My hour of freedom was over. I was desperate to hear Father's voice and to chat with Mother. I wanted them to know I was having a child, their first known grandchild! I thought deeply about the pregnancy and knew I desperately wanted it, maybe to compensate for the loss of Jonathan in my life. I considered that rearing an infant on a godforsaken cattle station was certainly not ideal. I also hoped our child would not inherit Stephen's moody character but have the soft, gentle nature of Mama. As I walked along the street, Stephen appeared. I was hoping he had not seen me in the telephone box. He sauntered toward me saying, 'Did you buy yourself a nice evening dress, darling?'

'I couldn't see anything I liked,' I gulped.

'Come on, sweetheart! I'll take you to a little shop I know of! We will get you something special for Richard Sullivan's fiftieth birthday party. I want you looking your most enchanting.'

He escorted me into a nearby arcade. I looked forward to attending the party of our nearest neighbours, one hundred miles away. It was Stephen's intention to fly us there in 'Silver Lady' the following evening. He purchased me a little black dress which fitted well and looked extremely good but again it was *his* choice!

After the shopping expedition, we visited Wally and Lizzie by taxi and spent a few hours in their company, the men talking business while Lizzie and I chatted. Lizzie sported a black eye, the excuse being that she had walked into a door. Other fresh bruises on her body pointed to Wally. I was convinced he was physically abusing her. She was such a sweet person. No wonder Wally and Stephen were friends. They say birds of a feather flock together.

'They seem to have a lot to talk about,' I observed.

'You can be sure whatever they are discussing, it's illegal!' Lizzie commented, 'Know anything about jewellery or paintings?' she asked.

'A little,' I said. 'Why?'

'Well, I heard a snippet of conversation. Wally and Stephen are trying to offload some ill-gotten gains.'

Before I could ask more, Stephen appeared. Wally had insisted Lizzie drive us to our plane at the airstrip.

She safely delivered us to 'Silver Lady'. As we parted she whispered, 'Be careful. Things are not always what they seem.'

'Who was the woman I saw last time we visited your house?' I asked. 'She looked familiar.'

'Oh, you mean Wally's sister. She is a greedy, stuck-up cow! She is Stephen's—'

My husband interrupted, grabbed my bags and insisted I board the plane. I smiled and waved at Lizzie as I left, not realising it would be the last time I saw her.

We returned to Masters Valley, and Stephen was euphoric that he had hired four new workers who would arrive by road. We ate a hearty meal prepared by Bindi. I settled down with a glass of fruit juice, while Stephen poured a tot of rum. Sitting together, with the workforce occupied elsewhere, provided a good opportunity for me to break my exciting news to him.

'Stephen,' I whispered. 'Can I tell you something?'

'What is it, sweetie?' he droned.

'I am pregnant.'

I waited for him to take me in his arms and hug me at the wonderful news, but instead he turned, glared at me disdainfully and shouted, 'You stupid cow! Do you realise what this means? You won't be able to help me with mustering the cattle. I need your riding skills, you bloody little fool!'

My heart sank. I stood up, tears in my eyes, and I left the room. He grabbed my arm, saying, 'You will have to have an abortion!'

I was horrified at his outburst. 'I am not having an abortion!' I bravely announced. For me an abortion was totally out of the question and something I would not agree to, no matter what! I could not contemplate a backstreet abortionist. I locked myself in the bedroom. Later Stephen insisted on me opening the door. He prepared himself for bed, and before getting between the sheets, threw a bundle of bank notes at me, saying, 'Get it done and get it done soon. I will take you into Darwin!'

I tried my utmost to put on a brave face for the fiftieth birthday party of our neighbour, Richard Sullivan. We arrived in 'Silver Lady', me in my new black dress, Stephen in the suit he had afforded himself in Singapore. We were greeted with open arms.

'Hello, Maria!' said Peggy Sullivan, shaking my hand. 'And you must be her husband, Christopher,' she said, facing Stephen.

He returned her greeting, standing there looking devilishly handsome, sporting an immaculately groomed, newly grown brown goatee beard and fashionable moustache. I had to admit to myself it suited him but gave him a totally different appearance to the man I had married three years previously. We were immediately introduced to Richard, passed on our good wishes for his milestone birthday, and presented him with a gift. Introductions over, we were whisked into an adjoining room where a number of people from surrounding communities had gathered. Richard announced, 'Ladies and gentlemen, our new neighbours, Christopher and Maria Masters!'

Everyone descended on us to meet the recently arrived 'Pommies'. To say we were overdressed was an understatement. Several women eyed my outfit with envy. There was dancing, to a band made up of various guys who had not clapped eyes on one another before that evening. Stephen soon charmed himself around the room, with an array of females flocking to him in the hope they would be asked to dance. I heard the words 'dishy', 'typical well-educated Pom', 'sexy' and 'good-looking guy' spoken by various females and envious males. He was in his element, lapping up all the attention. I was inundated with requests to dance, but Stephen made sure he kept a close, beady eye on me. I took to the floor and began enjoying myself, but the 'resident' band seemed to be on another planet as far as their music was concerned, and at least one hundred years behind the times. I excused my dance partner when the lead guitarist could no longer control his fellow players and stepped in to add a bit of a swing to the evening's proceedings. Marcus would have been proud of me.

Huge amounts of home-made food and refreshments were served, and there was a lull in the proceedings while guests ate and chatted. Stephen approached me, advising that I should not spend more than one dance with any partner. Richard Sullivan asked a Miss Elsie Brabbington, senior resident of the area, to play the piano, but she had to decline due to an arthritic condition afflicting her fingers. Stephen offered my services, simply so that he could watch me closely, making sure I behaved as he wished. The guests, having been isolated and years behind the times, requested songs from a bygone age. I played World War Two songs which Mama had taught me as a child, including her favourite, 'My Heart and I', which brought a tear to my eye, knowing it was my father's favourite too. Everyone joined in a singalong, including Stephen, who appeared to be enjoying himself immensely in the company of females who were expatriates from the UK. The party continued far later than anticipated. As we were about to depart, numerous people turned their attention to me and said, 'When we have another party we insist you join us. We enjoyed your playing so much. You really gave the party an excellent boost with your entertainment. It was brilliant!'

The lead guitarist kissed me, thanked me for rescuing him from a tricky situation, and said he hoped we would meet again soon. I replied likewise, much to Stephen's disgust.

On our return flight, Stephen had other ideas. From conversations with him, it appeared I'd had too entertaining an evening and received far too much attention. He was jealous! He told me we would not be accepting further invitations to any event. I disliked my husband intensely!

I could not have an abortion. I returned Stephen's bank notes to him, and despite threats from him, I explained I was adamant and would do nothing to harm the child. In retribution, he had me on horseback, mustering our huge herd of cattle for most of the season, hoping I would miscarry. As the time for the birth became imminent, we were hardly on speaking terms. On one occasion he caught me trying to send information over our radio to an operator in the hope they could contact Harrington Hall, for which I received a beating. He could take away my dignity but not my soul. *He was Maura incarnate*!

The following day he was all sweetness and light to me, and tried making amends for his disgusting behaviour of the previous day.

Stephen was on one of his regular flights to Port Keats and Darwin when my labour pains began. My intention was to give birth to my child at home with the help of Bindi and the communication of the Treager radio should anything untoward happen. A room had been prepared and labour progressed quite rapidly. Bindi, with the help of Big Al, who held my hand and whispered words of comfort in my ear, delivered a beautiful dark-haired baby girl who I immediately named Anna-Sophia. I wanted to hold my child, but Bindi was reluctant to place her in my arms.

'Maria. I must tell you…'

I looked at her solemn face, a tear trickling down her cheek as she spoke. I heard my darling daughter cry.

'Please hand her to me,' I begged. 'I need to hold her in my arms.'

Big Al had disappeared and I heard him conversing on the radio.

'What on earth is wrong?' I asked, as Bindi swaddled the child in a soft towel.

Big Al reappeared, informing me that the Flying Doctor Service would be arriving to transport me and my daughter to hospital in Darwin. Anna-Sophia was showing signs of jaundice and other complications. They both looked extremely fraught.

I hated Stephen for having left me with the birth so imminent. He could have transported us swiftly in 'Silver Lady'. The time waiting for the Flying Doctor seemed like an eternity, but luckily they had attended a situation at the Sullivan station and were with us promptly, immediate attention being given to Anna-Sophia. I was prepared also for the flight and for post-natal problems. Bindi packed a case with toilet items and clean clothing. It was en route to hospital that I learned from medical staff that my darling daughter had been born severely handicapped. I was naturally devastated and could not be consoled.

During the following two days in the hospital, I saw nothing of Stephen. Daily, I was taken in a wheelchair to visit my precious daughter, and allowed to touch her for a short while. After two days, Anna-Sophia's condition worsened. She passed away during the night. Nurses fetched me, allowing me to hold her for a considerable time after her untimely death. They were supportive and sympathetic in my loss. I was heartbroken and at an all-time low. She would have been a light in a very dark tunnel, and I would have loved and adored her with all my heart. Stephen did not appear and I was thankful. The paediatrician approached me, explained the seriousness of what had been Anna-Sophia's condition, and stated that her passing would have been a happy release. At least she had been spared life with a drunken brute for a father. The next bombshell to fall was the news from the gynaecologist that I would not be able to have another child. My life was crumbling around me. As I began recovering from my loss, I realised this could offer the opportunity I needed to get away, a chance to release myself from the husband I hated.

It was three days after Anna Sophia's death, and although extremely depressed, I had a plan. When the ward was busy with mothers feeding their babies, I'd disappear with my clothes, to the toilet, dress and walk out. I waited until the coast was clear. In the toilet I dressed myself and followed signs saying 'WAY OUT'. With my head down, I stole along numerous corridors until I reached the main doors. I was thrilled my plan was coming to fruition. My nightmare had almost ended.

'Hello – and where are you going?' was the question. The voice was all too familiar. I raised my head to find Stephen standing in my path.

He grabbed my arm in a painful grip and led me, protesting and shaking with fear, back to the ward. We sat with the staff and made arrangements for Anna-Sophia's funeral. It was arranged she would be flown to Masters Valley and be buried in a specially selected plot near the house. Not once did Stephen offer me any sympathy or hold me close to comfort me. He seemed relieved at the turn of events. Nothing had to stand in his way – not even his child.

On my return to the homestead, Big Al and Bindi were marvellous. They were more than understanding of my plight and lifted me from the depths of despair, helping me through the following days. Solomon had such wonderful views on life and death and helped me come to terms with my loss. He also helped me resolve the repugnance I felt inside for Stephen. I had begun despising him with feelings I never thought it possible to experience.

Once she had been buried at the ranch, I visited Anna-Sophia's grave daily. At least I could talk to her for a short while, even if I could not hold her in my arms or give her the love and attention I had reserved for her and her alone. To occupy my mind, Solomon, the adorable character, insisted on teaching me the fundamentals of tracking and hunting, although he assured me these were not a woman's task. We camped out overnight. With Sol, there was never a fear we would starve or be prey to any animal lurking about. I had been told Aborigines were experts when it came to bush craft and hunting. I would not dispute the fact for one moment. I was treated to fish for breakfast. He speared it with a tea tree branch, then cooked it on an open fire; and despite complaints from me we ate emu and kangaroo meat on occasions, which I have to admit was pretty palatable. What on earth would Marcus have thought had he seen me? He couldn't stand a fox being killed, so the consumption of kangaroos and emus would have infuriated him. Emus were often cooked outside the house in a hole in the ground by the Aborigines. Sol made a fire in the bottom of the hole; the earth became hot and was covered with live coals. Grass and branches of shrubs were placed in the hole, then the emu on top. It was covered with boughs, grass, earth and a fire lit on top. The head and part of the neck were exposed. It was left until steam came from the mouth. This was a sign it was cooked. The emu was retrieved and allowed to cool for a day, then eaten. Looking back, I feel queasy at the thought of this fare, but I suppose it was no different to the lamb, beef or pork we had at Harrington Hall. Solomon was quite protective of me, especially when Stephen enjoyed scaring me with snakes or spiders. Nothing ruffled Sol. He was a great young man and taught me many things about how his race perceived life and death. It was a great comfort to me. Aborigines have a great respect for the earth and everything contained therein, and this in turn keeps the balance of nature even. They do not destroy it as we do! Sol's hunting skills with a boomerang were unbelievable. He taught me to throw it and 'take out' an animal or bird in one throw. I truly adored the man and we became close friends.

I waited in anticipation for the arrival of my furniture from England, which seemed to be forever in transit. I had given up hope, when, the day after the wet season ended, the road became passable. A huge truck unexpectedly arrived with crates containing possessions Stephen had carefully packed, and which had been collected from Harrington Hall. They had been delivered to a warehouse in Perth belonging to Edmund Remington until the transporters arrived to collect.

The piano Father had purchased for me was part of the delivery. I was anxious to establish which crate it was in. Stephen had again flown to Darwin to discuss business with Wally. Knowing he would be gone for two days, I asked the delivery drivers to unload the crates into the barn. Heinz prowled around inquisitively. I marvelled at how quickly my furniture was deposited and feared the drivers were anxious of Heinz's fierce demeanour. I forgot to mention that he wouldn't hurt a fly! I was anxious to see my piano and get down to constructive playing, before the first muster of the season. I asked Big Al and Tim if they would undo the crate and help me unload the piano. It had been extremely well packed and was in excellent condition considering the miles it had travelled. Once it was out of the crate, I stood and marvelled at it, shedding a tear in appreciation of the gift my darling father had given me.

'Mrs Masters, that is one lovely piano,' Big Al observed. 'I take it you are a pianist!'

'I adore my piano, Al!' I confessed.

'Ach! Play me a tune, lassie,' he asked, and I began to play 'Auld Lang Syne'. Together we sang with Heinz howling in accompaniment. It disturbed me that certain dampers in the piano were ineffective. I investigated. Extending my arm inside the piano frame I used my fingers to detect obstructions. All appeared well until I withdrew my arm. My fingers touched something. I explored further and, looking inside the piano, I could see a package taped to the frame. I carefully released it cupping the offending article in my hands. The item was expertly wrapped in padding. Heinz jumped up to investigate and Big Al was as intrigued as I was to know where the package came from, or what it contained. I stood hypnotised by the contents sparkling in the sun.

'Mother's sapphire and diamond necklace!' I exclaimed. 'How on earth did it get in here? It was stolen from the Hall on the night of my engagement to Mr Masters.'

Big Al was spellbound. My head flooded with thoughts about how it could have become attached inside the piano, when the piano had been purchased a considerable time after the robbery. Who was the thief who had access to my piano? He obviously wanted to get the necklace out of the UK. I reflected on events leading up to and after the robbery. The only disturbing conclusion I could come to was that the thief was my own husband. This instilled in me a hatred I didn't think possible. I asked Big Al if it were possible to put the piano back in the crate and secure it so that it looked as though it had not been opened. He offered to make as secure a job as possible. I re-wrapped the necklace and considered where I could hide it. Stephen used all parts of the homestead and I was at a loss to know where to place it. Hopefully he would think it had gone missing in transit. I thought hard and long about where to hide it.

The Treager radio was the answer. I unscrewed and lifted the back off and carefully taped the necklace inside so it did not touch any components. He would never think to look in there. I wouldn't confess to having seen it no matter what my husband did to me. I guess it was his intention to sell the priceless heirloom, leaving me high and dry once he had realised the money. My dear friend, Big Al, a source of protection, needed an explanation. I outlined the circumstances of the Harrington Hall robbery. He was sworn to secrecy. He was a good man; I knew without doubt I could trust him. I went to bed, with Heinz for company, wondering just what kind of monster I'd married. My mind wandered to the post office robbery in the Yorkshire village and the murder. Knowing my husband as I was now beginning to, I believed he was capable of anything. Paranoia on my part? I thought not!

He arrived home two days later and appeared exceedingly anxious when he noticed our furniture had been delivered; yet he was equally keen to offload the passengers from the plane, namely a stockman and a blonde bimbo known only as Ellie, who was to be his secretary. I had been demoted. He made no attempt to bring the piano into the house for two days, but Ellie was quickly installed in the office, and his bed. He adored ridiculing me in public as well as private, but I would retaliate when he least expected.

Several days passed before more stockmen and jackaroos arrived by truck and were safely installed in their sleeping quarters. Bindi and I concentrated on cooking. It was the following weekend before the piano found its rightful place in our sitting room. I was too busy to begin playing due to the extreme workload. Alone in my room that night, I tried to find sleep. I heard footsteps in the hall and climbed out of bed, opened my door slightly and looked out. By the light of the lamp in the sitting room, I saw Ellie and Stephen investigating the inside of the piano. His arm moved slowly along the frame, his face a picture of disappointment when he found nothing. He had Ellie on her knees, her long painted fingernails exploring around the pedals and the underneath of the piano. I wanted to giggle, but refrained. I had never seen such an entertaining performance. When they realised the necklace was not inside the piano, an argument between them ensued. They tried again, carefully searching every inch of the instrument, making sure I couldn't detect any sign that they had been searching for an object. This continued throughout the night. I hid under my bedclothes stifling my laughter. Ellie left by mail plane the following day. Perhaps she had been promised a sum of money for services rendered when he finally sold the necklace. He would *never* retrieve it to sell – *never*! The moods that followed were unbelievable. Stephen was his usual Jekyll and Hyde character, hitting out at everything in his path, including me, but I said nothing.

On his next visit to Darwin, Stephen returned with Eva. She was German and his new secretary. She would sit with him, at night, on the sofa, running her fingers through his beard, laughing at me each time I passed by. Bindi could not understand how I tolerated such disgusting behaviour, but I didn't care a damn and spent my spare moments playing the piano. As I did so she catcalled, but I continued to play. Stephen flew Eva to Darwin days later, with a purse full of money to allow her a two-day shopping spree. Leaving her at a local hotel, he returned to the ranch and allowed himself a drinking spree with the stockmen and jackaroos in their quarters. By midnight, when Big Al checked, they were all totally inebriated. I crept across to the bunkhouse to find Stephen lying there out of his mind from the after-effects of rum. How I despised him!

Safety razors just had to be the invention of the age. Removing one from my apron pocket I approached him, sidled up to him on the bunk and touched him. He was far removed from this planet and didn't flinch. With a bar of soap and a basin of water, I carefully removed his right eyebrow, trembling as I did so. He did not move. The removal of the left half of his moustache was even easier, although the right side of his beard was far more demanding. I removed as much as I could with scissors first. He sighed, changed his position slightly, but I did the job without waking him.

The following morning Stephen stormed into the homestead, anger written over his mutilated face. I faced him, trembled, and yet looked serious.

'Where is Big Al?' he stormed.

'In the stockyard,' I replied. 'Problems?'

He stormed out of the kitchen, slamming the door. Bindi and I roared with laughter. Later in the day I caught up with Big Al. Stephen had approached him in an aggressive mood.

'It was you, wasn't it?' he accused, waving his fist at Al.

'What was?' asked Al, keeping a straight face.

Turning to the rest of the workforce, he said, 'OK, so which one of you was it?'

'Me!' said a young jackaroo.

'No, it was me!' announced Tim.

'It was me!' said Solomon.

'It was me!' stated a stockman.

And so it went on. All workers by now were sick of Christopher Masters and his continual bad moods and unsavoury behaviour. What choice did he have? He could sack one or all, but could not manage without one single worker, as mustering was due to begin. Poor Eva! My heart bled for her. What would she do on her return? How would she cope with running her fingers through one eyebrow, a part beard and half a moustache? It was a strange situation. For over a week they didn't grace the sitting room. I played Mozart in peace.

Every day my thoughts would drift to Harrington Hall. I cried when I thought of Mother and Father, sobbed at the demise of darling Alex, and became anxious when my thoughts focused on Marcus. Had he eventually returned to the Hall to help? What of dear Ben? Daily I visited the grave of Anna-Sophia.

The thing puzzling me most was what work Stephen actually did. Everything fell on my shoulders. I knew the loss of the necklace was insufferable, although he tried not to show it, but it badly affected his moods. He continually took off in his plane. No woman he returned with lasted long. Maybe he was not the lover he purported to be, but a sad drunken gambler, whom I no longer cared for.

Leaving Bindi once more to ensure the smooth running of the homestead, I took my horse, Sabre, and accompanied by Heinz I joined the stockmen droving cattle down to the main gate, fifty miles away. We camped out overnight, Heinz and Solomon sleeping close by to protect me. Exchanging our existing herd for new stock, we began our return to the station. It was a problem keeping them on the move. They were slow and dozy. I knew Stephen would be angry if it took too long for our return. Finally reaching the house, I was saddle sore, tired and exhausted. I learnt on arrival that Stephen had been drinking and gambling our hard-earned money. I was desperate!

Talking at length to dear Al, Solomon and Tim, I confided I could no longer cope with life and had to get away. We conjured up a plan that would see 'Sky-High Pete' helping me escape from that godforsaken place. They all agreed I should leave Mr Masters. Bindi was in agreement too. Pete promised to take me on the mail plane. I intended going straight to the Australian police to explain my dilemma.

The scene was set. Stephen was on his regular 'away days'. I said my emotional farewells to Bindi, Al, Tim and Sol, and kissed my beloved dog, Heinz. And with few possessions and Mother's necklace in my bag, I made my way to the plane. As I climbed aboard, Heinz bounded up and sat whimpering, knowing I was leaving. I climbed down and embraced him. He licked my face and buried his head under my arm. He'd been my constant companion and had protected me from Stephen on numerous occasions. I couldn't have survived some of those situations without him. He knew more about me than any human. As his big, brown, soulful eyes looked into my face, I shed a tear. I could not leave him. Stephen would vent his anger on my dearest companion and would possibly kill him. I asked Pete to hand me down my bag and I returned to the homestead, replaced Mother's necklace inside the radio, retired to my room and sobbed. Big Al and Bindi comforted me.

The years passed, and more women than I care to mention graced my husband's bed and our home. Harrington Hall became a distant memory, but my homesickness never lessened. I had a life of sorts, and survived the only way I knew how, with the help of my dear friends at the station.

Chapter Twenty-five

Stephen had taken to disappearing for days at a time on so-called business trips, but in fact he frequented gambling houses and bars, spending more money than I cared to imagine. There were constant letters from the bank pertaining to the large loan he had and the lack of monthly repayments on his part, yet he continued to live far in excess of our income, while I worked unstintingly, keeping the station running smoothly. He was certainly not interested in me as a woman, for which I was thankful, but as a workhorse to cover for his inability to manage the day-to-day running of our business.

It was Christmas Eve, 1974, and I awaited his return with a certain amount of trepidation. The difficult times and lack of money were my biggest worry, and Stephen's drink problems escalated with the constant consumption of Northern Territory rum.

I had, with the help of Big Al, Bindi, Solomon and Tim, decorated the rooms of the homestead and cooked a special meal to celebrate Christmas in some small measure.

I focused on the sky as the weather deteriorated before my eyes. Grey-black swirling clouds appeared over the hills, and it looked as if the world had come to an end. Through the crackle and static of the radio I learnt that Cyclone Tracy had hit Darwin, reducing the town to rubble. My thoughts went out to the residents and the pain and loss that so many were experiencing. I received no communication from Stephen, leaving me in an uncertain state, not knowing whether he was dead or alive. Although circumstances were extremely difficult, I made Christmas as pleasant as possible for the workers at the station. A small part of me worried for my husband's safety but a large part of me wished that he would not re-appear in my life. I hated myself for the awful thoughts that ran around my brain about him. I soldiered on, Bindi supporting me in the house, Big Al organising what workforce there was, and Solomon seeing to other necessities. The inclement weather lasted for almost two weeks, and how we survived that time I do not know. I realised that if Stephen had been killed I would eventually receive news of his demise. At least it was a peaceful time, and I was not fearful that he'd suddenly appear drunk and physically or mentally abuse me.

It was three weeks before I discovered what had happened. The first I noticed of anything untoward was the sound of a plane passing overhead. At first I thought the mail delivery had arrived, but then I recognised the distinctive engine sound of 'Silver Lady'. Stephen was at the controls. He cruised down the runway – not his usual mad, acrobatic self, frightening the living daylights out of me, but an extremely sober landing. He climbed from the aircraft, which appeared battered and almost battle scarred and as I walked slowly out to meet him, wiping my hands on my apron, he pushed past me without uttering one word and hurried inside.

'Stephen, I—' I began, but before I could finish he approached the drinks cabinet and poured himself a large tot of rum. I acted warily, having experienced his menacing moods so frequently. This time he had taken on a distinctively evil persona. His facial expressions were full of hate for me and I was scared of what was about to befall me. He placed his drink on the table and threw himself into the chair which stood nearby.

I lied and said, 'I have been fearful for your safety.'

He appeared not to have heard me and stared ahead, downing his drink. He poured another almost immediately and downed that too. With his head rested in his hands he murmured 'Everything has gone! She's gone!'

'What has gone? Who has gone?' I asked, but he ignored me and consumed more rum.

'Just about everything!' he groaned, as he consumed yet another drink. He then folded his arms, leant on the table and rested his head. He didn't talk for a few minutes, but then he looked up and muttered, 'The paintings, the artefacts, all destroyed in the cyclone! Susan – she was killed! I have just buried her!'

I understood nothing of his ramblings. He quickly downed the rest of the bottle of rum in an attempt to blot out his apparent misery, but it eventually loosened his tongue further. He staggered up from the chair to fetch another bottle and opened it. I offered to cook him some food but he refused my offer, stating that he couldn't eat a morsel and just wanted to consume more drink.

I learnt things that day which would break my heart and sever any ties I had for the animal of a husband who had threatened, cheated, abused and humiliated me, destroying any relationship I could have had with my family in England. During his drunken stupor, he continuously spoke of Susan!

'I take it you are referring to Wally's sister, who I had a glimpse of a few years ago!' I asked.

'Of course!' he snapped. 'She's gone! Killed in the cyclone! What on earth will I do without her?'

I appeared puzzled and could not understand how the loss of this woman he hardly knew could affect him so much. The drink was talking. I sat opposite him at the table.

'I cannot see what—' I began, but he interrupted me, pointing his finger in my face, saying, 'You stupid cow! She was my wife, you fool!'

I thought I had heard incorrectly and said, 'Stephen, *I* am your wife! We've been married nine years.'

He laughed in my face, staggered from the table, grabbed the bottle of rum and carrying it, poured more into his glass, spilling a great deal of it. He slumped once more into his chair.

'You're stupid, Sophia! You always were far too trusting,' he hissed. 'I'm not married to *you*! I was already married when I went through our ceremony – to Susan, Susan Wilkins – your father's demure little secretary! Now she has gone! She was killed in the cyclone!'

He poured more rum, downed it in one gulp and buried his head once more in his hands. I did not understand his confession and reckoned he was just drunk and talking nonsense.

'You, married to Susan Wilkins? What a ridiculous statement!' I challenged.

He leaned over, breathing fumes into my face saying, 'Good old trusting Sophia! You always did let your heart rule your head! Never could see what was staring you in the… Too bloody trusting by half!' He sank his head on to the table and rested.

'When did you marry her?' I asked, desperation in my voice.

'Long before I met you! Susan was not like you. You were always contented with life. Susan was greedy – very greedy – wanted more than I could give her on an estate manager's wages.'

I suddenly realised she was the woman I had vaguely recognised on my first visit to Wally's homestead.

'But my father paid you excellent wages! He was a good employer!' I said.

'Not enough money, lots of debts… She wanted the best of everything. I had to get extra money… she was expensive to keep… so I took things from the Hall!'

'And because you had a greedy wife that gave you the right to steal from my beloved father? That makes it all right, does it?' I yelled.

In an instant it all became apparent. She and Stephen had obviously planned the Harrington Hall robbery, she having access to the Hall in her capacity as Father's temporary secretary, a position Stephen had recommended her for.

'My father was so good to you, gave you everything you ever wanted,' I said, trying to calm my sense of outrage.

273

'When I was in his squadron I visited Harrington Hall several times. It was wartime. I discovered how affluent he was when everyone else was struggling. After I married Susan it occurred to me I should have some of what I saw at Harrington Hall. I knew things about your father, things he wouldn't want Mary Harrington to know – bad for his image – disastrous for Alexander and Ben.'

'What on earth are you talking about? What do you know about my father?' I snapped.

He simply placed his finger on his nose as if to say, 'Mind your own business,' which infuriated me.

'So you pre-planned everything? You took my father into your confidence so you could steal from him!'

He laughed in my face and waved his fist unsteadily at me. 'And you were the icing on the cake, Sophia!' he sniggered. 'When I first approached Oliver, after the war – when there were too many pilots and not enough jobs – he sent me on an estate management course to get me out of the way so I could not cause trouble with what I knew. Then when Alex decided on a RAF career like his father, Douglas, I worked for your father in the newly vacant management position. Susan was living in Leeds and it was impossible to plunder things without me being under suspicion. Susan continually wanted more so we organised, with Wally's help, the post office robbery! Went wrong... so wrong. Simon Phillips came back – too soon!'

'So you killed your golfing friend for lousy money?' I snapped. 'God, I hate you, Stephen Howard or Christopher Masters or whatever your damn name is!'

He mocked me, which sent shivers running down my spine. 'So you see, Sophia, I can kill, no problem! You'd better watch your step, hadn't you?' He waved his empty glass at me and poured another tot of rum.

'See... to get at paintings, jewellery, antiques, had to make a play for you – get engaged, married! No one would suspect your husband!'

In a moment of hatred, I leaned over and hit him, first on the shoulder and then the chest. He recoiled from the blows, but regained his balance by grabbing my arm.

'Only problem was Alex! He continually got in the way. Saw how in love he was – with *you* – but soon sorted him. The snow was a good excuse... pushed him off High Ridge, Sophia darling!'

I could not believe his confession. *He had killed my darling Alex!*

I could stand him no longer. I struggled free from his grasp, opened the drawer and pulled out a kitchen knife. I wanted to kill him at that moment. He was turning me into the kind of animal he already was.

Before I could use it, he grabbed the knife, gashing his hand in the process. Blood trickled down my clothing and onto my skin.

'Didn't you... wonder... why I visited Alex... in hospital? Had to make sure... he didn't tell what happened... still, thank God he's gone – can't say anything now, can he?'

I loathed this evil creature and was filled with revulsion at the sight of him – a revulsion I had never known before! I shook with rage and sank to the floor in despair.

'On our engagement night... put sedatives in the bedtime drinks. Ha! Stored many paintings and jewellery... in furniture... knew no one would look there! It would eventually be shipped to Australia. Lots of other pieces were placed in the priest holes which you told me you had hidden in as a child... put them inside crates when no one was around. It was important after our wedding you agreed to emigrate... I could offload many items on the other side of world. This place is far enough from anywhere not to be found... or recognised. Gave Oliver false address – ha! Stay here until I got money from sales. Then sell up... leave you to go to hell!'

'Why don't you go now – right now?' I screeched. '*Go now*! You're the one who will go to hell!'

He pointed the blade of the kitchen knife in my face.

' 'Fraid I can't. Was relying on your mother's necklace to meet mine and Susan's needs... but en route someone stole it from where I'd hidden it.'

I managed to show no emotion as he made this statement. It was obvious Susan had followed him out to Australia and lived near Wally and Lizzie in Darwin, but had perished in the cyclone. Poetic justice, I thought. Many of the treasures he'd stolen had been damaged beyond repair in Cyclone Tracy. Wally was unhurt, from accounts that I gleaned, but Lizzie was missing, presumed dead.

'Where do I go from here?' he drawled.

As if I cared! I was so outraged that I shouted, 'To hell! To prison! Anywhere – as long as it's out of my sight!'

He released me and collapsed onto the floor. I wanted to kill him there and then, but that would make me no better than him. I picked up the kitchen knife, cleaned it and returned it to the drawer. As he drifted into a sleep where he had fallen, he said, 'You see, Sophia, once the British police realise it was me, they will suspect you too! Silly cow – you're in this too – right up to your pretty little neck! No going back to England for you.'

I could take no more and headed for the paddock. I saddled up Sabre and rode off. I did not know where I was going, but I rode until I found a spot of ground and threw myself from the horse. I screamed and flailed around in the thick mud. I wanted to contact the police, but who or what would they believe? Stephen was a charmer, and could talk his way out of any situation. I wanted him out of my sight and out of my life but how? I was trapped in a loveless relationship with this evil monster, and unable to leave.

Following the night of the horrendous revelations, Stephen and I lived separate lives, with me in charge of the day-to-day running of the station. The only item out of my control was money – which Stephen continued to lose at poker. He had also lost his sense of reason. No news was ever forthcoming concerning the whereabouts of Lizzie Jenkins, and I continually wondered if they would find her body in among the rubble as they continued clearing the devastation that was Darwin. She had apparently been visiting friends when Cyclone Tracy struck the town, according to the information Stephen gleaned from Wally, but she never appeared in our lives again.

I returned one afternoon in 1975 from work on the station to find Stephen in his office, making considerable changes. Radio Wyndham, our faithful Flying Doctor base, had closed and we'd been transferred to Darwin. For the past ten years it had been our lifeline, but everything had changed over the last year. I stared in astonishment when I found Stephen replacing our old Treager radio with a new two-way system with a push-button microphone. We were now in touch with the outside world on a 24-hour basis. Trying not to appear too inquisitive about the Treager's fate, I said, 'What a splendid new radio! What have you done with the old one?'

'Who wants to know?' he snarled.

'I just wondered,' I said casually.

'It has been thrown out – discarded!' he replied.

My heart sank into my boots. Mother's necklace, I thought. Gone!

I left him fiddling with his new acquisition and helped Bindi in the kitchen.

'You look upset,' she declared. 'What is wrong, missus?'

I explained about the new radio and how I'd been informed by Stephen that the old one had been discarded.

'Mr Masters, he gave it to Big Al to get rid of,' she said, winking at me.

I placed my arm around her shoulder and she could sense how anxious I was to find it.

'Where do I find Big Al?' I questioned.

'In the small barn. He has something important to do!' She smiled as she announced the fact.

I hurried out to the barn. There stood Al, looking immensely pleased with himself.

'I have thrown the old radio away,' he said, 'if that's what you have come to ask me.'

My heart sank, but he added, 'O' course, I kept this!' He waved Mother's packaged necklace at me.

'You darling wee Scot!' I joked and kissed his ginger beard. He laughed. 'You are an angel,' I told him.

He grinned and handed it to me. 'Aye, lass! I know what this necklace means to you!'

I hugged his enormous frame then slipped out of the barn, intent on finding a new hiding place for the priceless item. When the coast was clear, I discovered a new haven for the necklace. I returned it to its original hiding place on the inside of the piano, where Stephen would never look, not in a million years. I chuckled to myself as I realised that Schubert, Mozart and Handel would be in excellent company!

While the 1976 cattle season was in full swing, Stephen had an accident. He was mustering cattle with a new toy he had acquired, a Piper Cherokee plane, purchased with yet another loan he had secured from the bank, having eventually made satisfactory repayments from small winnings he'd had at poker. He misjudged some trees and crashed. He was confined to the homestead for four months after release from hospital. I dreaded having him under my feet, watching my every move. He had taken over from Charlie Tungate, spying on me. He continued drinking and yet his behaviour became more reasonable because of his dependency on Bindi and me. He knew that his outward respect for us was important. Once mobile, he pottered around the place and helped with small tasks. Having no woman to keep him company at night, and not being able to fly out and collect his 'comfort', he turned his attentions toward me. I avoided his advances like avoiding the plague. Work on the station was a top priority, with excessive amounts of catering taking up our time. I managed to avoid his nightly confrontations, the rum frequently loosening his tongue. One evening, he joined me on the sofa as I consumed my nightly bedtime drink, placing his arm around me. I shuddered and tried to move away.

'Ah, darling,' he said, resting his head against my neck. 'You have been so good to me, caring for this poor, injured body.'

He kissed my cheek and I moved my head quickly in the opposite direction.

'Come on, Sophia! You loved me once! Can't we get it together again?' he asked reaching for my blouse and placing his hand inside.

I pushed his hand away and stood up. 'No, Stephen! There's no going back, not now, not ever! I'm not here as a replacement for the tarts you can't get access to!'

'You sanctimonious bitch!' he snarled. He hit out at me, but missed.

I removed myself from the room, taking myself off to bed and locked the door behind me. I heard him pottering to and from the drinks cabinet and then stagger to his room, when he'd had his fill of rum. Thank God he was settled for the night. I crept into bed, having said my prayers. I thought of my family, praying that they would be kept safe.

My mind dwelt on Jonathan, wondering how and where he was. Suddenly, without warning, Stephen put his foot against the door with such force that he broke the bolt. Before I could lift myself up the bed, he launched himself at me and tore at my nightdress.

'Sophia, come on! Be a good wife!' he grunted, leering at me.

In anger and frustration I spat, 'But I am *not* your wife!' – which made him extremely angry.

'Damn you! I want you! Need you!' he slurred.

He held me, forcing himself on me as he lay on top of my body.

'Leave me, Stephen!' I pleaded and tried to push him away. 'No! *No!* Please go!'

I implored him to stop but he ignored me. With his heavy, drunken body pinning me to the bed, he finally did as he wanted. I tried desperately to fight, bite, kick and punch him, but he mocked me as he cruelly satisfied himself and his needs. Once he had got what he came for he removed himself from the room, taunting me as he went.

'You have forgotten how to make love, Sophia! You are useless, but then you always were! Give me a sexy woman – any day!'

I lay there quivering and afraid, totally humiliated and feeling nauseous. I took myself to the bathroom and scrubbed myself until my skin bled. I wanted to wash every trace of the evil monster from my flesh. I couldn't cry. No way would he ever touch me again. I would kill him first!

The following morning I arose early and went in search of my beloved Heinz to feed him, but he was nowhere to be seen, which was unusual. I assumed he had gone to work with Big Al. I waited all day. Just as the workers arrived for their evening meal, Big Al took me to one side. I left Bindi in charge of the catering; she was more than capable of seeing to the workforce. He rested his arm around my shoulders.

'Mrs Masters,' he said, his green eyes flashing, 'Can you come to the paddock with me, lass?'

I walked with him and ahead I could see my beloved Heinz, lying prostrate on the ground. I rushed forward.

'Goodness, Al, has he been injured?' I cried, but as soon as I drew closer I realised he was not injured. He had a single gunshot wound to the head.

'I found him in the bushes,' said Al, trying to comfort me amid my tears. 'It takes verra little to figure out who did this, lass.'

I sobbed into his chest. Stephen, the evil bastard, had taken my faithful, loving companion away from me, with just one shot from his rifle, for being unwilling to please him the night before. My only consolation was that Heinz had not suffered, as Stephen was a crack shot. Big Al and I buried him not far from of Anna-Sophia's grave.

I caught up with Stephen some hours later, but did not speak or give him the satisfaction of knowing I was heartbroken. I hid my feelings well, but I noticed he was sporting bandages on a large leg wound, which I later discovered had been inflicted by Heinz before his untimely death. Stephen left for Darwin the following day, to receive necessary treatment for an infected dog bite.

As I knelt at the grave where Anna-Sophia lay, I was approached by Tim, our New Zealand mechanic. He looked sadly into my eyes and said, 'Mrs Masters, we are all worried about you. We are more than aware of your treatment at the hands of the boss, and we think you should leave before he causes you more harm. With his increasingly violent moods, there is no telling what he is capable of. We've put our heads together and conjured up a plan for your escape.'

I was flabbergasted at his concern and that of my dear friends. We sat on the ground by Anna-Sophia's grave and talked.

'We can cope with Mr Masters once you have left, but our priority is to get you away from here and safely to Darwin.'

I thanked him for his concern but explained I had tried to leave on numerous occasions, without success.

'You can make it this time!' he assured me. 'Tomorrow, Mr Masters is off to Port Keats and will be gone two days. Solomon has to go by road to Darwin to collect some necessary supplies in the truck. Charlie Tungate has fence repairs to do a good distance away from the house. One of the jackaroos is going to dress in some of your clothes and sit on the porch, so Charlie thinks you are lazing in the sun. Meanwhile, Sol will bring the truck to the rear of the house and you can hop in and he will drive you with him to Darwin.'

It all sounded like a marvellous idea, but I faced it with a certain amount of trepidation, knowing that all my attempts to leave in the past had been thwarted.

After considerable discussion, I decided to give it a try. I knew I couldn't stay on the station any longer and I feared for my life. Eventually I agreed, and it was decided their plan would be put into action.

When Stephen departed for Port Keats, I packed a few items in a bag, enough to see me through whatever fate had in store – plus Mother's necklace which I retrieved from the piano – and waited for Sol to appear in the truck. The only light-hearted moment of the morning was when the jackaroo I knew only as Monty dressed in items of my clothing and placed himself on the porch with one of my straw hats framing his face. I laughed, and he acted in a girlie fashion to bring a moment of humour to the proceeding. Sol arrived. I said my farewells to Big Al, Bindi and Tim. They were emotional moments, as I was leaving my trusted and true friends. I promised I would seek them out at a later date, and thanked them for their care and love of me. Storing my bag in the front of the truck, I climbed in and crouched down until I was well away from the homestead. We travelled a short distance when Sol slowed down. I heard a familiar voice – Charlie Tungate.

'While you're in Darwin, get me some six-inch nails, Sol and lots of 'em!' he ordered.

My heart beat rapidly as I curled into a ball and sank to the floor of the truck.

'Will do, Charlie! See ya!' Sol replied, as he put the truck into gear and drove towards the road. We travelled a short distance and, when instructed by Sol, I unwound myself from the cramped position I was in and sank into the comfortable old seat that was to be my resting place for many hours to come. Bindi had prepared drinks, food and necessary items for the journey. Sol and I travelled a distance of 150 miles, with another 250 to cover before arriving in Darwin.

As we travelled Sol's eyes looked skywards.

'Oh, no, Mrs Masters! Get down on the floor of the truck! Mr Masters is in the sky above. He must have forgotten something. He's on his way home! He must not see you!'

I crouched down once more. 'Silver Lady' flew past and Sol breathed a sigh of relief as he turned to watch the plane disappear in the distance. I returned to my seat, breathing a sigh of relief. We travelled a short way before we again heard the drone of the engine. Stephen had circled back and was making a beeline for us. He flew so close overhead that it frightened us both. Sol stared above, then tried to keep the truck positioned on the road, but Stephen continually circled around us, swooping down in an attempt to frighten us. Sol gathered speed, taking his eyes off the road for an instant. Without warning he hit a large boulder at the side of the highway and lost control of the vehicle, rolling it over and over in the process.

I don't remember anything of what happened for a while. When I awoke I could sense blood trickling down my face from a head wound. I could hear shouting and screams. Stephen had landed the plane on the road. He'd dragged Solomon from the driver's seat and was giving him the beating of his life with his brown leather belt. Sol was in no position to retaliate. I could see he was injured. He had blood oozing from a head wound and injuries to his arms and legs.

How I managed to struggle from the passenger seat of the overturned truck I do not know. I climbed across the gearstick and driver's seat and out through the open driver's door. I hobbled to where Stephen was and surprised him with a barrage of blows and abusive language. He stopped inflicting punishment on Sol, who by now was lying semi-conscious on the ground, and turned his evil gaze toward me. He raised his arm in an attempt to beat me and then suddenly withdrew it and simply stared at me.

'You bloody bitch, Sophia! Do you ever think you can get away from me? Not alive, I can assure you!'

I didn't answer but ran and knelt down beside Sol, who I could see was in untold pain and misery.

'Leave your bloody Aborigine lover alone!' Stephen shouted.

'No, Stephen! He is badly hurt and he is *not* my lover. He is my dear friend! We're not all animals like you!' I yelled. 'Give me a hand to get him on the plane. He needs urgent treatment. Bindi will know what to do!'

'You stupid little fool! He's going nowhere in my plane!' he screamed. 'Neither are you!' He turned and walked off to the aircraft alone.

'Stephen!' I shouted. 'You must take us back! We both need treatment!'

He turned and screeched, 'To hell with you, Sophia. You got into this bloody mess – you get out of it!' And with that he approached the plane, while I shouted, 'Please, Stephen, don't leave us here. We're miles from anywhere!'

'Bloody hard luck!' he shouted. He climbed aboard the aircraft and, using the road as a runway, took off. He was completely mad!

What on earth could we do? Strangely, I was no longer scared, without

Stephen in our vicinity. I was calm with Sol by my side. He was badly injured and constantly repeated, 'Help me… help me…' I sat by him, comforting him, but knew I had to take action. I ventured back to the truck and reached into the compartment where the first aid kit was stored. It only contained the bare essentials, but sufficient to give temporary treatment to the wounds Stephen had inflicted. There were containers of water and food too, and blankets to keep us warm when night approached. I hoped and prayed that a vehicle would pass by and offer assistance. We needed shelter if we were to spend time under the stars. When Solomon had been treated to the best of my ability, I attempted to help him toward the overturned truck, so we could at least shelter in or around it. I continued to hope that a truck, plane or helicopter would spot us on the ground, but none came. I cradled Solomon in my arms and talked softly to him. At times I thought he was unconscious but when I removed my gaze I would find his huge black eyes staring at me.

'Sleeping?' I queried.

'No, missus, dreamtime!'

I did not understand him but knew that his pain had subsided quite dramatically. Not once did he complain. He was a credit to his people and had nothing but concern for me. As we talked of my family in England his shining, shrewd, penetrating eyes fixed on me and seemed to explore the very depths of my soul. Although outwardly anxious, I was calm and peaceful within, a feeling I had not experienced in a long while. He pointed skywards and I was amazed when I turned and viewed a beautiful rainbow in the sky – which totally took me by surprise, as we'd had no rain.

We continued with our conversation. He said, 'You have a dark-haired man in your family.'

I looked at him with a bewildered expression. 'How did you know Marcus had dark hair?' I asked.

'This man, he is close to you, blood ties…'

'No! Neither Marcus or my father are blood ties,' I revealed.

'This is a young man. He is close, a son, he will help you!'

'But I do not have— ' I stopped in mid-sentence. What on earth was I saying? Of course I had a son – Jonathan – but I knew nothing of his whereabouts and was never likely to set eyes on him in my lifetime.

'He will help you! You and he are as one. He will bring you much happiness!'

I looked intently at Solomon and realised he was delirious. I gave him further sips of water and then stroked his brow and mopped the perspiration from it.

Night beckoned. We were alone in the wilderness, not knowing what our fate would be, and yet a peculiar atmosphere began to surround me. I was not my usual scared, trembling, fearful self, but strong and fearless in the face of what had happened and what might be. Solomon, with his powerful aura, had instilled in me a peace I had not known in a long while. I wasn't scared about the outcome of our accident, and if I had to leave this earth that night, so be it. I would accept what was to come. At least I would not be alone. Night closed in around us, and I could hear the sound of animal noises in close proximity, but none came near. I stayed awake watching over Sol. He appeared to sleep soundly and awoke at daybreak, weak but alive. The sun rose and I knew that in no time we would be victims of its rays. We had sufficient water and a little food, but Sol could not walk. As I was administering more water to him, I heard a vehicle in the distance. A truck, similar to our own, drew up, and I immediately identified the driver as our mechanic, Tim. How thrilled I was to see him! He had brought along a jackaroo to help. They carefully laid Sol in the back of the truck; they'd had the sense to bring a canopy. I sat with him in an attempt to comfort him.

When we arrived at the homestead, Stephen was there and he was drunk. I knew I had to face him, yet I didn't care. I felt strong and in control of myself.

We settled Sol in a room where Bindi and I took turns to care for him. She was marvellous with herbal remedies and knew how to treat his injuries. He was so grateful, yet it was I who owed him so much. Stephen appeared later in the day, surprised to see us, and insisted that Bindi and I remove Sol to the bunkhouse; but I stood my ground, and in front of Big Al, Tim and Bindi, I insisted he stay put.

Within the week, Sol had improved dramatically. I feared that although Sol was gentle in some ways, Stephen had finally abused the wrong person. The morale from then on among the workers was at an all-time low, and they despised Stephen as much as I did.

Chapter Twenty-six

I understood from conversations Bindi and I overheard that I was the laughing stock of Masters Valley and beyond. The whole territory was aware of Stephen's female liaisons, and of one girl in particular in Port Keats. Paula was renowned for her bedroom skills and flaunted herself in my home and in the streets of her own neighbourhood. The workers could not understand how I continued to tolerate Stephen's behaviour. He deliberately introduced her into our lives at the station on numerous occasions. He arrived home the day before my thirty-fourth birthday and insisted on the trollop accompanying him.

I thought back to birthdays at Harrington Hall and the wonderful parties darling Mother had organised to make every birthday so special. There was music on Father's birthday, precious presents for Mother on her special day, and the lads and I were always given an exceptionally good time on our anniversaries. Now I was in the middle of this god-forsaken country, with no hopes or plans to make my birthday different from any other day. I don't suppose Stephen even realised it was my special occasion.

He and Paula arrived, but neither of them had the decency to acknowledge my presence, and she set about installing herself in the house as though she owned it. It was then that I decided that Bindi, Big Al, Tim, Sol and I could at least enjoy the following day together, and set my sights on making a delicious birthday cake. My favourite had always been the chocolate one Edith produced, and this is what I decided to bake. No candles, just lashings of chocolate icing and decoration. Bindi was an enormous help with the preparation of things. We made lots of party food and prepared the sponge mixtures. She seemed inquisitive that I intended making two, but I explained that chocolate cake was Mr Masters' favourite, and I would ice two so that there was sufficient for all the workers to have a slice. She was mildly disgusted that I could even think of allowing Mr Masters a piece when he didn't care a damn, but I simply said that all was fair in love and war!

He and Paula entered the kitchen as I attempted to ice one of the sponges.

'My favourite!' he exclaimed as he scooped chocolate from the bowl with the end of his finger. 'Yum! This is delicious! Paula and I will have a few slices of the cake when it's ready.'

'But it is my birthday sponge!' I announced and he frowned as he said, 'Your birthday? So how old are you tomorrow?'

'One year older than last year!' I pointed out sarcastically.

Paula helped herself to some of the food I had cooked, without giving me the courtesy of asking.

'Oh, by the way, I won't be here tomorrow. I am going away for two days. Paula and I are flying to Darwin to a boat exhibition. I am meeting Paula's friends and I may buy some sort of sea-going craft. I will be leaving first thing in the morning!'

As if I cared! The only thing bothering me was that he was again spending our money, but as I had no jurisdiction over our finances, I ceased worrying.

I struggled up to the top of the kitchen cupboard when I had insufficient icing to coat both sponges, and had to make a fresh batch for the second one. It was way past bedtime when I finished, but I had to admit they both looked superb. I was totally exhausted and decided to retire. I carefully hid the sponges. I did not want Stephen or the trollop snacking during the night.

I awoke quite early and ploughed into doing numerous jobs, before the sun began to rise. Stephen and Paula came into the kitchen later for breakfast, as I was icing one of the sponges with a '34', in white icing, followed by 'HAPPY BIRTHDAY!'.

'Well, cut me a piece!' demanded Stephen.

'Not at breakfast,' I implored, but he became decidedly angry at my refusal and took a carving knife and sliced the sponge in half.

'Please don't do that! You have spoilt the cake! It took me such a long time to make it!' I cried.

He laughed the smug, arrogant laugh which he continually used to intimidate me.

'Here, Paula!' he said, handing her a large piece. 'You have this, darling. Maria makes excellent cakes.'

She looked at me and with a sanctimonious grin, devoured the piece within two bites.

'Lovely!' she remarked wiping chocolate from her nose, mouth and chin.

I stared at them and showed them in no certain terms how upset I was. They had ruined the cake I had spent so long making for my special day. I began sobbing and ran outside. They laughed heartily at my tears.

In no time they had packed and flown away to the meeting with their friends in Darwin. I walked back into the kitchen to find Bindi surveying the few morsels that were left of the sponge, looking angry and dejected.

'Oh, Mrs Masters, how could they? Your lovely cake has gone!'

'Don't fret, Bindi,' I said. 'We have another cake for ourselves. Anyway, I don't think the pieces of sponge they devoured will sit too well on their stomachs.'

She gave me a puzzled look. I handed her two little wrappers from my apron pocket. One said *'Cleansing Herbs for those little constipation problems'* and the other read, *'Laxative Chocolate for inner cleanliness'*.

'I don't think their days out will prove much fun. You see, I added the herbs to the mixture, coated the sponge in laxative chocolate and laced the sponge mixture with liquid aperients to help things flow – and my goodness, they will flow! I think more time will be spent in the loo than anywhere else. That will teach our greedy pig and his trollop.'

We laughed hysterically as we imagined 'my husband' and Paula constantly running to the nearest loo if they even made it to Darwin before Mother Nature called.

The workers and I sat down to a wonderful thirty-fourth birthday tea, ate the goodies and savoured the chocolate sponge. It was delicious!

During 1978, before the approach of the wet season, it was apparent Stephen was coming to the end of any funds received from the sale of his ill-gotten gains. He had, from all accounts, a few pieces of my dearest Mother's jewellery to offload. I hunted high and low for the items, but could not detect their whereabouts. By this time in my life the only ties binding me to this awful creature were ties of extreme fear and daily I was anxious for my life. I knew once he had sufficient money he would leave, but not before he had 'taken care' of me!

I was listening to news from the radio when I heard a bulletin that astounded me. I had always been given to understand dear Lizzie had been killed in the cyclone of 1974. Listening to snippets of information, I heard her name mentioned.

'Elizabeth Jenkins, who in 1974 was reported missing by her family and suspected of having been a victim of the Cyclone Tracy, which destroyed much of Darwin, has been found. Her body was discovered by visitors at a desolate area in the Northern Territory. A post-mortem has revealed that she had been poisoned and her body dumped in undergrowth,' said the broadcaster.

I gulped. Wally! It had to be Wally!

Perhaps she knew too much about what Stephen and Wally had done. I was horrified and decidedly scared. I wanted to call the police but feared for my own life.

'We are looking for a man in connection with this case, which is being treated as murder. Police would like to interview Walter Symonds, formerly Elizabeth's common-law husband. Anyone knowing of his whereabouts should contact the following number.'

I couldn't stop to listen to the end of the broadcast. I ran to the loo to vomit.

I did not consider it strange when Stephen invited me to join him on a trip to Singapore, which I reckoned would serve a twofold purpose. It enabled him to be out of the country should the police connect him with Wally and needed to ask questions and it was his intention to meet with Edmund and Adele Remington, with the sole purpose of offloading the last of the items of jewellery. It was obvious I was needed to act as hostess while he attempted to dispose of the gems to Edmund. How I hated him and all he stood for! But any opportunity which presented itself for me to get away from the godforsaken station was a bonus, and it gave me a chance to plan another escape. I insisted we had separate rooms at the hotel, but this was not an option for Stephen, as he wished to monitor closely my whereabouts and activities, so his promise of twin beds had to suffice. We left Big Al and Bindi in charge while we flew to Darwin and then boarded an aircraft bound for Singapore.

On arrival we were transferred from the airport to our hotel on Orchard Road. No sooner had we booked into our room when Stephen began emptying the minibar.

Adele and Edmund arrived in the nick of time, and we left for supper in the hotel's revolving restaurant. After supper, Adele, decked in fine jewellery, chatted with me while the men propped up the bar. Adele, like me, was terrified of her husband, and consistently did as he instructed. The evening was peaceful, and when Stephen and I retired to bed, my trepidation of what he might attempt to do to me disappeared. He kept his promise to leave me alone and left our room at 11.30 p.m. to go on a gambling spree. Here was my one chance to telephone home and the police.

I called the reception desk and asked to place a telephone call to England, but was informed that Mr Masters had left strict instructions that no outgoing calls were to be made.

The bastard! I thought. Oh, well, Stephen. There are other days and other ways!

I retired to bed, slept well and did not hear him return. When I awoke the following morning Stephen was in his usual stupor from the previous night. I sat on the balcony and read for a while, then took a bath. As I was finishing, my heart sank as I looked up and saw him standing in the doorway, a towel draped around his waist. I was extremely vulnerable lying in the bath, but he simply said, 'When you are finished I will bathe,' and disappeared into the bedroom. I quickly dried myself as he re-entered the room and poured fresh bath water.

'Did you have a successful night?' I asked.

'Great!' he said. 'I won a little at roulette, and it looks like I've made a good deal with Edmund for the sale of *my* jewellery.'

His comment infuriated me. I did not stay around to listen to more.

'When you're ready, we will go down to breakfast,' I snapped, leaving him to soak.

We finally arrived at breakfast and were faced with the most delicious selection of food. It was a self-service affair. I walked up and down the tables, eyeing the huge selection. Stephen had finished his first course and was serving himself a huge English breakfast while I decided what I would have. I poured a tumbler of fresh pineapple juice and began putting muesli into a bowl when a soft voice whispered in my ear, 'I thought it was you, Sophia! Good God, it *is* you!'

Having been addressed as Maria Masters for so long, I was shocked to hear my true name mentioned. Turning, I came face to face with Molly Danvers, the village gossip from Yorkshire, who had been the first to notify me of the post office murder all those years ago. I just stared at her, utterly speechless!

'Oh, Sophia, where on earth have you been? Your family have not been able to contact you for years! Your father has spent a fortune enlisting the help of private detectives to try and find you! Where are you living? I will tell him I have seen you when I get home! Oh, it's so good to see you. I am visiting my son. He is stationed with the Royal Navy here! Oh, Sophia…!'

'I am in—' I blurted out, but a hand roughly grabbed my arm and a voice said, 'Come on, Maria! We must go!' Stephen had seen the conversation taking place and had left his half-eaten breakfast on the table.

'But Sophia—' began Molly Danvers.

'You are mistaken, madam! She is not Sophia! Her name is Maria!' And with that outburst, Stephen gripped me tightly and dragged me out of the restaurant, leaving Molly with her mouth wide open in amazement.

He rushed me to our room shouting, 'Pack your bags, you stupid little bitch! We've got to get out of here.'

Our clothes were thrown into cases. Stephen was rough and unrelenting. The bellboy arrived to collect our luggage and we made a beeline for the reception desk, where he asked to be booked onto the next available flight to Darwin. Stephen pushed me into the lift, as he stormed, 'Wait until I get you home. You will pay for this!'

We arrived at the main entrance, and as I turned I saw Molly Danvers talking to the concierge. She was pointing in our direction. Could she have been asking for details about us? Would they explain to her where we were headed? The taxi took us swiftly to the airport and within three hours we were airborne, leaving Edmund and Adele high and dry.

During the following months I succumbed to physical and mental abuse. Stephen blamed me for the fact that his sale of jewellery had fallen through. I continued hunting high and low for the gems in question, but nothing was forthcoming.

On reflection, I realised Stephen had purchased Masters Valley cattle station at a sensible time, but as crops failed in America, cattle feed soon commanded an extortionate price and the sale value of our cattle had plummeted to such an extent that we were continually fighting for survival. Any plans Stephen had of leaving me became less and less feasible, and he had resorted to living off the proceeds of the items he'd sold from the robberies. I had struggled on knowing at some stage we were going to have to find another source of income. It was then Stephen decided to turn a huge barn into sleeping accommodation for paying guests, with him providing – for a fee – trips across the valley in 'Silver Lady' as a lucrative sideline if he could curb his drinking and remain sober! They would also go horse riding, experience general station life and engage in aerial photography of the Northern Territory – in fact anything that would earn us a crust. Yet another bank loan was taken out by Stephen in order to finance this project.

Our first visitors were Heidi and Chuck Peterson, Americans from West Virginia, followed by the Bryant family from Adelaide. They were enthralled by station life and all it entailed. Stephen enjoyed taking them on trips in 'Silver Lady', and captivated them with exaggerated tales of World War Two exploits in Bomber Command.

He engaged in aerobatics, which went down well with male guests but frightened the females. It was certainly a good earner, having guests stay, and large tips were always forthcoming – not that they ever reached my purse. We were suddenly accommodating twelve people each week during the cattle season. I enjoyed meeting the guests, but the hours were long and exhausting. We employed extra help in the kitchen but new female staff always managed to find their way into Stephen's room! He insisted I did not get too involved in conversation with our guests, but I endeavoured to be a good hostess in spite of this. It took my mind off more pressing matters and provided light relief.

As the 1979 Christmas season loomed, we were expecting our mail delivery when an unknown private charter plane cruised down the airstrip. A man of approximately fifty years of age, medium in height, with a clean-shaven face, but slightly balding, alighted from the aircraft, followed by a young lad in his late teens. I ran over to them, thinking they had landed at the wrong airstrip. The senior passenger extended his hand and said, 'Mrs Masters? I hope you were expecting us!'

'I'm afraid not,' I exclaimed, shaking his hand in a warm welcome.

'We did send you a letter, which contained a cheque as a deposit for our stay.'

'I am afraid it hasn't arrived yet, but we do have accommodation available if you wish to stay,' I said.

He acknowledged they would like to spend a month at the property with a view to capturing the vast wilderness on camera.

'I am David Williamson and this is my son, Paul,' he announced. I greeted them cordially.

'I am pleased to meet you, Mrs Masters,' Paul said. 'My father and I thought we would take time out. I am on a year off work and Father has retired. We considered spending time together, exploring Australia, and here we are.'

'Well, I hope you will be happy with us,' I concluded. 'Follow me, and I will show you to your accommodation.'

Father and son were warm, friendly natives of Kent, in the south England.

'You do not have an Australian accent, Mrs Masters. I would say, by your complexion, you are an English rose!' observed David Williamson, but before I could answer, Stephen arrived and commandeered the conversation.

David and Paul Williamson began unloading luggage from the aircraft with the help of the pilot and Stephen. I noticed a violin case.

'Do you play this?' I asked David.

'I am afraid not, Mrs Masters. That is my son's domain. He is the violinist.'

'Mrs Masters plays the piano,' Stephen explained to Paul in a charming manner. 'You will have to accompany her, young man. We often have musical evenings.'

Do we hell! I thought. Stephen, with his frequent drunken antics would do his utmost to prevent me playing. However, occasionally we had guitar solos from jackaroos or stockmen and accordion sessions from Big Al. Now we would have a violin. How I had missed the authentic sound of the instrument, the sound I so frequently heard in days gone by when Father and Alex played together!

As we walked toward the visitor's accommodation I asked Paul, 'Have you been playing violin long?'

'Since I was five!' he explained.

They began unloading their photographic equipment and all the luggage needed for their stay. I left them to settle in and explained that lunch would be served at 1 p.m. in the house. I bade farewell to the pilot and ventured to the kitchen to inform Bindi there would be two extra guests for lunch, which quite excited her.

During the following two weeks, Stephen built up an unlikely rapport with David Williamson which, for Stephen, was unusual. He took him by plane to parts of the Northern Territory, enabling David to photograph wildlife and the wilderness.

Meanwhile Paul stayed at the station and I taught him how to ride. Within the first two weeks he attained such excellent riding skills that he rode with me often. I liked the young man immensely. He told me of family life in England, of his younger brother, Jeremy, of his dear mother, Catherine and his beloved Dalmatian, Lucky. For me it was an exhilarating time.

Catching up with me one morning, as I walked out to Anna-Sophia's grave, he asked, 'Do you object to me walking along with you, Mrs Masters? I notice you walk in the same direction each morning.'

'Why, no! I'm just on my way to visit my daughter's grave – although you are more than welcome to accompany me, if you wish.'

'Oh!' he gasped. 'Perhaps you would rather be alone!' But I assured him I was very happy to have his company. We sat on the ground, inspecting the wooden cross with Anna-Sophia's name engraved on it.

'These are wonderful names, Mrs Masters.'

'She was named after my darling mama,' I told him.

'Have you any more children?' he asked.

'No, there's just Mr Masters and myself.'

I confided that Anna-Sophia had been born severely disabled and had died after two days. I began to shed a tear. He touched my hand and said, 'I am sorry for you. You must miss her dreadfully.'

'I know she has been gone for eleven years, but I miss her as if it were yesterday,' I said, choking. 'Losing a child is the worst fate to befall a woman, whatever the circumstances. You never forget the child for one moment. They are with you during your waking thoughts and you dream of them when asleep. I was told I can have no more children. That is also a difficult thing to come to terms with. I will never be able to hold another child of mine in my arms.'

I continued fighting back the tears. Paul did not know what to say to console me and I apologised for the embarrassing situation I had placed him in.

'Think nothing of it, Mrs Masters,' he said. 'I am thankful I was here for you to talk to!'

We sauntered slowly homeward, this extraordinarily kind young man and I.

Evenings were spent around the piano. As I played, Paul accompanied me. He was an excellent musician. It reminded me of the days when Alex and I performed our music together. It warmed my heart to hear a nineteen-year-old with an outstanding talent.

'You should have been a professional pianist, Mrs Masters,' he observed.

'Don't make me laugh!' said Stephen in his usual derogatory tone.

He and David were drinking partners. David was not a heavy drinker like my so-called husband, but Stephen often ended up inebriated, and humiliated me in front of our guests in the process. I apologised profusely on his behalf, but they always kindly excused his behaviour.

Christmas with our guests was excellent. Big Al, Bindi, Tim and Sol joined us.

After further trips with Stephen to Darwin and Port Keats, David and Paul returned with expensive perfume or delicious chocolates, something Stephen would not dream of doing.

The wet season approached, and the Williamsons asked if they could stay until it was over. I warned them there was very little to do and we would not be able to venture far, but they were happy in our company and the friendship continued. David and Stephen were by now very close, and I feared that in his drunken moments Stephen confessed to David things he should not have been divulging. It bothered me a great deal.

The money earned from giving them accommodation was extremely handy, and they were more than willing to lend a hand within the house. I had to admit I enjoyed having young Paul around for company. He was warm-hearted and fun. I caught David on several occasions, late at night, writing up a diary of his exploits while supping hot chocolate in our kitchen. He carefully hid it as soon as I entered the room. I hoped he was not writing too many awful details about me to show to his family on his return to England.

Suddenly the season changed, and Stephen was off to Port Keats in search of new workers. My heart was heavy with the thought that the Williamsons would soon be departing. Our carpenter, Charlie Tungate, the wretched little Welshman whom I detested, was being paid sums of money by Stephen to spy on me while he was away. He frequently followed me around like a whimpering pup, and I was sure he reported back detailing my every move.

Stephen and the Williamsons took off in 'Silver Lady' for a trip to Port Keats and Darwin. I had reached an all-time low with the volume of work at the station, and the knowledge that David and Paul would be departing for England upset me. Bindi had me concentrating on more pressing matters, and put a smile on my face with her laughter. She was a tonic, and by the evening I had begun to feel life was worth living once more. At the evening meal the workers were ravenous and got through our haute cuisine in minutes, like an army of soldiers returning from an assault course. They were complimentary of the food, although I am sure several of the men did not know what they had hurriedly consumed. Charlie Tungate viewed me suspiciously across the table and watched my every move.

With the return of the Williamsons from their trip, the day was complete, until Stephen walked in. He was sullen, even before his meal, and sent workers scurrying from the table. He seemed hell-bent on causing trouble. I assumed his visit to the bank in Darwin had not gone well. He was verbally abusive but I managed to keep my head down and continued going about my chores. David and Paul sat at the table, Stephen joining them. He banged his knife and fork repeatedly on the table, indicating he wanted his food at that precise moment, but I made him wait until last, which did not please. Bindi served his food and returned to collect the plates from David and Paul.

When Stephen ate his first mouthful, he immediately spat it on the tablecloth, shouting, 'Rubbish!' He then made tracks for the drinks cabinet, where he consumed two tots of rum, one after the other. He returned to the table and poured another. He shouted, 'Trying to poison me with your food, Maria?'

If only I dared, I thought.

He returned to the drinks cabinet and poured himself some whisky. David followed him across the room, saying, 'Come on, Chris! I think you've had enough!'

'*Enough*? Who are you to tell me I've had enough?' David tried unsuccessfully to reason with him, but Stephen downed glass after glass until he finally slumped across the table. I was embarrassed, not only for myself but for young Paul.

With Paul's help, David dragged Stephen into the bedroom, where he flaked out on his bed in yet another drunken stupor. At least no physical and mental abuse would be forthcoming, and for that I was thankful. David and Paul helped wash dishes and tidy the kitchen, and insisted I ate a small meal. They watched over me until I consumed it. Bindi was given the rest of the evening off to do as she pleased. These Englishmen were my silver linings. David soon fell asleep in the armchair and Paul disappeared to his sleeping quarters, returning with his violin.

'Shall we make music, Mrs Masters?' he asked.

This wonderful young man was my lifeline. He adored music as much as me. Surely my guardian angels had sent him to me to save me from insanity! Around the piano, we sang and played English and Irish melodies. David awoke and joined in. Paul could make his violin talk. David had an excellent singing voice, inherited from his Welsh ancestors. Bindi returned and joined in too.

By 10 p.m. we were exhausted and slumped into easy chairs. David retired to bed, and Paul chatted in his usual attentive fashion. He explained he intended making a career of the violin on his return to England. I was pleased at this, and said so.

'You play the piano with such feeling, Mrs Masters. Why on earth do you waste your life here?' he asked, a puzzled frown on his handsome features.

'I have tried to leave on many occasions, but I have nowhere to go!'

'Go home to England,' was his reply.

'Paul, if only I could. I have dreamed of the moment for so long.'

He could see how emotional I had become. He was so young, so how could he possibly understand the implications of trying to leave?

'Stop putting obstacles in the way! You can't go on living with Christopher – it would be suicidal! We have seen how he treats you and observed the bruises you've sustained. Have you no family to go to in England?'

I had tried to project myself to guests as a brave, adventurous Englishwoman in this wilderness, but my defences were down and the wine I had consumed since dinner was overtaking me.

'Yes, I have a wonderful family, but Christopher prevented me from contacting them and gave false addresses to them. It has been thirteen years since we were in contact. It has been a cloak and dagger lifestyle.'

He looked inquisitively at me. 'I suppose it's just as well you do not have children to worry about,' he said.

My defences were shot down completely. In one second I began sobbing.

'I apologise, Mrs Masters. I didn't want to make you cry.' He tried desperately to comfort me, but crying seemed the only relief from all the pent-up tension I had suffered over the years.

'I have a son!' I confessed. 'A beautiful son somewhere in the world!'

Goodness, I had blurted out my well-kept secret!

'He would be almost nineteen now!' I added.

I saw a deep, painful expression on Paul's face as I related the story of Alex and me, of his accident, and of the convent and the Magdalene Laundry. Then I explained about my marriage to Stephen.

'My son was Jonathan Bertucelli!' I admitted.

It was the first time I had talked to anyone other than Stephen of his existence, but suddenly I wanted to shout it from the rooftops. Paul held my hand, and in that revelatory moment stated he and David would help me all they could.

'Don't tell Christopher I have confessed these things to you,' I pleaded. 'He would kill me!'

Looking at him, he reminded me of myself so much at that age: full of hopes and ideas, thinking I had life weighed up, when in fact I was not at all worldly-wise.

This very kind young man had allowed me to unburden myself, and he listened patiently and quietly to what I had to say.

'Have you never attempted to find your son?' he asked.

I explained that I had, but all doors had been closed to me. He commiserated.

It was late, and time we withdrew to our respective sleeping quarters. He bade me goodnight and put his arm around my shoulder, kissing me fondly on the cheek. It was the first show of affection I had experienced in a long while and I took it upon myself to throw my arms around this handsome nineteen-year-old, with his olive skin and black curly hair, and I held him close to me, wishing he were *my* son. How fortunate David Williamson was to have such a wonderful child!

Chapter Twenty-seven

I saw nothing of David and Paul for a couple of days. Again they had gone to Darwin with Stephen on one of his so-called business trips. Unfortunately, I was suspicious of David Williamson, although he was a pleasant enough fellow. I don't know what it was that perturbed me about the man, but he had become uncomfortably close to Stephen.

Meanwhile the station was a hive of industry. I endeavoured to keep the day-to-day running on a smooth and even keel. Without Stephen, it was peaceful and I did not need to worry that one step out of line would find me suffering at his hands. It was the last trip over the Northern Territory for the Williamsons, and in days they would be gone.

Stephen and the Williamsons returned. The plane flew low over the homestead, and in a wild moment Stephen came close to touching the top of the building, impressing his passengers but frightening me. They disembarked safely but the peace was soon shattered. For once in his life Stephen appeared happy, which was something I had not experienced in a while, and at least he was sober! David returned looking joyful, his camera in tow, leaving me in no doubt this amateur cameraman had acquired excellent shots of wildlife, aerial views of the territory, and some basic holiday snaps which he promised I would see one day. Paul had little to say except to enquire after my well-being. They both retired to their accommodation, leaving Stephen and me to catch up on matters relating to the business.

'Everything OK here?' he asked, making tracks for the cabinet to pour himself a double rum.

'Yes, everything, except for Sabre. I went to fetch him from the paddock yesterday, but he had cut his mouth rather badly,' I said nervously. 'The vet had to fly out and administer treatment.'

'How the bloody hell did that happen?' Stephen glared at me. 'More bloody vet bills! Did you *really* need to call him out?'

'Yes, Stephen, I did! It was an extremely deep gash. I could not have the horse suffering. He cut himself on a broken bottle!' I tried to play down the cause.

'Broken bottle? *What bloody broken bottle?*' His cheeks were crimson and he was spoiling for an argument.

'The one you threw at me when we last had a barbecue! Some of it was obviously left behind after we cleared up.'

He stood up, and I did not sense them coming, but I reeled from the blows as they reigned down on my face. I lost my balance and fell to the floor. Not satisfied with his latest humiliation of me, he kicked me, first in the spine and then on my buttocks. I tried defending myself with my arms, but they too received the brunt of his boot! He carried on hitting me with his fists, followed by his footwear. When satisfied with the pain he had inflicted, he walked out, slamming the door. How badly I handled the whole scenario. Why could I never learn that everything that went wrong was *my* fault? Almost immediately I fainted with pain and laid prostrate on the floor – for how long I didn't know. Eventually I woke, to find Paul kneeling over me, looking distressed.

'Mrs Masters! What on earth has happened to you?'

He helped me gently to my feet, placed me on a chair, and began examining the cuts on my eyes and cheeks. Blood had spattered onto my clothing, skin and the floor.

'How on earth did it happen? It was *him*, wasn't it?'

I nodded my head, my face desperately painful. I felt the room spinning around as I tried to gain my balance.

'He's an absolute bastard! You have to leave him! You have to!' he insisted.

I knew Paul was right! I had to be strong – strong enough to do something constructive to leave – but I feared he would follow me and seek retribution.

Paul cleared away the blood from my face, dressed my wounds, then drew up a chair and sat facing me.

'I wish I had arrived earlier this evening, Mrs Masters! I had waited until the coast was clear before coming to see you. I saw Christopher disappear with a few workers to go drinking in their bunkhouse. I think he'll be gone for a long while!'

'Thank God!' I whispered. 'Please keep him away from me! *Please*!'

'Wipe your tears, Mrs Masters. I have lots to explain to you.'

He looked at me with a doleful expression on his face, his eyes searching mine. For one moment I was mesmerised by his features. His warm eyes, his mouth...

For one moment I thought...

I stopped thinking and dropped my gaze to the floor, but Paul placed his hand gently under my chin and lifted my head until his eyes came firmly into contact with mine once again.

'This really is important, so you really must try and concentrate on what I have to tell you!'

'I am listening, Paul,' I whispered, but my arms, legs and body ached and I shook so uncontrollably that I had to take refuge on the sofa with his help. He insisted on making me comfortable and then we both concentrated on what he had to say. The door opened. David stood there, looking extremely smug. His mood changed when he saw my dressings.

'Don't tell me that swine attacked you! I will swing for the bastard!' he said, fury showing on his face.

Paul summoned him to the sofa, and with a man on either side of me I felt reasonably safe for a while. David took over the conversation.

'These last three months have proved the most challenging and rewarding of my career so far, Mrs Masters!' he announced.

'Career? What career?' I asked, having been told by Paul that he had retired and was taking time out with his son.

He continued, 'Mrs Masters, I owe you an awful lot of explanations.'

He pulled his wallet from his jacket pocket, opened it and held it close enough for me to read. I read the card and peered at the photograph within.

Inspector Williamson, Special Branch, New Scotland Yard? Oh, God, what on earth…?

'Yes, Sophia! I am sorry I could not reveal to you my real identity until now, but I was sent here by Scotland Yard, and with the cooperation of the Australian police I managed to book in here for a holiday with Paul, so that I could get close to Stephen Howard. Yes, I know who he is,' he said, looking at the puzzled expression on my face. 'We have been hunting him for years. By getting close to him I have collated sufficient evidence to bring an airtight case against him, for a murder in England and two robberies. We still have to find his partner in crime, Walter Symonds, but that should not be too difficult. There is a manhunt underway even as we speak.'

Years of torment and abuse were suddenly lifted from my shoulders and a great tide of relief came across me, knowing that the suffering at the hands of this monster was hopefully at an end. But how on earth would they manage to arrest him?

'I can assure you I had nothing to do with the post office murder or the robberies,' I said, my body quaking.

'We never thought for one moment you had,' David replied.

I spontaneously threw my arms around Paul in a state of hysteria. I cried! I laughed! Both men comforted me. I wanted to thank them for the part they played in the future arrest of Stephen.

'Of course, as you may already know, Paul is not my son. He came along to help me with the enquiries and collection of evidence,' David explained.

I looked at the young man and thanked him deeply for his help.

'It was my pleasure, Sophia. I wouldn't have missed this case for the world – excluding the anguish you have suffered, of course. I would have wanted to prevent that at all costs, but Stephen Howard is a sly one. He always manages to carry out his evil deeds when there is no audience. But now that we have evidence enough to convict, I am the happiest person alive.'

I thanked them graciously once more and said that I thought Paul would make a good detective.

'But how did you find us after all these years?' I asked.

'Oh, a Mrs Danvers contacted your father to say she had spoken to you in Singapore. The police contacted the hotel, were told where you were flying to, your name and address, and it was left for us to collect the evidence we needed to submit a case. Christopher – sorry, Stephen – is very talkative when drunk. We have some amazing tapes! Now young lady, we have a plan for your return to England, and for bringing in police officers to arrest Stephen. We do not want you here when that happens. You have to trust us to finalise the details so that Stephen won't suspect anything.'

I suddenly trusted them implicitly to arrange the downfall of the man I had lived with for the last fifteen years.

The scene was set. Stephen received a telephone call and approached me saying, 'What a surprise! I've just heard from the Sullivans. Richard has called to say he has a business proposition to put to me, and would like me to go to his station tomorrow!'

I tried to appear surprised at the turn of events.

'What proposition?' I asked.

'Something to do with a land deal. He wasn't forthcoming, but reckoned it was a once in a lifetime opportunity, so I am flying over there tomorrow.'

I dismissed the conversation as though I did not care, but knew that once he landed on the Sullivan property he would be arrested by the police. Meanwhile an aircraft would land at our homestead and remove me to Darwin – where, it was explained, I would face intensive questioning before being allowed home to England.

I did not sleep that night. My stomach churned. I was as vulnerable as I think I had ever been, waiting for the escape plan to unfold and praying nothing would go wrong.

I watched Stephen eat his breakfast, trembling as I did so. I had collected up as many things as I could, without raising suspicion, ready to throw into a bag as soon as he departed. He was in a strange mood; excited at what prospects the Sullivans had to offer and ashamed when he saw the injuries he had inflicted on me. I had once been in a similar state twenty-eight years previously, when Maura vented her anger on me for having seen her in bed with Greg, one of Father's farm workers.

Stephen approached me to apologise and make amends, but I withdrew from the room, not wishing to give him the satisfaction. I heard him leave the kitchen and collect his briefcase, then walk out to the airstrip. I watched from the window and with tears of relief hoped that this was the last I would see of him until I faced him in an English court of law.

Within minutes of his leaving, David and Paul arrived. I threw everything into a bag that I needed and waited for the aircraft to collect me. In no time I heard the roar of an engine and relief swept over me.

'This is your moment, Sophia! The plane is here.' David Williamson, a pleasant look on his features, helped me gather together my last few items.

'Would you see that this gets back to Harrington Hall, David?' I asked, and handed him Mother's sapphire and diamond necklace. 'Make sure it gets to my mother. I cannot see customs allowing me to take it through, but I am sure you can arrange it!'

He examined it and laughed. I had told him about it, and how it was my mother's precious heirloom that Stephen had stolen.

'I will see it gets home to England,' he promised.

The pilot of the aircraft entered the kitchen and I made myself presentable for the flight, although I found walking and moving very difficult.

'Now, Sophia, Paul is going to accompany you on the flight to allow you to feel more secure and less frightened.'

He could see I was shaking from head to toe and needed help on the journey.

The pilot suggested we make a move and I thought of Stephen flying into a trap, but I had nothing but hatred for him and wished for his early imprisonment. I said my goodbyes to my beloved Bindi, Al, Sol and Tim, and promised I would find them, wherever their futures took them. Sol gazed into my eyes and said, 'Your man will get what he deserves, I promise you!' and I nodded. We were all tearful, and I turned and walked slowly away when I could no longer cope with our farewells.

A very pleasant police officer helped me to the aircraft; I boarded it and slouched into the rear seat, Paul climbing in beside me. He placed his hand on mine and offered what comfort he could. As I sat in the aircraft beside him, I gazed out over Masters Valley. Hopefully, this was the last time I would set eyes on it. I turned to look at the spot where Anna-Sophia was buried and wanted to shed many tears, but thought of Sol and his view of death. It gave me great comfort. As he explained, she was not there in some forsaken hole in the ground, but in my heart, where she would remain always. Paul could see I was fretful and stroked my hand. He was wonderful! I would miss him. I was much more at ease having him accompany me to Darwin.

'Are you comfortable, Mrs Masters?' asked the pilot.

'Please call me Sophia,' I asked. 'My real name is Sophia Bertucelli, and I want to be known by *no* other name!'

He apologised.

'Will you return to Harrington Hall immediately?' Paul enquired.

I explained I didn't know how long I would be questioned by the police, having to explain about Stephen, Wally and Lizzie. I certainly could not venture home in my present state, bruised and battered from my last assault.

'We will not keep you any longer than necessary,' explained the police officer in the front seat, who accompanied the pilot, 'You will soon be returned to England and your family.'

'Does my father know I am due to arrive home?' I asked, but no answer was forthcoming.

After a fretful journey, Darwin came into view. I sighed with relief. Now I had to face some intensive questioning.

Instead of the formality of an interview room, I was taken to a four star hotel and given an extremely comfortable room, where I was able to take a relaxing bath and inspect the numerous injuries Stephen had inflicted. I may have been broken in body, but my mind and spirit were totally intact.

A woman police officer was seconded to me for my protection and occupied an adjoining room. She collected anything I needed for my well-being. An officer stood guard outside the door. The police were hospitable and understanding.

Paul was given a room in the same corridor, where he awaited David Williamson's return from Masters Valley. I would then learn about the success of the operation to capture Stephen and the possibility of his extradition to London to face charges. Wally was being hunted, as was Edmund Remington in Singapore.

Interviews took place within my room, where senior police officers from Darwin and New Scotland Yard amalgamated in their quest to bring justice not only to my family, but those of Simon Phillips and

Lizzie. Questioning was extensive and they left no stone unturned. I tried to remember as much as I could of what was said, and things that were not said but intimated at. I dreaded having to face Stephen in the courts in England, but it was something that had to be done, and he would go down for a very long time. Life, hopefully!

During the questioning, I brought up the subject of Alex, explaining that it had been Stephen who had pushed him to his death from High Ridge, but although they did not divulge their findings they were well aware that Stephen had been the perpetrator of the supposed 'accident', and were taking all this into account.

Within three days the questioning was over and I was free to go. WPC Daphne Jackson presented me with a passport in my name, containing a photograph taken days earlier, with make-up disguising my bruises. I was given an airline ticket for an overnight stop in Singapore and then a further flight to Penang, where I would stay for seven days to allow me to recuperate before the last leg of my journey to London, where arrangements had been made for me to be met and taken to my beloved Yorkshire.

As I finished packing my few things, Inspector Williamson appeared.

'Sophia – so you are free at last! How does it feel?'

'Marvellous!' I replied. 'I have slept so well these past few nights. The doctor has been wonderful and attended to my injuries, patching me up so I can face the flight to Singapore. How did things go, David? Where are you holding Stephen?'

He frowned and said, 'I am afraid we're not!'

'Oh, *no*!' I gasped, the news taking away my breath.

'Do not fret, Sophia! Let me explain. Firstly I must ask you what state Stephen was in when he left the station to visit the Sullivans.'

'You must have seen him, David! He was fine – excited about the prospect of business discussions. I had not seen him so good in ages. Why?'

'That is exactly what I thought! I am asking, because Stephen never arrived at the Sullivans. His plane went down en route. Investigations have shown there was no engine failure, no fuel leak, and no outside force, as we know it. The aircraft was recovered intact, as were these.'

He held out his hand and opened it. Mother's gems! The ones Stephen had been so intent on selling to Edmund Remington. So he had hidden them in the plane – the one place where I never got a chance to look!

He continued, 'Stephen made an emergency landing for no apparent reason, close to where he drove you and Solomon off the road. His body was in the seat, and they suspected a heart attack; but on closer examination they discovered he had spear marks in his torso. Strapped in his seat, we could not understand how he had the appearance of a spear having entered between his shoulder blades, which penetrated his chest and another which appeared to have entered under his arm, passing through his ribs and piercing his heart. But you will not believe me when I tell you there were no spears, and no means of access to the aircraft.'

'*Solomon!*' I gasped.

'What was that, Sophia?' he asked.

'Oh, nothing!' I said, but I remembered what Solomon had said on my departure: 'Stephen will get what he deserves, I promise you!'

'How very strange!' I muttered.

'Very! But I must not delay you. You will receive the necessary reports in due course! Now you must go, because your aircraft is waiting and we have to continue our search for Walter Symonds. He's still evading capture, but we have some new leads.'

He placed his arms gently around me, and I thanked him with all my heart for rescuing me from hell.

'Visit me sometime when you return to England!' I said, and he assured me he would. We parted company. As I was escorted from my room and was walking slowly with WPC Jackson toward the car that was waiting, a voice called me. It was Paul! He was standing there with his wavy, dark hair neatly groomed, clothed in immaculate shirt and shorts. I walked toward him.

'Thank you so much for your help and support, Paul. I would not have made it here without you! Please accept my eternal thanks and visit me when—' I said, extending my hand.

A voice called, '*Please*, Miss Bertucelli, your car is here and the aircraft will not wait. You *must* leave now!'

I shook hands and kissed Paul's cheek, then turned tearfully away and walked to join the WPC as Paul said, 'But there is something I need to...'

It was then that I heard a word that caused me to freeze on the spot.

'Mother!' he called! 'Mother, I am your son, Jonathan! Don't go! Please, I need to talk to you!'

I turned abruptly and saw him standing there, his arms outstretched. We hurried toward each other, my heart beating fast in my breast.

'Sophia! I am your son! I am Jonathan Bertucelli-Parker!'

'But you cannot be! How can you be? You are Paul!'

I cupped his face in my hands and looked closely at his features.

There was no denying that he favoured Alex. He took me in his arms as I looked into his eyes and sobbed. 'But of course. You have my black hair and your father's enchanting smile. Are you really the son who was taken from me?'

'I am! I can assure you with all my heart that I am – and very proud to be so!'

I held him close as the years rolled away. It had been nineteen years since I had held him so lovingly in my arms, stroking his tiny fingers and his soft hair, and promising I would make life good for him! And here he was all those years later facing me in a hotel corridor in Australia!

'But how did you know where…? Oh, there are so many things I need to ask you! I do love you, my darling. Not a day has gone by when I did not think of you or miss you! I loved you in 1960 and I love you just as dearly today. You were my firstborn, my special child!'

'I know darling Mother! I know! I cannot explain everything to you now, but I will visit you when I return to England.'

'Have you had a good life?' I asked, stroking his hair. 'I do hope so!'

He nodded, tears falling down his cheeks, he trying unsuccessfully to wipe them away.

'Have you been to Harrington Hall?' I asked excitedly.

'Yes! I was welcomed with open arms!'

'Sir Oliver knows of your existence?'

'He does! He was amazing!' he said.

'Is Ben OK?'

'Yes, he is fine!'

'Did you meet dearest Marcus, and my darling mother?'

'*Please*, Miss Bertucelli, we *must* leave!'

Officer Jackson took my arm and began leading me away.

'How was my beloved father? Was he well?' I asked, turning around once more.

'He was really good, Mother!'

'Why didn't you tell me who you were?' I asked.

'I couldn't! I was instructed by Inspector Williamson not to reveal my true identity. It would have been too risky. I will explain everything later!'

'Your love of the violin comes from our Italian ancestors!' I said, excitedly.

'I know, Mother. Laws in the UK changed in 1975 which allowed me to begin a search for you, and in doing so I learnt all about you and our Italian family.'

He explained he had visited Harrington Hall for the first time just as word came through from Molly Danvers. Everything snowballed from there, and my father paid his fare to search me out in Australia. He threw his arms around me and together we cried. I stroked his cheeks and held him close to me.

WPC Jackson had by now lost patience. '*Miss Bertucelli*! I must insist. The plane will not wait! You will miss your flight.'

With those words I released my grasp, and as I departed I shouted, '*I love you, Jonathan*! Please visit me soon!'

He nodded, blew a kiss, and with tears running down his face shouted, 'Safe journey. I love you too, Mother! See you soon!'

Chapter Twenty-eight

My pre-arranged stopover in Singapore for one night and then Malaysia for one week proved to be the welcome rest I needed. After a night at the Mandarin Hotel, Singapore, I boarded a plane for Penang. This was the icing on the cake, with a flight and hotel accommodation at Batu Ferringhi organised by the Australian police. I needed to recuperate before flying to Heathrow and the first meeting with my family in years. This was my sanctuary for the next seven nights.

Penang was exquisite, its warm, sun-kissed stretches of golden sand bordering the Indian Ocean. Coconut palms stood tall against the hotel façade, with no breeze to dislodge their fruits. Local Malaysian traders flocked to the beaches, selling their wares, whether it was watches, rugs, paintings, batik or other handmade artefacts. They adored conversing in broken English, asking about life in the United Kingdom, but I could tell them nothing of life there. They waved battered photographs of their families under my nose, eager to chat about their wives and children. I could tell them nothing of my beloved father, mother and 'the lads' of Harrington Hall.

During mornings at the hotel I visited the beach, reclining on a sun-bed, taking in the fresh air and the sun's rays. I kept my body well covered with cotton clothing, hiding my bruised, battered frame. After a lunch, eaten at the poolside, I visited Salma, a young, attractive masseuse. She had a treatment room at the hotel, and she came to the rescue.

'What happened to you?' she asked, on my first visit.

I shyly began removing my clothing.

'You poor lady. You been hurt! Did your man do this?'

'No, I am afraid I fell,' I lied, trying to cover my injuries.

'You not fall!' Salma was adamant. Her long, slender fingers pointed to my contusions. 'These are made by shoe or boot! You been kicked!'

I began to cry. She caringly helped me remove my dress, provided a tissue and assisted in helping me climb onto the couch, where I lay, discreetly covered by a small cotton sheet, giving me a modicum of dignity.

'You need help! Trust me – I make you well!' she said comfortingly.

What would I have done without her total care and commitment? Would she ever realise what an extraordinary human being she was, to have performed the healing miracles she did, on my flesh, over the following six days? Far Eastern remedies, combined with massages, were an answer to my prayers. Money and sincere thanks did not seem enough, but the young Malaysians are such a delightful race, and that alone affected in me the ability to adore her.

At night-time I sat by the lantern-lit pool and watched the sun as it set, disappearing below the horizon. I savoured Malaysian cuisine at its finest. I had gone from hell to heaven in just days. My mind fixed daily on Jonathan. I could not wait to see him and hold him close once more! As each day passed I became stronger. On the seventh day I was ready for departure. Salma was in reception to bid me farewell. I vowed that one day I would return with my family to visit her.

I settled in my economy class seat of the magnificent Boeing 747, ready for a 10 p.m. take-off, but the pilot and crew apparently had other ideas.

'This is your pilot speaking, ladies and gentlemen. I apologise for the delay in leaving the airport. I am notified by ground crew that due to engine problems we must ask for your patience while we address the situation. We hope to have you airborne and safely on your way to London Heathrow soon. Meanwhile I am sure the cabin crew will do everything to make you comfortable. Thank you!'

London Heathrow – it was music to my ears! That was where I had said goodbye to Marcus when he was seventeen and starting life in the London. He would be thirty-one now. I was newly married and on my way to what I thought was going to be a happy life, but the hopes and dreams I had were never fulfilled. What of Marcus? Did he realise his dreams, or did he return to Harrington Hall? Thinking of the shy, scruffy, frightened teenager, I could not envisage where he would be now. He had always relied on me so much for help and support in the past, but I had let him down when he needed me most. My mind drifted to Mother and Father. I wondered how they had coped with the loss of Alex. He had been far too young to die. I considered how they would react to my return. Would they welcome me with open arms? Ben would be thirty-five, like me. I longed for their closeness. In thirteen hours I would be in London, and hopefully someone would meet me and drive me to Yorkshire.

'Your eye shield, earphones and sleeping rug, madam,' announced the attractive Singaporean hostess as she handed me a package across the passengers to my right. I accepted it graciously. Condensation was forming on the bulkhead of the aircraft, sending droplets of water onto my shiny black hair. I had occupied the window seat and gazed out into the night sky, watching the lights of unfamiliar aircraft encircling the airport. Glancing down at the runway, I could see the ground crew racing against time to ensure that our aircraft would soon be airborne. I huddled into my sleeping rug, pulling it up around my neck. It was then I made a promise to myself I was going to live life to the full once I got home. I stared up at the luggage locker, knowing all the possessions I had were in a single bag above my head.

I was cold and tired. I pulled the rug even further around my face to protect me from the world and peered over, looking at the other passengers. My new-found freedom seemed too good to be true. I reclined my seat, raised a pathetic smile for the guy next to me and continued staring out of the window. I caught sight of my reflection, which did me no justice, and then fell asleep.

As anticipated, the aircraft arrived at Heathrow approximately five hours late.

I had become anxious that the person designated to collect me might have grown tired of waiting – and left. Those feelings were heightened when I entered the arrivals hall to find there was no one holding an eye-catching little placard with my name on it. How things had changed! There were new buildings and a different outlook. A row of seats nearby beckoned me. I sat on a seat and waited, hoping someone would eventually arrive to collect me.

Fifteen minutes passed and then a warm voice said, 'Hello, Miss Sophia! I apologise for not being here when you arrived. The plane was very late, so I went to get a meal.'

I had never been so glad to hear the voice or set eyes on the lovely face of John Roberts, smiling his inimitable smile. He had aged and his hair had turned grey, but he was a wonderful sight in his grey uniform and peaked cap.

'John! You cannot imagine how wonderful it is to see you!'

I threw my arms around his neck which surprised him. He reciprocated with a kiss on my cheek.

'There, there, Miss Sophia! We are all so very pleased that you are home!' he said, patting my arm as I shed a tear.

'Me too, John! I have waited for this day for so long!'

Picking up my small holdall, he asked, 'Where are your suitcases?'

'I have this bag – nothing else!' I explained.

I saw the look of astonishment on his face. He said nothing as he escorted me to the car park opposite the main entrance. I could not wait to sink into the luxurious seats of Father's Rolls-Royce, especially after the 'sardine in a can' experience of the economy class seats. John stopped by a Range Rover and opened the door.

'No Rolls-Royce?' I queried with a look of disappointment.

'Lots of things have changed, Miss Sophia! Your father sold his Rolls.'

'But it was his pride and joy!'

'He cannot drive now, miss,' he said as he helped me into the vehicle.

I chose to sit in the front so we could converse. We left the car park and joined a seemingly endless line of traffic.

'Is Father well?' I asked.

'As well as he can be, under the circumstances. He had a stroke three years ago and was unable to walk for a while, but manages now with a stick for support. He has improved greatly, but is not allowed to drive. We have this instead. It is more practical for me for driving around in.'

'I hope he is looking forward to my return!'

'Miss Sophia, he is over the moon. He has been a new man since he knew you had been found and were coming home. He searched for you for so long! We began to believe you were dead!'

'Dead? Well, John, in some ways I think I was! I have so much to explain to you all. But Mother must have found it difficult coping with Father's illness.'

We stopped at traffic lights. John turned and stared into my eyes.

'Of course, you do not know. Your mother caught pneumonia three years after you left. Despite the best treatment money could buy, she never recovered.'

John detected the look of horror on my face.

'We couldn't contact you, Miss Sophia!'

I felt sick, and asked John to pull into a lay-by so I could leave the vehicle and breathe some fresh air. He kindly obliged. I sat on the grass verge for half an hour, shedding tears at the fact I had not been with darling Mother when she needed me most!

I slept during much of the journey. As we reached the last fifty miles, John appeared pensive. I attributed his silence to the concentration needed to cope with the volume of traffic on the motorway. In the years I'd been in Australia, with little traffic to contend with, motoring violations were all too apparent on English roads, motorists rushing to and fro without time to breathe. John glanced at me often, observing the difference between the twenty-two-year-old who had departed to the other side of the world, and the mature woman who now sat beside him. I was thin, tired and shattered, like an old car in need of urgent repair. My stomach churned and my heart leapt at the thought of facing Father. I wondered how he had coped without his beloved Mary. In many ways I was thankful he had outlived her, him being stronger physically and mentally. Mother would not have managed life alone. How would he greet me? With open arms or distant feelings? Stephen had so much to answer for!

How had Marcus coped with Mother's early demise? They were very close.

The vehicle turned into Bakers Lane. Immediately I noticed changes. The perimeter of Harrington Hall was now marked by a huge brick wall, with electric fencing on top; no doubt a drastic measure after the robberies of previous years. There were huge wrought iron gates at the entrance, which were firmly closed. The gatehouse was occupied and the small garden well tended. With a remote control, the gates opened, and then promptly closed once we were through. I nodded approvingly and thanked John for driving me safely home. A dirt track no longer faced us, but crunchy shingle underfoot. Neat grass borders displayed daffodils, poking their heads through as if to welcome me. Wooded areas alongside the track housed carpets of bluebells. Spring had arrived at Harrington Hall, and so had I!

I had visions of myself years previously, being driven down the same path by Peter Smyth as the ambulance drove by carrying Papa to hospital. I had noticed nothing of the beauty of the Hall that day, but on this occasion I noticed everything, including the stray pheasant which ran dementedly across our path.

We passed Starbeck Cottages. How different they looked! Great renovations had taken place. I hardly recognised the landscaped gardens that Papa and I had tended. I observed that the six cottages were now one and named 'Starbeck Row'. I mentioned this to John.

'Mr Marcus's idea, Miss Sophia,' he explained. 'He has made many changes. All of them for the better.'

Dear Marcus! He had obviously taken to estate work and saved the Hall from dilapidation.

'Where do you live, John?' I enquired.

'In the gatehouse, Miss Sophia! Mr Marcus had it completely renovated for us.'

Our last part of the journey held more surprises. Stunning lawns framed the Hall. Bowls enthusiasts would have died for them. The Hall itself had received a massive facelift, restoring it to its former glory. It stood in all its magnificence, ready to invite all into its medieval interior. How thankful I was to be home!

John drove to the large oak front door, helped me from the vehicle and unloaded my bag. I had a flashback of me running across the lawn on the day darling Mama had been taken ill. Sir Oliver had accompanied me back to the cottage to lend assistance. What a terrible mistake I had made along the way, in marrying Stephen. However, those years were not a total waste of time. I had learnt so much and had managed to survive against the odds. I think I was a stronger, more understanding person, able to face whatever life threw at me.

Once inside the Screens Hall, John took my bag to my old room. He explained that Father would be in his study. I walked pensively toward the door, smoothed my hair and clothing and quietly entered. I noticed immediately the lack of tobacco smoke. Father had obviously been advised against smoking since his illness, and had complied with doctors' wishes. The only scents invading my nostrils were those of wood polish and aftershave. I glanced toward Father's desk. He was sitting in a wheelchair with his back to me. His hair was now grey, his shoulders slightly bent. I wanted to throw my arms around him, but he appeared to be asleep. I did not wish to startle him, so I turned and crept gently toward the door. He must have heard me and said, 'Hello, Sophia!'

In a split second I turned and was faced with a charismatic smile that could have belonged to only one person. Coldness invaded my body, from my head down to my toes. I could not speak. It was as if my life blood had drained from me and I became faint. I shrieked out, a long, desperate, piercing scream…

'*Alex*! *Alex*! Oh! A…l…e…x!

I collapsed on to the leather sofa, not believing what my eyes saw or my brain told me. Before me sat darling Alex, greatly aged, his face scarred, but still handsome. The sobs began; long, hysterical sobs. Tears revealed a woman cheated out of years of her life by a monster of a 'husband'. Alex wheeled his chair alongside the sofa and tried his hardest to comfort me. I wanted to hold him, caress him and kiss him! So many years had passed. He had possibly forgotten what we had meant to one another. I, on the other hand, had not! I could feel all those poignant emotions surfacing again from where I had hidden them for so long.

'Please, Sophia! Don't cry,' he pleaded.

'Stephen, the bastard, cheated me out of fourteen years of my life, Alex!' I cried, over and over. 'Things could have been so different!'

'Darling, Sophia, please don't be bitter. I should be angry too. Stephen took away years of my life and left me confined to this wheelchair. When I awoke and remembered what had happened, I wanted you here with me, but you were gone.'

'But when did you—?'

He interrupted before I could finish, saying, 'The day you left for Australia, I woke and uttered my first words. No one was more astonished than the consultant who attended me. It took two years before I could walk, talk and dress myself. I had to learn the basics again. I cannot walk now, but I get around the estate in an adapted vehicle and use the wheelchair at home.'

I controlled my sobs, having waded through half a box of tissues kindly provided by him.

'Let me look at you, darling Sophia!' His sad blue eyes explored my face.

'I have altered so much Alex!' I confessed, but he looked at me and said, 'You are still beautiful, but maybe a little more mature!'

How subtle and kind he was.

'I am not the man I was, Sophia! My health is not all it could be. I suffer seizures from time to time and experience awful headaches, but I manage to lead a working life and absorb myself into estate business. I am content – but what of you, dearest Sophia?'

I realised this was going to be the confessional of a lifetime, and I talked at length of my life with Stephen, of Australia and the friendships I had formed. The subject of Ireland came to the fore. I explained about life in the convent, and about Maura's intervention with regard to Jonathan, and her untimely death.

'Do you remember the night before your accident, Alex?' I asked.

'I didn't at first, Sophia, but gradually the memories returned. One day about two years ago, a young man telephoned the Hall. Father and I had a meeting with him, and he asked for you. I explained you were not here. It was then he admitted he had been born in a convent in Ireland and was taken from his natural mother when only a few days old. He said he believed you were his birth mother, and it was then I realised the young man was my son. Dearest Sophia, he is a—'

'A violinist!' I interrupted.

I knelt down in front of Alex, rested my head in his lap and cried. I cried for him, for Jonathan and all those lost years. He kissed my head and stroked my hair, sending tremors through my body.

'Does Father know all the details about Jonathan and me?' I asked.

'Yes, he does, Sophia, but do not look so worried. They talked a while. He is very au fait with the situation and has welcomed Jonathan with open arms. There are things Father needs to tell you himself. Leave it until tomorrow. Tonight belongs to us, Sophia. Father wanted it this way!'

I lifted my head and looked into those doleful blue eyes, which had small smile lines.

'I really should have heeded your words about Stephen from the outset, Alex!'

'We cannot turn the clock back, Sophia. We must move forward and enjoy our lives.'

'I still love you, Alex. I have never stopped loving you,' I confessed. 'There was not a day that passed when I did not think of you and Jonathan.'

'I love you too, darling Sophia, but there is something I must tell you. You see, Sophia, I am married! I married Caroline Godber, the daughter of the owners of Witherington's, the Jewellers in York. You must remember her. She came to your engagement party to Stephen. We married just after Mother passed away. We have been married eleven years.'

I stood up abruptly, saying, 'Oh, Alex, I am so sorry. I have made a complete fool of myself. What on earth must you think of me?'

He looked up at me and, holding out his hand, grasped mine.

'Please, Sophia, sit down. You have done no such thing. I will not retract what I said. I loved you as a boy, as a man of twenty-one, and I love you now! I have never stopped loving you, but we thought you were dead. I married Caroline and we have existed together for eleven years; but those eleven years have been nothing compared to one hour with you!'

'No, Alex. We cannot begin where we left off. You have a wife, so please let us be good friends. I ask nothing more of you. Both of us have had enough heartache to last a lifetime!'

He nodded in agreement, sighed and said, 'Then come and meet Caroline. I am sure we can all be friends. She knows about Jonathan, and is not happy with the situation, but I am sure she won't let this affect our friendship. The least said about the subject to her, the better.'

With that wonderful news, we retreated into the drawing room for me to have my first meeting with Caroline Harrington, née Godber.

Caroline Harrington had certainly changed! She had once been a pretty blonde, but was now plump, with her fair hair hanging straight down to her shoulders. She had an extremely poor sense of style.

'Ah, Sophia! I don't suppose you remember me,' was her greeting.

She spoke with her back toward me, and I thought how impolite she was.

'I remember you well, Caroline,' I answered. She handed me a cup of tea.

'I take it you are going to have supper with Alex and me!' she said.

I thanked her and said I would be pleased to, if it were acceptable to them.

'Of course you will,' Alex insisted. 'We have so much to talk about.'

We sat a while and Caroline asked me about life in Australia, but I didn't wish to talk about one of the worst experiences of my life and certainly not on my first day home.

She glared at me and said, 'Now, let's get one thing straight! I know about this child you and Alex have between you. I am afraid I will not entertain him at Harrington Hall! He is a bastard child, and I—!'

Before she could continue, I stood up and, knocking my cup flying, said, 'How dare you, Caroline? Jonathan is *our* son, and it is not my fault he was taken from me. I never want you to refer to him again as a bastard child. He is a wonderful young man, born out of my love for Alex. If it were not for him, I wouldn't be alive now. He saved me from the brute I lived with. I won't have you talk of him in such a manner!'

'Sophia is correct, Caroline! Jonathan is my son too, and I will not have you speak of him in this way!' Alex added.

'While I am in charge at the Hall, I say who comes and goes,' Caroline announced. 'He is not welcome here.'

'But you are not "in charge" here, Caroline, as you so sweetly put it! My father says who can and cannot enter this place! Jonathan is his grandson!'

'Neither you nor Alex is related by blood to Sir Oliver. Therefore Jonathan is *not* his grandson.'

'I do not think my father will see it that way,' I retorted.

'And another thing, Sophia, I don't want you staying here at the Hall. If you think you have come back to steal my husband from me, then you are very much mistaken! He is mine, and that's the way it is going to stay.'

I couldn't believe what I was hearing from this vindictive, crazy woman.

'Your comments are totally out of order, Caroline! How dare you speak to Sophia in this way? It is not for you to say who stays here!'

Alex was exceedingly angry and showed it in no uncertain terms.

'I am so sorry, Alex,' I said. 'I cannot share a meal with your wife. She obviously hates me. I will retire to my room and tomorrow I will leave. I care about you too much to have you hurt over this stupidity.'

With my comment I passed a sad, furious Alex and left the room.

I hardly slept after the outburst from Caroline, but I sympathised with Alex. He was dependent on her for so many aspects of care. I wanted to search for Marcus and Ben. So far I had seen neither of them. Father was elusive too. It was with a heavy heart that I arrived down to breakfast, bumping into darling Edith.

'Sophia! How good to have you home, lass!'

She flung herself at me, surveyed my thin frame and passed comment on how undernourished I looked.

'We will soon have you built up again,' she stated as an elderly figure appeared in the doorway. It was my father, walking slowly, with the aid of a stick.

How he had aged! He stood there mesmerised by my presence. Holding out his arm he said, 'Sophia, my darling. It has been so long. Come here – I want to look at you! I began to lose hope I would ever see you again. Oh, God, how I have missed you!'

I left the table and ran to him, embracing him, holding my head close into his jacket. We hugged one another for what seemed like hours.

'Father, you cannot imagine how long I have waited for this moment,' I said, choking. Holding his arm, I guided him toward the table, poured him coffee and prepared him a plate of food.

'Not too much, darling! My appetite is not what it was!' He looked up at me and said, 'Let me look at you again, Sophia!'

I explained how saddened I was to hear of Mother's passing. He wiped his eyes as I commented on what a wonderful wife and mother she had been. We chatted and both had so many questions we needed to ask one another.

'Let's finish breakfast, Sophia. Then we will retire to the library. It is peaceful there. So much needs to be discussed!'

We finished our meal in silence. I helped him from the table, to his beloved library full of books, and sat him comfortably in one of his favourite chairs.

'I am so anxious to see Marcus and Ben!' I said enthusiastically.

Father could not take his eyes from my face. It was as though he were dreaming.

'Ben is married to Marianne,' he explained. 'They have a daughter, Rosie, who is eight. Ben manages the carpet factories. Marianne is an excellent wife. She supports him wholeheartedly. You will have seen Alex last night. His recovery is nothing short of a miracle, but his wife is a tyrant. I have never disliked anyone so much!' he commented.

I told him about my altercation with her and mentioned that she had asked me to leave the Hall.

'Pay no attention to her, darling,' he said bluntly.

'I cannot stay, Father. She will make Alex's life a misery. I do not want that.'

Father promised to arrange alternative accommodation for me on the estate.

'Now, Sophia, I have met your son, Jonathan!'

My cheeks became flushed and my heart beat rapidly. I explained about Alex and me, and what had happened when I went to Ireland under the auspices of Maura. I described having met Jonathan in Australia without having a clue who he was, although he had stayed in the homestead for two months.

'He is so wonderful, Father!' I said enthusiastically.

'You should have told me at the time that you were pregnant, Sophia. We could have worked something out.'

I explained it was not my wish to have brought shame on the family, and resorted to taking help from Maura. I apologised for the fact Stephen had stolen so many things from the Hall, and said that I had luckily retrieved Mother's necklace, which I hoped was now in his possession. It was, and the other gems too. A few items had been returned to Father over the years, by the police, but his favourite paintings were still missing.

'Father, Maura told me something before she died. I think now is a good time to ask you if what she said is true. Stephen also hinted of a… situation between you and him.'

He looked at me and was transfixed. I realised he knew what I intended asking.

'Firstly, you are going to ask if your mama and I were lovers.'

'Yes, I really would like to know,' I pleaded.

'Sophia, there is so much I need to explain to you, so that you won't get the wrong impression of myself or your mama. I have been writing my memoirs, hopefully for you to read. It covers my war exploits and those of other members of my crew. It also covers the relationship between your mama and me. In it there are also revelations about my friendship with Douglas Hastings, Alex's father and the subsequent hell that Stephen Howard put me through, because he thought he knew about the background to our friendship. He was hell-bent on causing trouble. You shall have it to read before too long. I think you will be able to relate to your relationship with Alex now you have grown older and wiser. It was history repeating itself.'

I seated myself comfortably as Father began relating the circumstances of his closeness to Mama.

'Sophia, I was a twelve-year-old on holiday in Cremona, Italy, with my father James and my stepmother Constance. My father was an ardent violinist and insisted that I learn the instrument from an early age. He was intent on obtaining the best violins money could buy, so we visited the home of the Stradivarius. I was more intent on purchasing a box of the famous nougat the Italians produce than an instrument, and while Mother and Father viewed the bell tower, the Terrazzo, I stole into the confectionary shop to buy some. As I left the shop I was apprehended by a small, dark, curly-headed child with amazing big brown eyes and olive skin. She tugged at my trousers and with tears streaming down her cheeks, she sobbed, "*Mi sono smarrita!*"

'I did not know how to answer. My understanding of Italian was non-existent. She wiped her tears with her tiny hand as I removed a handkerchief from my pocket and handed it to her. I tried to explain I could not speak Italian but she repeated, "*Mi sono smarrita!*" and continued to weep.

'I offered her a piece of nougat. She readily accepted, but found the piece too large to eat. I removed it from her sticky fingers. More tears followed. As a last resort I gave her the box of nougat to hold, picked her up and transported her across the Piazza del Commune to my parents. Father was flabbergasted at the sight of me holding a small child and asked where I had found her. He chastised me greatly for having carried her from the said spot. Once more she said, "*Mi sono smarrita*". Father understood that she was explaining she was lost. My parents thought she was the most beautiful child they'd ever seen.

' "*Come ti chiami?*" Father asked in Italian, and the child answered, "Anna!"

'Father took her in his arms and insisted we return to where I had found her. He suggested looking for a policeman. As we were crossing the Piazza del Commune, a voice from behind shouted, "Anna! Anna!"

'Constance, Father and I turned and were confronted by a lean, dark-haired stranger. The child held out her arms and called, "Papa! Papa!"

'She was handed over and gently rested her head in his neck.

' "*Molto grazie!*" said the man. He explained his wife was ill, and while he was looking after the child in his workshop she had wandered off. He spoke only a little English. Father and he conversed in Italian. The man was grateful for the return of his beloved daughter, and invited us to share a meal with him the following evening. He gave his address and bade us farewell.

'We accepted his invitation and arrived at the apartment off the main thoroughfare in Cremona. We discovered he was a violin maker. He introduced himself as Vincenzo Tipaldi. Sophia – he was your grandpapa! The small child was your mama!'

I listened intently to his story, anxious to know of my mama and her family.

'We were welcomed by your grandmama, Christiana. We had a delicious Italian meal, with plenty of Chianti to drink. On that night in 1920 a rapport was established between my father and Vincenzo. Father was invited to the violin workshop to witness violin making at first hand, and was able to play the instruments for sale. He bought me the most exquisite violin, and a magnificent instrument for himself. After our return to England, Constance and Father kept in touch with Vincenzo and Christiana. We spent endless holidays in Cremona, watching Anna grow into a beautiful young girl. The last holiday took place when I was nineteen and attending Cambridge University. Anna was twelve. She was an extremely talented pianist. It was hoped she would attend the Conservatoire of Music in Milan. During the late 1920s Mussolini had begun taking control in Italy. It was becoming a dictatorial state. Vincenzo was increasingly worried how life would develop for his family. It was then my father suggested they came to England. Vincenzo's long time friend, Mario Bertucelli, was already in Ancoats, Manchester, but finding life difficult, so my father suggested they both take up residence on the Harrington estate. He would provide premises for their violin making. My father had extensive contacts in the classical music world and could put huge amounts of work their way—'

I interrupted my father, saying, 'Now I realise how Mama, an Italian, came to be living in Yorkshire. It's something that has often puzzled me. So your father was instrumental in bringing her family to England?'

'Yes, but not for the reasons that were initially mentioned – but that is another part of the story which you can read about in my memoirs. My father was a devious man who revelled in controlling other people's lives. Vincenzo and Mario set up a workshop on the estate in 1928 and lived happily at numbers four and five, Starbeck Cottages; Vincenzo with Christiana and Anna, and Mario with his wife, Flaminia, and son Alberto (who had been born in Manchester and had British citizenship). Alberto was later to become your papa.'

'So Mama married Alberto, and I was their only child?' I asked.

'Please, Sophia darling, try not to interrupt. I will explain all. Anna grew up here on the estate and went to the Royal College of Music in London when she was sixteen. Alberto followed in his father's footsteps, learning to make violins. Meanwhile I worked as a private pilot after university, which displeased my father greatly, returning to Harrington Hall occasionally. You will understand when you read my autobiography how it was I learnt to fly at such an early age. It was with the help of Douglas's father, "Pinky". We were all great friends – Anna, Alberto, Douglas, his wife Mary and I – in those days. Eventually, to please my strict father, I joined the RAF. A few years later war broke out. Alberto had enlisted in the army and I was seconded to Bomber Command.

Anna was by now a well-known and respected concert pianist, having travelled to America, Canada, Austria, and many other places in Europe. I must confess to you I had been in love with her since she was sixteen. I sometimes collected her from the railway station on her weekends home from the Royal College. I knew there was no chance for me in the marriage stakes, as her parents intended she should marry Alberto.'

As he paused, I asked, 'Was Mama in love with you?'

He looked at me sadly and said, 'Yes, but it was a difficult situation that we were both in. So many traumas happened regarding your grandparents during the war years, which you can read of when I have finished my memoirs. To add to her distress, Alberto was reported missing at Dunkirk. Anna turned to me for comfort and understanding during these devastating times. I was there for her when she needed me most. We were very close. Our relationship continued through our love of music. I continued flying missions over Germany and saw many members of my squadron killed and their aircraft destroyed. Believe me, Sophia, when I tell you it was a harrowing time. I was one of the lucky ones to survive the war. News of Alberto was not forthcoming, and Anna and I found comfort in each other's arms on my return after bombing raids. Alberto eventually returned, injured. Anna nursed him here at the Hall. The west wing had been turned into sickbays for wounded soldiers and airmen. She cared for him tenderly but would not marry him. In 1941 Anna agreed to perform at a piano recital at my base station. It allowed us an opportunity to see more of one another. We spent the weekend together; we were already lovers.'

Father could see the look of disapproval on my face as I asked, 'How long did this relationship last?'

'Until your mama died!' he admitted.

Father noticed the look of disdain on my face and reprimanded me.

'Please, Sophia darling, don't scowl at me in such a manner. I need to explain the situation to you so that you can understand.'

I began to voice my doubts about that but Father interrupted me.

'We had many intimate weekends together, your mama and I. One day I was prepared, with my crews, for a vital bombing mission over Germany. Anna and I had arranged to meet, as she had something important she wished to discuss with me, but I couldn't keep the appointment. My aircraft went down over Germany that night and I was reported missing, presumed dead. Anna realised she was pregnant with you, and had wanted to talk to me about what she should do. I was a prisoner, during which time I escaped once but was recaptured. Anna was told by my father I was dead. My father, separated, was in love with

Anna and wanted her for himself. When Alberto discovered that she was pregnant she had the offer of marrying him so that he could bring you up as his child, and your mother would not have to bear the shame and degradation that you did in Ireland.'

'What is it that you are trying to tell me, Father?'

The tears had begun to flow down his cheeks as he announced, 'You are *my* daughter, Sophia. You are the child of Anna and me and I love you with all my heart.'

It took time for me to absorb the news, yet in my heart I knew he and I had a bond that was so great, it was as if we were one. It all made sense. I could see why Maura had the wherewithal to blackmail him. He extended his arms and I fell into them as we embraced. I could feel his heart pounding furiously in his chest at the revelations taking place.

'I suppose our mother, Mary, never knew I was your daughter when you took me in?' I asked looking into his sad eyes and he shook his head.

'I couldn't bring myself to tell her, Sophia, and somehow I shall never forgive myself for that! Alex's father, Douglas, was fatally wounded and burned in his aircraft during the war – not killed instantly, as Mary was told. I managed to pull him clear but he died in my arms. It broke my heart. He and I had been friends since the age of six. I really loved that man. Part of me died with him that day. As he took his last breath he asked me to watch over Mary and his sons, Alex and Ben. I promised this, and after my return from prison camp, I saw lots of Mary and the boys – but I continued my relationship with your mama although she was married to Alberto. We were so in love, but in the end I was deceiving the man who was bringing you up as his own child. You had grown to love him as your papa, so I took Mary and the boys under my wing. I waited three years before marrying Mary, just a few months before your darling mama died. You are *my* daughter, Sophia, and I am so proud of you. You cannot imagine the number of times I wanted to take you from Starbeck Cottages and bring you back to the Hall, but I couldn't. Alberto was a gracious gentleman and allowed me to see you whenever I wanted. We remained good friends, despite the situation. He accepted it because he loved Anna himself. I never stopped loving your mama. I loved her then and I still love her now. I always will. Every time I look in your face I see her staring back at me. You have her hair, eyes, smile, laugh and her amazing looks. While you are on this earth, Sophia, Anna will never be gone.'

All these confessions took a great deal of comprehension on my part. Father trembled. Looking very frail and vulnerable, he buried his head in his hands. My heart went out to this man, whom I loved so dearly. I could relate his love for Mama to the love I had for Alex. No matter how many years passed I knew my love would always remain the same. I placed my arms around his neck as he rested his head on my shoulder and cried unashamedly. He seemed exhausted, yet relieved, at the revelations.

'These confessions make no difference to the love I have for you, dear Father. It is unconditional. You have been such a wonderful parent to me, and I can never thank you enough for what you have given me in terms of love, care and devotion.'

He looked at me with his sad brown eyes as he wiped his tears. He suddenly seemed so weak. I smiled and said, 'Come on, Father, cheer up! You can take me to see Ben!'

'I am very tired, Sophia. Would you mind awfully if I go to my room and rest? We can talk again later and then find Alex and you can ask him about Marcus! He can explain to you about him. I never liked his music, as you are well aware, but despite this his talent has proved instrumental in me being able to hold on to our heritage. He is the most marvellous, loyal son anyone could wish for, and I can assure you without his financial help we would have had to vacate Harrington Hall long ago. You were right, Sophia. His talent has been phenomenal.'

I was puzzled by his comments, but helped him from his chair, escorted him up the staircase to his room, settled him on his bed, and stroked his greying hair. Then, after placing a rug around him, I kissed him and went in search of Ben.

Ben lived in a newly-built Tudor-style detached house situated in the grounds. He was elated when I walked in. He and Marianne were planning a day out with Rosie. Rosie was a cute, pretty child, who had the distinct look of her grandmother, Mary, the same eyes, hair and features. Unlike Caroline, Marianne was a wonderful hostess and welcomed me with open arms, insisting on making me coffee. I refused her kind offer, agreeing I would catch up with them later.

'We are so thankful you are home safely,' Ben said. 'I knew there was something suspicious about Stephen, and after the way he treated you I cannot feel anything but revulsion for the man.'

I replied that I understood, and we mentioned him no further. Stephen's evil deeds had reaped poor rewards. He was gone. Now I could start my life again. I could shed no tears for him and was just thankful to be home.

Ben, Marianne and Rosie drove off for a day out together, and I returned to the Hall in search of Alex to ask where Marcus was hiding. Hopefully I would not fall foul of the dragon, Caroline, breathing her fire.

Chapter Twenty-nine

Alex was deep in paperwork, but was relieved to see me as I entered the study. I sat opposite him and we spoke at length about Marcus. Although I was sure Alex was not a great lover of the kind of music Marcus played, he was an ardent admirer of his achievements and began telling me about his life from the day we said goodbye at Heathrow until the present, and how his vast financial contributions to the estate had kept it alive and in the Harrington family. I was astounded by Marcus's career, especially since I thought he had returned to the Hall to help Father.

Alex apologised profusely for the jealousy Caroline had shown toward me the previous evening. I realised he was in a 'no win' situation, trying to pacify an irate wife, while endeavouring to find me suitable accommodation on the estate. I was grateful when he announced I could stay at Starbeck Row, a place I had not lived in since the age of eight. Marcus had taken over the six cottages and converted them into one large building, using the accommodation as a retreat from his hectic lifestyle, but he had not been home for almost a year. I gathered that he was extremely elusive.

How could Caroline have been so consumed with rage at my presence at Harrington Hall? She had been married to the love of my life for eleven years. Of course I envied her, but Alex was a devoted husband and in no way would I attempt to cause a rift between them. He seemed happy, and that in turn made me happy too. I made it quite clear that he should think no more of Caroline's behaviour, and the least said about the events of the previous evening, the better.

Alex handed me a bunch of keys and the code for the alarm system at Starbeck Row.

'It is a haven there, Sophia! Marcus rarely visits. He is too busy. I can't keep abreast of his movements and we're never able to catch up with him, but I know he will be happy you are using the facilities.'

I thanked him and stated I was truly grateful for the accommodation.

'You need not be grateful, Sophia! Harrington Hall is your home and you belong here.' He raised his tired eyes as he said, 'Sophia, if only life had treated us differently, I...'

'Please, Alex, don't even go down that route, it is all too painful!'

He understood, and with one glance we knew our love for one

another had not died and could flare up once more, given the chance, but neither of us could allow it to happen. The situation was indeed history repeating itself, I realised, as I pondered on Father's earlier revelations.

With the enormous bunch of keys, the programme for the alarm and my holdall, I walked across the lawns and entered Starbeck Row. I immediately stood spellbound at the outstanding décor, furniture and artefacts in the room, all with a North American Indian theme. I knew as a child Marcus had favoured the American Indian and was speechless at the tasteful way in which handmade rugs, vases and throws were displayed. Nothing bore any resemblance to the cottages I had known as a child. I was more than comfortable with the atmosphere of the building. Along the walls of the largest room were framed gold, silver and platinum discs. I paused at the first. One million copies sold of 'Now I Know She's Gone', Marcus's first number-one hit on both sides of the Atlantic, achieved at just nineteen years of age. There were numerous awards in huge glass cabinets and cupboards full of recordings of performances in the UK and the USA. It was too much to comprehend, but I would no doubt have plenty of time on my hands to watch and listen in the future. I thought of the day at Heathrow when he had pleaded with me to stay, but despite his susceptibility, introversion and lack of confidence in himself, he had as promised stayed focused on his music and made it to the top. I hoped my tuition and encouragement had played a part in his success, for I had always recognised his potential.

As I ran my fingers across the top of the picture frames, I sent specks of dust into the air. A woman's touch was what was needed. After unpacking my bag, I would see the whole place polished until it sparkled. On reaching the upper floor, I searched around for what I thought was Marcus's room and then chose a room from the other four available ones. All were beautifully furnished and carpeted. Each had an en suite bathroom, shower and toilet. I chose a room with a huge brass bed, and stared at the lavish covers. This was sheer luxury, and far removed from the old sheets Maura had made me sleep in as a child. The windows had fine drapes and there were magnificent views over the Dales. A few sheep grazed in the field – unlike my childhood days, when there were sheep as far as the eye could see. So many things had changed in the years I had been away.

Edith Roberts knocked on the door and arrived laden with food. She had baked me my favourite chocolate cake. I laughed, but she couldn't understand why. My mind crept back to my birthday in Australia and the chocolate cakes I had made. After a light lunch I ventured into the garden, picked armfuls of daffodils and forsythia, and arranged flowers for the rooms. I then began the task of brightening the place up. I donned an apron, picked up the polish and set about bringing a sparkle to each room.

By evening I was exhilarated at what I had achieved, and after supper I explored the cabinets and found a cine-film of one of Marcus's first television appearances in the UK. I managed to find the projector and screen and assembled them both. I watched in great anticipation his debut. My eyes were fixated. There was Marcus, in brown boots, check shirt, corduroy pants and a patched jacket, alone on stage except for his guitars, harmonicas, a piano and a chair. I would not have recognised him with his hair so long. He had grown it to below his shoulders and it shone like black velvet. His eyes were those chocolate brown soulful eyes I knew so well, and he had developed into the most handsome of men. His frame was tall and slim, and gone were the trademark spectacles. He played some songs on 'Soapy' and during the performance, introduced his guitar to the crowd, stating that an extremely dear friend had given it to him as a present, years previously. I could feel emotions stirring within me. His harmonica playing during the performance was absolutely unforgettable and instilled in me wonderful memories of his earlier teenage years when we composed and played our music together in Doggett's Barn. His inimitable charming smile was there and he held the audience in the palm of his hand for a whole hour. He had a wonderful, unusual voice, and sang his own compositions which were deep, meaningful and thought provoking. He played piano during three songs with tremendous feeling. Marcus appeared at ease with the audience and spoke to them between each number. He appeared very open and honest about his life and career. Marcus was a true artist. He sang his number-one hit, 'Now I Know She's Gone'. I really envied the girl he had written it for! She must have been very special, and maybe was his first love, but I knew nothing about his relationships or his personal life and didn't feel it was my place to ask the family. Maybe one day he would arrive home. Then I would be bold enough to ask him personally. Unfortunately there was a long distance between us. I did not know if I would even see him in the foreseeable future.

I received a telephone call from Inspector Williamson of New Scotland Yard, who informed me that even after all this time they had not been able to apprehend Walter Symonds and that they would continue pursuing him across Australia. For this news I was extremely grateful.

He seemed delighted I had integrated back into life at the Hall and would visit when work and other commitments allowed. He wished me well.

Caroline annoyed me at every possible moment. When I lunched at the Hall with Father, Alex, Ben and family, she created an awful atmosphere. I discovered her wearing the ring Alex had brought home for me the day before his horrific accident, which indicated she had rifled through the drawers in my bedroom at the Hall. When I asked for its return, she couldn't remove it from her plump finger and had to go along to her father's jewellers shop and have it removed, which almost ruined the beautiful ring. An argument between her and me ensued. I thought it best if I did not go to the Hall again for any meals. Alex was distraught at her behaviour toward me, and so was Father. Ben commented too. It was not like him to pass judgement, but he called her a 'conniving, scheming, manipulative bitch'.

I invited Lucy – the girl Alex was once engaged to – her husband and children to the cottage for a Sunday lunch. Alex arrived in his wheelchair to see them, accompanied by Caroline, but again an argument took place, with her targeting Alex this time, for wanting to spend hours in the company of his 'two ex-tarts'! The air was blue as he insisted on her taking him back to the Hall, but I noticed the delight on her face as she attempted to push him across the lawn. The woman was trouble, and I found it difficult to control my dislike of her or of the way she treated dear Alex.

Despite all Caroline's bad behaviour, life continued in a relaxed manner and I adored staying at Starbeck Row. I was busy gardening when I heard the telephone ring. I left my trug of roses in the flower bed, and with dirty hands I ran into the cottage and proceeded to pick up the telephone receiver. It was Alex, and he sounded devastated.

'Speak slowly, Alex. I can't understand what you are saying. *Gone*? Who has gone?'

He caught his breath and announced, 'Caroline! She has packed her bags and left me!' He was distraught.

'She helped me out of the shower, picked up her case and went! I cannot dry and dress myself and—'

'Please don't fret,' I interrupted, moving into action. 'I will wash my hands and hurry over to you straight away.'

Without further ado, I replaced the receiver, cleaned my fingernails, scrubbed my hands to remove every trace of dirt, and then scurried to the Hall to find Alex in his dressing room, looking cold and shaken. I hurriedly finished drying his body and his wavy grey hair, and hunted for suitable clothes for him to wear. As I finished dressing him he said, 'What am I going to do, Sophia?' His expression was one of sadness.

'I don't know, Alex,' I commiserated, 'but first things first. Have you had your breakfast?'

The answer was, 'No'.

I cruised down the stairs on Alex's stairlift, hopped off and soon reached the kitchen, where Mabel, a kitchen hand, was washing dishes. I asked if she could prepare a breakfast tray for Mr Alex, and coffee, toast and marmalade for us both.

By the time I returned to the dressing room, Alex had managed to struggle into his wheelchair. I pushed him to the table by the window in his bedroom, drew back the curtains and cleared the books so Mabel could put the breakfast tray down. Then Alex and I could share breakfast. It was a gloriously sunny day but he did not notice. He was deep in thought. When the tray arrived I poured coffee and passed Alex his favourite bacon, sausages and eggs. He seemed uninterested in the food but sipped the coffee.

'What I find difficult to comprehend is the fact that Caroline has gone off with Richard Hanson, a merchant banker, who has a wife and three children. He and his wife have been entertained here at the Hall on numerous occasions. His wife is a sweet little thing. What on earth could he have seen in Caroline?'

'Perhaps he likes dragons,' I quipped, trying to bring a little light relief into a serious situation. '*You* must have liked her once,' I added, but Alex explained it was she who'd set her sights on him. He realised, too late, that Caroline simply wanted to be mistress of Harrington Hall after Mother's passing.

'You see, Sophia, when you came back to the Hall, she was angry and felt threatened by your presence, because of our past relationship, Jonathan and our love for one another. I am as much to blame for having married Caroline, as I needed someone to take care of my needs.'

'So I am not totally to blame for the break-up of your charade of a marriage?' I said, smiling.

He laughed, and together we realised perhaps life would not be as dreadful without Caroline as he had at first anticipated.

'I saw the way Caroline treated you, Alex. She had no love or care in her soul. Perhaps now you can find someone to look after you who's concerned about what happens to you.'

'Could you arrange a private nurse for me, Sophia? Someone to live in?' he asked.

I explained I could, but it would mean having someone in the Hall on an everyday basis whom we would know nothing about.

'You are thinking about Maura, aren't you?' he sighed.

I nodded, and asked if it were not possible one of the servants could take on the role of carer, but he feared there was no one of suitable experience.

'Then *I* will care for you, Alex!' I announced.

He was shocked by my statement.

'Sophia, this is a twenty-four hours a day, seven days a week situation. I could not ask you to give up so much of your time to see to my needs.'

'Why on earth not?' I asked. 'Those are about the same hours I worked on the cattle station. If I could run that place, I am sure I could take care of you, Alex, no problem!'

A deal was struck, and after seeing Alex tuck into his breakfast, I settled him in Father's study with all the relevant paperwork and hurried to Starbeck Row to collect a few personal items. I would be able to move back into my old bedroom at the Hall. How wonderful!

Alex responded greatly to having care and attention lavished upon him, and we soon had a viable routine in place. Difficulty arose at night when he required a change of sleeping position in his king-size bed. The estate electricians constructed a bell system between his room and mine, my room being a considerable distance away. Alex suggested I move into the room Caroline had occupied for the last eleven years. I was amazed she had not shared his room since the day they married, leaving him to his own devices, unable to do for himself the tasks most people would not have had to think twice about. I was not happy with the change, simply because it had been *her* room, but it was a practical solution. Alex had all traces of Caroline carefully removed from the room, and her personal possessions were packed into boxes and stored ready for her to collect at her convenience. For Alex, there was no going back to his old life or to Caroline. He seemed quite relieved she had gone.

I moved my few belongings into the room, and while emptying my drawers I came upon two items I had forgotten were there: the nightdress and negligee Alex had bought me the Christmas of his accident. I had carefully stored the items in the hope I would wear them on our wedding night, but that day never materialised. It was an emotional moment, uncovering the beautiful silk bedroom wear, and it stirred up memories I had hidden away for numerable years.

Time and time again Alex explained how excellent my care and attention of him was and thanked me continuously. We obtained equipment for lifting him, and I enjoyed giving of my time and energy to this gracious man. For the first time in a long while I considered myself needed. Days passed, and with each day our relationship became closer. We were trusted friends, making the most of a very difficult situation, trying to bring happiness and purpose into one another's shattered lives. It upset me to see the once sporty, athletic Alex so physically dependant on others, but I knew he would cringe if I displayed one ounce of pity toward him. He needed care and attention, and I gave it willingly; but pity, definitely not!

Over the following months, his whole demeanour improved and he was noticeably carefree and happy. Gone were the anxiety and unhappiness that had been etched on his handsome features. At night I would settle him comfortably in bed, making him a cup of hot cocoa. The position he most favoured was lying on his back with his head propped up on pillows. I would sit in a chair by his bed and read newspaper articles to him or help with paperwork concerning the smooth running of the estate. He often found difficulty reading newsprint and printed books and reports, suffering double vision and extreme headaches, but until the night in question I had not experienced him having an epileptic fit.

I had settled him into bed and fetched his pillows. It happened without warning. Having had no dealings with such things I was totally shocked. I shouted for Haynes, Father's butler, who immediately acted. He treated Alex swiftly. His airway had become blocked, giving him cyanosis but he dealt with this, and when the seizure had subsided, he put him gently into the recovery position. We stayed with Alex for what seemed like ages, and when he had recovered he wanted to do no more than sleep. Haynes and I ensured he was comfortable, and then withdrew to our sleeping quarters. I learnt so many procedures that evening, and knew I could cope in the event of further problems. I prepared myself for bed and began reading a book. My concentration was non-existent. I crept into Alex's bedroom and checked that he was peacefully sleeping. He was. Returning to my bed, I once more opened the book and read the words on the page over and over. They meant nothing. I didn't have a clue what I was reading. I closed the book and turned out the bedside light, tossed and turned and continually worried about Alex. Nothing would pacify me. It was no good; I could not leave him. What if he had another seizure and I was not aware?

I crept into his room once more and quietly dragged a chair to the side of his bed and curled up in it. Two hours passed. As I catnapped I became cold and uncomfortable. It was then that common sense prevailed. I abandoned the chair and crept to the vacant side of the bed, lifted the duvet and snuggled under the covers. Alex did not stir. I rested on my elbow and watched him lying peacefully there. What on earth would be his reaction when he woke to find me in his bed? At least I was in attendance should he need help, and I would rest easily. I settled on the pillows and placed my arm across his warm body. It felt so good, making gentle, physical contact with this lonely man!

For goodness sake! I thought, 'Why are you feeling so guilty? You and he were once so in love. You had a child together! If circumstances had been different you would have been married to him by now!

I wondered what Father would say if he were aware of my actions or Caroline – damn her – or Jonathan. All I knew was that I loved this wonderful man, and being there when he needed me was my top priority. I would deal with the consequences of my actions as and when they arose. I slept for a considerable time, happy in the knowledge that Alex was by my side. He slept too, very deeply. On waking he lay there staring at me in disbelief.

'Dearest Sophia, what on earth are you doing in my bed?' he exclaimed looking so surprised, yet a trifle smug.

'I hope you are not cross with me, Alex,' I whispered as I placed my arm down his body in an affectionate gesture.

'Cross? Of course I'm not cross with you. This is absolutely wonderful.'

I felt his body tremble. I looked into his eyes, which were brimming with tears, and realised he too was stifling his inner feelings.

'My darling Sophia, this is the first time I have had the closeness of a woman since we shared those precious moments the night before my accident. Caroline did not share my bed!'

'I adore lying here with you, Alex,' I confessed shyly.

'And I absolutely adore you being here with me,' he murmured.

I raised myself up and kissed him sensually on his lips. He reciprocated with a long, lingering kiss and then eased me away gently. Gazing at me, he said, 'Darling, I cannot enter into a sexual relationship with you. You see, since the accident—'

I placed my fingers on his lips to interrupt him saying, 'I know, Alex, but it really does not matter. I have thought deeply about this.'

'But Sophia, I have nothing to offer you,' he said softly.

I peered into his soft blue eyes and said, 'Alex, you have already given me so much. We have a wonderful son together in Jonathan, and daily you show me kindness, love and respect. That is something I have not had in years and I ask for nothing more, if it is acceptable to you. I will love you as dearly as I know how!'

He nodded, tears trickling down his cheeks and onto the pillow.

'Good! Then I will take care of you, Alex, for the rest of our lives together.'

He clutched my hand tightly and we drew closer together. He enveloped me in his arms and we lay there, happy in the knowledge we had the love and companionship of one another and were together at last. How I loved this adorable man.

I was returning with Alex from his hospital appointment, John driving us in the Range Rover, when a small clapped-out Mini erratically passed us on Bakers Lane, stopping abruptly at the closed gates at Harrington Hall. We drew up behind the tiny neglected car. John removed himself from the vehicle in an attempt to speak to the driver, and asked what business he had at the Hall. By now the driver of the Mini had got out, and stood looking pensively up at the gates, scratching his head and wondering how on earth he would gain access to the grounds. Becoming aware of our presence, he turned, and I shrieked in astonishment. 'Jonathan! Alex, it's Jonathan!'

I opened the door and rushed toward him.

'Mother, dearest Mother, I am so pleased you are safely home and settled. You look so well.'

I hugged him affectionately. It was delightful, holding my darling son in my arms. What more could a woman want than to have her beloved man – and the child of that relationship – together at last? Jonathan looked lovingly into my eyes as John stood there in amazement at my outburst of emotion for this handsome young man.

I patted John on the shoulder and whispered, 'I will explain everything to you and Edith later.'

I took Jonathan by the hand and said, 'Come and see your father!' and led him toward our vehicle. John stood there in a complete state of shock at the mention of the word 'father'. Opening the rear door of the vehicle, Alex extended an arm and they embraced one another.

'We had an exciting meeting once before, didn't we, Jonathan?' Alex exclaimed, blissful at being in his son's company.

Turning to face me, Jonathan remarked, 'I am thrilled to be here with you both! I would love to stay over at the Hall with you for a few days, if that is acceptable to you, and of course Sir Oliver!'

Studying him carefully, John explained he would open the gates to allow him through, and we would follow him to the main entrance of the Hall. My father, having spotted the cars approaching from a distance, stood proudly at the entrance, leaning on his stick, intrigued by our visitor. John swiftly lifted Alex's wheelchair out of the Range Rover and, putting his arms around Alex, lifted him into the seat and wheeled him to the Hall. I excitedly ran to Father, dragging Jonathan with me.

'Look, Father. Look who is here at Harrington Hall. It's Jonathan, my son!'

Father stood there, captivated by the presence of this warm, kind, handsome young man. He held out his arms and drew Jonathan to him in an enormous show of affection and then, taking his arm, led him inside where an excellent tea was served. We all chatted about anything and everything, but I changed the subject on numerous occasions when Alex and Father referred to my time in the Northern Territory, and wanted to know what life had been like for me with Stephen. I did not want them to know about the physical and mental abuse, and discreetly shook my head at Jonathan when questions were fired at him. He understood! We spoke of Catherine and Robert – Jonathan's adoptive parents – and expressed a wish to meet with them at some time in the near future so that we could all thank them personally for the wonderful way in which they had raised our son, and to pacify them with the knowledge we were not there to take him from them, but rather to share him for a short while from time to time.

The following morning, after breakfast, Alex wished to take Jonathan and me to a place on the estate he knew we would find interesting. It was a short walk across the grounds, and Jonathan happily pushed Alex in his wheelchair to our destination. Alex directed us to the enormous buildings where estate vehicles were housed.

What a place to bring us, I thought. We entered and stopped to speak to one of the mechanics, and went to a part of the building which housed a magnificent blue Bentley owned by Marcus. We managed to squeeze past carefully. Behind the Bentley, there she stood in all her glory, just as I had remembered her – Alex's Riley! Memories of my teenage years flooded back. Jonathan and I stood spellbound by the sight of the beautiful cream Riley with its red leather interior, which the estate mechanics had attended for so many years.

Alex and I looked lovingly at one another as we watched Jonathan run his fingers carefully over the shiny paintwork. I smiled as I thought of the day when Alex had allowed me the honour of driving the Riley – under supervision – along one of the estate roads.

'Do you like my car, Jonathan?' Alex proudly asked.

Jonathan turned and with a captivating smile answered, 'She's a real beauty!'

He opened the door and peered inside.

'Your mother and I had some great times in her. We ended up in the middle of a haystack on one occasion – your mother was driving, of course!' he chuckled.

Jonathan was thrilled at being shown the vehicle and was hypnotised by it. Alex wheeled himself nearer to the car and remarked, 'Your Mini seems to have seen better days, Jonathan!'

'I'm afraid so, Father! It was all I could afford at the time, but it has served me well, getting me from Sidcup to the Royal College,' was the reply.

Alex stared at Jonathan, who by now had finished giving the Riley a thorough inspection and said, 'I believe, my son, that you'll soon be twenty-one, so will you please accept this car as a birthday present from your mother and me – with our undying love?'

Jonathan's face expressed utter disbelief, and he said, 'But I could not accept this splendid motor car. It is extremely valuable!'

'Look at me, son,' said Alex, appearing sombre. 'I am never going to be able to get into my beloved car again, let alone drive it! I am only going to have one son – *you* – so we would like you to accept this car from us!'

The look said it all, and Jonathan was ecstatic. He hugged and kissed us gratefully, and before leaving the building Alex arranged with the mechanic that the car should be ready for our son to collect the following morning. Meanwhile we returned to the Hall, where Alex arranged insurance so that Jonathan could drive the car back to the Royal College of Music. We were thrilled he could enjoy the Riley as we had done. He would certainly turn a few heads, especially female ones.

Chapter Thirty

It was midsummer and the estate was relatively quiet.

We saw little of Ben. He was taking considerable pressure off Father now, by managing the carpet factories which were still in existence. Jonathan telephoned and announced he had hired a large vehicle and would like his father and me to accompany him to North Wales for a holiday. He explained on his previous visit to us that he thought I looked extremely tired. My father had also expressed his concern that I was possibly 'overdoing things' and needed a rest. This was when his idea became action. He insisted on taking us with him to Wales. I tried to say that I could not manage Alex without his equipment, but he would not allow any obstacles (foreseen or otherwise) to spoil his plans. He said that with his help we could manage to care for Alexander quite comfortably. I had to admit we desperately needed a change of scenery, and after Jonathan confirmed to us that he had booked a cottage specifically designed for a disabled person, I was won over – his father too. The holiday came at a crucial time in Alex's life. Caroline had approached him via her solicitor for a 'quickie' divorce on the grounds of non consummation of the marriage. It was due to be finalised on our return, and respite from the solicitor's tedious letters would prove a blessing. We were off to Wales with our wonderful, caring son. On our return, Alex would be free from the institution he had known as marriage and agreed we would not discuss it or even think of it during our two weeks away from the Hall. Father was delighted we had taken Jonathan's kind offer, and we arrived in North Wales determined to have the holiday of a lifetime and that is exactly what we had.

Mount Snowdon was our first port of call, after we'd settled in to the comfortable accommodation. It was spectacular, and although I am sure Jonathan would have preferred to have hiked to the top, he graciously accompanied us on the railway. Snowdon, with all its surrounding scenery, was spectacular. The Welsh streams, mountains and waterfalls were magnificent. We were in seventh heaven. Neither Alex nor I had laughed so much in ages. Jonathan was quite a comedian, with an enormous sense of humour. He helped me every step of the way with his father as we toured and visited places of profound interest. The holiday was a resounding success, for which I was deeply grateful.

On our return the decree nisi was waiting and relief was experienced all round. Caroline could now move forward with her life and be with her merchant banker, and Alex and I could settle down to a happy, contented life, offering companionship and love to one another. It suited us both very well.

The following months were idyllic and we savoured every moment together, sharing and caring.

After a busy day attending to estate business, Alex and I settled down to a wonderful evening together, listening to recordings of Rachmaninov. I played for him his favourite piano concerto on the Steinway grand piano in the Great Hall. He had some of his favourite tipple, whisky, and was happy, relaxed and attentive. We were both at peace with the world and with one another. We retired to our bedroom at a reasonable hour but Alex sat for a while in his wheelchair, reading a book, while I showered and prepared myself for bed. I wore the nightdress and negligee he had given me so many moons ago.

As I appeared in the room, Alex gazed up from his book and said 'Sophia! You really look beautiful. Is that the—'

'Yes,' I cut in, 'the nightdress you bought me over twenty years ago.'

'You look astounding, darling! I am so glad you're wearing it! And it still fits!' he teased.

Laughing, I kissed him tenderly.

'Sophia, I love you so much!' he murmured. 'Thank you for the wonderful life I now have with you, and for your care, concern and adoration of me. Eighteen months ago I would have not believed it possible for me to be so idyllically happy, but I am, and I want it to last for ever.'

I knelt down in front of him, resting my head in his lap as he fondly stroked my hair. He lifted my head and kissed me gently on my lips. I responded by saying, 'This is not a one-sided devotion, my darling. You have brought such happiness into my life too, Alex, which I never thought could be. Nothing lasts for ever, darling, but we can savour the love we have for one another daily and treasure it dearly.'

I looked attentively into his mesmerising blue eyes as he caressed my cheek and I sat awhile as he enveloped me in his arms. Alex eventually decided he would bathe and I prepared a bath of warm water for him. With the help of the hoist I lowered him carefully into the water. I knelt and washed his back, kissing his handsome body. How I loved this man! Looking into my eyes he said, 'You have brought such excitement and comfort into my life, Sophia.'

'Alex, I love you more than you could imagine, darling,' I whispered as I continued to wash his gorgeous physique.

The bedroom telephone rang.

'I think you should answer it, Sophia! It may be important.'

I lifted myself up and glanced at his watch on the bathroom shelf, muttering, 'At this time of night? I think not!'

'If you don't answer it, you and I will wonder all night who was calling,' he chided. I handed him the soap and sponge and went to answer the call. The caller took my breath away.

'Caroline! To what do we owe this honour, at ten o'clock in the evening?' I asked.

In her usual arrogant manner, she asked where the items she had left behind in her room many months previously had been put.

'They are carefully packed for you to collect, but couldn't this call have waited until tomorrow?'

She told me it was her intention to stop by for them the following morning, and that she wished to speak to Alex when she fetched her possessions. Surely she was not experiencing guilt at leaving Alex so abruptly after so many months?

'I'm not sure there is anything he wishes to talk to you about, Caroline. There really is nothing left to say! You left Alex in a difficult state without a soul in attendance. That was a hateful and spiteful thing to do!' I reprimanded. 'You certainly owe him a profound apology.'

She explained she was extremely upset by her actions and wanted Alex's forgiveness, but reading between the lines I was afraid the relationship with her merchant banker was at an end and that she hoped to return to Alex and the Hall. I promised I would ask Alex if he would meet with her the following morning to discuss things.

'I must go, Caroline! Alex is bathing and will need my attention.'

I excused myself from the conversation and replaced the receiver. What a cheek the woman had! But I would speak to him, as promised, to see if he would converse with her. Perhaps it would benefit them both to clear the air. I collected two bath towels from the airing cupboard as I passed by and hurriedly returned to the bathroom.

'That was Caroline on the telephone, Alex and she wishes to… *Alex! Alex!* What is wrong?'

I leaned over the bath. Alex had slipped down into the water and turned blue. He did not appear to be breathing. I ran frantically to the telephone and dialled 999 for an ambulance. I was beside myself! The young woman on the other end of the telephone was extremely helpful and guided me through what steps I should take. An ambulance arrived in super-quick time and the attendants were fast in their actions. Father and Haynes had by now arrived on the scene, both horrified as we watched as Alex was laid on the bathroom floor, where they performed resuscitation on him. I paced up and down the room and pushed Father away as he tried to comfort me.

'He will be fine, won't he?' I asked the ambulance men. 'Please tell me Alex will be all right! He has seizures from time to time as the result of a head injury sustained years ago, but he always recovers after a while. *Please*, tell me he will be fine!'

One of the attendants arose from his knees, took my arm and said, 'I am so, so sorry, but this was not a seizure, my dear. It looks as though he may have had a brain haemorrhage.'

I sank to the floor in hysteria as Father bent and cradled me in his arms. With the help of Haynes and an attendant, he placed me on the chaise longue and covered me with a rug. Then he asked Haynes to call Simon Marsden.

'Father, he is going to be OK, isn't he? Please tell me all will be well with Alex. You know how much I adore him.'

Father looked at me with tears brimming in his eyes and said, 'Sophia, darling, you have to be very brave. I am afraid that Alex is no longer with us!'

I lunged forward throwing off the rug. I knelt beside Alex. *My Alex.*

I kissed him and talked to him softly and took his hands in mine, my tears rolling down his fingers.

'Come on, Alex. You are going to be well soon,' I whispered. 'We have so much living to do. We are going to have such fun together. We always have great times. I need you. I cannot live without you!'

Father tried to drag me gently away, but I shrugged my shoulders from his grasp. I kissed Alex's cold, clammy fingers.

'I love you, darling! Please do not leave me. You cannot leave me! I need you so much. What on earth will I do without you? Please open your eyes!'

Only a short while before he was professing his undying love for me and what we meant to each other, but suddenly common sense prevailed and informed me that the spirit of this wonderful, charismatic man had already left his body. A feeling of desolation and loneliness invaded my senses. At that precise moment I wanted to die too! I knew my idyllic world of happiness was at an end. I would never experience such contentment and love again. I buried my head in his chest and sobbed. I was inconsolable.

Within a short while Simon arrived to give me a sedative, and after considerable deliberation on everyone's part I agreed to take it to blot out the pain and devastation I felt. I spent the night in the bed Alex and I had shared, hugging desperately the pillow Alex had slept on only that morning. It had the distinct aroma of his favourite body oil. I slept deeply under the influence of medication, and woke to find Edith sitting by my bed, her arms ready to comfort me. It was indeed a consolation to be able to share my pain with this devoted woman who had shared so much grief with me in the past. She listened, although grieving herself.

'It is my fault, Edith! I blame myself for this tragedy – I shouldn't have left Alex alone in the bath while I answered the telephone.'

She held my hand and insisted, 'You mustn't blame yourself, Sophia! This sad loss is not of your making. It could have happened at any time, anywhere! You must live with the knowledge that you brought more happiness to Alex in the last two years than he'd had since his accident. We all commented on how peaceful and relaxed he was in your devoted care.'

I knew she was correct, but I could not face the reality of what had happened. I realised my idyllic life had ended abruptly. My head ached; my eyes were stinging from the many tears I had shed.

I asked her, 'Edith, what of Father? He must be traumatised!'

She looked at me and calmed me by saying, 'Ben and Marianne are with him. Yes, Sophia, your father is shattered. Ben has notified Jonathan and he will be here tomorrow. He also contacted Marcus's manager in Los Angeles, to get word to him. As you know, he is on tour somewhere in Canada. I expect he will fly home very soon.'

I knew in an instant I had to be strong for my father, for Jonathan and for Marcus, when he decided to grace us with his presence. Alex and Oliver had been so close, and Jonathan was just beginning to know his father. I was thankful that Jonathan had come into our lives when he did. At last he and Alex spent precious moments together, moments that Jonathan could take with him for the years to come.

I found life extremely difficult in the days that followed. Moving around the Hall I saw constant reminders of Alex: his wheelchair, his equipment, his clothes. I would stop and sit for hours cuddling his sweater, nursing it, feeling it close to my skin; but I knew I could not carry on in this way. After offering what comfort I could to Father, I asked if he would be upset if I returned to Starbeck Row. I needed time and space to be alone with my thoughts and grief. Marianne, Rosie and Ben moved temporarily into the Hall. I returned to the cottage, where I buried myself in housework, cleaning every nook and cranny, preparing rooms for the hasty return of Marcus. We were informed a post-mortem would take place. This upset me deeply, but the verdict was that Alex had had a brain aneurism. Now it was for us to place him safely to rest with former Harringtons in the churchyard of St Michael the Archangel, close to his mother and my mama and papa.

An air of despondency crept quietly over the estate at the untimely passing of Alex. Father was in a state of desolation. No matter how strong I tried to appear on the surface for him, he withdrew into himself and wanted to be alone with his thoughts and memories. Preparations were in hand for the funeral to take place. It had been designated that Ben and I would attend to all arrangements and with support from Jonathan we were able to plan a celebration of Alex's life. Caroline was notified of the plans but made no attempt to contact us or put in an appearance. The most upsetting situation was that Marcus's manager had been contacted at his office in California, but Marcus was touring and had not responded to the news. We were all unhappy at his lack of communication. Several estate workers approached Ben with a request to take part in the service with the reading of scriptures, poetry or kindly words. We were honoured to accept. I wanted to show the congregation my love for a very special person, and to Jonathan just how much I loved and respected his father. For this reason I chose a song Marcus and I had written together in 1960 called 'Love Lasts For Ever'.

The day before the funeral florists from Leeds arrived to decorate the church with white chrysanthemums, carnations and Alex's favourite roses. After a lot of effort the church looked stunning. I quietly stood and stared at the white walls, the beautiful stained glass windows, the highly polished pews and the gleaming brasses at the altar. In the quietness and solitude, emotions invaded my senses. I knelt in a pew, closed my eyes and encouraged my mind to produce a picture of Alex, smiling, but his image escaped me. I tried again, but without success. Panicking, I jumped up from the hassock and left the church, running dementedly across the churchyard and lawns until I reached Starbeck Row. I dashed to my room, where I went through a box of photographs until I stumbled upon a smiling photograph of Alex, taken on our last Christmas together. I stared at it, absorbing every minute detail, kissed it and held it close to my breast, then threw myself on to the bed and sobbed into the quilt. It was terribly important I should never forget my precious love.

As Father, Ben, Jonathan and I were coming to terms with our terrible loss, the day of the requiem mass arrived, stirring up more memories and opening wounds we were trying hard to heal. There was still no word from Marcus. Had fame distanced him from those he had grown to love as his family? He had not been home in almost three years.

In the church, every pew was filled with estate workers, friends and RAF personnel. Only one pew was left, that reserved for family. Father held my arm as we walked down the aisle. Moving slowly to our seats, I observed he was a heartbroken shadow of his former self. Jonathan assisted his grandfather as Ben and I sat at the end of the pew. The coffin was carried by pall-bearers from among the estate workers and was decorated by dozens of white roses called 'My Love'. The support and devotion Jonathan, Ben, Father and I had for one another was overwhelming in those moments together. We were a family totally united by grief. The service began with a hymn and a reading from Corinthians; but the words of Jimmy, the groom, were so moving I was consciously aware of Father crying. I too was overcome by emotion.

In no time, sentimentality faded and every ounce of courage I possessed took over. I found myself sitting on a chair, guitar in hand, as I faced the congregation. The piano stood, waiting for me to play it, but my guitar had taken preference. I tuned my guitar and played a few chords, then began to sing but after a moment the words began to evade me. I could feel my throat tightening. I really could not utter a note. Then the main door of the church opened to let in a late guest, which unnerved me. The congregation turned round to view the latecomer, which gave me an opportunity to control my emotions. Head down, I went over the introductory bars once more, but again my feelings took over. I could not sing. Tears began welling up in my eyes, when, from nowhere a voice started singing the song I had chosen. Only one person on earth could have known those words. *Marcus*! I looked up, and walking slowly down the aisle was a tall, lean dark-haired man, his hair cascading over his shoulders. The handsome face which met my eyes was none other than Marcus. I could not comprehend how he had changed. No longer were there spectacles to peer over, but here was an extremely charismatic guy with a charming smile and vivid, soulful, chocolate-brown eyes.

'Marcus, oh, Marcus! You came!' I whispered.

He stared at me saying, 'Sophia! It *is* you!'

Without further ado he settled himself at the piano and began to play. The congregation gasped in awe as together we sang in harmony, the years rolling back in just a few moments of time. As we finished he stood and moved toward me, taking my hand in his. With exceptional grace, he walked with me toward the coffin, bowing his head in acknowledgment, tears trickling down his cheeks. He faced the gathering and with phenomenal kindliness, spoke generously of the young Alex who had taken him into his heart and under his wing when just a small frightened three-year-old boy, newly installed in the Harrington family. He spoke of Alex, the young man who had stood by him and nurtured him with great care throughout his life at Harrington Hall. Speech over, he once more bowed his head toward the coffin, straightened himself to his full height, released my hand, strode down the aisle and went out of the church. As quickly as Marcus had appeared he was gone.

The funeral cortège entered the churchyard. Near the graves of former Harrington's, Alex was laid to rest. Father, Jonathan, Ben and I comforted each other throughout this ordeal, but Marcus was nowhere to be seen. I placed six white roses on Alex's coffin, and Ben and Jonathan supported me as I came to the realisation of the finality of the situation. There was great comfort in the fact that Jonathan was there with me. We spoke to mourners who had assembled at the grave. They made their way to the Hall. I asked Father if he would excuse me. I needed to find Marcus and I knew exactly where he would be – in Doggett's Barn. On entering, I found him facing the wall, his arms extended, hands placed on the plaster, looking down at the floor. He was grieving desperately.

'Marcus,' I whispered, 'I am so delighted you are home.'

I ran toward him. He turned abruptly, opened his arms and I threw myself at him. He held me as if I were a porcelain doll, easing my head into his warm chest.

'Sophia! I could not believe it when I walked into the church and you were there. We all thought that you were—'

'Dead?' I finished the sentence for him.

He paused and again gazed intently into my eyes. I could not accept the transformation in the once spotty seventeen-year-old I had said goodbye to all those years previously. Gone was the dreamy look, the boyishness. I was faced with the charm and manliness of this tall, thirty-three year old successful rock star.

'We were desperately worried for you, Sophia! I really thought I would never see you again. It was so difficult coping with that possibility. Oliver spent thousands of pounds trying to trace you.' He held me close to him once more.

'It's a long story, Marcus. Too long to tell now! Another time I will explain everything that has happened, but I need to savour this moment. My goodness, how you have changed in looks. You are so handsome!'

He blushed before replying, 'God, Sophia, *you* are still as beautiful as ever.' He cupped my face in his hands. 'Oh, how I have missed you! I am totally devastated at the passing of Alex. We were all extremely close as children – what fun we had! I think it will take us all a long time to come to terms with his death. He was one very special guy, my brother, Alex.'

He hugged me tightly, and then released me and I looked into his eyes. They dazzled me with their intensity but he appeared so tired. I stroked his cheek and wiped away a tear.

'I see that you made it in the music world, Marcus. I have listened to all your beautiful songs, and I am so terribly proud of you and your achievements. I knew you could do it!'

'Yes, I made it, dear Sophia. You always had such faith in me and I wanted to prove myself to you. With your tremendous help and encouragement, I made it – but at what price?'

I looked at his exhausted features, not understanding his comment. He gave no indication of what he meant. I explained I was residing presently at his cottage. He was more than happy with the arrangement.

Cutting short the conversation, he said, 'Sophia, I hope you will excuse me. I have so much I need to talk to you about, but not today. I must go. I have something very urgent to attend to. Tomorrow we'll meet and spend time together, but at the moment I must leave.' Kissing my cheek, he released me and disappeared once more in the direction of Starbeck Row.

I woke the following morning, showered and dressed. Nothing had been disturbed in the kitchen. There was no coffee pot sending a delicious aroma around the room. Marcus was either sleeping or had got up early and disappeared around the estate.

I made myself toast, poured a cup of instant and sat at the table with the daily newspaper, when he arrived on the scene dressed in black leather jacket and pants.

'Wear leathers, Sophia!' he announced. 'I am taking you out on one of my motorbikes.'

'I don't have any leathers,' I protested. 'And I am not sure I could ride pillion!'

'Then you shall have a set of mine. You will soon get the hang of motorcycling. There is nothing like the fresh air in your lungs and cold winds to encircle you!'

He retreated to find a set of leathers, gloves and an assortment of various sized helmets. Dishes washed, I found myself a pair of black jeans which swamped me, but I certainly looked the part of a biker's moll when they were teamed with necessary accessories. I tucked my long hair into a French pleat and carried the helmet to a large building set aside solely for Marcus's bike collection. It was an experience in itself. I was taken aback at the vintage bikes he had stored. I was given a guided tour and an explanation of dates and reason for manufacture. The names Francis Barnet, Royal Enfield, BSA Bantam, Vincent Black Shadow, Velocette Venom, AJS, Matchless, and many others were introduced to me. He selected a Vincent Black Shadow, and I nervously seated myself on the pillion. We set off for Hardraw Force in Wensleydale. In no time at all my nervousness had disappeared and I began enjoying the venture more than I could have imagined. We arrived at the magnificent waterfall, parked up, then wandered into the ravine below to watch water tumble and cascade over the glacier-cut gorges. It was an awesome sight. As we ventured further on foot we were captivated by the beauty in every leaf, wild flower, and droplet of water.

'There is no place like England, Sophia! This is magnificent!'

Marcus was enthralled by what he saw. I agreed wholeheartedly.

'I will be coming back to England to live soon. I've had the decision made for me by circumstances. I need to talk to you about it sometime and ask your advice.'

He said no more, but it pleased me that I would have his company on a regular basis.

We enjoyed walking, but I was utterly surprised no one recognised him. I supposed that the shades he wore hid his features well. We returned to the bike and set off toward home. Eventually we came to a coaching inn on the road and decided on lunch. It was a quaint place, centuries old, with a generous English menu. There was a small corner alcove which we selected to occupy. After ordering I asked how long I could stay at Starbeck Row.

'I am happy for you to stay as long as you wish,' was the reply. 'You have certainly brought life and a woman's touch to the place. The atmosphere is great. Treat the cottage as your own, Sophia. If you are happy there, please stay.'

I thanked him as he announced, 'I'm afraid I have to return to America in three days.'

He could see the look of disappointment on my face. We had just been reunited and again he was travelling thousands of miles away.

'I shall miss you, Sophia, but I have to return to the States on business. My ranch is for sale and I have difficult negotiations with my record company. There is a great deal to attend to, but I will return in about ten days. Then you can give me some advice.'

I thought how tired Marcus looked. He appeared not to have had the sleep he so desperately needed. When he removed his shades, his eyes were glazed, his pupils dilated, making his brown eyes look larger than life, but they were encircled with dark rings. It seemed he was not as happy as he made out. He trembled on occasions and appeared to be in a world of his own at times. We sipped white wine as we waited for our meal.

'I understand you were married,' I said, my inquisitive nature getting the better of me.

He hesitated before answering. 'No, not married, Sophia, but I've been in two relationships. The first relationship, with a make-up artist, lasted a year by which time we realised what a terrible mistake it had been and we decided to go our separate ways.'

After careful thought, I asked, 'The second relationship – how long did that last? Were you happy?'

'My relationship with Suzi lasted three years, Sophia. I met her at a photo shoot in London. She couldn't abide me being on the road for long periods, or the fact I was constantly hounded by groupies who would have killed to get close to me. She was extremely jealous, and the rows that followed were bad, although I gave her no reason to mistrust me. Suzi was like you in looks, but that's where the resemblance ended. She had a heart of steel, but had me convinced that our relationship would improve dramatically if we were married, so after lengthy discussions a date was set. I arrived at the church with crowds outside to witness the ceremony. I heard the organ begin playing the Bridal March and turned to watch her glide down the aisle. I had invited Oliver, Ben and Marianne over to the States to attend the wedding. As she walked down the aisle on the arm of her father I suddenly realised that I was making a terrible mistake. As she drew closer, I turned and rushed out of the church. You can imagine what reaction I received from Oliver. That was when I wrote the song, 'The Biggest Mistake of My Life', which became a hit in the States. The press had an absolute field day,' he said.

'In time, foolishly, we recommenced our relationship, but after a while she and I parted once again, although I tried hard to make the relationship work. Happy? I don't think I was happy with either of them. I entered into the liaisons because it seemed the right thing at the time. I was so very lonely. I was a solo artist at the time, and it can be a real solitary existence on the road. I needed a peaceful, secure base to return to but neither of them seemed able to create that for me. Still I had my ranch eventually. That provided the solace I needed between tours.'

'Did you sleep with many groupies?' I boldly asked.

'Goodness no! It's not my scene. I did once when I was drunk – a big mistake. It hit the newspapers almost instantly. I received an angry call from Oliver, chastising me for my obscene behaviour.'

'I can imagine!' I laughed. 'What about drugs?'

'Ah, that's another story,' he said hesitantly. 'I guess I had my fair share of amphetamines and LSD and drink! Had to, to keep going when on extensive tours. It's a hard life, Sophia, and not all it's cracked up to be. Anyway, what is this? The Spanish Inquisition?' he joked.

'No, I simply wondered,' I replied.

The meal arrived and we ate, chatting in between mouthfuls.

'Do you have any children, Sophia?' he asked.

As I tried to begin explaining about Jonathan and Anna-Sophia, the waitress interrupted and asked if we were satisfied with our food. The conversation moved on to another subject.

'What about women in your life now? Are there any?'

He looked dauntingly at me saying, 'No, Sophia! I was in love with a beautiful woman. She was all I ever wanted: sensual, gorgeous, talented. She came into my life like a breath of fresh air, but left it suddenly. I lost her a long time ago. She will never return to me now!' He appeared saddened as he sipped his wine.

'I am sorry, Marcus. Please forgive me for bringing up the subject. I simply want you to be happy.'

'I am happy, I guess. I've fame, money, cars, and bikes – and of course I've my retreat at Harrington Hall when I can get home. I'm not interested in forming any long lasting associations again. Too much hassle, and too painful. Please don't concern yourself about me. I have all I could possibly need – but not everything I want.'

The conversation ended abruptly as we finished our meal. I thought how one very lucky woman had had a number-one hit, 'Now I Know She's Gone', written for her. She must have been quite a woman! I realised I had ventured too far into his personal life and quickly changed the subject. Our conversation began opening my eyes to the life of a rock star, but I don't think I had even begun to scratch the surface of what it was really like. I knew in time I would discover things about Marcus I had not considered possible.

Chapter Thirty-one

As we returned to Starbeck Row, I stepped off the motorcycle and asked, 'Will you join me for supper? I'm making steak and kidney pie. It used to be your favourite.'

He smiled as he said, 'I'd love to, but right now I must go. Something urgent beckons!'

Marcus gave me no chance to explain that Father and Jonathan would be invited too. I needed to explain about my relationship with Alex, and how Stephen had blackmailed me into going to Australia because of it. It was important I introduce Marcus to my son, and I decided that having Father there would calm a difficult situation.

Marcus gave the impression of being perturbed. I knew from his conversation that his record company were giving him hell. It was beginning to show in his actions. With the motorcycle locked, he set alarms to the building and beat a hasty retreat to the cottage, leaving me to saunter along at leisure. He obviously had important things on his mind which needed immediate attention.

'Seven thirty?' I called, and he raised his hand in acknowledgement.

I dropped in on Father at the Hall and found him playing a violin concerto with Jonathan. I applauded their efforts and interrupted them, saying, 'Will you both join me for supper?'

'Sorry, Mother, no can do! Grandfather and I are going to a concert this evening.'

Jonathan was spending precious time with his grandfather, so my plans had been thwarted.

'Enjoy your evening,' I called. 'I will invite you to dine with me another night.'

They returned to their practice and I hastily returned to the cottage. Marcus was nowhere to be seen. As I stood in the kitchen I heard footsteps overhead and knew he was in his room. I prepared a pie, cooked an assortment of vegetables, opened a bottle of Chianti and set two places at the table. I viewed the kitchen clock. It was 7.25. There was no sign of Marcus and no longer a noise from the room above. It had been my intention to eat at eight o'clock. When 8.15 arrived I called up the stairs, 'Marcus! Supper!' But there was no reply.

This was unlike the punctilious boy I used to know. I called again and ascended the stairs. His door slowly opened at the sound of my footsteps.

He looked dishevelled, pale and sleepy, mumbling, 'I do apologise, Sophia – I fell asleep! Give me fifteen minutes and I will be with you.'

Fifteen minutes turned into thirty as I constantly checked and re-checked the food.

I heard footsteps approaching, and, 'Damn!' as he missed the last two stairs and crashed against the wall.

'Sophia, I am so sorry!' he apologised, as he sat at the table and poured two glasses of wine.

'I hope my food is not spoilt,' I said. I was concerned, but he looked at the plate placed in front of him and said, 'Delicious!'

'Are you OK, Marcus?' I asked. I smiled at him, but his eyes stared at me. He looked dreadfully tired and exhausted.

'I'm fine!' he barked. 'Eat your meal, Sophia! For goodness sake stop fussing!'

He seemed ill at ease. I made an effort to eat as he poured more wine for himself, topping up my glass in the process.

'You are an excellent cook, you know!' He seemed to find it an effort to create conversation. There was a detectable atmosphere in the room. He ate slowly. I picked at my food, nervous of my impending confession.

'Pile the dishes in the sink and let's talk, Sophia…'

Marcus withdrew from the table, taking my plate. I produced a cafetière of coffee and we collapsed on to the sofa. I felt relaxed from the wine and was ready for conversation.

How I wished Father and Jonathan were there.

'You seem to have something on your mind, Sophia. I can sense it! What do you want to tell me?'

'There are issues I need you to understand. I don't know where to begin.'

'I am all ears. Fire away!' he said. Marcus seemed genuinely concerned, just like old times. Taking the last sip of coffee, he placed his cup on the table, reclined against the cushions and gave me his undivided attention. I coughed; I paused.

'Um! Where shall I begin?' I asked, but he just shrugged his shoulders.

'I will never forgive myself for having left you years ago to make your own way in the world, when you desperately needed my help!' I began.

'Think no more of it, Sophia! I was determined to show you I could make it, because you had such faith in me.'

'The truth is, Marcus, Stephen blackmailed me into going with him to Australia when I did not want to go!'

He looked puzzled.

'I confided in Stephen that I had a son, unbeknown to Mother and Father. He threatened to tell Father. It would have broken his heart.'

'But Sophia, you had a *child*? When?' he said, totally knocked off balance.

I replied, 'Yes, Marcus I have a son. When I went to the convent in Ireland, it was to give birth to my son, Jonathan, who was taken from me and adopted against my wishes.'

He stared at me, aghast by my revelations. 'But Sophia, I don't get this! You never had any serious boyfriends before Stephen! You were always so wrapped up in your friendship with Alex…' He suddenly fixed me with laser-like eyes. '*Alex*? No! Not Alex?'

I nodded and confessed, '*Yes*! Alex was Jonathan's father!'

Marcus pulled himself up from the sofa, swaying as he did so.

'Excuse me, Sophia! I must go. I feel sick…'

He rushed to the door, staggering as he left the room. Marcus had not changed. He was running away from situations he could not handle or would not accept; just as he had done during childhood. The anguished look in his eyes led me to believe I had suddenly lost a friend. As he climbed the stairs, I called out, 'Marcus, please let me explain!' but he chose to ignore me. I collapsed on the sofa, buried my head in my hands and sighed. How could I have been so foolish as to think that he would have taken my news lightly? Pondering on a situation close to my heart and too late to change, I slouched into the kitchen and buried myself in the task of washing dishes until they sparkled. I sighed, 'Oh, Marcus, this time I fear I have lost your friendship for good.'

It was late when I retired to bed. I halted by his bedroom door, intent on knocking. I wanted him to listen to my explanations, but everything was quiet. I withdrew to my room, showered, then slipped into bed, hoping sleep would calm my heavy heart, but I could not find sleep. I twisted and turned, viewing the alarm clock intermittently. At two in the morning I switched on the bedside lamp and leaned over, searching the bedside table for a book to read. I heard noises in the hallway and investigated. There was a strip of light under Marcus's door. I floated swiftly along the carpet and knocked on the door. He was obviously having difficulty sleeping too. There was no answer, so I knocked louder, but still no answer. I turned the handle and found it unlocked and entered. The bathroom was lit; clothes lay scattered around the room where they had fallen. Talcum powder had been spilt over the floor and the tops of the bathroom units. Everywhere was in a frightful mess. Something was definitely amiss. I peered into the dimly lit bedroom. Marcus was lying on top of the quilt, with the minimum of clothing on, in what appeared to be a sound sleep. I crept quietly toward him. He was perspiring profusely and had involuntary movements of his arms and legs. On closer inspection I came to the conclusion he was having a nightmare, as he mumbled nonsensical words. I retreated, leaving him with his demons. What a devilishly handsome guy he was, but a crazy, mixed-up one! I left the bathroom in its state of disarray, returned to my bed, and eventually drifted into sleep at 6 a.m., my brain tired with churning over events of previous years.

It was the sun that woke me from the bewildering dream I was experiencing. Its intensity directed rays of light through a gap in the curtains onto my bed. I rubbed my eyes, yawned and peered at the clock, trying to focus on the hands.

Goodness, its lunchtime! I thought. I shot out of bed, tripped over the bedtime book, threw on my dressing gown, strode to the bathroom and viewed myself in the mirror. I was not a pretty sight! My hair was tangled from moving around the bed. I had forgotten to remove my make-up. I washed my hair, ran a bath and soaked myself until I was rejuvenated from head to toe. Having dressed, I was determined to track down Marcus and try to explain about Jonathan. We had so much unfinished business; I had to do all in my power to redeem our friendship. I hurried along to his room. The door was ajar, so I called his name but there was no reply. I called once more. Taking myself into his room I noticed his bed had been roughly tidied, but he was nowhere to be seen. Several drawers were half open. I investigated the bathroom. Clothes and towels littered the floor. Talc spotted the carpet. I placed some discarded clothing into the linen bin, wiped a cloth around the sink and picked up various items of interest.

On closer examination it was clear what had happened in this room, and why Marcus had chosen to run out on me the previous evening. It was not my news which had disturbed him, but more pressing matters. I examined the evidence.

'I see, Marcus! So this is your game!' I said, horrified. I decided I would stop his behaviour in its tracks. I placed certain items in the pocket of my jeans and scurried down the staircase, calling, 'Marcus!'

He had to be somewhere, but seemed elusive. I ventured across to the Hall and discovered Father in the library, researching from his beloved books.

'Marcus – have you seen him?' I enquired.

'Sophia, darling, you are too late. He left for the States after breakfast.' Father seemed puzzled that I was unaware of his whereabouts.

'Gone? He wasn't due to leave for another three days!'

'He phoned to say goodbye. He has important business to attend to but will be home again next week. Is there anything wrong, my dear?' he asked.

'No, Father. What I need to discuss with him can wait a week.'

There was going to be a showdown when he returned. Marcus was not going to like what I had discovered.

I waited – not one week, but four – before he finally returned to Starbeck Row, his long unruly, black hair hanging around his handsome features, a five o'clock shadow on his face. His eyes were puffy and glazed. He looked like a ghost. Placing his luggage on the floor, he shot me a smile and said, 'It was a hell of a journey, Sophia! I had a body and luggage search at the airport. Long-haired types always get a rough deal. I am totally exhausted. Excuse me if I crash out. I'll see you later.' He started walking toward the stairs.

'No, Marcus, you're not getting away from me! You and I are going to talk until I get answers to the many questions I intend asking you.' I beckoned to him and said, 'Sit!' and pointed to the sofa. He looked quizzically at me and planted himself in an armchair. I opened the trophy cabinet housing many of his awards and removed what had been the contents of my jeans pocket. I asked for his hand. 'Well,' I said, placing the contents into his open palm, 'what have you to say about this?'

He looked horrified as he asked, 'Where did you get this, Sophia?'

'From the bathroom on the day you left for the States. You'd better explain – and no excuses!'

I watched his face. He was like an animal cornered. He knew that this was the time for confessions. 'It's heroin, isn't it? I've seen it before. We had a stockman on the station who tried supplying it to workers. He was immediately sacked.'

He nodded, bowing his head.

'Marcus, you lied to me! You told me you didn't touch drugs.'

He interrupted me, trying to explain his possession of it. It was then I realised what he meant when he said that 'fame came at a price'.

'That is why I was late arriving for Alex's funeral, Sophia. I tried for nearly two weeks to clean up my act before flying over, but I couldn't. I am an addict. I am thirty-four years old and all burnt out.'

'You have to let the family help you, Marcus,' I pleaded.

'No, Sophia! I don't want anyone else to know! Oliver would be so disappointed in me. I would absolutely hate it. I could never face him.'

'Father would *not* be cross or disappointed. He would want to help too,' I assured him.

I tried to tell him we were all there for him, but my words fell on stony ground.

The situation petrified me. I could not work out what effect it was having on his physical and mental stamina.

I asked him, 'How on earth did you get to this state?'

'Pressure, Sophia! Pressure from everyone! My last album flopped, my record company have demanded I produce a more marketable album, like back in the late sixties and seventies, but I cannot write. I seem to have lost the ability. In turn I've taken comfort in heroin. It's a vicious circle.'

I tried to place my arms around him to comfort him, but he rejected my advances.

'Now, with the death of Alex, there is this place to run. For years I've put thousands into the estate to prevent the Hall from being sold. There are two greedy ex-lovers to keep in the style to which they have become accustomed, and I must provide money somehow.'

'I will help you find a way Marcus if you will let me,' I promised.

'If only you could.' He was not impressed by my offer. 'I have only a small following of fans in this country now. I've been in the States too long. People soon forget you. The proceeds from the sale of my ranch have to go into making sure this estate stays in the family.'

'Then it's about time I got off my butt and did my fair share. Firstly, you have to get clean. Then we will devise ways of making lots of money. There has to be a solution. There always is! From this moment on you have my full, undivided help and attention – just like when we were children.'

'Sophia, how on earth can you help me? I want to change, get back on track. I desperately want to get off heroin. Can you help me, Sophia?' he pleaded.

He sank to the floor in a crumpled heap, grabbed my skirt and buried his head in my lap and cried frenziedly.

'Marcus, this is not like you,' I told him. 'Remember how we used to fight against the odds as children?'

He nodded.

'Well, we can do it again, you and I!'

I watched him as he began to shake uncontrollably. He excused himself. I was sure he was going to his room for a fix. The situation was desperate. He needed help and needed it immediately. This gorgeous guy, capable of holding the attention of an audience of thousands of people with his music, was suddenly weak, depressed, vulnerable and totally helpless. I had to find a way to save him from himself. I would spend every waking moment, and more, finding solutions to his problems and those of the estate which Father had hidden from me for so long.

I asked the surgery receptionist, 'Could you please ask Simon to call me as soon as he is free on 21725 at Starbeck Row – *not* at Harrington Hall? Please tell him Sophia would like to speak to him on a matter of great urgency!'

The secretary proved a hard nut to crack. Simon was engaged with a private patient, but she made notes of my call and I assured myself I had finally convinced her about the urgency of the situation. Meanwhile I checked, at intervals, on Marcus, but I wasn't sure whether or not his sleep was drug induced. This caused me great anxiety!

Doctor Marsden did not ring. He came immediately to the cottage, letting himself in through the front door, observing that I was deeply distressed.

'I am so relieved to see you, Simon. You cannot imagine how much! But now I need your advice – well, your professional help – but I must ask you say nothing to the family,' I pleaded.

'Whatever you tell me, Sophia, is in the strictest confidence. It is just between you and me!' he replied.

'And Marcus!' I added. I explained the circumstances for requesting a visit. He sat quietly, listened intently and wrote notes. He appeared extremely sympathetic and understanding. No judgement was made on his part whatsoever.

'You are going to need a controlled withdrawal programme for Marcus. He will have to be admitted to a private clinic.'

I explained that I could not make those decisions for him and asked him to talk to Marcus about the available options, offering my help in whatever capacity I was needed.

We woke Marcus from his deep sleep and he joined us to consider his future drug rehabilitation. Lengthy discussions took place, while Simon explained fully the options available.

'A private clinic is out of the question!' Marcus insisted. 'I have been to one before and it did not work!'

'But Marcus, this is serious business! The wanting to get clean has to come from you! You have to approach this with every drop of will power you can muster.'

'Simon, why can't I stay here and do my withdrawal programme at home?' he asked.

'That's possible, Marcus, but you are going to need terrific support from nursing staff, a doctor and Sophia. She has offered her services, but how you will keep this from Oliver I cannot imagine!'

'That is the way I want it! You will help me, Sophia, won't you? If you are here with me I can cope!'

I offered to do anything I could, and promised Marcus I would be there for him throughout his programme. Simon, efficient in the extreme, had medical associates in France; one in particular was a Professor Bachelet, a known advocate of natural withdrawal therapy for drug addiction. Armand Bachelet telephoned Starbeck Row in response to Simon's request for help, explaining his rehabilitation programme, and we were intrigued this process did not involve the use of methadone. Marcus and I naturally had reservations about the effect of the treatment and the long uncertain road ahead, but we knew his heroin addiction could not be allowed to continue.

Simon was intensely enthusiastic about Armand's programme, and had seen results of his methods in Paris the previous year. We were prepared to accept his observations, and Marcus immediately gave the go-ahead for treatment to begin. The existing sauna at the cottage would prove useful in the programme, and I had opted to cater for the nutritional food required. Massage therapy was also on the agenda and an expert was drafted in. I would need to attend Father daily to prevent him from visiting the cottage while the programme was in place. Two bedrooms were turned into treatment rooms and two elderly nurses were assigned to us in order to advise and help establish a routine. Their help and constructive advice would be invaluable. Neither Marcus nor I expected an easy ride, but we were totally unprepared for what was to happen.

As the procedures began, with them came the effects of withdrawal, which were horrendous, but somehow we faced it together. It was so difficult for Marcus and equally as traumatic for me having to stand by, watch, and be able to do little but give support and promises of great things to come after it was completed.

One night, I crept into his dimly lit room and placed a jug of fresh water on the bedside table. Observing his eyes were closed, I began my exit.

'Please, Sophia, stay with me and keep me company!' Marcus pleaded as I began to steal away.

'I thought you were asleep,' I explained, but he grabbed my arm and I knew he desperately needed reassurance to help him through the impending darkness. There seemed a need on his part to talk; to offload the many situations troubling him so sorely.

'Of course I will stay. Perhaps we can build a few bridges before the night is over,' I said, knowing our relationship had been under a great deal of strain during the past weeks. I pulled up an armchair by the side of the bed and curled myself into it.

'I need to talk to you about Jonathan,' he said, lifting himself up to rest against the mound of pillows. 'I am sure you think I ran out on you the night you told me about him and the fact Alex was his father. It was not for that reason I left the room abruptly. It was the heroin making me ill,' he explained.

I looked at him, took his hand and said, 'I know, Marcus. Please don't give it another thought, but at some stage I would love to introduce you to him. I know you would have so much to talk about. You really would like him. He is exceptional, like his father.'

I explained about my time at the convent in Ireland and what life had been like. He found it hard to believe I had been through such torment.

'I am sure I would like your son immensely, Sophia, but now we are having confession time, I have something I wish to tell you. Like you, I have a son!'

I thought my ears had deceived me.

'You have a son?'

He nodded and whispered, 'Yes, his name is Freddie! He is a good-looking ten-year-old who goes to boarding school in Somerset. He is the son from my relationship with Suzi.'

'How often do you see him?' I enquired.

'Not as often as I would like! When I was in the States he stayed on my ranch once during school holidays. It actually suited his mother. She lives in London. I have never had a chance to get to know him. I hate to think I have missed out on so much of his life. It gets to me!'

'Why don't you invite him to stay here for the summer?' I suggested.

My idea seemed to send shock waves through him.

'That would be a great idea, but I really would not know how to handle him. I have lost touch with him as a person, and with his likes and dislikes.'

'Then you owe it to yourself and Freddie to get well as soon as possible and approach your ex-partner to ask if he can stay. I will help you to take care of him and entertain him. You can renew your ties. It will be terrific!'

He looked at me in astonishment. 'You really wouldn't mind caring for a ten-year-old?' he queried, resting his head on his hand.

'I'd love to,' I enthused. 'Get yourself well, and Freddie can stay for the summer.'

The look of pleasure on his face was astounding. He rested on his pillows and gave what I considered a sigh of relief. One of his problems was due to be resolved, if he could find it in himself to kick his heroin habit. The ball was now in his court. He slept for a considerable time leaving me a chance to doze myself. When I finally awoke he was staring at me with his vivid brown eyes.

'What are you staring at?' I asked.

'You, Sophia! I was thinking how all my young life you were my saviour. Now you are here for me again, when I need you. You are one special woman, you know! How did I cope without you during my years away from the Hall?'

He stared into my eyes. At once I saw the young, shy, vulnerable Marcus of childhood days, and I knew I had to help get his life back on track. I assured him we would turn all his problems around. I hoped I had the strength and determination to cope with difficulties the following weeks would bring. For one brief moment I missed Alex more than it was possible to imagine. He would have known how to bring order into the chaos around us.

'There are times when I feel lost and do not know who I am,' Marcus murmured.

'But you are Marcus Walker – star!' I quipped, but he was not amused.

'That's my stage persona, Sophia. I mean the real Marcus Walker, with all his demons and insecurities.'

'I know you had a traumatic start in life, Marcus. Like me, it must have had a huge impact on how you think and feel. You are wonderfully talented, Marcus. Father has taken you to his heart as if you were his own. To him *you are his son!*'

He frowned in disbelief, rested on his pillows and closed his eyes. He was crying. His emotional defences were down. Difficult though it must have been for him, the tears flowed. He suddenly opened his eyes and said, 'Look at me, Sophia. Take a good look. Superstar or grovelling heap?'

'You are bound to feel like nothing on earth on this programme. Each day is one step nearer to your complete recovery. By mid-July you should be well enough for us to entertain your son.'

He paused and lifted his head. Then he gazed at me and said, 'What I cannot get my head around is being rejected by my own father. It eats away at me.'

'It is something you have to live with, Marcus. For all we know there may have been a genuine reason for his so-called rejection of you. After all, how often have you been a father to your son?'

I had overstepped the mark. The comment caused anger, so I quickly changed the subject and said, 'Although you are not far into the programme, I have been trying to arrange activities which can bring money into the estate. I hope to put forward some proposals to you when you are well enough. Please try to adopt a positive attitude.'

'Why are you prepared to do so much for me, Sophia?'

'Simply because I care what happens to you. We go back a long, long way. You have enormous talent, and I want to help you back to where you belong, at the peak of your professional career. You have taken your musical style into unknown territories over the years and not held onto what was a safe option. You are ahead of your time, Marcus. That time will come soon and you will set a new trend. No matter what happens I will be there for you!'

It was evident Marcus was uncomfortable, and I rearranged his pillows.

'What was life like in Australia, Sophia?'

He could see his line of questioning affected me deeply, by the look of dismay on my face.

'If it makes you unhappy to talk about it, then forgive me for mentioning it.'

It did hurt me to contemplate what happened during those years, but like Marcus I found there were many things about my past I needed to unburden to a sympathetic listener.

Spending so much time together gave us the chance to help each other through our nightmares. I explained about Masters Valley cattle station, the house, the staff and Stephen. I related what I had learnt of cattle ranching during my time there. There was a traumatic few minutes when I spoke about Stephen's Jekyll and Hyde character, about his treatment of me and his part in the robberies at the Hall, the post office and his involvement in the murder of the postmaster.

Marcus asked, 'But why did you stay with such a complete animal?'

I described the various threats made to me by Stephen, if I attempted to leave, and added I was sure Stephen would have no qualms in carrying them out.

'He was already married when he married me, to Susan Wilkins, the demure creature he had offered as secretary to Father. She was not the dumb blonde she portrayed herself as, but a manipulative, greedy woman.'

'So you were not legally married?' he exclaimed.

'Correct. I am a single woman, and that's the way it is going to stay. I am free, thank God.'

'And what of Stephen?'

'The police tried to arrest him but he escaped in his plane. They discovered him miles off course with signs of injury on his body which defied explanation. He was dead when they found him! You see, Marcus, I court disaster wherever I go.'

'Don't say such things, Sophia!' he said, taking my hand. Then his trembling began. The shaking, muscle cramps, pain, hallucinations and torment. I held him in my arms, trying to soothe him. He needed reassurance but it was a difficult, dependent time for him. By 6 a.m. Marcus and I were totally exhausted. I tried to allay his fears and bring some semblance of order into his very troubled life.

As each day progressed I looked for signs of improvement. There were indications that life for Marcus was beginning to take a turn for the better. He stuck religiously to the meals I prepared, which were extremely nutritional. He had saunas to help with detoxification via the skin. However, his mental attitude was at an all-time low. He could not see a return to his former star status, and I had to constantly instil in him how it was possible. His mind wandered to many situations continually haunting him. He explained about the loss of a very dear friend from heroin addiction, and could not erase the memory of discovering the body from his mind. Simon suggested counselling, but knowing Marcus the way I did, there was no possibility he would succumb to sharing his demons with another person in that way. I asked Marcus if he would consider it, and his reply was, '*No*! I have you, Sophia! I can talk to you! I know you understand. You will not judge me.'

I did understand, but the anguish of the withdrawal and its consequences were taking their toll on me also. I needed to be extremely strong.

I approached Marcus one morning with a view to suggesting we tackled his ex-partner, Suzi, to discuss about a possible holiday for Freddie at Starbeck Row during the summer months. Somehow the subject never arose. Marcus had his mind on more pressing matters, namely his nurse.

'Please tell her to go, Sophia! She sits in the corner, surveying me as if I were a caged animal, wondering if I am going to leap for the nearest light fitting and swing from it! Any moment I think she is going to throw me a few nuts!'

'Don't be so rude, Marcus!' I remonstrated. 'Nurse Thompson is following Simon's instructions, and if you don't keep your voice down she will hear what you are saying!'

Marcus sat cross-legged in the corner of the bedroom, perusing old sepia photographs. He was not in a mood to be argued with. 'I don't want her here! We don't talk the same language! Why can't you stay with me again, Sophia?'

I thought for a moment and then politely asked Nurse Thompson if Marcus had had all necessary treatments. If so I would take over from her. She sighed, raised her hairy eyebrows, and withdrew to an adjoining room, stating he was impossible to care for, but assured me she would be there should the need arise.

'Thank goodness,' he muttered. 'Now I can breathe at last! I tried to talk to her about music but the conversation drove me mad. She hadn't a clue what I was talking about! I would have got more sense out of one of Oliver's sheep.'

'She is elderly, Marcus, and maybe she does not like your kind of music!'

He grunted and said, 'Huh! It's her loss!' and continued to work his way through more photographs.

'Being rude does not become you!' I mocked, but he smirked at my observations.

'Look at you! You haven't shaved or combed your hair! You're a mess! Why don't you go and have a shower and put on some fresh clothing?'

He rolled his eyes at me in disgust and murmured, 'She-devil,' as he rose from the floor and made a hasty retreat to the bathroom. I sat in a comfortable bedroom chair and handled the photographs he had strewn across the floor, and which I suspected he had left for me to pick up. It was obvious that these were the remaining few photographs he had of Frances, his mother, and his father, taken perhaps before he was born. Mother had passed them down to him. How like his father he looked! He was also tall, with coal black hair and very handsome features. In fact the mirror image of his son, apart from that long, often unruly hair that Marcus sported. His father looked immaculate in his Canadian Air Force uniform. Frances too, was a good-looking, delicate creature, and they appeared extremely happy, if the photographs displayed the truth. What on earth could have happened for Mr Walker to have abandoned Frances and his son? I guessed that this was the answer to a question that we would never discover.

Chapter Thirty-two

'Marcus Walker, please!' the voice announced.

'Who is speaking?' I asked.

'Tell him it's Sam Dreyfus, Scorpion Records, Los Angeles.'

I swallowed loudly, not knowing how to answer. I froze on the spot.

'Hello? Hello?' The voice sounded frustrated at the lack of communication while I searched for an answer.

'I am sorry. Marcus Walker is not available today. He's unable to take your call. Can I give him a message?'

'Who am I speaking to?' he queried.

'Mr Walker's secretary,' I lied.

'Yes. Tell him I need to speak to him real urgent! It's about Scorpion Records. I'm selling the damn company!'

'Selling?' I screeched, sounding flabbergasted. 'I will get him to telephone you as soon as possible.'

'Make sure you do, ma'am! It is very important.'

Marcus was showering. I called through the door. He finally surfaced, wearing a bathrobe.

'Sam Dreyfus, Scorpion Records—' I said, but before I could finish the sentence, he asked, 'What on earth did Sam want?'

'He is selling the company! Said it was important you telephone him.'

'Not another setback now that I'm beginning to get back on my feet, I hope!' he muttered.

'Please, Marcus, stop being so negative! Wait until you have spoken to him and see what he has to say! Maybe things are not as bad as you think.'

I tried to instil hope in him but he appeared worried about his future. Marcus finally called Dreyfus in LA, and they chatted for a considerable time. When he reappeared he seemed stressed. I feared this setback would wreak havoc with his future plans. He withdrew to his room saying little. I couldn't decide whether to speak to him about the situation or leave him to think things through, but I left him deep in thought. Meanwhile, I walked across to the Hall in search of Father.

'What are you so engrossed in, Father?' I asked, slipping quietly behind him as he sat at his desk.

'Sophia, darling! You gave me such a fright!' He dropped his pen to the floor. I crouched to retrieve it and noticed he had been writing furiously. He placed his arm across the page, not allowing me to read what he'd written. As I handed him the errant pen, he gave a coy smile and announced, 'These are my memoirs, Sophia, for your eyes only, long after I am gone.'

'So you are writing about events of which I know nothing, are you? I hope they make exciting reading,' I teased.

'It is for you to judge, my darling, but I don't think you will be disappointed.'

'Can't I have a brief glimpse of what I hope is an eye-opener?' I asked.

He smiled gathered together his manuscript and I read, *Expecting to Fly*.

So that was the title. I couldn't wait to read it! He placed it in a drawer and locked it carefully away.

'You can read it when it's finished!' he said, winking at me. Then it will be yours to do with as you will!'

'Marcus is writing his autobiography too. What a wonderful idea! Perhaps one day I should do something similar for Jonathan.'

As we continued our conversation, we were interrupted by Haynes, serving morning coffee and a plate of Edith's delicious home-made ginger biscuits, which Father happily indulged in. I poured him a cup of coffee and one for myself, and distributed the culinary delicacies before settling down to further talks.

'Before we engross ourselves in what I deem to be serious discussions – an assumption on my part, Sophia, provoked by the expressions on your face – I have some excellent news. In fact it is exciting news! Drink your coffee, then I will take you to see something!'

I was intrigued. I chomped on my ginger biscuit as Father devoured his in record time, savouring every tiny morsel.

'No one bakes biscuits like Edith,' he chirped, and I had to agree.

'What is the good news, Father?' I asked, finishing my last sip of coffee.

'Come with me, Sophia!' he instructed.

I helped him from his chair and he walked toward a hidey-hole – a priest hole where Alex, Ben, Marcus and I had hidden many times as children. He cautiously opened it and there, perched on an easel, was Father's favourite painting: the portrait of a sixteenth-century ancestor – the Titian, stolen by Stephen so long ago.

'Where on earth did they find—'

Before I could finish my question, Father covered the painting, closed the priest hole and informed me it was awaiting immediate collection to be taken to an unknown place of safety.

'I am delighted you have got it back, Father!' I said, as I observed the immense pleasure on his face.

'Now Sophia, let us go to the drawing room, make ourselves comfortable, and you can ask me what it is you are dying to ask!'

Father knew me better than I knew myself and could detect what my thoughts and feelings were. I helped him to his armchair and sat facing him. I broached the subject of Mother's diamond and sapphire necklace. It was all I had of any significant value. I wanted it to be put to what I considered the best possible use.

'I came to ask you if you would allow me to sell the necklace Mother willed to me. I know how dearly she treasured it, but I really do need the money at this moment.'

Father's face bore the expression of one very disgruntled man at such a proposal.

'Your mother absolutely adored the necklace, Sophia. She insisted you were to have the pleasure of wearing it on special occasions,' he said.

'When, Father? I have no social life, and no female children to hand it down to. Mother adored Marcus. I am sure she would approve of what I want to do for him.'

'It would not take a genius to guess where the money is going!' he snapped.

'If you will let me explain, Father, I can assure you it hurts me to ask this of you, but I really do need the money the sale of the necklace would yield, in order to purchase a record company.'

'Record company? Are you out of your mind Sophia? *Record company?*'

I had not seen Father in such a volatile mood since announcing my intended departure to Australia.

'How much is the record company going to cost, Sophia?'

I couldn't furnish him with a sensible answer to such a searching question, so he waved his hand at me as if dismissing the idea.

'Father, Marcus's record company is up for sale. I want to purchase it. If I could own it there would be no question as to the kind of music he could record. He could do as he wished.

'I thought Marcus would be involved somewhere along the line. He has been home now for four months and I have hardly seen hide or hair of him.'

'He has not been too well, Father.' I leapt to Marcus's defence. 'He has provided this estate with huge amounts of finance for its upkeep, but money is going to run out unless we can think of ways to save his career and branch out into the music world. I am pleading to you for your help.'

Father calmed himself, knowing that if it had not been for Marcus, the Hall and estate would have been past history for us all. I explained my plan. If it went ahead, I would purchase Scorpion Records. We would produce music which we thought would meet the needs of the present generation. After extensive talks, Father agreed I could sell the necklace. He realised what faith I had in Marcus's ability, and he offered to approach Jacob Godber at Witherington's to see if he could find a buyer. I explained that time was of the essence, and he understood I wanted this move very badly.

Father rang Jacob while I mulled things over in my mind. Jacob, ever his obliging self, stated he would enquire of potential buyers on our behalf and would return with some news soon. Despite being Caroline's father, he was a true friend to my father. I kissed Father's brow and retreated, leaving him time to calm down. All I could do was to wait and hope.

I returned to the cottage. Marcus was pacing up and down, desperate to know where I had been.

'Sophia, I wanted to talk to you! I have been thinking. The sale of the record company is going to spoil any chance I have of restarting my career, you know.'

'Please sit down and let me explain, Marcus. First of all I need to ask you something.'

Puzzled at my request, he sat and viewed me with a puzzled look.

I asked, 'How much do Scorpion Records require for the sale of their company?'

'Sophia, why are you asking?' He was bemused at my line of questioning.

'Because I am going to buy the record company!' I announced.

He looked in sheer astonishment at my declaration and pointed out that we had no money.

'I am trying to arrange something!' I said.

'We're not borrowing money, Sophia! *No way!*'

He was most emphatic. At his comment I thought it wise to let the subject drop. I feared that any announcement that I was prepared to sell Mother's necklace would send him into a frenzy. I decided to telephone Sam Dreyfus in LA myself to discover the asking price when Marcus was not within earshot.

'If there are to be negotiations of any kind, I will buy myself out of my contract with Scorpion,' Marcus insisted.

'With no money?' I queried, but he walked away.

Within days, Father notified me that Jacob Godber had telephoned to inform him that he had a potential customer for the necklace. My heart leapt at the thought of facing Marcus with good news. Father mellowed after the conversation, and deemed it a tremendous success in that Jacob had an influential client willing to pay in excess of £1.6 million – a fortune! I thought, with hindsight, that it was sensible not to mention my negotiations to Marcus, as any disappointments at this early stage in his recovery would possibly cause further problems rather than alleviate them. I kept all negotiations between Father and myself.

Within a week the sale of the necklace was finalised, and I approached Scorpion Records with a firm bid for the company; but to my dismay I was told that some unknown buyers had put in an exceptionally high bid, and they were not at liberty to refuse their marvellous offer. There was no way I could top it. I was devastated. My plans had disintegrated and I was sitting on £1.6 million but no record company. I begged to be allowed to approach the new owners, but was told no names would be forthcoming and that contracts had already been exchanged. It was a difficult time, trying to explain to Marcus he was now under new management, and this did not sit comfortably with him. We began to feel we were climbing a ladder that was going nowhere. If the new owners wanted a certain kind of music, we would, against our better judgement, have to produce the goods. At least the money from the necklace could help fund running expenses for the estate a while longer.

There was a noticeable decline in Marcus's health. I feared he was not going to make the recovery that we had anticipated. Then a letter arrived from America. It was from Scorpion Records. Reluctantly we opened it to be informed there had been extensive changes within the corporation and that they would now be known as 'Phoenix'!

I thought what an appropriate name it was, as I considered Marcus needed to be rising from the ashes and reinventing himself. What a great name for a first tour in the UK: the 'Rising from the Ashes' tour! On reading further, we discovered that the management, knowing about Marcus's work, was prepared to give him carte blanche with his music, and let him produce albums he thought suitable for the market he wished to attract. We were amazed at this turn of events. We considered all our prayers had been answered in one letter. Phoenix wanted him to sign a new contract, and together we read and reread the letter, going over each point made. I began putting my plans into action.

Although he was continuing his treatment for heroin addiction, Marcus had many down moments. Nights were his most traumatic times. I would sit with him hour upon hour, while his demons invaded his space and took him to new lows. I began to feel totally useless. We would talk and revisit old ground, dealing with everything that was troubling him so much.

The following morning the telephone rang incessantly. I struggled out of the shower, wrapped a towel around me and, dripping water across the carpet, I reached for the receiver.

'Hello? Jonathan? How are you, darling? Are you keeping your grandfather amused? Good!'

'I am fine, Mother, but look, I am really anxious to meet Marcus. I have been here for one day and have to leave for London tomorrow. May I come over and meet with him?'

I hesitated. How on earth would I avoid telling Jonathan about Marcus? I wanted nothing of his addiction to get back to Father.

'Well, darling, he's still asleep. I think perhaps you should leave it, today.'

He sounded disappointed and thought me evasive but could not understand why.

'Is he ill, Mother?' he asked.

'He is a bit under the weather!' I added as an afterthought.

'But Mother, I am going to London tomorrow for an interview with an orchestra. I wanted to ask Uncle Marcus for his advice on how to handle myself at the interview.'

'How wonderful, Jonathan. I am so pleased for you!' I remarked, trying desperately to move the conversation away from Marcus.

'Yes, this could mean a long term engagement if I am successful!'

'I am sure you will be!' I remarked. 'I wish you all the luck in the world. Not that you will need luck – your talent will see you through.'

He continued, 'I am anxious to meet the famous Marcus Walker before I go. He spoke so well of my father at the funeral, and seems like a really great guy. There is so much I need to ask him about my father when they were growing up together. Can I please come over, Mother? *Please?*'

I was at a loss for further excuses to deter him from a visit. It was difficult to stonewall such a vibrant, enthusiastic young man who missed his father dreadfully.

He added, 'I want to see you too, Mother. I have something for you!'

'Well, if you can make it for tea at around 4 p.m. you will be most welcome to join us. I will make sure that Marcus is around. See if you can beg a cake from Edith. I am fresh out of such things!'

'That isn't like you, Mother. No cake? You're slipping! I will see what I can do! Shall I bring Grandfather?'

'No, not today, darling!'

He hung up, leaving me to explain my actions to Marcus. I had been apprehensive about their first meeting, and hoped he had not detected it in my voice. I was at a loss to know how to handle the introduction to a recovering heroin addict.

I returned to my room, went swiftly through my wardrobe and selected a blouse and trousers. I needed to make myself presentable before confronting Marcus. He was asleep, having had a horrendously disturbed night, but I woke him with a tray of tea and his favourite home-made jam, toast, and pot of coffee for me. He looked dreadful. I do not remember a time when he looked so ill. Not even during childhood days when measles, mumps and rubella had taken hold of us all. With great effort he raised his tired, weak frame up on to the pillows. I made him as comfortable as I could.

'Sit with me, Sophia!' he begged, patting the side of the bed. I handed him the tray and sat. 'Here, have a slice of toast and jam!' he offered.

I perched on the bed and he plied me with toast and my own home-made strawberry jam. I readily succumbed to the temptation. I asked after his health, but he rolled his vivid brown eyes, which penetrated me as if reading my every thought.

'Jonathan rang me a short while ago. He is with Father at the Hall and will be leaving for an interview in London tomorrow. He is anxious to meet you and talk about Alex. I have explained that four o'clock will be fine.'

'Honestly, Sophia, I can't! Look at me! I am in no fit state to meet with anyone.'

I dropped my head and he could see my disappointment. I explained that it was important to me that they got to know one another, and that he couldn't go on avoiding potential visitors, particularly special ones.

'I just cannot face anyone at the moment!' he protested.

'Forget it, Marcus!' I snapped, jumping up. 'I will tell him today is out of the question!'

He caught my arm as I was ready to leave, saying, 'Very well, Sophia. I will meet him. I will attempt to make myself look presentable just for you!'

'Oh, thank you, Marcus. Thank you!' I kissed his cheek, sending his coffee flying. He gave a sly smile as I mopped the tray and removed it from the room. He realised how happy his agreement had made me.

At 3.40 Jonathan arrived, clasping a small package and one of Edith's delightful coffee cakes.

'For you, Mother,' he announced, hugging me. He presented me with a prettily wrapped gift. I carefully opened it and discovered it to be my favourite perfume, which Alex had often bought me in the past.

'How wonderful – and very thoughtful of you, Jonathan.'

I held him close, my firstborn. How I loved the closeness of my son and his loving, gentle ways. I was so fortunate to be able to share my darling son with two doting adoptive parents. Jonathan and I had found one another, and that was fine. A wonderful part of Alex existed, and it pleased me greatly. We chatted for a while. I prepared our tea and fussed over him, listening to his dreams of appearing in an orchestra. I thought his talent on violin far exceeded a position in any orchestra, but he was happy to follow this route and I knew his interview the following day would be successful.

Marcus arrived downstairs promptly at 4.15 p.m., his black hair washed and gleaming brightly in the afternoon sunshine. His lean figure was impressive, dressed in jeans and shirt. Jonathan and Marcus embraced enthusiastically, and I nodded approval at Marcus for the way in which he had made tremendous effort to meet my beloved son.

In no time they had devoured, with minimum help, the coffee cake and two pots of Earl Grey and were deep in conversation about music. Marcus introduced Jonathan to 'Soapy', and it was the first time I had watched him handle a guitar since his return to the UK. There was a spare violin in the study, which Marcus promptly produced, and soon the cottage rang out with music. Jonathan seemed mesmerised by Marcus. I took a back seat in the afternoon's proceedings and excused myself to do an assortment of jobs my 'rock-star sitting' had not allowed, while they made fantastic music together.

After a while I rejoined them.

'I think the formation of a band will be the next item on the agenda,' I remarked, visualising Marcus interviewing new band members, and for the first time in weeks Marcus showed an enthusiasm I could only have dreamed of.

Jonathan stayed almost three hours. They were the happiest Marcus and I had experienced in weeks. I did not realise then that my son would not be attending his interview the following day. He was aware of what Marcus was going through with his heroin addiction. Uncannily, he knew, and approached me to offer his help and complete discretion. We could call on him at any time. My son was an extremely sensitive young man and his support and understanding were of the utmost importance when I found days I thought I could cope no longer but Jonathan was there for us both. Meanwhile, I had to help Marcus face his demons, return to the stage and appear for those fans who loved his music, and for the many followers his music would produce in the future. He could have a whole new career ahead of him, if only…

During the daytime, when Jonathan relieved me of my duties with Marcus's recovery, I sought interviews with various county council officials, the local parish council, and most important of all, long, arduous hours with Father, trying to instil fresh ideas into him with a view to saving our heritage, Harrington Hall. He became increasingly suspicious about why he had not seen or heard from Marcus. I tried unsuccessfully to pacify him on numerous occasions, but not once did I succumb to the temptation of telling him what the problems were. Only Jonathan, Simon, the nurses assigned to his recovery – and me – knew the facts and it was imperative we kept all details away from prying eyes, especially the press. A bad press would take away any chance of getting a foothold on the British music scene, and I certainly did not wish to jeopardise Marcus's recovery and career or my hopes and plans for the future.

Father, in his advancing years, did not succumb easily to change, but knew if we were to save the estate, steps needed to be taken which he normally would not have considered. As he was hostile to modern music, I knew my ideas would not be readily accepted, but drastic times called for drastic measures. He was a difficult man to persuade, but when confronted by the evidence I found he began viewing situations in a different light. I told Marcus nothing about the plans I had in mind, until I had safely secured approval from Father and received sound financial advice from my accountant as to the feasibility of my ideas. The accountant rubbed his hands gleefully at my proposals and considered them an exceptional money-making idea. I would need a substantial loan from the bank initially, but with over £1 million deposited with them this proved no problem. It was reckoned that with my financial genius I could have the loan paid after a year of the projected ventures. My time in Australia running the cattle ranch had not been totally wasted, and the business procedures I had learned stood me in good stead for the propositions I had for Marcus. Approval given, I decided to face Marcus with my plans, in the hope that my schemes would be agreeable and set him on the road to full recovery, kick-starting his career in Britain once more.

With my briefcase under my arm, I climbed the cottage stairs and knocked on Marcus's bedroom door. On his instructions I entered to find Harry Underwood, the experienced physiotherapist to the City football team, administering massage to him. The thrice-weekly visits were exceedingly useful in helping him return to health after his detoxification programme, which was in its latter stages.

'Oops!' I exclaimed, 'I will come back later!' I was mildly embarrassed.

Marcus lifted his head from the portable couch and insisted, 'No, Sophia, please stay! Harry is just finishing. I'll take a shower and then we can talk. I can see you have important things to discuss.' He pointed to the briefcase tucked under my arm. 'Sit by the window and I will join you shortly.'

He got up from the couch, a towel around his hips, and disappeared into the shower. Harry collapsed his couch, packed his bag, bade me farewell and, with a cheeky wink, left the room. I sat on a chair by the dressing table and was confronted by a photograph in a frame of Marcus's mother, Frances, at about thirty years of age. The original photograph had been cut down the centre, obviously removing any trace of his father from view. I picked it up and stared intently at it.

'You are interested in my mother's photograph, I see!'

I turned to be faced my Marcus, leaning against the dressing-room door, his bronzed body wrapped only in a scanty towel, his long, wet black hair cascading around his face and shoulders. I could see why so many women fans found him extremely sexually attractive. I tried hard not to let my eyes rest on his athletic body as I asked demurely, 'Would you like me to dry your hair?'

'That would be great, Sophia!' he murmured softly. 'Fetch your hair-dryer and I will put on some clothing.'

Resting the photograph back in its rightful place, I dashed to my bedroom door. Trembling, I searched in my room for my hair appliances. I returned to find Marcus clothed in jeans, but no top, sitting cross-legged on the floor – a favourite position of his – with his hair in need of a great deal of attention.

'You are trembling, Sophia,' he observed, taking hold of my hand. 'Are you cold?'

How could I tell him that I too, as a woman, found his physical presence exciting? I politely said, 'No. I am just nervous about the plans that I have to put to you, hoping you will find them acceptable.'

I tried to put the ridiculous feelings that had welled up inside me into the background.

He gazed at his mother's photograph and exclaimed, 'Wasn't she beautiful? How could my father have deserted us and gone back to Canada?'

'Marcus! You cannot go on beating yourself up over this!' I told him.

'Actually, Sophia, when I was on tour in Canada last year and giving TV interviews, I asked viewers if anyone knew of a wartime Canadian pilot named Bruce Walker. I wanted to meet him to tell him what an absolute shit he was for abandoning me and my mother, and how much I hated him for being instrumental in my mother's death; but no news was forthcoming.'

He observed the pained expression on my face.

'Let it go, Marcus! That's in the past! You can't change it, but it will surely affect your future if you do not come to terms with it. It will eat away at you. I came here today to talk about your future, so let's get down to business!'

I dried his hair until it shone like black velvet and he thanked me for my efforts. God, he was handsome! Looking at my watch I declared, 'Marcus, can you make an effort and put on some riding clothes? I have asked Jimmy to saddle up Nelson and Achilles for midday. I'd like us to take a ride. There is something I wish to show you.'

'I'm not sure I feel—' he began.

I interrupted him in mid-sentence. 'It really is important to our future, and anyway I think it is about time you got some fresh air!'

His curiosity had got the better of him. I toddled along to my room to find my riding gear, leaving him to finish dressing. Jimmy had saddled the horses and Marcus and I rode over to Hardy's Wood, and a considerable distance beyond.

'Hold on, Sophia!' he shouted, hard on my heels. 'I am finding it difficult keeping up with you.'

I looked back. 'Not far now!' I called, and within minutes I had come to a halt and dismounted. Marcus followed suit and stood looking at me. I surveyed acre upon acre of open land that had once been a park.

'I see nothing of any interest here, Sophia!' he commented, disappointment showing on his face.

'There isn't at present, but there will be. Father has given us this land and it is far enough from the Hall not to cause too much of a disturbance.'

'What kind of disturbance?' He looked decidedly puzzled.

'For open air concerts in summer!' I announced.

'Not another Woodstock!' he mused.

'Goodness, no! It will be far more wonderful. There are so many young people wanting outdoor concerts in this country. We can have one on a two-monthly basis, with a classical concert every other month to please Father!'

He looked at me and threw his arms into the air. 'But Sophia, you can't just take a piece of land and have a concert. There are so many factors to consider: car parking, security, access roads, safety, permission from various authorities…'

I took his arm, saying, 'I know, Marcus. I have been in touch with all the necessary authorities. The access roads are acceptable; the camping and parking facilities are going to be dealt with, and the parish council is fully in favour of the idea, as it will bring good business to a dying village. Father has been tremendously supportive to villagers in the past, and now they are returning that support.'

'You really have done your homework, Sophia!'

'I have – truly I have! Back at the cottage I have a briefcase full of letters of authorisation and plans. My accountant considers it to be an extremely viable proposition financially,' I explained, 'as does the bank!'

'And who will appear?' he asked.

'*You* will be the main attraction!' I giggled. 'And I'm sure that you have considerable contacts in the music world. There must be bands and groups out there who'd love to appear.'

'Let's go back to the cottage and talk this through, Sophia. It sounds like a marvellous idea. I won't ask you how you managed to persuade Oliver to give up this land, but then you always managed to wrap him round your little finger!'

I ignored the comment and mounted Nelson. Marcus and I rode back toward the cottage at a leisurely pace.

'I guess you realise this venture is going to take thousands to set up, and I do not have that kind of money any longer. The Hall is taking it faster than I can make it.'

'I have money,' I declared.

Marcus looked at me uneasily, saying, 'But it is common knowledge you had no money on your return from Australia, hence you're living at Starbeck Row. Where has the money come from?'

'It doesn't matter!' I answered indignantly.

'It *does* matter. Where is the money coming from, Sophia?'

'I sold the necklace Mother willed to me,' I confessed, 'with Father's blessing, of course.'

Marcus brought Achilles to an abrupt halt. I stopped too. His expression was one of anger.

'No, Sophia! *No!* You have to get the necklace back from whoever you sold it to! What on earth were you thinking of?'

I quickly explained that I'd sold it to raise money to buy the record company, but was pipped at the post on the deal, and so still had substantial funds deposited in the bank.

On the homeward journey Marcus was extremely upset and made this obvious as we walked from the stables.

'I really cannot take your money, Sophia! It's out of the question!'

'Please, Marcus, we need to talk extensively about this. There will be the cost of equipment, setting up of concerts, and tour buses when you take to the road to promote your album,' I pointed out; but he strode ahead, not listening, and I found it increasingly difficult to keep pace with him. He made tracks for his daily sauna while I prepared lunch.

After lunch, we resumed our discussion. He was still angry I had sold Mother's necklace and insisted I attempt to buy it back. I retrieved the briefcase from my room and we spoke in detail of concerts in the park area on a monthly basis and of touring the UK and Europe in the winter, after the release of his first UK album in many years, which he would hopefully have completed in time for the Christmas market.

After some considerable displays of anger, Marcus confided in me that it had been his intention to raise money by selling his beloved motorcycle collection to fund the tour; but I made it clear that the sale of the necklace was a deal completed, and that I would discuss it no further. I insisted his beloved motorcycle collection should stay intact.

Chapter Thirty-three

I forged ahead with my intended plans and eventually noticed vast improvements in Marcus's health. It was as though unseen forces were taking control of many situations and steering us onto a set path. At every step of the way, people were appearing in our lives, intent on contributing to the objective we wished to achieve.

The telephone rang constantly and I tried to be on hand to take calls.

'Hi, ma'am! I would like to chat with Marcus Walker. Tell him it's his old buddy, Rick Chambers, speaking. I understand he is getting a new band together.'

I acknowledged that this was true, and called Marcus to the phone. His enthusiasm at the call was astounding.

'*Rick*! It's been a long time! A new band? Why, yes, of course! You want to fly over for an audition? I am sure it will be OK.'

Marcus caught my eye. 'Can we accommodate a prospective band member, Sophia?'

I nodded obligingly.

'Yes, it will be fine, Rick! When are you arriving? Heathrow, Friday, midday? Yes, we'll send a chauffeur to fetch you. Witherspoon? Can't say our paths have crossed, but I have certainly heard of him. His reputation precedes him! Ray "Young Blood" Witherspoon, yes, bring him with you. I can't promise we will engage him but we will audition him. We certainly need a pedal steel guitarist on this new album I am compiling. Oh, before you go, it's a definite "*no*" to drugs. I am totally clean and that's the way it has to stay. Any drugs and you are out of the band, man! You may like to pass the message on. It applies to anyone and everyone. Good! As long as we understand one another. I will see you on Friday. Bye, Rick!'

Marcus turned toward me with enthusiasm plastered over his features and filling his voice.

'I take it from your conversation that we are expecting two guests?' I asked.

He smiled and nodded. 'Rick Chambers is a bass guitarist, one of the best in the States and this Ray "Young Blood" Witherspoon, well, I have never met him but he is a great pedal steel guitarist. He's been in the business for ever, according to Rick. He's the absolute best.'

Marcus disappeared to his room to work on the ever-flowing lyrics of new songs (mostly written in the early hours), while I planned what rooms our guests would occupy.

Friday was an exceptionally busy day. I baked good English fare in the hope the evening meal would be a special occasion, at which Marcus, Jonathan, Father and I could welcome our 'American cousins'. My greatest shock came when Rick Chambers alighted from the car, followed by Ray Witherspoon. Ray was a larger than life character, over six feet six inches in height, with the most enormous full set of black whiskers I had ever set eyes upon! His beard could have housed a family of chipmunks without them having seen daylight for a week. His eyes were dark brown and vivid. His hair hung below his shoulders. It was unruly and held in place by a bandanna. He was good-humoured and a delight to be with. Marcus and I gelled with him immediately. I considered him to be approximately sixty years old, give or take a year or two.

Rick Chambers was a pleasant forty-year-old, averaged sized, good-looking guy, but he had a quick temper, an extra large ego and considered himself God's gift to women.

Father and Jonathan appeared promptly at eight o'clock. Their expressions on being introduced to Ray were very revealing, but in no time they chatted as though they were long lost friends. Father appeared to be captivated by him. On two occasions I whispered in his ear that 'it was rude to stare', but he smiled and continued to do so.

Rick was from San Francisco and Ray lived in Chicago. Auditions had been planned, by Marcus, for the following day. Until then, it was 'get to know one another' time.

Rick was free with his life story, but I found Ray reticent about his past. I did learn that he was part Sioux Indian on his father's side. Marcus found this fascinating, having a great affinity with the culture of the North American Indian. Ray was quite taken with the way in which Marcus had collected huge amounts of Indian artefacts, which he'd used to decorate Starbeck Row. The get-together ended at midnight. Marcus was insistent auditions began at 9 a.m. on the dot.

The following morning saw me cooking breakfast at 8 a.m. for three hungry musicians. The barn bore witness to the first audition, which lasted no more than ten minutes and had Rick firmly installed as bass player. When the time arrived for Ray's audition, Marcus insisted I accompany them on piano. Ray was given a free rein to bring his own style and interpretation into the proceedings. It began with one song, then two and I began wondering when Marcus would finish! Without lifting his eyes to look at us I could tell he had a sullen expression on his face, which had me worried. Suddenly he stopped playing mid-way through the fifth song, and for no apparent reason shouted, 'Enough! Enough!'

Ray and I ceased playing as Marcus gathered up his music and stood there. Ray looked at me, frowned and I returned his gaze. I shrugged my shoulders. Marcus was obviously disturbed. I moved to within feet of him and said, 'Well?'

He looked intently into my eyes and said, 'Well what?'

'What do you think of Ray's playing?' I asked meekly.

He smiled and said, 'Same as you, Sophia! I think the man is a genius. He is so open. He gives so much of his soul to his playing, just like you and me. He is fantastic! Don't dare let him get away! Book him immediately.'

'Don't you think it's your place to hire him, Marcus?' I implored.

'Ray, buddy,' he laughed, 'Welcome aboard the "Phoenix Rises from the Ashes" experience!'

They shook hands and the deal was done. As Marcus left the barn, Ray turned to me and said, 'What a strange guy he is. Is he always so eccentric?'

I laughed and said, 'I am afraid so, but you'll get used to it.'

'You are one very special lady, Sophia,' he said. 'May I be bold and ask if you and Marcus are a couple?'

I shook my head and smiled. He apologised for his personal line of questioning.

Auditions over, we retreated to the cottage, and then I toured the estate with Ray and Rick, showing them where they would be residing for the next few months. I particularly wanted to show them the estate worker's cottage which would be their home for that period – and longer – if all went well.

As the following days passed, more band members arrived. Donald Dickerson, drummer, flew in from Scotland, and Jed Richardson, rhythm guitarist, arrived from East Anglia by road. The new band was complete and together they took shape in a most incredible way. All it took now was for Marcus to appoint a manager, producer and production crew, road manager and sound crew. Telephoning to and fro saw the meeting between him and Roger Ellison, his old manager from the days when he first formed Marc Walker and the Dream Catchers. Roger possessed a magnetic personality and was a straightforward guy. Marcus perceived him to be the most sincere and open of people he had dealt with in all his time as a performer, and knew he could rely on him for total honesty and respect, something he considered the most important factor in an artist/manager relationship. Surprisingly, all the band members gelled exceptionally well with each other which was unusual. There were arguments of sorts, and Marcus could at times be abrupt and impatient, but there was nothing that the calm, uplifting nature of Ray could not smooth out in his inimitable, patient way. Eventually a whole team of helpers and advisers were on hand, and we were ready to start our long uphill battle to return to the music scene in England.

The time was fast approaching for Marcus's son to stay with us for the summer holidays.

Freddie Walker breezed into our lives one sunny July afternoon, and we knew then that life at Starbeck Row would never be quite the same again. It had been my intention to travel with John in the Range Rover to collect Freddie from his Catholic boarding school in Somerset. Marcus became increasingly apprehensive about his first meeting with his son in a long while, and decided he could cope with the reunion under less controlled circumstances in the comfort of Starbeck Row. It was agreed that Marcus and I would await his arrival. We prepared his room – the one with magnificent views over the Harrington estate – and close to my room should he need help. Marcus appeared agitated throughout the morning, and I assumed that the ordeal of Freddie's arrival was weighing heavily on his mind. It had been almost four years since they had met and I thought Marcus was anxious as to what kind of reception he would receive.

After a snack lunch we waited for John to arrive with his special passenger. I felt an air of nervousness creep over me too. It was important for Marcus that everything went well during this visit. Suzi, Freddie's mother, had reluctantly agreed he could stay during summer holidays, leaving her freedom from the task of having to accommodate a child she hardly knew or had little contact with.

We walked along the path as he alighted from the vehicle. Freddie rushed forward to greet Marcus, his arms outstretched.

'Daddy! Daddy! How good it is to see you!' He flung his arms around Marcus in a bear hug. 'I am so glad to be here with you, Daddy!'

Marcus was taken aback by the greeting but the look of delight on his face was worth a million spoken words. He placed his arms invitingly around his son and held him close saying, 'My goodness, Freddie, how you have grown!'

The ten-year-old lad was tall, with wavy hair and angelic features. He was the breath of fresh air we both badly needed. Turning to me, he held out his hand, and with a firm shake he said, 'You must be Sophia! I have heard a lot about you from mummy. I would like to thank you so much for inviting me to stay!'

His manners were impeccable, his clothing immaculate. He was the mirror image of his father at that age, except for his wavy hair, total confidence and superb dress sense, and of course the lack of spectacles. It was obvious from first impressions I was going to adore this child. Marcus relieved John of the enormous mountain of luggage which accompanied his son, and I escorted Freddie into the cottage.

'Can I make you refreshments?' I asked.

'Actually, Sophia – can I call you Sophia? – I would prefer to have a bath and be allowed to unpack,' he said politely, a beaming smile stretching from ear to ear.

I had no hesitation in stating I preferred to be addressed as Sophia, and took Freddie to his room, while Marcus staggered up the stairs with the suitcases.

Young Master Walker agreed that his room was impressive and luxurious and that the views were breathtaking, explaining it was a far cry from his dormitory at boarding school. My mind travelled back to the dormitory at the convent in Ireland and I hoped he was happier at his school than I had been, but then the circumstances for me were so different.

Having unpacked his luggage and bathed, Freddie joined Marcus and me in the kitchen.

'Ah, Freddie! I thought we would go across to Harrington Hall to introduce you to Sir Oliver, and have supper with him. I am anxious for you to meet him!'

'How wonderful, Daddy! I am really looking forward to meeting Sir Oliver. He is my grandfather, is he not?' he enquired.

Marcus explained, 'Not quite, Freddie! Sir Oliver took me into his home when I was a small boy of three, so I regard him as my father. Therefore I guess he is, in some respects, your grandfather. I am sure he would like to be considered as such.'

Freddie was happy with the explanation and delighted at joining us in the visit to the Hall. Haynes, the butler, on hand as always, greeted us with, 'My goodness, Mr Marcus, how your son favours you in looks!' and then politely ushered us into the drawing room, where Father was engrossed in the music of Mendelssohn.

We stayed at the Hall for a considerable time. Father was overjoyed at meeting Freddie for the first time. They had good-natured conversations, and Father commented on how worldly-wise Freddie was for a ten-year-old. I agreed he was a bright, articulate boy. On our return to the cottage, Freddie asked if he could retire to bed, as he was quite exhausted. I went with him to his room, gave him fresh towels and showed him where various items were stored should he require them.

'This is my room across the hall,' I said, pointing to the door opposite. 'If you should need anything Freddie, just knock!' I explained.

'Thank you, Sophia! If I need anything I am sure Daddy will come to my aid.'

I explained his daddy's room was at the end of the corridor, should he need him.

'Don't you and Daddy sleep together?' he asked, his large brown eyes searching mine for an answer.

'Oh, no, Freddie!' I explained. 'We have separate rooms. We are just good friends.'

'Oh!' he sighed. 'Well, you see, Mummy has quite a few men friends, but they sleep with her when they stay overnight at her apartment.'

I tried to disguise the smile creeping across my face. He was grown up in many ways, yet saw many things in total simplicity through the eyes of a child.

'Do you love Daddy, Sophia?' he asked.

The question came as a total surprise.

'Well, Freddie, I suppose I do, but not as perhaps you… Well, you see, your daddy and I have known each other since childhood and we were always good friends, always there for one another. I adore his talent and well, I adore him for the person he is, underneath the rock star image.'

Suddenly I realised I was out of my depth, unable to explain my feelings for Marcus. I immediately changed the subject.

'Do you like your boarding school?' I asked.

Freddie stopped for a moment, looked toward the ceiling and answered.

'It's all right, Sophia.' He sat on the bed. 'It is not ideal. There is bullying by older boys. I suppose I miss family life. You know, being part of a real family; but then you can't miss what you've never had.'

'I am so sorry,' I said.

'Don't be, Sophia. Mummy is not a homemaker. She likes to shop, look beautiful and go to parties. There is no room for me in her life, if I am honest. Daddy is constantly touring, trying to make enough to pay my school fees and keep Mummy in luxury, but I do miss him. He is a great person. Don't you think so?'

'I do, Freddie, I do!' I exclaimed.

I looked at this boy in astonishment, at the way he considered his lot. He accepted life as it was, with all its ups and downs. It was then that it made me determined, during his stay, that I would not only be there for Marcus, when he needed me, during rehearsals and recordings, but introduce Freddie to a stable family life. I liked the boy so much and wanted him to be happy; but I suddenly feared I had bitten off more than I could chew.

Ray 'Young Blood' Witherspoon was a true gentleman, a big, gentle, hairy giant, a fantastic musician and, unlike Rick Chambers, an introvert. Rick constantly provided details of his families, past and present, and all the female conquests in between. Marcus would often tell him to 'shut up', especially when Freddie and I were in earshot.

Ray had taken a particular liking to the company of Freddie and began teaching him the basics of the pedal steel guitar. He found this fascinating and was quick to learn. In no time he was a musician in the making. On most days Freddie and I managed a hack, me on Nero, he on Samson, a nine-year-old gelding with a mind of his own. Freddie claimed to have ridden extensively on Marcus's ranch in California years previously, but had forgotten far more than he had remembered. I endeared myself to him with the time spent teaching him to ride. He was quick to learn; we were soon galloping across the many fields within the estate. Some days were fraught with difficulties, but however many times Freddie was thrown from the horse he would pick himself up, dust himself down and mount the horse once more mumbling, 'Stupid horse! The horse is stupid, Sophia!'

I agreed but wanted to laugh. We named the horse 'Stupid Samson'. During these periods, Marcus was at work in Doggett's Barn, rehearsing and recording. He was hoping to complete a demo tape for Phoenix Records. He played and recorded, mostly at night, slept until 4 p.m., then spent several hours with Freddie and me before returning to the barn. Freddie adored every moment of the attention received from his daddy, especially when introduced to the acoustic guitar. When not receiving tuition, we would invite Father to Starbeck Row for a game of Monopoly. Freddie was a good loser, unlike Marcus at his age, who always threw all the pieces to the four winds.

We had all become extremely attached to this young man. Freddie loved riding pillion on any one of Marcus's motorcycles. I do not think I had ever seen Marcus more happy and contented than during the month of August, despite the fact that he was under pressure to produce an album. He was off heroin, at peace with himself and the world in general. His band were an amiable bunch, and I realised for once Marcus was listening to and being advised by someone other than myself – and that someone was Ray! That was a breakthrough in itself. I sensed he and Ray had become close friends through their love of music, despite a thirty-year age gap. Ray was gentle whereas Marcus could be fiery if things were not going as he expected. They complemented one another. The lyrics and music were flowing from Marcus like water from a tap. He wrote a song called 'Freddie', dedicated to the son he was learning to adore all over again, and hoped to release it as a single. He asked my advice on the music to accompany the lyrics. I played piano on two recordings and sang harmony on three. The tide of change was turning for us all.

Life with young Freddie Walker was exhilarating. He was the most outgoing, vibrant child it had ever been my fortune to meet, with oodles of energy and a real love for everything and everyone. He possessed a great voracity for life. In no time I adored the boy, but time was fast approaching for his return to boarding school in Somerset.

It was early September. Marcus had been busy all night in the recording studio, working on his album. I was expecting him home for breakfast. I woke early, threw on a dressing gown over my nightdress and prepared breakfast for Freddie, who was going to the Flamingo Park in Pickering with Marianne and Rosie. It was their intention to make an early start. I watched Freddie chase his cereal around the bowl with his spoon. He appeared deep in thought when he suddenly focused his eyes on me and said, 'Do you like having me stay here, Sophia?'

'What a funny question to ask,' I began. 'No, I don't like having you here. I *adore* having you here! The place is so alive with your presence!'

He jumped excitedly up from the table and threw his arms around my neck, his brown eyes twinkling as he gave me an enormous hug. How often I had seen that look in his father in days gone by, when Marcus hoped I would help him out of some awful fiasco and spare him from Father's wrath.

'Well,' he asked, 'would you ask Daddy if I can live here with you both permanently? I do not want to go back to my dreadful boarding school. *Please*, Sophia! I love living here with you and Daddy. For the first time in my life you both make me feel special.'

There was the Walker look, the deep penetrating eyes, the pleading gaze.

'I will certainly ask him, Freddie, but I cannot judge what the outcome will be. It is not really up to your daddy. He will have to speak to your mother and see what she has to say. She is your legal guardian.'

'I am sure she won't care where I am as long as I don't get under her feet. She has a new man in her life, and has never been a mother to me anyway. I have got so close to you and Daddy, Ray and Sir Oliver. Please let me stay!'

I assured him I would speak to Marcus while he was away for the day in Pickering, with Rosie and Marianne. It would give me time to talk to his father alone.

Marcus returned a short while after Freddie had departed for the Flamingo Park. He slumped onto the sofa looking pale and tired, but ecstatic at his night's achievements. I prepared him breakfast and as we sat drinking coffee, I broached the subject of his son. He listened and then snapped, 'Suzi will never let me have him live here! You must understand that, Sophia. She was loath to give me visiting rights, and that was when I had a court order allowing me access to my son. She is one aggressive, volatile woman. Suzi is simply not interested in Freddie, but in the money I pay in maintenance for him.'

'Then you have to do something to change the situation,' I said angrily. 'You can at least speak to her. Freddie so wants to be part of this family and live here with us! He really loves you, Marcus. He loves his grandfather too, and he also adores Ray.'

He looked at me, his eyes flashing.

'I blame this situation on you, Sophia! You have shown him what real family life is like, and this has spoilt any chance of him getting back into boarding school life again. You are not able to have children yourself, so I believe you are compensating for this fact by wrapping yourself up in Freddie!'

I was dumbfounded at his remarks and extremely hurt. I stood up at the table and shouted, 'How dare you be so rude? How dare you? Lady Mary always insisted we were day pupils at school and were not brought up by outsiders. She loved and comforted us when we were ill and was always there for us when we were troubled. *Well, I have* – at the Magdalene Laundry! I know what hell it can be. I do not think Freddie should be subjected to boarding school life any longer.'

He looked in sheer astonishment at me, never having seen me so angry.

'You either love Freddie, Marcus, or you do not! For goodness sake do something. He needs you. He needs us both!'

The look on Marcus's face was mind-boggling as I turned and stormed out of the door.

I retreated to my room and flung myself on to the bed. It hurt me to think that the boy who had stolen my heart was to be sent away from those he loved and I cried unashamedly. Within ten minutes my bedroom door opened. There stood Marcus, hair hanging loosely over his face and around his shoulders, looking stunned at my outburst. He walked over, sat on the bed and reached for my hand as I sniffed into a tissue.

'I really am so sorry, Sophia! I apologise profusely for what I said. It was hurtful and unnecessary. I apologise from the bottom of my heart! My comments were totally out of order. Can you please forgive me?'

Tearfully, I said, 'I accept your apology but you have hurt me very deeply. You can't imagine what it is like knowing you cannot have children.' I wept. 'My darling daughter, Anna-Sophia, just three days old, lies in a godforsaken plot somewhere in Australia, while I am here.'

Marcus could understand neither my reaction nor the fact that my second child was dead.

'You have never explained about Anna-Sophia,' he replied.

In the next twenty minutes I revealed everything to him. I poured out my heart, releasing feelings that had been buried for years. He consoled me with comfort and reassurance of better times in the future. Marcus teased away my tears with his fingers.

'Please, Sophia, I know how much you have grown to love Freddie, but you haven't a clue what Suzi is like. She gives me so much grief. She is like hell on two legs. If I handle this badly the chances are it will be an awful long time before I get to see Freddie again. It would break my heart.'

He wiped away more of my tears.

'Then will you let *me* speak to her?' I urged. 'I have seen how special the last few weeks have been for you, having Freddie here. I know what a tremendous difference your love and attention have meant to him.' I continued to sniff into my tissue.

'Please, Sophia,' he begged, 'no more tears! Yes, I'll give you my permission to speak to her. I will give you her telephone number in London, but please – for all our sakes – handle her with great care. She is one very tough cookie!'

I thanked Marcus and began lifting myself up on the pillows. He stared at me, his eyes piercing my very soul.

'I want so much to thank you for all you have accomplished with me and my son. We will never be able to repay you Sophia! *Never!*'

He leaned over and gently placed his lips on my cheek, kissing away a runaway tear. Softly he placed his lips on mine and kissed me longingly. I should have pushed him away, but I did not want the kisses or the physical contact to cease. The excitement and feelings running through my body were unbelievably poignant. I began to speak but he placed a finger on my lips and said, 'Ssh,' as he lifted me into his strong arms and carried me from my room. As I nestled against his muscular frame I asked, 'Where are you taking me, Marcus?'

He did not answer but smiled and entered his bedroom, closed the door and removing my dressing gown and nightdress, placed me gently under the duvet. Shedding his clothing, he crept in beside me. I should have protested, but I did not want to. I wanted his arms around me, feeling the warmth of his gorgeous body next to mine, his lips, his caresses, his kisses. I wanted Marcus Walker, and I wanted him there and then. How could I have been so foolish and not realised what had been happening to me? He was gentle, sensitive and sexual. It was as if I were in a dream I did not want to wake from: just Marcus and me, shutting ourselves away from the outside world, locked in a loving embrace. He kissed me so tenderly and his huge, vivid brown eyes looked longingly at me. I could not contain the urgency with which my body wanted him. I adored this guy and reached out to him, running my fingers through his shiny black hair as I returned his kisses. He held me close, my heart pounding in my breast. I became light-headed with a happiness I hadn't known in years. Again his lips moved over mine, his tongue parting them as he explored my mouth, inciting in me feelings I had long since forgotten. I wanted his kisses and his touch so desperately. Why had I not realised my immense feelings for this sensitive, sexy man? He caressed my back, sending ripples of excitement down my body to my toes. I had not experienced longings of this nature since my teenage years with Alex.

'Marcus, I... I... want you,' I murmured.

'You will have me, darling Sophia, but not yet. I want to make love to you for hours.'

The words invoked in me a passion I found difficult to control. His hands cupped my breasts. His mouth encircled one nipple, then the other, as he teased them with his tongue. He looked at my naked body, his big brown eyes feasting on me, his own body filled with an intimate purpose.

'God, Sophia! You are so beautiful. I need you so much!'

'I need you too, Marcus,' I whispered, my hands exploring the contours of his chest.

I slid my fingers down his gorgeous slim body to his abdomen and then to more intimate parts and instilled in him an urgency he did not appear to be able to control.

Deep sensual emotions penetrated every fibre of my being. I wanted to please him so much. We were as one, loving, giving, and sharing of each other.

As we finally lay, fulfilled by our lovemaking and enveloped in one another's arms, I learnt so much. There had been no other woman for whom he had written his songs, as I had imagined; not former lovers, as I had suspected; but his lyrics and music had been for *me* and me alone. It was then I realised he had loved me since childhood. He explained he had been too frightened to approach me in those days, for fear of rejection, something he always found difficult to handle, no matter from what source it came. Dear, sensitive Marcus.

One lesson I had learnt from my many life experiences over the years, was that you cannot turn the clock back, however desperately you wish to, but I hoped I could at least persuade Suzi to part with Freddie. Then Marcus, his son and I could have a future together as a family.

'Marry me, Sophia!' he begged, but however much he pleaded I said no. I was quite content to live with him as his partner, sharing his life in whatever form it took. This satisfied him to a degree, but I realised that this was far from the end of the subject.

As we lay there the subject of Alex arose. Suddenly I began to think of him and realised I had betrayed him and his memory. A cold shiver invaded the whole of my being. I got up from the bed as Marcus lay contentedly there, threw on my nightdress and dressing gown and ran from the room. Marcus lifted himself up, looking horrified at such a dramatic exit. He called, 'What on earth is wrong, Sophia?'

Before he had even thought of following me I had left the cottage and charged across the lawns to the Hall, running barefoot. I did not stop to see if anyone noticed me in my state of undress, but crept in the rear door of the Hall and climbed the stairs to the baroque chapel at the top of the building. In a state of disarray, my hair hanging loosely over my shoulders, with tears streaming down my face, I knelt at the altar rail, clasped my hands together and rested my head on them as I wept.

'Please forgive me, Father, for I have sinned!' I croaked. 'I have betrayed my darling Alex's memory. I hate myself for what has happened. I desperately need your forgiveness.'

My voice began to fail me. The muscles in my throat became taut, and I wanted to ask again for help but words evaded me as I choked back tears. I heard the door open. Someone entered the chapel. I wiped stray tears with my fingers and gently rose from the altar rail. With my head bowed I made a beeline for the door. I glanced up swiftly and came face to face with my father. He had obviously seen me enter the Hall and realised where I had gone, and had bravely tackled the stairs to the chapel. He seemed breathless but held his arms out to me.

'Sophia, my darling, what on earth is the matter? You are in a dreadful state. Come. Sit here!' He pointed to the pew. I did as instructed. He placed his arms around me as I cradled my head in his chest.

'Oh, Father, I have betrayed Alex's memory. I hate myself. I need forgiveness. I will never let it happen again.'

He looked puzzled, and without further thought I found I had unburdened myself to him. He listened without interruption, his sad eyes watching every change in my facial expressions.

'Sophia, my dear one,' he said soothingly as I gazed into his face, 'please wipe your tears.'

He handed me his large white handkerchief and I mopped my face.

'I understand what you are telling me about Marcus and yourself. You must have been aware that this was inevitable.'

'No, Father,' I pleaded. 'This is as much a surprise to me as I am sure it is to you.'

'It has come as no surprise to me, darling. Marcus has loved you for so long. Surely you were aware. Mother and I used to discuss the very subject years ago, and realised that although you are nearly five years older than he, you were meant for one another.'

I looked up at my father, at his forthright awareness.

'You see, Sophia, you are a wonderful young woman, but you have always let your heart rule your head. You were a wonderful companion to Alex and saw him through the most difficult times in his last years. You were there for him twenty-four hours a day. I know the lack of a sexual relationship was something you both adjusted to, but you are young and should have a husband and family to care for.'

I explained I had been told that I could have no more children so it was of no consequence.

'But it is, Sophia!' he remonstrated. 'There is a young boy called Freddie at the cottage who desperately needs a mother. Can you be the mother he needs?'

'Yes, Father, I can. I know I can care for him. I love him dearly.'

He looked at me, a smile creeping across his face, and said, 'Then you must go and be his mother. And don't forget that Marcus needs you desperately too!'

I hugged him, but explained how I still loved Alex, and thought his memory would always be there to come between Marcus and me.

'Sophia, please listen to what you are saying! You don't need to forget Alex. You never will. The heartache of his passing will get easier, but you are here, and I knew Alex well enough to know he would want you to be happy with Marcus.'

'But I can't tell if I love him enough to spend all my days with him,' I sniffed.

'Dear one, you are very silly. Look at the love you have given him in the last few months during his recovery programme!'

I interrupted Father by saying, 'How on earth did you know about that? Simon was supposed to have kept it a secret!'

'Simon did not tell me. No one told me. I haven't reached my age without knowing what is going on around this estate. I admire what you have done for Marcus. You could not have faced that incredible journey if you had not loved the man. I think you are confusing love and sex, Sophia, they are two very different things, but when combined, can be the most magnificent experience in life.'

My father was like a wise old owl. He was so frail, and yet was always there for me with such excellent advice. I wanted to sit and hold his hand, draw strength from him and his great knowledge of life.

'Take your happiness while you can, Sophia. If I could have turned the clock back I would have done many things differently, with hindsight. I would never have let your mama slip through my fingers. I would have taken her away and lived with her and provided for you both somehow, family wishes or not. You would have been my child to love and care for. Don't mess up your life any more. Go back to Marcus and Freddie. Be a family. They love and need you, and I know you need them!'

We sat for what seemed ages savouring precious moments together.

'None of us know how long we have on this earth, Sophia. Grab all the opportunities you can and help Marcus back on his feet. You are strong. I know you can do it. Make sure Freddie stays here where he belongs. Now go!' he said, patting my arm and kissing my cheek. 'I have lots to do today, so run along!'

'I love you, Father,' I murmured as I left the pew.

'I love you too, Sophia, so very much!'

I quietly opened the door to the chapel and as I turned, I observed my father, kneeling at the altar rail in prayer.

Chapter Thirty-four

As Marcus had warned, Suzi was a self-opinionated, difficult, arrogant woman. I soon realised, while deep in conversation with her on the telephone, that her middle name should have been 'cash'. She was obstinate, rude and asked me nothing about her precious son and his welfare, except to demand he be returned to his boarding school at the beginning of the new term, which was days away. I soon realised the only Achilles heel she had was money or the lack of it. I subtly suggested that there were surely possessions she would like in life, and received a positive reply detailing her wants. After considerable persuasion, and the promise of a large sum of money from me to her, she was prepared to sign the necessary papers for Freddie to be handed over to his father's care and the boy would be resident with us for as long as he wished. Our solicitors would agree the legal terms and draw up the appropriate documentation. How strange that money can persuade certain people to do anything, even give away a child! The agreement was to be strictly between her and me. No one would gain knowledge of this fact, not even Marcus. I hated the secrecy but realised that this was the only way of securing his future happiness.

Marcus was amazed I had managed to get him guardianship of Freddie so easily, but thankfully asked little about my dealings. He was too excited at the fact that he, Freddie and I would finally be the family he had desperately wanted for so long.

As we prepared for sleep that night, Marcus explained it was his intention, with my approval, to have a memorial erected to Anna-Sophia, in the churchyard of St Michael the Archangel, close by the graves of Mama and Papa, so that I could visit it regularly. His decision met with my full approval.

Marcus arranged for Freddie to attend the Grange Catholic School, where he had attended as a student himself. In no time Freddie was installed at school as a day boy. He adored life and agreed enthusiastically to evening get-togethers and family weekends, welcoming the fact that Marcus and I were now in a very special relationship. It was just what he had hoped for. Father greeted our union with open arms and remarked, 'Sophia, you just couldn't see what was obvious to everyone else. You were undoubtedly in love with Marcus and he with you.'

He was correct in all his assumptions and was extremely happy for us both. Marcus and I were totally absorbed in one another's lives. My life was so very different and far removed from that of a cattle rancher's wife. Glorious music governed most of our waking hours, and by the October of that year, Marcus's album material was complete. A demo tape had been accepted and approved enthusiastically by the new London-based chief executive, Nigel Regis, and other important personnel, and he was excitedly given the thumbs up. He signed a deal for a yearly album over the following four years at an enormous fee per album. Phoenix Records had other star performers on contract, and were obviously making vast sums of money, which could have been ours had I been speedier in my dealings with Sam Dreyfus.

When released in late October, the single 'Freddie' was a resounding success and entered the charts at number one, where it stayed for twenty weeks. It remained in the charts for a following twelve weeks. The album entitled *Where Angels Fear to Tread* made its way to the top of the charts and sold millions of copies worldwide. The UK leg of the tour began late in October and was due to last until Christmas Eve, when we would head for Harrington Hall to spend Christmas with Father.

Our first gig in the October took place in Glasgow. We arrived at the rear of the theatre and met with Ray, Rick, Donny and Jed, for a rehearsal before the evening show. Marcus, ever the perfectionist, went off with the road manager and sound crew in attendance to make checks, while I made small talk with Ray and the band. We all eventually shared snacks in Marcus's dressing room. Marcus returned earlier than usual, deep in thought. The band retired to the stage to run through a few numbers with Bonny Matthews, a sweet, likeable, attractive backing singer whom Marcus had known years previously, leaving us alone for a while.

'Tonight is going to be so great, Marcus,' I murmured enthusiastically. 'The first night of the tour is here, and do you realise all seats are sold out?'

He turned and looked at me as he prepared coffee, without commenting; then slumped into a chair and with head in hands announced, 'Sophia, darling, I cannot go on stage tonight!'

'But Marcus...' I pleaded, trying to console him.

He looked up and said, 'It's no good. I realise now why I needed heroin. I cannot face the audience! No – I simply cannot do it. I need a fix. I really do need a fix, Sophia!'

'Marcus! How can you say such a thing? Not after all those months of rehabilitation and the effort we've all made to initiate your return to the stage.'

He buried his head once more in his hands, obviously in great distress.

'Sophia, I don't want to let you all down, but…'

He began shaking, saying, 'Please leave me. I need to be alone! I need to think. My head is in such confusion.'

He was emphatic, so I removed myself from the dressing room and searched out Ray, who was sorting out last minute details.

'What on earth is wrong, Sophia?' he asked, observing my frightened expression. I explained the state Marcus was in. 'Please, Ray, go and talk to him. He will listen to you. He won't listen to me in the condition he's in, but I know he respects what you have to say. I really don't know how to pacify him!'

He could see I was devastated by Marcus's behaviour.

'Leave it with me. I will sort him out,' he assured me, and, squeezing my arm, made tracks for the dressing room. I practised harmonies with Bonny but it was difficult trying to focus on what I was supposed to be doing. After we were satisfied with our efforts, I turned to leave the stage and came face to face with Marcus. He flung his arms around me.

'Sophia! I am so sorry, darling. Forgive me?'

'Of course I forgive you, but you gave me such an awful fright!' I gulped, feeling his obvious pain as well as my own. 'I forgive you.'

Ray had talked at length to him. The next two hours before the gig were an anxious experience, wondering if at any moment Marcus would change his mind about appearing.

Finally we were called on stage. As he surfaced, screams, waving and general hysteria began. I looked in his direction, winked, blew a kiss and we settled down into 'I'm Nobody's Fool', which had fans dancing with delight. Ray sat close and I could see him mouthing words to Marcus throughout what could only be described as a stupendous, electrifying night. He played, in all, for almost three hours, during which time fans continually tried to climb on stage, but security was tight. The evening ended with a great get-together backstage, and the media jostled for a chance to interview Marcus and the band. It had been a total and utter success, without one iota of heroin!

We arrived home early on Christmas Eve after a splendid first leg of the tour, to spend time with Father. We were on a high. The band members had all gone their own separate ways for the festive season. Marianne, Ben and Rosie had travelled to visit Marianne's parents in Scotland. Jonathan was with Catherine and Robert, which left Father, Marcus, Freddie and me to enjoy celebrations at the Hall. Ray had intended staying with a woman he had met the previous month on tour but their relationship had unfortunately foundered the previous week, so rather than him spend Christmas alone, we insisted he join us and on Christmas Eve. He said, 'Yes', which pleased us all greatly, especially Freddie. As was usual at this time of year, no expense had been spared, and a tremendous effort had been made by all the staff to ensure our Christmas was thoroughly enjoyable. Freddie had a Christmas Eve get-together with school friends in the Great Hall, a far cry from the parties we had known as children. Father allowed popular music to resound throughout the building, but he had a fair supply of earplugs on hand. Marcus entertained with 'Soapy', which appeared to get the party swinging, and a good time was had by all. On Christmas Day we invited Edith and John to join us at the Hall for lunch, tea and supper. They too, readily agreed and the usual rituals took place.

Firstly it was down to breakfast, which Edith insisted on cooking. She was remarkable, and still as buoyant and enthusiastic as ever. We were summoned to the drawing room, where a huge pine tree had been imaginatively decorated, and a log fire added to the splendour and comfort. Presents adorned the foot of the tree. It was present opening time. As I entered the room, Marcus caught my arm and spun me around to face him.

'Please come with me, darling,' he pleaded. He took my hand and led me to the kitchen. The catering staff looked in amazement as we invaded their territory, but smiled and wished us a happy Christmas before Marcus asked if they would disappear for a few moments while we talked.

'Here, my darling,' he said, handing me a small box. 'I know that for you marriage is out of the question, but I wanted to give you this while we are alone. If you have no intention of marrying me, perhaps you will wear this instead.'

I opened the box to display a gorgeous sapphire and diamond ring.

'It is an eternity ring, Sophia. I chose it myself. Say you will wear this ring for me and love me for all eternity!' He removed the ring from the box and placed it on my wedding finger. It was a perfect fit.

'Of course I will wear it, Marcus, for ever, darling,' I said, admiring the beautiful stones. He placed his arm around me and drew me close to him, and we kissed passionately. From the corner of my eye I spotted Elsie and Freda, the kitchen maids, smiling and nudging one another at our obvious show of affection. They realised I had spotted them and made a hasty withdrawal.

'I have a present for you too, Marcus,' I announced, 'but I am afraid it isn't ready yet and you're going to have to wait for a while for it.'

He gave me a puzzled look. 'Is it not finished?' he asked.

'Not yet.'

'I am intrigued!' he said, and smiled. 'Is it being made? How will it be arriving? By post?'

I stood on tiptoe and cupping his head in my hands, drew him close to me, whispering in his ear, 'By stork!'

'By stork?' He flashed me an entrancing smile.

'Yes, my darling, we are having a baby – but it will not be arriving until June,' I giggled.

The look on his face was one of utter astonishment.

'But I thought you said…'

'I did. The gynaecologist in Australia told me, after I lost Anna-Sophia, that I would not be able to have more children; but to my delight Simon confirmed my pregnancy yesterday.'

I cannot describe the emotions which followed, but I had never seen Marcus so euphoric. He kissed me, hugged me, lifted me up, twirled me around, jumped up and down and shouted, 'Yeehah!' He wanted to dash into the drawing room to announce the news to everyone, but I suggested we leave our exciting announcement until after lunch. We did, and while Father, Ray, Edith and John downed a glass of port and Freddie supped orange juice, Marcus stood and announced, 'There is something I am bursting to tell you all.'

Every face in the room followed his movements.

'I cannot wait any longer. Guess what! *I am having a baby!*'

He watched the startled expressions before adding, 'What I mean to say is, Sophia is carrying our child.'

Everyone stared in utter disbelief. I was afraid Freddie would not take the news well, but he was the first to jump up from the sofa, fling his arms around my neck and say, 'Gosh! This means I am going to have a brother or sister. How wonderful!'

Father was overjoyed at the news and hugged me so tightly I could hardly breathe, whispering, 'I am so glad you took my advice to return to Marcus. Now you have the blessing of a child to enhance your love for one another.'

Edith and John were over the moon at the news. Ray was speechless, but as thrilled as anyone else in the room. He kissed my cheek, tickling me with his black whiskers.

Marcus and his excitement could not be contained until Father had issued Haynes with the request to enter his wine cellar and bring out the finest bottles of champagne. Haynes readily carried out his instructions and joined us in a glass of bubbly to toast the expected arrival of the latest addition to the Walker clan. This was just what Marcus wanted and needed: a complete family of his own. I was at last able to happily provide him with one of his dearest wishes.

As each one of the family and guests went their separate ways that evening, Marcus, Freddie and I returned to Starbeck Row, elated and happy with the day's proceedings.

Freddie retired to his room and showered before I climbed the stairs to bid him goodnight and make sure he was comfortable and had all that he needed.

'Thank you for a lovely day, Sophia,' he remarked as he climbed into bed.

I sat by him and teased his dark curls with my fingers as I explained how wonderful it was that we had shared our Christmas with him, which it was quite clear he had thoroughly enjoyed. He grabbed my hand and staring into my eyes said, 'You cannot imagine how happy I am for you and Daddy that you are going to have a child of your own. I realise there will be lots of changes taking place over the next few months, and I was thinking that if I will be too much of a nuisance for you to take care of, I could go back to boarding school.'

I released his hold and took him in my arms, nestling his head on my shoulder as I stroked his hair.

'Darling Freddie, you are going nowhere of the kind. I want you here with us, and your daddy does too. A nuisance? How could you possibly be a nuisance? You are our son, our precious son, and we always want you with us. We love you more than you could possibly imagine and no little child is going to take away the affection we feel for you, Freddie. In fact, I have been talking to Daddy and we think it unfair you have to stay with Ben and Marianne while we are on the road, and see us only at weekends and holidays.'

He lifted his head and replied, 'I miss you and Daddy so much Sophia, when you are gone.'

'I know, darling,' I replied. 'How would you like to go with us, on tour, after Christmas? We have considered getting you a private tutor so you can accompany us wherever we go.'

'Will that be possible, Sophia? I would love it. Can I really join you?'

'Yes, Freddie. Daddy is in the process of sorting out all the necessary details with your school and a tutor. We want you with us always, Freddie, or until such time as you decide what you want to do with your life and branch out on your own. Then we will be there to help and encourage you, always.'

Tears trickled down his cheeks and I knew then that he realised how dearly he was loved and needed by both Marcus and me. He rested back on his pillows and fell into a deep, contented sleep.

Jonathan telephoned on Boxing Day and was delighted at the news of our expected arrival. He had joined a violin quartet in London and was busy with bookings around the country, bringing classical music to a wider audience in the way it was presented. My father was delighted at the news; especially when I explained that Jonathan would be appearing at the first of the 'Classical Recitals in the Park', which were due to begin the following spring.

Before leaving on the final leg of our 'Phoenix Rises from the Ashes Tour' in the New Year, Father called a meeting of the family to discuss his business propositions.

We arrived in his study – Marcus, Ben, Marianne and I – to discover that it was his intention to sell the remaining carpet factories. Ben was shocked at the news and saw his livelihood slipping through his fingers. Marcus came to the rescue by appointing him as his Promotions Manager, as he had an extensive knowledge of Marcus's thoughts, ideas and movements. It was decided that all employees of the factories involved would be offered alternative employment within the estate, working on ticket sales, promotions, security, car parks, seating, etc., which pleased us all greatly.

Marianne agreed to become Marcus's fan club secretary.

Marcus made it clear that he did not wish to spend his free time on the road with the band, and it was for that reason a tour bus was ordered so that Freddie and I could travel separately with him. The tour bus was a magnificent piece of engineering equipment, with a large phoenix rising from the ashes painted down each side. The inside, built to our specifications, had a spacious bedroom area, a bath/shower, toilet, powered sunroofs and a kitchen with fridge/freezer, cooker, padded benches and table. The driver's area was curtained off to allow for privacy. An underneath sleeping area on the bus housed a small cabin bed for Freddie. How thankful I was for the money from the sale of Mother's necklace! Marcus was not sure I should tour with him and the band in the New Year, owing to my pregnancy, but I insisted I was perfectly healthy and could be with him until the tour ended in April. It would then give me two months at Starbeck Row to rest and prepare myself for the arrival of our first child. Simon concluded that this arrangement would be fine, and we toured Europe, taking in many cities and playing to full houses. The tour was an unquestionable success. I had so much attention from the band, kindly treating me with kid gloves, Ray especially.

The months flew by and June drew closer. The 'Concerts in the Park' began and were extremely well attended. The Harrington estate was a hive of industry, with staff attending to all aspects of the entertainment. We returned from Europe to Starbeck Row, and I wallowed in the chance I had to see my son Jonathan appearing on stage with the quartet to which he now belonged. They were rapturously received by the audience, and Father was in his element, mixing with old friends from the classical music world.

The last two weeks before the birth seemed to drag. Marcus had been asked to perform in a Sunday evening live show for television from London, but was reluctant to appear with the baby fast approaching. He had expressly wished to be with me when our child arrived, but I thought he should not miss such a great opportunity to be seen by millions and insisted I was fine. He travelled with the band by light aircraft, taking Freddie, who wanted to view his daddy from the wings during his performance.

I pottered around the cottage quite happily collecting things needed for my impending visit to the clinic where I was to give birth, and thought I would have a long, hot soak in the bath before settling down to rest for the afternoon. It was my intention to watch Marcus's live performance on television later in the evening, and I grew increasingly excited as the hours passed. I was enjoying the warm water rippling around my large lump when I was suddenly taken unaware by pain –quite regular pain – which I knew to be contractions. I phoned Father to tell him I thought labour had begun. He said he would notify Marcus at the theatre and promptly sent John Roberts to the cottage with the Range Rover to drive me to the clinic. On arrival at the clinic, I mentioned to the midwife that my partner was presently in London but would be returning for the birth; but she simply laughed and stated, 'I'm afraid he will not be here in time, Sophia. You are due to give birth any moment!'

I had to admit to feeling sad, as Marcus had expressly wished a desire to see his child born. As labour progressed, I heard a most unusual noise and was informed that a helicopter had suddenly landed on the lawns outside. It was Marcus. He had flown from London. He ran across the grass and burst into the delivery room. He made tracks for where I lay, clutched my hand, kissed me, mopped my brow and offered words of comfort as I gave birth to the most beautiful baby boy. The gynaecologist, midwives and nurses just stared when he removed his shades and they recognised Marcus Walker!

'Look, Sophia! We have such a beautiful son!' he repeated over and over. 'Oh, darling you really are so clever!'

'Marcus,' I reminded him, 'women give birth to babies every day, darling.'

'Not this one, Sophia, not this one!' he said, his eyes glowing with pride as he waved our son around for everyone in the room to see. 'God, he is so gorgeous. Just like you, Sophia!'

He could not contain his pleasure at holding our son. He took the child once more in his arms and stood mesmerised by the perfect little boy he held so carefully. It took me back to the day of the birth of Jonathan. How different things were then, with no one available to give a word of comfort or support. It all seemed like a lifetime ago.

The midwives asked for Marcus's autograph. He handed me our son while he signed good wishes on face masks, arms, charts, anything available.

'If you go now, Marcus,' I urged, 'you can make it back to London in time to appear on the show.'

'But Sophia…'

'This performance in London is such a great opportunity for you, Marcus. Millions watch the show. Go on, darling, get in the helicopter. Please! You can return immediately afterwards, and you, Freddie and I can take baby home.'

He agreed, and with that he kissed us both and dashed out to the helicopter – but not before pressing his face against the window of my room, shouting, 'We'll call him Oliver! Is that OK with you?'

I nodded, smiled blissfully and held up our son. I heard the helicopter blades rotate and he was gone. I sat in bed that night cradling Oliver in my arms. Father visited the new arrival, thrilled with the name we had chosen for him. With a group of nursing staff and midwives, we were glued to the television set watching Marcus and his band perform live at the London theatre to an overenthusiastic audience. After his first song he took the microphone to his lips and announced, 'Hi! How are you? I am really on top form tonight. You see, three hours ago I watched my son being born. It was the most moving experience I have ever encountered. I need to tell his mummy I love and adore her and thank her for the wonderful gift of my gorgeous boy, Oliver.'

The audience clapped and cheered.

He continued, 'I also have a wonderful son, Freddie, watching me from the wings, and I need to tell him I love and adore him dearly too.'

With that, he turned to the band, and on his instructions they performed 'Now I Know She's Gone' – the very first song Marcus wrote for me. There was not a dry eye in the room and, I would guess, very few in the audience. I looked down at Oliver, who was sleeping peacefully, unaware that his father was performing to millions of people in many countries. He peacefully slept his way through the whole thing.

During the months that followed Marcus began lyrics and music for yet another album and Freddie attended the Grange once more. We were living at Starbeck Row, taking in several venues around the country when asked to do so, and Marcus attended numerous interviews for television, radio and the press.

Excitement rose when he was notified that he had been nominated in four categories for the approaching Music Awards in London. Preparations were under way for us to travel to this prestigious occasion, where stars would be out in full force, to be seen and hopefully heard. The day prior to the awards ceremony, exhilaration rang out in Starbeck Row. Marcus, having achieved star status with his first album, *Where Angels Fear to Tread*, and the 'Rising from the Ashes' tour, for which he received critical acclaim, had been nominated for Best Male Singer, Best Band, Best Single (for 'Freddie'), and Best Album.

John was given the honour of driving Ben, Marianne and Father to London, while Marcus, Freddie and I followed to the city in the Bentley. Edith kindly babysat Ollie.

Freddie was excited as we carefully placed our luggage in the boot. Our evening wear was already awaiting us at the hotel. The band was due to join us at a venue in the evening, where a party had been arranged for members, wives and girlfriends.

We had an exceptionally good evening in a happy, relaxed atmosphere, wallowing in our new-found success. Nigel Regis, Chief Executive of Phoenix Records, joined us for the evening festivities, but the owner of Phoenix did not have the decency to appear, and I was extremely hurt, Marcus too. We had consistently made him substantial sums of money over the previous year, and I thought he would at least have had the decency to wish us luck for our all important evening. Ray, accompanied by a woman he had met at our last tour venue, seemed content in her company, receiving the affection and companionship he had lacked since joining the band. He did not however stint on his time spent with Marcus, and gave a great deal of thought and attention to him. He also spared a great many hours encouraging Freddie with the pedal steel guitar, which I thought was extremely generous of him. He was a good friend.

We returned to our suite at 2 a.m. and in no time Marcus and I had fallen asleep. We awoke at lunchtime. Pangs of excitement began as we realised the evening awards were fast approaching. Appointments had been arranged for a masseur, manicurist and hairdresser to attend to my needs. Marcus was quite happy for me to groom his hair. As evening approached, Freddie was sent by Father to ask me to visit him in the hotel room they shared, wishing to see me urgently.

'Is there something wrong? I asked.

'No, Sophia,' he said, as he held the door open for me and informed me that my father was in the adjoining room. Freddie escorted me through to where Oliver sat waiting.

'Are you sure my father is all right, Freddie?' I enquired.

'Yes, he is fine, but he has something urgent on his mind.'

As I entered the room I was met by two officious-looking security guards.

'Goodness, Father! What on earth have you been doing?' I enquired.

'Don't worry your pretty head, Sophia. They are here to oversee this. I would like you to wear this tonight for me and for dear Mary.'

He handed me a long, black case which I carefully opened. It was Mother's sapphire and diamond necklace, the necklace which had been sold to raise the finance for Marcus's return to the music scene!

'But, Father!' I gasped, unable to take my eyes off the sparkling diamonds. 'Where on earth did you get the necklace?'

'It is a long, long story Sophia. I will explain it to you at a later date, but for now it is my greatest wish you should wear it. It will make me so proud, and I am sure Mary will be watching over you both on this special night.'

'I will, dearest Father! It will go beautifully with my white sequined gown.'

I smoothed my fingers very gently across the stones, admiring them in great detail, then kissed Father and thanked him for 'hiring' it for the evening. To think the necklace had been across the world and back again, then sold. Now it was in my possession once more for an evening. The security guards put it back in the hotel safe until required later, and I returned to my room, accompanied by Freddie. The look of surprise on Marcus's face when I related what had happened was incredible. How proud Mary would be if she could see me wearing the necklace for the glitzy occasion that her beloved Marcus and I were attending!

I tried to stay in the background as we alighted from the limousine onto the red carpet. Screaming girls waved autograph books and cameras flashed as they chanted, 'Marcus! Marcus! Over here!'

He stopped to talk and sign autographs, have his photograph taken with adoring fans as Ben, Marianne, Father, Freddie, Roger (his manager), Nigel and I, along with the band, made our way to the champagne reception. There were so many recognisable faces from stage and screen, and Freddie gave Father a running commentary on just about every guest in the room. It was ages before Marcus joined us, having stolen away from fans and the national press. We were escorted to our table, where we had an excellent view of the stage area, from the centre of the room. Helping seat Father at the table, Freddie leaned over and asked, 'Do you think Daddy will win one of those coveted awards Sophia?'

'But of course!' I exclaimed. 'I am positive he will.'

He smiled and seated himself beside his grandfather, explaining the proceedings of the night. Father leaned toward me and, apologising, said, 'Sophia! I am becoming a stupid, forgetful old man! I did not tell you how beautiful you look tonight. I have seen the many admiring glances coming in your direction. You look stunning! Your gown is a sight to behold as are you! The necklace complements it so well.'

I blushed and agreed.

Marcus, seated by my side, held my hand and nervously squeezed it at intervals. I glanced at him and gave him a reassuring smile. Ray, Donny, Rick, Jed and Roger occupied the adjoining table. Ray called over, saying, 'Hope you've brought a huge bag for your awards, Marcus!'

We all laughed, but nerves had kicked in and we applauded as the compère appeared on stage to begin the evening's entertainment. TV cameras circled the tables, filming our reactions to those awarded trophies.

A new group were introduced and entertained us with their latest hit – a catchy melody, if I could only have deciphered the lyrics. These were compounded into ten words repeated continually. The audience applauded, so I reckoned it must have been entertaining. Father simply raised his eyebrows with a look that said, 'Rubbish!' Announcements from two well-known faces from the theatrical world listed the four contenders for 'Best Single'.

There was 'Isa Gonna Get Ya', 'Two Worlds Apart', 'Love in the Mist' and 'Freddie'.

Each performance was shown on screen. I heard, 'And the winner is… 'Freddie'!'

Everyone on our table – apart from Father – jumped up and hugged anyone in handling distance. Marcus threw his arms around me and I whispered in his ear, 'You deserve this, darling. Go get 'em, partner!'

He smiled and shuffled his way to the podium but not before dragging Nigel Regis and Roger Ellison on stage with him. He looked so handsome, yet so vulnerable, standing there.

'Gee, I really do not know what to say, except that this was so unexpected. I would like to thank Nigel of Phoenix Records who had such faith in me and my work, and to the boss whom I have yet to meet and who seems to keep a low profile.'

The audience laughed.

'Thank you too to Roger, my manager, my production crew and everyone involved and to my son Freddie, who inspired me to write this song. You know, I almost lost touch with this incredible young man. Freddie! Stand up! Let everyone see what a handsome young man you are.'

Freddie, blushing, stood as the crowd acknowledged his presence by clapping.

'You know, ladies and gentleman, Freddie has been a ray of sunshine in my life and has given it new purpose and meaning to what I do. In this industry it is too easy to lose contact with those who we are closest to. If you have a child out there that you do not see often, then go and visit. Make contact, and tell him or her what they mean to you and see how different your life becomes.'

He held his award statue high above his head and, looking in our direction, said, 'Freddie! This one is for you, son!'

The audience stood and applauded loudly, and I caught a glimpse of Ray from the corner of my eye, wiping away a discreet tear. Ruby, the new woman in his life, patted his hand affectionately. Marcus returned to the table amidst pats on the back and handshakes, to receive untold praise from my father, which pleased me greatly. They hugged. It was wonderful to watch. More entertainment followed from an American group who had toured with Marcus on numerous dates in previous years in the USA. Then commenced the award for 'Best Female Artist' which was won by a girl who had been a backing singer for Marcus in the States. She took it upon herself to blow him a kiss and comment on how great it was to see him back where he belonged, at the pinnacle of his career. As nominations were read out for 'Best Male Artist', I watched Marcus nonchalantly sipping wine, quite content with his award for 'Freddie'; but one could not describe the happiness on his face as his name was once again called. He stood as if hypnotised by the events going on around him, and moved again to the stage to receive his award.

'Hi! Here I am again – quite unexpectedly, I can assure you. I must say I am proud that you like my music and lyrics.'

Loud screams came from female guests.

'Again I must thank Phoenix Records for their belief in me, to my band for their loyalty and backing, to everyone involved and especially to Sophia for her constant encouragement. I love you, Sophia!'

As the evening wore on, yet another accolade graced our table, the award for best album, 'Where Angels Fear to Tread'.

Marcus's speeches by now had become very emotional, and few words were forthcoming except to give thanks to all concerned. When Marcus and his band won their category, it was left to Rick and Ray to accept the award on his behalf. Ray spoke graciously of his musical relationship with Marcus and fellow members, and gave a heartfelt thanks to all the family at Harrington Hall who he now classed as 'his family'.

'There, I told Marcus to bring a bag for the awards, Sophia,' he joked as he returned to the table.

As the evening drew to its conclusion, Marcus looked lovingly at me and said, 'Sophia, darling, none of these awards would have been possible to achieve without you.'

'But Marcus, you are the star, the talent! I am just a keen helper in the background, and am quite happy to be that person.' But he shook his head.

The head of broadcasting was announced and walked onto the stage bearing an unusual and exciting statuette. He began:

'Ladies and gentlemen, it is a great honour for me to be here tonight to introduce this award. It is a new and exciting award which is a tribute to my late father, who himself was an eminent musician.'

Father nodded in my direction, whispering that he had known him well.

'This award will be given yearly to the artist showing the greatest outstanding contribution to his or her musical field. It will be known as the Christopher Martingale Award. This year it is being given to an artist who has, you could say, risen from the ashes, with such dedication, innovation, inspiration and overwhelming success in his art. The man is truly a genius! Whether he sings ballads, folk, blues or rock and roll, he has a charismatic personality and an outstanding talent that so rarely manifests itself in one person. I am pleased to announce that this award is going to none other than… Marcus Walker!'

On hearing his name, I believed Marcus would have collapsed with the intensity of it all, but I helped him gently to his feet and kissed him as tears brimmed up in his eyes. His body shook. Father stood, arms outstretched as their hands held one another. Ray jumped up and embraced Marcus, Freddie too. Marcus turned once more to me and gave me a long, lingering embrace, whispering, 'Thank you, Sophia! Thank you so much, darling!'

As he walked slowly to the stage, my heart went out to him. The audience rose and gave him a standing ovation which lasted a considerable time. He'd reached the top once more. He was a star! A true star!

As he was presented with the award, he seemed fixated on it and appeared lost for words, overcome by the moment. He stood as the cheers and applause died down. Marcus focused on the statuette seemingly not knowing what to say. Eventually he coughed, placed the award on the lectern and stared into the audience. What on earth was amiss? Was he so overcome that words failed him? Slowly he began to speak.

'Well, I have to say that I am so proud and honoured to be standing here, having been given this very special award, which, believe me, I will truly treasure. You know, I'd always been interested in music, since a young age, and over the years, with tremendous encouragement, I began to focus on my dreams. When I moved to London in the sixties I played my guitar on the streets, earning enough to see me through. I was eighteen when Roger decided to manage me and with my group, the Dream Catchers, we had our first hit 'Now I Know She's Gone' written on a napkin at Heathrow, for the love of my life. Now, almost twenty years on, I can tell you it has, for the most part, been an exceedingly lonely journey. There have been highs and lows. When the down times come, the fear of rejection in any form is devastating, and it has made me feel like jacking it all in. But then I realised that I know nothing else and that music is my life and without it I am nothing! So I kept on trying to return to my glory days when I churned out hit after hit. I have had my fair share of highs and I admit to having been lucky in the past. Then, three years ago, I succumbed to the depths that only this industry can induce in you. I could not see myself going anywhere at all. I was in despair. Then there appeared my guardian angel – *Sophia*! She returned to my life and turned me into the star I have become today with her unceasing support, love and devotion. Without this I would not be standing here tonight. Therefore I ask that *you*, Sophia, join me and jointly accept this award for without you I would be nothing. *Please*, Sophia, come and join me on stage.'

I looked at Father and said, 'Father, I can't!'

I stared at Marcus and shook my head, but he held out his hands to me and the audience stood and began chanting, 'Sophia! Sophia!'

Father took my hand and said, 'You must go, Sophia!'

'Go on, Sophia!' urged Freddie. 'Join Daddy on stage. *Please!*'

I stepped slowly along the carpet in a daze as Marcus walked down the steps to meet me and support my body, which I thought would collapse at any moment. He kissed me and escorted me to the podium.

'This, ladies and gentleman, is my guardian angel and the mother of my gorgeous young son, Oliver and stepmother to our dear son, Freddie!' announced Marcus.

I stood there speechless! The audience rose once more in adulation and I blushed shyly.

'Sing us a song, Marcus!' someone shouted.

'Yes! Yes!' came another voice.

He sang 'Nowhere Fast' – the lyrics he had written when trying to free himself from the depths of heroin addiction – and I provided harmony as the band joined us on stage. It was an exceptional end to a truly spectacular night.

It looked as though Marcus and I would be shopping in Harrods the following day for a large enough glass cabinet to house the statues, before returning to Starbeck Row. As he left the stage he concluded by saying, 'I would like to thank, with all my heart, Oliver, the man who took me into his home and his heart when I was a small boy of three. He showed me devotion and care when I needed it most, although at times it went against the grain. Thank you, Oliver, for your care and commitment, for everything!'

Chapter Thirty-five

Marcus and I had returned from a family day out with Ollie and Freddie, when he and I were unexpectedly summoned to the London office of Phoenix Records by Nigel Regis. Ben had been asked to join us too, which was strange, as Nigel's dealings had always been with Marcus and Marcus alone. We were anxious, especially when he chose not to tell us why the meeting had been called. Nigel had been in awe of the first two albums released under their expertise, which had both been colossal earners. He had promised he would be in attendance to receive us, and wished to show thanks and appreciation for Marcus's outstanding achievements.

The day of reckoning arrived, and although apprehensive of the visit I was quite excited at the chance of a trip to London to take in a little shopping expedition. Father had learned that his chauffeur, John, was driving us in the Bentley, for our midday appointment with Nigel, and asked if he could venture into the City with us, as he had various business commitments to attend to himself. We would then all meet at the Ritz for a late lunch.

This agreed, we set off, leaving our sons with Marianne, who had a day arranged at Scarborough. Marcus took with him a demo tape for his record bosses to approve, which, in my opinion, contained the greatest songs of his career to date. Marcus was now constantly pushing the barriers of his music, and this in itself made him a truly exciting artist.

Traffic in the city was unyielding and manic, but John eased through in Marcus's Bentley without too much difficulty. This saw the three of us comfortably seated in the waiting room of Phoenix Records in good time for our appointment. John drove off with Father to see he met his engagements, while we waited impatiently for Nigel to appear. I flicked through a magazine nestling on a coffee table in front of us, and Marcus and Ben talked about recording deals and their ideas for marketing the next album. Nigel appeared in the room on the exact stroke of midday and escorted us into his office, which was a lavish room with sumptuous leather seating. We were directed to a long table and were introduced to two other representatives, who had nothing but praise for the two albums. Marcus handed over his demo tape and they disappeared to absorb the contents.

'Well,' announced Nigel, 'it is an honour to have you all here, together, in this office, and for me to have time to spend with you. Marcus and I are usually griping at one another down the telephone,' he remarked, flashing a cheeky smile.

'I am so thrilled you were all able to attend this meeting and I hope we can soon get down to business of a serious nature which will affect you all.'

I gazed at Marcus and he stared at me, and in unison we stared at Ben, who wriggled uncomfortably in his seat. I suddenly became quite nervous, wondering if Nigel had, in fact, lured us there under false pretences.

'As you are aware—' he began.

He was interrupted by the door opening. We all turned to see my father walk slowly into the room, aided by his walking stick. I excused myself from the table and hurried to his side.

'Father, dearest,' I said, taking his arm, 'let me escort you to the door!' I turned him around, adding, 'I am afraid you should not be here. We are involved in a very important meeting with Phoenix Records. Had you forgotten to tell John that we were all meeting at the Ritz for lunch?'

He shook his head.

'But Sophia, I…' he said, as I walked him gently toward the exit.

Nigel Regis strode up to us and spoke to my father.

'How good it is to see you once again, Sir Oliver. What a remarkable evening we experienced at the Music Awards! You must be so proud of your son and his terrific talent.'

'I am, young man, I am!' he announced, his chest swelling with pride.

I apologised to Nigel for the fact that my father had gatecrashed the meeting, but he laughed and said, 'Now, Sir Oliver, allow me to escort you to a comfortable chair.'

Without further ado, he took Father's arm and helping him to the table, drew out a chair and helped him to sit comfortably.

'Coffee for everyone, I think!' Nigel said and buzzed his secretary to bring refreshments and a bottle of brandy. Father sat quietly eyeing each one of us as we sat transfixed by his every move.

'Well, dear family, this is a pleasant experience. Don't look so shocked at me being here at your meeting. I expect by now I have blown my cover! You see, I am the head of Phoenix Records!'

We must have looked a sight, sitting there with our mouths wide open. We were totally speechless. Marcus looked across at me and I stared at him. Our eyes moved toward Ben, who simply sat and shrugged his shoulders at us both as if to say, 'Father has finally gone gaga!'

'You see, Sophia,' Father said, speaking directly to me, 'when you came to me, asking to sell your mother's necklace to finance a record company, I didn't want you to sell something so precious, but you were most intent on helping Marcus with his career. I contacted Jacob Godber at Witherington's to ask him to value it. I then arranged to sell the Titian, which had been returned to me, to a private collector. I also sold two more of my favourite paintings. With the proceeds I bought the record company, and gave you an excellent price for the necklace so that you would have funds to finance whatever it was you wanted to do. I still have the necklace, as you must now realise. That is why you were able to wear it at the Music Awards ceremony. I will return the necklace to you when I feel the time is appropriate.'

I rose from my chair, moved toward Father and embraced him.

'Oh, Father! You are so wonderful. But you loved the Titian!'

'I love you more, Sophia! I had been without that painting for fifteen years. The most precious thing I had in my life was returned to me: *you*, Sophia! After your return, the Titian suddenly meant nothing.'

He looked across at Marcus. 'You see, Marcus, although I cannot abide your music, you have been a wonderful son to me, and without your unstinting financial help Harrington Hall would no longer be our home. I knew that Sophia had great faith in you and your music, and I thought if she could see a great future for you then I should do my utmost to help. When you get to my age, possessions are not worth that much. It is the true love of family that counts, and I have that in abundance with you all and my gorgeous grandsons.'

I kissed Father as Marcus stood and said, 'I really do not know how to thank you enough, Oliver. I am sure we have not let you or Phoenix down, and I know we will bring you even more monetary success in the future.' Marcus was visibly moved.

'Marcus, you and Sophia have made Phoenix considerable sums of money, and that is one of the reasons I have brought you all together today. You see, my entrepreneurial skills are not what they were, and I would like to hand Phoenix Records over to someone younger and more able than myself. I know that you, Sophia, have inherited my skills.'

We all looked at one another, fearing he had decided to hand everything to me, which I did not want. My life was wrapped in Marcus, Freddie and Ollie, and no way could I find time for such a huge commitment; but we knew that whoever Father chose would have to appreciate the kind of music we wanted to record, music that we knew in our hearts would be successful. There was a feeling of anxiety in the air.

'Nigel, have you the papers at hand?' Father enquired.

Nigel, so efficient, placed huge amounts of documentation in front of Father.

'Everything is here, Sir Oliver. The solicitors have been through it with a fine-tooth comb.'

'Good!'

Father perused the paperwork as the secretary arrived with coffee and brandy. Father twiddled his moustache nervously with his fingers, something I had witnessed so often during childhood, when important matters were at hand.

'Well, Marcus and Sophia,' he said, looking up. 'I have tried to help you, and as a team you are doing the most incredible job. You are making vast sums of money, so if you are both in agreement I would like to sign Phoenix over to Benedict! This is my way of helping him, and I know that with Nigel's guidance he will make a great success of the company.'

Ben almost choked on his coffee. Marcus stood up immediately. He embraced good, reliable Ben and I rushed to kiss him.

'Oh, yes, Ben! This will give you such wonderful financial stability for Marianne and Rosie!' I enthused.

'Guess I'm gonna have to find a new Promotions Manager,' quipped Marcus.

Ben was totally overwhelmed and overcome with emotion. He signed, in front of witnesses, shook hands with Father, and the deal was done.

'Excellent! Excellent! Let us keep all our dealings in the family,' remarked Father.

We all retired to the Ritz, and over lunch discussed Marcus's new album *Seasons of the Heart*, to be released the following year.

Our journey home proved fruitful as we chatted about future plans and the success of Jonathan's new album, which had reached number three in the Classical Charts. We were so proud of him and his uncle, Ben, would now be in charge of managing his recordings. We decided to stop at a small restaurant for tea and heartily ate delicious pastries and supped Earl Grey. I did not realise what was happening, but suddenly Marcus reached forward and, gathering up numerous paper napkins, tried stemming the flow of blood that trickled from my nose. The waitresses were marvellous and came to my aid, but could not control the flow however hard they tried. Eventually the manageress summoned an ambulance and I was taken to the accident and emergency department at a nearby hospital. Marcus accompanied me, while Father, Ben and John followed in Marcus's car.

The nursing staff was a delightful bunch who took blood pressure readings and declared that I was fine. Suddenly, after almost two hours, the bleeding stopped and after a short rest I was allowed to go, without the need for further treatment. I considered the emotional events of the day had possibly triggered the nosebleed and thought no more of it. As we left the hospital, the young nurse who had attended me approached Marcus and said, 'Gosh! Has anyone ever told you that you are the image of the rock star, Marcus Walker?'

'No,' replied Marcus, 'but then there could be a reason for that! You see, don't tell anyone, but I *am* Marcus Walker.'

She stared in amazement, not knowing whether to believe him or not. He kissed her cheek and wrote a small message on an empty chart. She was thrilled and we bounced toward the exit doors, happy and relieved my little fiasco was nothing more than a hiccup in the day's proceedings.

Our darling son, Ollie, was growing into a bundle of fun, and while recording we would take him into the studio so he was close at hand. Set in his playpen with numerous activity toys, he would reject them and stand, shaking the bars, jogging to and fro to his daddy's music. Marcus spoiled him and he found his way around the band members frequently. Freddie, now quite an accomplished guitar player, was keen to play at gigs in the village hall (which we allowed), and appeared to be following in his daddy's footsteps also. Life was beautiful, and we prepared for the launch of the album at Christmas with a five-month tour to follow starting in the January until late May. This pleased us greatly, as it allowed us time with Father before and during the Christmas festivities.

In October, Marcus and I were out riding when my horse was startled by gunfire in the distance and I was thrown. Marcus came to my rescue but was kicked trying to restrain the horse, and we both ended the day in hospital beds. Within the week we had been released to Starbeck Row, me in a plaster cast on my arm, with severe bruising – and Marcus bandaged in the most unlikeliest of places! But this did not deter him from rehearsing with the band, nor me from handling Ollie one-handed, despite great offers of help. Freddie was excellent, in that he helped at every available moment he was not at school or involved in homework. The media went into a frenzy at the accidents, and published the most horrendous articles about us having been crippled, and that we would not be able to walk again when we were in fact pottering quite happily around the closely guarded estate.

Christmas was a terrific affair with Father, Marcus, Freddie, Ollie, Ben, Rosie, Marianne, Ray, the band, and Jonathan and his adoptive parents, Catherine and Robert, gracing the table. It was a true family get-together, and once again Edith and John joined in the festivities. Christmas was complete with the release of the album *Bright Lights, Big City*, which entered the charts at number four. By New Year it had reached number one, and we commenced our nationwide five-month tour, taking Freddie and Ollie with us in the tour bus. Freddie loved his sleeping quarters, from which he frequently viewed the night lights of towns and cities when we were travelling.

We had called the latest tour the 'Phoenix Rises Again' tour, and were graciously received at all venues, with Marcus receiving rave reviews in newspapers and on television. The culmination of our five-month exhaustive tour was a date at Wembley for two nights. We were happy, and also relieved that these would be our final dates, as everyone appeared tired. It was May and everyone looked forward to a well-earned rest. Harrington Hall was calling us home, and Freddie and Ollie were anxious to see their grandfather. I was too, although he did appear at several concerts and spent time with us afterwards, but he looked frail and I felt his health had deteriorated. I wanted to go home. Although luxuriously furnished, the tour bus proved a trifle claustrophobic at times, and we craved the fresh air of the Yorkshire Dales and the comfort of our huge cottage. The outdoor 'Concerts in the Park' had begun once more, and Marcus was due to appear in one in June, July, August and September.

The music critics had been overwhelmed by his stage presence in his latest tour and raved at his ability to attract young and old alike to his music and lyrics, or, as they wrote:

> Marcus Walker is the most compelling figure on the music scene. His music and lyrics are so original, uncomplicated and evocative. His unusual but distinctively appealing voice continues to mesmerise his audience. His guitar work is magnificent in that it is crisp and stark, and there is no one on the music scene both at home and abroad who can play harmonica with such a depth of feeling that this star has. He aims at the heart and soul of every person in the audience, giving the impression he is playing for that person and that person alone. This guy has outstanding ability and instinct for what his fans require and expect of him. He delivers the goods every time.

Marcus had performed to full houses at all his venues, had a number-one hit single in both the American and UK charts with 'Flying High', which stayed at the top for a period of sixteen weeks, and his latest album had reached number one in the UK charts. Life could not have been more rewarding. We were riding high at home, in Europe and in the States, which we hoped to tour in 1989.

The tour bus arrived in Wembley and Ray, Marcus, Ben, the band and the sound crew were soon engrossed in a check of all their equipment, which had already been installed, and I awaited the arrival of Marianne, bringing Rosie down from her school. Our darling son, Ollie, was fast approaching his third birthday. He was in good spirits, knowing that his attentive brother, Freddie, to whom he seemed to be joined at the hip, was there for him – as was his daddy at every available moment he could spare. He played happily in our dressing room, knowing he would have not one, but two very attentive playmates the moment Rosie arrived. I pottered around, preparing my stage wear for the evening. Even now after three years off and on the road with Marcus, I found it difficult coping with the influx of young female fans and groupies waiting for the slightest opportunity to sneak into our dressing room to touch, caress or proposition him; but I realised from the outset that this was part of the circus that surrounded us, and before and after each concert I tried to disappear into the background. Marcus was quite philosophical about his fame, and the fans, realising that it was they who had made him into the icon he was, and knew they could just as easily destroy him. That also applied to the British press who, as Marcus put it, 'tried to muck-rake at the least little opportunity.'

He jealously guarded his private life from both, and offstage he wanted no more than to be at home with Freddie, Ollie and me. We were a complete, happy family, doing things normal families did, and somehow we achieved this despite Marcus's enormous success. To us he was Daddy, my lover, and most certainly my best friend. I guess that having known each other since childhood, we had built up this good, solid foundation on which to create our close relationship. We adored one another's artistic talents, which in turn brought another dimension into our lives. Our love and companionship for one another was both satisfying and fulfilling in all aspects. I gave Marcus the space he needed to craft his hits, but also provided an abiding love that nothing and no one could sever. I was there for him always.

At every venue we'd had the protection of bodyguards to and from the stage, but taking us totally unaware the previous week, several fans had bombarded us at a concert in Manchester and I had been pushed to the ground in the fracas that followed. Marcus was furious and threatened to cancel the performance but persuasion on my part, and expert first aid, resulted in me being able to join Bonny as a backing singer. Thankfully the evening went without further incident, and was a great success, but the bruises I sustained did not disappear as quickly as the adulation of the night.

I had hoped Jonathan could have joined us for the last two evenings of the tour, but he was finishing a tour himself in Europe, which had been rapturously received. He was, however, in frequent contact and hoped to visit us soon.

Marianne arrived at Wembley at 6 p.m., accompanied by Rosie and with Marcus, our children, Ben and other members of the band, joined us for snacks in the dressing room before the stage beckoned. Freddie was his usual exuberant self, delighted to be able to watch the performance from the wings with Rosie, while Marianne babysat Ollie. These were the most crucial two performances of the tour and the most physically demanding. The time arrived, and we received our last call to take to the stage. The crowd went wild as Marcus appeared. It was hectic, but in no time he had the audience eating out of his hand. Word for word they sang along, arms waving as they screamed and cheered. It was deafening and the atmosphere was electric.

I did not sense it happening. First there was blood trickling from my nose onto my clothing. Then came the feeling that the audience were a million miles away, accompanied by a sinking, hollow, heady feeling of losing control, and I collapsed to the floor. I remember nothing more until I awoke in the tour bus, having been carried there by Ben and Freddie, who had seen my predicament from the wings. Even Marcus was not aware of the drama unfolding behind him as he continued to entertain his fans.

The ambulance arrived and I was speedily transported to a private room at a London hospital, arranged by Ben. After examination and blood tests were taken, the doctor in attendance, Doctor Simpson, seemed concerned about the bruising to my body.

'I was knocked over by some rather enthusiastic fans last week,' I explained, 'hence the assortment of bruises.'

'Sophia,' he asked, gazing at me over his spectacles, 'have you noticed that you bruise easily?'

'Now that you mention it, Doctor, it seems that I do these days. After I broke my arm in a horseriding accident late last year, the bruises remained for a considerable time.'

'Any nosebleeds before this evening?' he asked, making notes.

'One, some while ago, which lasted about two hours, and was as severe as this,' I explained.

'Do you feel tired or weak?'

'Of course, but wouldn't you if you had been on the road for five months without a break? I'm tired from all the work that touring and singing entails. I did notice recently too that my gums bleed when I clean my teeth. Is this natural?'

He surveyed me once more and examined my gums, but did not reply. He wrote a large amount of words down on a sheet of paper. He proceeded to examine my neck, and my eyes and grimaced.

'Can I go back to Wembley now? I asked 'We have a final performance tomorrow evening, and there is no way I want to miss it!'

His answer was a definite 'No, Sophia! I am not at all happy with your condition. I would like to do more tests so we will keep you in overnight.'

No sooner had he left the room than Marcus burst through the door and pounced on me like an injured puppy.

'My darling, what on earth has happened to you? You look awful!'

I explained what had happened and managed to calm him.

'Are you able to come back with me now, Sophia? The children are asking for you!'

I explained that it was necessary for me to stay in the hospital until the following day, when I would get the result from tests that had been taken. He sighed and left the room, looking concerned. He returned a short while later and informed me he had arranged with staff that he would have a second bed brought to the room, enabling him to stay close to me and a security officer to attend to the door, for fear of press intrusion. He thanked Ben for his care of me. Ben returned immediately to Marianne who was caring for the children.

'You have appointments with the press and television tonight, Marcus,' I reminded him, 'and they will wonder why you are not there.'

'To hell with the press and television interviews, Sophia! You are my main concern, and the most important person in my life. I want to be here with you.'

He was unyielding, and I knew it was useless to protest against his non-attendance at the interviews. He catnapped by my bed, being both attentive and reassuring. I so badly needed his reassurance and his love.

Morning arrived, and Doctor Simpson appeared to be somewhat evasive. He did not appear until after lunch, to the disgust of Marcus, who had taken to pacing the floor, waiting for answers, giving nursing staff lots of grief. Doctor Simpson entered the room, pulled up two chairs to the side of my bed and insisted Marcus sit quietly and understand the results of my tests. Quite how much I remembered of the following conversation I cannot say, but I remember vividly the words, 'I am sorry, Sophia but the tests categorically point to you having…'

Did he say leukaemia – an acute form? Or was I imagining it?

I froze on the spot and could not speak. I glanced at Marcus. His face was ashen yet expressionless, but I noticed a tear trickling from the corner of his eye, which he casually wiped away when he thought I was not looking. I heard him speaking to the doctor but I could not grasp what was being said.

Chemotherapy? Transfer to a hospital near Leeds? Was I dreaming?

'I just want to go home to Starbeck Row, Marcus,' I murmured, not quite coming to terms with what I had heard. 'Please take me home. I want to see Freddie and Ollie.'

He looked caringly at me, took me in his arms and declared, 'Darling, it is vital you have immediate treatment. The doctor is arranging for you to be flown to Leeds by air ambulance.'

Suddenly I was no longer in control of my life. It was being organised from a concerned medical source.

In no time I was lying on a stretcher in the helicopter, Marcus sitting beside me, holding my hand.

'What is happening to Ollie and Freddie?' I asked.

'Marianne is taking care of the boys until you have completed your treatment. Please, darling, stop worrying and concentrate on getting yourself well.'

The journey was strangely quick, and in no time I was transferred to a bed in a private room at a Leeds Hospital. Marcus was informed I would commence treatment the following morning. Taking his hand in mine, I insisted, 'Please, Marcus, you must fly back to London and appear at the final concert tonight. Your fans are expecting you, and you can't let them down. There is nothing you can do here, and I am in good hands. I don't want anyone but immediate family to know I am ill.'

Marcus wouldn't hear of flying back to London initially, but after heart-to-heart talks between us, when I pointed out that whatever was happening to my body I would fight it with all my might, he succumbed. I realised how crucial the final concert was, and I pleaded with him to return. A few phone calls later saw him flying back to London by private plane. He had telephoned Father, who arrived promptly to sit with me and offer comfort and understanding before my treatment the following day.

'Cheer up, Father!' I chided. 'I know things are looking bleak at the moment, but I have so much to live for and I don't intend going anywhere just yet!'

He leaned over and rested his head on the bed. I stroked his steel-grey hair and thought how difficult it was for him, coming to terms with what was happening, but I knew once the initial shock was over we could talk, my father and I.

Marcus had organised security for my room so there would be no intrusion of press, and the hospital staff were sworn to secrecy. He phoned late in the evening to explain he had arrived at Wembley and that he, Marianne, Ben, the children and band would be returning to Yorkshire immediately after the concert by road. The last performance of the tour had been a tremendous success, although how he had coped on stage that night beggared belief. I actually slept well, primarily because I was totally exhausted, and secondly due to large doses of medication.

The telephone in my room rang shortly after breakfast to let me know that Marcus and family had arrived at Harrington Hall. He said they would see me later in the day and that he loved me deeply.

Chapter Thirty-six

My treatment started promptly the following morning.

An intravenous line was placed in my chest for the drugs to be administered in an effort to combat my illness. It had not occurred to me at any time to ask about my prognosis. I knew Marcus had spoken at length to the specialist and was confident he would inform me of anything I needed to know. I realised too, that any drugs given to alleviate my ongoing pain and distress had to be a bonus. My first therapy was given after explanations about possible side effects. Everything happened so quickly, and I had no time to question as to the feasibility of such treatment, but understood it was vital for my long-term recovery.

'Sophia, I don't think you realise how ill you are,' said the sister who arrived to oversee my medication; but I was too tired and weak to dispute the course being taken. I was totally in their hands.

Father arrived early in the evening looking pale, tired and fraught. I imagined he had slept very little. I had observed him through the glass window in my room, talking to nurses before entering. He sat by my bed, holding my hand, saying very few words. Something bothered him. I looked intently at the door waiting anxiously for the arrival of Marcus. I knew if he could just place his strong arms around me I would draw energy from his body to help me through the nightmare I was experiencing.

Freddie opened the door and peered in, but on seeing his grandfather, offered to visit later. Oliver beckoned him and said, 'Stay, Freddie! Have a quick chat with Sophia. She is only allowed one visitor at a time. I will go and get a cup of tea in the restaurant and meet you there in a short while.'

Father kissed me and squeezed my hand and, with mild relief, left the room. I imagined how awful it must have been for him, sitting there knowing that almost forty years previously, he had helplessly watched my darling mama fight her terminal illness.

Freddie had arrived laden with flowers from the walled garden and requested a vase from a nurse. Arranging them he placed them on a table and sat quietly by my bed, constantly patting my hand in an act of reassurance.

'We cannot believe what has happened to you, Sophia,' he said. He appeared extremely subdued. 'Please get well soon. Ollie and I miss you so much. Starbeck Row seems so empty without you there!'

I leaned to one side and kissed his cheek. 'I will soon be well, Freddie,' I assured him. 'Please look after Daddy for me. He has so much on his plate at the moment.'

He refrained from making eye contact with me, which was unusual.

'Is Daddy outside?' I asked, wishing to see darling Marcus and hold him close.

Freddie turned away and softly muttered, 'No!'

'You surely have not come here without him?' I queried.

'Oh, Sophia, I have been told not to say anything that is likely to upset you, but I am so worried about my daddy.'

He explained that Marcus had returned to the Hall the previous evening and had gone straight to his recording studio, locking himself in. Ray, Ben and Father had gone to talk to him, without success. He wouldn't allow any of them access and had been heard smashing equipment in a fit of anger.

'Why is he acting like this, Sophia?' he asked, looking concerned about his revelations. He wiped a tear from his eye.

My heart went out to Freddie. I had been down this road so many times before with Marcus, and I tried to allay his son's fears as I said, 'Try not to worry about Daddy. I am afraid he has always reacted like this when he is not in total control of a situation. He can do nothing to help me at present and is very frustrated, so he will lock himself away until he comes to terms with what is happening. He will appear at some stage, but until then you have to be brave and wait patiently until he gathers his thoughts together!'

He looked at me with a serious expression on his face saying, 'But you are the one who is suffering, Sophia!'

'But Freddie, your father is in great pain too. Please try and understand what I am saying.'

He changed the subject by informing me that Ray was in the corridor, waiting to say hello to me. Unable to comfort me, Freddie decided to join his grandfather in the restaurant. Appearing sad, he kissed me as he left the room. I bade him farewell and, although extremely tired, I needed to speak with Ray. I knew that if anyone other than me could help Marcus, it would be dear Ray. I raised myself up on my pillows as he entered the room. The gentle giant rushed forward to assist in making me comfortable.

'Dear Sophia, what on earth have you been doing?' he quipped, trying to make fun of a serious situation.

'I'm just taking a few days off!' I joked, and ran my spindly fingers through his bushy beard. His chuckles warmed my heart.

'Freddie was reluctantly telling me that Marcus has locked himself in the recording studio. He is so worried about his daddy and I am too!' I confided.

'We are all worried about him, Sophia. He has taken the news of your illness very badly. I don't know what to do to help him through his turmoil.'

I looked fixedly at the gentle, hairy giant and announced, 'Well, Ray, I think this is the right time for you to approach Marcus and tell him the truth, don't you?'

I watched his expression as he bowed his head. 'The truth, Sophia? What truth?' he asked.

'You know very well what I'm referring to, Ray!'

He raised his large eyes and attentively fixed his gaze on my face.

'How long have you known?' he asked, looking totally embarrassed.

'When you had been in the band about a month,' I explained. 'It was those vivid brown eyes that gave you away and the way you looked at me. I had experienced the Walker stare so often before, in Marcus. I made enquiries about you and, although you live in Chicago when in the States, you were born in Ontario, Canada, and Ray "Young Blood" Witherspoon is your stage name. Your real name is Bruce Walker. You're Marcus's father, aren't you?'

His lips quivered as he fought back the tears which welled up in his eyes. He held his head in his hands and began crying. I put my arm around his shoulder as he said, 'Forgive me, Sophia! I have been such a fool! Such a damn, stupid fool!'

'There is nothing to forgive, Ray!' I said, trying to offer words of comfort.

He began to explain that he had initially joined the band in an effort to get closer to his son through their love of music, while he still had the chance, but as the months passed and they built up a friendship and healthy respect for one another, it had been impossible for him to confess who he was, for fear of losing that respect and friendship and his son. He explained too that Father had recognised him after their first meeting and was sworn to secrecy, although the decision did not sit comfortably on Father's shoulders. I asked if it was he who had arrived in England when I was ten years old, to fetch Marcus, and he offered further explanations.

'I really did not abandon Frances and Marcus, Sophia! I loved them both deeply. I would never have done that. You see, when I left Canada to come to England during World War Two as a pilot, and joined your father's squadron, I had already divorced my wife, Grace. I met Frances, fell in love, and we lived together in London. Marcus was the welcome addition to our loving relationship and I adored him and his mother. In 1949 I was summoned to Canada because Grace was dying from tuberculosis. I had two young sons, Robbie and Michael, from my marriage, who were in danger of being taken into care; so Frances agreed I should return to Ontario to look after them all. She knew it was my intention to send for Marcus and her when Grace had passed away, and she was quite happy about being mother to my two sons. In 1950, shortly after Grace's passing, Canada had an epidemic of polio and Robbie became sick. I rushed him to hospital, where he was quarantined and diagnosed with polio. Mikey and I were quarantined at home, and as the days passed Robbie became desperately ill. He passed away just after his birthday. As you can imagine I was devastated. Meanwhile Frances was dejected at being stuck in England without any communication, and had convinced herself I had abandoned her and Marcus. She took the fatal overdose of pills in a moment of depression. I was mortified when the news reached me from London.

'Marcus was almost three, and I desperately wanted him with me, but the Canadian authorities would not allow him access until the quarantine had been lifted. He was taken into the care of a children's home. I wrote to Oliver Harrington, and he and Mary offered to take Marcus and watch over him until the time when I could fly to England and take him home with me. When I did eventually get to England, bringing Mikey with me, we found Marcus was so happy, and adored being with you at Harrington Hall. Oliver and I decided it was in his best interest for him to remain with you. I returned to Canada and made a life of sorts for Mikey and me, taking to the road doing the only thing I knew apart from flying – playing pedal steel guitar in various bands!'

'But Ray,' I interrupted, 'you should be explaining all this to Marcus! He needs you now more than ever, not just as his friend but as his father. He is having a difficult time coming to terms with what is happening, and only you can pacify him and give him the support he so desperately needs at the moment. Go to him and tell him who you are!'

It was agreed he would approach Marcus with Father and Freddie, and speak openly to him. As he left the room I called, 'Tell Marcus I love and miss him dreadfully, and I insist he listens to what you have to say to him! Tell him I need him here with me.'

He nodded and, looking relieved that I at last knew his reasons for supposedly abandoning Marcus, he blew me a kiss and shuffled out of the room. I lay there mulling over in my mind all that Ray had told me, and wondered how his son would react when told who he was. It was then that the feeling of queasiness came over me and the side effects of the treatment began. Jonathan appeared, laden with gifts, anxious and unhappy to see me in such a state. He was due to fly to Berlin early the following morning with his quartet, but promised to telephone regularly, and would return promptly should I need him.

My night was restless and uneasy, my mouth excessively dry. My head ached. I slept very little. By morning I had the feeling of having been run over by a double-decker bus, but it was simply the after-effects of the drugs. The daily paper delivery boy poked his head around the door and asked if I would like a newspaper. Reading was far from my thoughts, but I asked him to leave a copy and that I would perhaps read it later. Breakfast arrived, but I was not in the least interested. I toyed with everything on the tray before pushing it to one side. I reached over and managed to retrieve the newspaper, dragged it onto the bed and turned the pages. The front page declared in large letters:

LOVER OF ROCK STAR DYING...

And lo and behold, there was a picture of me, lying in bed at the hospital receiving medication. I could not believe it! There was a screed about Marcus and me, all of which was rubbish, taking up the following two pages. I reached for my bell and rang it furiously. I threw the paper at the staff nurse, who hastily arrived.

'Explain this!' I snapped.

She retrieved the paper from the floor.

'Marcus paid very dearly for security to be placed outside my room, so how on earth did these photographs and intimate articles find their way to the press office?'

Totally unaware of what I was referring to, the nurse looked at the pictures and read a small section of the offending article, before trying to calm me then raced to fetch Sister. She appeared forthwith.

'This article states that I am dying! Am I?' I challenged.

'Please keep calm, Sophia,' she said quietly.

'*Keep calm* – with my face plastered all over the daily papers?'

Doctor Pajwani, who was in charge of me, arrived, but between them they could not figure how the press had got hold of the photographs and the material for the write-up.

'I want who ever did this sacked. It must have been a member of staff!' I frantically announced.

They promised there would be a full investigation immediately.

It was then I decided that once I had received the necessary treatment

I would discharge myself and recuperate at home. Father arrived early for his visit, his intention being to stop me seeing the national newspapers, but he was too late. The damage had been done. Enquiring about Marcus, he explained to me that Ray had managed to persuade him to open the doors to the recording studio. Apparently the conversation between them lasted a considerable time and was extremely heated. Voices became raised, mostly on Marcus's part, leading to a culmination of anger and physical abuse being rained on Ray. Ray had retreated for the sake of self-preservation, leaving his son in utter turmoil. Marcus would certainly feel the sharp end of my tongue when he decided to put in an appearance.

Father stayed for a short while and then returned to Harrington Hall, but there was no sign of Marcus that morning, afternoon or evening. I closed my eyes and tried to sleep but continually wondered how he was faring after Ray's revelations. I was deeply anxious about him and his state of mind.

After the release of the newspaper article, steady streams of cards, flowers, soft toys and balloons began arriving from fans of Marcus, both at home and in Europe. People were sending flowers via the telephone services from as far afield as America, and I had apparently made world news. It was a crazy time, with more flowers than I was able to cope with, but it gave me a feeling of being cared about and prayed for. I had a number of bouquets distributed around the hospital and toys sent to the children's ward. I prayed incessantly, and for every prayer I said, one of the nurses released a 'good luck' or 'get well soon' balloon from the window of my room. They disappeared up into the sky, and I hoped that if there were angels out there, then perhaps they would contact 'head office' for me and place a few good words on my behalf. Sister popped her head into the room and admitted that the nurse who provided the press with the photographs had been found, and a disciplinary hearing would take place almost immediately.

Nurses attended to my daily hygiene, and during my shower one day I noticed long strands of my hair falling into the tray below – another side effect of the treatment.

'Will you cut my hair?' I asked the astonished nurse in attendance.

Reluctantly she agreed, and my locks were parted from me, put into a plastic bag and placed in my locker for old times' sake. Goodness, what an odd new look I had! But it had to be done at some stage, and now the problem was dealt with. Having dressed with a fair amount of help, I sat in a chair by the window and stared out, admiring the flower beds with their magnificent displays of colour. It was a warm, sunny day, yet I was unable to be out there to enjoy it.

The door opened, and as I slowly turned, I saw Marcus sheepishly standing there. He leaned against the door frame, looking tired, scruffy and unshaven. He reminded me of a vagrant, with his dark glasses hiding his bloodshot eyes. He sauntered slowly toward me and sat at my feet, placing his head in my lap. I stroked his lifeless, greasy hair as he murmured, 'Can you forgive me, Sophia, for neglecting you? I am trying so hard to come to terms with—'

'Ssh, Marcus,' I soothed, continuing to caress his long hair. 'I understand what you are going through. Really I do!'

He stared into my eyes with a look of utter hurt and despair, but I lovingly kissed him and said, 'Please, darling, don't be afraid. I have been giving my illness lots of thought. I have so much to live for. With you, the children, Jonathan and my father by my side I am strong enough to be able to fight this damned invasive "thing" that wants to take me over. Well, I won't let it happen. I am going to fight it tooth and nail and return to the old Sophia you know so well and love.'

'But I love the old *and* the new Sophia! I will always love you, always,' he declared.

That was all I needed to hear, and we kissed and hugged one another for what seemed like an eternity.

'I want to go home, Marcus!' I pleaded.

'As soon as the treatment is finished,' he promised. He looked at my hair and commented that I looked 'elf-like' with the new style. I explained I wanted to leave it as it was and let it grow naturally and not wear the wigs that had been offered to me. He ran his fingers over my soft scalp and we laughed together. Then he explained to me that Ray had been to see him, and they had talked extremely heatedly.

'You knew he was my father, didn't you, Sophia? How long had you known?'

'A few weeks after he joined the band,' I admitted.

'Why didn't you tell me?'

'Because it was not my place. It was for him to tell you.'

'I still cannot believe it. Oh, Sophia, I have treated him so badly! I was in utter turmoil when he told me last night. I hit him! I guess he won't even be around today. Chances are he will have left for the States!'

'I don't think you are going to get rid of him that easily, Marcus. He adores you and his grandsons, Ollie and Freddie. I am sure he is here to stay.'

'Thank God. I really do love the man. It's going to take a bit of adjusting to, him being my father as well as my friend, but it was wonderful learning he wanted my mother and me, and that I was not abandoned. Did you know I have a brother called Michael?'

'I did! He came over to England with your father in 1953, I think, and spent time with you. You gave him a real hard time!'

'Did I? He's a bass guitarist, Sophia!' he said eagerly.

'Oh, so it looks like we have another prospective band member!' I quipped.

'Ray explained he came to England to fetch me when I was five, but he could see I was settled with the family and adored you, following you everywhere, so he decided I would have a better life in Yorkshire than what he could give me in Canada.'

'I guess I am to blame for so much,' I mused, and he placed his arms around me, kissing me tenderly. He smiled his hypnotising smile and I realised then that Marcus was back on track and beginning to cope with my illness and his newly discovered parent.

'Ray tells me my grandfather was a Sioux Indian.'

'I am not surprised. You have inherited his dark, mesmerising looks, obviously.'

'What on earth would I do without you and your love, Sophia?' he asked, and we kissed and caressed once more.

'What about the newspaper reports? I understand from Oliver you have seen them! I wanted to protect you from all this and I failed you.'

'Please don't fret. I should be used to all the lies they continually print, but it can still be hurtful, especially right now! But then we did discuss this before I began living with you. We knew there would be many smears printed and that we had to dismiss them as being pure fabrication and take no notice,' I said.

'Good girl. Just ignore anything they write. We know the truth, and that is all that matters,' he said sensibly.

'I am not going to die, am I, Marcus?' I asked, looking for answers in his facial expressions.

'Of course not!' he said, fixing me with a stare. 'Nothing is going to part us, Sophia! *Nothing*!'

Marcus told me he was lost without me, and as soon as possible he would take me back to Starbeck Row. I explained I needed to set myself goals, and had had so much time to reflect on my illness. I affirmed that I wanted to achieve much more in my life, but Marcus insisted I had already accomplished a great deal.

'What can I do for you, Sophia? I will take you anywhere you want to go,' he pledged.

'There is nowhere I want to go except home. But I would like to give a piano recital in the Great Hall. I am sure you and Father could arrange for an audience of guests, and if Jonathan is available I would like him to be there too.'

'Your wish is my command, darling, but first you have to get well.'

We held each other close. My beloved Marcus was back in my arms and that was all that mattered. I loved him more than life itself. I was going to ensure I recovered in record time and give the concert of my life as a pianist – as Father had always hoped I would – in the Great Hall.

'And last, but not least,' I continued, 'I have realised through this illness that life is very, very precious, and tomorrow is not promised to anyone. So I have made this big decision: *I will marry you, Marcus Walker on Christmas day*! That will give us six months to make the necessary preparations.'

The expression on his face was one of astonishment and disbelief at my change of heart, and shouts of 'Yippee!' resounded around the hospital corridors and rooms. I had made one very special guy ecstatically happy!

Starbeck Row had never appeared more beautiful as I arrived home from hospital. Ollie ran excitedly down the path as I alighted from the Range Rover, helped by dear John Roberts. Marcus followed Ollie in hot pursuit, as our darling little son called frantically, 'Mummy, Mummy!' and threw his arms around my legs, before I could bend down to touch him. He looked up and frowned at my spiky hair. Marcus lifted him so he could hug and kiss me and we hurried inside, where I was pounced upon by Freddie, who was so excited to see me. How good it was to be home with the love and comfort that surrounded me! They were the greatest drugs available.

As each day passed I became stronger, and on my first induction to the fresh air, Marcus had arranged for Father's horse-drawn carriage to transport us around the estate. I sat, with rugs placed around me, facing two excited children and my father with darling Marcus by my side. The sun shone brightly and the estate had a warmth and serenity about it I had almost forgotten. A huge picnic hamper, placed strategically behind the carriage, housed the most lavish food and champagne. Edith and the staff had surpassed themselves once more. The carriage ride was magnificent. Eventually we stopped by the lake and rugs were spread out and the picnic hamper opened. We sat, laughed, chatted and watched Ollie carefully, ensuring he would not fall into the water, as Marcus had done at his age. Father seated himself beside me and whispered, 'Marcus tells me you have agreed to marry him on Christmas Day.'

'Yes, Father, I have. Are you happy for me?'

'Happy, Sophia? You cannot imagine how happy I am. You belong together always. You have my blessing!' He held my hand and drew it to his lips, kissing my fingers affectionately. 'And it is good to see you becoming stronger by the day.'

'Then you will give my hand in marriage?' I asked turning to view Marcus, who was deeply engrossed in a ball game with Freddie and Ollie.

'Most certainly, Sophia! You seem so radiantly happy!'

'I am, Father. I really am. My illness has made me reflect on so many aspects of life, and I realise you only get one chance, so I am going to grab it with both hands.'

'Good girl! You are my precious daughter. I love you deeply!' he said, a quiver in his voice.

Picnic over, Marcus lifted me into the carriage and instructed the driver to take us to the field where the first outdoor concert of the season was due to take place within days. Construction had already begun on the stage area and I was informed that all tickets had sold out. Marcus promised I could watch part or all of his performance from the wings, depending on how my health was on the day.

'Plans are well under way for your piano recital at the Hall,' he announced as we viewed the construction. 'So many people have declared an interest in wanting to attend. It has been booked for six weeks from now on the Friday evening. I do hope you will be well enough to take on the challenge.'

'I most certainly will be, Marcus. I thought for the first half I would perform Handel and then during the second half I would ask the audience to choose pieces they would like to hear. Will Jonathan be able to attend?'

'Yes, that is why Father and I have chosen that particular date.'

'Good! I hope that at the finale, you, Jonathan and I can perform together. Father would be delighted with that arrangement.'

He seemed intrigued at my idea, saying, 'Draw up a programme, Sophia and I will get 400 copies printed.'

'400? You don't think there will be 400 in the audience, do you?'

'Of course, the interest has been enormous.'

I settled back into the luxury of the carriage seats and contemplated playing to 400 people, on the platform, alone! I was scared. Yet Marcus, Ray and the band were preparing for 200,000 or more to attend their gig at the weekend.

With safety, security and first aid in place, the outdoor concert went ahead. The weather was delightful, and Marcus and the band were a resounding success. Reports in the newspapers and on television deemed it to be an explosive and well-organised event, singing the band's praises as never before. I watched Marcus during all of his performances and had nothing but admiration for his sheer energy and tenacity, but I returned to Starbeck Row when my body informed me it could no longer sustain me. He joined me later with the band in attendance, and I am afraid to admit that my head did not rest on the pillow until two o'clock in the morning because we were celebrating; but Marcus, the band and I were deliriously happy.

The days that followed saw me becoming stronger. Every day John Roberts would fetch me and I would practise on the Steinway grand piano that Mama had willed to me, while Marianne cared for Ollie. Freddie attended school and Marcus and Ben discussed the next album, *Childhood Days*, which they hoped to release for the Christmas market. Marcus and the band were in and out of the studio most nights, recording or occasionally hopping off for the day to record at other venues, and had a tour planned in the New Year from January to May. Hopefully I would then be strong enough to go on tour with them. Father sat while I practised and offered his advice and observations, which I found invaluable. My hair was growing and Marcus, Freddie and Ollie nicknamed me 'Henrietta Hedgehog', which caused mild amusement among my nearest and dearest. I had begun writing a book for my dearest son, Jonathan, and in my spare moments – and with Marianne's help – I forged ahead in the hope I would have it finished in time to present to Jonathan on my wedding day. Marcus frequently requested my help and advice with the music and lyrics he was writing, and I willingly offered my input, feeling honoured to have been asked. It was good to be back in the business of making music. The songs were great, and it seemed to me he had a choice of these that he could release as a potential number-one hit and enough good material for another number-one album. He always finished his writing and recording so that he was there for Freddie, Ollie and me after school hours, and if television or radio interviews encroached during those times, we would all go along with him for moral support.

The day of the piano recital drew near. I became increasingly nervous. Marcus arranged that he would be there to give me the support I so desperately needed. He insisted I had breakfast in bed and saw that Freddie arrived at school on time. Ollie and he brought a tray of delicacies to the bedroom, enhanced by a rose from the garden called 'My Love'. It had been Alex's favourite, and it was as though he were wishing me good luck too. He would have approved. Ollie and Marcus sat on my bed while I ate. I offered Ollie buttered toast and Marcus joined me for a cup of coffee. Breakfast eaten, the tray was removed. From his pocket Marcus removed a small box and laid it on the quilt in front of me.

'Here, darling, this is for you. Wear this for me tonight!' he whispered, and he kissed me softly.

'Oh, Marcus, you shouldn't have—' I began, but he interrupted me saying, 'Please, Sophia! I want you to wear this at the recital!'

I picked up the box. I had planned on wearing a pale blue long silk dress and Edith's brooch in the shape of an 'S', but he was so insistent. I cautiously opened the box and hoped what it contained would complement my dress. I lifted the lid and stared. I began crying as I gazed down at the gold locket.

'Where on earth did you get this, Marcus?' I asked, wiping my tears as I opened the locket to reveal four little photos of Marcus, Ben, Alex and Father which had been given to me the day after I rescued Marcus from the lake. Ollie crawled along the bed with a tissue for me and nestled into my breast, looking up at my tears. Marcus fixed the locket around my neck.

'I left this behind at the convent when I escaped!' I explained.

'I know, Sophia! It's a long story but I managed to contact the authorities in the Catholic Church in Ireland and traced the necklace. Oliver and I took extreme measures to get this returned to you as its rightful owner, because I knew how much it meant to you.' Ollie looked into my eyes and nestled even closer as I sobbed and put my remaining arm around his daddy and laid my head on his chest.

'I thought it would be your good luck charm for tonight, Sophia. And another good piece of news is that the Magdalene Laundry near Dublin has been closed down.'

'Thank goodness! But this necklace is the greatest present I could wish for Marcus, and of course I will wear it tonight.' I sighed. 'And tonight I will excel at my music!'

Jonathan arrived mid-afternoon, happy to see a vast improvement in my health. He remarked on how well I looked, and introduced me to other members of the quartet, who were anxious to see his mother in action on the piano. He was ecstatic at being able to tell me he had secured another record deal with Phoenix. He and his fellow players were in great demand both at home and abroad, and were taking classical music to an extremely wide audience. I was convinced his handsome looks and personality attracted female admirers in the audience as much as his superb playing. His adoptive parents, Catherine and Robert, were also due to attend my recital in the evening. Butterflies began to appear and I was becoming stressed.

We had an early supper at the Hall with Father, but I could not eat. Like Marcus, when a concert was looming, I needed space to prepare myself. I excused myself and went to the room I had occupied as a child and which still housed many of my treasured possessions. I bathed and dressed my hair, which was growing but needed very little attention. I slipped into my flowing blue dress and fastened my precious locket carefully around my neck. I sat quietly, my eyes closed, drifting slowly into another realm. I could see Mama so clearly, sitting at the grand piano in the Great Hall, with Oliver in attendance. She looked radiantly happy and beautiful. She held out her arms and spoke softly to me. 'Give your life to music, Sophia! Promise me!'

'Yes, Mama, I will!' I answered gazing into her dark brown eyes. Tears trickled down my cheeks as two strong hands embraced my shoulders. I turned and buried my head in Marcus's chest. He held me closely and I could feel his strength and love flow gently into my being. He gave me the energy, strength and will to walk into the Great Hall to play for my audience. I would play as Mama would have wished, and I would make Marcus, my father, Jonathan, Freddie and Ollie extremely proud of me.

As I walked toward the piano the audience rose and began clapping. I bowed my head in acknowledgement and moved towards the Steinway. I felt at ease with the dignitaries and guests. Every seat was filled. Several people stood at the rear of the Hall. Flowers were sympathetically arranged and placed strategically around. A small orchestra of old friends were there to accompany me. I waited for complete silence and began to play. It was as if my hands were being guided by an unknown, unseen entity. I sailed through my repertoire and completed the first half to a standing ovation.

It had been decided as guests arrived that they would be asked to request their favourite piece of music to be played during the second half. I worked my way through a long list and chose Tchaikovsky, Schubert and Mozart. Twice there were requests for the *Moonlight Sonata*, but I ignored these requests for fear of stirring up emotions in Father. I explained at the beginning of the second half that I would play as many requests as time would allow. The recital ended, and I received yet another standing ovation. Father appeared on stage. Speaking to me and to the guests he requested he would like me to play the *Moonlight Sonata* for him. I was happy to oblige. It was an emotional experience for us both, but Father, sitting next to Marianne, maintained control throughout. The audience clapped and stood once more in praise of my efforts.

Before he could return to address the audience and give his closing speech, Marcus moved to the piano. Jonathan promptly appeared with his violin, and I made my way to the microphone. Between us we performed 'O My Beloved Father' just as Marcus and I had performed it years previously at the Grange School Theatre. On this occasion Father succumbed to his emotions, but Marianne was on hand to offer comfort and understanding. Guests flocked in droves to speak to me. It was then that I realised from their comments what a wonderfully successful evening it had been. Catherine and Robert were the most difficult guests to free myself from. They continually praised my playing and thanked me for giving them the gift of my son, Jonathan. Marcus finally managed to prise me away from engaging guests, and I returned to Starbeck Row, elated, fulfilled but dreadfully tired.

Chapter Thirty-seven

September arrived, and with it the last of the open air 'Concerts in The Park'. Each had taken on its own momentum. I was well enough to have accompanied numerous songs on piano. It was a wonderful feeling, returning to the stage with Marcus. The pleasure and happiness at being part of the performance was exhilarating and a healing process in itself. Marcus was outstanding and at the absolute peak of his career and I was deeply honoured to have been part of the last concert of the season. As it ended, the crowds slowly scattered and I proceeded to our mobile dressing room. When Marcus had finished signing autographs and talking to fans, he returned swiftly to me. We desperately wanted to go back to Starbeck Row to our sons, who were being cared for by the capable Marianne. Entering the dressing room, Marcus pointed to me and said, 'Sophia, look! Your blouse! Oh, no!' He seemed dismayed as he dashed forward. I had not been aware that blood had begun to trickle from my nose onto my clothing. He handed me tissues and took control of the situation.

Marcus immediately sent for Simon, who was semi-retired but 'on call'. He quickly arrived, and when the flow of blood eventually ceased he insisted I go straight to bed at Starbeck Row and ordered tests for the following morning. He initially wanted to send me to the hospital, but I made it perfectly clear I had no intention of returning there and wanted to be given any treatment at home. After results of tests taken the following morning, this was considered impractical, and hospital was the only alternative. I received further chemotherapy, and the side effects were even more unpleasant than before; but at least my hair did not suffer as with previous medication, simply because I had so little that could be affected.

How I missed Marcus, Ollie and Freddie! But Marcus and Freddie appeared on a daily basis, except that neither of them wanted to leave, and I too needed their presence to reassure me. Father, Ray and Jonathan visited as often as possible, and I spent my days talking into a tape recorder, which allowed Marianne to type sections of this book for me. Within three weeks I had made enormous strides and returned home. The cottage looked charming. Marcus had filled the rooms with massive sprays of flowers. Freddie had crafted me a new pottery bedside lamp in art class at school, which I proudly displayed in our room. Ollie was intent on leading me straight to see his new pet, a hamster, aptly named 'Big Bertha', which he had acquired, as the request for a puppy had been refused by his daddy.

I rested far more than I wanted. Marcus thought it a good idea to hire a private nurse, but the suggestion was totally out of the question and I managed with the help of friends and family. Ben made one of his rare appearances to see me, but I knew he was hostile to illness; a state of affairs developed during his numerous visits to Alex years previously, which had left a marked impact on him. Ray was tremendously supportive of his son, his grandsons and me. Marcus coped with me, the children and his music in the most remarkable way. I had nothing but admiration and praise for him.

Our wedding was beginning to appear on the horizon, and thankfully in a few weeks we would be man and wife. I so wanted this marriage, and it was important I maintained my health and did not push myself as I had done in the past. I needed to know my limitations. It was for this reason I cancelled the next piano recital I had planned, in the Great Hall, but I allowed myself time to be with Marcus and the band in the barn recording studio, helping with vocals and piano on the last songs for the album, 'Childhood Days'.

We recorded and re-recorded until Marcus was completely satisfied with the end result. Spike Collins, the producer – and his crew – were in danger of tearing their hair out, but Marcus needed perfection on this special album. Containing many songs we had written during childhood, this was his most important work to date.

I had to admit there were times when I suffered bouts of extreme tiredness, and at other times sheer exhaustion. Marcus would take the day off, allowing us to spend time with each other and with Freddie and Ollie. Ollie was a little chatterbox, encouraged in his various antics by Freddie. They were joined at the hip, and Freddie adored his little brother. Laughter was not far away when they were around.

Wedding plans were well under way and the dressmaker arrived for my final fitting. My dress was to be in ivory silk. It was brilliantly styled to enhance my figure, except that I no longer had a curvaceous body, and extensive alterations were needed. I did not realise I had shed such a substantial amount of weight, but I didn't look in the mirror very often. Christine, the dressmaker, was obviously amazed at the weight loss, but handled the situation in a delicate manner and advised me that the dress would be ready in good time for my special day.

Flowers were ordered, by Marcus. Orchids from Singapore were the choice of us both. A reception was being planned by Father in the Great

Hall for a large number of guests. Marcus was in charge of invitations, but the numbers of people invited changed so frequently that I ceased asking how many would be attending and left all the arrangements to him. We talked, and it was decided that on the wedding evening immediate family and a few very close friends would return to Starbeck Row for a small celebration.

On waking one morning, I felt a great need to ride Nero, and for once Marcus was not overprotective and thought it a good idea. He was involved in last minute preparations for his album, and so was unable to accompany me; but Freddie offered his companionship on the hack to our favourite wood. Freddie and I rode along, chatting amicably about school, music and life in general. There was an autumnal feel in the air and the trees were shedding their glorious leaves in abundance. It was so good to experience all the pleasures that nature had to offer. At Hardy's Wood, we stopped, sidled down from our horses and sat under the trees watching all manner of wildlife.

'Look, Freddie,' I said pointing into the tree, 'a woodpecker!'

'Ah, yes! A green woodpecker!' he observed.

'You certainly know your birds,' I commented.

'That is Grandfather's influence! He often brings me here to view the birds. There are so many wonderful creatures to watch in this wood.'

'You really love your Grandfather Oliver, don't you, Freddie?'

'Yes, I do, Sophia! And now I have Grandfather Ray and Daddy to help and advise me with my dreams. I would like to be a musician, Sophia!'

'I am so pleased you have a career in mind, Freddie. We will do all we can to encourage you in your chosen path.'

'You have been a tower of strength to Daddy, Sophia. He is so lucky to have you by his side.'

'No, Freddie, I am the lucky one. I have you, Ollie and your wonderful daddy to love and protect me. I have such a wonderful, happy, contented life.'

He stared at me with his piercing eyes and said, 'Are you frightened of dying, Sophia?'

I was taken aback by his line of questioning.

'You certainly shoot straight from the hip, young man,' I said, laughing, but the serious look on his face made me realise I needed to reply with a sensible response.

'No, I am not frightened of dying, Freddie. I *am* frightened of the chaos and unhappiness I would leave behind. I am forty-five years of age and I still have lots of living to do. I have a splendid wedding coming up shortly, to your beloved daddy, and no illness is going to prevent that wonderful day from coming to fruition. I want to stand there and in front of the world, make my vows to him. Why do you ask me this?'

He watched my facial expressions then said, 'Well, I have observed you an awful lot lately, Sophia, and although you smile and joke continuously, I know that inside your suffering is far greater than you allow us all to see. I get the impression at times you feel you cannot cope with what is happening to you. I try to speak to Daddy about this, but he always manages to evade the subject.'

Darling Freddie was so aware – sensitive to my pain and how I was actually feeling. I believed Marcus was too, but he wrapped himself in his music and tried not to think about anything other than the day in hand and our future life together as man and wife.

I looked at dearest Freddie and said, 'There are days, darling, when I feel I can't cope any longer, but I intend fighting this illness with every ounce of strength I possess. I want to watch you develop into a fine musician like Daddy, and watch Ollie grow into a handsome young man, with a wife and children; so I don't plan on going anywhere other than with you all for the foreseeable future.'

'Thank goodness, Sophia! We all adore you so much and could not bear it. I know everyone has to die one day. That is the only certainty there is in life, but I pray you will live for a long while and grow old gracefully. You are still so beautiful and I am so thankful you are my mother.'

I threw my arms around him and we huddled together. He had grown into a caring, observant young man, with a heart of gold, just like Marcus.

I concluded, 'It is inevitable that one day I will pass from this world to another realm, but when the time comes I will never be far away from you. I will be in the very fibre of this estate and the wonderful Hall and cottage. You will sense me in everything. I will always be part of Harrington Hall and of you all.'

He hugged me once more, and as the horses were getting restless I suggested we return to the stables before someone came anxiously looking for us. He agreed. As I rode with him toward the Hall I experienced a feeling of relief that I had been able to talk about how I was feeling, and that we finally had this deep understanding between us. I hope I had allayed all his fears.

Three weeks before the wedding I had to return to the hospital for more treatment. It was imperative we discouraged the press in every way we could, and Marcus arranged for extra security staff at the hospital and in and around the Hall and estate. He wanted our wedding to be a close family occasion, with guests of our choosing. I hoped he had managed the guest list successfully, but unfortunately I had had to designate all this to him.

The doctors seemed pleased with my progress. I returned home once more, happy in the knowledge that my wedding was almost imminent. My health seemed improved, although my joints ached at times and I found walking a little difficult, but chemotherapy had given me strange side effects in the past so I was not unduly worried. Within I felt extremely good, I had all I could wish for and more. Marcus was extremely attentive as were Freddie and Ollie. Their love was unbelievable. The boys would creep into our room as soon as we were awake and we would share breakfast together. Then, after a short rest, we would spend time in their company. Freddie was on school holidays, allowing us to lavish time and attention on him.

The days were wonderful. Marcus had finished his album, *Childhood Days*, to be released in time for the Christmas season. It entered the charts at number five. The single 'On Tour' went straight to number one. No one was more delighted than I was. All our hopes and dreams had come to pass. In my spare time I carefully prepared two scrapbooks with photographs of Marcus and me on tour, and with newspaper reviews of us when we were young, at the Grange School concert. There were press cuttings and photos of Marcus on stage with the Dream Catchers, and then alone at Carnegie Hall in the USA. Each book came with a box too, of various mementos. A lock of my hair, a snippet of my dresses I wore on special occasions, leaves and flowers I had pressed from my various walks with Alex, a few remaining photos of Mama, Papa and their families from Italy and snaps of Alex and me that Father had given me. I wanted these precious things to be handed down to Freddie and Ollie sometime in the future. There were mementos too, of Marcus, which we held dear; simple little things, but precious to us.

★

I have continued writing this book but my fingers ached dreadfully when I penned the words, so I have resorted to the tape recorder once more. It is important that Jonathan should receive this book. I want him to know why I did what I had to do as a teenager. I don't know, with hindsight, if I would have arranged things differently. I do know that no one would have parted me from my beloved son had I not been ill at the time. I am thankful he was adopted by a marvellous, loving couple who gave him the confidence and support to follow his musical career, and become the stupendous grown-up he developed into.

I would not want one moment of my time again with Stephen, but that episode in my life certainly made me into a stronger person. Therefore those years in Australia were not totally wasted.

I continually savour the wonderful memories I have of dearest Alex. Marcus and I speak of him often, and precious times spent with him will remain with us both always. Part of him continues to live on in Jonathan and for that I am thankful. I will always be eternally grateful for the abiding love I now share with my beloved Marcus. No two relationships are the same, but I know with shy, talented Marcus I have the relationship that most women would die for. Together we have made music, given life to our precious son, Oliver, and raised dearest Freddie for the last five years, to become the special son Marcus and I love unconditionally. Marcus, the children and I are a complete family. I have had the marvellous experience of the love of my biological father, who nurtured and guided me through many of the obstacles in my life. His love is always there, and I adore and respect him greatly. My mother, Mary, was a truly wonderful soul who gave me love and attention during my growing-up years, and for the experience of her caring nature I will always be grateful. To my mama and papa I give thanks for the gift of music, which runs through my veins and in my soul; to my mama I give blessings for the gift of life.

The greatest time in recent years was the reunion with my son Jonathan, my cherished firstborn, who is now himself a star on the continent. I have always loved you, Jonathan, more than you could possibly imagine.

In recent months Marcus has discovered in Ray 'Young Blood' Witherspoon, his long lost father, Bruce Walker. They are extremely close, and I know that Ray and his son Michael will be there for Marcus, Freddie, Ollie and me, whatever befalls us in the future.

Now I am to marry the love of my life, Marcus, to whom I owe so much. He has brought a peace and contentment into my life that I never thought possible. We are as one.

What more could a woman want?

Epilogue

Starbeck Row
Harrington Hall
North Yorkshire
England
January 1989

Dear Reader,

So much of this book, which my beloved wife Sophia wrote, is directed at me; it was therefore agreed, with Jonathan (for whom the story was told), that I should write the final chapter for you.

Christmas Day 1988 was indeed the most wonderful day of my life, basking in the knowledge that Sophia would finally become my wife, making me the happiest man alive.

The day began with Freddie and Ollie invading our bedroom with their Christmas presents for us all to see. Freddie was astonished with his gift of an electric guitar, which he had set his heart on. After unpacking this and cosseting it, inspecting every minute detail, he left the room and staggered back into the bedroom with a large cardboard box, followed closely by Ollie.

'Look, Mummy!' shouted Ollie as Freddie placed the box on the floor. 'I found this in my room!' (I myself had placed it there an hour earlier.)

Bleary eyed, Sophia lifted herself up in the bed, with my help, and we watched our small excited four-year-old open the box. He knelt, viewing the contents in disbelief.

'Look!' he said excitedly, 'Father Christmas has given me a puppy!'

He gently lifted out the small, whimpering creature and put it on to our bed, much to the amusement of Sophia. My mind travelled back to the Christmas years previously when Sophia had persuaded Oliver to allow me a puppy, and how excited I had been. Here at Starbeck Row, years later, our son Ollie was behaving in exactly the same fashion.

'What shall I call him?' he asked.

'He is such a beautiful puppy, Ollie,' she remarked, tenderly stroking the bundle of fur. 'Why not call him Deefa?' She looked in my direction and stifled a giggle.

Freddie said, 'What a funny name for a dog! What does it mean,

Sophia?' as Ollie struggled to catch the puppy before it began its descent to the floor.

'Why, it is D for dog!' she remarked, winking cheekily in my direction.

And so another Deefa had joined the family. I hoped my son would have the love and companionship from his own dog that I'd had from my beloved Deefa years previously.

Freddie thanked us both individually for his present and was exhilarated by the acquisition of his guitar. We voiced our hopes that this handsome son would progress to become a superb musician. He seemed destined to follow in my and my father's footsteps. Our sons kissed Sophia as I disappeared to the kitchen to prepare a hearty breakfast for those who wished to have it, Ollie following closely with his puppy. Freddie stayed with Sophia and they chatted. As I returned to the bedroom to tell them that breakfast was prepared, I heard a conversation which took my breath away. Sophia was speaking softly to Freddie, saying, 'Dearest Freddie, you cannot imagine what a huge place I have in my heart for you! I want you always to remember this. I love you as if you were my own flesh and blood. You have brought more happiness into this life of mine with your presence than you could imagine.'

Freddie coughed nervously and, holding Sophia's hand, said, 'Thank you, dearest Mother, for your unconditional love. The last five years of my life have been the most contented and blissful I have known. I owe so much to you and Daddy.'

'No, darling,' she replied, 'Daddy and I owe so much to you. Your loving ways and caring attitude make you one very special young man in our eyes. Remember that no matter where you go or what you do, I will always be there.'

Freddie embraced her and they enjoyed a few close moments together.

'If I may be so bold as to return to the conversation we had in Hardy's Wood a week ago,' he said, 'your words have given me such a lot of food for thought, Mother. Please, if you can no longer cope and I know instinctively that you cannot, I want you to do what is right for *you*. Not what pleases me, or Ollie or Daddy! I want you to do what you have to do *for you*. It would be selfish for us to allow you to suffer simply because we cannot let you go. I love you too much for that, and I know you will be there for me, somewhere, somehow!'

He choked on his last words, and I casually, yet despondently, walked into the room and announced, 'Breakfast is served,' not allowing them to know I had heard their conversation. Sophia grasped his hand, held it to her face and then kissed his fingers softly. Helping Sophia from her bed, I gently carried her downstairs where she joined us, to eat a small meal. She commented on how wonderful it was to have been called 'Mother' by Freddie. She remarked too on what an 'aware' child he was, and reckoned he had an 'old head on young shoulders'.

After breakfast she returned to her room to rest. I took the boys to the Hall so they could get cleaned up and be dressed in readiness for our wedding. Edith, with Marianne, was on hand to help them put on their superb outfits.

I returned to the cottage where Sophia and I shared our last cafetière of coffee together before our wedding service. We were so excited. Within the hour the manicurist and hairdresser had arrived, followed by the dressmaker. I realised this was my cue to leave the cottage and head for the Hall so I could prepare for the ceremony, and I politely excused myself.

In my pale cream suit I waited anxiously at the church as midday approached. There was no sign of my intended bride, which was unusual for Sophia, as she was always so punctual. As was customary, she managed to keep me waiting an extra fifteen minutes. She appeared at the church door to the music of the 'Bridal March', and guests gasped in awe. As I turned, Oliver escorted her down the aisle. She looked the most enchanting picture of fragile radiance in the ivory silk dress which adorned her slim frame. Sophia carried a small bouquet of Singapore orchids. The hairdresser had arranged a spray of these in her short black hair to complement the bouquet. Her gold locket took pride of place around her neck. As she approached my side, I took her hand and gazing deeply into one another's eyes we made our vows, vows we had written for one another. The church was filled to overflowing with relatives and friends. My band were in attendance, and as we wandered slowly down the aisle they played 'You Are My Love' – a song written by me especially for our wedding day – for my beloved wife. I watched the expression on her face as she viewed the guests. Her smile lit up the scene.

I had traced and invited Niamh, the girl from the convent who had befriended her in Ireland in 1960. Niamh was accompanied by her husband and daughter, Angelique, whom she had searched for over many years and eventually found. There was Salma, the Malaysian masseuse who had attended Sophia in Penang, on her return stopover to England from Australia. My long lost half-brother, Mikey, had flown in from Canada (and was intent on taking Rick's place in the band, Rick being set to join another band in the New Year). Big Al had flown in from down under with Bindi, Solomon and Tim; her dear friends from the cattle station in the Northern Territory. Inspector Williamson of New Scotland Yard had joined them at the church. Sophia stopped, affectionately embracing each one in turn. The guests included all those who had played a part in her life. Lucy, who had once been engaged to Alex, had arrived with her husband and three children, along with all the staff who had attended Sophia in some way during her life at Harrington Hall. Sophia turned to me and gently kissed me as she said, 'Thank you, Marcus, for making this a truly special day. I love you so dearly!'

'And I you,' I murmured as I tenderly returned her kiss.

In no time we stood at the church porch, covered in confetti and rice, and after a photographic session we hopped into the car which was to take us across to Harrington Hall, where the guests would be welcomed by us on their arrival.

The reception was an affair beyond our wildest dreams. Oliver had employed outside catering staff to prepare the most extravagant champagne wedding breakfast imaginable. This gave Sophia and me a tremendous amount of time to mingle with our very special guests and to chat. We introduced our sons, who behaved during the reception with great decorum. Oliver had given Edith a break from normal duties so that she, John and all staff could enjoy the wedding. Champagne flowed, and this was a truly happy time. I noticed Sophia becoming tired yet she insisted on speaking to every guest who attended, thanking them for the part they had played in her life. I was amazed at her tenacity. Harrington Hall was to host a dinner for all special guests in the evening and accommodate many, but immediate family and special friends would be at Starbeck Row. We finally explained that Sophia needed to rest, and they were delighted and happy in the knowledge they had attended our magnificent wedding and had spent time with the woman they so obviously adored. They toasted her full return to health in champagne.

Sophia, the children and I returned to Starbeck Row. A few close friends were to meet there for an evening get-together. She was exhausted, and retired with Ollie to his room to read a story before settling him down for the night. I heard her talking to him and reciting with him 'Twinkle, Twinkle, Little Star' as they gazed into the night sky, with her pointing out the various constellations. She kissed him goodnight, spoke gently to him of how precious he was to her, and in no time he was settled and asleep.

Sophia appeared downstairs an hour later, dressed in a long black sequined dress, looking spectacular as she entered the room. Our special guests and family had drifted back to the huge, crackling log fires in the cottage and we enjoyed an evening of drinks, food and lots of laughter. Sophia was the perfect hostess. She and Jonathan chatted at length and she presented him with the book she had written. A long conversation was also entered into with Oliver, Ray and my half-brother, Mike, whom she seemed to have a great affinity with. She eventually returned to me, clutching my hand tightly, as if to harvest my strength to see her through the long day. God, I desperately loved this special woman I had married! We embraced and she sat with me on the sofa, when Ben shouted, 'Marcus! Play the song you wrote for Sophia when you were just seventeen!'

I looked around the room to huge nods of approval, then retreated to collect 'Soapy' and returned to the room. Everyone seated themselves in a half circle as I sat on a chair facing Sophia. Oliver joined her on the sofa, his arm around her shoulder holding her close to him. I wanted her to see me singing the words to her, words that were always meant for her and her alone. She smiled with approval and sang the first two verses of 'Now I Know She's Gone' with me. I marvelled at the woman who had been the backbone of my life. During her years of absence from the UK, the memory of Sophia and her love of music were what had seen me through the difficult times and taken me to the top of my career here and in the States in the late sixties and early seventies.

I sang three verses and she nodded with delight. I don't think I had ever sung it as hauntingly as I did that night. Sophia rested back into the cushions, embracing her father. She savoured the harmonica accompaniment that she always insisted was one of my greatest achievements, and I could see small tears in her eyes. I reached the last verse and guests, mesmerised by the song, hummed in the background. I cannot remember an evening when the room was filled with such love and affection. The atmosphere was electric.

Sophia insisted on joining me at the piano for the Christmas carol, *'Adeste Fideles'*, and then we sang together an Italian carol she had taught me when I was a boy of ten. It was an emotional time for us both. We ended the evening with Freddie entertaining us with his own songs, played on guitar. He gave a brilliant performance, and then guests once again toasted us both for a long and happy life together.

After the guests had dispersed and Oliver had spoken to us both, once more blessing our union, I carried Sophia to her room and allowed her time to prepare for bed. She insisted on calling Freddie to her side and wished him a peaceful night. They embraced a while and eventually he returned to his room. When I re-entered the bedroom, she was already snuggled under the duvet, her huge, brown eyes observing me as

I arrived. I showered quickly and crept into bed, taking her tenderly into my arms, trying carefully not to hurt her small fragile body.

'Can you see her?' she asked, pointing to the corner of the room.

'See who?' I replied.

'My mama. She is standing in the corner of the room with her arms outstretched!'

'I am sorry, darling, but I cannot see her!' I said peering over the covers.

'But she's there, Marcus. Anna-Sophia is with her. You must be able to see them. They are smiling at me!'

The only explanation I could give to myself was that perhaps exhaustion was having an effect on her, or she had maybe had a glass too many of champagne.

We lay enveloped in one another's arms for some considerable time, talking of the future, when she suddenly said, 'Marcus, what would you do if anything were to happen to me?'

I found great difficulty in answering such a ridiculous question.

'You must carry on with your music, you know! It is your life!' she implored.

'*You* are my life, Sophia,' I said, 'and nothing is going to happen to you! Nothing!' I choked.

'But what will happen to Ollie and Freddie if I don't get better?'

'You *will* get better,' I insisted. 'Anyway, I would stay home and look after them.'

She looked at me with her large, piercing brown eyes and said, 'No, Marcus, no! You must promise me you will *never* give up your music or your touring. You love the audiences. The fans have made you, and you must go on giving your music to them. They need your music and you need them!'

She held me so closely I could hardly breathe. I couldn't make eye contact, for I did not want her to see my tears. There was desperation in her voice as though she was waiting for a positive answer. I realised then how frightened she was, and for the first time in my life I saw her vulnerability. It scared me senseless. I needed to pacify her.

'The fans did not make me, Sophia! *You did*! I owe my career to *you*. You turned my life around with your love and devotion. I would never neglect our sons for my music. You and I have managed them on tour, to date, and we will do the same again, take them with us, our family, all together, as always.'

'I love you, Marcus, with all my heart,' she whispered and we kissed.

She looked lovingly at me and said, 'I promised Mama, when I was young, that I would give my life to music! Do you think she would be disappointed in me for not fulfilling my promise?'

'But you have fulfilled your promise, my darling,' I assured her. 'You see, you have given your life and all your knowledge of music to me, to allow me to become what I am today. She would be so proud of you Sophia! So very, very proud!'

'Thank you, Marcus, for all your devotion, love and care of me. I am one very lucky woman. In you, I have everything a woman could want. I love you deeply.'

We caressed and as I held her in my arms, she found sleep. I quietly prayed with all my being that Sophia would not suffer, as she had quietly done of late, but that she would make a complete recovery. I could not lose someone so precious. She was my life, my soulmate. The doctors were pleased with her progress, and there was no reason for me not to have faith in their judgement. Tomorrow would be the first day of a long and happy life together as man and wife.

I do not know what it was that woke me from the deep sleep I was experiencing. Something in my dream must have troubled me, and I turned to make sure Sophia was sleeping comfortably. She lay in my arms, a peaceful smile on her beautiful features. As I looked at her I could not believe what my eyes told me. I was devastated to realise that my darling wife had left this earth for what I hope is a far greater place, where her suffering is no more. Not once had she complained of the pain she had tolerated, not wishing to cause us unnecessary worry and I blamed myself for days for not realising how ill she really was; but knowing Sophia as I did, I know she would have hated my pity. I know in my heart she would have wanted me to forge ahead with my career, the career she had so carefully nurtured until her very last day, and this is what I intend to do in her memory.

I miss her more than anyone can possibly understand. Strangely enough, Freddie is seeing me through these difficult times, with his quiet yet profound strength and words of wisdom; and when I broached the difficult subject of her passing to our son Ollie he simply said, 'Mummy is a star up in the sky, Daddy,' and sang 'Twinkle, Twinkle, Little Star' as Sophia had taught him. I am wrapping myself up in my sons and my music in the hope the pain will lessen with time, but at present it is intolerable.

This year I am going on tour in the UK, Europe and the States, taking the children with me. I will have the companionship of my father, Ray, and brother Mike, and Ben and Marianne. The tour will be in

Sophia's memory and will feature songs from the album *Childhood Days* – lyrics and music which we had written together as children. A substantial percentage of the proceeds will go to her favourite organisation to assist talented musicians to further their studies.

While I have my music and my children, Sophia will never be far away. I hear her in the song of the birds, in the whisper of the trees, in the sun and the flowers, in the laughter of children – in my very soul. I see her in Ollie's twinkling eyes and smile.

I do not know how to do justice to my one and only love. She was such a beautiful human being, and our relationship was one of excitement and continual encouragement. She was always fun to be with and yet was as solid as a rock, giving her all to me and my career. She allowed me freedom to be myself. Anything I try to write about her could never compliment her enough. She was my love and she will always be. She filled my soul with love and laughter.

Cards and messages of condolence have been arriving daily from all across the world, and it is a great comfort to know that my sons, Oliver and I are in so many people's thoughts and prayers.

After a celebration of her life, Sophia was laid to rest in the churchyard of St Michael the Archangel, Harrington Hall, North Yorkshire, on 3 January 1989, wearing her wedding dress and locket. She is buried close by her mama, papa, dear Alex and mother Mary Harrington and next to the memorial to Anna-Sophia.

In days that followed I found lyrics and music she had written called 'I Gave You My Today' which will appear in my next tour and album.

Until we meet again, dearest Sophia, may the Great Spirit watch over you and keep you safe.

Your devoted husband,

Marcus Walker

Appendix

Hit Songs written by Marcus Walker:

- 1989 You Are My Love
- 1986 Freddie
- 1983 Nowhere Fast
- 1980 Flying High
- 1978 You and I
- 1976 On Tour
- 1974 The Pianist and the Star
- 1973 The Biggest Mistake of My Life
- 1968 Nobody's Fool
- 1966 Now I Know She's Gone
- 1961 Brotherly Love
- 1960 I Don't Wanna Be a Man

You Are My Love

You held my hand
When life was dark and stormy,
You dried my tears
When things I failed to see,
You gave me hope,
When all others shunned me.
You are my love,
And you will always be.
You took my life,
And turned it round and made me
Into the star I always longed to be.

We climbed the heights
And faced the depths together.
You are my love
And you will always be.
I miss your warmth,
Your tender care and beauty,
Your wayward smile,
The heart you gave to me.
I miss your love
Your praise and understanding,
But most of all, my love,
I desperately miss you.

Marcus Walker, New Year 1989

Lyrics formerly written for wedding of Sophia and Marcus on 25 December 1988. The last verse was altered to enable it to be sung at Sophia's requiem mass.

Freddie

Travelling in my tour bus
From venue to venue,
Taking in places,
Some old, some new.
Peering through the window
While my band sleeps,
Seeing passing buildings,
My memories start to creep…
Creep… creep.

Staring at the window
Your reflection I see –
My precious Freddie,
Estranged from me.
My firstborn, I watched you
Taking your first breath,
Marvelling at your tiny features.
How I was blessed…
Blessed… blessed.

Your mummy and you, son,
Went your separate ways;
You were left out in the cold,
As music filled loveless days.
I quit the rocky relationship
So I could pursue my goal,
But I wanted you in my life,
This stupid inadequate fool…
Fool… fool…

No one loves you more, son,
No one has more care.
When I'm on the road
Or at home,
In my heart you're always there.
Always there… there… there.

Freddie, you've taught me many things,
I simply failed to see.
You showed me what it was to love
And just to simply be.
I was the man who knew the price
Of everything in store,
But you have made me wiser
And taught me so much more.
I now know the value
Of the love that is the core,
Of you and me… you and me…
You and me.

No one loves you more, son,
No one has more care.
When I'm on the road or at home,
In my heart you are always there.
Freddie, in my heart,
You are forever there…
Forever there… forever there.

Marcus Walker, 1986

Nowhere Fast

The greatest part
Of me
That used to be…
I now can see…
Is going nowhere fast.
Nowhere fast,
Nowhere fast…
My life is going
Nowhere fast.

The pain, the sorrow,
Loss of face,
No one else can
Reach this place.
I'm going nowhere fast.
Cannot face the light
Of day… oh, no.
Lost in darkness so remote,
Lost my way,
Going nowhere fast.
Nowhere fast,
Nowhere fast.
Hell is going
Nowhere fast.

A light appears and
Stays with me
Consoles, awakens, comforts me,
Sets me free.
I'm going *somewhere* fast.
Your kind and tender

Care of me
Finally has set me free,
But my all-consuming
Love for you,
Is going nowhere fast.
Nowhere fast,
Nowhere fast,
But my love is going
Nowhere fast.

*Written by Marcus Walker in 1983
during rehabilitation from heroin addiction.*

Flying High

I'm waiting for the aircraft,
Is my plane ready to go?
Did you reach your destination
Or dreams of long ago?

Luggage on the carousel,
Pressmen at the gate.
Fans around the perimeter fence,
The aircraft landed late.

Flying high in my life,
I'm finally at the top,
Flying high in my life
And it ain't gonna stop.

No word, no communication,
No ring of the telephone bell,
No letters in the mailbox
And I am going through hell!

My dreams came to fruition,
I made it to the top –
Did you reach your destination
Or did your dreams all flop?

Flying high in your life,
Or are you flying low?
Did you reach that 'somewhere' –
Have you still a way to go?

Another venue, another place,
Another step in time,
I can't shake you from my mind
You're with me all the time.

No word, no communication,
No ring of the doorbell.
No letters in my mailbox
And I'm going through hell…
Flying high… flying high… flying high.

Marcus Walker, 1980

You and I

You and I,
We were friends
For as long
As I can remember.
Playing games,
Having fun,
Growing up,
Secure and loved.
Changes came,
You were gone,
And I struggled
On without you,
Seeking fame
And my success
Lost and insecure.
Took my chance
I found love…
I'm afraid it was
Not your love.
It wasn't true,
Not like you,
So I sent
That love away.
Reached a point,
In my life,
Where I could not
Live without you.
Took a chance,
Then opted out
And I threw
My success away…
Please return
Into my life and

Give me hope –
Give me signs
And stay with me.
Be my love, and
Please, please don't
Ever go away.

Marcus Walker, 1978

On Tour

I leave the bus and, sound checks done,
I await my cue, yet feel so alone.
Thirty thousand fans crowd in to see
The Star – the person that's not me.
I sing the songs that we once wrote
I smile, I play and also tell a joke.
I leave the stage after taking my bow
They scream, they chant, and yet I know,
I'm lonely,
Lonely without you.
I'm swept along, this famous star,
I've reached my goal, I've journeyed far,
I should have told you how I feel.
Nothing in my life is ever real.
You were my love, I let you go,
I need you now like you could never know.
I move from venue, town to town,
A different stage, this famous clown.
I sign my name, give my autograph,
I'm interviewed, I make them laugh,
I play the fool and try to be,
The kind of star I'm expected to be.
I miss you so – come back to me.
I need you now so desperately.
What good is my fame? It seems like a game,
My love for you still stays the same,
I'd let this fame and stardom go,
To have you here, to let you know
I'm lonely,
I'm lonely without you.

Marcus Walker, 1976

The Pianist and the Star

You had talent in you fingertips,
Since the day that you were born,
But you gave it up to nurture me
And help me become a star,
You did,
You helped me become a star.

For hours and hours we'd sit right there
The piano keys, you and me,
Playing composers old and new
And I yearned to become a star,
I did,
I yearned to become a star.

You introduced me to guitar and harp
And taught me all you knew.
Against family wishes and hopes
You saw in me the star,
You did,
You saw in me the star.

Fame and fortune could have been yours,
But you left it all behind,
To encourage, love and comfort me,
To mould me into a star,
You did,
You moulded me into a star.

I thank you for all the work you did
To get me to where I am.
I wish you could share it with me now
The pianist, the fame, the star.
You could…
The pianist, the fame, the star.

You must be such a long, long way,
From where it once began,
And I never, ever hear from you
But I thank you now I'm a star,
I do,
I thank you now I'm a star.

One day I hope you'll reappear,
And I will take you by the hand
And introduce you to this crazy world
And you will be the star,
You will,
And you will be the star.

Marcus Walker, 1974

The Biggest Mistake of My Life

I'm standing at the altar,
In my white suit and tie.
Hair long but neatly combed,
Flowers arranged nearby.
Pastor's silently waiting.
For the bride to appear –
I'm dreading this big moment.
The biggest mistake in my career.

I cannot turn the clock back
To before the day we met.
I'll make my vows and try,
Try so hard to forget,
Wishing you'd not told me
That you would be my wife –
I'm dreading this big moment,
Making the biggest mistake of my life.

The organ has started playing
And you walk down the aisle,
You stop and hold hands with me,
And kiss me for a while.
I have known it since the day.
I asked you to be my wife,
That I was honestly making
The biggest mistake of my life.

Don't ask me to love you,
The way that I love her,
Your hair and eyes are just the same,
But you'll never be like her.
I will respect and honour you,
Honour you as my wife,
But I know that I'm making
The biggest mistake of my life.

How I wish that she'd come back
And give this empty heart a stir!
I look at you in your white gown,
And wish that it was her.
If she would only enter now
And stop me ruining my life,
Stop me from being a fool and making
The biggest mistake of my life.

Please come back and stop me making
The biggest mistake of my life…
Come back and stop me making
The biggest mistake of my life.

Marcus Walker, 1973

Nobody's Fool

Think I'll leave these English shores
And fly off to LA…
Journey along the California Coast,
Take in Vegas on the way.
I hear that's where the action is
And the Flower Power zoo
When I reach San Francisco
I'll become a hippie too.
I'm gonna take my old guitar
And though it's plain to see
I'm the new boy on the scene
They'll soon have heard of me
'Cause I'm nobody's fool,
Nobody's fool, nobody's fool.

I'll sing my songs and sell my wares
I'll drop before I stop.
In a year or two you'll find me
On my way up to the top.
I'll make you all so proud of me
As I try to reach my goal.
I'll show you what I'm made of
I'll be nobody's fool.

I may take a trip to Memphis
Search out Elvis on the way,
Stop and visit the Grand Ole Opry,
Do that country stuff some day
'Cause I'm nobody's fool,
Nobody's fool, nobody's fool.
I'm nobody's fool.

Marcus Walker, 1968

Now I Know She's Gone

Today I held you in my arms,
Then watched you walk away,
Will I see you in this lifetime,
Will I hold you again and say,
I love you?

You never saw the lover in me,
You only saw the child.
My feelings leave this ache inside
Which forever drives me wild.
You've gone…

Your gentle ways,
Your loving glance,
Are meant for just another,
It breaks my heart,
To watch us part
And for me to discover that
I love you.

Life will never be the same
Without your tender touch.
Your smile, comfort, loving arms,
Can you imagine how much
I adore you?

Your love is now a million miles
From where we once were friends,
I want no other,
Wish I was your lover
Come home, come home,
And fill my dreams…

Oh, she's gone… gone… gone.
She's gone.

Written by Marcus Walker, April 1966
on a napkin at Heathrow Airport.

Brotherly Love

As you lie in a deep sleep,
What kind of vigil should I keep?
Do angels hover in your room
Combating parental gloom?
Do your thoughts go out to me?
If only I could set you free,
Free… free…

Blood does not tie us
It's love that binds us
Love that binds us,
Binds us, binds us,
In brotherly love.

End my heartache, end my tears,
I live my life with silent fears,
That you will not return to us,
But forever dwell in the abyss,
Abyss… abyss.

Chorus: Blood does not tie us…

No one knows just what you mean,
To your family and to me
Silent gratitude for all you've been,
Makes me wanna set you free,
Free to love and feel again
That wondrous loving touch
That fate has taken from you
And those you love so much.

Chorus: Blood does not tie us…

Marcus Walker, 1961

I Don't Wanna Be a Man

I Wanna Stay a Child

I don't wanna be a man
I wanna stay a child.
Not responsible or sensible,
I'd rather stay just wild.
Why should I be rational?
Why can't I be free?
Why must I be someone else?
Why can't I be me?
I don't wanna be a man,
I wanna stay a child
I often wonder who I am
This notion drives me wild.

Do I have to be a puppet?
I'd rather stay afloat.
Do I have to run with the sheep?
I'd rather stay remote.
Must not have an opinion,
Have to accept others' views.
Do I live the life *they* want –
Or live the life *I* choose?
I know I sound complaining.
You can tell it in my tone.
Need I agree with others' thoughts?
Just wanna have my own!
I don't wanna be a man
Just wanna be a child,
Help me keep my sanity.
Just let me run free awhile.

Marcus Walker, aged 12, 1960

Acknowledgements

Mike Stych, for introducing me to a musical sphere which had, until recently, been undiscovered and for planting the idea for this book, unknowingly.

Marie and Charles Bryant (South Australia) for their help and encouragement.

Gil Stevens (South Australia) for advice and help.

Rita Barclay for the services of a listening ear and a beady eye.

Jean and Brendan Smith for their expert help, biscuits and coffee.

Kay Lyon for allowing me to bend her ear on numerous occasions.

Margaret Benns for her invaluable comments.

Billy Lund for advice on musical material.

Jamie Scott for his input on songs and lyrics…

Lesley Grist for giving her valued opinions and support.

Marjorie Griffiths – I need say no more than a very special thanks.

John Wharton for friendship, help and kindness when needed most.

And last, but not least, the staff of Athena Press and their associates for their help, patience and encouragement in the publication of this book.